Saigon

Anthony Grey is the author of five previous books: *Hostage in Peking*, the story of his two years' solitary confinement during the Chinese Cultural Revolution; *A Man Alone* (1972), a book of short stories; and three novels, *Some Put their Trust in Chariots* (1973), *The Bulgarian Exclusive* (1976), and *The Chinese Assassin* (1978). He has made television documentaries for the BBC and ATV and from 1974–9 was a regular presenter of 'Twenty-four Hours', the BBC World Service programme on international current affairs broadcast daily from London.

Also by Anthony Grey
in Pan Books

The Chinese Assassin

Anthony Grey

SAIGON

Pan Books London and Sydney

First published 1982 by George Weidenfeld and Nicolson Ltd
This edition published 1983 by Pan Books Ltd,
Cavaye Place, London SW10 9PG
9 8
© James Murray Literary Enterprises Ltd 1982
ISBN 0 330 28042 2
Photoset by Parker Typesetting Service, Leicester
Printed and bound in Great Britain by
Cox & Wyman Ltd, Reading

The author is grateful to J. M. Dent & Sons Ltd Publishers
for permission to quote excerpts from
"Of Chastity" in *Thus Spake Zarathustra* by Friedrich Nietzsche,
translated by A. Tille and revised by M. M. Bozman.

*This book is dedicated with love
to my dear, valiant mother Agnes Grey,
my sister June, my lovely wife Shirley, and
my blessed little daughters Clarissa Jane
and Lucy-Emma.*

What's past is prologue

— William Shakespeare,
The Tempest

CONTENTS

PART ONE

C'est la Vie Coloniale!

1925

By 1925 present-day Vietnam was divided into three parts under French colonial rule. The southern region embracing Saigon and the Mekong delta was the colony of Cochin-China; the central area with its imperial capital at Hue was the protectorate of Annam; and the northern region, Tongking, was also a separate protectorate with its capital at Hanoi. The Annamese emperor, Khai Dinh, in theory ruled the two northern regions from Hue with the benefit of French protection, while Cochin-China was governed directly from Paris — but in effect all three territories were ruled as colonies. Some backward tribes inhabited the remoter mountains and jungles but the main population was of the same race; today they are known as Vietnamese but then the outside world knew them as Annamites or Annamese. They had detached themselves from the torrent of peoples that in prehistory had poured out of China onto the countless islands of the Pacific and, settling the eastern coastal strip of the Indochina peninsula, they had named their country Nam Viet — Land of the Southern Viet People. This was changed to An Nam — The Pacified South — by the Chinese who conquered them, occupied their territory for eleven centuries, and called them Annamese. During this time they absorbed the Chinese imperial system and Confucian philosophy, but after winning their freedom on the collapse of the Tang dynasty they flourished as an independent nation. Called at different times Dai Nam — The Great South — and Dai Viet — Country of the Great Viet People — they repulsed an invasion by Mongol hordes and successfully resisted new attempts by the Sung, Ming and Manchu emperors of China to reconquer them. Late in the nineteenth century, however, they were not strong enough to resist European troops. It was then that France, after two centuries of increasing penetration by its missionaries and traders, decided to establish dominion over the Annamese lands and the separate kingdoms of Laos and Cambodia by force of arms and set up the French Indochinese Union. About sixteen thousand Frenchmen ruled the fifteen million Annamese, and their government was harsh and uncompromising. They appointed their own French administrators down to the lowest levels, leaving the Annamese powerless and humiliated in their own land. Rice, coal and rubber were sold abroad for the exclusive benefit of French shareholders in Europe, and Annamese coolies were driven hard in the mines and on the rubber plantations for paltry pay; peasant rice growers, too, were frequently robbed of their lands on flimsy pretexts so that bigger holdings could be granted to French *colons* and the few rich Annamese who collaborated with France. While exploiting the conquered territories France constantly proclaimed in public that it had come to Indochina on a "*mission civilisatrice*" to help the backward nation into the light of the twentieth century. Leading Annamese scholars and mandarins, aware of the French hypocrisy from the start, had always refused to cooperate wholeheartedly with their colonial masters and held those of their countrymen who did in contempt. Some tried to organize patriotic resistance groups without much success. Like other colonial nations of the day France believed its subject peoples were inferior to the white European races, and this belief conditioned all areas of daily life in 1925 — whether they were political, economic, social or sexual.

1

Crinkled quiffs of white foam spurted from the steel bows of the five-thousand-ton French passenger freighter *Avignon* as they parted the warm, tropic-blue waters of the South China Sea. The ship which had left Hong Kong two days earlier was heading south towards the equator under a fierce afternoon sun, and in the sweltering darkness between decks, three hundred Chinese coolies and their families jostled together in silence, straining up towards the fresh air currents playing beyond the iron grilles that confined them.

On the upper deck outside the half-dozen first-class cabins, green-and-white-striped awnings fluttered gently in the breeze of the ship's movement, and in their shade Senator Nathaniel Sherman sprawled at ease in a canvas deck chair, his long legs splayed comfortably in front of him. Tall, ruddy-faced and tending to corpulence in his early forties, he had about him the self-satisfied air of a man who has already achieved some measure of public acclaim; he wore his thick shock of fair hair brushed across his forehead from a center parting in two matching wings, and his upper lip was thatched with a fashionably luxuriant mustache. He had removed the jacket of his white linen suit but the sense of decorum bred into him by his aristocratic Virginian upbringing compelled him to retain its matching vest and a cravat of maroon silk held in place with a small diamond pin. The same ostentatious pride in Southern good manners also prompted him to sit up immediately when one of the ship's white-uniformed junior officers appeared at his side bearing a tray of iced drinks for him, his wife and two sons.

"This sure is mighty civilized of you, m'sieur, to look after us like this," he drawled, letting a gracious smile play across his face. "Especially when you've already got your hands full running this tidy little ship."

"Please don't mention it, senator. The captain sends you these refreshments with his compliments." The young Frenchman inclined his head deferentially, speaking his English with the caution of one unused to employing it. "We have never before had the honor to carry such an important representative of the United States of America to Saigon."

"Please thank your captain most kindly for his consideration. Your legendary French hospitality promises to make our stay in your colony a memorable one."

The boyishly handsome officer inclined his head once more, then turned his back on the senator to offer the tray to his wife, Flavia, a strikingly beautiful woman in her late thirties. Her pale, oval face framed with raven-dark hair and her slender, high-breasted figure betrayed the Louisiana French blood in her veins, and the officer smiled directly into her eyes as she lifted a glass of fresh lime juice and *glace pilée* from his tray with a white-gloved hand.

"*Merci beaucoup, monsieur*," she murmured, smiling back at him for a fraction longer than necessary. "*Vous êtes trop gentil.*"

The Frenchman, before turning to her sons, let his glance fall pointedly for a moment to the swell of her breasts tightly bodiced beneath a new Fifth Avenue day dress of sheer white silk chiffon; then he smiled secretly at her again and this undisguised expression of passionate interest brought a faint flush to her face.

Across the table her younger son, Joseph, saw her cheeks burn, and she looked up to find him gazing at her in mystification. To hide her embarrassment she fumbled in her handbag for a little mirrored compact backed with tortoiseshell and turned away to repowder her face. Joseph took a glass from the officer's tray but didn't drink; instead he continued looking in his mother's direction, ready to smile in sympathy. To his puzzlement, however, she kept her eyes averted and wouldn't look at him.

"I wonder what he would have said, Chuck, if I'd told him he'd just served a drink to someone who's probably going to be much more important one day than a run-of-the-mill Democratic senator from Virginia?" Nathaniel Sherman chuckled and leaned confidentially towards his elder son's chair as the Frenchman departed. "What if I'd told him that the *Avignon* was carrying a young man named Charles Sherman who's destined one day maybe to become the *President* of the United States?" He squeezed Chuck's forearm, then glanced across at his younger son. "That would've made him sit up and take notice, Joey, wouldn't it?"

Joseph nodded and picked up his drink. "I guess it would, Daddy," he replied shortly and drained the glass without looking up.

Six years separated the two brothers, and although both were fair-haired, Charles Sherman at twenty-one bore the strongest resemblance to the senator. As tall as his father and with the slender, broad-shouldered build of a natural athlete, he had regular features of that open, well-chiseled handsomeness that also suggests unusual strength of character. Already he sported a blond mustache that was a passable imitation of the older man's, and he twisted a strand or two of it between finger and thumb as he shot a comic grimace of pain in Joseph's direction to convey his discomfort at the extravagant declaration of faith in him. Joseph grinned ruefully back at him for a moment, then sensing the senator was warming to a familiar theme, he picked up a history of French Indochina that lay open on the table before him and sank down in his chair behind it. Of slighter build than his brother, at fifteen Joseph still had the unfinished face of a growing boy, but his features were already set in a more thoughtful, reflective cast than Chuck's and there was a hint of his mother's sensitivity in his smile. When his father began talking again, a little irritated frown wrinkled his smooth young brow, but although he made a great play of concentrating fiercely on his reading, he still listened carefully from behind the book to what was being said.

"I know you come over a little shy when I talk about you this way, Chuck, but I do it for a good reason," continued the senator, lighting a Havana cigar with elaborate care. "It's never too soon to get a big idea planted in a young head. I believe there's nothing a man can't do once he's made up his mind. If you start early enough, there isn't a thing on this earth that can stand in the way of real determination — remember that. The Commonwealth of Virginia is famous as the birthplace of American presidents, isn't it? Washington, Jefferson and six other Virginians besides have led our nation; so why shouldn't President Charles Sherman in about thirty-five years' time — say round about nineteen sixty — be sitting in the White House? I've told you before — you've got to set your sights high." He paused and pointed his cigar at his elder boy in friendly admonition. "If you do, the impossible will start to seem probable."

Chuck Sherman squirmed in his deckchair and frowned humorously at his mother. "Oh boy, here we go again — you will come and visit me in the White House sometimes, Mother, won't you, so I don't get too lonely there?"

"Nothing would give your mother greater pleasure, I'm sure, Chuck, than to see you bring distinction to yourself and your family," cut in the senator reprovingly before his wife could reply. "She wants to see you succeed as much as I do."

Flavia Sherman smiled sympathetically at Chuck for a moment, then turned to her husband with an ill-concealed sigh of exasperation. "Wouldn't it be better, Nathaniel, to let us all relax and enjoy our expedition for a few weeks? Can't we leave Washington and Virginia politics at home just this once?"

"I certainly want us all to enjoy this rare journey, my dear," replied her husband, smiling and waving his cigar in front of his face in an expansive gesture. "Particularly you. You look most delightful this afternoon in that new frock. I think the trip's been a tonic for you already. It was lucky for us all, wasn't it, boys, that that fancy new Saks store opened up on Fifth Avenue just before we came away?" He directed an exaggerated wink at his two sons, then dropped his voice and reached out to pat his wife's hand on the arm of her chair. "I hear there's a rumor going around Manhattan that they had to close down again the day after you shopped there because they'd run out of Paris fashions; is that true?"

Flavia Sherman forced herself to smile while recoiling inwardly from his touch. During the past three days of the voyage her first contact for many years with French life had begun to stir long-forgotten feelings in her. The gallant compliments of the captain and his officers particularly had reminded her that the beauty so widely admired in her youth had not yet faded. The many deadening years spent bringing up a family in the narrow society of Tidewater Virginia seemed to be evaporating rapidly from her memory in the heat and excitement of the tropics. She had been lonely from the start of her marriage, despite the presence of a small army of black servants in the Queen Anne plantation house overlooking the James River, and several years had passed before she understood fully that her husband had used his frequent absences, at first on plantation business, then in Washington, to conceal an almost total lack of physical interest in her. Eventually she had become resigned to a dull, passionless existence; her husband had masked his indifference to her real feelings with elaborate public courtesies, and her only role outside of motherhood had been to act as a decorative hostess at his political functions. In the end she had become so used to living the lie of marital contentment that she had perhaps come to believe it herself. But now that her once-passionate nature was reawakening and she was beginning to feel vibrantly alive again, the cold perfunctory touch of her husband's fingers seemed suddenly more repugnant than ever before, and she withdrew her hand hastily from his and picked up her glass to conceal the real reason for breaking the contact.

"I shall be much happier, Nathaniel, if you don't bother Chuck every few minutes about his future," she said quietly without looking at her husband. "I'm sure he's very excited about the hunting. Why not just let him enjoy himself?"

Nathaniel Sherman removed his cigar from his mouth and patted her hand patronizingly once more. "You're right in one way of course, my dear. We certainly intend to enjoy the hunting and bag ourselves some of Cochin-China's rare game animals. But we *are* traveling to a little-known corner of the globe, remember. Life in a French colony in Asia will be very different from anything we've seen back home. Every journey, wherever you go, is a new education — that's what my father taught me! Chuck — and Joseph too, of course — might learn something here that will be useful to them later. I aim to help them learn to look at things right, that's all." He paused to smile at Chuck. "Even a Harvard man has still got an awful lot to learn from life. You don't get all the wisdom of the world from a library, no matter how good a scholar you might be. . . ."

The sudden snap of Joseph's history book closing caused the senator to glance up briefly but he didn't pause in his monologue; his abstracted gaze followed the younger boy for only a moment as he sauntered away along the deck. "The fact is, Chuck," he said turning back to his elder son, "just seeing what's happening around you isn't enough. Whether in Indochina or Washington you've got to learn to interpret events correctly. . . ."

Joseph kept walking until the slow drawl of his father's voice became inaudible to him. Then he stopped and leaned on the rail at the top of the companionway, staring with unseeing eyes at the deck below. He found he was angry with himself for leaving his seat; he had badly wanted to hear what his father was about to say, but the all-too-familiar sound of him praising his brother had produced its usual feeling of agitation. Not for the first time he wondered why it should affect him like that, when he himself was fond of Chuck and admired him, too. No answer suggested itself, however, and after a minute or two he became aware that as these thoughts whirled through his mind he had been staring down at the grilles confining the Chinese coolie families. They seemed to come into focus only slowly, a silent mass of tightly packed yellow faces glistening with perspiration; scores of dark eyes had been watching him unwaveringly all the time, but their expressions remained uniformly blank. He realized with a shock that they reminded him of steers he had once seen in a railroad siding back home in Richmond, Virginia, crowded uncomprehendingly in trucks bound for the slaughterhouse. He was wondering whether the slaves who had been shipped to America had looked like this, when he felt his mother's gentle touch on his shoulder and turned to find her smiling fondly at him.

"Don't brood about it, Joseph," she said softly. "You know your father gets a hornet in his hat every now and then about Chuck. But I'm expecting great things of you, too."

Joseph nodded and managed to smile back at her, relieved that they were communicating again. "It's nothing," he said quickly. "There's no need to worry about me."

At that moment the French captain of the *Avignon*, a stocky, spade-bearded man, appeared beside them smiling and holding a pith helmet in his hands. "You must always be careful, Monsieur Joseph, not to expose yourself unduly to the sun in the tropics." He placed the helmet squarely on the American boy's head and glanced at Flavia Sherman, who had put on a wide-brimmed sun hat of white felt decorated with colored ribbons. "Your *chapeau* doesn't look as pretty as your mother's but it will save you from sunstroke just as effectively."

Because the captain had spoken French, Joseph thanked him haltingly in that language, then motioned towards the lower deck. "But what about those people down there, monsieur? They must be feeling the heat worse than any of us — and there are women and children among them."

"They're potential troublemakers, young Joey, that's why they're kept under lock and key."

The French officer half turned at the sound of Nathaniel Sherman's voice as he came up behind them with Chuck, and nodded in agreement. "You are perfectly correct, senator," he said switching to English. "There are three hundred Chinese on board and only a handful of us. They are illiterate coolies from Canton mostly, emigrating to Cochin-China. But there may be pirates hiding among them. The waters of the China coast are full of pirates. Only last week a gang boarded a British ship disguised as steerage passengers. They attacked the bridge in the dead of night and when the crew barricaded themselves in, they set fire to the decks."

Joseph's innocent eyes widened in alarm. "What happened? Were they all burned alive?"

"Fortunately not." The captain smiled at the eager intensity of Joseph's inquiry. "The British master of the ship turned her to windward and the fire was blown back towards the pirate mob. They all had to jump overboard and a lot of them drowned."

"Wow, that was a smart trick," breathed Joseph, his face alight with excitement at the thought of the drama. Then his expression clouded again. "But all the Chinese down there can't be pirates, can they? Isn't it a bit unfair on them?"

"It's only for the voyage, remember," said the captain smoothly. "There is no other way. Certain things have to be done differently in the colonies." He lifted his shoulders in a little Gallic shrug of helplessness and smiled. "*C'est la vie coloniale*, Monsieur Joseph. You will soon get accustomed to it."

Joseph's expression remained dubious for a moment, then his face lit up again and he pointed westward over the captain's shoulder. "Isn't that land over there?" he exclaimed excitedly.

The Frenchman peered through his binoculars for a moment. "Yes, Monsieur Joseph, you are right. That is the coast of the most beautiful and prosperous French colony in the world." He glanced at his watch and offered the glasses to the American boy. "Would you like to look? We shall probably be landing in Saigon sometime after lunch tomorrow."

With his naked eye Joseph had glimpsed only a faint smudge of coastline, but through the glasses he was able to see more clearly some of the rocky peaks of the thousand-mile-long mountain spine that linked the rich southern rice lands of the Mekong delta and Saigon with the fertile plain of the Red River around Hanoi in the north. From the book he'd just put down he knew that vast tracts of virgin tropical forest covered those mountainsides and large areas of the lowlands too; in the book there were sepia-tinted photographs of primitive tribesmen who still hunted with stone-tipped arrows and poison darts in those same forests that also teemed with elephant herds, tiger, buffalo, black bears and countless other rare species of animal life that had been left undisturbed by the march of civilization. Joseph had devoured the contents of the book avidly during the long Pacific crossing and had begun reading it again after they left Hong Kong.

As he peered through the binoculars he felt a tremor of excitement course through him at the prospect of seeing the printed images come to life. For a moment he let himself imagine he was some great explorer about to enter a hostile, unknown land on which his name would later be stamped for all history. Then he wondered if great explorers ever felt as he did — excited, yes, but more than a little frightened too! Remembering suddenly that Chuck and his father were standing behind him, he blushed inwardly at the thought. Could they detect the excitement he felt? Could they read the apprehension of his expression? The last thing he wanted them to think was that, at fifteen, he was immature. As he turned and handed the binoculars to his elder brother he frowned in what he hoped was a manly, intent manner and tried to make his voice sound casual. "Looks a bit like Virginia Beach in a heavy haze, if you ask me," he said and attempted to shrug like the French captain.

Chuck Sherman, who had noticed the excited gleam in his

17

young brother's eyes, grinned and punched him affectionately on the arm as he took the binoculars, but before he could lift them to his eyes a tumult of shouting and screaming broke out suddenly among the throng of Chinese pressing up against the iron grille below them. All the Shermans turned to watch in alarm as the captain dashed away down the companionway, dragging a revolver from inside his white uniform tunic. Beside the grille he dropped to one knee and fired three quick shots into the air. The sound of the gun silenced the Chinese for a few seconds, then a lone woman's voice began wailing again and the Shermans saw a thin ragged body forced up against the underside of the grille.

After a muttered exchange through the bars, the captain ordered two of his officers to stand by with pistols drawn while he unfastened the padlocks. When the grille swung open he called two or three seamen to his side and ordered them to haul the corpse out onto the deck. He allowed a thin, ill-clad woman to scramble out behind it, and immediately she fell to her knees beside the body and began wailing once more. Ignoring her, the captain ordered his men to carry the body aft, and the woman eventually rose and hobbled after them, still sobbing piteously.

Flavia Sherman turned her back to the rail and closed her eyes; her face was pale and she was trembling. "How dreadful," she said at last. "It's a wonder any of them survive in there."

"I shouldn't lose too much sleep over it, my dear," said the senator in a soothing voice. "Chinese coolies are tough. They live hard lives. They don't crave the same bodily comforts as we do. Life is cheap to them." He leaned over the rail to peer down onto the lower deck. The captain's party had disappeared, and the Chinese beneath the grilles had grown quiet again. "You might say, Chuck," he said over his shoulder, "that you've just witnessed a very clear demonstration of the principle on which every empire in history's ever been built. Julius Caesar and Alexander the Great knew it, and so did Britain's Queen Victoria — 'might is right.' Here and now the French have the power, so the Asians on their ship and throughout Indochina do as they tell them. That's the way of the world. The rich and the powerful call the tune. If you can muster superior strength, you can impose your way of thinking on others — even if they don't like what you do or the way you do it. If you've got bigger muscles and the will to use them, the others have to go along with you. Nothing's ever going to change that." He paused and glanced about him to check that no French crew members were within earshot. "The French have a heavy hand. They like to use an elephant gun to stun a flea. You'll see that when we get ashore. I'm told they behave here as if they expect their empire to last forever. We know different in America. The French way isn't the American way. We do things different, boys — and do things better. . . ."

The senator took his elder son by the elbow and, still talking, motioned him to stroll with him along the deck. Joseph watched them go, then he glanced back at his mother with a troubled expression in his eyes. "Do you think those people down there are really so different from us, Momma?" he asked, keeping his voice low so that it wouldn't carry to his father's ears.

Flavia Sherman brushed away a strand of hair that had fallen across his eyes and smiled fondly at him. "Life is full of impossible questions like that, Joseph. They're very different in many ways, no doubt. But we're all still made of flesh and blood, aren't we?"

His face remained creased with thought and she could see that the answer hadn't satisfied him. To distract him she put an arm around his shoulders and moved away from the rail. "Don't worry about it any more for the moment. Let's go back and sit together in the shade, shall we? Then you can tell me some more about that book you've been buried in for the past week."

2

"Oh boy," breathed Chuck Sherman, gazing longingly at the impenetrable green wall of tropical foliage slipping past only a few yards from the ship's rail, "this is going to make the mountains of West Virginia seem a bit tame. How d'you think you're going to feel, Joey, when we come face to face with a herd of elephant or a tawny tiger out there?"

"I thought we weren't out to shoot elephants or tigers," replied Joseph absently.

"We're not going looking for them, genius — but they don't know that, do they? If they come looking for us with tusk and fang you'd better be ready with that Winchester peashooter of yours."

"I suppose so." Joseph nodded automatically.

They had left their cabins early to enjoy the fresh morning breeze, and Joseph had perched himself on a coil of rope beside Chuck at the rail to finish his reading. The clear, blue water of the river mouth had given way to a brown muddy flow as the ship moved inland, and both banks were now lined with natural stockades of tall, fleshy-leaved trees that trailed tangled creepers over the water. In occasional clearings the American boys caught sight of slender natives in conical, palm-leaf hats bending over fishing lines or snares for river fowl, but they rarely looked up; only the naked, potbellied children paid any attention, staring at the *Avignon* with brown, expressionless eyes as it swung past the low banks on which they stood. Sometimes the sudden screech of an unseen bird startled the brothers, but otherwise the brilliant green tropical forest through which they were gliding remained eerily silent.

"I'll bet you don't know, Chuck, how Saigon got its name, do you?" exclaimed Joseph at last, closing the book and jumping to his feet. "It's really quite interesting."

"I don't know how it got its name, no," replied the older boy smiling patiently, "but no doubt some book-reading bore is about to inform me."

"In old Annamese it means 'Village of the Boxwoods,' after the trees that originally grew there. It wasn't much more than a fishing village until the eighteenth century when French Jesuits and a few merchants demanded the right to build a city. But its name could also be based on the Chinese characters '*Tsai Con,*' which mean 'Tribute paid to the West.' "

"Fascinating," said Chuck facetiously. "You're still king of the useless-information department."

The *Avignon*'s captain, strolling down from the bridge in a crisp, freshly starched uniform, smiled on hearing their banter and approached to greet them both with a formal French handshake. "No matter what the Annamese named it, my dear young sirs, you'll find that we French call the city you are about to visit 'the Pearl of the Orient' or sometimes even 'the Paris of the East.' And it won't take you long to see why."

"But why are all these Chinese going there?" asked Joseph, dropping his voice and nodding towards the sea of silent yellow faces still pressed against the underside of the grilles in the deck below.

"Saigon has a twin city, Cholon, a mile or two away across the plain — that's where they're making for. 'Cho Lon' in Annamese means 'Great Market,' and they hope to make their fortune there as many Cantonese emigrants have done, by exploiting the lazy Annamese. There are already two hundred thousand Chinese living in Cholon and you can buy everything there from a pipe of opium to a slant-eyed 'singing girl.' " He paused and winked surreptitiously at Chuck to emphasize his innuendo. "Your father will have to go to Cholon to buy all your hunting supplies, too. Warn him to be careful. Bargain hard! The Chinese are the Jews of Asia."

"How much longer will it take us to get there, captain?" asked Chuck impatiently. "This jungle seems to go on forever."

"The journey from the river mouth to the city takes six or seven hours normally, Monsieur Charles. It's about sixty miles. All too soon, I regret, we shall be forced to say *adieu* to you and your distinguished father."

"It can't come too soon for me, captain." Senator Sherman advanced smiling affably across the deck, still getting into his jacket. "I mean no disrespect, of course. We've been greatly flattered by your generous hospitality on board. But we're mighty anxious now we've come all this way to get out into that jungle just as soon as we can and start hunting."

"What will you be going for, senator? A tiger skin for your floor? A pair of tusks for the wall?"

"Neither, captain. We're not souvenir hunters. Before he died my father set up a trust to endow the Sherman Field Museum of Natural History in Washington. Natural history was a special interest of his, you see. He died five years ago but the museum's only just been finished on the Mall below Capitol Hill. It's really a pretty sight, captain, built of Tennessee marble like one of those old palaces in Florence. So we want to put only the best wild animals in it, and here in these jungles of yours you've got some of the rarest animals in the world. . . ."

The senator paused to light his first Havana of the day and as he got it going he studied the matted vegetation of the riverbank through its smoke. From the corner of his eye Joseph saw his mother emerge from her cabin. As she walked down the companionway to the lower deck the breeze molded her couture suit of cream silk bouquette against the contours of her body. On the bridge he saw the third officer raise his hand to his cap in a debonair salute, and she waved gaily back. Joseph noticed that she avoided passing close to the iron grilles closing off the between-deck areas of the ship and when she reached the stern she gazed into the jungle for a moment, then closed her eyes and lifted her face to the gentle warmth of the morning sun.

". . . We're going mainly for wild water buffalo, banteng and seladang," said the senator, his resonant Southern drawl sounding loud in the stillness that lay over the river. "And we don't just want the big bulls. We need a pair of each — and calves, too, where we can. That will require some fancy shooting. We'll skin them right here and preserve their hides so they can be shipped home and stuffed. Then they'll be put on show in what we call 'habitat displays' so that all the people of America who won't ever come here will be able to see them in our nation's capital just as they once lived in these jungles. We'll send other expeditions to India and Africa for tiger and elephant later. You see, captain, I want to make the Sherman Field Museum the finest of its kind in the United States, maybe even the finest in the world."

"And who is the family's leading marksman?" asked the captain, glancing inquiringly at Chuck and Joseph in turn.

"Chuck here is a deadeye," replied the senator, ruffling the hair of his elder son. "He's learned everything that I can teach him. We hunt in the mountains of West Virginia every fall and he shoots now nearly as well as his daddy."

"And Monsieur Joseph is a budding 'deadeye' too?" asked the captain, rolling the unfamiliar expression off his tongue with a grin.

"Well Joseph isn't too sure yet what he's going to be. He can shoot well enough if he wants, I think, but just can't seem to make up his mind whether he likes the idea that much." The senator's smile faded and he leaned over the rail to let the ash that had formed on his cigar fall into the muddy river. "His mother isn't that keen on hunting, and he maybe sides with her a little. I guess we'll find out for sure what Joseph's made of here in Cochin-China."

The captain saw the corners of Joseph's mouth tighten momentarily, then the American boy's eyes widened and he pointed excitedly over the starboard rail. "Captain, what's that out there? Is it a native temple? It looks enormous."

Two pointed spires of stone had become visible, seeming to sprout from the middle of the jungle, and the captain laughed again. "It's a native temple of sorts, I suppose, Monsieur Joseph. Dedicated, you will find, to the main religion of my own native country. Those are the steeples of Saigon Cathedral — the first sight any traveler ever sees of 'the Pearl of the Orient.' "

"But we aren't going towards them, captain," protested Joseph, standing on the bottom rail and craning his neck to get a better view.

"That's right — not at the moment. The Saigon River now begins to wind like a serpent. It's like sailing through a maze. Every time I come here I begin to worry that I have somehow crossed into another stream and am sailing back in the opposite direction."

The *Avignon*'s bows had begun to swing rapidly through all the points of the compass as the river meandered on through the jungle, and the tips of the cathedral spires seemed to dart around the ship, popping up first in one quarter then another like the ears of an inquisitive rabbit trying to follow its progress. Joseph saw them one minute to port, then the next minute to starboard, and once they even appeared dead astern as the river turned back on itself. After an hour the ship emerged from the jungle, and the Shermans found themselves gazing across an open alluvial plain dotted with isolated clumps of palm. Rice paddies stretched away endlessly on either side of the ship, and they saw crowds of Annamese in cone-shaped hats of palm leaf already at work, sometimes wading waist-deep in the muddy water.

For a while Flavia Sherman joined them at the rail and stood with her hand resting on Joseph's shoulder; but she seemed restless and soon tired of watching the peasants at work in the fields. As the sun climbed higher in the sky, the heat grew gradually more oppressive, and Chuck and his father also retreated to the shade of their cabins. Joseph joined them briefly to gobble down his lunch then rushed back on deck alone, wearing his sun helmet, and stood at the rail eagerly devouring with his eyes each new detail of the ever-changing scene.

The *Avignon* sailed in and out of thick belts of marshy, deserted jungle, and sometimes he caught sight of villages of stilted houses with matting walls built in the clearings. He waved his helmet in greeting at several groups of Annamese squatting in the dirt before their doors, but they gazed back at him unmoving. When the river broadened, the *Avignon* began to encounter other craft that had started downstream from Saigon on the favorable tide, and Joseph wondered why the battered-looking Chinese junks, with their shabby, patched sails, didn't sink as they lumbered past among a succession of grimy workhorse freighters from Europe and Latin America. A long French liner slipped majestically by with a mixture of European and Asian faces staring curiously from its rails, then the *Avignon* was pushing its way through a swarm of sampans moving downriver on local errands, most of them rowed, to Joseph's surprise, by women. Gradually the water emptied of departing traffic and the *Avignon* glided on along the muddy river in the deep silence of a blistering noontide.

The white stone wharf, when it appeared, took him by surprise. It ran beside a broad, shaded boulevard of feathery pepper trees, and the sudden sight of European-style buildings made him reflect that the jungles, fields and villages through which they'd been moving for the past few hours had remained unchanging

23

throughout many centuries. But there without doubt were the elusive twin spires of Saigon's cathedral that he'd seen from far off, stationary now and clearly visible, standing sentinel over the wide, tree-lined avenues. They had really arrived at last at their destination!

Then Joseph realized why they had come upon the city so completely by surprise; it was the uncanny silence. No sound of any kind rose from the hot deserted streets — no traffic noise, no hustle of people, no children, no animals. There was no movement either, along the quay in front of long rows of deserted customs sheds. It was with a sickening sense of shock that his eyes fell at last on the heaps of bodies lying in the shadows of the dock buildings and beneath the pepper trees. He grabbed his binoculars with trembling hands and swept the long quay as the *Avignon* drew nearer, scrutinizing each pile of bodies in turn. There was no doubt about it! The men lay crumpled and motionless, open-mouthed, their thin legs tangled together. Through the lenses he could see clearly that their faces and clothing were covered with blood.

"Captain, captain!" he called frantically, running towards the bridge. "Come quick, there's been a terrible massacre in Saigon."

The captain, to his horror, emerged from the wheelhouse smiling. "A massacre, Monsieur Joseph?"

"Yes. Yes. You can see the blood — look! On their faces! Everywhere!" His own face had turned pale.

The captain followed the direction of the American boy's pointing finger for a moment, then lifted his left wrist and showed him the dial of his watch. "Look, Monsieur Joseph, it's almost two o'clock. It's still siesta time. Nobody in the tropics moves between eleven-thirty and two in the afternoon. Their very lives would have to be at stake first. My countrymen are all dozing at home by their electric fans, but the natives aren't so fortunate." He waved his hand along the dock. "They have only the shade of the trees."

"But why have they got blood all over them?"

The captain laughed. "That isn't blood, Monsieur Joseph. The Annamese all chew betel nut. It's a mild drug. It dulls the senses but the juice stains their mouth and their clothes — even the street when they spit."

Joseph stared at him in disbelief. Then he looked back again at the blinding quayside. In the shade beneath the trees he saw that the "massacred" Annamite coolies were beginning to come to life; they untangled themselves from one another with painful slowness and staggered to their feet. The ship's engines ceased and the crew began throwing down ropes to a white man in a pith helmet who had emerged from one of the quayside offices. Like sleepwalkers in a dream the coolies began advancing out of the shade towards the ship. As they came, many of them spat repeatedly, leaving behind them a trail of crimson, betel-stained saliva on the burning concrete of the wharf.

3

"*Pousse-pousse! Pousse-pousse!*" yelled Chuck Sherman and sprang down the steps of the Continental Palace Hotel into the Rue Catinat with his arm raised in the manner of a French *colon*. Immediately a swarm of coolies rushed towards him, dragging their wire-wheeled rickshaws behind them, and he leaped into the nearest one with a loud whoop. "*Allez! Allez! Vite! Vite!*" he yelled, clapping his hands, and the coolie set off instantly at a frantic gallop along the boulevard.

Joseph clambered aboard his *pousse-pousse* more tentatively. Both brothers were dressed in neatly tailored white tuxedos and black ties in preparation for the formal reception being given in their father's honor at the palace of the governor of Cochin-China, and it was Chuck who had insisted that they travel separately by *pousse-pousse* rather than in the official Citroën sent for their parents. "This way we'll get to see more of the real Saigon," he said loudly for the benefit of their father — then he winked confidentially at Joseph and whispered in his ear: "And the last one there is a horse's ass. It's a race, okay?"

Before Joseph could agree or disagree, his brother had mounted up and was laughing loudly as he urged his coolie along the boulevard at top speed. Joseph could see tufts of grizzled hair protruding from beneath the sweat-soaked turban wrapped around the head of his aged coolie and he didn't have the heart to order him to gallop. He was stripped to the waist and as he jogged along between the shafts a few coins — obviously his meager earnings for the day — jingled pathetically in a leather pouch fastened to the back of his belt.

Before he'd gone a hundred yards Joseph saw a burly French *colon* cuff an Annamite coolie roughly about the head at the curbside after descending from his *pousse-pousse*. The American boy turned in his seat and stared, expecting to see a fight, but the cowering Annamite accepted his beating meekly and none of the European passersby spared the man a second glance. Half a minute later another Frenchman sent his *pousse-pousse* puller staggering in the gutter with a blow to the head after an apparent argument about the fare, and Joseph realized with a shock that such beatings were merely routine. Outside the hotel he had fought down misgivings at the idea of allowing an old man to drag him through the streets when he could easily have walked, and he began to wonder if he should dismount. But when he caught up with Chuck, who had at last relented and allowed his breathless coolie to slow to a trot, he found the older boy grinning and lolling casually in his seat, obviously suffering no such pangs of conscience.

"I don't find these little oriental chariots altogether unpleasant as a mode of transport, Joey," he said, affecting an exaggerated Harvard drawl. "How about you?"

"Not bad — not bad at all," replied Joseph hurriedly and he tried to lean back against the cushions in the same careless fashion as his brother while the two rickshaws rolled on together side by side through the light traffic.

The approach of evening and release from the heat had transformed the city through which they rode, and the tree-lined streets that had been scorched and deserted on their arrival were coming rapidly to life. Saigon's main boulevard, the Rue Catinat, linked the docks and the cathedral, symbols of the twin goals of commerce and religion which had led France to colonize the land, and in its fashionable sidewalk cafés they saw deferential Annamese waiters in black turbans and linen gowns darting among the marble-topped tables, serving aperitifs to languid groups of their European colonizers. Beneath the tamarind trees white-suited Frenchmen and their women strolled with an indolent confidence through the native throng — goateed mandarins in Chinese long gowns, younger Annamese wearing round caps and black knee-length silk jackets and occasional groups of shabby peasants arrayed in dark calico, cartwheel-sized straw hats and wooden sandals. Bright red betel juice, the brothers noticed, stained the lips of all the Annamese, low- and high-born alike.

But evidence of the betel habit was no longer the most striking sight for the two Americans. Among the slow-moving crowds slender, graceful Annamese girls wearing traditional silken *ao dai* caught their eye again and again. The pastel-colored costumes were at once demure and provocative; fitted tight from throat to hip, they clung to every line of the delicate, high-breasted figures, heightening the allure of slender shoulders, tiny waists and the swell of young flanks; below the waist, however, the gossamer-light, side-split skirts and billowing trousers of white silk shrouded legs and thighs in secrecy, and to Chuck and Joseph the exotic girls of Saigon seemed not to walk but to float gently beneath the tamarinds on the evening breeze.

Chuck peered intently at each girl they passed, but without exception they avoided his gaze. "The local flappers appear most agreeable, if unduly maidenly, don't you think, Joey?" he called, grinning wolfishly across at his brother from his moving rickshaw.

"Indeed they do, Charles!" Joseph laughed and smacked his lips loudly, feeling very grown up. He had felt sure when he left his hotel room that every eye in Saigon would be on him that evening because he was wearing a white tuxedo for the very first time in his young life. The Continental Palace orchestra had been playing the new popular melody "Tea for Two" as he came out onto the terrace, and he had been faintly surprised in the event that nobody had turned to stare at him. He had noticed the eyes of one or two French matrons stray wistfully to the tall, spectacularly handsome figure of his brother, and as the rickshaws bowled on side by side he darted a glance at him and decided it must be his new blond mustache that set him apart. Enviously he raised his fingers to his own top lip but could still detect only the finest thistledown there.

"You look just great in that new white tux, Joey," called Chuck suddenly, as though reading his mind. The rickshaws moved together and he leaned across and punched his brother affectionately on the biceps. "I'm sure you're going to be the belle of the Saigon ball tonight."

Joseph leaned outwards and aimed a violent retaliatory blow at his brother's midriff, but at that moment both rickshaws swerved apart and skidded to a halt. Joseph looked ahead and saw that their side of the boulevard was blocked by two carts with big, iron-rimmed wheels. One had overturned and they stared in amazement as a swarthy-featured European lashed out with a thick bamboo cane at what they first thought was a small animal collapsed between the shafts. When they looked closer they saw that he was whipping, not a fallen beast, but a spindly-legged Annamese; both carts, they could see, contained refuse and had shafts front and back that terminated in *cangue*, big wooden halters that were locked around the necks of four sweating Annamese. These human beasts of burden also wore heavy leg-irons chained to thick steel bands clamped around their waists.

The Americans watched the bamboo rod rise and fall and heard the sickening thud of wood on flesh and bone; as the fallen Annamese struggled to raise himself from the dusty road they saw blood welling from the crimson weals on his back. His eyes were squeezed tight in agony, and he and the other three men locked in the shafts grunted loudly with exertion as they strove to get the heavy carts rolling again. Gradually they began to move and the *colon* flayed each of them in turn once more to increase their speed. As the carts came abreast of the Americans seated in their stationary rickshaws, the Annamese who had fallen opened his eyes, and his pain-clouded gaze locked for a moment with Joseph's. Then his lids fell closed again and the veins in his neck and forehead bulged as he strained afresh against the neck halter.

When the carts had moved on Joseph turned a horrified face to his brother. "Those poor devils looked nearly dead, Chuck."

The elder boy nodded grimly. "That certainly wasn't betel juice on their backs this time."

A thin, stoop-shouldered Frenchman wearing a pince-nez, who had been watching and listening from the curbside, stepped into the road suddenly and leaned close enough to Chuck for the American boy to smell the garlic on his breath. "They are prisoners! Convicted criminals! They deserve nothing better. Don't feel sorry for them. All outsiders make that mistake." He spoke heavily accented English, screwing up his pinched sallow face in disgust. He carried a silver-topped malacca cane and he waved this vaguely in the direction of the strolling crowds all around them. "These people are not like the white races. Don't think that. Most of them are idle, work-shy, good-for-nothing. Don't waste your sympathy on them." He peered belligerently through his pince-nez from one brother to the other, then turned and stumped off, shouldering his way roughly through the oncoming crowds of Annamese.

The Sherman brothers looked at each other in silence. Then Chuck shrugged dismissively and raised his eyebrows. "Like the captain of the *Avignon* said, it's another world — different from ours."

When his coolie picked up the shafts and broke into his loping stride, Joseph found he couldn't look at the narrow, sweat-streaked shoulders bobbing in front of him without seeing the bleeding welts caused by the French *colon*'s cane. A sudden surge of compassion washed through him, and when they reached the governor's palace Joseph rashly thrust two piastres into the coolie's cupped hands, thanking him over and over again in French. This was more than three times the normal fare, and the astonished

Annamese stood between the shafts of his vehicle staring after Joseph in amazement until he and Chuck disappeared inside the palace.

4

The white stone *palais* of the governor of Cochin-China was built in the grandiloquent, neoclassical style favored by those fervently patriotic Frenchmen who had erected the great public buildings of Paris in the late nineteenth century. Surrounded by formal gardens in a square off the Rue de la Grandière, its imposing façade of fluted Doric columns and carved balustrades had been designed to serve as an enduring testament in stone to the colonial nation's confident pride in itself. A high-domed cupola of glass and wrought-iron crowned its roof, and from a flagstaff on its summit the French tricolor fluttered in the faint evening breeze as Chuck and Joseph Sherman arrived. They found their parents waiting for them at the top of a wide terrace of marble steps, and the governor's aide-de-camp conducted them to the reception through a series of lofty, marble-floored chambers forty feet high.

In the *grand salon* white-robed Annamese servants glided silently among the potted palms with silver trays, serving chilled champagne to a big crowd of *colons* already gathered there. The French men were identically garbed in black trousers and "*le smoking*" — a white dinner jacket cut away at the waist — while the women wore dresses from shops in the Rue Catinat fashionable enough to allow them to forget that the Rue de la Paix was a twelve-thousand-mile sea journey away. The governor himself stood waiting to greet them beneath a large, gilt-framed portrait of the Emperor Napoleon. A tall, haughty man with luxuriant black whiskers and beard, he wore a formal uniform of horizon blue trimmed elaborately with gold. On the left breast of his tunic the insignia of the Légion d'Honneur glimmered among a broad cluster of medals, and his plumed tricorne had been placed ostentatiously on a table at his side. He didn't smile as the Shermans approached but waited with his left hand resting on the hilt of his ceremonial sword, his aloof expression suggesting that he estimated the dignity of his person to be at least equal to that of the fabled hero of France looking down from the wall behind him.

"*Bienvenu à la plus belle colonie de la France!*" The governor offered a formal, white-gloved hand to each member of the Sherman family in turn, but when the affably smiling senator began to say how pleased they were to be there, the aide-de-camp immediately cut him short and motioned the family aside so that the governor could begin a formal speech.

"Senator and Madame Sherman, I am highly honored to welcome such a distinguished family as yours to French Indo-china," he said, speaking sonorously in his own language. "You have come here chiefly to hunt the rare wild animals in our jungles so that the people of America will be able to see them on display in the Sherman Museum in Washington. We wish you good fortune and good hunting while you are in our colony — but of course that is not all." He lifted his head and gazed unseeing towards the ceiling while his aide read a translation of his remarks from a sheet of paper. Then he resumed in the same imperious tone. "We are all very proud of the progress that has been made by France in Cochin-China and the other lands of the French Indochinese Union in recent years. Here I hope you will see some evidence of the high moral purpose with which the government of France is endeavoring to fulfill its civilizing mission." He slowed his delivery to linger emphatically on each syllable of the French expression "*mission civilisatrice*," gazing proudly around at the assembled gathering as he did so. "We have brought new roads, railways and the telegraph to this backward corner of the globe that would otherwise have continued to languish in the toils of an unprogress-ive past. We have developed rubber plantations, coal mines and other modern industrial amenities in cooperation with the hard-working Annamese, and all these ventures serve the best interests of both the French and the Annamese peoples. We hope our American visitors will have an opportunity to appreciate some of these achievements during their journeys here. We wish them all a pleasant and successful stay."

While the aide translated these remarks Joseph Sherman took the opportunity to glance around the room and noticed for the first time that groups of diminutive Annamese were standing quietly with their wives among the taller European men and women. Some wore brightly colored Chinese long gowns and black mandarin bonnets, others, shorter black silk coats and white trousers. Only a few were dressed in European suits, but each of them cultivated a wispy goatee, the mark of the Annamite man of consequence. All, in differing degrees, Joseph noticed, appeared ill-at-ease, looking neither at the governor nor at each other but directing their eyes most frequently towards the floor.

"If the lovely boulevards of Saigon are anything to judge by, *Monsieur le Gouverneur*, you have already brought great civilizing benefits to this tropical colony of yours," Nathaniel Sherman was saying. His public voice was richer in its Southern tones than normal and he was delivering his words in the slow, measured cadences that he normally employed on the floor of the Senate. "Your fine capital fully justifies its appellation, 'the Pearl of the Orient,' and the people in its streets seem content and happy and are obviously at ease under your benevolent governance. . . ."

Joseph frowned, then looked at Chuck in puzzlement. He had told his father about the *pousse-pousse* coolies being beaten by their passengers, and he had seemed to listen. "Do you think he didn't believe me?" whispered Joseph, but Chuck merely shrugged in reply.

"Our two nations, monsieur, hold many beliefs in common," the senator continued smoothly. "We both are ready and willing to shoulder the responsibilities and duties which fall upon the rich and powerful nations of the world. Once the United States was itself a colony and fought hard for its freedom and independence. I'm sure your enlightened civilizing mission which is bringing modern communications and industry so unselfishly to the Annamese people will make sure that no such conflict will ever be necessary here. . . ."

The aide-de-camp was quietly providing a running translation of the senator's remarks and the governor looked up sharply at the mention of the word "independence." But he found the American rocking on his heels and smiling back at him engagingly, and the slow drawl of his address continued without pause. "I think I should point out too, monsieur, that there are other closer links between our family and France." He flourished his hand in the direction of his wife like a showman introducing his star attraction of the evening. "My lovely wife, Flavia, was born in an old French colony that the great man in that picture on the wall behind you, *Monsieur le Gouverneur*, sold to the United States for fifteen million dollars in the year 1803. The Emperor Napoleon got a good deal because France would have had to give it up sooner or later anyway, and I got a good deal because Louisiana gave me a lovely companion for life with all the legendary charms of your people."

He turned a dazzling smile on Flavia and she smiled back, her cheeks flushing faintly. She already knew from the sour expressions of the French wives among the gathering and the open admiration in the eyes of their sallow, perspiring spouses that she had achieved an outstanding success with her greatest extravagance, a simple couture gown of lilac organza. She had dressed her hair daringly with ivory combs, sweeping it straight back from her face to emphasize her high cheekbones, then letting it fall behind her in a dark torrent that contrasted sharply with the pale silk of her gown. Her cheeks were already aglow from a combination of the heat and the exhilaration of being the center of attention, and this had lent an extra, youthful radiance to her beauty.

"She gave up on me a long time ago, but she made sure that my two sons, Charles and Joseph, speak the language of her forebears, and that will stand us in good stead in your colony." He paused and beamed affably at his host once more. "We thank you most heartily, *Monsieur le Gouverneur*, for your kind and hospitable welcome."

When the aide finished translating the senator's remarks the assembled *colons* applauded politely and an Annamese servant hovering nearby offered champagne to the group. The governor immediately raised his glass in Flavia Sherman's direction and complimented her elaborately on her French ancestry and the "astonishing combination" of her beauty and her two fine sons. "I trust you will not spend all your time hunting, Madame Sherman," he added, smiling for the first time. "Your presence would greatly enhance the dull routine of colonial life if you chose to attend any of our social occasions."

She returned his smile, then darted a quick glance at her husband; seeing he was engaged in conversation with the governor's aide, she allowed a confiding note to enter her voice. "Life in Virginia is very limited, monsieur. The social and cultural horizons are very narrow. I've been looking forward to this visit for a long time for that reason. My youngest son, Joseph, is very interested in history, and we are going to Hue to look at the Imperial City and watch the emperor perform the traditional ceremonies of Tet."

"Then I will hope to have the pleasure of meeting you again in the ancient city of the Annamese emperors," said the governor, smiling again. "I too shall be attending the ceremonies prior to a few days' relaxation at the hill station of Dalat."

At that moment the senator's wife sensed the eyes of another man upon her and turned her head quickly to find a tall, lean-faced Frenchman in a white dinner jacket standing beside the governor's aide, watching her intently. Because she turned unexpectedly she surprised him in an unguarded moment of frank sexual appraisal, but his dark, unsmiling gaze continued to hold hers steadily until she looked away again. The governor's aide, who had noticed her turn, saw his chance and ushered the silent Frenchman into the circle.

"Senator and Madame Sherman, may I present the man who will be your guide and mentor in the jungle, Monsieur Jacques Devraux. Monsieur Devraux was formerly an officer of the Infanterie Coloniale but he is now our most accomplished hunter of big game."

Jacques Devraux pressed her fingers briefly and bent his dark head for an instant over her hand. She felt his lips brush against her skin and heard his murmured "*Enchanté*," but he didn't look at her again before greeting the senator.

"I'm glad to meet you, Monsieur Devraux," cried Nathaniel Sherman, treating the Frenchman to a warm, vigorous handshake. "We've got a lot to talk over. How soon do you think we can get our supplies together? When might we think of making a start?"

The governor raised his shaggy brows at Flavia Sherman in a theatrical expression of sympathy as her husband launched into a detailed discussion of his hunting plans, and taking her by the elbow, he guided her away towards the waiting throng to begin introducing her.

As they departed an Annamese servant appeared soundlessly at Joseph Sherman's elbow, offering him another glass of champagne. The American boy stared at his empty glass, which he had drained nervously at a gulp, and looked uncertainly towards the figure of his mother fast disappearing among the crowd. She had admonished him before they left the hotel to drink no more than one glass, and his brother, Chuck, who was sipping his own wine confidently without the restraint of any such embargo, looked down and laughed good-naturedly at his indecision. "It looks like Momma's upstaged you — she's the real belle of the ball after all, not you. So take another one and drown your sorrows — I'll be responsible."

Joseph scowled back with mock ferocity at his brother as he picked up another glass and he was sipping it more circumspectly when a grinning dark-haired French youth of about eighteen approached them, holding out his hand.

"*Bonsoir, messieurs*, I'm Paul Devraux. I help my father and I was very glad to hear that you speak good French. The only English phrases I have learned so far are: 'You have a beautiful figure' . . . 'Will you go to bed with me?' . . . 'I love you.' . . . And I don't think these expressions would be much use between us."

Both brothers laughed out loud at the deliberately comic

delivery of his English phrases as they shook hands. Paul Devraux's features bore a strong resemblance to his father's, but his dark eyes twinkled mischievously in his sunburned face and he affected a droll, cynical expression.

"I hope you enjoyed our governor's speech," he said, leaning confidently towards them. "But don't believe everything he says. Some people claim it is not really a *mission civilisatrice* at all that the French are conducting here. There were no brothels in the colony you see before we came — but every town now has a fair selection. So perhaps it should really be called a *mission syphilisatrice* — in English a 'mission of syphilization,' yes?"

Chuck guffawed uncontrollably and Joseph laughed too, but a little uncertainly, wondering whether he correctly understood the French boy's irreverent humor.

"It's really true then, Paul, is it, what we hear about Frenchmen?" inquired Chuck in a low voice. "That they are all sex maniacs?"

"It certainly is not true!" Paul Devraux allowed himself to look outraged for a moment. "Only *most* of us are sex maniacs." He smiled and twirled one end of his black mustache in a little gesture of bravado, and the Americans laughed again.

"I must say from what we saw on our way here tonight the local female population seems fairly unapproachable," said Chuck, "even though they look good in those snazzy little silk dresses."

"You're absolutely right, *mon vieux*," said the French boy, gravely twirling his mustache again. "They are very unforthcoming. The mandarin classes, you see, have very strict morals. When an Annamese girl gets married, her husband spreads a square of snowy white silk on the bed on the first night of their honeymoon. If she fails this test he's allowed to send her packing and make a public announcement saying why."

"So how do all you French sex maniacs manage to preserve your sanity then?"

"Ah," said Paul, raising a didactic finger. "You obviously haven't heard of the noble institution of the *congaie*?"

"No," admitted Chuck, "I haven't. What is the *congaie*?"

"The *congaie* is the house girl, the houseboy's sister — or sometimes even his wife. Peasant girls from the countryside mostly." He flourished his hand around the rest of the gathering. "See how few wives there are in the colony. Most French *colons* come here alone — for the *congaie*. That's why there are forty thousand *métis* in the colony."

"*Métis*? What are they?" asked Joseph quickly, anxious not to be left out of the intriguingly adult discussion.

"People of mixed race, *mon ami* — half French, half Annamite. In French they are called *poules-canards*, you understand? 'Chicken-ducks,' neither one thing nor the other. They get left behind when the French *colon* goes home to France. If she is lucky, the *congaie* and her *métis* children are passed on with the furniture to the next occupant of the house. If not, too bad. Nobody worries. '*C'est la vie coloniale*,' they say and shrug their shoulders."

"But your mother makes sure you keep clear of the *congaie*, I'll bet," added Chuck, laughing again.

"My mother is unfortunately dead," said the French boy quietly. "She drowned in an accident four years ago."

"I'm very sorry," said Chuck hastily.

The French boy dismissed his apology with a little motion of his hand. "But in any event I don't admire those of my countrymen who treat the Annamese *congaie* so badly. I came to Saigon eight years ago when my father was in the army. After my mother died he decided to stay on and make a living hunting, so I've grown up here with Annamese boys and girls of my own age. Perhaps I have a different point of view from the older generation." He glanced up for a moment towards the senator and Jacques Devraux. "I don't always see eye to eye with my father for instance about the way things are done here."

Joseph tugged at his brother's sleeve suddenly and nodded across the room. "Look, Chuck, there's the man we met on the boulevard tonight." Chuck followed his gaze and saw the stoop-shouldered Frenchman, dressed now like all the others, conversing with a smaller, pallid man with dark-ringed eyes like his own. "We saw some prisoners being beaten," explained Joseph, turning to Paul Devraux, "but he told us not to feel sorry for them. He said all Annamese were idle and good-for-nothing."

The French boy glanced at the man for a moment, then shrugged. "He and his friend are typical representatives of the old guard. See the dark half-moons beneath their eyes? That's the sure sign of the habitual opium smoker. I have met your 'friend' once — his clothes always smell musty from the fumes. I believe he's an inspector of mines or some such." Paul Devraux lowered his voice and leaned closer to the two Americans. "And as it happens opium is not the only vice of that particular pair. When they leave here they will probably stroll down the Rue Catinat to the riverside. On the quay opposite the Café de la Rotonde you'll see poor Annamese boys parading there for such men, with rice powder on their faces. Or they will pick a young rickshaw coolie and ride around all night watching his little golden rump bobbing in front of their eyes — and beat him if he refuses their advances." The French boy pursed his lips suddenly in an expression of disgust. "Those types are far too common. The men who come to the colonies from France are not always of the best quality. Let's not talk anymore about them."

"Then tell us a bit more about the natives," said Chuck lightly, sipping his champagne and glancing around at the little groups of Annamese who were tending to draw closer together as the babble of noise from the French around them grew louder. "Who exactly are the slant-eyed oriental gentlemen who've come among us in their gaudy silk dressing gowns and funny hats?"

"We call them '*collaborateurs*' but the Annamese who don't want anything to do with the French call them the 'licensed pirates.' "

"Why 'licensed pirates'?" asked Joseph with a mystified smile.

"When our mighty French warships sailed in here sixty years ago the old Annamese scholars kept their distance. But we were very cunning — we bought loyalty. The lower-ranking mandarins who agreed to work as interpreters were rewarded with big tracts of good rice-growing land in the Mekong delta, and the idea soon began to catch on that collaborating paid. Over the years *collaborateur* families have become very rich. Because they've been good boys we've helped them extend their landholdings and they lease it back to their own peasants at exorbitant rates — *that's* why their own people call them pirates." Paul Devraux paused and nodded across the room. "Take the Tran family over there who've just been introduced to your father, for instance. They're very big landowners — probably worth quite a few million piastres."

The Sherman brothers looked up to see the governor and their father talking to an old Annamese with a long gray goatee, who was wearing a black-winged Ming dynasty mandarin's bonnet and a long embroidered gown of brilliant sea-green silk. They noticed that he kept his hands clasped inside the voluminous sleeves of his gown and rarely raised his eyes to the face of the governor or the senator. At his side a middle-aged Annamese dressed in a darker mandarin's gown followed the conversation with a watchful expression.

"The venerable-looking Annamese with the beard is unusually shrewd," said Paul. "He has retained his post at the imperial court in Hue. The family comes from the central region of Annam, I believe. But his son, Tran Van Hieu — that's him in the darker gown — lives here in Saigon as the court's Imperial Delegate. This

36

allows him to supervise all the family's vast landholdings in the delta. That way the family keeps a foot in both camps."

"They don't look much like American millionaires," said Chuck facetiously. "Our tycoons back home tend to look a mite less submissive."

Paul Devraux laughed humorlessly. "It's not surprising, is it, in the presence of dignitaries of the master race? The French government allows the Annamese almost no say at all in running their affairs. There's a lot of discontent beneath the surface."

"But what happened to all that famous French *liberté*, *égalité* and *fraternité* that you fought your revolution for?" asked Joseph in astonishment. "Doesn't that apply at all out here?"

Paul Devraux gave a little hollow laugh but didn't reply. Glancing up he saw the senator beckoning for his sons to join him. "I think your father wants you to meet the mandarins," he said. "You'd better go."

"But what's the answer to my question?"

Paul Devraux grinned at him for a moment, then raised a cynical eyebrow. "Unfortunately, Joseph, the *égalité* and the *fraternité* get left at home. But in her colonies France reserves the right to take whatever liberties she chooses."

5

Nathaniel Sherman looked at his sons and beamed proudly as they joined the group around the governor. "May I have the pleasure, monsieur, of introducing my two sons," boomed the senator, smiling into the wizened face of the Annamese mandarin while the governor's aide translated for him. "My elder boy, Charles, and his young brother, Joseph. . . . Monsieur Tran Van Lung is a high official in the Ministry of Rites at the imperial court of Hue," he added for his sons' benefit.

Joseph reached forward eagerly to shake hands, but the mandarin, after a moment's embarrassed hesitation, closed his right hand over his left fist, clasped them to his gown and bowed his head towards Chuck and Joseph in turn. Only then did the American boy notice his extraordinarily long curling fingernails, the mark of a high-ranking courtier that would have made a Western-style handshake awkward and discomfiting for both parties. Flushing to the roots of his hair, Joseph dipped his head in greeting as he realized the more circumspect Chuck had done.

"The Annamese never shake hands among themselves," declared the governor as if the mandarin and his son were not listening. "Equals simply bow from the waist with their arms at their sides. And the traditional form of greeting you've just seen" — he paused and grasped his left hand loosely in his right fist in imitation of the Annamese — "is employed to denote respect from an inferior to a superior."

The casual offensiveness of the governor's remarks was evident to the senator even before his aide finished his translation; he glanced sharply at the Annamese, but it was impossible to gauge their reactions from their impassive faces. "The American South where I come from is mighty proud of its good manners, messieurs," said the senator, flashing them a smile of exaggerated charm. "But I think all of us here still have a lot to learn about civility and courteousness from your own ancient world."

The old mandarin allowed his eyelids to droop fractionally in acknowledgment of the American's compliment when it was translated but otherwise held his face expressionless. The governor, who had only half listened to the senator's response, failed to notice the barb in the remark. Nodding absently he opened the palm of his hand to gesture towards Tran Van Lung's sea-green gown. "You might be interested, senator, to note that this robe is a unique piece of silk. Its pattern and hues are both very rare indeed. It was given as a personal gift to Tran Van Lung by the father of the present emperor, Khai Dinh." The governor gestured towards the Annamese as if he were a museum exhibit. "Near the hem you can see the delicately embroidered imperial dragon in gold. Beautifully worked. The world has much to thank the Chinese ancients for, don't you agree?"

"Indeed I do, governor. And we also have Monsieur Tran Van Lung here to thank, do we not, for reminding us of the great and unshakable dignity of the Orient."

The governor looked keenly at the American for a moment, but encountered only the senator's disarming smile and turned away again. "Speaking of rare things of the Orient, senator, let me show you my most treasured piece of *chinoiserie*." He touched the American's elbow and moved off in the direction of a single Ming vase standing on a pedestal nearby. "It is from the Lung Ching period, and I'm fairly confident that it is one of only two perfect examples of its kind left anywhere in the world."

It was clear from the governor's demeanor that his invitation did not extend beyond the Americans, and the elderly mandarin remained standing apart with his son and his son's wife. Chuck followed his father towards the pedestal where the wide-necked Ming vase, decorated with blue phoenixes and lotus sprays, glowed under a direct light, but Joseph hesitated. Seeing that the Annamese would otherwise be left abandoned, he remained beside them, shifting uncomfortably from one foot to another, searching his mind frantically for something to say. The face of the elderly mandarin above the long gray wispy goatee remained dauntingly blank, and Joseph turned in desperation to the younger Annamese, realizing that no formal introduction had been made with them. "I'm Joseph Sherman. I'm fifteen, six years younger than my brother Chuck, you know. He's twenty-one. I have a sister at home. Her name is Susannah – but she's only nine." Relieved at having thought of something to say, Joseph gabbled his small talk in a rush of unpracticed French, stumbling here and there over his pronunciation. "Susannah is much too young of course for a big journey like this. She had to stay behind with one of my aunts."

The old Annamese, possibly hard of hearing, gazed unblinkingly into the distance above his head for a moment then turned and shuffled away, but his son nodded gravely. "My name is Tran Van Hieu, and it is indeed a pity for your sister, Monsieur Sherman, that she couldn't accompany you. I hope she speaks the language of France as well as you do?"

Joseph laughed. "Nobody could speak it worse!" Infected by his laughter the wife of the younger mandarin smiled, and Joseph looked at her for the first time. Slender and demure, she wore a simple *ao dai* of brown silk, and the serene beauty of her delicate golden face belied her years. "Do you have sons and daughters, madame?" he inquired politely to draw her into the conversation.

"Yes, monsieur, two sons and a daughter."

Joseph glanced hopefully around the room. "Are they here?"

Tran Van Hieu shook his head. "They are still too young for such an occasion." He waved behind him towards one of the French windows that led out to the formal gardens surrounding the palace. "They asked if they might come to see the *palais*, but they had of course to remain outside in the gardens with their nurse where they can do no damage."

Joseph looked out through the windows and saw three small Annamese children dressed in traditional silk tunics like their parents walking on the lawns below the terrace in the company of a plainly garbed Annamese servant.

"Would it be possible for me to meet them, monsieur?" Joseph hesitated, then laughed. "You see, I'm not allowed to drink any more champagne. My mother made me promise to have only one glass — and I've had two already."

The Annamese mandarin looked at Joseph's eager face for a moment, then his eyes lost their watchful look for the first time and he smiled. "*Pourquoi pas?*" He turned to his wife, who was smiling too. "Why not?" he repeated and led the way to the French windows. Outside on the terrace he waved and called to the children, and a moment later they arrived panting and breathless at the top of the broad flight of marble steps.

"This is Joseph Sherman. His father is an important visitor from the United States of America," Tran Van Hieu told them in French. "That is an important country far away across the sea."

Remembering the earlier misunderstanding, Joseph kept his hands pressed to his sides. Smiling broadly he bowed stiffly from the waist and greeted each of the children in turn. "*Je suis enchanté de faire votre connaissance.*"

"Tam is twelve," said the Annamese, pointing to the taller boy. "Kim is eleven, and my daughter, Lan, is just ten years old."

The girl's serious little face was delicate, rounded, promising that she would soon flower into at least as striking a beauty as her mother; in an attempt to make her smile Joseph winked theatrically at her, but this made her draw closer to her mother and she continued to gaze gravely back at him with the curious, unselfconscious eyes of childhood. Her brothers had intelligent, mischievous faces, and they giggled and jostled one another constantly, refusing to stand still. The younger of the pair, Joseph noticed, held his arms unnaturally high across his tiny chest, and looking closer he saw a little bulge rumpling and moving beneath his silk tunic. "Are you hiding something interesting under your jacket, Kim?" asked the American, dropping playfully to his knees and pointing to the moving lump.

Both boys immediately burst into peals of embarrassed laughter, and Tam ran shamefaced to his father's side and whispered loudly in his ear in French: "Kim has brought Lan's gibbon, Papa! I told him he shouldn't, but he wouldn't listen to me."

The mandarin chided his younger son in rapid Annamese and immediately the giggling stopped. Kim unbuttoned his jacket, and when the head of the frightened baby gibbon appeared, Lan let out a little cry of protest and gathered the tiny animal tenderly into her arms.

"May I stroke him please, Lan?" Joseph spoke softly and leaned towards her. Not fully understanding his intent, she shrank away from him protectively and the animal, sensing her unease, began snickering and struggling in her arms.

Joseph started back immediately, anxious to cause no offense, but the nervous gibbon, taking fright at his sudden movement, tore itself free and bounded from her grasp. The two boys, shrieking excitedly, chased it around the terrace, panicking it further, and to escape them it darted through the open doors into the *palais*. Tran Van Hieu and his wife stared after it aghast, and the boys, halting on the threshold, stopped shouting and fell silent. Lan's face had turned pale with apprehension and she stood open-mouthed, one tiny hand raised to her check, her face trembling on the brink of tears.

Their anxiety rooted Joseph to the spot for a moment; then, desperate to make amends for his clumsiness, he flung himself through the doorway in pursuit. Inside, the tiny creature skidded to a halt on the marble floor, terrified by the sudden din of the gathering. Joseph lunged toward it, but the sight of him terrorized the gibbon further, and it set off frantically towards the only visible refuge.

The governor had moved his guests back from the illuminated pedestal to show the line and glazing of the Ming vase to its best advantage, and because he had turned his head in their direction to explain a point, he didn't see the gibbon streak across the marble floor on all fours. His eye fell on it for the first time as it sprang onto the marble plinth and clutched at the neck of the vase to steady itself. The governor's white-gloved hand froze in mid-flourish and for a second he stared horror-struck at the chattering animal. Then he started towards the plinth with a cry of alarm, and the gibbon, sensing a threat, leaped two feet into the air and disappeared inside the vase. The darkness of the interior only increased the animal's terror, and immediately it began to struggle frantically to free itself. The vase rocked back and forth on its base for an instant, then toppled towards the floor. Realizing he was too far away to save his prized possession, the governor could only stand and watch it fall, speechless with anger.

Several nearby Frenchmen started belatedly to the rescue, but the guilty knowledge of his responsibility for the impending disaster had lent Joseph's legs extra speed. He sprinted desperately towards the plinth and, as the vase fell, launched himself towards it in a lunging dive. His shoulder hit the floor with a thud that knocked the wind out of him but he managed to get one hand under the vase at full stretch and slithered across the marble floor juggling the smooth-glazed porcelain above his head. He almost lost it as he came to rest, but at the last moment he twisted onto his back and with both hands pressed his prize thankfully against his frilled inside shirt front.

In the hushed silence that followed he scrambled to his feet, his face and neck flushing scarlet. Reaching inside, he hauled the monkey out by the scruff of its neck and replaced the vase carefully on its pedestal. Then without a backward glance he fled towards the French windows, clutching the offending animal under his arm.

The moment Joseph stepped out onto the terrace the worried faces of Tran Van Hieu and his wife relaxed with relief. Their two small sons stood apart with their nurse, already contrite and tearful, but Lan clapped her hands delightedly and ran towards Joseph. The American boy apologized haltingly in French as he knelt to return the shivering pet to her, but once the animal was safely in her arms again she turned and fled shyly back to her father's side without speaking.

When the governor's uniformed aide appeared silently in the doorway behind Joseph, he took in the scene at a glance and his face darkened with reproof. "The governor is ready to take dinner with his invited guests, Monsieur Joseph," he said, pointedly ignoring the Annamese.

Joseph smiled and apologized once more and watched as Tran Van Hieu shepherded his family off the terrace. At the foot of the steps Lan stopped for a moment to turn and stare back at Joseph. She was still whispering to the gibbon to soothe it, but her innocent face was puzzled, as though she could not quite grasp everything that had happened. Joseph smiled hesitantly and waved, but this embarrassed the little Annamese girl and she turned and ran as fast as she could to catch up with her parents.

6

The main living room of the Imperial Delegate's official residence on a tree-shaded street north of the Saigon Cathedral betrayed little evidence of the great wealth amassed by the Tran family through three generations of collaboration with the French. Sparsely furnished in keeping with the austere, scholarly traditions of the Annamese mandarinate, it was dominated by the family's ancestral altar, which consisted of three tables of different heights lacquered in red and gold. Beyond the windows, tropical trees and shrubs that bore guava, pawpaw, mangosteen and pomegranate sprouted in profusion from the moist earth of a walled garden, and heaped bowls of fruits picked from their branches were clustered on the altar, along with tiny dishes of spiced meats, fish, lotus seeds, vegetables and porcelain beakers of tea and rice alcohol. A gilt-framed portrait of a venerable-looking mandarin attired in court robes occupied the place of honor on the highest level of the altar, and as the light began to fade, the wizened Annamese to whom Senator Sherman had spoken an hour earlier entered the room and bowed solemnly before it.

He was dressed in a wide-sleeved ceremonial gown of dark silk and a soft hat embroidered with colored threads partly hid his face from Lan and her brothers as they followed him through the doorway, walking barefoot between their father and mother. A stream of other relatives followed, and from the shadows they watched the old man touch each of the tall red candles surrounding the portrait with a lighted taper; when four tiny buds of flame bloomed above the altar he sank to his knees and pressed his palms together.

"In lighting these candles," he murmured in a reverent voice, "we extend an invitation to the spirit of my greatly esteemed father to come among us and bless us." For a moment he remained motionless, his eyes closed, then he lifted his joined hands in front of him in a graceful arc and bent to press his forehead against the floor in silent prayer.

Because she had spent much of that day watching her mother supervise preparations for the traditional *Gio* ceremony observed by the family on each anniversary of her great-grandfather's death, Lan knew the altar held all the favorite foods and beverages that the high-ranking courtier had enjoyed during his lifetime. The little girl had been allowed to help with the setting out of the banquet, and noticing suddenly that there were six dishes of each delicacy and six pairs of chopsticks, she had asked her mother why this was so.

"We provide extra food and drink so that your great-grandfather can bring the spirits of other famous patriots and scholars to join our celebration," her mother had explained in a whisper, and Lan, remembering this, found herself peering apprehensively at the spare chopsticks to see if any of them showed signs of moving. She and her brothers had always found the idea of ancestral spirits appearing during the *Gio* ceremony an awesome prospect, but her sense of unease had been greatly heightened on this occasion by the fear of unknown punishments that seemed certain to follow the incident involving her baby gibbon at the governor's palace.

Already their father had given an indication of his deep displeasure by ordering all three of them to remain in the room throughout the ceremony. It would last, they knew, about half an hour — until the single joss stick planted in a bowl of white rice on the altar burned down to the level of the cereal. Normally after offering their silent prayers all three children were dismissed to play in the garden and were not recalled until the offertory food was removed from the altar at the end of the ceremony and eaten along with other dishes at a festive family supper. In addition their father had told them that he wanted to speak to them in his study afterwards, and although he had given no indication what chastisement he planned, they knew from the severity of his expression that he was angrier than they had ever seen him before. Their mother had warned them to beg for forgiveness when their turn came to pray to their great-grandfather's spirit before the altar, and it seemed certain to Lan's ten-year-old mind that if she and her brothers had angered their father so deeply they must also have offended the spirits of their illustrious ancestors too.

Beside her Kim was struggling to hide his feelings, but Lan could tell from the paleness of his face that he was apprehensive and on edge. In Annamese families of their rank supervision of the home and the children was left largely to the mother; like most Annamese fathers, however, Tran Van Hieu kept a sturdy bamboo cane locked in a lacquered cabinet in his study to reinforce where necessary the Confucian notion of filial piety. He had never used the cane before, only the threat of it, but all three children were well aware that Kim's flagrant disobedience earlier that evening had caused him acute public embarrassment. On Lan's other side Tam shot an accusing look at Kim from time to time as if to make unmistakably clear to his father that he had done everything possible to dissuade Kim from his folly. Lan, for her part, hoped fervently that her innocence would be self-evident, and as she watched her prostrate grandfather's lips moving soundlessly she began to phrase in her own mind the plea for leniency she intended to submit to the ancestral spirit.

Three times in all her grandfather prostrated himself on the altar mat, then he rose slowly and stepped aside to make way for his son. In his turn, Tran Van Hieu knelt to perform the same silent acts of obeisance as the older man, but after prostrating himself for the third time, he remained on his knees and to his children's surprise began to pray aloud.

"Above all, help us never to forget the teachings of the great sage, Confucius, which remind us of our daily obligations towards our parents, our ancestors, our emperor and all those set in authority over us," he said, speaking in a firm voice that carried clearly to his children's ears. "Help us, too, to live in closer harmony with the great forces of nature and the world of spirits so that you and all our ancestors may continue to dwell restfully and happily in our midst. If we fail in these duties we know that we risk forfeiting the protection of your spirit and all the spirits of our nation's past heroes. . . ."

Kim bit his lip and stared at the floor as his father rose to look meaningfully in their direction; Tam and Lan also shifted uncomfortably under his gaze, which remained on them unwaveringly throughout their mother's act of devotion. When she had finished, he motioned Tam forward first because he was the oldest, and the twelve-year-old boy rushed eagerly across the room to fling himself down on the altar mat.

"Great-grandfather, you must know already that I did all I could to stop Kim taking the gibbon," he said, whispering aloud in the hope that his fervent words might be audible to his father and grandfather standing a few feet away. "I always obey my father without question as I did today, and all I ask is that you help me to continue to do that." He pressed his forehead fiercely to the floor and hurried obediently back to his place, taking care not to look at Kim.

To Lan's astonishment her father signaled for her to approach the altar next; as she was the youngest she had expected to go last, but her father was clearly singling Kim out for special treatment by allowing her to precede him. Her bare feet made no sound on the polished wood floor as she approached the altar with her head bowed devoutly over her clasped hands. "Please, Great-grandfather, don't let my father be angry with me for what Kim did," she prayed silently, closing her eyes as tightly as she could in an effort to add force to her thoughts. "I only ever wish to please him and I'm very sorry my pet gibbon was taken to the palace. But because I am a girl I can't stop my brothers from doing wrong, so please help Kim to behave better so that there is no more trouble." She remained bent towards the portrait of the dead mandarin for several seconds to show the spirits how deeply repentant she was, and when she rose to return to her place she kept her head bowed so that her dark hair fell across her face and hid the tears of remorse in her eyes.

When his father motioned him forward, Kim approached the altar more slowly, his lips pursed in a determined line. For a long time he remained bent over his hands without uttering any form of prayer. Then a moment before rising to rejoin his brother and sister, he clenched his teeth together hard. "If my father decides to beat me for what I did," he whispered fiercely to himself, "please help me to endure the pain and not to cry. That is all I ask."

From the back of the room where they were made to stand apart from the family for the rest of the ceremony, the three children were able to hear only snatches of their grandfather's words as he conducted a long discourse praising the virtues of his dead parent. When at last the joss stick on the altar burned down, their mother ushered them to their father's study and arranged them in a line before his writing-table on which the bamboo cane had already been laid out.

"You all know how disrespectful your behaviour was this evening," Tran Van Hieu said severely when he had seated himself, "both to the French governor and to your parents. And though I am well aware that you, Kim, are the main cause of the trouble I have no alternative but to punish all three of you."

Tam's face fell and Lan felt tears start to her eyes again, but Kim received the news without showing any visible sign of emotion. "Tam, because your responsibility for what happened is not so great as Kim's, you and your sister will kneel in the corner of this room for one hour with your faces to the wall. If you remain perfectly still and keep your backs straight, you won't be punished further. Use the time to reflect on your disgraceful behaviour — and resolve never to disobey me again."

As the elder boy and Lan turned away in relief, the mandarin let his hand fall on the bamboo cane; he rolled it between his fingers for a moment before glancing up at his younger son again. "Your punishment, Kim, will depend on the quality of your answers," he said, speaking in a quiet voice. "And I want you first tell me why you took the gibbon to the palace when you knew it was wrong."

For a long time the boy maintained a defiant silence and didn't look at his father.

"If you don't tell me, I will beat you without mercy," said the mandarin at last and rose from his chair with the cane in his hand. Still the boy didn't speak, but when his father advanced around the table and stood over him, he looked up into his face.

"I did it because some of the older boys at school dared me! They said I was too frightened of our long-nosed French masters to do

46

such a thing. I wanted to show them I wasn't afraid!"

Tran Van Hieu's eyes glittered and the muscles of his jaw tightened. "Why should you need to show you are not afraid? You know very well you should accord the French governor and his officials the same respect you show to me and your grand-father. They are the ruling authority. Our position and our wealth depend on their goodwill."

"Some of the older boys at school say we are nothing more than dancing puppets of the French!" The boy blurted his words in a rush, his pale face flushing suddenly. "They say we've sold our souls to France in return for rice fields over which the crane might fly all morning without encountering barriers. They call us 'licensed pirates' behind our backs!"

In the tense silence that followed, Tam and Lan, who had their faces to the wall, heard their father draw a long shuddering breath; then the first crack of the bamboo cane rang through the quiet room like a pistol shot. As the sound was repeated again and again the tears that had been brimming in Lan's eyes spurted down her cheeks, and beside her Tam listened rigid with horror, waiting for the sound of his brother's wailing to begin.

But although the cane continued to rise and fall with a terrible regularity, and they continued to hear the awful blows landing, no sound came from their brother. Once Tam darted a terrified glance over his shoulder and saw Kim sprawled across the writing-table; white faced and trembling from head to toe, he had his eyes closed and his fists were clenched tight as he summoned up every last ounce of courage in his eleven-year-old body to endure his father's beating without weeping or crying out.

7

In the bright, clear sunlight of the morning that followed the governor's reception, the three-mile highway linking Saigon with Cholon was aswarm with almost every form of land transport that had ever served mankind. Drawn by light-stepping ponies, lowing bullocks, sweating, yellow-skinned men or smoking petrol and steam engines, unending processions of carriages, carts, rickshaws, trams, trains, cars, and motor buses were plying urgently back and forth across the drab plain of treeless rice fields, hurrying to complete their business before the heat of noon drove their passengers to seek shelter and shade.

Perched on the tailboard of a tiny wooden *malabar* pulled by two short-legged Cambodian ponies, Senator Nathaniel Sherman was puffing reflectively on a Havana cigar as he surveyed the early morning scene. "It's worth remembering, Chuck, that without the white man's know-how this road would be nothing more than a dusty cart track today. And the only vehicles on it would be those native ox carts. Maybe even this quaint little matchbox on wheels wouldn't be here."

Chuck and Joseph were hunched on facing seats in the covered interior, their sun helmets touching the underside of the curved wooden roof. As they jolted along they grinned at each other, letting out little exaggerated groans of pain every time the un-sprung wheels hit a bump in the road. A line of the *malabars,* named after the Indian immigrants who had brought them to the colony, had been drawn up under the trees in the square outside the Continental Palace Hotel when they emerged to go to Cholon with Jacques and Paul Devraux to buy the last of their hunting supplies. On learning that the French called them disparagingly *"boîtes d'allumettes"* — matchboxes — and that they were usually only used by poor Annamese, the senator had suddenly elected to ride in one with his sons and meet the Frenchmen at the market.

"I'm saying this, Chuck, to remind you that it's the rich and powerful nations that call the tune around the world," continued the senator through a burgeoning cloud of pale blue cigar smoke. "And I thought that maybe a few bruises under the seat of your pants might make sure you remember something else that's important. Wealth and power go hand in hand, at home too, as well as in the big wide world. Men from families like ours have always governed America — and the great countries of Europe. But I don't want you to make the same mistakes the French make here. High-handedness and arrogance are their trademarks, as you saw last night at the governor's palace. But no American politician, especially a wealthy one, is going to last two minutes if he's caught looking down his nose at folk the way the French do. It's the ordinary folks at home who vote you into office, remember — and out of it. So first and foremost let everyone see that you make common cause with the common people. And never be too proud to be seen riding in a little buggy like this, instead of a limousine. The people like it — especially in the South. That's how they want it there. It makes them feel close to you and they like that."

"I don't think *I'll* ever feel anything ever again with the region I

48

sit on," grinned Chuck as he continued to bounce up and down on the plank bench. "I sure won't forget this *malabar* ride in a long while."

The senator drew hard on his cigar and studied the glowing end. "I guess you saw through the governor's speech last night, Chuck, did you — all that hypocritical talk about the civilizing mission?" The senator glanced up inquiringly at his elder son.

"Yes," said Chuck uncertainly, "I think so. He did paint a kind of rosy picture, didn't he? But I guess they have got something to point to if they've built good roads and railways and so on."

"But what's the point of building all those roads and railways?"

Chuck hesitated and peered out at the teeming streets of Cholon, which they were entering. Beneath the shady colonnades built out over the pavements, fat Chinese stripped to the waist like living Buddhas sat flicking their abaci behind high mounds of fruits, foodstuffs, silks, porcelains, hardware and a dozen other commodities. Wooden-wheeled ox carts trundled through the dense throng and the air was heavy with the pungent reek of salted fish, oriental teas and spices. Reluctantly Chuck turned his eyes back to his father.

"To improve their communications, I guess . . . ." said Chuck, his voice trailing off without conviction.

"Isn't it to help them transport the rubber and coal and rice and all the things that they export from the colony?" Joseph made his suggestion diffidently in the uncomfortable silence. "Don't the French really get more benefit from having roads and railways than the Annamese?"

The senator nodded at Joseph. "Exactly. And all that talk about the hardworking Annamese people was a mite misleading. The American consul told me they still force the peasants to do *corvée*. Every man jack has to work ten days each year for nothing as a kind of tax. They build those roads and railways or canals — working like the serfs did for their feudal lords in Europe in the Middle Ages."

"So why did you say, Daddy, last night, that the people in the streets seemed content and happy?" asked Joseph eagerly. "After I told you what we'd seen."

"Perhaps you've figured that one out, Chuck?" said the senator, turning to his elder son with a self-satisfied smile. "A little bit of wide-eyed innocence is good for lulling your opponents into a false sense of security. If you listened carefully to what I said, though, most of it could be taken two ways. A lot of folks drop their guard when they think they're dealing with a man of simple mind — and if behind that kind of pose you hide the steely determination I've been trying to drum into you, son, you'll do just fine." He leaned forward and patted Chuck's arm encouragingly as the *sais* brought the *malabar* ponies to a halt outside Cholon's biggest covered market.

Jacques Devraux and his son were waiting beside a baggage truck that was already loaded with the rest of their hunting equipment, and leaving their sons to stand watch, the two men disappeared into the shadowy interior of the market to haggle over a purchase of several hundred pounds of salt and arsenical soap that would be used for drying and preserving the hides of animals they hoped to shoot. At the pavement's edge Joseph stood surveying the crowd with fascinated eyes; in Cholon's narrower streets, Europeans were far rarer than on the boulevards of Saigon, and the vast majority of the faces were Chinese. Gleaming French cars nosed along the cluttered roadway bearing corpulent Chinese and their bejeweled wives or concubines in their curtained interiors, and the staccato, unmelodious babble of the Cantonese dialect had entirely replaced the softer, sibilant tones of the Annamese language.

"Look there," whispered Paul, draping his arms around the shoulders of both American boys and turning them to face across the street. "Do you see the Chinese beauty with her little *mu tsai*?" He pointed to the straight-backed figure of a striking Chinese girl in an embroidered silk dress before whom the crowds were parting as she made her way slowly along the opposite pavement. Her face was powdered and rouged, and beside her trotted a younger, plainly dressed girl holding a parasol above the delicate head of her mistress.

"What is a *mu tsai*?" asked Joseph, staring.

"She's a little slave girl," said Paul, a lascivious note creeping into his voice. "But she can still be very important. In an arranged marriage the husband often insists that his wife brings a pretty little *mu tsai* along as part of her dowry. Then if the wife displeases him he can distract himself with her little slave."

"And have you got a little *mu tsai* tucked away somewhere, Paul?" inquired Chuck, grinning broadly.

"Unfortunately not," sighed the French boy.

"What, no *congaie*, no *mu tsai*?" asked Joseph precociously, straining to bridge the gap of those few years that seemed to separate him from the world of adult banter inhabited so effortlessly by Paul and his brother. "And the Annamese girls are all virgins? How on earth do you manage?"

The French boy turned on one of his fierce expressions of shock and outrage and leaned back from the waist to subject the American boy's now-blushing face to pantomime scrutiny. "There are ways, my dear young Joseph," he said at last, his eyes twinkling merrily, "that even your audacious mind has not yet dared to conceive. Since you're obviously a young man of ardent passions, perhaps I'll have a chance to show you personally what I mean — and sooner than you think."

8

The incandescent flowers of roadside flame trees blazed like orange candles overhead as Jacques Devraux's gleaming black Citroën B-2 landaulet slid through the shadows they cast on the road leading northeast out of Saigon. Devraux himself was sitting in the front beside his Annamese driver while Senator Sherman shared the rear seats with his sons and Paul Devraux. Flavia Sherman had elected to spend the day shopping on the Rue Catinat and was to join them for the first hunt next morning. With their baggage truck trundling fifty yards behind they were heading towards the junction of the Dong Nai and La Nga rivers sixty miles from Saigon, where wild water buffalo and other rare animals of Southern Asia roamed freely through a low-lying region of jungle and plain.

Outside the city the road passed through a broad expanse of flooded paddy fields where swarms of Annamese *nha que* were bending and straightening, belly-deep in the sludge. To tend the rice shoots all wore broad, mollusk-shaped hats and identical trousers and tunics of black cloth that made men and women indistinguishable to the eyes of the Americans in the car. Domesticated buffaloes lumbered through the flooded fields, too, hauling tiny wooden plows, or wallowed at rest in deeper hollows with only their scimitar-shaped horns and noses showing above the water. Endless streams of similarly clad peasants hurried barefoot along the dikes and roadsides, moving with the same tireless rhythm as those workers in the fields. In baskets slung from shoulder poles they carried paddy seedlings, husked rice, fruit, vegetables, matting and even, as Joseph once delightedly pointed out, two live piglets squealing and squirming in separate nets at the pole ends. As in Saigon the mouths of the men and women alike

51

oozed with betel juice and the roadsides there too were stained with red saliva blotches.

"This is the other side of the coin," said Jacques Devraux in English and gestured peremptorily toward the windshield. "In Cholon you saw the fat Chinese millionaires taking their ease. They set up the mills to husk the rice and charter the ships to transport it to the best markets — then sit back. These gullible Annamese peasants are the ones who do all the hard, dirty work to make them rich. Sometimes to me Indochina looks like a Chinese colony run for the fat men of Cholon by courtesy of France."

The Frenchman's voice betrayed no trace of humor, and his tanned, leathery face remained set in unsmiling lines as he spoke. The hardness of his tone produced an uncomfortable silence in the car, and Paul Devraux, sensing this, hastened to lighten the atmosphere. "We say in French, senator, that the Annamese are the 'rizicultivateurs' — the rice growers — and that the Chinese are the 'usuricultivateurs' — the cultivators of usury," he said with a laugh. "That's neat, isn't it?"

The senator laughed and patted the French boy on the arm. "Whatever you call them, Paul, I wouldn't mind having a hundred or two of these peasants come over to Virginia to work my plantation." He gazed out of the window at the jog-trotting crowds of peasants moving in both directions along the road. "They seem to have fancy little engines driving them, don't they? They never seem to stop running."

"They're a very hardworking people," said Paul earnestly. "They have a surprising amount of energy in those frail-looking bodies."

"Then how come they don't make anything for themselves out of all this hard labor?" inquired the senator politely.

"However much they earn seems to make no difference. They constantly get themselves in debt." Jacques Devraux spoke quietly without turning around. "Then they have to go to the Chinese to borrow money at highwaymen's rates. Sometimes the Chinese charge thirty-six percent and the peasants are foolish enough to agree. Often they lend as little as ten piastres knowing they will be able to take the borrower's scrap of land, his house — and his wife and daughters too, probably — when he fails to repay."

"But that's not the whole story, Papa," protested Paul hotly. "The peasants have a hard time of it all round, it seems to me. We robbed them of their land in the first place to reward the Annamese who collaborated with us. Now those landowners have become greedy and demand high rents — and we help to exploit

52

the peasants by levying crippling taxes. Who can they turn to if the native landowners *and* the French are against them?"

Jacques Devraux did not reply immediately. Joseph, who was watching him closely, saw the muscles of his jaw tighten as he continued looking ahead through the windshield, and when he spoke there was a new undertone of coldness in his voice. "The Annamese were part of the Chinese empire for a thousand years, Paul, remember. They're a people who succumb easily to exploitation. It's in their nature. They seem to need it. If we hadn't colonized this country when we did somebody else would have. . . ."

The landaulet jolted suddenly as the Annamese driver trod on the brake, and Joseph, who was sitting directly behind him, heard Jacques Devraux curse softly under his breath. Glancing up the American boy saw a peasant pole-carrier, who had skipped across the road close in front of the Citroën, grinning triumphantly from a roadside ditch. As they accelerated away Joseph turned to stare out of the window and saw the peasant jump up and break into a little celebratory caper in the middle of the road.

"You will have to get used to that, I'm afraid," said Paul Devraux in an apologetic voice. "It happens all the time."

"Why do they do it?" asked Joseph in alarm. "Are they trying to kill themselves?"

"Not quite. They're trying to kill their *ma-qui*. But unfortunately they sometimes do kill themselves, too."

"What are their *ma-qui*?"

"Their evil spirits. All Annamese peasants — and that's about eighty percent of the population — worship invisible spirits. House spirits, hearth spirits, river spirits, tree spirits — in the jungle you'll sometimes see little offerings of food in the fork of a tree. Their *ma-qui* are the two spirits which they believe live in their shadows. One is good and one is bad. The bad one leads them into temptation and they believe that the only way that they can get rid of it is to drag it close to danger. If they narrowly miss death themselves and their shadow is 'hit' by a car, or 'gored' by a buffalo, they believe the evil spirit living in it will be destroyed. That's why the peasant was dancing in the road — we'd killed his bad shadow. It happens a lot at this time of year — it's Tet soon, the festival of the lunar new year, and they like to start afresh without any evil following them around."

The car slowed again more gently as the Annamese driver spotted another group of peasants gathering themselves at the roadside fifty yards ahead. From the back seats the Shermans heard Jacques suck in a long irritable breath. "Don't slow down every time, Loc," he told his driver curtly in French. "Otherwise we shall never get there."

The Annamese pressed the accelerator and the landaulet gathered speed again; it didn't falter as three more young peasants darted white-faced into the road, and Joseph found himself holding his breath until they got clear.

As the Citroën began to climb away from the crowded rice paddies into the red-soiled rubber plantation region, Joseph studied the face of the driver in the rearview mirror, trying to guess his feelings. He wondered if he'd understood what Jacques Devraux had said earlier in English about his country. But from his impassive, narrow-eyed face it was impossible to gauge his thoughts; like many Annamese he had the kind of boyish appearance that made it difficult for an American to estimate his age. He could have been anything between twenty and forty years old, thought Joseph. Jacques Devraux had not troubled to make him known to the senator, but while his father made a final check of the baggage truck, Paul Devraux had patted him affectionately on the shoulder and introduced him to them as "the great all-purpose Annamese genie Ngo Van Loc, who's houseboy, camp boy, chauffeur and indispensable general assistant to the humble Devraux family." Loc had giggled with embarrassment then shook hands and greeted them hurriedly in French before Devraux returned to the car. There seemed no reason why he should have known any English, Joseph reflected as they drove on and concluded in his own mind that the wary-eyed Annamese probably hadn't understood the earlier conversation.

For mile after mile the car ran on through the shadowy rubber groves where the straight-trunked trees with herringbone scars and metal latex cups stretched unendingly into the distance on either side of the road. The repetitive, uniform appearance of the soldier-like trees made it seem as if the car was scarcely moving, and their silent, gloomy shade gradually eased the tension created inside the Citroën by the earlier near-accident. But then as the car sped out of the rubber groves and down a steep hill towards another village Joseph stiffened in his seat again. A big crowd of peasants had gathered around the slimy village pond to wash their clothes and themselves in the gray, brackish water. They had spilled halfway across the road, and although most of them shuffled quickly aside when they saw the car approaching, four boys gathered themselves quickly into a group and remained standing defiantly in its path. Ngo Van Loc instinctively eased his foot from

54

the accelerator again, but Jacques Devraux lifted his open hand in a gesture of admonishment and leaned across to press the horn in the center of the steering wheel.

"They will never learn to get out of the way if you slow down every time," he said sharply. "Keep going."

As they drew nearer Joseph could see the flat peasant faces of the four Annamese boys clearly; they were wide-eyed with apprehension, but obviously determined to remain rooted to the spot until the last moment. Jacques Devraux's face was visible in the rearview mirror and his cold expression did not flicker as he held his hand firmly on the blaring horn.

When the large chromium headlamps of the Citroën were only five feet from them, the first boy flung himself into the roadside ditch and let out a yell of triumph as he tumbled into the filthy water. Two of the others stumbled but managed to leap awkwardly over the offside fender of the car. The fourth boy, however, slipped and fell to his knees and was only beginning to scramble upright again when the fender caught his chest with a thud that shook the vehicle. His arms and legs flew wide as he cartwheeled over the hood and fell in a motionless heap in the dusty road behind them.

Ngo Van Loc started to slow the car, but to the surprise of the Americans Jacques Devraux motioned him to keep driving. The Frenchman studied the scene behind them in the rearview mirror for a second or two but did not turn his head. Joseph and the other occupants in the landaulet twisted in their seats and watched the rest of the villagers rush to surround the fallen boy. The baggage truck that was following slowed as the crowd in the road thickened, then stopped, unable to pass.

"Won't you turn back, Monsieur Devraux, to see at least if he's alive?" asked Nathaniel Sherman in a quiet voice.

"There is really no need to inconvenience yourself, senator," replied Devraux calmly. "I assure you this is a very common occurrence here."

"But shouldn't the accident be reported to your police?"

"There is no need. The most a French judge will fine you is the cost of the funeral expenses — twenty-five piastres if in fact the boy has died. And the judge will only do that if he really has to. Repeated warnings are given to the peasants to stay away from passing traffic. They ignore these warnings completely." He glanced briefly in the mirror again. "The baggage truck driver will take care of it. He is Annamese."

The Frenchman spoke the final words in a tone that suggested he would find it disagreeable to discuss the subject further, and the senator lapsed into silence. Joseph glanced at Ngo Van Loc, but although his knuckles were white on the steering wheel he made no comment, and nobody else spoke for the rest of the journey.

9

"You will never argue with me again in front of clients, French or foreign, is that clear?" Jacques Devraux held himself ramrod straight on the back of his stocky saddle pony and delivered his order to his son in a vehement undertone. "Your behavior was unpardonable! It's astonishing to me that a boy whose father and grandfather have both been soldiers before him should have such a poorly developed sense of loyalty and duty."

Paul bit his lip as he jogged at his father's shoulder along a trail that wound through fringes of jungle beside the La Nga River. His face had grown pale at the harshness of the rebuke and he drew a long breath before replying. "You can't expect me to agree with you on every single thing, Papa," he said, keeping his voice low so that it did not carry to Senator Sherman and his sons, who were strung out in single file on their ponies behind them. "But that doesn't mean I'm disloyal to you."

"Perhaps you will learn the meaning of obedience and respect at St. Cyr. I hope so. If you don't, you won't remain an officer cadet for long." Devraux didn't look at his son as he spoke, but stared straight ahead along the track, his face set in harsh lines. "After the Americans leave I must travel to Canton again. You will have to conduct on your own the party of French officials who want to shoot muntjac. I don't wish to hear from them on my return that you've been airing the kind of sentiments I heard from you today."

Paul rode without speaking for a minute or two, listening absently to the strident cries of unseen birds in the tangled roof of the tropical forest. He sensed that his father was silently demanding some expression of regret, but whenever he glanced at his grim, unsmiling face he found it impossible to summon an apology to his lips. "Are you going on Sûreté Général business?" he asked at last in a low voice after glancing around again to see if they could be overheard. "Is it to do with the bomb that was thrown at the governor general?"

"You know I can't discuss my work for the Sûreté with you,"

replied his father brusquely. Then he turned his head and eyed his son coldly. "But perhaps holding the views you do makes you feel no action should be taken against the enemies of France."

A faint flush rose to the French boy's face. "I'm as proud of our country as you are, Papa," he said softly. "But if we did things differently here there wouldn't be any need for resistance movements. And the Sûreté wouldn't need to spy on anybody."

"Life is not that simple," replied the older man sarcastically. "There are outside forces in Russia and China trying to stir up trouble for us here." Then he paused and looked more thoughtfully at his son for a moment. "But don't think there's any pleasure or satisfaction in such work, Paul. Many hours are wasted watching and waiting. And often there's nothing to show for it at the end. I do it from a sense of duty — for my country. For myself I would much rather be hunting — or even back in the army again."

Paul detected a faint note of weariness in his father's voice and for a fleeting instant his mask of grim detachment had seemed to soften. "I'm sorry, Papa," he said quickly. "It wasn't that clever of me."

Jacques Devraux continued to ride straight-backed in his saddle without acknowledging the grudging apology, and Paul was begining to wish he had left it unsaid when his father spoke again in a softer tone. "Your mother's death caused me great pain, Paul, you already know that. But having his only son turn against him is painful for a man too."

The French boy looked up sharply at his father, but the familiar expressionless mask had already settled back on his face. "You'd better ride back now and check the baggage carts," he said sharply. "Make sure the Moi haven't lost anything. And stay in the rear till we get to the camp."

Joseph Sherman saw Paul turn his pony and begin trotting back towards him. He had been riding in front of Chuck and his father, watching with admiration the erect, narrow-backed figure of Jacques Devraux jogging easily at the head of the column; the fierce-eyed Frenchman had quickly made a deep impression on Joseph's fifteen-year-old mind and he was trying to hold his own shoulders high and square in the same fashion. The Frenchman's dark aquiline features and unsmiling silences made him think of history-book pictures he'd seen of the warrior heroes of ancient Greece and Rome, and the dismay he had felt at first when their car had struck the Annamese villager had increased his sense of awe.

He had forgotten the incident, however, the moment they

entered the jungle for the first time, riding on the little saddle ponies which Devraux's Moi bearers had brought to the road from the hunting camp. One moment they had been crossing a burning glade of shoulder-high grass in the full glare of the sun and the next they descended abruptly into a dark, silent, mysterious world where the air was cool and moist, the earth soft and spongy underfoot, and dazzling orchids blazed suddenly among the deep green undergrowth. The change had been so abrupt that Joseph had been moved to speak only in hushed whispers of the thrilling sights and sounds that unfolded all around them. They had disturbed alligators in the shallows of the river, listened to unseen deer bark in the riverside thickets, and a herd of wild pigs had fled snuffling and grunting from a stagnant pool at their approach. He and Chuck vied to identify the exotic birds they saw: ibis, king-fishers, herons, white pheasants and once a peacock darted frantically across their path. A wide grin of delight had become a permanent fixture on his face, and Paul smiled at him in return as he cantered back to check the ox carts.

"*Regarde*, Joseph," said the French boy, suddenly reining in his pony beside him and pointing to the far edge of the plain that they were crossing. "Do you see the elephants?"

Joseph turned in his saddle in time to see a score of shuffling gray humps slip silently into the distant trees. "Those are the first wild elephants I've ever seen in my life," he whispered reverently, and his grin of delight spread from ear to ear.

He was still grinning when they rode into the camp which had been built by the Moi in a bend of the slow-flowing river. Four huts of palm thatch laid over jointed poles had been constructed, and cooking and storage tents were pitched nearby. Immediately the little mountain tribesmen, who seemed to have stepped straight out of the sepia photographs in his history book, began unloading the baggage, and Joseph saw them take their crossbows and arrows from the carts and carry them to their own huts a hundred yards away along the riverbank. "Moi," he knew from his reading, was an Annamese term derived from the Chinese word for "savage," and looking at the dark-skinned, low-browed men, he could see they were of a different racial stock from the Annamese; they wore only breechclouts that left their haunches naked and they grinned and chattered animatedly in their own language as they moved quickly about their work. Some of them had plaited scraps of cloth in their long black hair and all wore beads around their necks.

The women who waited to greet them outside their huts wore bracelets of tin on their wrists and ankles, but otherwise their only other garment was a long dark cloth wrapped round the hips, which left their jutting, dark-nippled breasts uncovered. Seeing Joseph staring at the women, Paul walked over to him and put an arm around his shoulder. "You like our Moi women then, young Joseph, do you?" he asked, grinning broadly.

The American boy colored and laughed. "They're okay, I guess."

"They're a branch of the Rhade tribe — but a bit ancient, wouldn't you say, for your youthful tastes? The chief in the next village has a dozen wives and a lot of juicy young daughters who would better suit a passionate young man like you." He slapped Joseph on the back and laughed again. Then he nodded towards the senator and Chuck who were helping his father and Ngo Van Loc supervise the unloading of supplies. "Everyone else is busy at the moment, so why don't we try to get something fresh for the pot. Nice little muntjac for supper, say." He winked broadly. "And if we have time I'll show you the Moi village, too."

Joseph looked doubtfully towards his father. "Hadn't we better ask?"

"Fetch your rifle. I'll go and check if it's okay."

He ran across to talk to the senator and his father while Joseph collected his light Winchester carbine from the hut he was to share with his brother. A moment later the French boy returned carrying a Mauser .350 slung carelessly over his shoulder. "It's all right. I've promised we'll bring back a young hog deer." He leaned close to Joseph and whispered, "That means we've got to shoot two, okay?"

Two of the Moi carrying short poles followed them to a dugout canoe moored by the camp, and they paddled across the river to the plain on the other side. When they landed Paul crept forward to peer out into the grassland from behind a tree. Then he waved Joseph forward. "See over there, look! There are about a dozen deer grazing."

The late afternoon sun was beginning to lose its heat, but under its fading glare the waving grass of the plain still shimmered in a gray-green haze and Joseph's unpracticed eye could detect no movement.

"There! Half a mile away; the red blotches close to the trees." Paul turned Joseph's head gently in both hands until he saw the deer. "And we're in luck, the wind's blowing straight towards us. We'll just walk quietly down behind the tree cover and bag two of those beauties. One for us, and one for the chief's daughters, eh?" He chuckled quietly and set off towards the feeding animals.

When they were only fifty yards from the herd the French boy came back to Joseph and raised a mischievous eyebrow. "Have you ever . . ." He nodded and winked exaggeratedly. ". . . before, Joseph? Have you?"

The American boy looked away, his cheeks burning suddenly.

"I thought not." Paul laughed and took his arm confidentially. "You know, at your age I had . . . well, never mind. Let's shoot the muntjac first. . . ."

He led them to within thirty yards of the unsuspecting deer, then motioned for Joseph to sit down on the ground at the edge of the plain. He squatted beside him and demonstrated how to prop his elbows on his knees to steady the rifle. "Take the little fawn nearest to us," he whispered, pointing to one of the young.

Joseph fingered his rifle and gazed at the pretty little muntjac. Its red flanks were flecked with white, and it stood broadside on to him, a perfect target.

"Go on, take aim," urged the French boy.

But Joseph didn't raise his rifle. "You shoot, Paul. I might miss and scare them," he said softly, his cheeks coloring again with embarrassment.

The French boy gave a grunt of exasperation and fired almost casually from a standing position. The fawn bounded forward instantly in a reflex action, then fell dead in the grass. He shot a larger doe on the run as the little herd began dashing for cover, and the Moi bearers ran out into the plain to hoist the two dead animals on their shoulder poles. Grinning broadly the French boy led the way into the forest, and for a quarter of an hour they threaded through the trees following a narrow trail.

The village when they reached it consisted of three dozen palm-thatched huts raised on poles ten feet above the ground. In the shade beneath them pigs, dogs, domestic fowls, horses and even a few ancient buffalos swarmed in a stinking congregation. Moi children who had heard the noise of their approach came running helter-skelter to surround them and began shouting excitedly when they saw the dead deer. Paul pulled several cubes of sugar from his pocket and tossed them among the children, and they squealed and fought among themselves, passing the prizes eventually from hand to hand.

"Ah, at last! Here comes the *pholy*." The French boy nudged Joseph as a tall, white-haired Moi who was obviously the village chieftain slowly descended the stepped tree trunk that led from his hut to the ground. Paul gestured towards the biggest muntjac suspended from the carrying pole and made an elaborate gesture of donation.

The old man, who wore a cloth bow in his long gray hair, looked at the French boy for a moment, then his weather-beaten face cracked in a slow smile and he raised his arm above his head. From inside the hut behind him came the sudden sound of gongs and drums being beaten and immediately a bare-breasted woman appeared in the doorway at the top of the stepped log, holding aloft a tall earthenware jar.

A sigh of satisfaction escaped the French boy's lips. "That's the *ternum*," he whispered.

"The what?"

"*Ternum* — the Moi's own special rice alcohol. Fermented for three years — very potent. Think you can take it?"

"I don't know."

"For a man who can catch a gibbon in a Ming vase it will be child's play." The French boy laughed loudly and followed the *pholy* up the log staircase into the gloomy interior of the long hut.

The moment Joseph stepped through the doorway he began coughing uncontrollably. Several fires were burning inside and their smoke stung his throat and eyes. The floor was made of bamboo strips laid haphazardly side by side, and he staggered several times as his feet slipped between the round poles. Maize had been hung to dry beneath the thatch, and he knocked his head against a bunch as he straightened up, bringing a shower of husks and crawling insects cascading down upon himself.

By the light of the fires he could see Paul already sitting cross-legged on a buffalo skin by the *pholy*, and he sank gratefully down on the other side of him. He heard the French boy whispering urgently, then the chief grunted and plunged a long hollow bamboo rod into the *ternum* jar and drank a deep draught. When he'd finished he wiped his mouth and passed the jar to Joseph. The American boy hesitated, then sucked hard on the bamboo. The harshness of the alcohol took his breath away and made him choke again, and Paul collapsed in a fit of laughter as he expelled half of it in a further bout of coughing.

It took several minutes for Joseph to recover his composure and only then was he able to see by the light of the fires that the rear of the communal hut was divided up into tiny stall-like compartments for the *pholy*'s wives and daughters. They were all empty, but rows of Moi females were seated along the other walls, banging the gongs and drums. All were naked to the waist, and their bodies quivered and trembled rhythmically to the beat of their instruments. The *pholy* passed the rice alcohol again, and this time Joseph gritted his teeth as the spirit burned a fiery track into his stomach. His eyes watered so fiercely that tears ran down his cheeks, but he fought down the choking sensation and his self-esteem soared.

They continued drinking from the jar in turn, but gradually the effects of the smoke, the alcohol and the clamor of the gongs made his senses swim. Only dimly, when the jar began to return to him more rapidly, did he realize he had been left alone with the mute *pholy*, and by then the women had begun striking their gongs and drums in a faster rhythm. One of them, her naked upper body glowing like bronze in the flickering firelight, advanced and leaned down beside him to replenish the alcohol jar. Her bare flesh came close enough to his face for him to inhale its pungent female odor and he peered around desperately into the gloom for some sign of his French companion. He thought he heard him chuckle from the shadows once, but his eyes could not penetrate the gloom.

When the woman standing over him returned to her place, Joseph rose to his feet and made his way unsteadily towards the back of the hut, calling Paul by name. But no response came from the darkness, and after swaying precariously back and forth for a minute or two, his feet slipped on the twisting bamboo rods and he fell to his knees. He felt unseen hands help him into one of the partitioned stalls and there he stretched out and closed his stinging eyes. His head was swimming and he began to drift into a drunken doze but the sense of a new presence in the stall made him open his eyes again. In the reflected light of the fire he saw the silhouette of an entirely naked Moi female kneeling at his side, and as he watched, her hands began working rhythmically at some unseen task. Was she, he wondered, trying to make another fire in the fashion of the ancients? He heard the tin bracelets jangling on her wrists and from time to time she bent her head close over her fists as though blowing on reluctant embers; but it was some time before he realized that he, too, was naked, and that the hands of the Moi girl were stroking and chafing his own body.

He followed all her movements with dreamlike detachment; an all-engulfing numbness seemed to have removed every trace of feeling from him. All the time her face remained in shadow, the attitude of her head intent and concentrated; no eyes ever sought his face. Only gradually did he become conscious of a commotion in the darkness beside him. Then to his astonishment he heard the voice of the French boy, grunting like an animal in distress. A moment later he heard his laugh, a low guttural sound released from deep in the throat.

"*Ça va, Joseph, heh? Ça marche bien?*" The words spoken softly close to the American boy's ear made him start. He heard what sounded like a stifled cry of pain from a shriller voice; then the commotion beside him resumed once more.

Joseph tried to rise, but the female crouching over him leaned closer and shifted her body clumsily onto his. It was then that he sensed her extreme youth; the twin globes of her dark breasts with their sharp, neat points were hard and solid, her skin, a deep indigo in the near-blackness, was velvet-smooth, entirely without hair. To the feral reek of buffalo, horse and fowl and the sour remains of human nourishment was added suddenly a smoky, faintly ammoniac odor of female flesh, entirely new to him. The bracelets on her ankles and wrists danced and rattled again more urgently and her pungent breath began blowing softly against his face as she spread her thighs and forced her smooth dark belly downward against his own.

The sublime memory of that first descent into the moist, mossy darkness of the jungle earlier in the day blazed again suddenly in his mind's eye for a moment, but then his numbness left him in a furious rush and a piercing surge of purity and sweetness flashed through the rank darkness of the hut. He cried aloud in agitation and tried to twist free, but the sturdy thighs of the anonymous Moi girl held him fast. Only when his struggling became more violent did she fall from him, and then with frantic hands he untangled himself from her and rose to crouch against the wall, his eyes closed, his breath rasping in his throat.

From the darkness beside him came a sudden wild shout of laughter. It rose and fell in time with the drums and gongs which continued to fill the hut with their relentless clamor. After a moment, Joseph Sherman, his fifteen-year-old heart pumping with a sudden new elation, began laughing uproariously too.

10

"Okay, gentlemen, today we hunt buffalo!" Senator Nathaniel Sherman stood in the middle of the camp clearing, his booted feet astride, clutching a hand-crafted Purdey .450 double-barreled rifle in one fist. He had jammed a solar topee squarely on his head and a broad confident grin creased his face. "This beauty here or its .375 twin will be firing hard-nosed bullets at any Annamese buffalo who comes within sniffing range of the Sherman family." He slapped his rifle butt against his leather boot and nodded to Chuck Sherman, who held a similar rifle easily in the crook of his arm. "And in the rare event that I should miss, young Mister Deadeye here will be raring to let fly with a deadly Holland and Holland cannon of the same caliber. Right, Chuck?"

His elder son grinned easily back at him. "Sure thing, Dad."

"In the unlikely event of us both firing wide — and that's about a million-to-one chance, I'd say — young Joseph here with his Winchester peashooter will be a big favorite to pick off the stragglers. Right, young Joey?"

Joseph looked up with a start and nodded vigorously although he hadn't heard a word his father had said. He was standing on the edge of the group that included Flavia Sherman, Jacques and Paul Devraux and half-a-dozen Moi trackers, but his mind was only half on the hunt to come. Since waking that morning his thoughts had returned constantly to the encounter with the unknown Moi girl, and every time he recalled what had happened he felt a surge of exhilaration course through him. The fetid stench of the darkened hut, the mind-dizzying rice alcohol, even Paul's mocking laughter had all fused into a delicious composite memory now. He had really *done* it! How many young fellows of fifteen in Charles County, Virginia, could say that? Whenever he thought of that first blind delicious sensation, as he had a hundred times that morning, he had to close his eyes. It had hardly seemed possible before: but now he knew for sure. He'd done it. And he could do it again!

". . . That is, if he's got over his '*ternum*' sickness."

The ripple of laughter that greeted his father's jocular reference to the previous night's adventure broke into his train of thought. He looked up guiltily to find his mother, his brother and Paul smiling broadly at him. There had been plenty of leg-pulling already about his return to the camp the previous evening slightly the worse for wear from the *ternum*. Paul had laughingly explained that they had taken one small pull only at the bamboo rod, purely out of courtesy to the Moi chief, but it had gone straight to Joseph's head. He had distracted attention from the incident by crediting Joseph with the killing of the fawn and therefore the capture of the expedition's first prize, since the senator had decided they should collect a group of muntjac. Joseph himself had attracted more laughter by excusing himself before dinner and going directly to his cot; there he had fallen immediately into a deep, peaceful sleep that lasted until the dawn cries of the jungle birds roused him, and when he rose he had felt clear-headed and exultant.

Jacques Devraux had ridden out to the road before it was light with a spare horse to meet the car that brought Flavia Sherman from Saigon. They had arrived back at camp before breakfast and when he greeted his mother, Joseph had wondered with a sudden stab of alarm if she could *tell*. He had blushed at the thought and turned quickly away, but as time passed he found that he desperately wanted to share his secret with her; until then he'd always confided in her unhesitatingly and it seemed strange that something should now make him hold back. But perhaps, he thought to himself, adults could detect such things without being told. Just by looking maybe they could pick out those who had, or hadn't. He noticed in himself a definite tendency to swagger as he walked around the camp that morning and he had tried consciously to suppress it. But at least if his mother could tell, he reflected, she had not made any sign.

In fact Flavia Sherman had paid less attention than usual to her two sons since her arrival at the camp. The dawn ride alone with Jacques Devraux through the breathtaking natural beauty of the tropical forest had first heightened the pleasurable feeling of pent-up excitement that had been growing within her in recent days, then eventually left her feeling tense and on edge. Since the evening of the reception at the governor's *palais* when she had turned her head to find him looking at her, the memory of the naked desire she had seen in Jacques Devraux's eyes had smoldered in her mind. Because she knew he would be meeting her at the road alone, she had risen very early and bathed and scented herself with special care in her suite at the Continental Palace that morning. She had dressed her hair with a dark, crocheted net beneath her sun helmet and put on new, snug-fitting breeches and a tailored bush shirt that flattered her slender, shapely figure.

When she stepped from the car he had greeted her with careful formality and his manner had remained stiff and impersonal as they began the ride; but she sensed a tension in him too and knew intuitively that it was not a lack of interest that kept his gaze averted from her. Inside her she had felt a little sense of triumph begin to grow as they rode side by side through the cool bright jungle glades; sometimes she had allowed her horse to drift towards his on the narrow trail, perhaps hoping he might give voice to the passion his expression had seemed to promise at the *palais*. But as they made their way towards the camp he had spoken only to point out signs of bird and animal life that he thought might interest her; in the mud at the riverside, he showed her the pug mark of a tiger that had drunk there the previous evening and at another point on the trail he drew her attention to torn-up grasses and leafless trees that marked the passing of a herd of elephant. Her eyes sparkled afresh at each new revelation and she hung on his every word, but his lean face remained expressionless, his eyes unchangingly distant.

"My sons told me you lost your wife in a swimming accident four years ago, Monsieur Devraux," she had said at last, speaking quietly in French. "I was very sorry to hear that."

She had chosen her words with calculation in an attempt to break the impersonal barrier the Frenchman seemed determined to keep between them. But if her words had any effect on him, he hadn't revealed it; instead he had continued to avoid her glance, riding at her side with his features frozen in the same expressionless mask.

"Do you still feel her absence keenly?" she had asked, determined to extract a response of some kind.

"I've chosen to keep myself to myself!"

The vehemence of his reply had taken her aback, and suddenly she heard the throb of her own heartbeat loud in her ears. A flush of embarrassment rose to her cheeks at her own uncharacteristic forwardness and she lapsed into an unhappy silence, which to her surprise the Frenchman broke a minute later.

"My work fills all my time. Colonial life is very predictable. French *colons* love only to gossip. I prefer to hunt — and keep myself apart." He had spoken his words with his habitual grim-faced detachment and still didn't turn to look at her.

"When I first saw you at the governor's reception I thought you seemed . . . unhappy."

He had abruptly spurred ahead of her then without replying, and they had ridden without speaking further for a long while. The coldness of his manner had convinced her they wouldn't speak again, but in the middle of a clearing he had reined in his horse and turned to wait for her. He had looked directly into her face for the first time, and she saw his dark eyes blaze with a mixture of anger and pain. "We took our car on a river ferry during a monsoon storm. My wife was reluctant to go, but I had crossed often before in bad weather. The ferry sank. I dived many times. Once I felt my hand touch her sleeve on the river bottom —

but I couldn't find her." The muscles in his face had flexed tight as he spoke and his breathing had become uneven. "Now perhaps you will be kind enough, Madame Sherman, to ask me no more questions."

He had ridden on ahead again, ignoring her apology, and remained in front until they reached the camp. Around the huts he had avoided all contact with her and although they stood side by side listening to her husband, he did nothing to acknowledge her existence.

". . . On the question of conduct, who does what, who goes where in the jungle," the senator was saying, "the word of Monsieur Jacques Devraux will be law. He knows the terrain and the animals. But I don't need to remind you that we're here to collect for display groups in the Sherman Museum. So it will be me who decides who shoots what, and when." The senator smiled broadly at all of them and lifted his hand towards the Frenchman, gesturing for him to lead the way. "If that's clearly understood, let's make a start, Monsieur Devraux."

They followed him out of the camp in single file and headed along the riverbank, making for watering places where buffalo liked to wallow in the heat of the day. Although they moved stealthily on Devraux's instructions, great flocks of black parrots rose from the tops of the trees as they passed below, darkening the sky and filling the air with the sustained applause of their flapping wings. Armies of monkeys marching through the jungle roof on swinging arms took fright, too, when they saw the little file of humans and they fled chattering through the upper branches almost as speedily as the birds. Every few minutes Jacques Devraux sent his trackers up the taller trees to scan the plain on the other side of the river, but each time they descended shaking their heads. None of the watering places they visited showed any signs of fresh tracks, and no animals were sighted in the first hour.

As the sun rose higher in the pale sky the temperature climbed steeply and patches of perspiration began to appear on the backs of the men's shirts. The jungle birds fell silent in the growing heat, and Jacques Devraux eventually called a halt and distributed flasks of cold tea that had been carried in satchels by the Moi bearers.

"I will go quickly ahead on my own to search for new tracks, senator," he said brusquely. "The animals don't seem to be heading for their usual haunts today."

A few minutes after they started again a movement out on the plain caught Nathaniel Sherman's eye. He motioned his family and Paul to halt and pointed silently across the river to a herd of muntjac grazing in the long grass. "Okay, Joseph, here's your big chance," he said in a hushed whisper. "Since we're not being led to any buffalo, take one of those muntjac does. Then that little fawn you shot last night won't feel lonely in the museum."

Joseph hesitated for a moment then sank to his knees. Pulling his rifle to his shoulder he squinted along the barrel, aiming at the broadest part of the deer's neck. He tightened his finger on the trigger but again the fragile, defenseless beauty of the deer prevented him from firing and he lowered his rifle immediately. "I can't shoot it, Daddy — even for our museum. It looks too helpless." He stood up and let his rifle butt slip to the ground. "And you might as well know that it was Paul who shot the fawn last night too, not me."

His father looked at him with a disappointed expression, shaking his head slowly from side to side. "Okay, Chuck," he said at last in a resigned voice, "show Momma's boy here how to shoot muntjac!"

Chuck fired from a standing position, and the deer sprang into the air then fell and lay still.

"Nice going, son," said the senator quietly and sent one of the Moi trackers across the river to retrieve the fallen doe.

Joseph hung back walking slowly as the others moved on again, and his mother, noticing his discomfited expression, waited for him at the side of the track. "There's nothing to be ashamed of, Joseph, in not wanting to kill a beautiful animal," she said softly. "I'm really rather proud of you."

He smiled back at his mother in gratitude, but when she made to put a consoling arm around his shoulders he moved aside. "We'd better catch up with the others, hadn't we?" he said quickly, gesturing along the track. Inside his head he could still hear his father's slighting reference to a "Momma's boy" and because this rankled more than his inability to shoot the doe, he hurried on ahead of her in case his father should turn and see them close together.

As Joseph caught up with the senator and Chuck, Jacques Devraux appeared on the track ahead, walking quickly back towards them. "What was that shot?" he asked in a sharp tone of reproof.

"Since we weren't being shown any buffalo," replied the senator, smiling easily, "we bagged a muntjac that I spotted on the plain — for one of our smaller groups."

"Your shot will make sure we see no big game for at least another hour," countered the Frenchman tersely. "It's better not to shoot smaller animals until you have the bigger prizes you seek. We'll have to cross to the other side of the plain now to find anything."

He led them to a dugout canoe half a mile downstream, and they poled slowly across to the other bank. There the grass was almost chest-high, and by the time they reached the far side of the plain the clothes of all of them were drenched in perspiration. While they rested, Devraux again sent his trackers to climb lookout trees.

Joseph found he couldn't sit still and he rose to pace back and forth at a distance from the others. The incident with the muntjac doe had distracted him for a while but gradually the sense of exultation in his deeds of the previous evening returned and blotted everything else from his mind. While crossing the grassy plain, the intoxicating heat of the sun had made him a little light-headed, and intense feelings of tenderness for the unknown Moi girl had begun to sweep through him. He realized with a stab of regret he had never once seen her face clearly, and if he went back to seek her out he wouldn't know her for sure among the many daughters of the chief. While watching the Moi trackers scurrying up the trees, he began to daydream of how he would return alone to compete with all the youths of her village in feats of strength and athleticism. There would be running races, mock duels with spears and shields, tree-climbing contests. . . . He would win them all, and by demonstrating his great prowess he would force the anonymous Moi princess to step forward and offer him her hand. . . .

When the Moi trackers again descended from the lookout trees shaking their heads, Joseph on an impulse asked Jacques Devraux if he might climb to take a look with Chuck's binoculars. The Frenchman nodded his assent without displaying any interest in the request, and Joseph bounded immediately into the lower branches of the tree nearest him. Thirty feet above the ground its boughs became too slender to support his weight, and he stopped and raised the binoculars to his eyes.

For several minutes he saw nothing in the shimmering haze of the plain. Then he thought his eyes must be playing tricks; a mirage of round-backed whales seemed to be sporting amid the waves of golden grass. He kept the glasses trained, and as he watched they turned into a herd of about seven buffalo filing slowly in their direction. They were still a mile off, but their gray-black humps were unmistakable. Joseph called softly to those below and pointed. The Moi immediately climbed other trees and peered in the direction of his finger; then they began chattering excitedly to Devraux in their own language.

The breeze was blowing from behind the buffalo, and if they remained quiet, Devraux counseled, the animals would have no inkling of their presence. The track of the animals seemed likely to take them within two hundred yards of their hiding place, so they should crawl out onto the plain to try to get a shot from half that range.

Nathaniel Sherman nodded his agreement and motioned to Chuck, and together they moved bent double into the tall grass. Joseph, although he had not been invited, followed, keeping low, his Winchester clutched in both hands.

Crawling through the thick grass with heavy rifles in the heat of the day left all three of them gasping for breath. Chuck was the first to recover, and when he pulled himself to his knees to peer across the plain, the closeness of the leading herd bull surprised him. It was no more than three hundred yards distant, and he could see the great flattened scimitars of its horns swaying above the grass as it advanced, scenting the breeze at every step. Its small herd included two sturdy calves, and he ducked down excitedly to report to his father what he had seen.

Nathaniel Sherman peered at his watch, his face puckering in concentration as he calculated the time necessary to allow the buffalo to move into the most favorable range. When two minutes had passed he motioned Joseph to stay flat, then nodded at Chuck, and they both stood up simultaneously, their rifles at their shoulders.

The herd bull stopped in astonishment on seeing two men rise abruptly from the grass only eighty yards away. It lifted its great horned head as though to bellow a warning, but in that moment Chuck Sherman's rifle roared and he let out a yell of delight as he heard the thud of the bullet strike home into the buffalo's broad chest. He fired again as the wounded bull turned and began galloping clumsily towards the safety of the trees, but this second shot went wide. Beside him his father's rifle recoiled, and they saw one of the two calves stagger, then begin stumbling after the bull.

"I think we've got the big boy and his calf, Chuck," breathed Nathaniel Sherman. "Now for a cow!" He took careful aim with his second barrel at a smaller buffalo that had begun circling in dismay, and they heard the dull thud of his successful shot echo clearly across the plain. The wounded cow, however, dashed frantically towards the jungle along with the other terrified animals of the herd and disappeared with them into the shade.

Only the dying bull stopped before it reached the trees. Staggering slightly, it turned to stare balefully back at them, standing broadside on. Chuck glanced around inquiringly at Jacques Devraux, who had moved out into the plain with his son and Flavia Sherman. "Shall I shoot again, Monsieur?"

The Frenchman shook his head and lifted a silent hand in a gesture that implied "Wait!"

For a minute or two they all watched the wounded bull swaying on its legs. "That was great shooting, Chuck," said the senator at last, growing impatient. "But I think we have to go forward and finish him off."

Once more Devraux raised his hand. "No. Shoot again from here."

Chuck reloaded and fired off both barrels with great care, and again he had the satisfaction of hearing his bullets slam into the stationary animal. But although it staggered once more, it still didn't drop. Instead it stood staring bemusedly at its assailants while blood dribbled from its jaws onto the grass. Only when Chuck reloaded and shot a third time did the animal slowly crumple to the ground and roll onto its side, leaving one great horn curving majestically upward above the tall grass.

Nathaniel Sherman slapped Chuck heartily on the back and, taking his arm, hurried him away toward his kill. Jacques Devraux followed more slowly with his son, Flavia Sherman and Joseph. Paul Devraux pointed to the fringes of the thicket into which the remnants of the herd had disappeared: the bulk of the small black calf was clearly visible lying dead on its side a dozen paces short of the trees.

As they approached the curved horn of the dead bull, Nathaniel Sherman began pumping the hand of his eldest son in congratulation. Jacques Devraux followed them, holding his rifle at the ready until he was certain the big animal was dead. Joseph and his mother, after watching them for a moment, turned and strolled away to inspect the dead calf.

Nobody was looking at the thicket at the moment the wounded cow broke cover. Bellowing with pain and leaving a bright trail of blood on the grass, the crazed animal galloped frantically towards its dead calf, over which Joseph and his mother were bending. When he looked up and saw the charging buffalo, Joseph raised his Winchester in an instinctive reflex action and dropped to his knees. Peering along its barrel he saw blood foaming around the cow's mouth and heard clearly the tortured rasp of its breath between each anguished bellow.

At the moment of firing he closed his eyes tight, but he never heard the crack of the Winchester discharging because it was

drowned in the roar of Jacques Devraux's Mauser. The Frenchman's bullet pierced the brain of the buffalo just behind its left
ear, and the impact twisted its neck and threw the animal down in
a swirl of dust only ten yards from where Joseph was kneeling
beside his terrified mother. A long shudder ran the length of its
body, then after one last explosive and bloody exhalation of
breath, it lay still.

In the ensuing rush of silence that gripped the plain and its
fringe of jungle, nobody moved; for several seconds the tableau
of scattered human figures stood as though spellbound among
the black and bloody bodies of the dead animals. They didn't
loosen and begin converging around the dead buffalo cow until
the first flock of ragged black vultures flopped clumsily onto an
outcrop of rock on the grassland fifty yards away.

Flavia Sherman was white-faced with shock but she managed to
smile at her younger son as he stood up. "You were very brave,
Joseph," she said quietly before the others arrived within earshot.
"Thank you for what you did."

Joseph's face was pale and his hands were trembling, but he
tried to hide this by gripping his rifle tightly as the others
gathered around them. In an uncomfortable silence Nathaniel
Sherman and the others gazed down at the dead buffalo cow.
Only then did they see the great livid gashes that no man could
have inflicted raked along both flanks.

"A tiger must have savaged her recently," said Devraux quietly.
"She was already half-crazed with pain. We've all had a lucky
escape."

"She is no damned good for display like that." Nathaniel
Sherman frowned down resentfully at the dead animal. "Not with
her hide all lacerated." He lifted his foot and touched the
buffalo's curved horns with the toe of his boot. "Still, I guess her
head will make us an unusual little trophy." He turned and
smiled at his white-faced wife. "A little souvenir for you and the
plantation house perhaps, my dear — of a moment we won't
forget in a hurry?" Each of the Moi carried a long-bladed
machete which had been dubbed a *coupe-coupe* in Annam, and
taking one from the nearest tribesman, the senator bent over the
dead buffalo. When she saw what he intended to do, Flavia
Sherman turned her head quickly. Holding onto one horn, he
hacked off the buffalo's head and handed it, still dripping blood,
to one of the Moi. Then he grinned and looked at Jacques
Devraux. "I guess we ought to get the ox carts here as quickly as
possible, Monsieur Devraux, to take our bull and the calf back for

skinning. Otherwise their hides won't last long in this heat, will they?"

Later in the afternoon Chuck Sherman ran excitedly into the hut he shared with his brother. Joseph was sitting quietly on his cot, his chin in his hands, staring out thoughtfully at the jungle. "The skinners found two bullets in your buffalo's head, Joey," he said excitedly. "Monsieur Devraux's went through her left ear, but she had another one — yours — right between the eyes!" He shook his brother's shoulder delightedly. "How about that? Now we know, don't we? When it really matters you shoot straight."

"Thanks for letting me know." Joseph looked up and smiled, but his expression betrayed no sign of real pleasure.

Chuck stared down at him in puzzlement for a moment. Then he shrugged and turned away. A moment later he was running eagerly back across the camp to help the Moi with the skinning of the massive bull he himself had killed, unaided.

11

At sunset, darkness enveloped the hunting camp in a sudden rush. The fading light gave way in a matter of seconds to a moist, velvet blackness, as if a curtain had been drawn swiftly across the sky, and the shadows beyond the glow of the hurricane lamps immediately began to come alive with the shrill vibrations of the jungle night. On the riverbank a small army of frogs croaked a hoarse descant to the incessant, high-pitched whine of unseen cicadas and from somewhere far off a bird screamed intermittently as though in agony.

In a shadowy corner of the cook tent, Ngo Van Loc crouched beside an upturned packing case that he was using as a makeshift writing-table. His face was clenched tight with concentration and he wrote *quoc ngu*, the phonetic rendering of Annamese into the roman alphabet, in a large, ungainly hand. Every now and then he stopped to peer out through a slit in the tent wall and check that Jacques Devraux was still seated with the American hunting party at the table in the center of the clearing. He had seized the opportunity while they dined to make another copy of a revolutionary tract calling for an end to French rule. It had been prepared originally by the secret society he had joined two years earlier after being forced off his own rice lands for nonpayment of taxes, and he had copied it out dozens of times already in trying to win new recruits for the society in remote jungle villages far from Saigon. He had been hurrying to finish this latest copy before the meal ended, and seeing through the slit that his wife was heading out across the clearing with his two small sons to begin collecting the dishes, he put aside his pencil and hastly read over what he'd written.

> O Brothers! O Brothers! For seventy years we have been slaves to the tyrannical French. They beat us down with duties and taxes and pitilessly steal the fruits of our labors. We are treated like buffaloes and horses in our own land. Under the pretext of accomplishing a civilizing mission, the red-bearded French barbarians have stolen our rice fields, our mines, our seas, our press, our commerce. All power, all profits, all our sources of livelihood are in their hands — but the one thing they leave behind will destroy them — the hatred of a million coolies! The time is coming, Brothers, for us to take the destiny of our nation into our own hands! United we are a vast army against a few thousand Frenchmen! O Brothers and compatriots, join our society today! Unite with all those who hate the French and revolt against their despotic rule. . . .

At the sound of footsteps outside the tent Loc quickly folded the copy and its master and hid them inside the packing case. Peering through the eye-slit he saw his wife, Mai, approaching, carrying the dishes from the supper table. Not yet thirty, she wore a long dark skirt and a pale scrap of cheap cloth above the waist that left her arms and shoulders bare. The sensuality of her broad, peasant face was heightened by her modestly downcast eyes and the long swathe of glossy black hair that reached to her waist. Barefoot, she moved with the natural sinuousness of her race, and looking beyond her, Loc saw Jacques Devraux lift his eyes momentarily from his plate to follow the swaying movement of her hips as she walked away from the table. For a second or two the expression of the Annamese camp "boy" hardened as he stared at his employer, then he moved away from the peephole and began to busy himself cleaning the pots and pans that had been used to prepare the meal.

"Devraux told me today he is going to Canton again soon," he said in an excited whisper when his wife came to plunge her arms in the suds beside him. "And he wants me to go with him this time — as his driver."

Her impassive face showed no sign of reaction and he leaned closer to emphasize the importance of his news. "Don't you realize what this means? I'll be able to meet other revolutionaries in exile there. We're very lucky to have positions of trust with Devraux." He glanced briefly towards the Frenchman, who was still seated at the table. "We must be very careful not to jeopardize them."

His wife nodded at his side but continued to clean the pans without replying or looking at him.

"Why aren't you interested in this good news?" he asked at last in an exasperated voice. "Don't you understand what I'm saying?"

"Yes, I understand," she said quietly.

"Then what's the matter?"

She scraped away at a pan in silence for a while. "He has been behaving differently today." She hesitated, seeming uncertain of what she wanted to say. "Normally he ignores me. But today he has looked at me two or three times — in a certain way."

Loc stared hard at her for a moment then glanced out across the clearing again, remembering suddenly the expression he'd seen a few minutes before on the Frenchman's face.

"I think the American woman has upset him in some way," she continued in a quiet voice. "He never talks to her at the table — but she stares at him strangely sometimes."

"You're probably imagining it," he said quickly. "I'm sure there's nothing to worry about."

From the corner of his eye Loc noticed Flavia Sherman rise from the table and begin sauntering back towards her hut. Although she walked slowly, he saw there was a noticeable agitation in her manner; she tossed her head frequently, as if finding the heat oppressive, and ran her fingers repeatedly through her long black hair. He watched her, frowning, for a moment but then a squeal of high-pitched laughter rang across the camp, distracting him, and he turned to see his two sons, Dong and Hoc, squatting at the side of the clearing beside Paul and Joseph. The far-off cries of the lone bird they'd been hearing since sunset had recently seemed to double in intensity, and Loc realized that Paul Devraux had been echoing its call by blowing on blades of jungle grass between his thumbs. The American boy, he saw, was puffing out his cheeks and making loud trumpeting noises in an attempt to emulate these feats, and it was this comic performance that was causing the Annamese boys to shake with laughter.

Fearing suddenly that their behavior might upset Jacques Devraux, Loc ran quickly across the clearing towards them. "Monsieur Paul, please don't excite them any more," he called in French. "It is time they both were in bed."

Before he reached them Paul and Joseph had hoisted the two boys, aged eleven and thirteen, onto their shoulders and were encouraging them to joust at one another with chopsticks from the table. When Loc, with another worried glance in Jacques Devraux's direction, insisted it was time for them to go to bed, Paul galloped across the clearing with little Hoc on his shoulders and dumped the boy squealing with laughter on his sleeping mat. Joseph followed suit with Dong, and when the commotion died down and they had bidden the Annamese boys goodnight, he and Paul stripped off their shirts and walked over to the bamboo skinning platform where Chuck was already back at work on his buffalo hide.

In her hut Flavia Sherman, distracted by the sounds of merriment, gave up trying to read by the light of a hurricane lamp and walked restlessly to the front opening. Her bush shirt was sticking to the small of her back and she could feel tiny rivulets of perspiration trickling between her breasts. In the distance thunder rumbled across the dark sky, and she suddenly raked her hands through her hair, holding both palms tight against her temples until the noise ceased.

In the center of the camp Senator Nathaniel Sherman was still seated at the table on his own, savoring his third post-prandial cognac. He had drunk a lot of wine during supper "to celebrate Chuck's mighty fine bull," and she had noticed that his manner had been louder and more expansive as a result. On the far side of the camp, she saw Jacques Devraux stripping to the waist in order to resume work at the skinning platform, and suddenly unable to remain in the hut any longer, she strolled out across the clearing again. By the ox cart that had been used to haul the dead buffalo in from the plain, she paused to watch the men working on its hide. The curly-haired Moi were wearing only breechclouts, and their naked haunches gleamed in the lamplight as they moved vigorously around the platform; beside her pale-skinned sons, their glistening bodies looked almost black. Chuck's broad back was bowed over his task, his pride in his kill visible in every movement, but the slighter figure of Joseph bent and straightened at his side with less enthusiasm. Once Chuck turned and grinned delightedly at her as he paused to mop his brow, and she smiled warmly back. Against her will, however, she found her gaze straying repeatedly to Jacques Devraux.

Without a shirt the Frenchman's body looked lean and hard, and she guessed he must be a man of her own age. The muscles of his arms and shoulders were tight and sinewy, flexing like knotted cords beneath a sheen of perspiration, and in the flickering light of the lamps she could see a livid white hunting or battle scar running down the base of his throat and across his ribs. The American woman watched him intently for several minutes, a commotion of half-forgotten sensations stirring within her, but if he had noticed her presence he gave no sign.

When they had scraped and gouged all the fat from the buffalo's hide, Jacques Devraux showed the others how to rub in arsenical soap to repel the hordes of flies that would otherwise blow on it, and gradually the pungent reek of arsenic mingled with the other rank odors of human sweat and animal fat hanging in the saturated air. Another distant roll of thunder added a bass note to the orchestrated shrillness of the tropical night, and Devraux lifted his head for a second to listen. Anticipating rain, he ordered the Moi to sling the hide on poles and move it into a canvas tent set up nearby. There he broke open some of the salt sacks and instructed the tribesmen to begin drying the skin. When he was satisfied they were doing it correctly he picked up the head of the dead buffalo and carried it to the river. Wading knee-deep into the warm, muddy water he drew a broad-bladed hunting knife from his belt and began hacking the flesh from it.

The American woman strolled over to the riverbank to watch him, and as the fragments of the raw flesh floated away downstream she saw the water churned to a white froth by shoals of ravenous fish fighting to devour them. Fascinated and repelled in the same moment she continued to watch the macabre spectacle despite herself, her lips parted, her eyes bright. Then she turned to look at the Frenchman and spoke softly in his language. "You honor us, Monsieur Devraux, by working so late into the night for our expedition."

"If we don't start drying the hides now, dampness and the heat will destroy all our efforts within a few hours." He stopped work long enough to look up directly into her face, then bent his head once more and continued cleaning the skull with neat, precise movements of the knife.

"I also wanted to thank you for what you did this afternoon," she said quietly. "It was a fine shot that killed the wounded buffalo."

The Frenchman scrambled out of the river and stopped in front of her. She had been standing on the bank above him with her booted feet apart, her hands jammed into the pockets of her tight-fitting breeches, and for a fleeting instant he looked at her appraisingly as he had done at the reception. Then he thrust his knife back into its sheath and spoke towards the gleaming skull he still held in his left hand. "I think, Madame Sherman, it might be more diplomatic if you were to return to your quarters now. We're about to rid ourselves of the blood and fat of the buffalo."

When he glanced up at her again his thin mouth had returned to its habitual unsmiling lines and she turned away immediately. From her hut she heard him call to the Moi and her sons, and a moment later they all plunged naked into the river. For several minutes she heard them splashing and laughing in the water, then gradually quiet returned to the camp. Chuck and Joseph, flushed and tousle-haired from their dip, looked in to bid her goodnight, and after they had returned to their hut she tried to resume her book by the lamp. But the words on the page didn't have the power to blot out the crack of hunting guns she was beginning to hear again inside her head, nor make her forget the sight of the blood trails on the hot plain. She saw too, in her mind's eye, the heaving bulk of the buffalo bull struggling in the grass in its death throes, saw once more the blindly charging cow and the ragged black vultures flopping down out of the sky, and all these images crowding through her mind heightened the vague sense of turbulence that was growing inside her with the gathering storm.

When she heard Jacques Devraux join her husband for a final drink at the table in the center of the clearing, she tried to listen to their conversation. What they said remained inaudible, but it was clear that the Frenchman was offering only an occasional monosyllable to punctuate her husband's rambling drawl. They talked in this desultory fashion for a few minutes, then when she heard them bid one another goodnight she ducked quickly under her mosquito net and lay down without undressing.

Inside his hut on the other side of the camp Ngo Van Loc also heard the two men take their leave of one another. He had been keeping a wary eye on Jacques Devraux while he made another laborious copy of the revolutionary tract and he stopped writing to watch the Frenchman walk back to his own quarters. In the rear of their hut his wife was bending over a bowl of water, naked to the waist, washing herself, and she snatched up a towel to cover her bare breasts when she heard Loc hiss a sudden warning. Glancing over her shoulder she saw him fumbling frantically to hide the pencil and paper he had been using, and a moment later Jacques Devraux ducked under the hut's front flap. Blushing furiously she turned away but still she felt the eyes of the Frenchman on her naked back.

"Send Mai to my hut in two minutes," she heard him say at last in a curt voice. "I wish to give her instructions for tomorrow's meals. Ask her also to bring needle and thread."

When he'd gone the Annamese woman turned to stare apprehensively at her husband. "He has never asked me to go at this time of night before," she whispered.

Ngo Van Loc avoided her gaze. "If we disobey him I may lose the opportunity to go to Canton," he said shortly. "And that's important for our movement. Get dressed and go quickly. I will find the needle and thread for you."

Taking care not to wake her sons, who were curled up together on their sleeping mats, she dressed and combed her hair then slipped out of the hut without looking at her husband.

Nathaniel Sherman stumbled slightly at the entrance of his hut, and his wife heard him cursing and fumbling for a long time with the flap fastenings. Once inside he removed his shoes and trousers very slowly then drew back her mosquito net and smiled lopsidedly at her before lowering himself unsteadily onto her cot. Outside, the thunder rolled more loudly, and a few drops of rain began to plop against the thatch above their heads.

"You're still a mighty beautiful woman, my dear," he said, slurring his words slightly. "I know I haven't always been what a husband should be to you — but that doesn't mean I don't appreciate and admire your beauty." He bent his head towards her until she could smell the cognac fumes on his breath. "You know that, don't you?"

She closed her eyes to hide her revulsion as he pressed his open mouth against hers and began fumbling with the buttons of her bush shirt. Eventually he pushed his hand inside her brassiere and began kneading one of her breasts, but instead of responding she lay motionless and waited as she always did; gradually the movements of his hand grew slower, the rhythm of his breathing more regular, and when at last he lay still she disentangled his hand from her twisted clothing and slipped out from underneath him. Immediately he sprawled sideways across the cot in a loose posture of sleep and began snoring loudly.

The rain at that moment became torrential, drumming noisily on the thatch above her head, blotting out all other sounds of the night. She hesitated for only a second or two, then without looking around, she ripped the ties from the front flaps and stepped outside. The rain was driving down with great force, swamping the dry ground, and within moments her hair was plastered flat against her cheeks. Lightning forked overhead, illuminating the camp like day, and thunder crashed deafeningly through the deep darkness that followed. In the glare of the lightning flashes she rushed across the flooded clearing and didn't stop until she reached Jacques Devraux's hut.

Inside, a lamp hanging from the apex of the roof was still lit, and because he hadn't closed his mosquito curtain, her eyes fell at once on the slender golden body of Ngo Van Loc's wife spread-eagled beneath him on his cot. Devraux was staring towards the front flaps as she entered and he froze when he saw her. She gazed back mutely into his eyes, horrified and deeply aroused in the same instant, and when she didn't turn away he began to move once more, slowly at first, and then with gathering force and swiftness. Again and again he bore down on the Annamese woman and as his movements quickened he kept his gaze fixed challengingly on Flavia Sherman's face.

She stood rooted to the spot, staring back at him as though hypnotized, watching the skin of his face slowly tauten across his cheekbones. Gradually the downward thrust of his naked loins became more urgent and uncontrolled, and in a final moment of spasm, his features spread and widened suddenly into a flattened mask. For a long time he remained motionless like this, his body arched backward, his teeth clenched, his lips drawn back in a silent rictus of ecstatic agony. Then the Annamite woman began to sob and he relented at last and raised himself from her; still moaning quietly to herself she scrambled from the cot onto the dirt floor, gathered her scraps of clothing together and fled past the American woman into the rain.

As soon as she'd gone, Flavia Sherman began to fumble with the buckle of her belt; but her hands shook uncontrollably and it took her a long time to undress. Jacques Devraux watched in silence as she stepped out of her sodden clothing. In the light of the lamp her naked body was glistening with rain and perspiration and when she saw the desire in his eyes she fell to her knees beside him.

With a tenderness that surprised her the Frenchman put his arms around her and lifted her onto the cot beside him. For a moment he held her head in his hands, searching her face with a strange expression in his eyes. Then he drew her against himself and kissed her roughly. She began to moan as he caressed her trembling body, and when he entered her she cried aloud as though in great pain. With the roar of the jungle storm filling their ears they abandoned their bodies to the hunger of many lonely years, driving in blind, frantic rhythms towards one furious ecstasy after another.

Sometimes Flavia Sherman wept as though with grief, and although the storm drowned most of her cries Joseph heard the faint sounds of his mother sobbing as he stood outside the hut in the torrential downpour. Unable to sleep he had drawn back the front flaps of his hut to watch the spectacular storm and had been startled to see her dashing across the flooded clearing in the glare of the lightning flashes. Thinking that she might need his help, he had dressed quickly and hurried after her, but outside the hut of Jacques Devraux he had stopped, suddenly afraid. When he first heard her voice she seemed to be in agony, and imagining she was ill, he had started impulsively forward again; then with a deep sense of shock he had sensed the awful intimacy of the strangled cries. For several minutes he stood outside the hut, drenched to the skin, listening to the muffled sounds with a growing sense of desolation. Then he turned away and splashed numbly back across the flooded camp to his own hut.

12

A vista of paradisiacal tranquillity opened up beyond the windows of Jacques Devraux's Citroën B-2 landaulet as the motor car swung over the summit of another of the many rolling hills along the Mandarin Way. On one side of the ancient north-south coastal highway linking Saigon and Hanoi steep cliffs fell away to a dazzling beach of white sand fringed with coconut palms, and on the mirror-flat surface of the South China Sea far below, bat-winged Chinese junks floated at rest like toys on a turquoise pond. Inland, the Annamite Cordillera thrust its purple peaks towards the afternoon sky, but neither Joseph Sherman nor his mother gave more than a passing glance to the spectacular mountain and ocean scenery outside the car.

They had remained wrapped in their own separate thoughts ever since leaving the hunting camp earlier in the day and had barely spoken to one another. Flavia Sherman was still wrestling with the turmoil of emotions that had kept her awake long after she returned to her own hut through the stormy jungle night. There she had found her husband still snoring on her cot, and she had stretched out on his; but sleep hadn't come, and long before dawn she had decided she must leave the camp at once. When Nathaniel Sherman awoke and saw where he was, he had looked at.

his wife shamefacedly and agreed immediately to her request to be driven to the imperial capital at Hue where the emperor of Annam was due to celebrate the Tet festival the following day. Joseph had accompanied her willingly, but she had soon noticed that his manner was subdued and cool towards her, and this had added a vague new dimension to her unease.

As Ngo Van Loc drove them northwards, her thoughts against her will returned constantly to the frenzy of that midnight jungle storm and the gnawing fear that she might not have emerged from her folly unscathed. A breathless, pervasive sense of heat possessed her body at every return of the memory and she was unable to remain settled and at ease in her seat for more than a few minutes at a time. She found herself searching back to her youth for reasons to explain the blind and selfish obsessions which had taken hold of her since they arrived in the French tropics and she wondered if her father's ruin and death by his own hand in the Louisiana cotton slump of '89, when she was only two years old, was the root cause. If he had lived, her hard-pressed mother might not have insisted that she accept the advances of the heir to the Sherman tobacco fortune. Perhaps the suffocating conventions of the Shermans' Queen Anne plantation house would not have been forced on an unknowing seventeen-year-old if her ailing mother had not been so shamed by their straitened conditions in a rented house on the borders of the Creole quarter of New Orleans.

The first of a series of world hunting trips to collect animals for the newly endowed Sherman Field Museum of Natural History — the latest public shrine to celebrate the force and virility of the male Sherman line — had seemed to promise her a refreshing diversion from the dull routine of Tidewater Virginia and the house of political convenience in Georgetown. But the strangeness of the tropics and the sophistication of the almost-forgotten culture from which she had sprung had greatly exaggerated her sense of release from the frustrations of the past. The sudden disturbing plunge into the jungle in the cloying heat of the Saigon River had made her more intensely aware of her body than at any time since the fevered days of adolescence. Perhaps too the journey had reminded her of the dreadful certainty that within a few years her beauty would fade, and all these inflated hopes and fears had combined to produce a mood of abandon utterly foreign to her that had found its culmination in that jungle storm. She closed her eyes as the memory rushed back vividly into her mind again, and a feeling of panic rose through her at the thought that a fierce spark of that madness might be living on within her as she approached the middle of her life. She shifted restlessly in her seat once more, imagining she could actually feel the angry pinpoint of fire burning deep inside her womb. . . .

In his corner Joseph found himself grappling with an over-whelming sense of bewilderment. He couldn't reconcile those terrible uncontrolled cries he had heard in the night with anything he already knew of his mother. To him until then she had always been a safe comforting haven; complete and seemingly self-sufficient in herself, she had always been an unfailing source of reassurance, ever ready to pour unquestioning love and affection on him in his moments of need. His father's favoring of Chuck had forced him to turn to her increasingly for solace, and that some unimaginable selfishness should have driven her to commit her dreadful act of desertion baffled and disturbed him deeply for reasons he didn't begin to understand. Although she was sitting only a foot or two away from him in the opposite corner of the seat and had frequently tried to smile at him, he felt inexplicably betrayed. He didn't really understand what had happened or why, but he sensed things would never be quite the same again. Some-thing alien had come between them, something that could never be removed. He felt irretrievably alone and the woman beside him seemed suddenly to be a total stranger.

Sometimes, as they encountered new crowds of pole-carrying Annamese peasants jogging ceaselessly between market and rice field, or spilling out of their tiny village temples and pagodas, he felt that what had happened was somehow inextricably bound up with the torrid, exotic country that was so totally unfamiliar to him in all its ways, and other distressing images of the recent past began to flood through his mind; he saw again the brutal French *colon* lashing the fallen prisoners between the shafts of the cart in Saigon, remembered the horror he had felt at the sight of what he thought were many massacred coolies on the river wharf on their arrival, and he heard once more the thud of the Citroën striking the peasant boy on the way to the hunting camp. The elation he'd felt the day before at his own breathtaking adventure with the Moi girl now also seemed suddenly shameful to him, and he began to wonder if his exaggerated pride in the deed hadn't been the direct cause of the danger in which he and his mother had suddenly found themselves on the plain. It had, he decided, certainly brought about the death of the unfortunate buffaloes. Before they left the camp he had seen the hides of the bull and its calf scraped clean of all life, suspended like limp black rags in the drying tent; their white, eyeless skulls were hanging close by, and he felt a sense of desolation suddenly at the thought that he was responsible. Only the day before, those noble, horned beasts had been filing unsuspectingly through the long grass of the plain, intending to wallow harmlessly in some cool place through the heat of the day. Then in his foolish exhilaration he had leaped into a tree and spotted them with his binoculars. If he hadn't been so puffed up with conceit, the buffalo that had not been noticed by the Moi might now be basking contentedly in the shallows of the river. . . .

"Joseph, is something wrong?"

The voice of his mother broke into his thoughts unexpectedly and he started inwardly. Because he knew he couldn't speak of what was in his mind, he pretended he hadn't heard her and continued to stare out of the window.

"Is it because you couldn't shoot the deer? Are you still upset because your father called you 'Momma's boy'?"

"Perhaps, a little." He kept his face turned away from her so that she wouldn't see that he wasn't telling the whole truth. "I was thinking too, about the buffalo. I feel like I sentenced them to death because I spotted them. Those skins are going to be shipped home and stuffed with sawdust and put in a glass case in our museum. But nobody would really care if they weren't. It would have been better if we'd let them live. . . ."

His mother leaned across the seat to squeeze his hand, but he felt an inner coldness towards her and didn't respond. Studying his profile she noticed that he looked pale and red-eyed, and a new fear made her temples throb suddenly.

"Did you sleep well last night, Joseph? The storm didn't keep you awake, did it?"

"No. I slept very well," he said quickly. "I was really tired after everything that happened yesterday."

She sat watching him for a moment, hoping he would look around and smile; but he kept his back turned to her and continued to gaze abstractedly out the window.

13

"We believe that living in harmony with natural forces of life is of the highest importance," said Tran Van Hieu gently, waving his hand towards the golden-roofed temples and palaces of the Imperial City inside the Hue citadel. "That is why the location for the Thai Hoa, the Palace of Perfect Concord, was chosen with such care."

Joseph gazed up wide-eyed at the snarling ceramic dragons that writhed along the ridges and cornices of the Thai Hoa; in the bright sunlight of the first morning of the Year of the Buffalo they glittered and shimmered like real gold. "It's very beautiful," said Joseph in a hushed voice. "But why was this particular spot found to be so favorable?"

They were crossing the Bridge of the Golden Waters and entering the ornamental esplanade in front of the palace where shaded, tree-lined walks led past lotus pools and balustraded flower gardens. Joseph was dressed in a formal gray knicker-bocker suit and the Annamese at his side was already wearing the stepped Ming dynasty bonnet, curly-toed boots and embroidered silk gown in which he would pay homage to the emperor of Annam along with hundreds of other mandarins at the annual Tet cere-mony.

"This was where the strongest forces of all were found to meet in perfect union," said Tran Van Hieu quietly. "The white tiger and the blue dragon, which are often in conflict, rest peacefully with one another on the precise spot where the emperor's throne stands inside the palace."

"What are the white tiger and the blue dragon?"

The mandarin hesitated, then smiled at the American boy. "We believe they are the male and female principles of existence. The white tiger is the female principle, which is negative and threatening, but the blue dragon, the male principle, is positive and benign. They also symbolize East and West."

"But how exactly can you tell that they are in harmony right here?" asked Joseph, glancing curiously about him. Other man-darins in bright silk gowns, booted and bonneted like Tran Van Hieu, were hurrying through the ornamental gardens towards the palace. Around the inner walls the Annamese soldiers of the imperial guard, who looked as if they'd stepped out of the pages of one of his adventure-story books, stood sentinel with their mus-kets. They wore mushroom-shaped hats topped with glittering brass spikes, and white cloths fluttered at their necks to protect them from the sun; all of them were barefoot, but Joseph noticed that their leg wrappings were yellow — the color, as Tran Van Hieu had already pointed out, which was worn only by the emperor and his immediate entourage.

"It is very difficult to explain quickly, Monsieur Joseph," said the mandarin. "Some wise Annamese sages devote their whole lives to

85

the study of *feng-shui*. Those are the Chinese characters meaning 'wind' and 'water.' A dwelling for the living or a tomb for one's ancestors should be sited only where it harmonizes completely with the forces of nature." He smiled again. "Let us start with something easy. You have already seen the serene beauty of the River of Perfumes that flows past the citadel walls. The scents of its rare grasses and reeds drift gently on the wind bringing calm and tranquillity to its banks. And many lotus flowers grow in our waters. The lotus is the symbol of purity, the symbol of Hue. Although it grows from mud, it turns into a thing of great beauty and smells very sweet. Under its influence we believe good men can resist evil. And see there!" He paused and pointed above the vermilion walls of the citadel to the dark bulk of an isolated mountain rising to the south. "That peak is called the Ngu Binh. It means the 'Emperor's Screen.' All bad spirits travel in straight lines from the south, and that mountain prevents them from entering the Imperial City." He paused again and waved his hand in several directions in succession. "But there are many other good signs all around us . . . a maiden holding a spray of blossoms . . . a serpent entwined around the root of a lotus . . . a phoenix in a prayerful attitude."

Joseph peered in the directions indicated by the mandarin but saw only the scented shrubs and trees of the formal gardens. "I can't see anything, Monsieur Hieu," he said smiling delightedly. "But it is very beautiful here. I'm sure what you say is true."

The American boy had begun to fall under the spell of the old Annamese city soon after crossing the lotus-choked moat into the Kinh Thanh, or Capital City, the first of three concentric "cities" within the citadel modeled on the ancient walled quarters of Peking. Although the citadel had been rebuilt by the Emperor Gia Long in 1802, its palaces and temples had been designed and constructed faithfully in the style favored by China's Ming emperors and at the entrance to the Dai Noi, the Imperial City itself, Tran Van Hieu had been waiting for him in the shadow of the Ngo Mon, the multitiered "Bull Gate" roofed in gold tiles like the Gate of Heavenly Peace in Peking. The governor of Cochin-China had arranged the meeting; on hearing of Mrs. Sherman's arrival in Hue he had invited them to join his official entourage for the imperial New Year ceremony and had also arranged for Tran Van Hieu to show Joseph the palaces beforehand.

Joseph's melancholy had begun to evaporate for the first time since leaving the hunting camp as the goateed mandarin, walking ponderously beside him in ceremonial boots, reeled off the mystical-sounding names of the shimmering buildings: the Can-Chanh, the Great Mansion . . . the Palace of the Spirits of the Six Emperors . . . the Temple of Generations . . . the Halls of the Splendors of the Moon and the Glory of the Sun — and most mysterious of all to his young impressionable mind, the guarded heart of the citadel, the Tu Cam Thanh, the Purple Forbidden City named after the Purple or Pole Star, the symbolic ruler of the heavens. As had been the case in Peking, Tran Van Hieu explained, the emperor dwelled in utter seclusion behind the walls of the Forbidden City, and no European ever entered those precincts.

Bronze griffins and gilded chimera stood guard outside the palace doors, and life-sized stone mandarins appeared silently among the scented trees as they walked. In a temple courtyard they came unexpectedly upon a troupe of imperial singers and dancers rehearsing a performance; garbed in dazzling costumes of gold, red, green and turquoise, the expressionless boys and girls were indistinguishable from one another in their close-fitting bonnets as they performed the mannered steps of a delicate oriental dance to the plaintive accompaniment of gongs and ancient stone lithophones.

All these sights and sounds alone would have fascinated Joseph's young mind, but the murmured talk of deities and devils beyond his imaginings coming from the grave-faced little mandarin pacing at his side established the walled city of palaces lastingly in his mind as a place of deep mystery and enchantment, and by the time Tran Van Hieu delivered him to the governor's aide outside the Palace of Perfect Concord he was almost ready to believe he would see a live white tiger curled up contentedly with a blue dragon around the emperor's feet.

His mother and the governor of Cochin-China were already waiting by the entrance with the Résident Supérieur of Annam and his official suite of guests. The military officers among them wore full dress uniform of horizon blue while civilians wore frocked coats and *chapeaux hauts de forme* — top hats. The rule that normally barred women from the ceremony had been waived after representations on her behalf by the governor, and in response Flavia Sherman had chosen her most sober clothes for the occasion. The full-length skirt of her modest navy blue suit brushed the ground and a veil and matching, narrow-brimmed hat of the same color partly hid her face. She was relieved to see that her son's tour of the palaces had left his eyes shining and he greeted her with something approaching his normal smile.

"It's all a little bit like a fairy tale, isn't it?" she whispered as they filed into the throne room with the other guests, and he nodded eagerly in reply. To Joseph's delight the Résident Supérieur led his entourage to the very front of the audience chamber and the American boy found himself standing only a few feet away from the throne where the Emperor Khai Dinh, a slender, almost feminine figure, sat swathed in a golden robe of richly embroidered silk. His feet, shod in the long black leather boots of China's Ming rulers, rested in the embrace of two reclining golden dogs carved in the throne's base and in his hands he held an ivory wand bearing a tiny mirror, which, Tran Van Hieu had explained, he used to shield his face and demonstrate his symbolic humility before the spirits of his ancestors. On either side of the throne two liveried Annamese eunuchs stood at attention holding long-handled fans of decorated feathers which they waved in slow, synchronized strokes above the emperor's head to cool the air that he breathed.

In the wall opposite the throne, screen doors had been drawn back and a blaze of early morning sunlight flooded into the chamber from the flagstoned courtyard, causing the emperor's gem-encrusted crown of beaten gold to flash and glitter with every movement of his head. Outside, all the foremost mandarins of the court were already assembled in lines that reflected their rank. In the first row Joseph spotted Tran Van Hieu's father standing just behind the two red-robed royal princes who were to lead the annual act of homage.

"You'll notice that we are standing to the left of the throne," said the governor, addressing Joseph and his mother in a stage whisper. "The heart side of the emperor, you see, is the place of honor in the Orient."

Joseph glanced quickly at the emperor to see if he'd heard and was surprised to find his expression uneasy beneath the bonnetlike crown that fitted close around his face. Once or twice as they waited for the ceremonial to begin he saw the eyes of the Annamese sovereign shift anxiously in their direction and he dabbed occasionally at his pale perspiring face with a silken handkerchief that he held concealed in one of his voluminous sleeves. When the Résident Supérieur finally stepped forward to face the throne, the Annamese emperor dropped his gaze to his brightly polished boots and listened without looking at him directly.

"Your imperial majesty," boomed the Frenchman in his own language, "it is my singular honor as representative of the *Nation*

Protectrice to extend the felicitations of the president of France to your highly esteemed imperial person and all your court on this auspicious and sacred occasion. . . ." The Résident Supérieur, a tall, barrel-chested man who wore a monocle in his left eye, was an imposing figure in his official blue and gold uniform. A ceremonial sword hung at his left side in a gilded scabbard and clusters of beribboned medals and star-pointed orders festooned both sides of his tunic. As he spoke, he let one hand rest on the hilt of his sword as though to emphasize subtly the ever-present might of French arms. "In the nine years since your majesty ascended the throne of Annam in 1916, your kingdom has continued to enjoy the unselfish and benevolent protection of France and it is our sincere hope that this mutually rewarding state of affairs will continue far into the distant future to the benefit of both our peoples. . . ."

From time to time as he read his salutation from a sheet of paper held before him in a white-gloved hand, the Résident Supérieur squinted at the emperor through his monocle; his voice was loud and confident and betrayed little outward sign of the extreme deference implied in his spoken words. In contrast, the Annamese monarch seemed to shrink deeper into the embrace of his gilded throne as though he was only too well aware that the diplomatic niceties of the Frenchman's address did nothing to alter the fact that he and his people were irretrievably beholden to the will and whim of France.

These subtleties, however, were lost on Joseph because the dryness of the speech had caused his attention to wander and he gazed round the richly furnished audience chamber with awe-struck eyes. A forest of scarlet, lim-wood pillars supported the roof, and the five-clawed golden dragons entwined around the length of each of them seemed to snarl fiercely at their reflections in the floor of polished ceramic tiles. Delicately wrought Ming urns and vases stood on tables at the foot of every pillar and to Joseph's surprise an impassive young mandarin appeared silently from a place of concealment behind one of them as the Résident Supérieur finished speaking. In a singsong tone he translated the address into Annamese for his emperor. When he had finished the mandarin disappeared again as silently as he had come, and Joseph saw the emperor take a rolled Chinese scroll from one of his sleeves.

In a sibilant, fluttering voice he read his reply from the throne in Annamese, but his delivery, unlike the Frenchman's, was hesitant and nervous and once or twice he stopped to swallow in mid-sentence. The moment he finished, an elderly mandarin with a white, whispy goatee appeared from behind another pillar beside the throne and translated the emperor's brief address into melodiously accented French. Several times the Résident Supérieur dipped his chin an inch and lowered his eyes in acknowledgment of a dutiful reference to "the great protecting nation of France," and when the translation ended he inclined his head more formally without bowing. He watched closely as the emperor rose from his throne, and when he saw him bow low in his direction, he allowed a little smile of polite acknowledgment to play across his face before he turned and strode majestically back to join his entourage.

With a little wave of his hand he indicated that his officials and guests should take a pace or two backward into the aisle between the adjoining rows of pillars to clear the way between the throne and the open doors, and the next moment the ranks of singers and musicians drawn up around the walls of the courtyard outside burst into a plaintive musical chant. On hearing this, the two royal princes prostrated themselves in the doorway of the throne room and pressed their foreheads to the floor tiles in a reverent attitude. The mandarins behind them, who all carried mirror wands like the emperor's, followed their lead and stretched themselves full length on the flagstones of the courtyard.

Joseph saw Tran Van Hieu and his father make their obeisance gravely beside other high-ranking Annamese. Three times they lowered themselves to the ground in response to commands chanted by the minister of rites and all the time the musicians and singers banged gongs and drums and continued their strangely discordant chanting. On his throne Khai Dinh remained unmoving, accepting their abject demonstrations of loyalty without a flicker of expression.

"The Chinese call it 'kowtow' but the Annamese term is '*lam lay*,' " said the governor deprecatingly at Joseph's shoulder. "But whatever you call it, it doesn't come easy to some of the older members of the fraternity. I sometimes wonder if some of them are going to get up again." He laughed unpleasantly at his own jest, and a number of Frenchmen around them smiled.

Joseph watched Tran Van Hieu's father lower himself to the ground with difficulty for the third time. He might have looked comic if his proud, wrinkled face had not remained set in a devout and dignified expression as he went through what was clearly a considerable exertion to his failing strength. As each group of mandarins finished their performance of the ritual they backed slowly to the edge of the courtyard to be replaced by others, and wave after wave of courtiers in silks of all hues flowed across the gray flagstones under the yellow glare of the early sun. When the last group had backed from the emperor's presence, the chant of the court musicians suddenly changed to a faster rhythm and the gateways filled immediately, to Joseph's astonishment, with the gray, swaying bulk of elephants. Decked in tasseled yellow howdah cloths and ridden by straw-hatted Annamese mahouts perched straddle-legged behind their ears, a dozen elephants lumbered slowly across the flagstones and lined up before the open doors. Urged on by their riders with short metal-tipped bamboo rods, the elephants lowered themselves slowly to their knees, facing towards the throne, and remained kneeling for a minute or two, their trunks curling and swaying in front of them in time with the cacophonous music. Then, with a lazy dignity, they rose one by one and backed out of the courtyard again.

The explosions started as soon as the last elephant had shuffled out of sight. To Joseph's startled ears they sounded like a simultaneous volley of a thousand rifle shots. Without pause the explosions became a continuous bombardment, and thick, white smoke engulfed the courtyard, blotting out the sun. Joseph looked wildly round the throne room, expecting to see the emperor and the Résident Supérieur bolting for cover. But the emperor remained impassive on his dais and the Résident Supérieur merely raised an amused eyebrow in the direction of one of his colleagues.

"Don't look so worried. It's only the traditional Annamese way of welcoming Tet." The governor had to shout into Joseph's ear above the din to make himself heard. "They believe that these very loud explosions will frighten away all evil spirits and make sure they have good fortune for the coming twelve months."

Looking outside again Joseph saw then that the smoke and explosions were emanating from tall bamboo poles set up around the courtyard. Topped by a few sprouting leaves, the poles were festooned to the ground with garlands of paper-wrapped firecrackers, which were all now detonating deafeningly. He let out a long breath and raised his hands to cover both ears. "That's a relief! I thought the Great War had begun all over again."

The celebratory boom of cannon echoing from another part of the citadel marked the end of the ceremony and the emperor descended slowly from his throne to shake hands in European fashion with the Résident Supérieur, and side by side they led the way into an antechamber. A band outside began to play the "Marseillaise" and iced champagne was served for the guests to toast the emperor and the New Year. Jeweled caskets of areca nut, betel leaves and little jars of lime were served by court servants to mandarins who wished to chew betel, and gem-studded boxes of cigarettes and cigars were offered to the French. As Joseph sipped his champagne, Tran Van Hieu appeared silently beside his mother with a younger Annamese man and bowed gravely.

"It gives me great pleasure, Madame Sherman, to welcome you and your son to the imperial court of Annam," he said politely. "I hope that you found our New Year ceremony of some interest."

"I'm very honored to have been present," replied the American woman, smiling in her turn. "Especially as I believe ladies are not normally permitted to observe the rites."

"Tradition is most important, but it is not good to live entirely in the past. The French have brought many advantages to our country as you no doubt have already seen." The mandarin turned and motioned the younger Annamese forward to introduce him. "May I present to you, Madame Sherman, a member of my wife's family, Monsieur Dao Van Lat. He is my wife's brother and he works as a journalist with a newspaper in Hue. He was educated in Paris, and when he heard that some Americans had been present at today's ceremonies he expressed a wish to meet you."

The handsome young Annamese in his early twenties who offered his hand promptly to Joseph and his mother had the piercing gaze and broad forehead of a scholar. Unlike the other Annamese present who wore court robes, he was dressed in the conventional short black gown and white trousers of an ordinary civilian and on his head he wore the traditional black turban of the region.

"Are you writing about today's ceremonies for your newspaper, Monsieur Lat?" asked Joseph eagerly.

"I shall write only that which was written last year and the year before that," said the Annamese with a sarcastic smile. " 'The traditional rites of homage to the emperor were performed in the Palace of Perfect Concord.' I shan't be allowed to say that we were really saluting the Résident Supérieur of France."

"My brother-in-law was educated in Paris but he is an idealist whose unorthodox views are not shared by myself or many of our countrymen," cut in Tran Van Hieu hastily. "You should not take what he says too seriously." The mandarin excused himself with a nervous smile and moved quickly away across the antechamber to talk with a group of French officials.

"What the Imperial Delegate says is not strictly true," said Dao Van Lat quietly. "Many people in this country do not share his affection for France."

"But why can't you write about the ceremonies the way that you want?" inquired Flavia Sherman politely.

The Annamese glanced over his shoulder for a moment to see if they were overheard. "You are not French, madame, so perhaps I may be honest, yes?"

The American woman nodded.

"We have no freedom of press here. Newspapers are closed and journalists are sent to jail if they displease our foreign masters." Lat's eyes glittered suddenly with the fervor of his words. "We aren't free either to pursue our political beliefs. We can't hold meetings or travel freely. We can't even send mail without its being intercepted!"

"But what would you write in your newspaper about the ceremonies if you were free to say what you liked?" asked Joseph. "I thought they were fascinating. The '*lam lay*' is a very old ritual that in other countries you can only read about in history books."

"Exactly, Monsieur Joseph," Lat glanced quickly around the room again. "The ceremonies taught us by the Chinese emperors ceased to be celebrated fourteen years ago in China itself when the revolution of Sun Yat-sen put an end to the Manchu dynasty. The precepts of Confucius only make sense if the Son of Heaven to whom we offer loyalty and allegiance represents the power and dignity of the people. The French have long ago destroyed the authority of Confucius in our old society. Today you have watched our mandarins banging their foreheads on the flagstones — but not for our emperor! That's what I would write today if I were free to choose. But instead I say only: 'The traditional rites were performed.' " Lat paused and smiled another glittering smile.

The firecrackers were still exploding intermittently in the courtyard and occasional salvos of cannon fire boomed out from beyond the walls of the Imperial City. Joseph noticed out of the corner of his eye that Khai Dinh had risen from his seat and was walking slowly in his ponderous Ming boots towards the door. Once he seemed to sway slightly and one of the red-robed princes moved quickly to his side and took his elbow.

"Our Son of Heaven unfortunately is a sick man," said Lat, seeing Joseph turn to watch the emperor. "Did you notice how often he mops his face with a handkerchief? He is only forty-two but it is feared he may have tuberculosis. We are not allowed to write about that in our newspapers, either."

All conversation ceased and the firecrackers quietened suddenly by some invisible command as the emperor took his leave of the Résident Supérieur and the governor of Cochin-China; the other French officials and guests immediately began lining up to file past and shake the sovereign's hand in farewell.

"If you go now, Madame and Monsieur Sherman, you too will be able to shake the hand of the emperor of Annam," said Lat in a low voice. "Although it is not our custom to shake hands, he likes to please his foreign overlords. But make the most of your chance, because soon our emperors will exist like those of China — only in the dusty pages of history books. *Au revoir*."

Dao Van Lat hurried out of the antechamber by a side door, leaving Joseph and his mother to join the line of departing guests. When the Emperor Khai Dinh offered his slim, feminine hand to Joseph it felt limp and damp, and although the American boy murmured his farewell politely in French, the sovereign didn't raise his head to look at him. Because Joseph was already slightly taller than him, his last memory of the Annamese Son of Heaven was a closeup view of the shimmering jewels in the top of his golden crown.

14

The raucous cries of wild jungle fowl welcoming the pale light of another dawn roused Chuck Sherman from a deep, refreshing sleep. He sat up immediately on his cot, feeling a surge of pleasurable anticipation course through him at the prospect of one more day stalking the great game animals of southern Asia through the beautiful tropical forest where he now felt almost at home. He pulled aside the mosquito net and in the gray light caught sight of his gleaming double-barreled Holland and Holland .450 propped against the wall of the hut. For a brief moment he experienced again the exhilaration he had felt on the plain late the previous day when he dropped a big red banteng bull with a single shot from nearly two hundred yards. The animal had been plunging towards the shelter of a riverside bamboo grove when he fired and it had probably been the best shot of his life. His father had wounded another bull in the same herd, but not mortally, and although they had tracked it by a faint blood trail for an hour, in the end, to the senator's ill-concealed irritation, they had been forced to abandon the search.

Chuck drew his hunting knife from its sheath before picking up his boots. He upended each of them in turn and allowed himself a grim little smile of satisfaction when a squirming scorpion tumbled from one of them. After killing it with the knife he dressed quickly. He had already learned his lesson by painful experience; the burnlike swelling on his left calf still throbbed occasionally to remind him of the morning a week ago when he had drawn on his trousers carelessly, to discover that a scorpion had spent the night nestling in one of the legs.

In his shaving mirror he saw a face burned a deep brown by two weeks of fierce tropical sunshine. His blue eyes were bright and clear and the frequent pump of adrenaline through his veins as he tracked and shot for fourteen successive days had left his senses sharpened, on a high edge of alertness. He felt fit and hardened by the spartan life of the jungle camp and he contemplated exercising the skills of stealth and lightning-sharp reaction again for one last day with a fierce relish. As he finished shaving he found he was grinning broadly at his reflection in the mirror; in that jungle dawn he knew he was as happy as he had ever been in his life.

On the other side of the camp he saw Jacques Devraux, already dressed, checking the hides the Moi had finished cleaning late the previous night. He had become accustomed to the grim silences that surrounded the Frenchman but he admired greatly his harsh efficiency in the jungle and had learned through him to identify the spoor of all the larger animals. Senator Sherman had shot marginally less well than his son and was openly disgruntled about this. But in the two weeks, as they moved slowly north into the forested hills and grassy uplands close to the hill station of Dalat, they had killed between them prime specimens of almost all the groups required for the museum. Paul Devraux had returned to Saigon the previous evening with the hides of buffalo, banteng, seladang cows and calves and a dozen smaller deer, to organize their shipment to the United States. Only a bull seladang, the giant wild ox of Asia, had so far eluded them.

When Chuck crossed to the cook tent, carrying his rifle for the early start they planned for the final day, his father was already sitting at a table in the open, sipping a steaming mug of black coffee. Torrential rains had fallen each afternoon in the past week, and three days before in the steaming jungle he had contracted a fever which he had kept at bay since with frequent doses of quinine. His face was still taut and sallow, and he looked as though he had not slept well.

While the wife of Ngo Van Loc served his breakfast and poured coffee the American boy peered anxiously at his father. "How are you feeling this morning, Dad? Got that fever beat now?"

"Fever and the jungle go together like a carriage and pair, Chuck," said the senator lightly. "It doesn't do to get too excited about it. I've been feeding it a goodly amount of quinine and aspirin in the night to keep it from going hungry."

Although his face was damp with perspiration he winked over the rim of his coffee mug, and Chuck, reassured, smiled back. As he bolted down his breakfast Chuck gazed around the clearing with delighted eyes. The first rays of the sun were gilding the grassy hillsides visible through the trees, and all around them the thick green roof of the jungle was gradually coming alive with the cries of darting, bright-hued birds. "I guess, Dad, this must be some of the finest hunting country in the world, isn't it?"

The senator nodded. "It's a hunter's paradise, Chuck. It makes a man feel like a *real* man. Makes you remember all men were hunters once — and only the fittest of them survived. It's a real pity it's so far away from America."

"It sure is. I haven't enjoyed anything more in my whole life than the shooting we've had here." Chuck watched Jacques Devraux enviously for a moment as he moved briskly about the camp, giving orders to the Moi. "You know, Dad, I'm not so sure that I'm cut out for what you want me to be," he said, and sipped his coffee with a pensive expression on his face. "I'm not sure I could do as well as you say in politics. I love the outdoors. I'd just as soon be doing what Monsieur Devraux does. That wouldn't seem like work at all to me."

The senator looked up at him sharply. "You're young yet, Chuck. You'll come around to my way of thinking before you're much older. I just know you will."

Chuck smiled at his father again, but without enthusiasm. "Maybe Joseph is a better candidate for the tricky world of politics, Dad. He's already got an old head on his young shoulders, you know."

The senator waved a dismissive hand and stood up. "I don't want to hear any more of this talk, Chuck. Let's keep our mind on the job at hand. I'm going to prove to you today what I've often told you before — that all you need in this life to succeed is real cast-iron determination." He turned away to swallow another handful of pills that he shook from a bottle, then picked up his rifle. "Come on; the sooner we make a start, the sooner you'll see what I mean."

Jacques Devraux and half-a-dozen Moi trackers were waiting beside the narrow river that flowed past the camp, and the senator put his arm lightly around his son's shoulders as they walked over to join them. "All we've got to do is convince ourselves that no matter what happens today we're going to kill a seladang bull for the Sherman Field Museum. Then it's as good as done, isn't it?"

"If you say so," agreed Chuck with a happy laugh.

When they reached the bank of the river Nathaniel Sherman motioned his son ahead into the waiting dugout canoe and laid a hand on Devraux's shoulder. "Chuck and me just want you to know, Jacques, that we don't aim to leave this jungle today without the hide and horns of the biggest bull seladang in all Asia. We're going to match up that cow and her little calf we got last week with a daddy — or go bust in the attempt."

The Frenchman peered intently into his face for a moment without replying. "Are you sure, senator," he said at last, "that you wouldn't be better taking that fever to your cot for the day?"

"No sir! Like I told you, we're determined to crown our collection with that seladang bull. So just lead us to him, if you please!"

Devraux shrugged and climbed into the dugout behind him. The tall grass on the other side of the river was still wet with dew and before they had gone fifty yards all the men were drenched to the waist. They trekked in single file for more than an hour, holding their rifles high in front of their chests, without sighting any animals at all. When they entered the jungle again, the Moi several times spotted banteng, but what few traces of seladang they found proved to be cold trails.

By nine o'clock Nathaniel Sherman was flagging. Beside a muddy pool in a shadow-dappled patch of jungle where faint feeding tracks had finally petered out, he lowered himself onto a fallen log. He was shivering again and he swallowed another handful of tablets from his waist pouch. Chuck noticed that instead of drinking the usual cold tea like the others he surreptitiously raised a hip flask to his lips a couple of times when he thought he was unobserved.

"Are you sure you're well enough to go on hunting, Dad?" he asked anxiously. "It sure looks to me as though that fever might be beginning to take hold."

"I can take my fever to bed for a couple of days back in Saigon," snapped the senator irritably. "There's no point wasting our last day." He rubbed the back of his hand across his eyes, then stood up impatiently as two of the Moi who had been scouting the region while they rested rushed into the clearing and began chatting excitedly to Devraux, pointing back the way they had come.

"They have spotted a group of seladang cows and calves grazing a half mile away," said Devraux when they had finished. "The bulls may not be far off. They're probably making for the cool thickets on this side of the river to avoid the heat. We must go carefully. There's no more dangerous animal in the jungle if you surprise him at close quarters."

"Okay, I'm ready," said the senator, picking up his rifle. As Chuck followed Devraux into the trees he hung back, pulled out his flask again and drank deeply from it. Then, treading carefully, he followed on behind the last Moi trackers.

The tall bamboo thickets fringing the narrow river rattled and groaned in the faint breeze as the file of men moved cautiously through the half-light beneath the dense overhead foliage. Every few paces they paused to peer ahead into the gloom, and when they reached a gap in the trees Devraux stopped and pointed. Two hundred yards away a group of about fifteen seladang were visible, the calves frisking and sporting around the cows that had borne them.

"The Moi were wrong!" breathed Nathaniel Sherman in an awed whisper, as he peered through his field glasses. "There *is* a big old hump-necked herd bull right in the middle of his wives and children. And he's mine!" Without waiting for the others he plunged down the bank into the stream, slipping and slithering heedlessly over the protruding roots and rocks. He waded across, scrambled up the other side and pushed through the undergrowth on the edge of the plain.

Devraux, his face stolid, looked at Chuck Sherman. "From here the wind is wrong," he said curtly. "You will see."

By the time they had splashed up the far bank Nathaniel Sherman was fifty yards away, moving erratically, breasting the grass, preparing to risk a standing shot at two hundred yards. But the swirling breeze was at the hunters' backs, and the big bull suddenly lifted his muzzle to scent in their direction, and a moment later the whole herd was running towards the shelter of the trees.

Cursing obscenely in his exasperation, Sherman set himself and fired. The crack of his first shot succeeded only in raising a screeching flock of parrots from the trees behind him and the herd ran on unharmed. The American cursed loudly again, then planted his feet more firmly and fired his second barrel — but still none of the seladang faltered. When his son and Devraux arrived at his side, however, he was still squinting through the sights of his raised rifle, watching the herd break up to enter the jungle. "Would you believe it, boy," he whispered softly, "I hit him with my second." Without waiting for Chuck he strode off in the direction taken by the herd, and halfway across the grassland he let out a roar and dropped to his knees. When he turned towards them, his son and Jacques Devraux saw that his fingers were bright with blood. "I told you I hit him! Nigh on two hundred yards and running away and I hit him!" He stood up breathing fast. "Come on, Chuck. Let's go and get him."

Devraux placed a restraining hand on the American's shoulder. Above the grasslands the air shimmered in the midday heat. "The blood trail is light. The animal is not badly wounded. To go on you must hunt through the hottest part of the day. It would be better to return to camp and resume when the sun begins to cool."

"If the rains come again today, hunting will be impossible later!"

"It would be dangerous for a fit man to pursue this animal now. In your condition" — Devraux shrugged — "it would be madness."

Perspiration was streaming down the senator's face and his eyes were bleary with too much quinine. "I've made up my mind to finish that bull, Jacques. I've hit him and I'm going to kill him!"

"Then I will take no further responsibility for this day's hunting," said the Frenchman with quiet finality.

Nathaniel Sherman jabbed a thumb against his own chest and his words came out in a fierce undertone. "That's just fine by me, Jacques. I will take the damned responsibility myself." Peering down at the faint blood trail staining the grass, he strode angrily away towards the jungle with his son at his heels. After a moment's hesitation Jacques Devraux followed at a distance with his trackers.

For half an hour they followed the telltale red blotches until finally they petered out in a glade surrounded by dense thickets of thorn and bamboo. "I'd guess we must be getting pretty close, Chuck. He's holed up somewhere around here licking that wound of his." Nathaniel Sherman removed his helmet to mop his streaming face and as he did so a movement caught his eye in the tangled undergrowth. "Did you see that, Chuck?" he asked in a fierce whisper, pointing to a thicket of thorns. "I think we've found him."

Although the denseness of the bushes prevented a clear view,

Chuck saw a patch of brown-black shadow move unmistakably and he immediately raised his rifle.

"Wait — it's mine!" His father motioned the weapon aside with a peremptory gesture. His eyes gleamed and he breathed noisily through his nose as he lifted his own rifle to his shoulder then fired both barrels at the shadow in quick succession.

A loud bellow rang out as the bullets struck home, then they heard a heavy body plunging wildly among the restraining toils of the thorn bushes. After a few seconds all movement ceased and silence returned to the glade. Grinning triumphantly at his son, the senator dropped two fresh shells into the magazine of his rifle. "Didn't I tell you, Chuck, that all you need is determination? Come and take a look at him with me."

Chuck hesitated as his father moved off unsteadily towards the thicket, and at that moment Devraux and the Moi trackers entered the glade. When the Frenchman saw what was happening, he shouted angrily for the senator to stop. But if he heard, he paid no heed.

"Wouldn't it be better to wait some, Dad?" yelled Chuck as his father reached a narrow defile between the thorns.

The older man stopped and turned. "It was me that shot the bull, son. You wait there with the trackers, if you're feeling nervous." Without waiting for a response he stepped into the thicket.

Stung by his father's words, Chuck dashed forward across the clearing.

Immediately inside the tangle of bushes Nathaniel Sherman was astonished to find himself face to face with the massive standing bulk of the black seladang bull. More than six feet high at the shoulder, the enormous, blue-eyed animal towered above him, swaying slightly on its legs. All around it the bloodstained undergrowth lay broken and flattened by its struggles, and as soon as it saw him, the animal lowered its needle-sharp horns that had grown in its prime to a length of nearly three feet. Although he had set his loaded rifle at his shoulder in readiness as he entered the thicket, before he could squeeze the trigger the wounded seladang was upon him. The bony excrescence between its horns knocked the wind from him and he collapsed onto its great hump-muscled neck. He hung there for a second before slithering sideways, and as he slipped towards the ground the seladang hooked blindly at his body, knocking it this way and that, until one of its long horns caught and held. Entering from under the pit of his arm it pierced and split his left shoulder joint, and his body swiveled slowly into an upright position, suspended on the horn. Bellowing and rearing on its hind legs, the massive bull lifted him bodily off the ground and shook him repeatedly like a rag doll.

When Chuck Sherman ran into the thicket, his father seemed to be bending over the great bull's lowered head in an attitude of extreme tenderness. The animal, sensing a new danger, shook its horns furiously to free itself from the encumbrance, and the already unconscious senator was catapulted into the thorns, where he lay without moving.

Chuck raised his rifle coolly and fired just as the bull launched itself on him. He had aimed carefully between its eyes, but its movement changed the attitude of its head and his first bullet merely grooved the glossy hide of its neck. It was an arm's length away and raising its head to hook at him with the horn that was already dark with his father's blood when he discharged his second barrel. The hard-nosed bullet struck home into the bull's chest, wounding it fatally, but it could not stop the lunging charge nor ward off the twin crescents of bone thrust upwards into his body with all the force of the seladang's powerful neck.

He fell gored through the abdomen, and the bull attacked him again as he writhed in agony on the ground. On the second thrust, one horn pierced his lung high in the left side of his chest and its tip reached his heart. As the animal roared and twisted above him, he saw close before his eyes the gray hairs of its broad black muzzle and felt the heat of its sour and bloodied breath. From below he could see that its skin was strangely pale and pink between its wide-straddled hind legs and the tight black bag of its scrotum, he thought, seemed incongruously small and toylike for such a massive, murderous animal. Distantly he heard the report of another gun and felt the impact of other bullets shudder the bull's body, but by this time its heavy black bulk was already sinking down upon him, lifeless from his own second shot.

Curiously, the last sensation of his own life was not the pain of the terrible wounds inflicted by the horns of the seladang. For a final moment the inflamed bruise on his left calf where the scorpion had stung him a week before seemed to blaze with new agonizing fire. He tried to move one of his hands to touch and soothe it but a great weariness engulfed him suddenly and his hand never reached its destination.

PART TWO

The Hatred of a
Million Coolies

1929–1930

The foundations of the colonial era, during which white
European nations dominated vast areas of Asia, Africa and
Latin America, were fatally undermined for the first time during
the turbulent second decade of the twentieth century.
Revolutions toppled first the Chinese emperor in 1911, then the
tsar of Russia in 1917; the Great War of 1914–1918 also
weakened the European powers drastically and at the same time
showed the colonized peoples that their seemingly invincible
white masters were capable of enormous self-destructive folly.
This undermining of the colonial system was accelerated further
by the formation in 1919 of the Communist International. The
organization was dedicated to the overthrow of capitalism
worldwide, and in the latter years of the 1920s Comintern agents
began working secretly in the vulnerable, far-flung colonial
territories of the capitalist nations to exploit the native
discontent. In the Annamese lands political dissatisfaction had
intensified following the premature death of the Emperor Khai
Dinh in November 1925. He was only forty-three when he died,
and the French, seizing the opportunity to reinforce their
influence, insisted that he should be succeeded by his son, Bao
Dai, then a boy of twelve still at school in Paris. They ensured
that the infant emperor continued to study in Paris for another
seven years and meantime the French Résident Supérieur in

Hue arrogated to himself the few remaining vestiges of imperial authority. This quickened anti-French feeling, and encouraged by the successes of Sun Yat-sen and Mao Tse-tung in neighbouring China, Annamese nationalists and Communists began to organize themselves more coherently. The Great Depression of 1929 sharpened the mood of rebellion when a catastrophic fall in the price of rice spread hardship and even starvation to many parts of Indochina. As a result of these mixed forces the resistance movements that had previously been the exclusive domain of irresolute Annamese intellectuals began, as the decade drew to a close, to stir the mass of the people toiling in the rice fields, the mines and the rubber plantations.

1

With its customary fury the northeast monsoon flung its nightly torrent of rain onto the close-packed ranks of rubber trees sprouting from the red-brown jungle soils of the Vi An plantation a hundred kilometers north of Saigon. In the midnight blackness the glossy-leaved trees stood silent, each with a beggar's cup of tin wedged against its straight trunk to catch the milky latex that oozed slowly from within. On the earth floors of the leaking, palm-thatched barrack huts dotted around the vast plantation, fifteen hundred Annamite coolies who would resume the unending toil of emptying the little tin cups in the gray light of the coming dawn shivered and drowsed fitfully in the downpour. To their untutored peasant minds it seemed that the endless rows of alien rubber trees marching with unnatural precision across great tracts of their wild ancestral jungles provoked the storm each night to new extremes of savagery.

In Village Number Three, where five hundred coolies were quartered, the men were packed so tight in their barracks that many of them slept and dozed seated upright. Ngo Van Dong and his younger brother, Hoc, huddled close together in the darkness in one of the long huts, their ragged clothes already saturated with the rain that streamed in through the inadequate thatch. Close beside them an older coolie, stretched full-length on the earth, was shaking and moaning uncontrollably with malarial fever.

Although they were still only in their teens, the two young Annamese had undergone a drastic change in appearance in the four years since the Sherman family had watched them gamboling around the cooking tent of their father, Ngo Van Loc, the hunting camp "boy" of Jacques Devraux. Woefully undernourished, their bodies were emaciated, pocked with sores, and eighteen months of unremitting labor in the dark, fever-ridden alleys of the rubber plantation had left their faces pinched and haggard. By day their sunken, listless eyes reflected the depth of an inner misery that would have been unthinkable to the exuberant youths of 1925.

In a lull of comparative quiet in the wind-driven roar of the rain, Hoc leaned towards his elder brother and put his lips close to his ear. "He's stopped shivering," he said in a horrified whisper. "Do you think he's died?"

In the near-total darkness Dong could not see the old coolie stretched out on the muddy floor beside them. He had been trembling violently for several hours but now no sound came from the place where he lay. Noticing that his younger brother himself was shivering, Dong, who was taller than the average Annamese, inched his long, thin body closer to him and put his arm around his shoulders. "Don't think about it. Maybe he's sleeping now. Let us try to get some sleep!"

The younger boy closed his eyes, but the sudden familiar gnaw of hunger pains drove all thought of sleep from his mind. It was six hours since they had shared their meager ration of black rice, boiled as usual in a rusting can on the communal fire inside the barrack hut. For cooking and drinking all the coolies had to use brackish water from the mosquito-infested streams that flowed sluggishly through the plantation, and Hoc wondered, as he did every time he found himself shivering, whether he too might have contracted the dreaded fever.

Dong, sensing his brother's fear, reached quietly behind him in the darkness with his free hand until his fingers brushed against the face of the malaria victim; the clammy flesh, already growing cold, was slippery with rain and the sweat of the fatal climatic fever, and in the moment that his hand recoiled from the contact Dong knew that they would not be able to avoid the horror of a burial this time. During their stay on the plantation more than a hundred coolies in Village Number Three had died of fever and malnutrition, or had committed suicide — but there had never been a death among their immediate neighbors.

Fleetingly Dong wondered whether the excursion into the jungle with the corpse might present them with another opportunity to escape. Then immediately he dismissed the thought. They had tried twice before, and on each occasion they had been pursued relentlessly through the forests by hostile Moi tribesmen who had stripped them naked, lashed their hands behind them and led them back to the plantation roped together at the neck with twisted creepers. The glowering Moi had been rewarded by the French plantation director with five piastres for each of them, and he and his brother had been publicly beaten on the soles of their feet by a group of overseers wielding heavy staves. Their swollen feet had bled profusely and they had hobbled painfully among the rubber trees for more than a month before they recovered. After the second escape attempt they were beaten again and flung into the blackness of stone-floored isolation cells in the nearby fort at An Dap. There they had spent fourteen days in solitary confinement, chained in heavy leg irons and fed only on dry rice. Never once during that time had they seen the light of day.

"Dong! We will have to bury him, won't we?" His brother spoke in a quavering voice close to his ear as though he had read his thoughts. The younger boy was trembling more violently now, and Dong feared he, too, was becoming feverish.

"Try to sleep, Hoc. I will make the grave. Don't worry."

A half-mile away in the plantation director's house a scratchy rendition of "Muskrat Ramble" played by Louis Armstrong and Kid Ory was struggling to make itself heard over the roar of the monsoon rains. Gauze screens fitted to the doors and windows were tightly closed as always to deny the plantation's malaria-bearing mosquitoes access to the presence of Claude Duclos, a heavily built Corsican in his early forties who was sprawled in a wickerwork chair under the cooling breeze of an electric fan. A glass of iced cognac and soda dangled from his right hand and he listened to the jazz with an expression of seraphic contentment on his face. When the record ended he sat up and drained the last drop of his drink, then banged the empty tumbler loudly on the low, glass-topped table beside him.

While he waited for a response he got up and moved ponderously to the wind-up gramophone housed in a carved oaken cabinet in a corner of the room. He lifted the chromium-plated playing arm and with some difficulty replaced the worn needle with a fresh sliver of sharpened steel from a tiny tin. As he restarted the record, the door of the room opened and a young Annamese peasant girl entered. He turned and watched blearily as she walked to the table, picked up the empty glass and departed again without once raising her eyes to look at him. Her bare feet made no sound on the polished pine floor, and she moved with the smooth, unbobbing grace of the peasant pole carrier. She wore the "uniform" of a house *congaie* — a long black skirt and a white blouse-cloth tied in the small of her back to leave her arms and shoulders bare; on her dark hair she wore a scrap of cloth, also of white. Swaying slightly and humming tunelessly in time with the tinny notes of the recording, Duclos waited until the door closed quietly behind her, then made his way unsteadily back to his seat.

In the kitchen his *congaie* began preparing him another drink without hesitation, although she had noticed he was swaying on his feet. He had banged his glass on the table and it was not for her to disobey. He had indicated already he wished her to stay in the house for the night, and she knew well enough that the continued presence of her widowed mother and four brothers in the servants' quarters in the rear compound depended on her strict obedience to all the wishes of the plantation director in his house. Even so, a little frown of apprehension clouded her face as her thoughts strayed to the hours ahead. Normally, although his massive body dwarfed her own, he showed her consideration in his bed, but she knew from the rare occasions when it had happened before that drinking heavily coarsened his sexual appetites. She had already refilled his glass five or six times but she had no idea why he was drinking so much. In the sudden hope that he might fall asleep without calling her, she poured a large extra measure of cognac into the glass before adding the soda.

In the main room of the house Duclos sat up suddenly in his chair, wondering why his drink was taking so long. As he looked about him his eye fell again on the telegraph message from Paris lying on the table beside him. Snorting angrily, he picked it up and read it aloud in a contemptuous voice: "Shareholders demand immediate explanation why production tonnage down last month. Essential you increase output at once to fill projected quota by year end."

He stared at the paper for a moment then crumpled it angrily into a ball and tossed it into a corner. Were the damned shareholders never satisfied? Average monthly production figures were higher than ever. Ten new vats had been installed since Christmas, there was a new dryer, the warehouse had been extended — and all this had been achieved despite the fact that twenty of the feeble "yellows" were still dying every month from malaria! Now because the output tonnage had fallen slightly for once, they wanted his blood! How did they think he could get more production from his work force if they allowed so little cash for its upkeep? If draft horses weren't fed sufficiently, they couldn't pull heavy loads, didn't they know that? If machinery wasn't serviced it broke down! He cursed the shareholders again, then looked up as the Annamese *congaie* appeared soundlessly beside him. She avoided his eyes as she placed the fresh drink on the table by his elbow, and the unchanging passivity of her face enraged him suddenly without reason. A European woman might at least chastise him about his drinking! As if the jungle and the heat and the blasted "yellows" were not enough to endure in the godforsaken tropics! His intense irritation with his distant superiors transferred itself with an illogical rush to the silent girl, and he caught her by the arm. She halted, helpless in the grip of his massive fist, but still she kept her eyes downcast. In his irrational anger he wanted to snap the lotus-stemmed wrist, and he tightened his grip until she winced. Then as soon as it had come, his anger subsided and he smiled.

With his free hand he pulled at the cheap cloth of her blouse until it slipped from her shoulders and bared her breasts. He stared at her for a moment, then motioned with his head towards the door. "*Va te coucher*," he said quietly. "*Et déshabille-toi!*"

Holding her arms modestly across her chest to cover her nakedness, she hurried obediently from the room. After she had gone he switched off the gramophone, drained his drink in a single gulp, then stooped to pick up the offending telegraph message. Smoothing out the paper he stood staring at it, reading it over and over again, all the while drumming his fingers agitatedly on the gramophone top. Then at last he straightened and squared his shoulders in resolution.

"All right!" he said vehemently, speaking aloud. "If Paris wants higher production this month at all costs, they shall have it! Let them learn the lessons of capitalism the hard way. The 'yellows' will have to start half an hour earlier from tomorrow and treat five hundred trees each — instead of three hundred and fifty! If they die faster, whose fault is it?"

He strode angrily from the room, slamming the door behind him, and when he reached the bedroom he found his lamp already lit. In blurred outline through the fine mesh of his muslin mosquito net he could see the dark shape of the Annamese peasant girl stretched naked on his bed. He pulled the net aside and looked down on her with greedy eyes. She had drawn one leg up so that her thigh hid the base of her belly from his view. Her head was turned away from him and she held her left arm across her face. Because she was reclining on her back, her small breasts lay flat on her boyish chest; only the nipples, purple shadows in the dull glow of the lamp, stood tautly erect, through fear.

Already distended in his excitement he had difficulty in removing his clothes. When he finally lowered the heavy bulk of his sweating body onto the bed beside her, his roughened hands pressed her small thighs wide and he forced himself into her immediately, ignoring her repeated cries of pain. For a few brief moments he reared and plunged on the bed, grunting like an animal, until his lust emptied itself into her. Then his corpulent body collapsed and gradually the noise of his drunken snoring drowned out the quiet sobbing of the Annamese girl.

2

A black mantle of pre-dawn darkness still cloaked the jungle and the rubber plantation villages when the Annamese *cai* who assisted the French plantation director and his European staff began sounding clamorous gongs outside the barrack huts. The coolies inside the fetid dens immediately began to stretch their stiffened limbs and drag themselves off their sodden mats, knowing that within minutes the *cai* would be among them flailing heavy staves to rouse the laggards.

Ngo Van Dong stumbled to his feet and helped his brother up quickly at the approach of the squat figure of Phat, the overseer of their barrack. He was one of a caste of brutish Annamese of low intelligence widely cultivated by the French colonizers to serve them as jailers, labor foremen and police. Phat was Duclos' particular favorite among the *cai* because the ruthless sadism with which he disciplined his fellow coolies was matched by the utter servility he showed to Duclos to ensure he retained both his approval and the necessary stamp of his authority. It was barely four o'clock when he entered the hut of the Ngo brothers and he waddled threateningly down the center of the earth floor towards them, shining his flashlight right and left, looking for any excuse to employ his cane. As he drew near they heard the sickening crack of the rod striking flesh; once, twice they heard it fall but it brought no anguished shout of pain in response. Phat struck the motionless corpse of the coolie who had died beside Hoc a third time before he realized that the wretched man had passed forever beyond pain and productive labor. Without pause or sign of remorse he swung his flashlight on the brothers and raised his rod again. "Fetch rope and a spade and dispose of this stinking carcass in the jungle! And be quick." The brutal face bulged as he yelled his order and he swung the rod again in a threatening arc. When they had gone Phat pulled a small notebook from his shirt pocket and with a little grunt of irritation made a mark in it beneath the number of the barrack hut.

Outside in the darkness Dong stopped and pressed his shivering brother against the flimsy wall of the barrack. "Stay here and hide! I will do the burial with Old Trung. Prepare our tools and take my dose of quinine at roll call as well as your own." He pressed into Hoc's hand the little ball of cold rice wrapped in a palm leaf that each of them always saved from the night before to give them strength to start the new day. "Eat my rice too — I'm not hungry this morning."

Hoc nodded dumbly as his brother sped away to fetch a spade and rope from the *cai*'s quarters. When Dong returned he found the dead man was not heavy. An emaciated rice cropper from the Red River delta who had been forced south like many others because typhoons had recently inundated the rice lands, he had worked in the rubber plantation for less than a month before succumbing to the fever. Shocked and exhausted by the severity of the work and his illness, he had spoken little of himself or the family he had left behind in the north.

Old Trung, a toughened three-year contract coolie compelled to stay on in the plantation beyond the term because he had no money or clothes to leave, knotted the cord Dong had fetched around the neck of the cadaver with a deftness that betrayed his familiarity with the task. He picked up the dead man's only possession, a straw mat, and together he and Dong dragged the body out of the barrack and through the mud towards the jungle half a mile away. Phat escorted them, scowling and flailing their shoulders with his cane from time to time to speed their progress. "Take him at least a hundred meters into the jungle," he yelled as he swung the cane across their shoulders one last time to urge them in among the trees.

Only the faintest streaks of light were brightening the sky to the east, and by the time the two coolies had gone thirty or forty yards into the jungle, the overseer was lost to sight. Trung stopped immediately and motioned Dong to dig. "Work quickly. The tigers are always hungry at this hour."

Dong dug frantically with the shovel, lifting the heavy rain-soaked clods of earth with difficulty. It took him several minutes to make a hole only two to three feet deep. When he stopped for a moment to wipe the sweat from his brow, Trung laid a cautionary hand on his arm. "Listen!" They stood with rigid tension listening to the brooding silence of the jungle all around them. "I'm sure I heard the rustle of an animal." Trung cocked his head for a moment longer. Then he looked back at the hole in the ground. "That's enough! Take his feet."

Dong looked doubtfully at the inadequate grave. "But it isn't deep enough. . . ."

From behind Trung the distinct sound of movement in the underbrush reached their ears. "Take his feet I say! And quickly."

Dong did as he was told, and they dropped the lifeless body into the shallow impression in the ground. Trung untied the cord and wound it around his waist to return later to the overseer. Then he covered the dead coolie with his mat and helped Dong fling clods of earth rapidly on top of it with his hands. When they had finished, one foot of the dead man still protruded above the surface. Seeing this, Dong picked up the shovel and made to dig again.

"No! Come; it's enough!" Trung grabbed him by the shoulders and turned him bodily in the direction of the village. "You are too conscientious. It's a better and deeper grave than any I've seen. Let's run now or we will wind up alongside him."

Dong took one last look back and shuddered at the sight of the disembodied foot poking from the red jungle earth. He closed his eyes and offered an anguished prayer to his own ancestors and those of the dead man, begging their forgiveness. Then he turned and ran as fast as he could to catch up with Trung. By the time they had run the half-mile back to their barracks the tiger that had been stalking them in the penumbra had emerged from his cover. Without difficulty the animal unearthed the dead coolie by dragging at the protruding leg and disappeared again into the undergrowth. In the comfort of its lair its powerful jaws were soon mangling the puny chest and shoulders of the dead Annamese into a bloody pulp.

3

When Dong and Old Trung fell into the roll call line on either side of Hoc outside their barrack hut, names had already been checked and the morning doses of quinine had been handed out. Hoc was pale, but shivering less violently. All five hundred coolies from Number Three Village were drawn up outside their barracks in long ranks; silent and apprehensive, they were wondering why they had been roused half an hour earlier and why the burly, intimidating figure of the plantation director, Duclos, was waiting to address the massed roll call beneath the single lightpole in the barrack compound.

Their bruised shoulders and backs reminded them that the *cai* and the French assistants had been particularly vicious that morning. Had there been another mass breakout attempt in the night for which they were all to be punished? Or perhaps another of the *cai* living quarters had again been burned down by coolies in one of the other villages? Clutching their *coupe-coupes*, their tapping tools and their collecting cans, they waited dumbly, their eyes flicking from Duclos to the cane of the overseer nearest to them.

The plantation director was standing on an upturned crate that had been placed in position for him beneath the light, and despite the early hour he was already wearing his customary pith helmet, the sleeves of his bush shirt were rolled high on his brown muscular arms and he was bare-legged in shorts, heavy jungle boots and short thick socks. Around his waist he wore a broad leather belt with a bone-handled knife clasped in a sheath and as usual in the presence of the coolies his right hand rested on its hilt as if it were a ceremonial sword. Filling his barrel chest with a deep breath, he glared around at the assembled crowd. "Twenty years ago there was not a single rubber tree in all Indochina," he roared. "Do you hear? Fifteen years ago this plantation where we live and work today was virgin jungle inhabited only by savage herds of elephants! We, the French, came twelve thousand miles across the sea. We built roads and villages and brought rubber trees and planted them for mile after mile through your wild land. We produced an oasis of civilized industry in this fever-ridden wilderness!" He stopped, jammed his hands on his hips and leaned forward from the waist in a belligerent posture. "And we worked for many years before we collected a single cup of rubber, do you hear? Storms blew down the trees, fires ravaged the plantation, dry years killed our saplings — but we did not give up, we labored on!" He paused and drew himself up proudly to his full height again. "Today our plantations here have become the finest in all the Far East!"

The coolies shifted uneasily, their gaze never leaving the Corsican's face. The older ones among them who had heard similar harangues before had already sensed they were about to experience some harshening of their conditions.

". . . I, Duclos, am responsible for the plantation of Vi An and I will not tolerate lazy, idle, work-shy 'yellows' here. . . ." His lips curled contemptuously as he used the abusive French term *jaunes*. "Last month our production fell because of your contemptible idleness. The shareholders in Paris are displeased. They expect 1929 to be the best year ever for rubber production. We have less than three months of the year left now, so from today the daily quota of trees to be treated by each one of you will be raised from three hundred and fifty to five hundred!" He stopped again and glared aggressively along the ranks of silent Annamese. "That is why you have been roused early. Five hundred trees each and every day you will treat from now on — or

113

you will be punished with fines, you will be beaten and you will be clapped in irons in An Dap."

A young French assistant, who had been holding the white horse on which Duclos ranged the plantation each day, stepped forward at a signal from him and steadied the animal while he mounted. Swinging the horse's head to face the massed coolies again, Duclos drew a long solid wood truncheon from a leather saddle scabbard and stood up in the stirrups.

"Go now! And don't return until you have completed your quota." As he shouted his order he spurred the horse forward suddenly towards the front ranks of the coolies, scattering them in the direction of the rubber groves.

It was still not yet five o'clock, and the trees themselves were scarcely distinguishable in the semidarkness. Dong and Hoc ran panting along the adjacent ranks allotted to them, calling out frequently to encourage one another and to check each other's progress. They had to run constantly to complete the first tapping of their three hundred and fifty trees in the five hours before ten o'clock. They spent only a minute or so at each tree, cleaning off dried latex, adjusting the collecting supports and making new incisions through which the day's latex could escape. They had to work fast but with care since poor incisions invariably brought a beating from the *cai* or the French.

At precisely ten o'clock a siren split the burning air above the plantation to indicate that collection of the latex was to begin. On hearing this, the brothers ran the two thousand meters back to the start of their rows and began visiting each tree in turn again to empty the cups into their carrying cans. When the cans were full they ran with them to one of the many collecting stations from which trucks transported the latex to the central warehouses.

By the time they had finished collecting it was midday: the sun was directly overhead and the rubber groves steamed with suffocating heat. Exhausted from seven hours of nonstop toil, the brothers flung themselves down on the red soil in the shade along with the other fifteen hundred coolies of the plantation and lay like dead men. When they had recovered they hurriedly cooked and ate the ration of cold rice they had brought with them from the barracks and swallowed a mouthful or two of water.

Usually they cleared underbrush and weeds from the rubber groves from one o'clock until sunset, but the new quotas ordered by Duclos that morning meant they had had to tap and collect from more than a hundred extra trees through the hot afternoon although their energies were largely spent. Hoc's fever began to return halfway through the task, and Dong ran frantically back and forth between their adjoining rows, working his own and his brother's trees while Hoc rested. This saved Hoc from the beating that would inevitably have followed discovery of his shortcomings when the scowling overseers dipped their yardsticks into the cans at the collecting station.

It was nearly seven in the evening and the sun was setting behind their backs before the two weary, footsore brothers were able to limp back to their barracks in Number Three Village with their joint quota fulfilled. At the gates they found the *cai* assembling the whole labor force before the barrack huts to witness the public punishment of those who had failed to meet the new demands. The exhausted coolies stumbled against one another in panic as the overseers marshaled them into a circle with blows about the head and shoulders. A group of thirty or forty downcast men stood apart in the center of this ring, their heads and arms hanging slack in attitudes of despair.

Dong put a supportive arm around his brother and pulled him deeper into the crowd. There at least they would not have to see and hear the effect of the blows as clearly as those in front. Duclos was watching grimly from astride his horse, and a hush fell on the compound when he rose in his stirrups and lifted his own stave from its leather scabbard as a signal to the *cai* to begin.

The first batch of five coolies were flung face downward in the red dirt, and under the direction of the burly figure of Phat, half a dozen of his subordinates began lashing at the exposed soles of their bare feet. Their staves rose and fell steadily, the men swinging them high above their heads with a measured and deliberate rhythm born of long practice. Each coolie received a hundred blows, and only their muffled cries of pain punctuated the regular thud of the staves.

Phat counted the strokes, darting an occasional glance at Duclos to ensure he retained his approval. On the hundredth blow he motioned his subordinates to cease and haul the moaning coolies upright.

"*Nhanh nhu tho!*" yelled Duclos, brandishing his own stave. "Now run like hares!"

The *cai* prodded the five men until they began hobbling on their swollen, bleeding feet around the edge of the circle formed by their fellows. One who fell was beaten again before being dragged upright and pushed on his way. The five Annamese, grunting with pain continued stumbling and staggering around the circle in grotesque imitation of bounding hares while the next group of victims were thrown down in the dirt.

As the punishments resumed, the sound of revving engines broke upon the scene and three open trucks crowded with new coolie laborers swung into the compound in a swirl of dust. A brightly polished black Citroën followed them in and drew up beside Duclos' horse. Phat looked inquiringly towards his master, wondering if the procedures should be halted, but the Corsican waved him on, gesturing peremptorily for the crowd to be moved back so that the new recruits could see what was happening.

Dong, because of his unusual height, had a clear view of the new arrivals above the heads of the crowd — and within a matter of seconds his startled eyes fell on two familiar faces that he had not seen for well over a year. The tall stoop-shouldered European in a white suit and felt hat who climbed from the gleaming car and offered a languid hand in greeting to Duclos he recognized first as Auguste Lepine, the director of the Indigenous Labor Recruitment Agency. Lepine had accompanied the *cai* who had lured him and his brother to the plantation eighteen months earlier, but despite the feeling of hatred the sight of him inspired Dong scarcely gave the recruiter a second glance. His astonished gaze was fixed on the second familiar face staring out at the public floggings from amid the crowd of frightened coolies on the first truck, a face he hadn't seen for even longer — that of his own father!

4

"Where on earth do you keep finding them, Auguste?" Claude Duclos wiped the champagne froth from his mustache with the back of his hand and refilled their glasses. "I heard a rumor you were deliberately smashing dikes in the north and flooding the paddies to drive the starving 'yellows' to our rubber trees. Is that right?"

Lepine's sallow features twitched and a sardonic smile flickered across his face, but he didn't reply. Instead he took a sheaf of glossy photographs from his portmanteau and pushed them across the table towards the Corsican. Duclos rattled the empty champagne bottle impatiently against the table-top as he picked them up. The oppressive heat was making both men sweat despite the breeze from the electric fan, and distant thunder presaged the early approach of the nightly storm. Duclos mopped his forehead with a handkerchief already soaked in perspiration before looking at the photographs.

Some showed neatly dressed Annamese families smiling from the doorways of houses set in small gardens beside groves of rubber trees. In other well-fed, well-clad workers were tapping trees while friendly, attentive Frenchmen in sun helmets looked indulgently over their shoulders. Duclos smiled grimly as he flicked through them. "Marvelous, *mon vieux*. Marvelous! You show them these, and then you have to put up barriers to stop them volunteering in their thousands, yes?"

"It's not quite as easy as that, Duclos," replied the recruiter testily. "It's very hard work. Last year I supplied the plantations of Cochin-China and Annam with thirty-five thousand northern coolies — and shipped another ten thousand to the New Hebrides."

The Corsican whistled approvingly. "Forty-five thousand bodies! And you make a fifteen-piastre profit on each one, don't you? That's nearly seven hundred thousand piastres. . . ." He closed his eyes to calculate then opened them and whistled softly again. "About seven million francs — not a bad profit for the year, Auguste." He smiled and made a little admiring gesture with his hand that took in Lepine's well-cut linen suit, his handmade shoes and silk shirt. "No wonder, Auguste, you can afford to dress now like an English lord."

"If your wastage rate on these plantations wasn't so high, there would be no need for me to supply you with new coolies all the time," said Lepine sourly. "If you treated them better, they wouldn't be mutilating their hands and feet at the rate they are, to escape your clutches." He glanced at another sheaf of papers. "Your fever deaths too are high again — or are they mostly concealed suicides?"

Duclos, taken aback by Lepine's hostility, sat up indignantly in his seat. "The fashion for voluntary mutilation is being stamped out, Auguste. They know that we send them straight to the cells at An Dap now, no matter how badly they injure themselves. And can I help it if so many 'yellows' die of fever in their own country?" He shrugged helplessly. "I have to drive them hard. Always the shareholders in Paris want higher production. Already they've had six million francs' profit from an investment of twelve million — but always they want more."

Lepine yawned and passed a hand wearily across his face. "You talk of the shareholders in Paris as though you yourself owned no shares in the plantation," he said slightingly. "Perhaps it is most convenient to imagine you are doing all that you do here at the behest of some distant ogre."

"My holding is very small, Auguste," protested Duclos with a little laugh of embarrassment. "Compared with the major share-holdings, it is nothing." He looked at the stiff unbending features of the recruiter for a moment: the dark hollows around his eyes and his dry, parchmentlike skin betrayed a long addiction to opium, and Duclos guessed that his irritability stemmed from this. "But why should we endure the hell of life in the colonies, *mon vieux*, if we don't enjoy ourselves a little and try to put something by for our old age at the same time, heh?" The Corsican, straining to inspire conviviality in his guest, picked up his champagne glass and held it towards him, inviting him to drink to the idea. But the recruiter steadfastly ignored him.

At that moment a clap of thunder exploded directly overhead as the storm burst and rain began beating noisily against the outside of the house. Both men listened to it for a moment, then Duclos stood up restlessly and walked over to his gramophone. "Perhaps we need a little jazz, Auguste," he said, winding the mechanism vigorously. "I find it is the only thing which will keep the *cafard* at bay when I'm alone. I try not to drink too much when nobody's here. Without my jazz I don't think I would survive the tropics. What would you prefer? Sidney Bechet's saxophone? I have 'Wild Cat Blues' or 'Kansas City Man.' "

Lepine shrugged indifferently, and the plantation director put on a record of his own choice. He stood listening attentively for a moment as the saxophone vied with the noise of the storm outside; then he returned to his seat, picked up his champagne glass and drained it. "Another fashion we are stamping out on the planta-tion, Auguste, is Bolshevism," he said, leaning earnestly towards the recruiter. "Did you hear about the trouble the big Michelin plantation at Phu Rieng has been having with 'red peril' agitators?"

"I've been in the Pacific islands for a month looking at the plantations there," replied Lepine in an uninterested voice. The jazz coming from the gramophone was irritating him and in his limbs the uneasiness familiar to smokers of opium was beginning to take hold.

"There was a mass breakout two weeks ago and the *cai* uncovered an attempt to organize a strike. Half-a-dozen coolies have been clapped in irons — assorted Bolsheviks and members of something called the 'Viet Nam Quoc Dan Dang' — the Nationalist Party." He snorted with contempt. "My overseers keep their eyes peeled here, I can tell you. The slightest suspicion of trouble and we run them into An Dap so fast their yellow feet don't touch the ground." He laughed mirthlessly, hoping to persuade Lepine to share his black humor. "You didn't bring any Comintern infiltrators with that load today, did you, Auguste?"

"Just getting coolie labor to you here is difficult enough, Duclos," snapped the recruiter. "I can't give you guarantees about their political purity."

At that moment the door opened to admit the barefoot Annamese *congaie* carrying a fresh bottle of chilled Perrier-Jouet champagne. She filled Duclos' empty glass unobtrusively and retreated silently towards the door. As he picked up his drink Duclos looked meaningfully at Lepine and raised an inquiring eyebrow in her direction.

Lepine dropped his gaze. "Can she prepare a pipe?"

"Of course."

"Then for that alone, I will require her." The recruiter spoke his words with careful deliberation, peering intently into the froth of his champagne. Then he added: "And do I understand correctly that you don't keep a 'boy' in your house?"

Duclos looked puzzled for a second. Then comprehension dawned and he bristled. "I have no need of 'boys' in my house," he said brusquely. "That's not one of my vices."

"Really, Duclos, you surprise me." The tone of the recruiter remained confident, unabashed. "It might perhaps be worth considering who controls your supply of coolie labor now. I tend to remember first the requirements of those plantations that care to provide the best hospitality when I pay a visit."

Duclos' eyes narrowed as he registered the undisguised threat in the recruiter's words; then he forced a laugh to his lips. "I am a man of the world Auguste, *mon ami*. I'm sure we can find a pretty young thing for you."

A hundred yards away across the rain-drowned compound Dong and Hoc were weeping openly as they embraced their father in the blackness of their leaking barrack hut. Huddled together on the muddy earth floor they were content for a long time to embrace one another without speaking.

"How did you find us, Father?" sobbed Dong at last. He strained his eyes but could make out no more than the vague outline of Ngo Van Loc's face in the darkness.

"The party helped me trace you — the Viet Nam Quoc Dan Dang. It's a new secret organization of nationalists and patriots working to free us from the French!" The older man paused and his voice took on a faint note of censure. "But how did you come to be here?"

Dong and his younger brother moved closer together. "After we ran away from you we traveled as far as Quang Nam — that's where we met the French recruiter who arrived here tonight with your truck," said Dong hesitantly. "He and his Annamese *cai* tricked us. They gave us six piastres and told us it was advance pay for work on a rubber plantation not far away. They said we'd receive eighty cents a day for six hours work and promised us good food, good houses to live in. They then put us on trucks to bring us here and anyone who tried to escape was beaten senseless." Dong's voice became tearful at the memory. "We tried to escape but every time they caught us and beat us. We tried to write letters to you — but they were taken away by the *cai* and burned. . . ."

Around them the coolies punished earlier whimpered and groaned in their sleep. Others snored and all the time the rain pounded loudly against the thin palm thatch above their heads.

"But why did you run away from the hunting camp in the first place?"

Both brothers shifted uncomfortably on the wet ground but did not answer.

"Why, Dong, why?" he asked again in a gentler tone.

After another long silence Dong found his voice. "We were ashamed, Father."

"Ashamed of what?" A slight break in the older man's voice suggested he already suspected what the answer might be and was afraid.

"Ashamed of what was happening. . . ." Dong's answer came in an almost inaudible whisper. "We hated what our mother was doing — and you knew!"

Loc let out a little moan of anguish. "I thought you were too young to understand! I should have tried to explain." He groaned again. "Now it is too late."

Hoc gripped his father's arm in alarm. "Why is it too late?"

"Because all I can do is to pray to the spirits of our ancestors for forgiveness. . . ."

The despair in their father's voice had sent a sudden chill of apprehension through the brothers. "What do you mean? Where is our mother?" asked Dong. "Why have you left her alone to come here?"

Ngo Van Loc reached out in the darkness and clasped both his sons' hands tightly in his own. "Your mother is dead."

"Dead?" Both brothers echoed the word in horror.

"Yes. She died two months ago — in prison."

"How in prison?"

Loc hesitated, then took a long breath. "We supplied information to different revolutionary groups for many years about Devraux's work for the Sûreté. I often traveled abroad with him as his driver when he investigated the activities of our revolutionary émigrés. When the Quoc Dan Dang was formed two years ago we joined secretly and agreed to continue spying on Devraux. . . ." His voice broke with emotion and faded to a whisper. "That's why she did what she did — so that Devraux wouldn't suspect us. She hated it! And I hated it too! It didn't happen often, but when it did, we tried to put it from our minds — to remember only what we were trying to do for our country."

Hoc buried his face in his brother's shoulder and began sobbing silently. For a long time the furious rhythms of the storm and the grunting of the exhausted men around them were the only sounds to be heard inside the hut.

"But why was she taken to prison?" asked Dong in a choked voice.

"I had to go away for several days and while I was gone your mother saw some papers in Devraux's desk. She hid them in our quarters, thinking they might be of use to the party, but Devraux found them and she was taken to prison. I was warned by the party and didn't return to the house." He paused, fighting again to control his emotions. "A month later I learned she was dead. The French say she died of ill health! But I know from the jailers that she was tortured! The French are terrified of the revolutionary movement and are torturing all prisoners for information, with electricity."

"He killed her!" breathed Dong. "Devraux killed her!" He pulled his sobbing brother to him and they rocked back and forth together making little moaning noises between their clenched teeth, trying to ease their agony.

A moment later the sounds of the storm were magnified suddenly in the hut as the door at one end flew open. A flashlight searched back and forth across the sleeping bodies of the coolies as the hulking figure of Duclos advanced down the barrack in a dripping black rain cape. The beam came to rest on the Ngo brothers, and after a moment's hesitation Duclos bent down and seized Hoc by the arm. "Come, my pretty lad, you're coming with me!" He hauled the sobbing boy to his feet.

"This is no time to sleep. There's a spot of extra work for you tonight."

Beneath the shelter of the plantation house verandah, Auguste Lepine was standing, his eyes glazed with opium, watching the rain. When he saw Duclos striding back across the compound dragging a young Annamese boy behind him, he smiled quietly to himself, stepped back into his bedroom and began fumbling with the buttons of his silk shirt.

5

The plangent notes of the dawn gongs rousing the coolies from their barracks faded and died as Claude Duclos drained his third and last cup of *café noir* on the verandah of the plantation house. The scowl of irritation on his face was more marked than usual, and the moment he replaced the cup on its saucer the *congaie*, who had been hovering behind the screen door, hurried out to remove his breakfast tray. Sniffing the moist morning air, he fancied he could still detect sickly traces of the opium smoked by his guest, and his scowl deepened. He found the personal habits of the coolie recruiter deeply repugnant and this only increased the resentment he felt at his helpless dependence on him for replacements to his dwindling labor force.

From inside the house the scratchy gramophone burble of "Muskrat Ramble" was providing an incongruous counterpoint to the screech of the wild birds wakening unseen in the roof of the surrounding jungle, and Duclos sighed and closed his eyes to concentrate better on the music. For a minute or two he relaxed; with something approaching a smile on his face, he sat drumming his fingers on the tabletop and tapping the toe of one of his jungle boots on the verandah boards. Then he opened his eyes again to peer at his watch and the expression of irritation returned.

From the nearby compound of Village Number Three he could hear the Annamese *cai* marshaling the shuffling coolies for roll call. He listened for a moment to their angry shouts and the occasional thud of their rattan canes, then he stood up and jammed his pith helmet squarely on his head; automatically his hand checked the presence of his bone-handled knife in its sheath. As he made to step down from the verandah he heard a footfall behind him and turned to find Lepine, already immaculate in his white suit, ready to leave. Although the recruiter had obviously bathed, he still exuded the faint mustiness of the habitual opium smoker as he pressed past Duclos to take his place at the breakfast table.

"*Bonjour, Auguste, mon vieux.* I hope you've enjoyed your first visit to Vi An," said the plantation director with a forced affability.

Lepine confined his greeting to a surly nod. Without looking up he poured himself coffee and sipped it noisily. "Your Annamite was scabrous — and he sniveled constantly," he complained in a sour voice.

"*Tant pis, tant pis!* Perhaps next time I'll have more time to prepare. I know what to look for now." Duclos offered his hand, anxious to be gone from the unwholesome presence of the recruiter. "Please excuse me — I must begin my work."

Lepine shook his hand perfunctorily without rising. "I trust from now on you will employ your work force sparingly. Replacements for your plantation won't be so easy to come by in future."

The recruiter's voice had become undisguisedly offensive and Duclos, after a moment's hesitation, stepped off the verandah and strode angrily away without replying. When he reached the barracks of Number Three Village the sky to the east was already lightening but the *cai* had still not finished handing out the morning quinine. Immediately the anger and irritation he had brought with him from the house erupted in a howl of anger. He snatched up a handful of the medicaments and began distributing them himself to the coolies in the front rank. Halfway along the line he came across the Ngo brothers, and his eye fell on Hoc. The Annamese boy was standing in an attitude of despair, his chin sunk on his chest. His *coupe-coupe* and his other tapping tools hung limply in his hands at his sides, and he didn't raise his head at the Corsican's approach.

The sight of the youth who had so displeased the detested recruiter and thereby jeopardized his future supply of coolies stopped Duclos in his tracks. Hoc's puny shoulders and bowed head reminded the furious Corsican suddenly of his own helplessness in the face of the unreasoning demands from Paris, and without warning he struck out at Hoc with his free hand, knocking him to the ground. "You sniveling wretch! Stand up straight and show respect to your superiors — or you will feel the irons of An Dap about your ankles again!"

Hoc struggled upright with difficulty. For a moment he stood gazing balefully at the Corsican's back as he turned away to pass on down the line. Then his eyes, red-rimmed from weeping, widened dementedly and he lunged from his place, swinging the long blade of his *coupe-coupe* high above his head.

One of the Annamese *cai* yelled a frantic warning, and Duclos was starting to turn when the sharpened edge of the heavy blade split his helmet. Because he was swiveling his head to look behind him, the blow skidded off his skull, severed his left ear and bit deep into vital veins and arteries at the base of his neck. The anguished force of the stroke drove the Corsican to his knees and, paralyzed with shock, he remained in this posture, groping ineffectually for the bone-handled knife as his blood spurted onto the red dust around him.

Hoc and his brother shrank back in momentary horror from the man dying at their feet; then Hoc began sobbing loudly. All around them the other coolies stared in disbelief at the sight of their tormentor so astonishingly struck down before their eyes; then the floodwaters of their hatred burst some invisible dam, and several men dashed forward screaming incoherently to slash at the kneeling man's head and shoulders with their *coupe-coupes*. He fell on his side under the onslaught, and one coolie wrenched the bone-handled knife from his helpless fingers. With a wild yell of triumph the Annamese dropped to his knees and plunged the knife to the hilt in the dying Corsican's chest.

The moment Duclos fell, his two young French assistants and the *cai* started instinctively towards him; but seeing the electrifying force of spontaneous, hate-inspired rebellion sweeping through the crowd of five hundred coolies, they froze where they stood, their faces blanching with fear. The coolies sensed their fright instantly, and in a moment forty or fifty of them were advancing menacingly on the little group of overseers, brandishing the implements they had used for so long to tend the rubber plantation under their ruthless tutelage.

Caught up in the hysteria of the moment, Hoc ran blindly with the milling crowd, still clutching the bloodstained *coupe-coupe* with which he'd felled the Corsican. His brother, Dong, ran yelling beside him, as shocked and bewildered as all the other coolies by their sudden freedom. Knowing they could expect no mercy from the revenge-crazed mob, the Annamese *cai* were the first to turn and flee, and the two terrified Frenchmen followed them. They reached the shelter of the brick-built *cainha* far enough ahead of their pursuers to lock themselves in, and for several minutes the coolies milled around the building, trying without success to smash the stout wooden doors and shutters. Then a voice yelled: "Burn them out! We must burn them out!" and Dong and Hoc joined a party of two-dozen coolies in a headlong dash to the tractor sheds to fetch drums of oil.

The two boys were splashing the fuel frenziedly over the walls and windows of the *cainha* when their father found them. Flushed and wild-eyed like all the others, they resisted at first when he tried to drag them away.

"The alarm will be raised soon! The provincial garrison at Bien Hoa will be called out! We can't take on the whole French colonial army — we must escape. Now!" Loc seized them both by the arm and forced them to run with him towards the jungle.

As they reached the trees they heard a wild burst of cheering and turned to see the first tongues of flame licking up the walls of the *cainha*. Several hundred coolies were surging round the building baying for the blood of the overseers inside.

"They will have guns in there! They'll shoot their way out!" cried Loc, urging his sons on again. "Many coolies will be killed. They are foolish to stay."

"But where are we going, Father?" asked Dong frantically. "Whenever we tried to escape before we were always captured by the Moi. It's impossible to get through the jungle to Saigon from here."

"We're not going south! Runaways from these plantations have always tried to reach Saigon because it is the nearest big city. That's foolish! We will go the other way — to Hue, to Hanoi. It's much farther but there we can carry on the fight. The Quoc Dan Dang is stronger in the north!"

A sudden flurry of shots rang out from the direction of the *cainha*, confirming the older man's prediction, and without further argument the two boys turned and followed him into the jungle at a run.

On the verandah of the plantation house Auguste Lepine heard the commotion in the compound but in the half-light could not see clearly enough to identify its cause. As a precaution he returned leisurely to his bedroom to collect the case containing his business papers and the revolver he habitually carried. On his instructions his luggage had already been carried to the Citroën by the *congaie*. When he stepped out onto the verandah again, to his astonishment a mob of twenty or more Annamese was swarming across the garden dragging between them drums of oil and petrol stolen from the tractor sheds, intent on firing the house.

125

They recognized him instantly and half-a-dozen coolies wielding *coupe-coupes* separated from the rest and dashed towards him. Snatching his revolver from his case, he emptied the gun into the advancing group from a range of only thirty yards; three or four of the coolies stumbled and fell, but the rest came on screaming with even greater frenzy.

Sweating with fear, Lepine dashed along the verandah and flung himself behind the wheel of the Citroën. The engine started first time and the car shot away down the dirt road, but he could not prevent the leading coolie from leaping onto the running board beside the driver's door. As the motor car gathered speed, the Annamese flailed wildly at the windshield until the glass splintered in the recruiter's face, blinding him. Revving fast in low gear the Citroën swerved in a half-circle and smashed into the bank at the roadside, flinging the coolie clear. Lepine was knocked unconscious by the impact and a few seconds later his head was hacked from his shoulders by a flurry of *coupe-coupe* blows rained on him in the driving seat by the surviving coolies. They tipped the contents of one oil drum into the car and threw in a burning rag. When its petrol tank exploded a few minutes later, the flames from the blazing car, the house and the *cainha* lit the dawn sky more brilliantly than the first rays of the rising sun.

6

Dao Van Lat studied his naked body in the long mirror and was seized afresh with an exhilaration of awe. For an instant, too, a detached sense of pity welled up inside him at the body's seeming frailty in the face of its task; could the slight, sloping shoulders carry the heavy burdens of leadership, the thin arms and bony wrists hold a long steady course? Would the sharp-jutting pelvis, the spindly, narrow-thighed legs support all the endeavors of the rest? His amber skin was suffused with the roseate glow of a red Tet lantern hanging from the ceiling, and because it cast a shadow across the dark valley of his groin he brushed his hand quickly down the funnel of his lower belly as though seeking reassurance of his completeness.

Poetic wishes for longevity and health written in Chinese calligraphy on blood-red streamers decorated the walls of the shabby room adjoining the printing shop of the Hanoi newspaper for which he worked. On the little altar to his ancestors beside the mirror, lighted candles stood amidst tiny dishes of fruits, pork, fish and rice, and behind him incense burners and small brass pans of aloe wood set on a low lacquered table sent perfumed smoke drifting in gentle spirals towards the ceiling.

When he raised his gaze to inspect his face, Lat found his eyes agleam with the intensity of his fervor. Round, high-cheeked, boyish but with a scholar's high brow, it was the face of a man of twenty-seven years of age nerving himself for an extreme deed, a supreme effort of will. It was a face that Joseph and Flavia Sherman would have recognized instantly from their encounter with the Annamese journalist in the palace of Khai Dinh at Tet exactly five years earlier because it had changed little, if at all, in the interval of time.

Lat searched his own eyes and saw reflected there the mingled emotions that haunted his mind. He was proud that the invisible spirit animating the slight frame had dared to conceive the intended deed as his duty; but he was afraid at the same time that he would lack the courage to endure the pain and carry it through.

"Our hearts are like iron and stone; they will never tremble!"

Between clenched teeth he quoted the words of the nineteenth-century poet Phan Van Tri. Written nearly eighty years before as marauding French forces seized their first tracts of territory in Cochin-China, they reflected his own deep conviction, derived from a totally different experience, in the ultimate supremacy of the spirit of man. Hadn't he studied in France and seen the men of this supposedly superior civilization living amid their mighty machines and their great institutions? Hadn't he read the philosophers of France, of Germany and of other European nations? Didn't they all agree with Phan Van Tri that the seeds of victory were to be found only in the spirit of man? And wasn't the disciplined, self-denying spirit of Nietzsche's Superman the finest expression of this high ideal? After all, hadn't the insuperable iron ships, the powerful weapons, the all-conquering engines of the colonialists been born first in the determined spirit of Western man? If Western nations could produce the philosophical Superman of Nietzsche, why not Asian nations too? The time had come at last for Confucius to bow to the sages of the modern world!

He nodded avidly in affirmation of his train of thought and turned so that the light fell directly on the front of his body. Again he ran his gaze down his reflection from shoulder to loins. The physical manifestation of his manhood, as always in repose, appeared a shrunken, insignificant part of him. He wondered anew that the great and glorious power of life could flow so fiercely and endlessly through such a shriveled and unbeautiful fountain-head. It hardly seemed possible that powerful, destructive pass-ions could spring unendingly from such an unpromising source! He shook his head in a little motion of disbelief but he knew there could be no turning back. If he was to rise above the constant lure of carnal lusts that distracted him daily, if he was to dedicate and devote his life to freeing his country from the monstrous rule of France, there could be no choice! He clenched his fists at his sides to strengthen his resolve. If he was to become the Asian Superman of Nietzsche's teachings, he must cast aside all thought of pleasure and sensual gratification and concentrate only on the task before him!

Closing his eyes, he forced himself to think of his hatred for the colonial French. Behind his back they called him a *"jaune"* — a "yellow" with its unmistakable implication of cowardice; if feeling more tactful they called him an "Annamite" — but wasn't that only in truth a man of China's ancient colony, the "Pacified South"? True, they had been vassals of China for nine long centuries — but hadn't their hearts "like iron and stone" enabled them at last to throw off the Chinese yoke when the Tang dynasty crumbled? Hadn't they hurled back the Mongols from their frontiers and defeated the invasion forces of the Sung and Ming emperors? And when their great Emperor Gia Long finally rose from the Mekong delta a century ago to unify all the peoples from Saigon to Hanoi, hadn't he triumphantly renamed his new empire "Viet Nam"? That was what they must keep in mind! The arrival of the French colonizers a few decades later had merely given them another chance to demonstrate their indomitable spirit. The white foreigners may have partitioned and ruled their land for seventy years, but that didn't make him and his countrymen "yellows," "Annamites" or "Annamese." They were men of "Viet Nam"! They were *Vietnamese!* And in their spirit lay the dormant power that could make them proud, free men again! That power must be released, allowed to gush forth. Yes, and he must lead them and inspire his companions by his example!

He opened his eyes and glanced at the clock beside his bed. In five hours' time it would be midnight. The first day of the first month in the Year of the Horse was at hand. In the Western calendar a new decade had just begun — it was the right time for a new beginning!

The intensity of the emotions evoked by his train of thought quickened his breathing and he rushed across the room to the bookshelves in the shadows beside the ancestral altar. He ran his fingers along the spines of the books he'd brought back from the other side of the world; books owned illegally since the French not only censored newspapers but decreed which books he and his fellow countrymen might lawfully read. There were the works of Flaubert, Kant, Plato, Nietzsche. . . . He plucked the little blue leatherbound volume of Nietzsche's *Thus Spake Zarathustra* from the shelf and held it towards the light of one of the flickering candles on the altar.

The well-thumbed book fell open at the single page headed "Of Chastity" and his lips moved as he recited a passage to himself in a hushed whisper.

"And behold these men! Their eyes confesseth it — they know naught better on earth than to lie with a woman.
The ground of their soul is filth. Alas if there be yet mind in their filth!
Would at least ye were perfect, as are the beasts. But to the beast belongeth innocence.
Do I counsel you to slay your senses? I counsel you innocence of the senses!"

Lat let the book fall closed in his hands and looked up at the altar. It consisted of three lacquered tables of different heights. Elaborate carved figures of clouds, dragons and trees intertwined endlessly across their surfaces and on the highest table stood a box lacquered in red and gold which contained a list of the names of his ancestors, stretching back over several centuries. His gaze fixed itself on the box with great intensity, as though he were willing the spirits of his forebears to understand alien thoughts. Then he closed his eyes. "Thus Spake Zarathustra!" he whispered fiercely, and as he did so tears squeezed out from beneath his closed lids and rolled down his cheeks.

He stood unmoving for several minutes and then opened his eyes and inhaled deeply until he had regained his composure. With something approaching reverence he replaced the book on the shelf and went into the kitchen and opened a drawer. The long knife that he withdrew glinted dully in the light from the altar candles and after gazing at it for a moment he took a whetstone from the same drawer and began caressing the already razor-sharp blade with it.

Less than a mile from the shabby little room where Dao Van Lat was contemplating his act of self-sacrifice on the eve of Tet, 1930, Jacques Devraux was working late at his new desk in the Hanoi headquarters of the French Sûreté Générale. Lines of anxiety furrowed his brow as he sifted through yet another batch of infuriatingly sketchy agents' reports. A new cache of crude native arms had been found in the Red River valley that day — cement grenades and homemade sabers again; that brought the total to six in the past fortnight. Plotting for a widespread uprising was obviously well advanced, but still no coherent plan was discernible from the Sûreté's intelligence.

Devraux swung around thoughtfully in his swivel chair to stare at the map of Tongking on the wall behind him. He had flagged the locations of the previous arms caches with red markers but they were scattered over a large area ranging from the lower delta near Haiphong to the limestone mountains of Upper Tongking. He got up and pushed a new flag into the map, then resumed his seat to study the result.

Newly installed as a full-time inspector three months earlier at the suggestion of the governor general, Jacques Devraux was not the only Sûreté officer working late on the eve of the Annamese holiday. Because increasing evidence of unrest was surfacing throughout the north, lights still burned in many of the other offices, and in the top security archive in the basement below his feet half-a-dozen clerks were busy updating the twenty thousand secret dossiers and the fifty thousand related cross-reference cards that Sûreté agents in Asia and Europe had painstakingly compiled over the past decade on those Annamese suspected of posing a threat to French rule in Indochina.

When the door of Devraux's office opened to admit the top-ranking officer of the Sûreté Générale in Indochina, the special commissioner for political affairs, the former hunting guide noticed immediately that the bulkiest file in the whole archive was clutched beneath his arm. Its "*Secret d'État*" designation — "State Secret" — was clearly visible stamped in big red letters on the cover and the commissioner dropped it on Devraux's blotter with an audible sigh of exasperation.

"Your wily adversary has given our Canton people the slip again, Jacques," he said irritably, perching himself on the corner of Devraux's desk. "Disappeared from his haunts yesterday." A lifetime of secret police work had given a permanently watchful, narrow-eyed cast to the commissioner's gaunt features, and through the smoke of his meerschaum he subjected Devraux to as careful a scrutiny as he ever gave any suspect.

The file before Devraux bore the title "Nguyen Ai Quoc" with its translation in brackets beneath — "Nguyen the Patriot." A list of half-a-dozen other Annamese and Chinese aliases known to have been used by the subject during twenty years of undercover revolutionary activity in Asia, Russia and Western Europe were also listed on the cover. Devraux knew them all as well as his own name; many of the reports that made the file so bulky, he reflected as he drew it towards him, were his own. He opened the dossier and glanced at the photograph pinned inside the front cover; it showed a thin-faced Annamese with intent, heavy-lidded eyes that had a curiously compelling quality. He had spent many days and nights watching for that face; he had tracked Nguyen the Patriot when he had gone shaven-headed and disguised in the robes of a Buddhist monk in Bangkok, had watched undercover while the Annamese sold matches all day on a street corner in Singapore, seen him mingle with Chinese peasants in Canton, humping a swing plow on his shoulder. All these disguises had been assumed by the Comintern agent in the course of his efforts to build Communist groups throughout the Far East, and Devraux's skill in dogging his footsteps accounted largely for what little was known of his activities to that date. Other Sûreté agents had not been so successful, and Devraux shook his head in exasperation as he ran his eye quickly over the newly decoded telegram from Canton on top of the file. It stated simply that Nguyen the Patriot could no longer be traced at his address there. "Interrogation of another Annamese Communist in Canton," the telegram added, "suggests he has departed for Hong Kong. He is believed to be under Comintern orders from Moscow to try to unite the warring factions of the Annamese Communist movement and form a cohesive Indochina Communist Party."

"I thought of sending you to Hong Kong, Jacques, to try to pick up his trail," said the commissioner slowly when Devraux finally glanced up at him. "You know his habits better than anyone. But I think it's clear enough that the Communists are too busy fighting among themselves just now to do us much damage. Perhaps you could just send our Hong Kong people a guidance brief. The need for you is far greater here." He glanced round at the little clusters of flags on the wall map. "Another Quoc Dan Dang arms dump has been uncovered today, yes? Do we have any clearer idea of how and where they mean to strike?"

Devraux shook his head quickly. "No. I thought this morning we might have a lead. We arrested a new suspect — a young girl, a teacher from a village just outside the city. I've questioned her myself, but so far she won't even admit she's a member of the party." He let out a long sigh of frustration. "Another informant has told us there's to be an important cell meeting tonight 'somewhere in Hanoi' — but the location isn't known."

The commissioner puffed on his pipe in silence, studying the ceiling above his head minutely. Then he glanced down at Devraux again, his eyes suddenly hard and calculating. "We're very glad, Jacques, you agreed to give up your hunting and come to us full time," he said quietly. "We're going to need every good man we can lay our hands on in the next few months. Things look bad — much worse than I've ever seen them." He paused and puffed fiercely on the pipe again. "We can't afford to treat the 'yellows' with kid gloves any longer. I've never seen anything like these arms dumps before. They're obviously out for blood this time, and we've got to get the ringleaders before they strike. Otherwise the whole thing might spread very quickly. It's no good being squeamish or worrying what we might do, or not do, elsewhere. French lives are at stake. It could be your head — or mine — that gets chopped off if we fail." The commissioner ceased looking at Devraux and puffed hard on the pipe again. "I know from your fine military record and everything else you've done, Jacques, that you're not just a strong man — you temper your strength with a respect for justice. But sometimes in this line of work you have to turn a blind eye."

Devraux, unsure of his superior's meaning, leaned back in his chair looking at him with a little frown of puzzlement on his face.

"What I'm getting at," the commissioner continued, avoiding his subordinate's gaze, "is that we can't afford *not* to make the most of every suspect we bring in. They have vital information — we need it badly. I've just had a special interrogator brought here from the police commissariat in Cholon — a big *métis*. He's got a fearsome reputation — they say in Cholon he can get a corpse to talk. I'll have him sent up." He blew a long spiral of smoke towards the ceiling, then rose from the desk and walked towards the door. "Use him, Jacques — he'll get the girl to tell you what you want to know." The commissioner opened the door, then paused as he was about to step into the corridor. "There's no need of course for you to be involved yourself," he said quietly. "You understand that, don't you?" Without waiting for a reply he turned and hurried away towards his own room, the smoke of his pipe slip-streaming over his shoulder behind him.

A few minutes later there was a respectful knock at the door and one of Devraux's French aides ushered in a heavily built French-Annamese *métis* who was holding in one hand what appeared to be a large carrying case for a French horn. His Eurasian features were heavily fleshed and he stood silently before the desk, his head tipped forward towards the Sûreté inspector in an attitude of guarded deference.

"This is special interrogator Lung, Sir, who's just come in from Cholon." The aide made the introduction in a flat voice without looking at the *métis*, as if he was anxious to disassociate himself from him, and withdrew immediately.

Devraux studied the new arrival in silence. Loose-limbed, heavy-browed and hunched at the shoulder, he held himself awkwardly as though uncomfortable inside his big, hybrid body. As he waited for his orders his eyes flicked uneasily from the Frenchman's face to the toes of his boots. To conceal the distaste he felt at his presence, Devraux half turned to face the map on the wall. "Lung, how much do you know about the Viet Nam Quoc Dan Dang?" he asked tersely.

"Only that it's one of the many secret societies dreaming of making a revolution." The *métis* spoke his French in a dull, sibilant monotone that only increased Devraux's irritation.

"Maybe that's how it looks from Saigon," he said testily. "Here in the north the Quoc Dan Dang is something more than a crazy secret society." He paused and gestured towards the map. "We've uncovered half-a-dozen arms dumps in the past two weeks in the provinces of the Red River delta. They are plotting some kind of bloody rebellion. We think the party may have possibly fifteen hundred members scattered through the region. They're organized in little cells of fifteen or twenty members that are hard to track down. And time is running out. Do you understand?" Devraux looked around sharply at the *métis*, who shifted uncomfortably under his scrutiny, then nodded.

"We believe a crucial cell meeting is being held somewhere in Hanoi later tonight — but we don't know where. We arrested a suspected member of the party this morning but so far we haven't obtained the information we require."

For the first time a spark of interest lit the dull gaze of the *métis*. "Is the suspect a man or a woman?"

"A girl — a village schoolteacher of nineteen."

A sudden smile loosened the heavy features of the *métis* and he moistened his lips quickly with his tongue. "Then it will be easy. I will soon make her talk for you."

Devraux eyed the man before him with open distaste. He still held the big bulbous case tightly in his hand although it was obviously heavy. "What methods do you use?" he asked quietly, looking away and shuffling some of his papers together on his desk.

The noise of the locks snapping open surprised Devraux and he looked up again to find the *métis* kneeling beside his open case. "I always carry my own instruments. I know how they feel in my hands, you see, and I'm confident then, because they've always worked for me in the past."

The voice of the *métis* had become suddenly animated, and Devraux saw then why he used the old French horn case; several long bull-hide whips were wound carefully around the inside of its large bowl and an assortment of other instruments were attached by hooks and fastenings to the velvet interior. As Devraux watched, the *métis* unhooked one of the whips and held it up so that he could see that it was bound around its entire length with fine copper wire.

"This is for stubborn suspects," he said, running his hand slowly along the tapering lash. "It can be connected to the mains and the electric current doubles the pain." He paused to check Devraux's reaction and found the Frenchman gazing expressionlessly into the case. Mistaking his uneasy silence for approval, he turned and laid a hand on a long steel corkscrew. "If this is inserted slowly into the male penis and withdrawn with sudden force, a confession is usually not difficult to obtain. And these tongs" — he indicated with one finger a pair of large metal pincers — "can be applied to the temples to give a suspect the impression his eyes are being squeezed from his head. Or there is this black box in which I carry an ant nest. If the arms and feet of a female suspect are securely tied, the nest of ants can be introduced into the vagina. . . ."

"That's enough! Close it up!" Devraux's sudden shout startled the *métis*, and he looked up in alarm.

For a moment there was a strained silence in the room, then the telephone at Devraux's elbow jangled. He picked up the instrument angrily without taking his eyes from the face of the torturer and unhooked the bell-shaped earpiece.

"Have you got anything new yet, Jacques, on that meeting tonight?" The voice of the special commissioner was curt. "Time's slipping away."

For a second or two Devraux continued gazing at the stooped figure of the *métis* as he refastened his case of tools; then his jaw tightened suddenly. "I hope to have something shortly," he said in a low voice and replaced the earpiece in its holder with unnecessary care. Motioning to the *métis* to follow him, he led the way out of the room, his face composed in grim lines.

They descended to the cellars of the building and an Annamese warder carrying a ring of keys led them along an echoing whitewashed corridor to the interrogation cells. Behind the door he unlocked they found a diminutive female figure crouched on the plain plank bed. She didn't rise as they entered but looked up at them with eyes that were both frightened and defiant.

The *métis* cast a practiced eye around the cell without looking at her, then returned to the corridor, walking along with his instrument case until he found an electricity supply point. He unreeled a cable until it reached back to the cell and without a word pulled the frightened girl to her feet to secure her wrists with handcuffs. Pushing her face-down on the plank bed, he wrenched off her cheap cotton trousers and underclothing, manacled her ankles and rolled her effortlessly onto her back.

The girl's eyes widened in terror as he uncoiled several loops of copper wire and fastened one terminal with clips to her bare upper arm. She let out a startled squeal of pain as he pushed the other end of the wire roughly between her thighs. Still without looking at her, he picked from his case a "hell box" that resembled in miniature a dynamite detonator, connected it to the wires and turned to look inquiringly at Devraux.

"Ask her in which pagoda tonight's cell meeting of the Quoc Dan Dang is being held," said the Frenchman, turning towards the door. "I'll wait outside."

The *métis* nodded and repeated the question in Annamese, holding the "hell box" close in front of the girl's face so that she could see its plunger clearly. "I will tell you the answer within three minutes," he said quietly and pushed the little plunger sharply downward.

As the Frenchman banged the heavy steel door gratefully behind him, he heard the girl's first high-pitched shriek of agony. He lit a cigarette with trembling fingers and stood staring hard at the whitewashed wall on the opposite side of the passage as the screams increased in intensity. It was almost exactly three minutes before the screaming stopped and the *métis* stepped smirking into the corridor to give him the information he had promised.

8

At normal times the narrow cobbled lanes of Hanoi's native quarter were jammed until late into the night with a noisy throng of people, produce carts, rickshaws, and occasional honking motor cars; even elephants bearing swaying loads of timber still sometimes plodded slowly through the confusion. But by eight o'clock on the eve of Tet, at the moment when Jacques Devraux was receiving his torturer's report in the Sûreté cellars, the ancient streets stood silent and deserted. Only the iron-wheeled rickshaw bearing Dao Van Lat to the secret cell meeting in a little pagoda behind the Street of Coffins broke the stillness as it clattered noisily across the cobbles.

Lat had known that most of Hanoi's ninety thousand citizens would by then be clustering around their ancestral altars to celebrate with traditional reverence the advent of the Year of the Horse. He had considered traveling more stealthily through the empty lanes in one of the new wire-wheeled rickshaws with pneumatic tires, favored by the French, but having decided that Sûreté agents would least expect a revolutionary to ride openly through the city by rickshaw, he had followed this tactic boldly to its conclusion and chosen the noisiest vehicle he could find.

The blue-and-white nameplates on the alleyways through which he rumbled still reflected the trades and crafts that had been carried on in the old quarter for hundreds of years. The Rue de la Soie — Silk Street — and the Rue des Médicaments — The Street of Herbs — linked and intertwined with the streets of Rice, Iron, Veils, Lacquer and many others named after the sources of their inhabitants' livelihood. In the Street of Coffins where gilded and lacquered caskets built for rich Chinese corpses were piled high in the workshop windows, Lat paid off his coolie and melted quickly into the shadows. He stood motionless in the doorway of a coffin-maker's for several minutes peering along the street in both directions, watching for signs of pursuit; when he was satisfied he hadn't been followed he slipped into a narrow, flagged passageway that led to the pillared entrance of a tiny Buddhist pagoda.

As he approached, a shadowy figure emerged suddenly from behind one of the pillars. "Lat, is that you?" whispered an anxious female voice.

The Annamese girl was wearing a dark coat of filmy black tulle over her paler tunic and trousers to help her blend into the shadows but there was enough natural light from the sky for him to recognize Lien and see the warmth of her welcoming smile.

"Yes, it is me," he whispered. "Didn't you hear me coming in my deafening rickshaw?" Leaning closer he pressed his cheek gently against hers and for a brief instant they allowed their breaths to mingle in the traditional kiss of their race; then they moved apart and entered the pagoda separately.

In the first hall where flickering candlelight illuminated the gaudy statues of Quan Thanh, the God of War, and Diem Vuong, the Lord of Hell, a doorkeeper waited to scrutinize them. While they were identifying themselves three other figures crept stealthily into the pagoda behind them, and Lat and Lien exchanged whispered greetings with Ngo Van Loc and his sons, Dong and Hoc. Like all the other members of the cell, the three Annamese who had escaped from the Vi An rubber plantation four months earlier were known to other members only by their secret code names. Ngo Van Loc was Son Thuy, or "Waters of the Mountain," his son Dong was Lam Giang, "Blue River," while the younger boy was Manh Tung, "The Persuader," Lat himself had been dubbed Giao Nhan — "The Educator of Men" — and Lien was Trinh Chinh — "Warrior Maiden."

When he was satisfied with their identities the doorkeeper beckoned them to follow and led them past the closed gates of the innermost shrine, where gilded images of the Amitabha and Maitreya Buddhas gazed down impassively on the festive mounds of fruit and flowers heaped on the altars around their feet. He motioned them towards a little room at the back of the pagoda normally used by the bonzes for informal meetings, and there they found a dozen other Annamese already huddled around a table. The darkness was relieved by only a single candle set in a wall niche, and individual faces were barely distinguishable in the gloom.

The cell leader at the head of the table was a bespectacled Tongkingese teacher in his early thirties. Known to the cell members as Thanh Giang — "Limpid Stream" — he still had the round cheeks and tilted nose of a boy. When the five newcomers had taken their places he nodded impatiently towards the last unfilled chair that waited for the girl who at that moment lay sobbing with pain in the Sûreté jail. "Can anybody explain the absence of Minh Quon?" he asked quietly.

When nobody replied, he glanced uneasily at his wristwatch. "We can't wait any longer. We may all be in danger now. Listen carefully to what I have to tell you." He paused dramatically. "The moment we've all been working for during the past two years has finally come, comrades. Our party leadership has decided we must strike at the French now — without further delay!"

The conspirators around the table leaned forward excitedly in their chairs, and one or two of them gasped in surprise. Behind his spectacles the eyes of the man they knew only as Limpid Stream suddenly gleamed more brightly.

"Two years of patient propaganda work among our brothers serving in the French military garrisons have prepared the way! All over the delta of the Red River they are ready now to rise up and turn their guns on their French officers. But they need us, comrades, to lead them in revolt. Each cell of our party has been assigned to a different garrison for leadership duties. If we all act bravely, we shall soon be marching together in triumph into Hanoi and Haiphong!" He paused and glanced down at a little sheaf of papers on the table before him. "Our cell has been assigned to lead the mutiny at Yen Bay sixty miles from Hanoi on the Red River. It is the headquarters of the Second Battalion of the Fourth Regiment of the Tirailleurs Tonkinois. We must raise a force of sixty partisans. Weapons have already been made and hidden close to the fort. I have visited the garrison myself and laid concrete plans. There are four companies of our brothers — a thousand men, all of them sympathetic to our cause!" He turned a page and held it towards the light. "There are only eight commissioned officers under Chef de Battaillon Le Tacon. Captains Jourdan and Leonnard, Lieutenants Caspian and Devraux command the companies. . . ." He raised his eyes again and gazed fiercely round the table. "Four days from now, comrades, all the Frenchmen and the noncommissioned officers too shall taste the steel of those sabers we have smelted in our secret furnaces."

As the list of French names was read out, Ngo Van Loc had stiffened in his chair. Now he felt his elder son, Dong, pluck at his sleeve and he leaned forward urgently to interrupt the cell leader. "Comrade, what is the full name and age of Lieutenant Devraux, please."

Limpid Stream glanced down irritably at his notes again. "Lieutenant Paul Devraux is aged twenty-three — a graduate of St. Cyr military academy; Yen Bay is his first post." He looked keenly at Loc for a moment. "Why do you ask? Is he known to you?"

Loc shook his head hastily. "Excuse me. I misheard. But I want to make it clear, comrade, that I and my two sons wish to be included in the first assault party."

"Good, good! Thank you, Son Thuy," replied the cell leader briskly, looking quickly round the table. "I hope everybody will be as eager as you to volunteer for their tasks."

"I think anyone who risks his life in this rash venture will be a fool," said Dao Van Lat in a gentle voice. "You are wrong. The time is not ripe for an uprising. The people are not yet prepared."

The naked hostility of Lat's words produced a stunned silence in the pagoda and the cell leader glared at him, suddenly white-faced with anger. "I have done the propaganda work at Yen Bay myself. Many other garrisons are ready to rise too. The party leadership has proof."

"The French have proof too, haven't they — of our intentions! It's no secret any longer that hidden stores of our arms have been found and confiscated. The French are on their guard now."

Furious at the sustained challenge to his authority, Limpid Stream banged his fist violently on the table. "Yes, all right, some of our hidden arms have been discovered! But that only makes the need for action more urgent. If we don't strike now, more weapons will be lost, more of our comrades will be arrested. If we delay, our people will lose the desire to rise against France!"

"If what you call 'our people' rise up now, they will surely die," insisted Lat quietly. "The Quoc Dan Dang membership is still only a few hundred people."

"It is better to die like brave men than live as you would wish us to — like cowards." The cell leader's voice rose to a shout. "If we fail we shall at least leave behind an example of sacrifice and struggle for others to follow."

"A wiser leader might decide it is better to wait — to live to fight another day. To bring destruction on ourselves before we are fully prepared achieves nothing. The Communists of Nguyen the Patriot have refused to join with us for that reason — because they can see the time for a national revolution is not ripe."

"Nguyen the Patriot is so patriotic that he hasn't set foot in his own country for twenty years." Limpid Stream spat his words out contemptuously. "He is a tool of the Bolsheviks in Moscow. He is frightened to come home. He is not fit to call himself a Vietnamese patriot. We want no agreement with his supporters."

Lat held the gaze of Limpid Stream steadily. "At least he knows something that you and higher leaders of the Quoc Dan Dang refuse to acknowledge — that numbers make strength. I am determined to arouse the whole of our people. If we can do that we are millions against a few thousand French. And then we must be victorious!" He paused and leaned back in his seat, his face pale but composed. "I refuse to join your uprising, Thanh Giang. That is all I have to say."

Limpid Stream saw Lien squeeze Lat's arm as he finished

speaking. Lat acknowledged her show of affection with an easy smile and the anger of the cell leader, who was not attractive to women, was sharpened to a new pitch by his unconscious envy. "The Quoc Dan Dang has no use," he said in an icy voice, "for those who seek only personal glory and strike vain poses. Those who wish above all else to be seen in a false heroic light by pampered bourgeois 'concubines' posing as 'Warrior Maidens' should exercise their empty powers of rhetoric elsewhere. Especially those who lack the courage to face pain or death for their country!"

Lat's fists clenched suddenly on the table-top in front of him and his voice shook with the passion of his words. "I love my country, comrade, more than life itself. Soon you will see. . . ."

The sound of frantic footsteps approaching at a run through the darkness of the pagoda halted Lat in midsentence, and several of the conspirators, gathered around the table, rose anxiously to their feet. A white-faced boy who had been posted as lookout at the entrance to the flagged passageway emerged into the light, gasping for breath and pointing behind him. "Two Sûreté cars have entered the street! They are heading this way!"

The cell leader rose without a word and ushered the group silently towards a side door. Each of the conspirators had his appointed escape route through the maze of alleyways, leading to a prearranged cellar or storeroom. Within one minute of the warning being given the pagoda was empty and there was no moving figure on the streets within half a mile of the meeting place.

When Jacques Devraux led two dozen armed Annamese Sûreté gendarmes into the candlelit pagoda, he found it deserted. Several chairs had been knocked over by the departing conspirators in their haste, and a cigarette still burned in one of the ashtrays on the table. Devraux stood in the incense-scented darkness for several seconds, cursing beneath his breath; then he strode angrily back to the car that had been parked to no avail a hundred yards away in the shadows of the Street of Coffins.

9

The moment they reached his room, Dao Van Lat locked the door behind them. Both he and Lien were breathless after their flight from the pagoda, and when they had recovered he took her quietly in his arms. Beneath the silken tunic he could feel the tantalizing softness of her small breasts against his chest, and a little groan of desire welled up in his throat. Standing motionless, neither sought to cover the lips of the other; instead they inhaled the delicate scents of each other's skin as their warm breath flowed back and forth in gentle rhythms between their two bodies.

When at last they drew apart Lien smiled up into his face, an expression of undisguised love lighting her eyes. "You spoke very movingly tonight," she whispered. "I'm proud to be the one closest to a man who's sure to become a great and famous patriot."

He gazed back at her unsmiling for a moment then dropped his eyes. "I intend to make this a very special night, Lien — for us and for our country. I'm very glad that you could be with me for Tet."

Alarmed by his grave expression she wrinkled her smooth forehead suddenly in a worried frown. "What do you mean, Lat?"

"Please wait and see. I would rather not talk of it now." He turned from her and moved to the big teak mandarin's bed that had been his father's. He had already covered the porcelain pillow and the wooden planks with a silken quilt and cushions. "Will you bring my father's pipe for me to smoke while you make tea for us?" he asked softly, settling himself on the bed and smiling warmly at her again.

Reassured by his smile she nodded, and he watched her as she went to the corner of the room and knelt beside an old lacquered traveling trunk. The movements of her body were deft and graceful, and his eyes brightened with desire as she bent over the chest searching tiny compartments and trays which had once contained Chinese pens and inks, visiting cards, betel leaves, lime, areca nut — all the small necessities of an itinerant mandarin's daily life. When she returned to him she was carrying a water pipe made of jade and bamboo. She pinched a strand or two of tobacco into its bowl and knelt at the bedside to ignite the tobacco for him with a match. The pipe bubbled quietly, and he sighed and closed his eyes as he inhaled the fragrant smoke. Lien remained kneeling, smiling fondly at him as he drifted into a reverie, then she rose quietly and placed two small carved tables at the bedside for the teacups before tiptoeing from the room.

When she emerged from the kitchen a few minutes later with two steaming cups of scented tea, she found him sitting cross-legged on the bed, wearing only his white silk trousers. Seating herself beside him, she averted her eyes from his bare chest with an exaggerated show of modesty and smiled into her teacup. "Are you so impatient tonight, Lat, to begin?"

He covered her hand gently with his own but didn't reply. When she looked at him again she found he was gazing around the room at the other ornaments and furnishings inherited from his father: lacquered boxes inlaid with mother-of-pearl, delicate porcelains, scroll paintings of Buddha strolling in the mountains, riding buffalo, meditating by a stream.

"Lat," she said quietly, moving closer to him, "your mood tonight is so strange. What are you thinking?"

"I was thinking we must never give up our vital essence, the essence of our race and nation," he said vehemently. "We must learn from the West, yes, to defeat the French! But we must always remain true to ourselves, remain true Vietnamese. Otherwise all our sacrifices will be in vain."

She shrank from him under the unexpected intensity of his words, and seeing this he put down his empty teacup and seized her by the shoulders. "Lien, I want you never to forget what I will tell you now!" He spoke more fiercely than before and pulled her face close to his own. "My love for you is greater than for any living thing. Do you understand?"

A new look of alarm entered her eyes. "Of course I understand, Lat. Why should I forget that you love me?"

He looked away from her. "Because there are things a man must do for his country. . . ." He paused and his voice broke a little. ". . . that a woman may not always understand."

She stared at him in bewilderment, and when he turned and saw her expression, he let his hands fall from her shoulders and stood up. "But this is no time to dwell on such thoughts, my beautiful Lien. Forgive me! It is the eve of Tet, the feast of a new dawn, the time for renewal and fresh hope." He gazed desperately around the room, searching for something to lighten their mood, and his eye fell on one of the red streamers bearing a poem in Chinese pictograms. "Do you like the words I have chosen from Ly Thanh Tong?" He turned to her eagerly and took her hand in his once more. "Shall we recite them together?"

Although deeply perplexed by his rapidly changing moods, she flashed him a little smile of relief and nodded.

"I open the shutters looking out onto the yard," he began and paused, waiting for her to continue.

"And find Spring has come back. . . ."

"Pairs of white butterflies. . . ."

"Beating their wings. . . ."

"Dance upon the enchanted flowers!"

He smiled into her eyes and moved closer to her on the bed.

"You are my 'enchanted flower,' " he said softly, nestling his face against her cheek until their breaths mingled again. "You are my enchanted lotus." He brushed his fingers lightly against the points of her silk-clad breasts and bent to kiss the soft curve of her neck. "The petals that adorn my enchanted lotus are so delicate that I hardly dare touch them," he whispered softly in her ear. "But tonight I want to undress you with my own hands."

Her cheeks burned with a sudden fire, and she nodded shyly without looking at him. Reaching behind her, she removed the combs which held her hair in an elaborate waved chignon, and when the glossy black tresses cascaded over her shoulders, he unfastened the buttons of her tunic and slipped the filmy material from her shoulders. But his own hands began to tremble as he unbuttoned her satin trousers, and he was unable to free the sleeves of her second tunic from the tight-fitting bracelets at her wrists. In his anxiety he tore the silk and with a little cry of regret he stood up.

"Forgive my clumsiness, Lien! The fingers of a gentle girl are required, not my ungainly fists. Please help me."

She rose from the bed and quietly removed the rest of her clothes. When she stood naked before him, he took off his own remaining garments and sank to his knees before her. Slipping his arms around her waist, he pressed his face against her trembling loins, but a moment later, to her dismay, he began to weep.

"What is it, Lat?" Her voice was suddenly frightened. "What's wrong?"

He lifted his tearstained face to look up at her. "I love you too much."

She smoothed the dark hair of his head with both hands and pressed his face against the swell of her belly in an effort to stem his bewildering tears. "But you can't love me too much! How can you love me too much?"

"I must love you enough tonight to last a lifetime!"

"Lat, I don't understand you."

Still on his knees he caressed her with shaking hands. "Your skin, Lien, is more beautiful than the velvet petals of the hibiscus rose. Your lovely body is smoother than polished jade." Letting out a little cry, he picked her up and carried her to the bed. With great tenderness he kissed her breasts, her thighs, her arms, her feet, all the time murmuring words of love and passion in an unceasing flow. Then he flung himself down beside her. "Do everything to me, Lien!" he whispered in her ear. "Do everything. Now!"

He shut his eyes and arched his back from the teak bed as she

143

played her breath on him, tantalizing his senses the length of his body. He felt her mouth close gently on him, felt her hands and fingers quiver lovingly against his skin and suddenly the realization that he was experiencing such pleasures for the last time produced an exquisite tremor of anticipation in his limbs. Opening his eyes he put his arms around her shoulders and drew her gently towards him. For a long moment he gazed fiercely into her dark eyes, then stretched himself beside her, moving very slowly, and they sighed in unison as their bodies joined.

Their lovemaking was subdued at first, mounting only slowly towards abandonment and Lat's sense of exhilaration expanded moment by moment. No pangs of remorse intruded until their passion entered its final throes and then the agony and the joy for a few fleeting seconds fused and flowed together, becoming indistinguishable in his mind.

When Lien at last opened her eyes again she saw only the flames of the candles flickering on his ancestral altar. Then slowly the rest of the room began to reform and refocus itself in her vision. It was in the moment that she realized she had been left alone that she heard the long-drawn cry from the adjoining room. She remembered then her earlier terror and rose shakily from the bed. In the kitchen she found Lat crouched beneath the open drawer. He was still clutching the knife in his right hand, and its blade was crimson; his courage had not failed him.

A speechless hysteria seized her and she watched petrified as Lat rocked once, then toppled onto his side in the spreading pool of his own blood. Then the door burst open and two of his close friends dashed white-faced into the room. One carried a medical satchel and he dropped to his knees and pressed a prepared dressing against the terrible self-inflicted wound between Lat's thighs.

The second man caught her by the arm and began talking urgently to her, repeating the same words over and over again. But because of her hysteria she registered nothing of what he was saying at first. Through the open door she heard the first volleys of firecrackers exploding to welcome the Year of the Horse and only gradually did the meaning of the man's words penetrate her brain.

". . . Lat asked me to tell you . . . he has done this for Viet Nam . . . for the new Viet Nam! . . . He has sworn to dedicate his life utterly to freeing our country from the French. . . . He feared his physical and emotional desires impeded him — he has sacrificed them for our cause! . . ." The bloodless lips formed the same shapes over and over again in the ashen face, repeating what was obviously a prearranged explanation for the horrifying deed. ". . . He had to forswear forever the company of all women. . . . He hasn't done this because he didn't love you. . . . He did it because he loved you too well. . . ."

When the hysteria finally broke, Lien began sobbing uncontrollably. Because she was still without clothes she was able to free herself easily from the man's grasp. Whirling around she stood staring disbelievingly at the naked body of Lat still prostrate on the floor. Then the room tilted suddenly beneath her feet and the next instant she collapsed unconscious in the pool of blood beside him.

10

As the clouded moonless night of February 9, 1930, slowly swallowed the Yen Bay hill fort and the curve of the Red River that it dominated, Limpid Stream led his band of sixty crudely armed rebels into the deep shadows of the lac trees below the citadel. "The French officers must be taken by surprise and put to death in their beds," he whispered in a flat, unemotional tone as his men pressed close around him in the darkness. "Those are the party's orders! You must attack barefoot in complete silence, using at first only your sabers and *coupe-coupes*. No quarter is to be given. Do you all understand?"

Although their faces were barely distinguishable in the gloom, Limpid Stream sensed their fear and apprehension as they nodded and muttered dutifully in response; an unfamiliar tightening of the muscles in his own chest and throat was making him feel breathless as the hour of the attack drew nearer. He noticed one or two heads turn uneasily in the direction of the pale-walled citadel on the crest of the hill above them and strove to keep his voice calm and reassuring.

"Don't let the sight of those high walls make you afraid, comrades," he said firmly. "Two corporals are waiting inside for my signal to open the gates and let us in. Only two companies of *tirailleurs* are quartered in the fort itself — and they will be waiting to welcome us and turn their guns on their officers." He paused and pointed towards the long, two-storied building at the foot of the hill. "The other two companies — five hundred of our brothers — are quartered in the caserne with the French NCOs. Other *tirailleurs* are ready to open the doors to us there, too. Many machine guns and rifles are waiting for us in the armory, comrades. Armed with these we shall lead the two companies up the hill to storm the fortress!"

The confidence of his words had their desired effect, and one or two of the rebels giggled suddenly with relief.

"But everything will depend on the surprise attack led by Son Thuy against the officers' quarters," he added, searching the faces closest to him. "Where are Son Thuy and the other heroes of Vi An?"

Ngo Van Loc, who had been standing quietly to one side with his sons, took half a pace towards the cell leader, his face set in determined lines. In hand-sewn pouches at his waist he carried two shapeless cement grenades and his right fist was clenched tight around the hilt of a rough-smelted saber; manufactured secretly in a makeshift village workshop these arms had been carried to Yen Bay in shoulder pole baskets buried under piles of onion and paddy.

"There's no need to look so worried, Son Thuy," said Limpid Stream quietly, turning again to point to a cluster of single-storied stucco houses set apart at the foot of the hill. "See how low the wall around the officers' compound is! No guards are ever set. The French are careless here in this sleepy backwater. In the forty years since it was built the citadel has seen no military action of any kind."

Ngo Van Loc nodded silently in acknowledgment, and beside him his youngest son, Hoc, tried to smile. He still carried the *coupe-coupe* he had used at Vi An, and in recognition of his deed there he had been chosen by Limpid Stream to carry an oriflamme, the long lance beloved of French medieval warriors, decorated now with double-pointed red and gold silk streamers of the Viet Nam Quoc Dan Dang. Like all the other rebels Hoc wore a band of red and gold silk around his forehead and on his sleeve a red armband which declared in blurred stenciled lettering: "Vietnamese Revolutionary Forces."

Limpid Stream himself carried a big furled flag of red and gold — gold to symbolize the people and red for the uprising — and he held it up suddenly above his head. "When the fortress is ours we shall fly our standard above it and seize all the military points in the town. Only women, children and priests are to be spared. All over Tongking tonight other groups of partisans will be helping our brothers in uniform to rise in revolt and seize the military strongholds of the French. The uprising will become general, comrades! You will be striking an historic first blow here at Yen Bay to help set our country free."

Limpid Stream flourished the flag above his head in a fierce gesture of determination, and all around him the rebels raised their sabers aloft in silent response.

"We shall attack on the stroke of midnight," he said in an undertone. "Until then disperse to your hiding places and rest. Rest well — and prepare yourself to do great deeds for Viet Nam!"

As the rebels were melting away through the lac trees, Lieutenant Paul Devraux, duty officer for the evening, was pacing briskly across the courtyard of the citadel, his routine rounds finished. Broader in the shoulder than in the days when he had assisted his father as a hunting guide, his proud bearing, the bright sheen on his belt and boots and his spotlessly whitened sun helmet all now reflected the uncompromising St. Cyr disciplines he had brought from Versailles to the hills of Tongking. Open-faced, ready to smile and more handsome than his father, he had emerged from three years at the French military academy as a young officer of high promise, but as he strode towards the guardhouse that night his brows were knitted in a persistent frown. Without knowing why, he had been left feeling ill at ease by the tour of inspection through the fort and the caserne, and as he walked he tried without success to pin down his apprehension.

During the past three months he had often found himself struggling to maintain the strict standards of St. Cyr in the hot, enervating climate of the remote fort town. To him the longer-serving officers and NCOs of the garrison seemed to have become unnecessarily lax in their military habits, but because he was the most junior officer he had decided to say nothing and pay greater attention to his own self-discipline. Some of his brother officers had taken to teasing him openly about his youthful enthusiasm, but tonight he was sure his suspicions were not simply due to overzealousness. At the guardhouse he asked the gray-haired French sergeant if he'd noticed anything unusual, but the NCO merely yawned and shook his head as he took his ring of keys from him. On the point of descending to his quarters he hesitated at the opened gates of the fort. In the town below a few fires still flickered here and there along the darkened streets and the lights were going out as usual — everything seemed normal, but the feeling that something was amiss persisted.

The fort was one of three built in an arc across the jungle-clad uplands of northern Tongking as a first line of defense for the city of Hanoi against invasion from across the Chinese border. Yen

Bay, he knew from his studies at St. Cyr, had been designed by Marshal Joffre thirty years before he led French forces to a famous victory at the Battle of the Marne in 1914. Joffre had been an eager captain of engineers then, and the young lieutenant found himself reflecting suddenly that if the marshal's reputation had been forced to rest solely on the construction of the Yen Bay fort he would hardly have become a hero of France. Standing in the open gateway looking down at the officers' quarters and the caserne, both standing unprotected at the foot of the hill, he realized with a start how vulnerable the garrison was to surprise attack.

"Are you still worrying, Paul, about how you might turn the smelly *tirailleurs* of Yen Bay into a glittering praetorian guard fit for ceremonial duties at the Élysée Palace?" A friendly hand slapped him on the shoulder, and he turned to find himself looking into the grinning face of Lieutenant François Clichy, a young married Breton attached to the Eighth Company whose pretty young wife had just traveled out from France to join him.

"No, not really," replied Paul, trying to force a smile to his lips. Then his face become earnest again. "François, have you noticed anything strange about the way the men are behaving tonight?"

"Strange? Don't our smelly *tirailleurs* always behave strangely?" asked the married officer flippantly. "We know *you* think they're human, but it's a minority viewpoint, you must admit. Still, we forgive you. Living six years in Saigon and speaking their language is probably enough to turn anyone's head."

"I'm serious," insisted Paul. "I can't help feeling tonight that there's something going on."

"I'm sure there is — about a thousand illegal gambling games."

"That's just the point, François. None of them *are* gambling tonight. And you know how they usually descend on the town and terrorize the local barkeepers — well, almost none of them left camp tonight. All the men of the Seventh and Eighth here in the fort were sitting quietly on their mats looking very subdued when I made an unannounced inspection. Some of them were already asleep — or pretending to be. Down in the caserne it was the same story with the Fifth and the Sixth. No noisy gambling groups at all. A few of them were sitting huddled together talking in whispers but the rest were asleep — two hours early."

Lieutenant Clichy shrugged. "It doesn't sound that unusual to me. Have you reported your suspicions to the old man?"

Paul nodded glumly. "Yes, he was very curt. Like you he told me I still had a lot to learn about the shiftless natives. He said he was going to bed early and suggested I did too."

"That sounds like pretty good advice to me, Lieutenant Devraux." The young Breton laughed and slapped him on the shoulder again. "Why don't you follow it? I think I'm going to. It wouldn't be fair to keep my Monique waiting when she's just come all this way from Paris to warm my sheets for me, would it?"

Paul smiled and wished him goodnight as he hurried off down the hillside. For a moment he stood peering into the shadows on the surrounding hills, but the clouds gathering in the night sky were beginning to blot out even the faint light from the stars. After ordering the sergeant to close and bar the gates, he walked down the hillside and, with his hand resting on the flap of his revolver holster, he strolled through the deserted streets of the town. But he saw nothing suspicious and returned slowly to his quarters. For half an hour he sat indecisively on his bed, cleaning and loading his revolver. Then he got up, pushed wedges under his door and dragged his wardrobe in front of it. Tucking his sheathed saber beneath his pillow, he lay down fully clothed on his bed and fell into a fitful sleep.

By midnight the shadows beneath the lac trees at the foot of the hill were as black as ink. When the Annamese rebels reassembled from their places of concealment, Limpid Stream had to use a shaded flashlight to check his wristwatch. At exactly twelve o'clock he glanced out between the trunks of the lacs. The citadel and the caserne were silent and dark; no window remained lit.

"*Giet! Giet!*" he whispered urgently in the darkness. "Forward to kill!"

Ngo Van Hoc was standing obediently at his side, and as the cell leader uttered his command he tapped the boy lightly on the shoulder. Hoc felt his heart throb violently in his chest, then he ran forward, thrusting his ribbon-decked oriflamme towards the sky. Immediately the band of sixty rebels broke from the cover of the trees behind him, clutching their sabers and *coupe-coupes*. Swiftly and silently on their unshod feet they sped through the darkness towards their sleeping victims.

11

Lieutenant François Clichy and his young wife, Monique, were peacefully asleep in one another's arms when Ngo Van Loc rushed into their bedroom with half-a-dozen of the Quoc Dan Dang assassins at his heels. Because the girl newly arrived from France was finding the dark silence of the Tongking uplands disquieting, she had taken to leaving a child's night-light burning on a bedside table while they slept, and the sudden commotion in the room set its tiny flame dancing and guttering wildly.

Monique was wearing the same sheer nightdress that she had worn during their recent honeymoon in France, and a moment before they wrenched her from her husband's arms she opened her eyes and saw them; the hate-crazed faces, the red and gold silk bandanas around their foreheads, the crude sabers raised to strike all seemed to her like the stuff of a childhood nightmare. On the walls and ceiling behind them their giant shadows dwarfed them in the flickering candlelight, and she began screaming in terror. One of the attackers, to silence her, covered her mouth with his hand and dragged her from the bed, and on the instant of waking the lieutenant imagined a crowd of his drunken *tirailleurs* were attempting to rape his wife.

"Take your filthy hands off her, you fiends," he yelled, frantically struggling to free himself from the bedclothes. "How dare you come into our house!"

The sudden, unexpected sight of man and wife lying intimately together revived vividly in Ngo Van Loc his own unbearable sense of loss, and it was he who lunged forward to strike the first blow. His heavy saber wielded with two hands split the skull of the French officer, and as he collapsed across the bed Loc's sons and the other rebels crowded in on him, the fear that had grown in them during the tense hours of waiting exploding at last in an uncontrolled burst of savagery.

Flailing at the lieutenant with their weapons in turn they ripped open his body from shoulder to groin and disemboweled him. They struck with such frenzy that the blood of their victim splashed on their own clothes and bodies, but still they didn't stop. When Ngo Van Loc finally pushed them aside, they turned wild-eyed in the direction of the girl they had just made a widow.

"No! Leave her!" shouted Loc sharply. "Remember the party's orders." He motioned for the man holding her to set her free, then led the assassins silently from the room at a run.

Left alone, the lieutenant's wife did not cry out. For a long time she stood paralyzed with horror, then she crawled to her husband's side and cradled his head protectively in her lap. Numb with shock she covered his bleeding body with blankets and pressed her fingers against the terrible wounds through which his brains were already oozing. Gazing fearfully towards the bedroom door, she waited only for her husband's murderers to return and kill her, too.

In the next house the rebels disturbed the children of the French adjutant living there as they searched through the darkened rooms for him. Rising from their beds two young boys and a girl watched terrified at their mother's side as the intruders hacked off their father's head; but again in obedience to the party's orders the murdered officer's family were left unscathed. In the sleeping quarters of the noncommissioned officers too, another group of rebels, moving swiftly and silently without lights, achieved total surprise. The gray-haired sergeant whom Lieutenant Devraux had been on the point of reprimanding for yawning in the guardhouse earlier was snoring so loudly beneath his muslin mosquito net that the arrival of his assailants at his bedside didn't wake him. They struck savagely at his body through the fine gauze and the sleep-stunned man twisted and jerked dementedly in its toils like a fish trapped in a trawl net, before he died. They killed another sergeant close by before he woke, then scalped both men and disemboweled them before chopping the limbs from their lifeless bodies.

All four of these Frenchmen — the lieutenant, the adjutant and the two sergeants — died in the first few moments of the raid. The speed and stealth of the attackers gave their first victims no chance to save themselves, but gradually the growing noise of the carnage roused the other sleeping officers. Paul Devraux heard the distant screams of the dead adjutant's wife and children as he lay dozing on his bed, and at first they seemed to be part of his troubled dreams. Then the rush of bare feet in the corridor outside brought him fully awake. The footsteps stopped before his door, and although the man spoke in a low subdued whisper, the fearful voice of his own Tongkingese batman carried clearly through the flimsy woodwork.

"That is the room of Lieutenant Devraux!"

He heard the doorknob squeak as an unknown hand tested the lock; then a muffled Annamese curse followed. Snatching up his revolver from the night table, Paul pressed himself against the wall beside the door and waited.

Outside, Ngo Van Loc motioned his sons and two other rebels to retreat to the end of the corridor, then tugged one of the homemade cement grenades from the pouch at his waist. Activating its rudimentary friction igniter with his teeth, he rolled it against the door and ran to take cover beside his sons. The grenade exploded in a flash of flame and smoke, but although it splintered the lower panels, it lacked the force to breach the barricaded doorway. When he saw how little damage it caused, Ngo Van Loc cursed softly again and ordered his sons and the other two rebels to stand guard by the door while he fetched a machine gun from the caserne.

Inside the room Paul rose shakily to his feet, coughing and retching from the effects of the grenade's acrid fumes. He had flung himself flat the moment he heard it roll against the door, and although he could see that his barricade had withstood the blast, he quickly manhandled his chest of drawers into position to strengthen it further. A minute or two later he heard the scrape of a machine gun's tripod on the concrete floor of the corridor and ran to crouch in the corner farthest from the door. Its woodwork cracked and splintered under the impact of the bullets when the heavy-caliber weapon opened up outside, but to his relief, after several sustained bursts the makeshift barrier still held firm.

While the rebels under Ngo Van Loc were attacking the officers and NCOs in their quarters, Limpid Stream raced up the hill to the fort with the main body of his men. The corporals in league with him opened the gates from inside as planned, and when their bugler sounded the "*Générale*" the French sergeant in charge of the armory, assuming one of his officers had given the order, rushed to unlock the gun racks. The two hundred and fifty men of the Seventh Company immediately grabbed their weapons and rushed into the courtyard. When their captain tried to rally them to resist the invaders, they shot him dead and swarmed down the hill to the caserne. There the Fifth and Sixth Companies had already been armed in response to the "*Générale*," and mutineers won over earlier by Limpid Stream flung open the doors to welcome the rebels and their fellow *tirailleurs* from the fort. In a mood of wild elation the Tongkingese troops and the rebels sang and danced together, firing their rifles aimlessly into the night sky. Some of them began racing through the streets of the town distributing leaflets brought from Hanoi and chanting the printed slogans aloud in unison. "All the French are massacred!" they proclaimed. "The uprising is general in Indochina! People of Yen Bay take part! Join in!"

Through the single small window high in the wall above his bed which he'd boarded up with his night table, Paul heard these distant shouts mingling with the jubilation of the mutineers, and his heart sank. The occasional muffled explosion of a grenade and the intermittent drum of machine gun fire from inside other buildings close by had convinced him that other French officers were trapped helplessly inside their rooms, too. The gun trained on his own door had stopped firing suddenly in the middle of a long burst a few minutes earlier, and he guessed it must at last have jammed. But the muted whispers still audible through the door told him that his attackers hadn't gone away.

In the corridor, Ngo Van Loc gave up trying to free the twisted cartridge belt and threw the useless weapons aside with a curse. He was squatting on his haunches staring helplessly at the unyielding barricade of the room when Limpid Stream appeared white-faced at the end of the corridor.

"Son Thuy, come quickly," he called. "I need your help! The *tirailleurs* of the Eighth have remained loyal in the fort. We must gather the men for an attack. Leave guards on these rooms."

Loc motioned to his two sons to remain by the door then dashed away with the other two rebels to join Limpid Stream. Behind his barricade Paul felt his spirits revive a little. He had heard enough of what Limpid Stream had said to give him a shred of hope. The men of his own Eighth Company had not joined the other mutineers! There was at least some small prospect of a counter-attack from the fort now. Standing motionless in the middle of the darkened room, he strained his ears to interpret the confused sounds reaching him from the night outside — and prayed.

It took Limpid Stream and Ngo Van Loc a long time to organize the first assault; the exultant faces of the mutinous *tirailleurs* fell in dismay when they were told two hundred of their brothers had decided to stand by their French officers in the fort. Running away to turn their weapons over to rebels from Hanoi was one thing; attacking back up the hill in the dark against their own comrades-in-arms of the Eighth commanded by the *chef de bataillon* was quite a different matter. Because of the reluctance of the *tirailleurs*, the first assault was ragged and confused. Although they used a few machine guns, the uncertain leadership of Limpid Stream did not inspire the *tirailleurs* and they were eventually beaten back. During the next half hour Limpid Stream led assault parties up the hillside again and again — but always they were easily repulsed.

Inside the fort the French *chef de bataillon* slowly recovered his nerve. He had been deeply shocked by how close he had come to death at the hands of his own forces when the mutiny began, but the success of his officers in throwing back the new rebel raids convinced him that he could stand fast within the citadel until daylight. His confidence grew when a native messenger found his way up the hillside through the fighting to report that the French civilians in the town were all safe. The *Résident de France* had managed to gather them together into a blockhouse of the Garde Indigène, which had remained loyal to a man. As the night wore on a trickle of *tirailleurs* from the three companies which had mutinied began to trickle back to the gates of the fort, beginning to be readmitted and offering their unopened ammunition pouches as evidence of their innocence. One of the officers who had barricaded himself in his quarters escaped up the hill at about two o'clock in the morning and the French commandant was sufficiently emboldened to send out a small patrol to seek other survivors.

In the caserne Limpid Stream slumped exhausted on a bench weeping with frustration at his inability to complete his conquest. Ngo Van Loc stood indecisively beside him listening to the sounds of sporadic firing coming from outside. Some of the rebels were still leading groups of *tirailleurs* up the hill against the fort, but Ngo Van Loc realized suddenly that although there were still several hours of darkness remaining, the revolt was now doomed to fail. He glanced down once more at Limpid Stream, who sat with his head buried in his hands, oblivious to what was going on around him, then turned and raced back towards the officers' quarters.

His two sons were still standing guard outside Paul Devraux's room, clutching their bloodstained weapons. The walls and door were pitted and scarred with bullet holes, but the barricade still denied them entry. In a fit of anger Loc kicked the jammed machine gun across the floor, and as he did so he saw the frightened face of the French officer's batman peer out of the kitchen door a few yards away to see what was making the noise. Loc stared at the little Tongkingese for a moment, then drawing his saber from the red sash at his waist, he beckoned the frightened man towards him.

Two minutes later Paul was startled to hear a gentle knocking on his shattered door. "It is safe to come out now, Monsieur Paul," called Ngo Van Loc in French. "The men who were here have all gone."

The French officer, half-recognizing the voice, stiffened. "Who is that?"

"Do you remember me? — Loc? Your father's 'boy' from the hunting camp. I can help you reach the fort now. Most of the other officers are safely gathered there. The men of your own Eighth Company have remained loyal to the *chef de bataillon*."

Paul's face registered his mystification. He recognized the hunting camp boy's voice despite a lapse of five years since he had last seen him but his presence at the fort aroused his suspicions. "What are you doing here, Loc? Are you with the rebels?"

There was a long pause outside. "Yes, I am, Monsieur Paul," he said, assuming a shamefaced tone. "But once you were a good friend to my sons and me. When I realized you were an officer here, I knew I must help you. I can make sure you get safe conduct to the fort gates." He paused and his voice took on a wheedling note. "Our rebellion has failed, Monsieur Paul. Perhaps if I help you now, you will be able to help me later. . . ."

"How do I know I can trust you?" asked the Frenchman suspiciously.

"Your batman is here with me. He will tell you." Loc tightened his grip around the man's puny shoulders and pressed his saber closer against his throat.

"Yes, yes, *mon lieutenant*, it's true," said the batman in a strangled whisper. "It's quite safe to come out now. All the others have gone!"

Paul buckled on his sword belt and took his revolver in his right hand before beginning to dismantle the barricade. The combined assault of the cement grenade and the heavy-caliber machine gun bullets had split and shredded the furniture, and as he moved the damaged wardrobe aside, the woodwork of the door itself collapsed inwards. It was then that he caught sight of his little batman, staring bulging-eyed at him from across the corridor. With one hand Ngo Van Loc was covering his mouth and with the other he pressed his bloodied saber against the terrified man's neck. The former hunting camp boy was holding the Tongkinese in front of him so that the frail body covered his own, and although Paul raised his revolver instinctively to fire the moment he saw he had been tricked, the risk of killing his batman made his finger hesitate on the trigger.

In the same instant Dong lunged from his hiding place beside the door and struck at the Frenchman's arm with his saber, shearing away part of his sleeve and knocking the revolver from his hand. His young brother, Hoc, appeared simultaneously from the other side of the door, swinging his *coupe-coupe*, and although the French officer twisted and ducked away from the blow aimed at his head, the *coupe-coupe* bit into the hump of his shoulder muscle and he staggered backwards into the room. He started to draw his sword but the two young Annamese pressed towards him, knocking it from his grasp, and together they forced him down onto his bed. They were lifting their weapons again, preparing to strike at his defenseless head, when Ngo Van Loc pushed between them, his features contorted with hate.

"Wait! Hold him for me. I will kill the son of Jacques Devraux myself!"

The two boys fell on the French officer and pinioned his arms. Paul's face was white with shock and blood from the wounds in his wrist and shoulder was already soaking through his uniform tunic. "Why, Loc, why?" he whispered, staring at them in horror. "Why kill someone who has been your friend?"

The Annamese lifted his saber and pressed its point against the base of the officer's throat. "Your father killed my wife!"

"Killed your wife?" Paul echoed the words of the Annamese in a horrified whisper. "That's not true!"

"He had her taken to jail in Saigon — his torturers murdered her." The Annamese drew the point of his saber sharply across the Frenchman's exposed chest, and a thin weal of new blood appeared.

"Loc, listen to me," said Paul desperately, trying to rise. "My father told me he found missing papers in your wife's quarters. The gendarmes *had* to question her. He left for a new post in Hanoi the next day. We had no idea Mai had died. . . ."

"Lies will not save your life!" Loc jabbed him viciously once more with the point of his saber. "Mai is dead — murdered by France and you're going to die for this crime! A revolution of blood and iron has begun!"

Paul turned from the hate-filled face of the father to look at Loc's two sons, who were pressing his shoulders against the bed. The blood of their earlier victims was drying on their clothing and the eyes that he remembered sparkling mischievously as he taught them to imitate the calls of jungle birds with blades of grass gazed back at him from their gaunt faces with the same expression of ferocious loathing.

"Hoc, Dong, please listen to me," Paul began, speaking quietly in Annamese, "you don't understand. . . ."

"Hold your tongue!" Loc's voice rose in a shout, and his features twisted into a snarl. Standing up to his full height he lifted his saber to swing it at the French officer's head.

Paul struggled frantically in the grip of the two young Annamese but his wounds were sapping his strength and he could only watch helplessly as Loc's saber began to descend. Because his eyes were fixed on the blade, he didn't see the French sergeant from the fort appear in the doorway leading two loyal *tirailleurs* of his Eighth Company; he only heard the flurry of shots from a revolver and at his side he felt Hoc shudder as a bullet struck him.

Then the tiny room was filled suddenly with stumbling, frantic bodies; the two *tirailleurs* lunged at Loc and Dong with their bayonets while the sergeant reloaded his revolver, but the two Annamese fought with great ferocity and succeeded in breaking out into the corridor. The sergeant fired after them as they fled, but both father and son made their escape from the building through a shattered window and disappeared into the confused melee on the darkened hill outside. Young Hoc struggled to his feet and tried to follow, but the wound in his shoulder had left him dazed with shock, and the French sergeant, on his return to the room, took one look at the bloodied uniform of his now-unconscious lieutenant, then knocked the Annamese boy to the floor. Although Hoc was already moaning with pain, the sergeant's face showed no sign of pity, and after staring down at him for a moment or two with hate-filled eyes, he began kicking him savagely about the head and body.

12

Rivulets of sweat trickled slowly down the face of Ngo Van Hoc as he crouched on the floor of his unlit cell in the Garde Indigène jail at Yen Bay with his hands covering his ears. It was four o'clock in the morning of June 17, 1930, and the fetid, stagnant air was heavy with the reek of putrefying foliage. It had been one of the hottest, most humid nights of the year in the Tongkingese fort town, but it was not just the suffocating heat that was making Hoc sweat; the agony of an uncontrollable fear was bathing the whole of his seventeen-year-old body in perspiration.

He pressed his hands more tightly against his ears in an effort to blot out completely the ringing knock of hammers coming from the field outside; he had hauled himself up to the barred window to peer out into the darkness when the noise first began, and it was the sight of the gang of coolies working in the center of the field by the light of the hurricane lamps that had filled him with dread. The tall, twin-pillared structure of wood and steel they were erecting was only partly visible in the light of the lamps, but it confirmed beyond any doubt the apprehension that had first seized him the previous evening when he and twelve other Quoc Dan Dang prisoners were taken from the Hanoi cells where they had spent the past four months and put on a heavily guarded train.

They were not told their destination, but when the clanking, five-hour journey up the Red River valley ended just after midnight on the platform at Yen Bay, the silent prisoners had begun to suspect the truth.

When the hammering finally stopped, Hoc uncovered his ears and stood up. For a minute or two he paced back and forth across the cell, massaging the spot just below his right shoulder where the bullet had struck home on the night of the mutiny; the wound had healed satisfactorily but it still ached if he allowed himself to get into a cramped position. From time to time he stopped moving to listen, but only the incessant shrill of cicadas in the trees bordering the field and the occasional croak of a toad broke the silence of the night.

He lay down on the plank bed and tried to sleep, but soon another commotion made him spring up to the window again. By the light of their torches he watched more coolies maneuver a heavily laden ox cart into the prison courtyard; they made no attempt to unload it quietly but flung what looked like long packing cases carelessly onto the flagstones. He didn't realize that they were cheap wooden coffins until they were all laid side by side in a neat row with their lids open. Then he counted them slowly and his heart lurched sickeningly in his chest — there were thirteen!

He released his grip on the bars of the window with a little moan of anguish and sank back into a crouch on the stone floor. He remained there for the rest of the night, hugging his frail body with his own thin arms, and just before dawn a fitful sleep brought his exhausted mind and body a few moments of ease. In dream he imagined himself back in the cold dark isolation cell at An Dap, condemned again to solitary confinement for trying to escape from the plantation. But despite the heavy leg-irons and the fever which shook his body, he felt exhilarated. He wasn't going to die after all! Soon he and Dong would be together again in the leaking hut, pressed close in the darkness, helping one another to endure the daily hardship of plantation life. Even the rough stone walls of the An Dap cell, which he could feel but not see, seemed friendly and familiar, and although his feet were swollen from the beating he had received, he had no bullet wound. He pressed his shoulder hard with one hand; see, there was no pain! All that had been a terrible nightmare. Only one thing was not familiar in the blackness of the An Dap cell — the muffled, rhythmic whisper of noise coming from outside. It seemed to be growing louder, drawing closer to him in the darkness, and his fear returned with a rush; he didn't know what the new sound was, but he was certain it was menacing to him.

He awoke trembling, to find the intensity of the darkness in his cell lessening. Then he noticed the new sound hadn't ceased with his dream. Wide-eyed with terror he listened to the muffled beat of a thousand bare feet scuffing through the damp grass outside the jail. Two companies of the Second Battalion of the Fourth Regiment of the Tirailleurs Tonkinois were marching down from the fort — the very men that Limpid Stream and the other Quoc Dan Dang rebels had hoped would help them begin a nationwide rebellion were marching and assembling obediently under their French officers to stand guard around the execution ground! He lifted himself to the window again and in the half-light caught a glimpse of them; with their rifles on their shoulders, their cone-shaped hats squarely on their heads, their legs wrapped from knee to ankle with blue puttees, they were taking their places in silence, staring mutely towards the center of the field.

As the scuff of the *tirailleurs*' marching feet quietened, from along the prison corridor Hoc heard the sudden crisp echo of soled shoes and the clank of keys. A cell door creaked open and the murmur of formal, dispassionate French voices reached his ears. After a minute or two the feet moved on, another door was opened and the voices murmured again. As the footsteps drew slowly nearer to him, Hoc rose from his bed and stood rigid with anxiety in the middle of his cell.

When the door finally opened it admitted the French Résident of Yen Bay, a thin bespectacled man with a straggling mustache. Without looking at Hoc, he raised a sheet of paper in front of his face and read from it in a dry, emotionless voice. "A presidential decree of June tenth has rejected all appeals for clemency. The sentence of the Criminal Commission of Inquiry will therefore now be carried out." The Résident waited impatiently while the Annamese interpreter translated the announcement, then turned quickly on his heel and left the cell. As Hoc stared after him the black-frocked figure of the Hanoi prison chaplain stepped smoothly forward to take the Résident's place. He murmured something that Hoc did not hear, raising his eyebrows at the same time in an expression of inquiry. When the Annamese interpreter offered a translation in his own language, Hoc still did not understand what was being asked of him, but he nodded his head numbly, hoping by his compliance to win a reprieve or at least a few minutes' respite. After motioning him to kneel before him, the priest sprinkled holy water on the trembling boy's forehead and deposited a few grains of salt on his tongue while murmuring the incantations of baptism into the Holy Roman Catholic Church. Hoc continued to nod uncomprehendingly during the perfunctory absolution that followed, and when he'd finished the priest asked quietly if he had any last wish to be made known to his family. "If you wish to write a letter, I will try to see that it is delivered," he added gently.

Hoc had heard nothing of his father and brother since the moment he was taken captive. In Hanoi he had been tortured with electricity until he revealed the address of the tiny room where they had all lived together above a carpenter's workshop in the city's old craft quarter. But other prisoners had told him later that Dong and his father had avoided returning to that address and were still at liberty. He was deeply ashamed of his betrayal and, suspecting this was some new trick to trap him into helping capture them, he shook his head fiercely.

As the priest left a barber entered, and warders held Hoc in a seated position while the barber lathered and shaved the nape of his neck. Tears of hopelessness welled in Hoc's eyes as the barber finished his work, and if he saw the traditional glass of cognac offered to him, he gave no sign. Other men came to dress him in a loose white smock and afterwards manacled his wrists behind his back. With a length of rope they hobbled his ankles so that he could take only short steps, then they left him alone again. By a quarter to five all the preparations for the mass execution had been completed, and an unnatural hush descended over the jail.

Outside a small crowd of Tongkingese had gathered on rising ground overlooking the field of execution, and in their midst Hoc's father and his brother, Dong, stood watching, gray-faced with anxiety. Stripped to the waist and wearing the dark turban of the upper Tongking peasant as disguise, they carried hoes like many of the other men around them. From where they stood they had a clear view over the heads of two companies of native *tirailleurs*, and the sight of the tall, mainly African troops of the French Colonial Infantry and the kepis of the Foreign Legionnaires, drawn up in a tight ring of security around the guillotine itself, were a disquieting reminder of their own frantic dash for freedom after the failure of the Yen Bay revolt.

The French officers with their loyal Eighth Company had routed the rebels with ease when they emerged from the fort at dawn, and the Colonial Infantry and men of the Legion came swiftly up the Red River valley by train to cut off their retreat. Limpid Stream himself had been captured, and Ngo Van Loc and his son were among the few who escaped downriver to the crowded safety of Hanoi's old quarter. There they learned for the first time that the Quoc Dan Dang's national leader, Nguyen Thai Hoc, code-named "the Great Professor," had tried to postpone the uprising at the last moment but his messenger had failed to reach the Yen Bay rebels in time. Other halfhearted raids launched that night in the upper delta had fizzled, and scattered grenade attacks against public buildings in Hanoi the day after had also failed to make any impact. The wave of revulsion that swept through Indochina and France in the wake of the bloody massacre of the fort's officers, however, had brought down a terrible retribution on the Quoc Dan Dang. The National Assembly in Paris rang daily with the name of Yen Bay, and many stern demands for retribution were made; the governor general of Indochina traveled to the fort for the funeral of the victims and made a ringing pledge of vengeance to their black-garbed widows at the graveside.

A few days later when "the Great Professor" launched a despairing attack against a post of the Garde Indigène in the lower delta, his own force of rebels became the victims of the first air attack to be launched in Indochina. Five wood and fabric Potez 35 biplanes of the French Armée de l'Air swooped on the village of Co Am, where they were hiding, and devastated the thatched houses with sixty twenty-two-pound bombs; when the rebels and the terrified peasants of the village fled from their burning houses, the pilots had strafed them indiscriminately with Lewis guns swivel-mounted on their cockpits. Some two hundred men, women and children were killed, and the French Résident Supérieur announced publicly next day in the newspapers: "We will bomb all villages like this without pity if they give shelter to the rebels."

"The Great Professor" himself was captured while fleeing towards the Chinese border, and after interrogating him and other party leaders, the Sûreté Générale arrested many hundreds of rank-and-file members. Eighty of them were condemned to death, and five hundred others were sentenced to long terms of imprisonment and forced labor. It was to put an emphatic and symbolic end to the Viet Nam Nationalist Party and its rebellion that the French colonists had decided to execute its top leaders and the Yen Bay rebels at the fort where their bloodiest revolt had failed.

The first prisoner to emerge into the pale light of that June dawn was a diminutive Annamese, and Ngo Van Loc and Dong craned their necks to catch a glimpse of his face as he reached the top of the long slope leading up from the jail. Handcuffed and dressed in a snowy-white smock, he was escorted by four tall black Madagascans of the Infanterie Coloniale who towered above him.

"It is 'Bui the Messenger,' " breathed Dong in a hoarse whisper, and beside him his father nodded grimly.

In total silence the little group moved across the field, led by the quick-stepping figure of the French Résident. Beside the macabre scaffold a squat, broad-shouldered Annamite *bourreau* waited with folded arms. In front of him the giant African infantrymen halted and stepped smartly aside, isolating the prisoner for the first time. The *bourreau*, who had been carefully trained by a French executioner, immediately grasped his shoulder and pushed him violently against the *bascule*; the hinged plank tipped forward with a crash under the impact of the prisoner's body and he fell face-downward into the lunette. The *bourreau* quickly slammed the upper half of this wooden collar into place and positioned his three-sided shield carefully so that it would protect him from any blood that spurted from the trunk of his victim's body.

In the deep silence that had fallen over the field the click of the sprung jaws in the crossbeam opening to release the blade was heard clearly by everyone watching on the hillside. The razor-sharp steel mounted in a wheeled, eighty-pound weight rushed noisily down its metal-lined channels and shuddered to rest at ground level, decapitating Bui the Messenger instantly without breaking its momentum. His severed head dropped neatly into the waiting bucket behind the scaffold, and two of the executioner's Annamese assistants hastily tipped the bleeding trunk of his body into the first of the waiting coffins.

Bui the Messenger died without a sound, without betraying any signs of fear, and on the hillside, women among the crowd began sobbing quietly. Ngo Van Loc closed his eyes for an instant to blot out the image of the grisly apparatus in the center of the field and put a trembling arm around Dong's shoulders; he knew that like himself his elder son must already be imagining how they would endure the sight of Hoc's neck trapped in the lunette.

Before the lid of Bui's coffin was secured the French Résident and his military escort were hastening toward the jail again, and as the sun brightened behind the eastern hills he scurried back and forth to the cells shepherding each successive prisoner to the scaffold with the brisk efficiency which he knew the French officials and journalists from Hanoi expected from a colonial administrator of his rank. Jacques Devraux was among the group watching from the balcony of the Garde Indigène barracks; one of three Sûreté inspectors who had volunteered to accompany the group of high officials led by the inspector of political affairs and the captain of gendarmeries, he glanced down at a list in his hand from time to time to name the prisoner they were watching or offer a few words of explanation. Nguyen the Pacifist . . . Ha the Laborious, Nguyen the Benefactor . . . Dao the Paltry. . . . One by one he ticked them off as the rebels marched straight-backed to the scaffold, their faces taut with the effort of mastering their fear. Beside his father on the balcony, Paul Devraux watched the grim procession in silence. He had already resumed light duties, but his right arm was still supported in a white sling and his pinched pale face continued to betray something of the toll his injuries had taken on him.

"From this distance, Paul, they all look like schoolboys, don't they?" The Sûreté inspector shook his head, musing to his son as the short quick-striding figure of Limpid Stream appeared at the top of the slope leading from the jail. "Perhaps we're lucky that they apply the romantic notions of boys at play to organizing a rebellion. Otherwise it might not have been so easy to defeat them."

"I'm not so sure there isn't something more ominous in their makeup," replied Paul quietly. "They seem to have an unshakable faith in their destiny. It doesn't matter how wild the scheme, how great the odds stacked against them — they still throw themselves in headlong without a second thought."

"But doesn't that only prove that they're foolish people?" The older man raised a cynical eyebrow at his son.

"Not foolish — fanatical," replied the young lieutenant evenly. "A much more dangerous quality."

His father shrugged and looked away without replying. For a moment Paul studied his profile; he fancied the lines of age in his father's face were suddenly more pronounced, and there seemed to be a new hardness about his mouth and eyes. "Did you ever find out, Father, how Loc's wife came to die in prison?" he asked quietly.

The older man shook his head without looking at him. "You know I'd left for Hanoi before it happened. I tried to make some inquiries from there. The death certificate said 'natural causes — heart.' That's all the information Saigon had."

"Could that be true?"

His father still didn't turn to face him. "There's no reason why we shouldn't believe the official explanation, is there? Prison cells are not healthy places. People do occasionally die in them."

"Yes, but Loc's wife —" The lieutenant broke off suddenly as the eerie silence in which all the executions had been taking place until then was shattered by a flurry of Annamese shouts from the center of the field.

"*Cho toi noi! Cho toi noi!*"

They looked up to find Limpid Stream struggling before the scaffold in the grip of one of the legionnaires, who had clamped a hand over his mouth when he began yelling in his own language: "I demand to speak!" The legionnaire managed to hold him silent while the Annamese *baurreau* forced him down into the lunette, but as soon as he was released the Tongkingese teacher opened his mouth and began shouting at the top of his voice: "Viet Nam! Viet Nam! Viet Nam!"

The rallying cry of the Vietnamese Nationalist Party rang electrifyingly across the hushed field, and as he heard the click above his head signal the blade's release, the leader of the Yen Bay revolt yelled even louder to drown the noise of its descent.

"Viet Nam! Viet Nam! Viet Nam!"

The words died abruptly as the guillotine severed his head, but his strident cries had already reached the ears of the remaining seven prisoners in their cells, and as each one was brought onto the field new defiant shouts of "Viet Nam! Viet Nam!" echoed from their throats. The Great Professor, the national leader of the party who had been one of the few to refuse baptism into the Catholic Church in his cell, marched silently to the scaffold and inclined his head in a grave salute to the crowd on the hill. Then he shouted "Viet Nam!" once in a loud sonorous voice before he died.

The silent Annamese spectators, believing that the party leader was the guillotine's last victim, had begun to break up and move away when Ngo Van Hoc appeared. For a few brief moments his father and brother had been seized by the hope that he might have been reprieved at the eleventh hour because of his youth; but the truth was he had been mistakenly left until last by the harassed French Résident, who in his anxiety to be done with his unpleasant task had overlooked Hoc's presence in the cells. As a result, his escort of Madagascan infantrymen had been ordered to march him to the scaffold as rapidly as possible, and Hoc had to keep breaking into a shuffling run to keep up with the long-striding African soldiers. This and the innocent whiteness of his smock cut away around his thin neck exaggerated his childlike appearance, and an Annamese woman in the crowd, deeply moved by the sight of him, cried out suddenly in anguish: "*Toi nghiep con toi* — Oh my poor little boy!"

Imagining in his agony that it was the voice of his own mother,

Hoc stopped suddenly in his tracks and tried to turn in the woman's direction. The soldiers behind him stumbled into him and one fell to the ground. In the confusion Hoc tried to break free and run towards the voice, but because his ankles were hobbled they caught him easily. When they tried to form up around him again, he began kicking and screaming hysterically, and one of the Madagascans eventually picked him up and carried him bodily to the guillotine.

The sight of the wing-shaped blade silhouetted against the glare of the rising sun at the top of the scaffold shocked him to silence and when the *bourreau* reached out his arms to take him from the soldier, Hoc offered no further resistance.

"Don't be afraid," said the Annamese quietly in their own language. "You will feel nothing."

The next instant he thrust him roughly against the bascule and Hoc tipped forward helplessly into the jaws of the guillotine. On the balcony of the Garde Indigène barracks Paul Devraux turned his head away to stare unseeing at the matted jungle high up on a distant hillside; in the crowd of watching Annamese, Dong and his father bowed their heads in anguish and prayed silently to their ancestors.

As the upper half of the lunette was slammed into place, Hoc closed his eyes tight and the face of his dead mother swam before him suddenly in the darkness. Then he heard the click of the mechanism and the frame rattled and shuddered about his shoulders. In the instant before the blade bit into the newly shaved nape of his neck he opened his eyes to stare into the sun-dappled dust before his face and screamed frantically, "Viet Nam! Viet Nam! Viet Nam!"

13

One of the gentle morning breezes of late August was ruffling the surface of the Lake of the Restored Sword in the heart of Hanoi when Dao Van Lat stepped onto the little ornamental bridge leading out to the Island of the Turtle close to its eastern shore. Leaning on the parapet he gazed fixedly down at the thick clusters of red and white lotus flowers stirring in the sparkling, jade-green water and tried hard to calm the pent-up sense of excitement growing inside him.

He had been awake half the night thinking about the clandestine meeting he was to have with the most celebrated Annamese revolutionary of his generation, and because of his agitation he had arrived a quarter of an hour before the appointed time. He had chosen the contact point himself on the same bold principle that had led him to take the noisy rickshaw ride to the Quoc Dan Dang pagoda meeting. The last place the Sûreté would expect revolutionaries to conspire, he reasoned, was beside the placid Ho Hoan Kiem in the full light of the early morning. But that was only part of the reason; the little coral pagoda on the Island of the Turtle that was just beginning to glow red in the rising sun was the enduring symbol of his people's love of freedom. Five centuries had passed, according to legend, since the lake had yielded up a miraculous sword to a fisherman on its shores; with the sword in his hand that fisherman, Le Loi, had raised a huge peasant army, repulsed an invasion from Ming-ruled China and founded a new dynasty that had opened a glorious era in his country's history. Lat had insisted that the meeting be held there to demonstrate his fervent conviction that now, in August 1930, the time was ripe for a new Le Loi to appear and lead a modern army of peasants against the invaders from France! He was sure there should be no further delay, and he was determined to throw down a challenge. Who was to be the modern Le Loi, the new hero of Viet Nam? Would Nguyen the Patriot return at last from twenty years of exile to march at their head — or would he continue to skulk secretly abroad for twenty more years? If he did, then the peasants must have a leader who would inspire them by his presence and he, Dao Van Lat, would take up the miraculous sword of revolution in his place!

Carried away by his train of thought he realized suddenly he was not being as watchful as he might about his security and turned quickly to scan the Boulevard Francis Garnier that bordered the lake on its eastern shore. He was searching for a telltale Sûreté Citroën or Peugeot that would indicate he was being followed, but he saw nothing and turned back to the lake. He was dressed neatly in the European style in a pale double-breasted linen suit and a white panama hat pulled over his eyes. From beneath its brim he scrutinized the roads along the other shores, wondering from which direction Nguyen the Patriot might come. He was rumored to be ingenious in his use of disguise, but how would he conceal his identity in the city where his arch-enemies of the Sûreté Générale had their Indochina headquarters? Or perhaps he would not come at all. The meeting had been arranged through intermediaries, and if, as was rumored, he had never once returned to his own country since working his passage to Europe on a French liner as a twenty-year-old boy, perhaps he would not have the courage to return at the age of forty now that many provinces in northern Annam and southern Tongking were suddenly and unexpectedly seething with popular rebellion. Or possibly Nguyen the Patriot too had been astonished at this unexpected turn of events.

Lat himself had watched with grim satisfaction in February and March as his predictions about the foolhardiness of the Quoc Dan Dang rebellion came true — but had then been amazed by the lightning speed at which conditions throughout the Annamese lands had changed and deteriorated thereafter. The Wall Street Crash had led to a rapid flight of French capital from all Indochina, and Annamese toiling in mines and factories were thrown out of work or had their wages slashed. There had already been a succession of poor harvests, and great tracts of productive land had been abandoned abruptly in the wake of a disastrous fall in the price of rice. Starvation had spread quickly and strikes and rioting followed. In some provinces the Garde Indigène and the Foreign Legion had been ordered to fire into the midst of crowds, and many demonstrators had been killed. With great energy and determination Lat had thrown himself into the task of expanding his own peasant movement, the Society of United Hearts, beyond his home province and his stature as a revolutionary leader had grown by leaps and bounds. Rumors of his violent act of self-sacrifice had spread, too, and many members of his movement as a result were openly in awe of him.

For the twentieth time that morning Lat checked his wristwatch. It was still a few minutes short of eight o'clock, the appointed hour for the meeting, and again he looked all around the lake in vain for a sign of the mysterious revolutionary he was waiting to meet. The sun was already hot on his back but because it was Sunday the streets of Hanoi were still quiet and with the exception of a bent rickshaw coolie hobbling painfully along the shore road two hundred yards away, the approaches to the bridge remained deserted. Resting his elbows on the parapet again he gazed into the sun-dappled lake and let his thoughts return to the slumbering jade dragon of national salvation that the legend claimed had chosen to make its mythical lair there.

He half closed his eyes and imagined the dark-clad figure of Le Loi casting his net into the water and withdrawing, in astonishment, the gleaming sword into which its genie had transformed itself; he saw it flashing colored fire across the waters, the *nha que* —

the peasants — surging from the rice paddies in their tens of thousands to follow the magical blade and its bearer in a bitter ten-year war of independence against the Chinese. A poet's words that he had memorized as a young boy chased the images through Lat's mind and he repeated them softly aloud:

> "The tyrannous invader fled in fear
> When his slave refused to kneel.
> From the deep lake the fiery sword of vengeance leapt forth
> Rousing the people to freedom."

The little bridge on which he stood must have been very close, he reflected, to the spot where the fisherman who became an emperor returned to offer a sacrifice to the genie of the lake a decade later. It was then that the sword sprang out of its sheath and, exploding in a flash of light, refashioned itself into a great jade dragon that roared and whirled through the clouds above the awe-struck crowd before plunging down to disappear into the green depths of the lake. At the same moment, the legend said, the little red coral pagoda materialized on the rock in the lake's southern reaches to mark the spot and Lat was turning to look towards the pagoda when a voice spoke quietly in Annamese at his shoulder.

"Our ancestors long ago established an independent nation with its own civilization. We have our own mountains and our own rivers, our own customs and our own traditions. . . ."

Lat turned slowly, recognizing the words uttered by the emperor Le Loi in his victory address at the lakeside. He started when he found himself gazing into the face of the bent rickshaw coolie, who still clutched the shafts of his vehicle behind him. But instead of the wizened, aged face he might have expected from the coolie's posture, he saw a pair of deepset eyes regarding him with a glittering intensity from beneath a smooth, high-domed forehead. A shock of dark hair swept back from the narrow, intelligent face belied the impression of agedness given by the cringing gait and the hairpin-thin body. The Annamese was not much more than five feet tall and clean shaven, and as he awaited Lat's response his piercing eyes softened into a faint, self-mocking smile at his assumed disguise.

". . . We have sometimes been weak and sometimes powerful — but at no time have we suffered from a lack of heroes," said Lat softly, completing the quotation which had been set as their secret password.

For a moment the man between the rickshaw shafts said nothing but merely glanced about himself in all directions with the practiced casualness of one used to being pursued.

168

"I can hardly believe I am at last face to face with the famous Nguyen the Patriot," said Lat quietly. "Are you really Nguyen Ai Quoc?"

"How should a humble *pousse-pousse* coolie answer that?" replied the Annamese, his eyes twinkling. "Only Nguyen Ai Quoc himself would be able to give an adequate reply."

Lat stared at him uncertainly. "If Nguyen Ai Quóc himself were really here," he asked, his voice suddenly challenging, "what would he advise our nation's best patriots to do?"

The Annamese fumbled in the pocket of his faded shorts and drew out black tobacco and papers to roll himself a cigarette. As if in response to the obvious tension in the man facing him, his movements were exaggeratedly slow and relaxed. He had positioned himself with his back to the rising sun beneath the overhanging fronds of a lakeside willow, and Lat had difficulty in discerning his features in the shadows. "Your name has gained much renown because of a courageous act of self-sacrifice," he said. "You have proved you have the determination to lead."

Lat, despite the seeming compliment, detected a clear note of disapproval in the unemotional statement and didn't reply.

"But determination is not enough on its own — it should always be tempered by good judgment. Weren't the leaders of the Quoc Dan Dang determined to make a rebellion at Yen Bay?"

"My judgment was good," replied Lat coldly. "I refused to take part. I warned them that the people weren't ready."

The dark eyes glittered in the shade of the trees and he nodded slowly. "That at least was wise. . . . But are the people really ready now, do you think?"

"Yes. I've worked among the peasants for six months. Many thousands have flocked to join my Society of United Hearts."

"Better known to its members as the Dao Van Lat Society, yes?" An ironic little smile tugged at the corners of the older man's mouth. "I found the oaths and the initiation rites of our secret societies exciting as a boy, too. It was like 'The Romance of the Three Kingdoms' come to life. I've heard your followers still prop their leader's picture on their altars and prostrate themselves before it like members of the old societies did, is that right?"

"I've forbidden that practice," said Lat sharply, "but our peasants respond best to traditions of the past that they understand."

"But do they really know your program? Do they have any idea along which path you are leading them?"

"To sovereignty, independence, freedom!" replied Lat hotly.

"They can't eat sovereignty or drink independence — or plant

169

rice in them either. They need a promise of land, something they can feel and touch — or they will lose interest when they're no longer starving."

"Their loyalty to my leadership is unshakable," protested Lat, his face flushing with anger.

The man between the shafts of the rickshaw sighed resignedly and lit the straggly cigarette he had rolled. He sucked the smoke noisily into his lungs for a moment, peering absently across the lake. "Yes, the old habits die hard. But we must fight modern oppression with modern means of resistance. Secret societies and ancient rituals are of little use against machine guns and bombs dropped from the sky."

"And what is so much better?" asked Lat in a sullen tone.

"About the time of the Yen Bay débâcle I held a meeting with representatives of three different Communist factions from our country — on the crowded terraces of a football stadium in Hong Kong!" He paused and smiled impishly at the memory. "With the crowd yelling all around us we succeeded in sinking our differences and formed a united Communist Party of Vietnam."

"And now all our problems are solved, I suppose," rejoined Lat sarcastically. "What magic genie is watching over the party born at a Hong Kong football match?"

The morning wind shook the trailing willow branches in little flurries about his shoulders as the older man leaned towards Lat. "We agreed to work to overthrow French rule and set up a government of workers, peasants and soldiers. But most important of all our new Marxist-Leninist party is supported by the international proletariat — by all the oppressed people of the world. The party and its goals will survive the death of individual leaders. If you are killed or imprisoned, what happens to your society?"

"A man with a will of iron is not so easily destroyed," replied Lat fiercely.

The man who called himself Nguyen the Patriot drew slowly on his cigarette, then suddenly his face lit up with a childlike radiance. "A true revolutionary cannot be a man of iron," he said softly. "An iron rod can be broken with a single blow. A revolutionary should be more like our own bamboo that bends before the wind and springs back again. Vietnam needs revolutionaries who are flexible, revolutionaries who don't try to cut themselves off from life — revolutionaries who are sensitive to the winds of events and needs of their people."

Stung by the rebuke, Lat glared angrily at the man before him.

"The greatest need of the people now is for a leader who will march bravely and openly at their head — not one who continues to hide abroad!" He paused, his chest rising and falling quickly in his agitation. "The provinces of Nghe An and Ha Tinh are seething with revolt. Do you intend to go there and lead the peasants?"

Before he replied the older man calmly studied all the roads leading towards the bridge once more. Then he turned the full brilliance of his gaze back to Lat. "I'm a professional revolutionary. The Comintern makes sure that every party in the world is strengthened by the support of proletarian internationalism. I am always on strict orders. My itinerary is carefully prescribed."

"So you don't have enough faith in our revolution to stay?" Lat couldn't hide the note of triumph in his voice.

"We've worked patiently for five years training our activists in Moscow and at the Whampoa revolutionary academy in Canton — some small results are beginning to show. But we must proceed carefully. Our organization is still poor." He stopped, and a rueful smile played across his face. "Many peasants still believe the hammer and sickle is the flag of the French government. So the road will be long — and you are right — we need many more good men to lead our movement."

He smiled again and his face radiated a warmth and simple-heartedness that the younger Annamese found strangely disarming despite his anger.

"What if I join your new party," said Lat brusquely, "and go to Nghe An to help organize the peasants? We lack arms now, but what could the French do if fifteen million Vietnamese could be persuaded to lay down their tools in the factories and mines and in the rice fields?" He paused, and his voice grew excited. "What if the cooks and the boys and coolies of the cities could be made to join them in peaceful protest marches? Even without arms they would become a great unstoppable tide!"

"We must proceed carefully," warned the man between the shafts of the rickshaw, staring over Lat's shoulder. "The movement isn't steady or continuous by any means. Don't take unnecessary risks." Then he smiled quickly. "And don't arrange any more meetings in daylight on the shores of the Ho Hoan Kiem."

Lat saw that the other man's eyes were fixed on the Boulevard Garnier, and swinging around to follow his gaze he saw a shiny black Sûreté Citroën nosing slowly along the lakeside. Nguyen the Patriot raised his hand in the direction of the red coral pagoda and immediately a bent peasant woman hobbled from the doorway, struggling with a heavy bag of vegetables. The Annamese removed his faded, threadbare shirt and wound it quickly around his head in a makeshift turban. Naked to the waist he trotted slowly towards the woman, and when she had climbed into the rickshaw, he turned with lowered head and brought her back across the bridge. Hobbling hunch-shouldered between the shafts, he had transformed himself in seconds into a bowed and shriveled figure, in appearance twice his forty years.

Lat leaned over the narrow parapet again, watching the rickshaw out of the corner of his eye. He saw the Sûreté car cruise slowly towards the shabby little vehicle, then pass by without pausing. In the rear seat Inspector Jacques Devraux was reading a newspaper and he didn't even glance up at the hunched figure between the shafts.

Lat remained on the bridge with his back to the road until the car had disappeared into the distance. Left alone he felt suddenly exhilarated and full of confidence. He would show Nguyen the Patriot who was right! He would show him that too much caution was as dangerous as too little. Millions of peasants now were crying out for strong, courageous leadership, and if Nguyen the Patriot wished to give priority to his secret foreign duties, he, Dao Van Lat, would show the way! And perhaps by his decisive actions he would even win first place in the hearts of the people as Le Loi had done five hundred years before!

Excited by this thought he turned and strode briskly away along the eastern shore, glancing from time to time into the shimmering waters of the lake. The jade dragon *was* there in the shadowy depths, he reminded himself fiercely, waiting to rematerialize as a mighty sword of vengeance. It remained invisible only to the eyes of those without sufficient faith and determination to see it! But as surely as the dragon of his own iron will lay coiled and waiting inside him, it was there, ready and eager to spring forth again soon!

14

The narrow road winding through the empty paddies of Nghe An province in northern Annam was lit only by the feeble glow of a waning moon as Dao Van Lat pedaled a bicycle furiously northward in the early morning of September 12, 1930. It was an hour before dawn, and to the west, the peaks of the Annamite Chain, dimly visible in the fading moonlight, resembled a dark jagged row of dragon's teeth. As always the sight of the mountains stirred Lat's emotions deeply; the mighty outcrops of gnarled rock that pushed down almost to the sea in places in the province where he had been born, he thought of as the strong roots of his own life. Sandwiched between the mountains and the sea, these stony rice lands, much less fertile than the rich deltas around Hanoi and Saigon, had over the centuries produced a tough, resilient breed of people from whom he was proud to be descended. They were accustomed to battling hard to survive, and all the leaders of peasant rebellions in his country's history had sprung from that region — including, Lat reflected grimly as he rode, Nguyen the Patriot.

His encounter with the Communist leader in a rickshaw coolie's guise had lived on vividly in his memory during the past three weeks; the strangely hypnotic physical presence of the man had left an impression that grew with the passage of time — but above all else his smiling, ironic criticisms had continued to rankle in Lat's mind. As a result he had flung himself into his new role in the Viet Nam Cong San Dang — the Vietnam Communist Party — with ferocious energy, and he had found his determination to prove Nguyen the Patriot wrong increasing daily during the furtive meetings of the party's Provincial Committee.

He had been appointed to the committee immediately on joining the party because of his reputation, and in the first ten days of September its members had been meeting in almost daily session in pagodas in and around Vinh, the capital of Nghe An, as they battled to control the great upsurge of peasant discontent that was shaking the province. By then it had become clear that starvation was affecting about a third of the entire population throughout the Annamese lands, and the unrest that had begun with Communist-led coolies hoisting a hammer-and-sickle flag above the *cainha* of a rubber plantation on May Day was obviously reaching a new peak. In Nghe An and the neighboring province of Ha Tinh, violence had become widespread; peasants armed with crude spears and *coupe-coupes* had begun burning down district government offices, murdering landlords and pro-French mandarins, and other terrified Annamese officials were fleeing to the provincial capital in increasing numbers. In many areas something close to anarchy reigned.

To bring the stamp of firm leadership to this growing chaos and provide a focus for the discontent, Lat had proposed a massive unarmed protest march into the city of Vinh and had undertaken to organize and lead it himself. He had worked day and night for a whole week, drafting fifty of the best members of his Society of United Hearts into the party to help him in the task. He was trying to assemble a column of ten thousand peasants, and as dawn approached on the day of the march he was racing from village to village by bicycle checking that they were being assembled in sufficient numbers, distributing crudely written petitions to be carried and giving last-minute orders.

He had already visited a dozen villages in the past two hours and to his satisfaction had found that behind the tall bamboo thickets which screened all the settlements of that part of Annam, the sleepy-eyed peasants were gathering obediently in groups several hundreds strong under the watchful eyes of his own handpicked leaders.

Lat himself was wearing a tunic and trousers of cheap red-brown peasant cloth, and a mollusk-shaped straw hat was tied about his shoulders. He crouched low over his handlebars as he rode, pumping the pedals in a fast rhythm, his anticipation of the march's success fueling his strength. Occasionally he disturbed a pair of long-legged herons rooting for frogs in the shallow water of the roadside paddies and the quiet plain echoed for a moment with a succession of eerie cries as the birds flapped away into the darkness. The rice fields through which he was pedaling had just produced their third bad harvest in succession, and he had found little difficulty in persuading the hungry peasants to march on Vinh to present petitions demanding abolition of the high rice taxes still being collected by the French. When he dismounted from his machine to wheel it through the bamboo groves rattling in the pre-dawn breeze around the fourteenth village on his list, Lat was pleased to see the familiar face of Ngo Van Loc materialize from the shadows.

"How many, Comrade Loc?" he asked sharply before offering any greeting.

The murmur of a big crowd could be heard coming from the clearing in the center of the darkened village, and Loc smiled. "Don't worry! Already seven hundred when I last checked fifteen minutes ago."

"Good!" Lat glanced down at his list. "Then you still have three hundred or so to come. Send out new messengers and hurry them up." He lifted his head and listened for a moment to the growing murmur. "And when they begin to move, they must all remain absolutely quiet. Is that clear? The march must be tightly disciplined. It must take place in total silence."

"Yes, Comrade Lat," replied Loc dutifully. "I have already told them. But I will get Dong to make a new announcement when they are all assembled."

Lat had persuaded the former hunting camp "boy" to accompany him to Nghe An with his son Dong when they had met by chance in the old quarter of Hanoi. After watching his younger son and the Viet Nam Nationalist People's Party itself die under the guillotine at Yen Bay, Loc had turned naturally in his agony to the new Communist Party to continue the fight against the hated French. He had welcomed the hard work and the responsibility of supervising one of the biggest assembly points for the march, and when Lat arrived, his eyes were alight with a subdued excitement at the success of his efforts to gather the large crowd together in secret.

Lat patted him on the shoulder and smiled as he pulled a sheaf of petitions from inside his tunic. "Now, Comrade Loc, you are really seeing the people rise up together. There'll be no more crazy, halfhearted military mutinies! This time the leadership is right!"

Loc nodded and took the papers he was offered. "These look very authentic, comrade," he observed, leafing through the pages by the light of his flashlight.

"I had them written by semiliterate peasants of my society. Give them to innocent-looking villagers. When the time comes, hide yourself in their midst — but make sure that they know you're there so that you can control them."

Loc nodded again.

"How many women and children have you got?"

"Over two hundred, I think."

"Good. Put them all at the front and along the sides of the column. Your group will lead the whole march, and the soldiers won't open fire if they see only women and children." Lat glanced at his watch. "Begin moving towards the road half an hour before dawn. And search them again before daylight for weapons. No bamboo lances, no *coupe-coupes*, nothing. Understand?"

"Yes of course, comrade."

Lat turned his bicycle and swung his leg across the saddle again, then he stopped and patted Loc quickly on the shoulder. "You've done a good job, comrade. Keep it up. Things are going well. Today you will be part of a mighty sea of protest — the biggest the French have ever seen!" With a wave of his hand he turned and pedaled rapidly away towards the next village on his list.

While it was still dark the village groups all began trickling out of concealment and heading for one of the main highways ten miles

175

from Vinh. By the time dawn broke the column had virtually assembled; filling the narrow road from edge to edge, it stretched for a distance of three or four miles between the flat patchwork of paddy fields. Moving slowly and in silence, it began heading for the provincial capital.

The sun was well up the eastern sky before the French detected the marchers and it was an *adjutant chef*, piloting a Potez 25 fighting biplane of the Armée de l'Air, who first caught sight of them. He was flying his first routine reconnaissance patrol of the day and from a distance he merely thought he was looking at a muddy brown river that he hadn't known was there before. Then as he drew nearer he saw with astonishment that he was looking at a silently flowing stream of human bodies. Wide, conical hats spread a multipointed roof of straw above the heads of the peasants, but as he flew in to take a closer look, the pilot saw the hats tip backwards in a long slow rippling movement; like an army of mollusks opening their shells in unison on the sea bed, the brims lifted to reveal thousands of soft, unprotected faces beneath. With their eyes narrowed against the glare of the sun the peasants of Nghe An stared blankly at the unfamiliar sight of the little French warplane as it flew along the length of the column.

Because the plane was on reconnaissance duties, its external bomb racks beneath the fuselage were empty and the two Lewis guns mounted in the rear cockpit were unmanned, but when the *adjutant chef* recovered from his astonishment he used his cockpit wireless to call his base near Vinh. "*C'est incroyable!*" he repeated over and over again into his tiny transmitter. "It is incredible. There are many thousands of peasants marching towards Yen Xuyen — but they have no arms, no banners. And they are marching very slowly — it's all very eerie . . .!"

On the ground Lat dismounted from his bicycle and stood still at the side of the procession, watching the little biplane disappear into the sky towards the east. "Retreating in bafflement," he thought delightedly and turned to look at the faces of the peasants trudging past a few feet away. Men, women and children alike were hollow-cheeked from hunger, but they were moving along the road with determined strides and he felt a tremor of elation run through him. It was working! The great tide of humanity flowing towards the French administrative capital had been conceived in his own mind, and by his energy and determination he had brought the dream to life!

As the peasants plodded by, they stared at him incuriously and he wondered if they knew that they were marching because he, Dao Van Lat, had decided they should. Then he realized a face beneath one of the wide straw hats was staring at him with unusual intensity. For a second or two because, like him, she was dressed in the dun-colored clothes of the region, he didn't recognize Lien. They had not met during the eight months that had passed since the eve of Tet, and she was staring at him with a pained expression in her eyes. Although she must have seen that he had recognized her, she turned away quickly without acknowledging him to whisper in the ear of a young Annamese marching beside her. For a moment Lat watched her retreating back, but she didn't turn her head again and he jumped on his bicycle to give his stewards new instructions.

As he pedaled along the column, however, he found he couldn't dismiss from his mind the naked expression of pain he had seen in Lien's eyes. Remorse welled up inside him with sudden, unexpected force, and when he had finished giving his orders he hurried back towards the front of the marching column. On spotting her he ordered one of the peasants to push his bicycle and slipped into the crowd at her side. "It's good to see you marching with us today, Comrade Lien," he said quietly.

She looked startled when she turned, but didn't speak. Despite her drab clothes and her cartwheel-sized hat of plaited banana leaves, the fineness of her features still betrayed the background of her upbringing in one of Hue's leading mandarin families. If anything, her plain garb accentuated the refined, gentle loveliness of her face, and Lat felt his pulse quicken at the memory of the love they had once shared.

"This is Comrade Hao," said Lien awkwardly, and the young Annamese at her side nodded and moved away so that Lat could walk between them.

"And have you come here *together* to join my march?"

"Yes." She nodded once but stared hard at the ground as she spoke.

"I take it you're an enthusiastic worker for the party, comrade," said Lat, addressing Hao in a curt voice. "Would I be right?"

"Of course." Hao, who appeared to be in his early twenties, looked steadily back at him, his eyes bright and eager in his boyish face.

"Then take my bicycle and ride two miles ahead to Yen Xuyen. Give me an idea how many Legionnaires are on duty there and how many local militia!"

"Very good, Comrade Lat." Hao turned and pushed through the crowd and mounted the bicycle immediately.

Even after he'd gone Lien still continued to march with her eyes turned from Lat, and because he found himself at a loss for words they walked side by side in silence for several minutes. Once, somebody ahead of them stumbled and fell, and as the crowd surged to a halt he was pressed roughly against her. Conscious of touching the softness of her upper arm and the curve of her hip with his own body, he felt a spasm of sweet agony shoot through him. Almost immediately the crush of those around them relented and they shifted apart but she saw at once how deeply he had been stirred by the brief moment of contact.

"Lien . . . ." he began then stopped, his voice dying in his throat. "Lien . . . I'm sorry." Impulsively he reached out and took her hand in his own, looking at her with burning eyes.

"It is too late to be sorry, Lat."

He felt something fall against his hand and looked down to see that a single gold bracelet, one that he had given her a year before, had slipped down her arm from its place of concealment beneath the loose sleeve of her peasant tunic. She glanced down and saw it, too, then looked into his face and tried to smile. But tears suddenly welled in her eyes.

"Comrade Lat! Comrade Lat!" The anxious voice made him turn, and he saw Ngo Van Loc struggling through the crowd towards him. "The Legion guardpost up ahead sent an Annamese messenger to ask about our intentions, and some women at the front of the crowd said we were carrying tax petitions."

"Yes, yes. What of it?" snapped Lat irritably.

"They say now that we must stop here and send a delegation into Yen Xuyen to deliver them."

"And if we don't?"

"Then they say they will fire on us."

Lat snorted contemptuously. "Are the women and children still leading the march?"

"Yes. The front ranks are solid. The first two or three hundred are women and young people."

At that moment Hao arrived back beside them and leaped off the bicycle, panting with exertion. "There are only about a dozen soldiers of the Legion, Comrade Lat," he gasped. "And fifty or sixty Annamese militia."

The column was moving up an incline, and looking back Lat could see the great swathe of marchers winding along the narrow road behind them for several miles. Visibly moved by the sight, he drew a long slow breath. "Twelve soldiers of France and sixty puppet troops against ten thousand peasants of Vietnam! How dare they command us to stop."

He glanced in turn at those around him. Loc's face was taut with anxiety, while the boy Hao was awaiting Lat's decision with a look of awed admiration on his face. Lien had bent her head so that her face was invisible beneath the wide hat, but he fancied that he saw her slender shoulders shake once in a silent sob. Suddenly a helpless rage seized him. "They will never be able to stop us! We go all the way through to Vinh as planned. Tell the Annamese messenger that!"

It was another half hour before the little Potez 25 biplane that had spotted the column in the early morning appeared again. By then the front ranks of the marchers were within a quarter of a mile of the roadblock set up by the French Foreign Legion, and on Lat's instructions the pace was quickening. But this time the fighting biplane was not on a reconnaissance mission. The two external bomb racks below its pinewood and fabric fuselage were fully loaded with a dozen twenty-two-pounders, and the rear cockpit was occupied by a sergeant observer who was traversing his Lewis guns in practice sweeps as they neared their target. Two more Potez 25s of the Armée de l'Air Vinh squadron were flying above and behind it and they too were fully manned and loaded with bombs.

The planes had been in sight, small specks in the sky dead ahead of the marching column, for a minute or two before Lat heard their engines. Although the peasants appeared to be marching in silence, in the midst of the throng a low murmur of muttered conversations was audible, and at first the distant airplanes sounded like an intensification of this muted hum of human voices. But gradually the angry, high-pitched buzz of their four-hundred-and-fifty-horsepower Lorraine engines became unmistakably clear as they drew nearer, and Lat and the marchers began screwing up their eyes to stare into the bright sky. The three aircraft were coming in from the east with the sun behind them, and Lat had difficulty in seeing them clearly at first; then suddenly Ngo Van Loc was beside him, yelling in his ear. "Remember Co Am, Comrade Lat! Remember Co Am!"

Lat glanced about himself in desperation. The marchers were wedged in a tight mass between a long stretch of flooded, tree-lined paddy fields. It would take an hour or two to disperse them along the narrow highway; even to scatter them across the adjoining rice fields would take more time than they had — and would end the march in defeat and humiliation.

He looked frantically at the sky again. The engine noise of the three biplanes was growing louder and when the pitch suddenly rose it became clear that they were starting to dive.

"Disperse them!" he yelled suddenly into Ngo Van Loc's face. "They're going to bomb us." He turned and ran into the water of the roadside paddy, screaming and waving his arms in both directions along the column. "Scatter! Scatter! We are going to be bombed."

Instead of following into the fields, the peasants all around him stood rooted to the spot, staring incredulously, first at him then back at the dark smudges of the three biplanes falling towards them out of the blinding sun. Four hundred feet above their heads, the *adjutant chef* in the leading Potez tightened his grip on the control column and eased it gently back towards his groin. As the biplane reached the bottom of its dive and began to pull up again fifty feet above the heads of the marchers, the first bomb slipped from its rack and twenty-two pounds of high explosive encased in cold steel rose and fell in a gentle arc towards the densest part of the column just behind the leaders. When it detonated on impact with the ground, it brought down a hundred marchers instantly. The explosion enveloped the front of the column in a pall of white smoke, and in this lethal fog survivors found themselves scrambling blindly over piles of torn and burned corpses that blocked the road. A moment later the other two planes released their bombs on the middle and rear sections of the column, and these explosions cut down another hundred marchers.

Horribly mutilated men and women not killed outright staggered into the paddies to die, and the flooded fields along the roadsides were soon stained a dark crimson with their blood. As the planes rose and dived, dropping more bombs and raking the marchers with long bursts of fire from their Lewis guns, Lat scrambled knee-deep through the sludge trying desperately to disperse crowds of peasants who were huddling close together in their terror. But shocked and hysterical, they refused to listen to his advice, and after a few minutes he stopped and stood still, gazing about him at the carnage with tears streaming down his face.

He saw Ngo Van Loc throw up his arms and collapse in a heap as one of the biplanes swayed across the fields at tree-top height machine-gunning those Annamese still stumbling among the dead and wounded. Another exploding bomb ripped up mud and earth in a fountain from the fields on the far side of the road, but Lat didn't bother to take cover. When its fumes cleared he began stumbling blindly back towards the section of the route where only a minute before the front of the column had halted. When he got there he found the road surface slippery with blood, and he searched with a sinking heart through the tangled mass of broken bodies.

Many of them were unrecognizable, their features obliterated by burns and blast, but even before he saw the single gold bangle on the anonymous stump of a handless arm, he knew that he would find her dead. The gruesomely truncated corpse of Comrade Hao, who had also fallen in the first explosion, half covered her, but when he rolled the dead boy aside he saw that Lien's long, lustrous hair was matted and clogged with blood. Part of her face and one eye were gone, and her mouth, a gaping animal's maw, was horribly contorted as though in one last formless scream of protest at such a hideous death. Lat realized then that a bullet or a piece of shrapnel had pierced his own side, and sinking to his knees, he lay uncaring with his head resting on the trunk of her dead body as the squadron of French planes roared back and forth through the smoke and din, dropping more bombs and strafing the road and surrounding fields again and again with their machine guns.

PART THREE

The River of Perfumes

1936

In 1936 the colonial territories of Indochina were enjoying a new era of peace and stability. The French had crushed all Annamese resistance to their rule by the beginning of 1932 and the economy had recovered. But beneath the surface calm, hatred of the French had intensified as a result of the atrocities committed against the rebels during 1930 and 1931. The world at large knew little of these events, but the Annamese calculated that more than ten thousand of their countrymen had been executed, tortured to death or killed with bombs, guns and bayonets during those two violent years. The bombing of unarmed marchers at Vinh in September 1930 accounted for more than two hundred dead, and another seven hundred Annamese were guillotined without trial. During the same period only two Frenchmen were killed. About fifty thousand Annamese nationalists and Communists were imprisoned or deported, but the true dimensions of the brutality emerged only when soldiers of the French Foreign Legion were put on trial; then it was revealed the Legionnaires often took ten prisoners at random from a village and killed nine before interrogating the survivor, sometimes interrogated prisoners in pairs, decapitating one and forcing the other to hold the severed head while they questioned him. On occasions Legion troops brutalized prisoners in their cells without reason, cutting off their ears, gouging flesh from their faces with their bayonets, and leaving them, according to one contemporary account, "marinating in an abominable mess of blood, urine and vomit." Atrocities, however, were not committed only by the French. The Communists set up rural "soviets" in some provinces, modeled on the peasant-ruled areas first created by Mao Tse-tung in southern China, and their "self-defense" forces, armed with sticks and knives, employed terror tactics against their enemies. Peasants who refused to join or who were judged to have betrayed the Communist cause were murdered in secret, pro-French mandarins and Annamese landlords were publicly hanged, garotted, or thrown into lakes in weighted bamboo cages, while particularly detested victims had their noses cut off, their teeth wrenched out and their beards set on fire before they were killed. Nguyen the Patriot, the elusive Communist leader of the insurgency, was eventually sentenced to death in his absence by the French for organizing the rebellion, but although he spent a brief spell in a British prison in Hong Kong, he continued to elude the Sûreté Générale, and realizing that the tide of the revolution was ebbing, he disappeared once more to the obscurity of Moscow where in 1932 he was officially reported by the Communist press to have died. Almost all the leading members of the Communist movement he had founded were arrested, and the crowded cells of Paulo Condore off the coast of Cochin-China became the training ground for a new generation of Annamese Communists. These prisoners might have languished longer in the island's dungeons, but Hitler's rise to power in Germany prompted the French Communist Party to join socialists and centerists in an anti-Fascist coalition in Paris. This new Popular Front Government legalized the Communist Party in Indochina and in the early months of 1936 declared an amnesty for the prisoners of Paulo Condore. As the prisoners began returning to Saigon, Hanoi and Hue, agents of the Sûreté Générale were again put quietly on alert to watch for new signs of anti-French conspiracy.

1

As he walked the darkened streets of Saigon for the first time since 1925, Joseph Sherman wondered whether his senses were playing him false. Above his head the tamarinds in the Rue Catinat drooped lifelessly in the stifling April heat, but in contrast the dank, saturated air filling his throat seemed to be producing in him an overexcited, breathless sensation that was both disturbing yet vaguely pleasurable; at the same time every nerve in his body seemed to be dilating and expanding to absorb as many new impressions as possible of the city that had lived on so poignantly in his memory during the eleven years that had passed since his last visit.

Tall, broad-shouldered and strongly built at twenty-six, Joseph's still-boyish features had broadened with the approach of maturity, giving his face the same kind of chiseled handsomeness with which his dead brother had once been endowed. Perhaps, he told himself as he walked, he had felt like this during that first unforgettable *pousse-pousse* ride with Chuck along the city's boulevards — he couldn't really remember. Or perhaps a reawakening of the grief he had suffered on hearing the news of his brother's death was in some way responsible for this strangely heightened sense of perception.

In the quiet residential streets north of the cathedral where he strolled after dining alone at the Continental Palace, he had fancied he could distinguish all the many pungent night odors that drifted from the lush gardens of the opulent French villas — the cellar-damp reek of mold that everywhere discolored their pale walls, the fetid perfumes of wet earth and fleshy leaves, the headier mingled scents of jasmine, lotus, cycas, papaya and countless other tropical fruits and flowers whose names he had never known. In his ears the liquid notes of a piano drifting down from an unseen balcony, accompanied by French laughter and the gentle clink of glasses, had lingered for a time, magnified by the moist air, as though to emphasize for him the civilized sophistication of Indo-china's colonizers.

In the streets of the native quarter too, around the central market, the pavements seemed to Joseph's eyes to teem with life painted in dense primary colors. The bodies of bare-chested Annamese peasants glowed like gold in the light of naphtha flares as they crouched beside brilliant green mounds of tropical fruits and vegetables, Indian women with gaudy red and yellow *sampots* wound about their brown bodies hovered in servile attendance on curbside moneylenders, while along the gutters other Annamese gambled noisily with dice and cards, and *pousse-pousse* coolies crouched at rest, scooping rice into their mouths with grimy hands. Before their open shopfronts fat Chinese merchants gabbled praise of their wares in guttural Cantonese, and amidst all this clamor Joseph caught a glimpse through a half-open door of a candlelit altar bearing brass Buddhist images and ancestral tablets; he stopped to peer in and saw a goateed Annamese donning a silken long gown to perform his evening devotions.

The reverent composure of the old man's face as he lowered his frail body to the floor brought back vividly to Joseph's mind the Tet ceremony of homage to the emperor that he had watched with his mother in the Palace of Perfect Concord, and in that instant he understood more clearly than ever before just how profoundly his callow, fifteen-year-old mind had been influenced by the experiences of that first visit; it had been those few enchanted moments beside the Emperor Khai Dinh's throne, he was suddenly sure, that had made it impossible for him to accept the soldier's life that his father had wanted for him. After gulping down those heady draughts of the exotic in the ancient capital of Annam, his early fascination for history had focused itself unshakably on the Orient, and he had elected to follow in his dead brother's footsteps and go to Harvard. His decision to major in Asian history could only have flowed, he realized now, from that fleeting contact with one of the spectacular rituals of Annam's Confucian past. He had studied the Chinese language so that he could work with the originals of ancient texts, and the great emperors of the Han, Ming and Ching dynasties of whom he had read so deeply had all come to life in his mind's eye, it was clear, only as variations of the bejeweled figure of Khai Dinh whom he had seen seated on his sumptuous throne in Hue.

An unquenchable obsession with his subject had led him after graduation into further study, and he had completed a successful doctoral dissertation on the "Middle Kingdom's" tributary states — Korea, Burma, Siam, Mongolia, Tibet and Annam — that over many centuries had acknowledged the supremacy of China's emperors with regular gifts of silver and other treasure. The study was to be published in book form, and as he strolled on through the heart of the sweltering city the thought occurred to him that even the choice of his doctoral subject might have been decided by that first fateful visit to the Annamese lands. Had he, in choosing to concentrate on the vassal states of Imperial China, been subconsciously seeking a reason to come back to the country that held both painful and poignant memories for him? It had been Joseph's own idea that he should do some final research in the archives of the École Française d'Extrême Orient in Hanoi to lend greater authority in the published version to his chapters on the Annamese, and it was only after the Harvard professor advising him on the project had approved his plans that he became vaguely aware that his desire to return might not have been motivated exclusively by academic zeal.

In the weeks before he set out on the long sea journey he had found his thoughts returning increasingly to the hunting expedition that had ended so tragically with the death of the brother he had both envied and admired. Before leaving America, Joseph had made a rare visit to the Sherman Field Museum of Natural History on the Mall in Washington to look at the groups of buffalo, banteng and seladang shot by Chuck and his father. Seeing the lifelike animals in their original jungle habitats again had begun to stir feelings in him that had lain buried for more than a decade, and during the long voyage from Vancouver to Hong Kong on a Canadian Pacific liner he had found himself growing increasingly restless. He had sailed on to Saigon in a steamer of the French Messageries Maritimes that had come from Marseilles, and when he caught a glimpse of the spires of the Saigon Cathedral dancing above the trees in the tortuously winding river, he had felt once again the spellbinding strangeness of the tropics that had first engulfed his young mind so many years before.

The sight of the voracious green jungle reaching to the water's edge on both banks had brought memories long held in check flooding back into his consciousness; tears had started to his eyes when he recalled how deeply his dead brother had relished the prospect of hunting there as they sailed up the river together for the first time, and in a happier moment he had remembered with a wry smile the great sense of exaltation that followed his own secret triumph in the Moi village. But he had an uneasy feeling, too, that other more ominous thoughts might be hovering in the outer darkness of his memory; a troubled dream on shipboard had jumbled together disturbed images of brutal French *colons*, slaughtered buffalo and mandarins kowtowing in golden palaces, and Chuck, along with his mother and father, had floated among them like disembodied wraiths, unable or unwilling to see him or communicate with him. Confused and left utterly alone in the dream, he had experienced again the same deep sense of shock and bewilderment that he had known during that midnight storm in the jungle hunting camp, and he had woken on his bunk in a cold sweat.

On arrival in Saigon Joseph had been surprised to find that the Sherman family's first ill-fated visit had not been entirely forgotten. An alert French journalist who kept a weather eye on hotel arrivals had remembered the famous American name that had figured in the tragic front-page stories of 1925, and Joseph had been promptly interviewed and photographed in his room at the Continental Palace for one of the colonial news sheets. A report had already appeared in the evening edition, accompanied by his picture, outlining the reasons for his visit and mentioning that the game animals shot by his father and late brother were now central exhibits in Washington's Sherman Field Museum. Joseph had carried a copy of the paper with him on his walk, and when he arrived back at his hotel he sank into one of the wicker chairs on the terrace and cast his eye idly over the story again while a waiter fetched him a drink.

"So you've come back to see if your little Moi princess is still waiting for you in her smoky jungle palace, have you, Joseph?"

The voice speaking heavily accented English close to his ear made the American start, and he turned to find himself looking into the grinning face of a captain of the French Infanterie Coloniale. For a moment Joseph stared uncomprehendingly at the darkly handsome face with its neatly clipped military mustache, the creaking, highly polished boots and belt, the immaculately pressed uniform.

"Don't tell me *le jeune Américain amoureux* doesn't recognize the companion of his first illicit encounter with the fair sex," said the captain, removing his white sun helmet with an indignant flourish to reveal a mop of dark curly hair. "Don't tell me you refuse to come this time. I have a motor car and horses arranged. The *pholy* is already uncorking the *ternum*. . . ."

The Frenchman's infectious laughter caused heads to turn in their direction all over the crowded terrace as Joseph rose uncertainly from his chair to take his outstretched hand. "I can hardly believe it," he said hesitantly. "Is it really Paul Devraux?"

The French officer gripped Joseph's hand warmly with both his own. "Indeed it is. When I saw your picture in the paper tonight I had to come straight over here." He leaned closer, still grinning, and spoke against Joseph's ear in a stage whisper. "I should perhaps warn you before we leave for the Moi village — those women age very quickly. She's run to fat, and is gray-haired like the *pholy* now. But she's still waiting for you in that same fragrant hut. Never forgotten you, never taken another lover. Told the *pholy* no other man could ever match her 'Amorous American.'"

He laughed delightedly again, but Joseph, uncomfortable under the stares of those around them, didn't join in. Seeing Paul's face for the first time since leaving the jungle hunting camp had catapulted his thoughts against his will back to that desolate morning after the storm; he felt a sudden flush of embarrassment enter his face and wondered bleakly if Paul had any inkling of what had happened during that night.

"I take it all this stuff in the newspaper about you going on to Hanoi to do historical research is just a cover," said Paul in the same loud whisper, grinning and tapping the newspaper that lay open on the table. "You couldn't very well admit to the press, could you, that you crossed the Pacific just to visit your old Moi girl-friend."

Paul's tanned, good-natured face remained creased in what was obviously a genuinely delighted smile of welcome, and Joseph's doubts dissolved suddenly under its influence. "You're as jealous as ever, Paul, aren't you — even after eleven years," he said, his expression still serious.

"Jealous?" The Frenchman's smile faded a little. "How do you mean, Joseph?"

"That I got the prettiest one!"

Both men erupted into a new round of laughter at the same moment, and Paul clapped Joseph warmly on the shoulder as he sank into a chair at his side. The waiter arrived at that moment with the modest glass of beer that Joseph had ordered for himself, and Paul, seeing this, waved it away with an expression of mock horror on his face. "Bring us a bottle of good champagne, *garçon, s'il vous plaît*," he demanded in a loud voice. "We are celebrating an historic event — the return to Saigon of one of the world's greatest lovers!"

They were still laughing boisterously at exaggerated reminis-cences of their visit to the Moi village when the waiter returned with a chilled bottle of Perrier-Jouet and two glasses, and they drank one another's health with gusto. Both men were equally surprised and pleased to discover that the long-forgotten bond of friendship forged so briefly in their youth had endured the passage of time; they felt as relaxed and at ease in one another's company in their twenties as they had been in their teens, and only gradually did their humorous banter give way to more serious inquiries about the years that had intervened.

"You have changed a lot in your appearance, you know,

189

Joseph," said Paul, grinning affectionately at him as he refilled their glasses for the second time. "You look much more like your brother, Chuck, now than you did as a boy — more handsome. For a moment when I first saw you, I thought . . ." Paul stopped pouring champagne suddenly and shot a worried glance at the American. "I'm sorry — we haven't seen each other since that dreadful accident. You left the expedition before it happened, didn't you?"

Joseph nodded quickly and waved a dismissive hand. "It's all right, Paul. It's all been said before." He paused in the midst of lifting his refilled glass to his lips. "But I must confess that coming back here has made me think more about my brother than I have for many years. You must have got to know him quite well during those weeks you spent hunting together, didn't you?"

"Yes, I did." For a moment Paul gazed reflectively into the evening crowds strolling beneath the tamarinds across the road from the hotel. "He was a very brave young man, your brother, and a fine shot. A most amiable companion, too. His death shocked me and my father very deeply."

A silence fell between the two men for the first time, and for a minute or two they sipped their drinks without speaking.

"We talked a lot together in the camp in the evenings," continued Paul at last, "and he said something one night which stayed in my mind for a long time afterwards."

"What was that?"

"He said that your father had very high expectations for him as a politician and hoped he might even be president of the United States one day. He grinned as he told me and admitted that he wasn't all that interested in politics — that's why I remember it, I think. It all seemed so sad in view of what happened later." Paul hesitated for a moment, then looked directly across the table at Joseph. "Has your father transferred those hopes to you? Will you be going into politics?"

"I don't think so." Joseph answered quickly, almost before his companion had finished speaking. He was vaguely aware that Chuck's death had produced in him a desire to shine in his father's eyes in his place, and that awareness still embarrassed him. He had thrown himself into sports activities at Harvard with a physical bravado which he often suspected might never have declared itself in the shadow of Chuck's athletic brilliance; he had become an outstanding member of the football squad and one of the leading swimmers and tennis players of his year, and to his surprise he had found himself able to shoot game without compunction when his father invited him to accompany him on his regular hunting trips. But even these successes had done little to change the nature of his relationship with his father, and for some reason he hadn't been surprised or especially disappointed. In the end he had seen the futility of trying to re-create a mirror image of Chuck's talents — but this realization paradoxically hadn't entirely removed the irrational compulsion to do so. "I think, like Chuck, I'm not cut out for politics either," he said at last, adopting an airy tone to conceal his sensitivity on the subject. "And, anyway, my younger brother tends to be the apple of my father's eye these days."

Paul's brow crinkled in a frown of inquiry. "Do you have a younger brother, Joseph?"

"Guy was something of an afterthought, I guess," said Joseph hurriedly, staring down into his glass. "He's ten now. He was born at the end of that year Chuck died. It helped my father a lot, I think, in getting over the tragedy. Stopped him brooding too much." He stole a quick look at the French officer's face, but saw no sign that he had read any special significance into this information.

"And did he make a complete recovery himself? — your father, I mean."

Joseph nodded without looking up. "He lost an arm, as I expect you know. But he's a very determined man — stubborn, even, I suppose you could say. He still shoots with his one good arm — and not badly either. Uses a very light rifle, of course, and never goes for anything bigger than deer anymore. He felt badly at first, I think, that he wasn't able to do more to save Chuck. It seemed to worry him for a long time that Chuck acted so much out of character. My brother was courageous as you say, but never foolhardy. For a while my father seemed almost to blame himself that he hadn't reacted quicker after Chuck insisted on chasing the wounded seladang into the thicket against his orders."

Paul leaned forward suddenly in his seat and took a quick breath as if to speak. Then he changed his mind and lifted his champagne quickly to his lips instead.

Joseph, who had been twisting the stem of his glass distractedly as he spoke, looked up in time to see the French officer's embarrassed expression, and there was a moment of unease between them. "But what about yourself, Paul?" he said, to bridge the silence. "What's been happening to you since we last met?"

The Frenchman shrugged and grimaced to hide his discomfort. "Much and little — the rather dull life of the colonial soldier. I left Saigon to go back to France — to St. Cyr — soon after you left. After my three years there, my first posting was back here, in

Tongking, at a place called Yen Bay. I went to Africa in 'thirty-two for a three-year spell and came back to Saigon again at my own request only six months ago."

"So you were here during the troubles of 'thirty and 'thirty-one then?" asked Joseph eagerly. "Some reports of the uprisings got into our newspapers." His brow wrinkled with the effort of recollection. "Wasn't there some kind of mutiny at Yen Bay?"

Paul nodded slowly but didn't offer to elaborate.

"I was talking to one of your countrymen on the boat coming here — he said it was all a storm in a teacup. 'Some of Joe Stalin's Bolsheviks trying to exploit a couple of bad harvests' I think was how he put it. He said they tried to foist a few hollow revolutionary formulas on the credulous natives but didn't get very far. Does that sound right?"

Paul shook his head and leaned forward again, lowering his voice so that they shouldn't be overheard. "It was much worse than anyone in the outside world ever knew, Joseph. There was a lot of unnecessary bloodshed. It all came as a great shock to me. The revolt almost succeeded at Yen Bay. The rebels butchered half a dozen of my brother officers and I saw for myself for the first time just how deep the hatred for France really is among many Annamese."

"Were you involved directly yourself, Paul?" asked Joseph anxiously.

Paul nodded. "Unfortunately, yes." He was scanning the crowded boulevard again, his face set in troubled lines. "I suppose I was lucky to escape with my life. I got a shoulder wound which still bothers me from time to time." He massaged the top of his right arm unconsciously as he spoke, and Joseph realized that he had noticed a stiffness in Paul's movements whenever he picked up his glass. "But perhaps the worst thing of all was to find Annamese I'd befriended suddenly transformed into the screaming enemy."

"You mean your own native soldiers?"

"No — worse than that." He paused and looked back at Joseph. "Do you remember our hunting camp 'boy,' Ngo Van Loc?"

Joseph nodded.

"Well, Loc and his two sons turned up among the rebels wielding machetes and yelling for my blood along with everybody else's. . . ."

Joseph stared in disbelief. "You mean those two little boys we played with in the camp?"

Paul nodded grimly. "It turned out that Loc and his wife had been working for one resistance movement or another for years. My father, you see, when we met you, was doing a bit of under-cover work for the Sûreté Générale, and they had been planted on us. My father became a full-time Sûreté officer when the troubles came along and he's deputy chief of the whole organization now, based in Hue."

"What happened to Loc and his sons?"

Paul looked at Joseph for a long moment with a pained expres-sion on his face. "Hoc, the younger boy, was captured and execu-ted publicly later by guillotine along with a dozen other rebels."

Joseph shook his head slowly from side to side in horror at the thought. "It seems unbelievable, Paul."

"Sad to say, that's not the whole story." The Frenchman rubbed the side of his jaw in a little gesture of agitation. "My father noticed some papers missing from his desk one day and found them in the servants' quarters. Loc was away at the time, so his wife was taken off to prison for questioning." He paused, clearly distressed by what he was saying, and glanced out into the street again. "She died later in prison — from 'ill health,' the police chief said. So you see, the Ngo family had grounds not to love us at the end of all that."

"What happened to the father and the older boy?"

"Loc joined the Communists later and was eventually wounded in a rebellion somewhere in the north, I think. He was captured and shipped off to the prison island of Paulo Condore eventually with thousands of other Communists four or five years ago. I don't know what happened to Dong."

"Has all this left you feeling bitter towards the Annamese, Paul?" asked the American quietly.

The French officer sipped his drink without pleasure and sat back in his chair with a faraway look in his eyes. "Strangely enough it's perhaps had the opposite effect. I wanted to get as far from here as I could after the troubles quietened down at the end of 'thirty-one — but in Africa I found myself thinking about the Annamese more often than the Africans." His face creased in thought as he searched for a way to convey complex feelings he perhaps didn't fully understand himself. "This place and these people, I discovered, had somehow got into my blood. I can't really explain it. Whatever it is, it made me ask to be sent back." He looked at Joseph and smiled ruefully. "It might seem crazy to you for an army officer to think this way, but I suppose I feel France has done a lot of things wrong here in many ways — and they could and should be done better. There have been improvements already, of course. The Popular Front coalition in Paris has legalized the Communist Party here and they are starting to free political prisoners from Paulo Condore. There are even four Communists on the Saigon city council now. That is only a beginning, I know. . . ." He shrugged by way of admitting his inability to explain his own feelings more fully. "There's maybe not much I can do on my own — but here I am anyway. . . ."

Joseph smiled, feeling himself warm to the French officer's honesty and frankness. "I think I understand, Paul. Now that I'm here, I can see that I've always wanted subconsciously to come back. Although I'm not involved in the way you are, I find there's something fascinating about the country and the people."

"So there was more truth in my joking than I knew," said Paul, grinning again. "You really have been drawn back by the memory of those naked Moi bosoms after all, eh? Or are you married already?"

Joseph shook his head, grinning in his turn. "No, I'm not married yet."

"Why not? A rich handsome young bachelor like you must be highly sought after by the *belles filles* of America, no?"

Joseph, embarrassed by the directness of the question, hesitated for a moment. "To be honest, Paul, I find most females too devious," he said, trying to make light of the remark but not really succeeding. "I don't think I've ever met a girl yet I'd trust enough to marry."

"Ah, so the perfidious female is a common species in America too, eh?" inquired the French officer, laughing again.

"Isn't it a worldwide phenomenon?"

"Perhaps, perhaps — although of course the well-brought-up Saigon *mademoiselle* still likes to take her chastity to the altar." He turned again towards the street to watch two slender Annamese girls parading past in high-necked gossamer-light *ao dai*.

Joseph, following his eye, smiled. "Do bridegrooms here still do that trick with the white square of silk on the wedding night?"

"Ah, you have an excellent memory, Joseph," laughed the Frenchman. "You remember something of what I taught you. Yes, indeed, the Annamese still put a high price on virginity and fidelity." He turned a mischievous face back to his American companion. "Perhaps I should confess and come right out and tell you that the only reason I came back was to watch these delightful golden creatures drift past my eyes every day on the gentle breezes of Saigon."

"It doesn't surprise me," replied the American humorously,

"after what you told us about yourself the last time I was here."

"I'm only half joking, Joseph," said the French captain, leaning earnestly across the table to pat his arm. "Take some advice from an old man three years your senior — you could do much worse than carry off one of these Asian beauties for a wife. I'm thinking about it quite seriously myself." He smiled broadly again as he tipped the remaining champagne into their empty glasses. "I'll let you see for yourself what I mean, if you like. Tomorrow afternoon at the Cercle Sportif they're playing the final of our annual tennis championships. It's a mixed tournament now and in keeping with the spirit of the times an Annamese player has reached the final of the men's singles for the first time. He has a very beautiful sister, and I'm escorting her to the match. Why don't you join me? You'll see how we're going about making our *mission civilisatrice* work in the modern manner — and you'll meet one of the loveliest girls in Saigon at the same time."

"All right," agreed Joseph, smiling and raising his glass to his lips. "Let's drink to that."

When they had drained their glasses, Paul smiled and held up an admonishing finger. "But this time I insist that the Amorous American be more discreet. I know our friendship, because of its special beginning, requires us to be utterly frank and honest with one another — but on this occasion please make no reference to escapades of the past. And there must be no attempt to share my stall this time." He stood up, laughing loudly, and clapped Joseph on the shoulder. "*Entendu?*"

"*Entendu!*" echoed Joseph, and shook him warmly by the hand. He stood and watched with a genuine feeling of affection as the evening crowds thronging the Rue Catinat gradually swallowed up the square-shouldered military figure. The French officer's erect bearing made Joseph aware of how like his father Paul had become and suddenly he saw again in his mind's eye that silent, mysterious hero figure awesome to the eyes of a fifteen-year-old boy, jogging stiffly upright in the saddle at the head of the pony train on their first enchanted ride through the jungle. The memory rekindled a new train of recollections that led back eventually to those terrible moments in the storm outside Jacques Devraux's hut, and long after the crowds had dispersed from the boulevard outside his window Joseph lay awake in his room in the Continental Palace, wrestling once again with the strangely disturbing echoes of his past.

2

On the afternoon of the tennis final Captain Paul Devraux had exchanged his military uniform for a civilian suit of white duck and a soft hat of the same color and Joseph had difficulty picking him out among the similarly clad crowd of French *colons* thronging the trim lawns and terraces of the Cercle Sportif. The club, set in tree-shaded parkland adjoining the grounds of the governor general's grandiose marble palace, was normally the preserve of the white colonial elite, but for the occasion of the tennis championship its normal regulations had been relaxed to admit non-members. Even so, as Joseph searched for Paul among the crowds he noticed that the young Asians present were well mannered and well dressed, obviously the offspring of wealthy Annamese and Chinese families.

The wives and daughters of the French members all wore cool white dresses and carried white sun hats or parasols to protect their pale complexions from the glare of the hot afternoon sun, and as he moved among them Joseph found himself wondering if they were dressed in accordance with some unwritten club rule to distinguish themselves more emphatically from the golden-skinned Annamese girls in their gaily colored *ao dai*. In his efforts to find Paul he had to peer beneath the brims of sun helmets and felt hats worn by the Frenchmen, and in the end the grinning officer spotted him first.

"I'm glad to see, Joseph, that you're paying close attention to the fact that Saigon society has now become thoroughly democratic," he said, arching an ironic eyebrow and glancing at the crowd around them.

Although racially mixed, the gathering was still preponderantly white and privileged, and the American acknowledged his wry wit with a smile. "As much as looking for you I was trying to get a sneak preview of the dazzling oriental creature who's head over heels in love with you." He scanned the faces of several Annamese girls standing shyly nearby with escorts of their own race. "Where is she?"

"Wait a minute, *mon vieux*, not so fast." Paul smiled and laid a cautionary hand on his arm. "That's putting it a bit high. Perhaps I was too hasty last night. I didn't say her heart was conquered and won beyond dispute. Momma and Poppa, as you would say, still have a big say in who their children marry here. Her father likes me, I think — he's very pro-French. But the idea may not even have entered her head yet. All I said was it had entered mine.

Courtship here still follows rigid rules of procedure — and the chaperon barrier still has to be broken down. Her mother always comes too, so far — or a friend." Paul touched Joseph's arm gently to draw his attention to a young Asian couple in their early twenties moving through the crowd towards them. "Or in this case, her brother."

Joseph glanced up to see a slender girl in a high-necked *ao dai* of pale turquoise silk walking demurely beside an Annamese dressed in European style. She carried a cone-shaped hat of plaited palm leaf and wore her long hair dressed tight at the nape of her neck in a simple clip that allowed it to be drawn in front of her left shoulder in a glossy black torrent. Even at a distance, the striking beauty of her golden face was apparent to the American, and a little murmur of admiration escaped his lips. "You weren't exaggerating, Paul," he whispered appreciatively before the couple came within earshot. "She's lovely."

Paul, obviously pleased, stepped forward smiling warmly. Raising the girl's hand to his lips, he murmured a compliment in French, then shook her brother cordially by the hand. "May I introduce Joseph Sherman, a good friend of mine from the United States of America." He spoke in French, smiling into the girl's eyes, then turned back to Joseph: "This is Tran Thi Kieu Lan . . . and her brother Tran Van Tam."

"*Enchanté, mademoiselle.*" Her fingers were as small and fragile as a schoolgirl's in Joseph's grasp, and his own hand seemed suddenly elephantine in comparison. Her cheeks were tinged with pink, either dusted faintly with rouge or from her own natural coloring, but otherwise, unlike the French women all around them, she wore no other makeup and the freshness and innocence of her young face caused Joseph to stare for a moment longer than he should have, and she dropped her gaze. In his anxiety to make amends he seized her brother's hand with extra effusiveness. "Congratulations, Monsieur Tam, on reaching the final!" he cried jovially, clasping the elbow of the Annamese as he shook his hand. "I wish you good luck for this afternoon's match."

"Unfortunately there's no chance at all of my winning," replied Tam, giggling loudly. "It's my younger brother, Kim, who is the tennis player, not me. He'll be here in a moment — he's parking our car."

Tam's sister and Paul joined in the general laughter, to Joseph's discomfort, but after a moment's embarrassment the American suddenly stopped and stared at them with an astonished expression. "Did you say your brother's name is Kim?"

The Annamese nodded, still giggling.

"Then if you are Tran Van Tam . . ." He paused and turned to the still smiling girl. ". . . and if you are Kieu Lan, your father must be Monsieur Tran Van Hieu, the Imperial Delegate."

The Annamese girl nodded again, smiling at him in mystification.

"Then we have all met before! Don't you remember the day your baby gibbon almost broke the governor's vase?"

The smile faded slowly from Lan's face and she raised a hand to her mouth as realization dawned. "You were the American boy who brought the gibbon back for us?"

Joseph nodded delightedly. "Yes. You were just a little girl then."

Paul slapped Joseph on the shoulder and roared with laughter. "*Bon Dieu!* Of course! How did I ever forget your monkey-saving antics — the hunter who preferred to use a Ming vase to capture his trophies live, rather than a gun."

They all laughed again, but when the laughter subsided it was Lan who spoke. "It perhaps seems funny now, Monsieur Sherman, but at the time our father was very angry. We were scolded severely and made to kneel with our backs straight for more than an hour. My father often said if it hadn't been for the young American saving the vase, our punishment might have been much worse — so you see, we're very grateful for what you did for those three unruly children. . . ."

At that moment another young Annamese appeared behind them, carrying a hand case and a tennis racquet in a press. Of slighter build than the pudgy, overweight Tam, his face was set in a surly expression, almost a scowl, and he shook hands with Paul without cordiality.

"Kim, who do you think this is?" asked Tam in an excited voice, gesturing towards Joseph.

The younger Annamese looked Joseph up and down quickly, still without smiling, and shrugged. "I don't know. Who is it?"

"It's Joseph Sherman, the son of Senator Sherman, remember — the American who rescued the baby gibbon you smuggled into the grounds of the governor's palace. Now's your chance to thank him."

Kim studied Joseph's face intently for a moment, then offered his hand with exaggerated courtesy. "Without your intervention, Monsieur Sherman, I'm sure the governor's precious vase would have been smashed beyond repair — and I, my father and my whole family would have been banished to the dark dungeons of

Paulo Condore for the rest of our natural lives." The glittering smile that flashed across the face of the Annamese did nothing to soften his sarcastic tone. "If it hadn't been for you, perhaps, we should still be there now and today's match and this reunion would not have been possible."

Tam shot an uneasy glance at Paul and forced a laugh. "The meeting might well have been possible, Kim — we would certainly have been released in the amnesty. The first boat sailed into Saigon last night, didn't it? And another is due tonight." He laughed uneasily again, watching Paul's face as he did so. "So everything would have been all right in the end."

Paul laughed politely in return and patted Tam's shoulder, but Kim's face remained set in unsmiling lines. Without looking at the French officer he inclined his head once more in Joseph's direction. "So thank you again, monsieur. Now if you will excuse me, I must go and get changed for the match. *Au revoir.*" Without acknowledging the French officer, he turned on his heel and walked away in the direction of the dressing room.

"I must apologize, Monsieur Sherman, for my brother's strange sense of humor," said Lan quietly as soon as her brother had gone. "He sometimes speaks without considering carefully what he says. And I think he's very tense today. This match is very important to him."

Moved by her troubled expression, Joseph smiled reassuringly. "There's no need to apologize at all, Lan. I understand perfectly."

"Like me, Monsieur Sherman, my brother enjoyed the great privilege of an education in Paris," explained Tam with another anxious sidelong glance at the French officer. "We both studied law, but he chose perhaps to misuse some of his time with people who muddled his thinking. They dabbled with the outrageous theories of Karl Marx, Lenin and even Nguyen Ai Quoc. I'm not sure how seriously he took it because he still seems happy to enjoy the pleasures of the capitalist life. But his study of Marxism sometimes colors his thinking in ways very different from my own." He turned to Paul directly and giggled nervously. "You understand that, don't you, Captain Devraux?"

The French officer smiled. "But of course, Tam. Don't concern yourself. Today in Saigon everybody's allowed to believe what they like — and there's nothing illegal about studying Marxist doctrine." He glanced about him and saw that the crowds were beginning to move towards the tiers of banked seats around the lawn tennis court that had been prepared for the final. "Come on. I think it's time we were taking our places."

As they made their way towards the court, Tam glanced anxiously about him at the faces of other Annamese. "I know Kim went out of his way to invite a lot of people from the staff of *La Lutte*," he said in an undertone as he fell into step beside Paul. "I hope they don't intend to make trouble."

"Relax, Tam," said Paul lightly, as he guided Lan into a seat between himself and Joseph. "Everything will be all right. Just enjoy the game."

"What is *La Lutte*, Paul?" asked Joseph in a whisper when they were seated.

"A left-wing journal published in Saigon. Most of the writers are young Annamese intellectuals who favor Communism of one kind or another. Some are Trotskyists."

Joseph glanced around the stands that were rapidly filling to capacity with French *colons* and scattered groups of Asians. Twenty or thirty youthful Annamese were seated in the row behind him, but like the rest of their countrymen their behavior was subdued in the unfamiliar surroundings and they made no attempt to converse with the French around them. When the two players came onto the court, they applauded Kim enthusiastically but they didn't call out.

As the players took up position on their respective baselines, there was a little amused buzz of comment among the French spectators about the difference in size of the players. The French champion, Jules Pinot, was a tall, muscular assistant planter from one of the tea plantations near Saigon, and because Kim was only of average height for an Annamese, he appeared small and frail in comparison. As they warmed up, the French player made it clear he was intending to make no concessions to his opponent's diminutive stature; he served and drove the ball deep, forehand and backhand, using the full power of his broad shoulders, and Kim, who employed a heavily cut spinning serve, had to scurry about the court to return the ball with his more delicate, wristy shots.

"Your man looks very confident, Paul," said Joseph after he had watched for a minute or two. "He plays a strong game."

Paul nodded, then directed a sympathetic smile at Lan. "Unfortunately Kim could not have met a tougher player. Pinot has won this championship three years running. You can see that he does not expect to lose."

Lan watched the wiry figure of her brother for a moment; although they were still loosening up, his face was grim with concentration as he dodged back and forth across the court, scooping up the long, raking drives of the Frenchman. "Yes, I fear that Monsieur Pinot will prove too powerful for Kim," she said with a little sigh. "But he is very conscious that he is the first Annamese to reach the final — he won't give up without a fight."

The opening games conformed to her predictions, and from time to time between points she smiled resignedly at Paul and Joseph. The Frenchman raced to a three-love lead in the first set, his fast service and sweeping ground strokes swamping Kim's defenses, and all around Joseph and his companions the French *colons* applauded Pinot with unbridled enthusiasm; on the rare occasions when Kim gained a point they clapped politely to show their sympathy with the underdog. The young Annamese, however, continued to contest each point with great tenacity. He darted swiftly from one side of the court to the other, never tiring of his fruitless pursuits, and as the set advanced he began to anticipate better the pace and direction of his opponent's shots. He lost the fourth game to go four-love down, but the fifth game hung in the balance for a long time as he saved a series of set points with delicately cut returns which fell dead close to the net. The French player's face darkened as he dashed forward from the baseline repeatedly to deal with these tantalizing shots, and by varying his direction cleverly, Kim was able to deceive his bigger opponent with increasing frequency. In trying unsuccessfully to prevent Kim taking the game with yet another cleverly flighted backhand, the irritated Pinot slipped as he lunged across the court and sprawled full length into the foot of the net. When he untangled himself and stood up, his white singlet was discolored with bright green grass stains, and the group of Annamese seated behind Paul and Joseph immediately rose to their feet, clapping and yelling their appreciation of Kim's guileful first victory. Some waved folded copies of *La Lutte* above their heads, and seeing this, Annamese in other parts of the stands got up to join in the noisy accolade.

Joseph, glancing sideways at Lan, saw her delighted smile fade slowly into an expression of unease as the ecstatic cheering continued. The rigid set of her head and shoulders betrayed her inner tension, and Paul, noticing this, took her hand in his in a little gesture of reassurance. A moment later, however, Joseph saw her withdraw it and she sat silently between them, staring fixedly at the court while the French spectators all around them glared stonily at Kim's gleefully cheering supporters.

Winning the game had increased Kim's confidence, while the heavy fall had shaken the Frenchman, and when the match resumed the Annamese began to flight the ball with ever greater accuracy. Each point that he won was greeted by his countrymen with renewed bursts of cheering, and many of the French *colons* began to scowl and mutter irritably among themselves. Kim won the next game, then the following two more easily to level the set at four-all, and again his supporters cheered him wildly.

In the ninth game Kim served his heavily cut services with great care, his face a mask of concentration. He dropped the ball short over the net again and again, then made the rattled Frenchman scurry to the rear of the court with delicately struck high lobs. With the rhythm of his powerful, free-swinging game broken, Pinot began to make error after error; the rallies stuttered and jerked in erratic patterns robbed of their traditional European flow, and Kim won that game and the next one easily to take the first set six-four amidst a new storm of delirious Annamese applause.

In the second set the pattern of the early part of the match was completely reversed. To hysterical cheers from his countrymen, Kim raced to a five-love lead, dancing nimbly around the court, stroking the ball artfully in unexpected directions to make the perspiring Frenchman appear leaden-footed and foolish. Pinot, growing red-faced with embarrassment, began shaking his head and muttering to himself between points, and the watching French *colons* fell silent, sharing visibly in the humiliation of their champion. Lan and her brother Tam, sensitive to the tension that was growing among the spectators, ceased to applaud their brother's points and sat silently beside Paul and Joseph, their faces serious and apprehensive.

At the start of the sixth game the increasingly desperate Pinot crashed to the turf again during an unsuccessful dive to retrieve a deftly flicked passing shot; when he rose to his feet he was limping badly and clearly doomed to lose. Kim, taking full advantage of the injury, continued to dart nimbly about the court, tapping and patting the ball with infuriating accuracy just beyond the reach of the handicapped Frenchman, and when he arrived at match point with another delicate drop shot, the Annamese in the crowd made more noise than ever.

In an effort to clinch the match Kim spun his service wickedly, then followed it with a new flurry of cunningly weighted wrist shots; another jerky rally ensued, and in the tense silence a monocled Frenchman in front of Joseph stood up suddenly and waved his arms at the umpire. "*C'est honteux!*" he yelled in an exasperated voice. "This is shameful! You must disqualify him! His play is *antisportive*."

Other Frenchmen in different parts of the crowd, as though

relieved that some lead had at last been given, leaped to their feet too, shouting complaints about Kim's "unsporting" use of *balles amorties* — the "deadened" ball — and his *service coupé* — his heavily cut serve.

Yells of "Disqualify him!" rose from French throats in all corners of the stands, and on the court Pinot stopped suddenly in the middle of the rally and turned an agonized face towards the umpire. Kim, his features stiff with concentration, chipped the ball accurately past the immobile Frenchman and, throwing his racquet ecstatically into the air, ran towards a large group of Annamese at the courtside with outstretched arms. The French umpire, however, shouting above the growing pandemonium, called a "let" and tried to order Kim back onto the court to replay the point.

"*Sales Français! Sales Français!*" suddenly screamed an Annamese close behind Joseph and Lan. "Filthy French! Filthy French! You can't stop and replay the game just because you've been beaten by one of your 'slaves.'"

Joseph turned his head in time to see two enraged Frenchmen rise from their seats and knock the Annamese down.

"All the French are dogs!" yelled another youth close by, struggling to climb across the seats to assist his fallen friend. "Even on the tennis court you want only to oppress the Annamites!"

Women began screaming in panic as struggles broke out all over the stands; in the seat behind Joseph a French fist crashed into the face of an Annamese and a flurry of blood from his broken nose splashed Joseph's white suit. Another French spectator in the same row began grappling with Tam, and seeing this, Paul lunged to his aid.

"Get Lan away from here, Joseph, please!" he yelled over his shoulder. "Take her home!"

Joseph flung a protective arm about the trembling girl and forced his way through the milling crowd to the gates. Outside he hailed a passing *malabar* and sat wordlessly beside her in the little wooden carriage as the trotting ponies drew it sedately through the quiet afternoon streets towards the walled residence of the Imperial Delegate, north of the cathedral square.

For a long time she sat staring in front of her without speaking, her fingers tightening nervously on the brim of the sun hat she held in her lap. Then at last she turned to him and smiled briefly. "Thank you, Monsieur Sherman, for being kind enough to take care of me. I'm sorry you had to see such ugly things happen. Unfortunately the hearts of many Annamese are filled with hatred." She bit her lower lip and looked away from him.

Sitting close beside the beautiful Asian girl in the tiny vehicle, Joseph felt a rush of tenderness sweep through him; while struggling in the unruly crowd with his arm around her slender shoulders, he had been deeply moved by her fragility. She had recoiled against him several times as he struck out to force a way past the knots of fighting men, yielding herself trustingly to his protection, and as he studied her profile in the *malabar*, the gentle exotic loveliness of her golden face seemed heightened suddenly by their unexpected intimacy.

"I'm delighted that I could be of help to such a beautiful girl as you, Lan," he said softly. "And I have to say that I envy Paul."

She turned to look at him with a faintly quizzical look. "Captain Devraux is a good friend, Monsieur Sherman — that is all."

"But he's very fond of you — he told me so," said Joseph, smiling at her again.

"My father admires him. He believes he's a fine officer. He has great respect also for Captain Devraux's father. He's the deputy chief of the Sûreté Générale."

Joseph's face hardened for an instant at the mention of Jacques Devraux; then with an effort he smiled again. "I'm sure Paul is an outstanding officer. Perhaps if more Frenchmen were like him, what happened at the Cercle Sportif this afternoon could be avoided."

The worried frown returned to her face immediately at his mention of the trouble. "My father will be very displeased," she said, speaking almost to herself. "He didn't wish Kim to enter the tournament at all. . . ."

"Please present my compliments to your father, Lan, will you," said Joseph gently, trying to guide her thoughts away from the unpleasantness of the riot. "I've never forgotten his kindness in showing me the palaces of Hue." He hesitated for a moment, then went on eagerly: "I would be very pleased to call on him, Lan. I'm writing about the history of your country and I would be delighted to have a chance to talk to him."

"How long will you be staying in Saigon?"

"I'm on my way to Hanoi to work in the archives there — but I can stay another day or two in Saigon."

"Then I'm afraid it will be impossible for you to see him." She smiled apologetically. "We are all leaving first thing tomorrow for Hue. The emperor, Bao Dai, is to make his three-yearly Sacrifice to Heaven later this week, and my father is taking part in the ceremonies."

Joseph stared at her in surprise: then a delighted smile broke across his face. "What good fortune! I didn't realize the ceremonies were due. I mustn't miss them — it's over twenty years since the last Chinese emperor performed the Sacrifice to Heaven in Peking before the revolution — I could travel to Hue quite easily." He paused, gazing excitedly at her, and suddenly in the confined space of the tiny vehicle he fancied he could detect the fragrance of perfumed jasmine on her skin or in her hair; they were passing through the dappled shadows of a street of banyan trees and the reflected flashes of hot sunlight playing across their faces inside the *malabar* illuminated her dark eyes and the beguiling Asiatic curve of her amber cheeks in a way that made his senses swim. "Would it be possible, Lan, for me to watch the ceremonies with you?" he asked, unable to keep a tremor of excitement from his voice.

For a moment she gazed back at him; the handsome American face, with its strong jaw and startlingly blond hair, was as strange and exotic to her as her own face was to him. The directness of his pale blue eyes and the unconcealed admiration in them caused a flush of warmth to rise to her cheeks without her knowing why, and she looked away from him quickly before answering. "I shall be with my family in Hue, Monsieur Sherman," she said shyly.

"But perhaps I could join you for part of the time," he persisted. "I could even come a day before the ceremony and we could look at the palaces again together. I've never forgotten my last visit. I stood right next to the throne! And the Emperor Khai Dinh shook hands with me before we left. Every time I read about the emperors of China I saw him in my mind — and every time I pictured a mandarin I remembered your grandfather and your father performing the *lam lay* ceremony in the palace courtyard."

His eager words poured out of him in a rush and she smiled at his boyish enthusiasm. "I love the ancient ceremonies of my country and I'd be only too pleased to explain them to you." She hesitated, and her smile faded slightly. "But any invitation must come from my father."

"Don't worry, Lan, I'll come to Hue anyway." He grinned delightedly again. "And could you do one other thing for me? Will you call me Joseph? 'Monsieur Sherman' is too formal, isn't it, for two people who've already known each other eleven years?"

"I will try."

She gave a little embarrassed laugh and turned her head away to peer past the *sais* as the *malabar* turned into the street on which the Imperial Delegate's residence stood. When she directed him to halt before a red-painted circular moon gate in a high wall, Joseph clambered out first. She allowed him to assist her briefly as she stepped down onto the road, and again her hand felt as delicate as a child's in his grasp. Moving gracefully beside him in her billowing costume of turquoise and white silk, she seemed suddenly to Joseph the embodiment of an almost divine femininity, both chaste and alluring in the same moment, and when she turned at the gate to thank him, impulsive words sprang involuntarily to his lips.

"Lan, since I've been here . . . I feel as if fate of some kind brought me back," he said, stumbling over the words. "I'd forgotten about meeting you and your brothers at the palace. . . . But perhaps it was . . . perhaps we were fated to meet again."

She blushed deeply this time, and he realized suddenly how foolish he sounded. "Lan, I'm sorry," he blurted as she turned away to open the latch. "That was a stupid thing to say — but I really hope we can meet again."

Before she closed the gate she paused and smiled shyly once more. "Whatever is meant to happen will happen, Joseph," she said softly. "*Au revoir!*"

3

"How can you say that I disgraced the family, Father — I beat the French champion fairly, don't you understand?" Kim's raised voice carried clearly through the open windows of Tran Van Hieu's study to where Lan sat beside the lotus pool. For half an hour or more she had been daydreaming idly about the handsome young American who had brought her home; the memory of his smiling blue eyes gazing so intently into her own had left her feeling strangely excited, but the strident, high-pitched tone of Kim's voice alarmed her, and she stiffened on the little stone seat and turned her head to listen. "I played according to the rules and I won," continued Kim insistently. "The silver trophy is rightfully mine!"

"The manner of your play offended the French deeply. It was unsporting and provocative — not in the tradition of their game as they play it." Lan could tell from the slow, deliberate tone of her father's voice that he was suppressing his anger with difficulty. "They are right to order you to replay the final, and I forbid you to employ those methods again."

"I can hardly believe my ears, Father! Are you trying to order me to 'collaborate' with Pinot in my own defeat?" Kim's words came out in an incredulous whisper, and Lan had to strain her ears to catch what he said.

"The disturbances in the crowd caused by your behavior have left a terrible stain on our family's reputation!" said Tran Van Hieu icily. "I leave it to you to decide how best to ensure that there is no repetition of that disgrace."

"I'm not responsible for what was done by our people in the crowd," protested Kim. "They were only responding to the blatant injustice of the French. I refuse to play again! I've won fairly and I've agreed to write a signed article for *La Lutte* attacking French oppression on and off the tennis court!"

"You have always been determined to disobey me. You entered the tournament against my advice. You wanted above all else to defy me — and to make trouble in the process."

The rising note of anger in her father's voice caused Lan to catch her breath, and she waited for her brother's reply in an agony of suspense.

"I can see it now," said Kim at last with a little hollow laugh. "You must have been hoping for me to lose all along! That's why you refused to come and watch. What a fool I was to think you might have been proud of me — proud that we'd at last won some genuine respect and admiration among our own people! You've never been proud of me no matter what I've done. And by winning even a small victory over our French overlords, I've disappointed you once again, haven't I?"

"Yes! Because it's always been your nature to seek success by defiance and confrontation. I've always tried to guide you and Tam as my father guided me — to have proper Confucian respect for your elders, for the sovereign and the governing authorities. Tam has learned his lessons well, but always you've chosen the path of the rebel — that's why I'm ashamed of you!"

"The ethics of Confucius promote exactly the kind of docile slave mentality that our French masters want us to have," said Kim, his voice rising almost to a shout. "We'll be their serfs forever if we listen only to those teachings."

The sound of her father drawing in his breath sharply at this blatant discourtesy brought Lan to her feet, her heart beating faster. Although the light was fading in the garden, through the open window she could see her father seated at his writing-table in front of two big red decorative wall silks embroidered in gold with the Chinese characters for "Peace" and "Harmony"; portly and graying faintly at the temples in his early fifties, he was wearing the dark gown in which he dressed every evening to perform his devotions before the family altar, and from the agitated movements of his head and shoulders she could see that he was fighting to control his fury. Tam stood at his side and Kim, still dressed in his tennis clothes, was glaring at them from the other side of the table. Fearing that they might turn and notice her, Lan stepped behind the foliage of a peach tree outside the window, where she could watch and listen without being seen.

"You make your offenses graver by addressing me in this fashion," said her father, speaking very quietly. "I suggest you go now and make preparations for our journey to Hue tomorrow. Perhaps observing the ancient ceremonial will remind you of our proud heritage and bring you to your senses. Reflect on your words and your actions, and I will talk to you again in a few days' time."

"I'm not coming to Hue with you!" Kim's voice trembled as he spoke, and Lan saw her father raise his head to look at him with a shocked expression on his face. "After what you've said tonight I see no point in concealing my real views from you any longer."

"So because of your devotion to the insane doctrines of Bolshevism," said Tran Van Hieu, his voice icy with outrage, "you not only dishonor your father and your ancestors — you are prepared to turn your back too on the country of your birth and all that it stands for!"

"No! That's not true! To love your country you don't have to love a gilded tailor's dummy performing ancient rituals that have lost all their meaning! You don't have to spend hours watching mandarins acting as clothes hangers for multicolored robes. Our people detest the corruption of the mandarins, don't you see? If the French had not come here, the tide of history would long ago have swept away the emperor and his depraved court — just as it did in China twenty-five years ago." Kim's face had turned pale and his fists clenched and unclenched at his sides as his impassioned words poured from him. "The people know that the emperor and his mandarins are mere puppets who dance obediently when the French governor of Cochin-China or the Résident Supérieur in Hue pull their strings. They know they have no real power on the Colonial Council or the Council of Ministers. They know well enough that the collaborationists have been richly rewarded for their betrayal of the people. The peasants hate absentee landlords like us, don't you understand? We've become nothing more than usurers and speculators battening on their misfortune. . . ."

The speed with which Tam moved surprised Lan, and the sound of his open-handed blow striking Kim's face made her flinch even in her place of concealment. Kim rocked on his feet but recovered quickly and stood his ground, glowering fiercely at his brother. For a moment it appeared that Kim would retaliate; then he relaxed.

"That, I know, is what my esteemed father longs to do to you," said Tam, his breathing ragged. "But he's too loyal to his code of honor which detests loss of control. So I gladly do it for him."

"You wouldn't dare to do it outside this room," said Kim in a low voice.

Tam hesitated and glanced uncertainly towards his father.

"That's enough, Tam!" Tran Van Hieu waved his elder son aside. "Your brother has forgotten that the wealth and position he so despises enabled him to go to France to be educated. He forgets it was in France that he discovered this new 'faith.' He forgets or he's too hotheaded and foolish to see that a weak country like ours must proceed cautiously. While our people are politically immature like him, the protection and guidance of France is greatly preferable to less scrupulous rulers from China — or even fascist Japan."

"If you had been the father of Le Loi, I'm sure you would have advised him to 'respect' the Chinese invaders he so gloriously defeated in the fifteenth century," said Kim, his voice now openly contemptuous. "You teach me to respect the great heroes of our past — but forbid me to emulate them. I know in my heart that the only course for a true patriot today is to become a revolutionary!"

"And you will become the savior of our country singlehanded, I suppose."

"The savior will not be one, but many," replied Kim confidently. "The Communist Party of Indochina supported by all the oppressed peoples of the world and led by Nguyen Ai Quoc will set us free. I hope that I'll be able to play my part — in that way, yes, I will try to become my country's savior."

"Nguyen the Patriot is dead," said Tam flatly. "It was reported in the Communist newspapers of Moscow and Paris."

"They were wrong. He's alive and the party is recovering," rejoined Kim.

"Then where is he now?"

"That's not important. What's important is that he won't be in Hue with you taking part in the futile charade of the Sacrifice to Heaven. He's still working with many other comrades to ensure that the modern theories of Marx and Lenin conquer the antiquated ideas of Confucius."

Lan saw her father raise his head, his expression suddenly pained and sorrowful rather than angry. For a moment he looked at each of his sons in turn. "There's nothing more dangerous than to reject the past completely," he said in a quiet voice. "The emperor is still important today as a symbolic focus of our culture and our national character. If our nation is to survive, we must try to combine the best of our Confucian ideals with the best of the new scientific teachings from the West. We must harmonize old things with new things and let the past and the present meet as equals. You've been won over, Kim, by the wild rantings of your uncle Lat. He's obsessed by foreign ideas — but if we let our national sense become submerged in an ocean of foreign knowledge, we will lose the soul of the nation." The mandarin employed the emotive Annamese term *quoc hon* with a sonorous gravity. "We've always retained our traditions although we've often lost our independence — first to China and now to France. If you and Lat sacrifice our national soul to Bolshevism in return for independence, you'll find afterwards there's nothing left of the true nation to revive. During the Red Terror of 1931 your 'friends' committed many atrocities, butchered hundreds of their own countrymen. They've shown they will not hesitate to tear out our nation's vitals to 'save' it."

Kim stared in silence for a moment, his expression uncertain, as though some small part of him still intuitively respected the wisdom of his father's words. Then his features contorted in a sudden grimace of irrational anger and he sprang forward and banged his fist violently on the writing-table. "You and Tam are blind — or you won't see. The doctrines of Lenin alone can make our people free! Only Leninism can free us from the humiliation of kowtowing all our lives to the insufferable French!"

Tran Van Hieu looked expressionlessly at his son. "You know well enough that the best Frenchmen — like Captain Devraux — have a deep affection for our country. Things are changing now. If we work quietly and methodically, the Emperor Bao Dai could become our first modern sovereign — advised by the French but governing with greater independent powers."

Kim snorted derisively. "The French will only ever use us, as we use the water buffalo. They love only the material riches they can wring from our soil." His eyes blazed suddenly as he stared down at his father, then he thrust a hand into the pocket of his shorts and pulled out some crumpled banknotes. He smoothed out a ten-piastre bill between his fingers, then waved it in front of him. "This is the only thing for which the French *colons* have a deep affection. And you have the same deep affection for it too. All else is hypocrisy!"

He turned the note in his hands and pointed to the engraved design portraying Mother France with her arms draped benevolently around the shoulders of two native Annamese. "Do you know what that picture is meant to convey? It shows a mother dragging her Annamese bastard sons to market — to sell them as slaves! And I'm the son of one of the middlemen who has grown fat on the proceeds." He paused and with a dramatic sweep of his arm flung the banknote in his father's face. "You may not be prepared to stop selling our people to France for private gain, but I am — I will no longer be a party to such shameful deeds."

Tran Van Hieu winced and closed his eyes as the banknote fluttered to rest on the table in front of him. When he opened them again his eyes fell directly on the engraving. For a long time he sat without moving. When he finally spoke, he kept his eyes averted from his son.

"You will leave my house immediately," he said in a barely audible voice. "And never return again as long as I live."

From outside the window Lan clearly heard Kim's sharp intake of breath. Beside her father, Tam stood motionless, like a wax figure, his face drained of all color.

"The family and the nation should be one," continued Tran Van Hieu in the same quiet voice. "If the family is lost, the nation will be lost too. In the end, Kim, if Bolshevism succeeds you'll bring down ruination on your country, your family and yourself! Now go!"

Lan could not prevent a little sobbing cry escaping her lips, and when Kim rushed from the room, she hurried up the steps into the house. She met her brother in the shadowy hall but he pushed past her without acknowledging her presence. Sobbing openly, she ran into her father's study and found him hunched gray-faced in his chair. Kneeling beside him, she seized his hand and kissed it convulsively. In the doorway her mother appeared silently, having come from the back of the house where she had obviously been listening all the time. Tam went to her and she put her arms around him and drew him close; tears were already streaming down her cheeks too.

4

The features of the ragged Annamese prisoners appeared uniformly gaunt and pallid as one by one they stepped onto the gangplank of the freighter that had brought them from Paulo Condore. Some carried a few scraps of clothing tied in a bundle, others nothing; all had the watchful, haunted look common to men who have been confined behind bars for a long time against their will. On the quayside Joseph Sherman studied the individual prisoners intently as the companionway sagged beneath their weight. He had retained a clear image in his mind of Ngo Van Loc's face in the jungle hunting camp, but as the first dozen or so men hobbled ashore, he began to doubt his ability to recognize him. Eleven years before, Loc's habitual expression had been the servile, respectful half-smile of the domestic servant, but none of the grim, resentful prison faces seemed to bear any resemblance to that memory.

The small freighter, the second to arrive in Saigon with Communists released under the amnesty, carried about fifty prisoners, and there were almost as many uniformed French and Annamese gendarmes stationed ostentatiously on the quayside, monitoring their arrival. To make their job easier arc lamps had been rigged along the berth, and the prisoners blinked uncertainly in the bright pool of light they cast onto the nighttime quayside. Across the broad boulevard that ran beside the river, another mixed group of Frenchmen and Annamese dressed in civilian clothes watched more surreptitiously from beneath the awnings of the Café de la Rotonde at the foot of the Rue Catinat. From time to time one of their number rose unhurriedly from his table and detached himself from the others to follow a particular prisoner or group of prisoners into the darkened streets of the city; always these agents of the Sûreté Générale took pains to keep a good distance between themselves and their quarry to ensure that they remained unobserved.

As Joseph scrutinized each successive face, he felt his chest tightening with the same kind of breathless tension he'd first noticed in himself on his arrival in Saigon; again the night was hot and clammy and he tried to dismiss the feeling as a natural reaction in someone unused to the dense tropical heat. But at the same time he suspected that the events of the day and his impulsive decision to come to the dockside had tautened his nerves. The riot at the Cercle Sportif and the subsequent ride in the *malabar* with Lan had left him feeling strangely exhilarated; his appetite had fled and he had not been able to face dinner alone at the hotel. Paul had telephoned to thank him for escorting Lan home and to report that the disturbance had been quelled without serious injury; because Paul was on duty that night, they had arranged to meet the next day for lunch, and it was while Joseph was sitting alone on the hotel terrace at sunset that he had seen a photograph in the evening paper of the first group of prisoners arriving from Paulo Condore. He had been peering closely at the blurred faces in the picture for some time before he realized with a start that he was unconsciously searching for Ngo Van Loc. At the end of the story the newspaper announced that a second group was expected to arrive some time that evening, and he had risen immediately from his table and hurried down to the quayside.

The next two hours had passed with an agonizing slowness, and as he paced restlessly back and forth along the darkened water-front watching ships arrive and depart, conflicting impulses and emotions had warred endlessly with one another inside his head; one part of his mind, his most rational self, urged him repeatedly to leave before the prison ship docked. What good could be achieved by seeking out the former hunting camp "boy"? The past was undeniably past — would anything more be achieved than the opening of old wounds? And would he, when it came to it, have the courage to fire painful questions at a man he barely knew and who had just been released from a harsh spell of imprisonment? He asked himself these questions a hundred times, but still he didn't leave the sweltering riverside.

During the long wait, the image of Loc's sobbing wife fleeing half-naked through the storm, and the sound of his own mother's faint cries returned to haunt his mind, and he remembered again with a disconcerting intensity the turmoil of shock and bewilder-ment that those events had caused him as a fifteen-year-old. Subconsciously the vague feeling of betrayal, instinctive in that jungle storm, had deepened as his knowledge of the adult world expanded, leaving him with a legacy of suspicion and wariness; but on that Saigon dockside he realized he had never entirely aban-doned the hope that perhaps some explanation beyond his imagining might have existed for what had happened, an expla-nation that somehow would relieve the disquiet that those terrible moments in the storm had implanted in him. He was half aware that such a hope was a forlorn one, but it was this slender chance, he knew, that kept him there, striding back and forth along the wharves in the sticky darkness, his shirt plastered against his back with perspiration.

When the prison ship finally appeared Joseph had hurried to join the little crowd of Annamese relatives who had anticipated its arrival, and it was then that the Sûreté agents across the boulevard noticed his presence for the first time. When he moved closer to the foot of the gangway to get a better look at the disembarking prisoners, the inspector directing the undercover operation from the back of the café gave quiet instructions to a heavily built Frenchman to put him under immediate surveillance.

More than half the prisoners had left the ship before Joseph saw a man who bore a faint resemblance to Ngo Van Loc; like all the others, however, his features were blurred by the ashen pallor of long confinement, making recognition difficult. His threadbare black cotton tunic and trousers hung loose on his skeletal frame, and Joseph noticed that his left arm dangled uselessly at his side. At the moment of stepping ashore the prisoner glanced incuriously into the American's face before turning away, and for a second Joseph decided he had been mistaken. Then on impulse he stepped towards the man and touched his shoulder.

"Excuse me, monsieur," he said quietly in French, "are you Ngo Van Loc?"

The released prisoner turned to look at him with a startled expression; fear and suspicion were mingled in his gaze, and he didn't reply. He glanced warily around at the faces of the uniformed gendarmes crowding the quayside, then back at Joseph again.

"Weren't you once the hunting camp 'boy' of Jacques Devraux?" asked Joseph desperately.

For a fleeting instant he fancied that the emaciated face of the Annamese registered surprise, but then he turned his back without speaking to catch up with another of the released prisoners. Joseph watched for a moment or two as they crossed the boulevard, then looked back again towards the ship. But none of the remaining faces aroused his interest, and making up his mind suddenly, he hurried across the quayside in the direction taken by the Annamese with the paralyzed arm.

The streets were crowded, and fearing he might lose track of the man, Joseph broke into a run. He caught sight of him and his companion as they turned into a street leading towards the central market, but the sound of his running feet caused the two Annamese to turn their heads, and to Joseph's dismay, on seeing themselves pursued, they began to run too. By one of the arched entrances to the vast covered market they turned and glanced frantically in his direction again, then disappeared inside. Joseph followed without hesitation, and although he could see nothing in the subterranean gloom, he clearly heard the scuff of running feet and the labored breathing of the two Annamese.

"Monsieur Loc, please wait," he called frantically in French. "I just want to talk to you."

His voice echoed and re-echoed hollowly in the cavernous interior of the deserted market, but the men didn't stop, and Joseph plunged on in the direction of their footsteps. When he paused to listen again, to his surprise he could hear nothing except the sound of his own breathing, and he walked on more cautiously through the silent darkness that reeked of overripe fruit and rotten fish. From time to time he called Loc's name, but still there was no response, and when an unseen arm encircled his neck from behind he was taken completely by surprise; in the same instant he felt the point of a knife pressed hard against the small of his back.

"Who are you?" whispered an Annamese voice in French, close to his ear. "Why do you follow us?"

"My name's Joseph Sherman," gasped the American, struggling to loosen the fierce arm lock clamped around his throat. "Jacques Devraux once guided my family on a hunting trip when Ngo Van Loc worked with him." He heard the two men mutter rapidly to one another in their own language, but the pressure on his windpipe didn't ease and the knife was jabbed harder into his back.

"And is Devraux living here in Saigon?"

"No, he's chief of the Sûreté Générale in Hue now. Are you Ngo Van Loc?"

"Yes!"

The headlights of a car passing one of the market entrances penetrated the gloom briefly as the hold on his neck was released, and Joseph turned to see Loc still holding the knife warningly in his good hand; beside him the other Annamese stood in a half-crouch, ready to move against him again if necessary.

"How did you know where to find me? How did you know I was a prisoner?" Loc's voice, still threatening, betrayed his curiosity.

"I've talked with Paul Devraux," replied Joseph, massaging his neck. "He's in the army here. He told me he thought you were in Paulo Condore." He hesitated and rubbed his neck again. "He told me, too, the tragic news about your son, Hoc. I was very sorry to hear that he'd died."

"He didn't 'die' — he was butchered by the French with their guillotine! Did he tell you that they murdered my wife too? And that I lost the use of my arm when their brave pilots bombed and machine-gunned defenseless peasants at Vinh? Did he tell you that the French killed ten thousand Annamese because we dared to defy their despotic rule?"

"Paul feels deeply sorry for all that's happened," said Joseph desperately. "He regarded you and your sons as his friends."

The Annamese snorted in contempt. "Did he send you himself to tell me these lies?"

"No. He doesn't know I've come."

"Then what did you wish to talk to me about?"

Joseph suddenly found himself unable to summon up the words he wanted. "It's a very personal matter, Loc," he said hesitantly. "I wanted to speak to you alone."

The Annamese muttered a few rapid words in his own language, and Joseph waited until the shadowy figure of Loc's companion had moved away through the gloom and taken up guard inside the nearest archway.

"Loc, do you remember that night of the bad storm in the jungle camp at the start of my family's expedition?" Joseph's voice shook slightly as he spoke. "Do you remember what happened?"

No reply came from the darkness, but Joseph thought he sensed an unseen tension in his listener.

"I couldn't sleep and wandered out into the rain. I was walking past Monsieur Devraux's hut when I saw your wife rush from there weeping. . . ." Joseph felt suddenly that his heart was expanding in his chest, threatening to choke him, and he became acutely aware of the sickening reek of putrefaction inside the darkened market. "I wanted to ask . . ."

"Don't ask me questions about that night!" The ferocity of Ngo Van Loc's words shook Joseph, and he sensed that the Annamese was trembling beside him in the darkness. "Every day for five years in my cell in Paulo Condore I've had to live with my own misery. And often I saw the accusing face of my dead wife in my dreams!"

For a long moment they stood facing each other silently in the evil-smelling darkness.

"What do you mean, Loc?" whispered Joseph at last.

"I forced her to do it. In the end it was my fault that she fell into the hands of her French murderers." He paused, his breathing agitated, and his voice dropped to a whisper. "So the senator and I have something in common, haven't we? Does he have bad dreams too?"

Joseph started at the unexpected reference to his father. "Why should he, Loc?"

"Because just as my stupidity led to the death of my wife — it was your father's stupidity that caused the death of your brother, wasn't it?"

"My father tried to save Chuck," said Joseph, his voice rising incredulously. "He was injured badly in the attempt — he lost his arm."

Loc's bark of humorless laughter startled Joseph. "Is that what he told you?"

"Yes."

"It was the other way round."

Joseph leaned forward anxiously; he had suddenly remembered the startled look on Paul's face when he mentioned the accident. "What are you suggesting, Loc?"

"I'm not 'suggesting' anything, Monsieur Sherman. Your brother was killed trying to save the senator. Your father was suffering from fever — he was too sick to hunt. He drank a lot of alcohol with the medicine he took and foolishly followed the wounded seladang into a thicket against Devraux's orders. Your brother lost his life trying to save him."

"You must be lying!" The words leaped to Joseph's lips before he considered what he was saying.

"What reason have I to lie?" asked the Annamese in an indifferent voice.

Another car passed one of the entry arches, and in the reflected glow of its lights Joseph saw the second Annamese turn and begin running swiftly towards them. Loc listened to his urgently whispered words for a moment, then leaned towards Joseph again. "Two Sûreté agents are watching the market entrances," he said accusingly. "So you are in league with them after all!"

Joseph started to protest, but the Annamese didn't stop to listen; after cursing him bitterly in their own language they ran off in opposite directions, and he was left alone again in the reeking darkness. For several minutes he stood rooted to the spot, grappling with the enormity of Ngo Van Loc's revelation; then he left the market in a daze and returned slowly to the Continental Palace.

He walked without seeing the streets along which he passed and didn't notice that both the Sûreté agents were following him. They entered the foyer of the hotel openly a minute or two after Joseph had gone up to his room, and the nervous Annamese clerk on the reception desk, after one glance at their stolid faces, made the hotel register available to them without question. Knowing from previous experience what was required of him, the clerk turned away and busied himself with some mundane task while the agents copied into a notebook the name and address of Joseph Theodore Sherman of The Sherman Plantation, Charles County, Virginia, U.S.A.

5

"Because the river is so peaceful and serene, the sages say the heart of Annam can be heard beating on its banks." Lan turned to smile warmly at Joseph as their sampan glided southwards out of Hue on the glittering waters of the Huong Giang — the River of Perfumes. "That's why the emperors chose these lovely glades outside the city for their final resting places."

Joseph smiled back at her and glanced around him, marveling inwardly at the richness of the natural color in the landscape. Under a clear azure sky the river was as blue as the silk of Lan's *ao dai*, and all along its borders willow trees bent as though in homage to trail their pale tendrils in its sparkling waves; to the west the river was sheltered by the Annamite Cordillera, and the dense emerald-green foliage cloaking the shoulders of the mountains tumbled extravagantly down their slopes and across the valleys to the water's edge.

"I expect you already know, Monsieur Sherman, that we Annamese believe that the spirits of our ancestors continue to dwell among us after their deaths," said Tran Van Tam politely from one of the rear seats. "But we believe too that the well-being of each family depends on the happiness of those spirits — and it's our responsibility to see that they remain content. It's the same for our nation too — and that's why this region where the emperors have their tombs is the most beautiful and sacred in all our land."

Joseph nodded and smiled his thanks. To make his duties as chaperon for the visit to the emperors' tombs less intrusive, Tam had brought along the girl he had agreed to marry at his parents' command; plain and shy, her chief virtue was that she was the daughter of another wealthy mandarin family, and she spoke only when Tam addressed her. In comparison, Lan's beauty seemed to Joseph's excited gaze more breathtaking than ever. A faint flush of color that he had seen rush into her cheeks on his arrival in Hue that morning had persisted; she had been visibly embarrassed by his appearance at her father's official residence inside the red walls of the Imperial City and was still reserved in her manner when he called again to collect her for the afternoon outing. But once on the river, her eyes had begun to shine, and as the coolie on the stern rowed the sampan beyond the city, she eagerly pointed out the ancient landmarks that became visible one by one in the surrounding hills.

"There's the Shrine to the Venerable Lady of Heaven . . . and that's the Tower of the Source of Happiness . . . and do you see the little Confucian temple almost hidden by the trees? It's the Van Mieu — the Pagoda of Literary Culture."

Joseph smiled back at her each time, scarcely taking in her words; he was above all else delighted to find himself close to her again so soon, and he had to make a conscious effort not to stare. Her glossy black hair tumbled loose around her shoulders, and the gentle wind ruffled it now and then, causing her to toss her head prettily and brush an occasional strand from her eyes with what to Joseph seemed movements of infinite grace and delicacy; she smiled at him sometimes in her exasperation with the playful breeze, and Joseph felt a simple glow of happiness take hold inside him.

His decision to travel to Hue by the first possible train had been taken during the sleepless hours that followed his meeting with Ngo Van Loc. Throughout the long night, as new tortured images of the past invoked by his conversation with Loc flickered through his brain, the memory of Lan's beautiful golden face in the *malabar* began to return more and more frequently until it assumed the force of an obsession; amidst the turmoil of deceit and suspicion in his mind, she seemed suddenly to personify the sweetness and purity he instinctively craved and before dawn he rose and packed his belongings to ready himself for the journey north. In the note that he left for Paul Devraux explaining his premature departure he had said only that no student of Asian history could possibly afford to miss the imperial ceremonies, and this half-truth had left him feeling guilty and ill-at-ease as he hurried to the railway station. The little wood-burning train that left before breakfast had taken nearly three days to cover the five hundred miles to Hue, stopping each night to deposit its passengers in wayside inns, and during the long, slow journey he had suffered renewed pangs of remorse at the thought that he was betraying Paul's trust. But as the train drew nearer to Hue, the growing excitement he felt at the prospect of seeing Lan again had gradually overshadowed these thoughts and they had been replaced by a growing anxiety about how he would be received in the capital of Annam. To his great relief, however, although he had neither announced his coming nor received any invitation, Tran Van Hieu had welcomed him courteously at his residence. After inquiring briefly about the health of his family and thanking him elaborately once again for his rescue of the gibbon eleven years before, it had been Tran Van Hieu himself who had suggested that a visit to the tombs might be of special interest to a student of Asian history.

"Don't imagine they are just gloomy sepulchres," he had warned with a smile. "Many of the emperors supervised the building of their own tombs and often used them during their lifetimes as country palaces where they could meditate in peace and tranquillity close to nature. There you'll discover the art and sculpture of the Orient wedded in perfect harmony to great natural beauty."

When the sampan coolie finally moored beside a long grove of sacred banyan trees, and they approached the tomb of Minh Mang, heir and successor to Emperor Gia Long, Joseph remembered Tran Van Hieu's words. A breathless hush seemed to hang in the air above the red-pillared pavilions built across the center of a wide, crescent-shaped expanse of water known as the Lake of Scintillating Brightness; lotus flowers clustered on its surface as thickly as freshly fallen snow, and in the distance pointed hills and mountains were visible, forested thickly with the same luxuriantly green trees that bordered the lake.

"I don't think I've ever seen anything more beautiful in all my life," said Joseph in an awed voice as he mounted the blue granite steps of the entrance gate at Lan's side. "It scarcely seems real."

"Whenever I felt troubled as a little girl I liked to come here with my nurse — and somehow my worries always went away. I wonder if it's lost its magic powers."

Her expression was unexpectedly sad and there was a faraway look in her eyes; glancing around, Joseph saw that Tam was already descending the steps in front of them with his future wife. "Is something worrying you, Lan?" he asked gently.

She shook her head quickly and smiled. "No — but so many things change as you grow up, don't they? It always makes me feel sad when I realize I can no longer go back."

The simple poignancy of her words moved Joseph deeply, and he took a step closer to her.

"The burial mound itself is beneath that green hill covered with tangled trees, do you see?" She shaded her eyes and pointed along the wide terrace that bisected the lake. "To get there we have to pass through the Gate of Dazzling Virtue. In that temple on the other side, we'll see the memorial tablets to the emperor and empress. The gardens have been laid out in the form of the

Chinese character for 'Eternity' . . ." She broke off when she became aware that he was gazing at her instead of following her pointing finger, and the intensity of the expression in his blue eyes made her blush.

"I'm sure no empress was ever more beautiful than you, Lan," he said softly. "Seeing you here among these lovely old palaces makes me realize why your father and mother named you after the heroine in 'The Tale of Kieu.'" He paused and smiled at her again. "Do you remember those lines describing Kieu . . .?

> 'Crystal-bright autumn streams, her eyes,
> Her brows curve like hills in spring,
> Flowers envy the brilliance of her face,
> Willows wish only for her grace,
> Compared to her beauty, the riches of
> An emperor's palace are without worth.'"

He continued to gaze wonderingly at her. "Those words could just as easily have been written about you, Lan. . . ."

She looked at him with startled eyes for a moment, then turned away and almost ran down the steps.

Alarmed that she might fall, Joseph hurried after her and took her elbow to steady her. "I've been thinking about you constantly, Lan, since I last saw you," he said breathlessly. "I've dreamed of you at night, too." She didn't reply or look at him, and when they reached the bottom of the steps he glanced anxiously ahead to check that Tam was beyond earshot. "I don't seem to be able to get you out of my mind even for a minute."

She blushed deeply. "It's not right to say such things to me, Joseph. We hardly know one another."

"But we've known each other for eleven years!"

He smiled again, a dazzling, delighted smile which seemed to Lan to draw her towards him with the force of a physical embrace, and she glanced with agitation around the formal gardens. With the exception of the red-robed imperial guardians patrolling the terraces, the tomb was deserted; occasionally a blue-gowned mandarin appeared, moving reverently among the temples on some errand aimed at soothing the imperial spirits, but otherwise the antique pavilions stood silent in the middle of the dreaming lake as though hanging on their every word. "You must promise me, Joseph, not to say such things again," she said distractedly. "Otherwise, I can't permit us to walk apart from my brother."

"Please forgive me!" Joseph felt a sudden, desperate regret. "I was so happy at seeing you again that I forgot myself."

She turned away abruptly and walked ahead of him. In the deep silence she was frightened that he might have been able to hear the sound of her heart racing inside her chest. A minute later she could still feel the touch of his hand, as comforting as his arm around her shoulders had been during those sudden moments of fright at the Cercle Sportif. Even in the sampan she had noticed herself suddenly at ease in his presence; she had become intensely aware of his strong, sunburned face, his good-natured smile, his broad shoulders that made him seem so powerful in comparison with the slight figure of her brother Tam. His closeness to her had produced again the same indefinable sense of physical well-being that she had first felt beside him in the *malabar*, but it had been the tender intensity of his smile as he quoted the lyrical passage of Nguyen Du's epic poem that had made her pulse race so bewilderingly, and she determined to keep herself apart from him to try to still the commotion inside her.

She bent with unnecessary concentration to study the inscriptions on the memorial tablets among the lim-wood pillars of the shadowy Sung An Dien, pretended to lay wondering fingers on the long-legged brass cranes before another altar, peered closely at the gold and jade ornaments, the urns and vases in each richly furnished chamber as though she had never seen them before; but during all this time there was barely a moment when she wasn't acutely aware of his presence, wherever he moved around her.

In his turn Joseph, anxious not to offend again, was careful to remain at a distance behind her as he wandered through the gardens and palaces. He too pretended to study the treasures of the tomb with care, but the motionless rows of life-sized mandarins and elephants carved from white stone drifted almost unseen past his eyes and the sculpted dragons and other mythological beasts entwined in the roofs and balustrades in reality received little more than a passing glance from him. As he followed her slowly across the lake towards the tree-covered tumulus known as the Mount of the Sun, the antique, weather-mellowed dwelling places of the imperial spirits remained beyond the real focus of his vision; to him the splendid pavilions were merely a sublime backdrop for the lithe, living figure moving beguilingly ahead of him, her long mane of hair flowing darkly down her back. In one of the shadowy temples when she thought she was unobserved, she knelt briefly before an altar in prayer, and coming in sight of her suddenly from the garden, his heart lurched inside him; with her head bowed over her hands, her kneeling figure seemed to radiate simple piety and goodness, and in that instant he knew he loved her.

The realization made him tremble inwardly, and he wanted desperately to rush to her side and tell her of his feelings. But remembering the startled, uneasy expression in her eyes minutes before, he fought down the impulse and waited out of sight until she rose to her feet again. Then he moved quietly to her side, feeling a new sense of pleasure in their closeness, and together they viewed Minh Mang's most intimate possessions — his great teak bed with its long pillow of decorated porcelain, his favorite jewels and weapons, the altars on which every morning fresh dishes of his favorite foods and beverages were set out by tomb guardians. They didn't speak again until they were standing outside in the Garden of Eternity where azaleas, orange flamboyants and frangipani blossomed around twin lotus pools; the sun was still pleasantly warm, and the deep, thrilling silence was broken only occasionally by the muted calling of waterfowl from the lake below them.

"This must be how paradise is, Lan," said Joseph in an awed whisper. "It hasn't lost any of its magic, has it?"

She shook her head, but there was still a hint of melancholy in her smile. "It's still an enchanted place — but perhaps as we grow up our worries grow bigger too. I don't really expect my prayers to be answered this time."

Joseph frowned. "Then there *is* something bothering you?"

"Yes." She looked anxiously along the terrace and didn't continue until she spotted Tam and his fiancée climbing the steps to the Gate of Dazzling Virtue. "I try not to think about it all the time — but my father was very upset by the trouble at the Cercle Sportif. Kim's hotheadedness has caused trouble between them before. But after the tennis match he and my father quarreled violently. . . . Kim insulted him and vowed to become a revolutionary. In the end my father ordered him never to return to our house." The recollection disquieted her, and she tugged agitatedly at the bracelet of translucent blue jade on her left wrist. "It's upset all my family, of course."

"I thought your father seemed a little distracted this morning."

Lan nodded, still tugging unconsciously at the bracelet. "It's affected him the most. The Communist troubles five years ago were bad for my country. I hoped all that had passed — but obviously it hasn't. My father's afraid that one day there might be a civil war." She sighed and gazed at the golden roofs glinting in the sun. "In this beautiful place those worries don't seem to be real. Coming here makes me wish I could get away from all those awful things."

"I wish I could show you my country, Lan," he said impulsively, seizing her hands. "Wouldn't you like to see America?"

He had spoken before he realized what he was saying, and again she looked uneasy. "Please let me go, Joseph," she said quietly, struggling to free her hands. "My brother might see us."

He loosened his grasp reluctantly and she turned and began walking away from him across one of the three little parallel bridges leading back towards the Hall of Venerated Beneficence. Realizing that within a few minutes they would be back in the sampan with her brother Tam, he caught her up quickly in the middle of the bridge and took her gently by the arm again.

"I believe you feel something for me, Lan — I think I can see it in your eyes. I know you need time — but I could come back to Saigon to work for a while. That way we might get to know each other better. Would you like to do that?"

"My father wouldn't approve of such a thing."

She half turned away from him to gaze across the lake, and he saw her tugging agitatedly once more at the jade bracelet.

"Why not?"

"Because of Kim! Perhaps you can't understand — but now my father needs the loyalty of Tam and myself more than ever. I can't think of myself at a time like this."

"But I don't see —"

A sharp cry escaped her lips suddenly, and she leaned out over the parapet, gazing horror-stricken into the waters below. Frightened that she might topple off the bridge, he seized her shoulders. "What is it, Lan?"

When she turned to look at him, her face was white and tears were brimming in her eyes. "My bracelet! It's fallen into the lake." She held up her bare wrist for him to see.

Joseph peered into the blue water twenty feet below but saw nothing. "Don't worry," he said soothingly, "I'll buy you another bracelet."

"You can't."

"Why not?"

"It can't be replaced. It was given to me by my mother when I became twenty-one. It's been passed down in our family from life to life, from mother to daughter for over two hundred years. It was a gift to one of our ancestors from the imperial court."

Joseph stared helplessly at her stricken face. "I'll try to find one just like it."

"It's another bad omen," she said in a horrified whisper.

They heard the sound of footsteps and looked up to see her

brother, who had obviously heard her cry out, approaching at a run.

"Please, Joseph, don't tell Tam," she pleaded. "My mother and my family mustn't know the bracelet's lost."

When Tam came up to them, she pretended she had twisted her ankle and leaned on her brother's arm all the way back to the sampan. During the journey downstream to Hue she scarcely spoke, and Joseph forced himself to exchange polite conversation with Tam about the tombs. The River of Perfumes was again as serenely beautiful as it had been earlier, but as the light faded, somber black shadows began to creep across the valleys, and in his dejection Joseph thought he suddenly sensed an ominous, brooding quality in the jagged mountains that hadn't been noticeable in the brightness of the afternoon.

6

The face of the Frenchman who stared incredulously at him as he entered the foyer of his hotel on the morning of the Sacrifice to Heaven seemed only vaguely familiar to Joseph Sherman. Then in a remarkable feat of memory he recalled a fleeting encounter with a stoop-shouldered stranger on a street in Saigon eleven years before while watching shackled Annamese prisoners endure a savage beating; the man in the foyer had the same unhealthy, parchment-like skin that hung slack on the bones of his face, his yellowing eyes were sunk in the same blackened sockets, and when he came close to him, Joseph's sense of smell was jolted back eleven years too, as he detected the same mustiness about the man's clothing that betrayed the addicted smoker of opium. Then with a palpable sense of shock Joseph realized he was mistaken; the aging, dissipated face was not that of the supercilious *colon* he and his brother had met briefly in 1925 — he was looking at Jacques Devraux.

The Frenchman didn't drop his gaze until Joseph stopped in front of him; then he held out his hand, smiling apologetically. "Forgive me, Joseph, for staring like that. But you looked so much like your brother as you came through that door. For a moment I couldn't believe my eyes."

Joseph hesitated, not wanting to have any physical contact with the man before him; illogically he had expected Devraux to have remained unchanged — to mirror still the silent, heroic image that had first scored itself so deeply in his impressionable, fifteen-year-old mind on that first ride through the jungle. The thought of seeing even that man again had induced a sour, sullen mood, but the startling deterioration in the appearance of the once clear-eyed hunting guide sent a new sensation surging through him — contempt. His instinct was to ignore the Frenchman's greeting pointedly, but in the end habit prevailed and, regretting it immediately, he allowed his hand to be shaken.

"There's no need to concern yourself," said Joseph, speaking with a deliberate coolness. "I've got very used to people telling me I look like Chuck. Paul said the same thing."

In the awkward silence that followed Joseph saw Devraux's gaze flicker over the wet swimming costume wrapped in a towel that he carried under his arm, then shift to his still-damp hair. "Even so, it can't be an enjoyable experience, Joseph. I apologize."

"It's really not important. May I ask how you knew I was in Hue?"

"Paul sent me a wire from Saigon. He told me you were writing a book." Devraux spoke his previously clipped English in a dull monotone as though he made the effort now unwillingly, and he stumbled occasionally over his words. "He urged me to make sure that you saw the ceremonies from the best vantage points. I left a note here yesterday to say I would arrange something. I trust you received it."

"Yes, I did — thank you." The typewritten note stating that the "Chef de Sûreté d'Annam" would call after breakfast had been waiting for him the previous evening when he returned to the hotel from the tomb of Minh Mang, and he had decided that if a meeting became unavoidable he would try to be civil but no more. Outside the hotel the streets of Hue, decked with national flags and banners bearing expressions of good omen, were filling rapidly with crowds of Annamese gathering to catch a glimpse of the Emperor Bao Dai, and Joseph gestured through the windows in their direction. "It's getting late. Perhaps it would be better if I made my own way there. It'll take me a few minutes to get ready."

Devraux shrugged. "As you like. But I've made special arrangements for the Tran family at Paul's request and would be glad to include you. You'll be able to see very little of the procession or the ceremonies on your own. The spectacle is greatest at the Bull Gate as the emperor leaves the Imperial City. If you go over there alone, you won't be able to follow the procession back to the south side of the river — the Clemenceau Bridge will be closed for two hours after the emperor passes. I've arranged a sampan to bring the Trans and myself to this bank. I've got Sûreté cars waiting here to take us all to a viewing stand at the Nam Giao. And I've reserved places for you and the Trans inside on the temple steps tonight for the climax of the ceremonies."

Joseph wavered for only a moment or two — then the prospect of seeing Lan again swayed his decision. Hue was the only city in the world where the three-thousand-year-old ritual of the Sacrifice to Heaven inherited from China's emperors had been celebrated since the overthrow of the last Peking dynasty in 1911; soon it seemed certain that the tradition must die in Hue too, and because the elaborate ceremonies were performed only once in three years, the opportunity, Joseph knew, was unique. To see the solemn procession emerge from the Purple Forbidden City and follow it across the River of Perfumes to the Nam Giao would be an unforgettable experience; the Nam Giao was the sacred walled compound, corresponding to the blue-roofed Temple of Heaven in Peking, where the emperor would spend the day in meditation before performing the sacred rites, and Joseph decided it would be foolish to pass up such a rare chance to witness all this pageantry from a position of privilege.

"If you don't mind waiting a moment or two longer," he said quickly, turning towards the stairs, "I'd be glad to accept your invitation."

The ramparts of the Citadel glowed a fiery red in the light of the rising sun when fifteen minutes later Joseph and Jacques Devraux stepped onto the modern bridge of latticed steel girders that spanned the river. Two imperial elephants decked with gold harness and ridden by Annamese in blue, ankle-length court uniforms stood guard at the entrance to the bridge, ready to close it to traffic as soon as the boom of nine cannon from inside the Citadel indicated that the emperor was ready to leave his secluded palace; this signal, however, was not expected for another ten minutes, and all around Joseph and the Sûreté chief a noisy, excited crowd was still pouring across the bridge towards the northern bank.

Among them a shabby *pousse-pousse* bearing the wasted figure of Ngo Van Loc attracted no attention. A wide hat of palm leaf hid his features, and his thin body was clad in the black tunic and white trousers of a middle-class Annamese clerk whom he and his son Dong had ambushed and robbed in a narrow side street in the Annamese quarter of the city the night before. Dong, stripped to

227

the waist, loped easily between the shafts of the *pousse-pousse*, a black peasant's turban wound around his head, but even if the Frenchman or Joseph had turned to look behind, they would not have recognized him as the shy thirteen-year-old who had once romped in their jungle hunting camp. He had grown into a tall, gangling youth of twenty-four who had to affect a stoop to hold the shafts of the *pousse-pousse* level, and the expression in his brown eyes, although watchful, hinted at the physical self-confidence his unusual height gave him.

"It's the American who told me Devraux was here in Hue — I'm sure of it." Loc leaned forward in his seat to murmur quietly in his son's ear. "It looks as though he's taking him to the Ngo Mon. Don't get close. There are too many people around to do anything here."

Dong nodded obediently and slowed his pace. They had been shadowing Jacques Devraux since he left his home that morning, and Dong had agreed before they set out that his father should decide when the best moment came for him to act. Behind him Ngo Van Loc settled himself in the *pousse-pousse* once more, shifting his paralyzed arm into a more comfortable position with his other hand, and as they continued across the bridge he glanced back towards the southern bank where they had watched Devraux station the two Sûreté Renaults before visiting the American's hotel. For a moment his brow creased in thought, then he touched the hard steel butt of the Beretta pistol concealed in the waistband of his trousers and searched ahead among the crowd until his gaze came to rest once more on the white-suited figure of Jacques Devraux.

"No copulation . . . no garlic . . . no wine . . . but plenty of hot baths and devout prayers — those are the rules of the 'Great Abstinence' the emperor's been practicing for three days now. Or at least he should have been." Devraux's ravaged features twisted in a sardonic smile as he glanced at the young American at his side. "After spending ten years of his youth in Paris, there's some doubt in court circles whether he's still capable of observing the Great Abstinence — even for three days."

They had come in sight of one of the carved stone bridges leading across the moat, and Joseph caught his first glimpse of the golden palace roofs that had so entranced him as a boy; the heady charm of the imperial tombs was still fresh in his mind too, from the previous day, and the Frenchman's cynicism about the ceremony suddenly deepened the offense he felt in his presence. "You say that, Monsieur Devraux, as though France has reason to be proud of the corruption it's brought to the Annamese."

The American didn't trouble to hide the animosity he felt, and Devraux looked sharply at him. For a moment Joseph saw again in the Frenchman's expression a hint of the fierce, soldierly pride that had once distinguished him; then he shrugged and turned away. "Times change, Joseph. Everything changes sooner or later."

"The force of the Sacrifice to Heaven has given meaning to these people's lives for three thousand years," said the American truculently. "To them Heaven and Earth have always been the mother and father of their existence. They've always believed the good favor of their great ruling spirits can pass to them only through the virtue of the emperor and his ancestors — that's why he has to be seen as a remote, magical figure when he makes his sacrificial offerings every three years. If France has endangered their faith by dragging their emperor off to Paris for half his life, it's hardly something to be proud of."

The Frenchman angered Joseph still further by smiling again. "Perhaps you're right. But the emperor himself doesn't seem to object. I suspect he might rather be playing bridge or poker right now. He's fond of cards — a useful golfer too for a young man of twenty-four. And he rushes around those mountains over there in a supercharged French sports car, dressed in sweaters and shorts, without seeming to worry too much about disturbing the evil spirits trying to clamber over into Hue." He touched Joseph's arm lightly to indicate a turn through one of the Citadel's gates. "He's a realist. He knows you can't really live in the past. . . ."

Joseph didn't reply. As they emerged into the esplanade inside the Citadel walls, he caught sight of the dazzlingly arrayed throng of courtiers waiting for the emperor outside the Ngo Mon, the golden-roofed "Bull Gate" designed in the style of the Gate of Heavenly Peace in Peking. Imperial troops wearing cone-shaped helmets with golden spikes jostled with gaudily clad mandarins, musicians and bearers of ceremonial regalia, and among them Annamese generals, resplendent in uniforms of violet and green brocade, trotted on sturdy, short-legged ponies. From beyond the inner walls of the Imperial City Joseph heard a high-pitched Tibetan temple trumpet begin to wail above a sudden clamor of drums and gongs, and he instinctively quickened his pace.

"The emperor's ready to leave," he said excitedly. "We've arrived just in time."

The moment Joseph and Jacques Devraux disappeared into the shadow of the Citadel gate Ngo Van Loc leaned forward in the seat of his *pousse-pousse* to tap his son on the shoulder.

"Head back across the Clemenceau quickly, before it closes! They must be using a sampan to reach the cars on the southern bank. That's where we'll strike!"

Dong turned immediately and broke into a gallop. He reached the bridge just as the sound of cannon fire began to echo from the fortified city, and his rickshaw was the last vehicle of any kind allowed to set out for the southern bank. A few seconds later the Annamese mahouts maneuvered their elephants into position to seal off the roadway.

7

The tolling of a single bronze bell high on the gilded balconies of the Ngo Mon heralded the arrival of the emperor's entourage, and a moment later Joseph saw its vanguard emerge from the deep shadow of the gate's central arch. Six shoeless bearers in belted court robes and tiny conical hats fringed with tinkling bells carried the Table of the Cult on their shoulders under the watchful eyes of a contingent of the Imperial Guard; behind them a group of mounted generals escorted other litters displaying the emperor's sacrificial robes and his personal ceremonial objects — incense burners, golden goblets, swords and lanterns. Great throngs of drummers, gong bearers and other musicians striking mournful notes on ancient stone lithophones followed the grave-faced bearers of the Symbols of Good Augury as they emerged blinking into the bright morning sunlight holding aloft the Table of the Wine of Felicity, the Chair of the Nine Dragons and representations of the Sun, the Seven Stars, Rain, Wind, Thunder, the Nocturnal Light.

The fragrant smoky scents of aromatic resins and aloe-wood swirled on the breeze from little wayside shrines, and as moment by moment new squadrons of richly robed courtiers marched out through the gate to the discordant beat of cymbals and gongs, Joseph felt himself transported deep into Asia's mysterious past.

The Imperial Coach drawn by eight stallions and the Imperial Chair — both empty on the outward journey from the palaces — appeared, followed by a jostling crowd of white horses from the court stable; although riderless, these favored animals were escorted by liveried grooms who held a forest of tall yellow parasols above their bare backs. More dancers, musicians and bearers bobbed through the gate in a moving tide of gaudy colors — then abruptly the drums and cymbals ceased their clamor, and the waiting crowds, recognizing the signal, craned forward to catch a glimpse of the emperor himself.

In the expectant hush Joseph couldn't resist the temptation to turn his head in Lan's direction. She was standing with Tam and her mother only a few feet away inside the enclosure that had been reserved for French dignitaries and the families of high-ranking Annamese; poised on the tips of her toes and shading her eyes with her hand, she was gazing intently towards the Ngo Mon, watching for the Annamese sovereign and, among the other senior mandarins who would follow him, her own father. She wore a pale blue *ao dai* decorated with pink floral motifs, and Joseph felt his senses quicken as he watched the fine tulle of the filmy outer garment, caught by the breeze, mold itself against her slender body. In his jacket pocket his hand closed round a jade bracelet wrapped in an envelope of silk, and he wondered if he were ever going to have the chance to give it to her. On her arrival Lan had greeted him as formally as did her mother and Tam, and afterwards avoided his glance. He had tried without success to catch her eye while they waited for the procession to begin and had sensed then her continuing anxiety. He had considered trying to slip the bracelet to her surreptitiously in an effort to bring a smile back to her face — but then decided against it for fear of embarrassing her.

A murmur of excitement rippling through the crowds drew his attention back to the ceremonial gate, and he turned in time to see the Imperial Litter shift out of the shadows of the archway on the shoulders of twelve tall Annamese bearers; a gift from Louis XVIII to the Emperor Gia Long, its glossy coachwork of black lacquer and gold filigree glittered and flashed whenever a shaft of sunlight penetrated the shifting glades of yellow parasols clustered around it. As the litter moved by him, Joseph caught a fleeting glimpse in the shadowy interior of the slender figure of Bao Dai resplendent in his yellow robes. He wore an elaborate silken turban of the same color on his head, but he remained motionless in his seat, looking shy and ill-at-ease and glancing neither left nor right as he proceeded; in the profound silence that had fallen over

231

the crowd the only sound was the faint scuff of the bearers' unshod feet on the metaled roadway. Other male members of the imperial family and the highest mandarins of his court followed the emperor at a respectful distance in hooded rickshaws, and Joseph saw Lan tug excitedly at her mother's sleeve as Tran Van Hieu, composed in his black winged bonnet and embroidered gown, glided silently past.

Her face was still alight with her smile of pleasure when she turned in his direction, and seizing his chance, he smiled back and moved quickly to her side. "Lan, please let me speak to you privately," he whispered. "Can you leave your family for just a moment?" Inside his pocket he clutched the bracelet once more as he waited for her answer.

For a second or two they stood side by side with their backs to her mother and Tam, watching the procession flow away from them across the esplanade; they heard the gongs and drums begin again as the front ranks reached the Clemenceau Bridge and started across the river — but still she made no reply. Then the harsh, incongruous sound of gasoline engines reached Joseph's ears and he looked around to see a cavalcade of shiny black Citroën motor cars driving out through the Ngo Mon, carrying the governor general of Indochina and his suite. The French officials inside the limousines stared straight ahead in the manner of the emperor, but the lofty hauteur of their pale features contrasted sharply with the uncomfortable expression of the olive-skinned Annamese sovereign.

"If you want to be at the Nam Giao in time to see the procession arrive," said Jacques Devraux, appearing suddenly at Joseph's elbow, "we must leave and cross the river now."

A moment later Lan moved away, walking between her mother and Tam, and Joseph could only follow behind disconsolately with the Frenchman.

Beneath the shade of a gnarled tamarind tree on the southern bank of the River of Perfumes, Ngo Van Loc straightened in the cushioned seat of his rickshaw when he caught sight of Devraux's sampan nosing out into the stream; the white-suited figure of the Sûreté chief was clearly visible seated beside the young American in the rear of the craft, and two hundred yards away along the waterfront boulevard, Loc could see that the two Sûreté drivers had come to attention beside their black Renault tourers. After looking round cautiously to see if anyone was watching, he tugged the Beretta pistol from his waistband and slipped it under the cushions of the rickshaw; then nodding meaningfully to his son, who was squatting on the grass by the bole of the tamarind, he climbed down from his seat and set off towards the Sûreté cars, walking slowly and casually in the shade of the riverside palm trees. When he had gone, his son put on a ragged shirt, picked up the shafts of the rickshaw and began trotting towards the two Sûreté Renaults as well.

On board the sampan Joseph saw the rickshaw moving along the waterfront without registering it. His distracted gaze kept returning to the slender figure of Lan who was seated beside her mother in the forward part of the craft. He had tried to force himself to watch the procession strung out now across the length of the bridge above their heads; he could still hear the jangling gongs and cymbals echoing across the blue waters of the river, and from that distance the marchers in their brightly colored costumes looked like a slow-moving tide of confetti; but for the moment their fascination for him was gone — his mind was lost to thoughts of Lan.

She was seated with her back to him, and because the sun hadn't reached its full heat she still held her hat in her lap. Her hair was dressed for the occasion in a formal chignon, pierced through with a tiny jeweled dagger, and he sat watching a stray wisp that had come loose in the river breeze elude the absentminded grasp of her fingers. Suddenly she bent and turned her cheek, the better to ensnare it, and caught him watching her; he smiled eagerly, but to his intense disappointment she again affected not to notice and turned quickly away.

"How has your father managed with the disability he suffered after the accident?"

Joseph started inwardly at the sound of Jacques Devraux's voice beside him. "He's always refused to have a false limb," he said guardedly. "But he's too stubborn to let it affect his daily life very much. He does most things that require two arms with only one."

The Frenchman nodded. "He's a very determined man."

Joseph stared for a moment at the Sûreté chief. "I never expected to see you again, Monsieur Devraux," he said quietly, trying to hide the sudden intensity of his interest. "But now that we've met, would you mind telling me exactly what happened on the day of the accident?"

Instead of answering, the Frenchman turned to look upriver in the direction of the procession and took his time lighting a cheroot. "I expect your father has already gone into all that, hasn't he?" he said at last, exhaling smoke slowly through his nose. "I wasn't directly involved."

"But wasn't his safety your responsibility?"

Again the Frenchman didn't reply immediately. "In normal circumstances, yes. But that day your father decided to take all responsibility on himself."

"Why?"

"He was suffering from fever. I advised him most strongly to stop hunting in the heat of the day. He chose to ignore that advice."

"And was that the cause of the accident?"

Joseph's voice shook a little as he put the question, and for the first time the Frenchman turned to look at him. "Have you discussed this with Paul?" he asked carefully.

"No — not at all."

The sampan's oarsman swung the craft broadside on as they neared the quay, and for a long moment the Frenchman studied Joseph's taut face. "They went on ahead on their own, your father and your brother, Chuck. . . . When I caught up with them it was too late." He drew hard on the cheroot once more, then tossed it into the water. "That's all I can tell you."

Fifty yards along the waterfront in the opposite direction Dong had just overtaken his father, who was still strolling casually towards the two Sûreté Renaults. Seeing that Devraux's sampan was about to moor, he stopped the rickshaw and fumbled under its cushion; when he straightened again his ragged shirt bulged above his belt where he had concealed the pistol. He broke into a trot when he saw Jacques Devraux help the older Annamese woman onto the low quay, then began to speed up with the light rickshaw as the Sûreté inspector led the way towards the cars. Dong thought for a moment that he had misjudged the distance, but to his relief Devraux motioned the two younger Annamese and their mother into the rear seats of the first car and held the front passenger door open for Joseph; he heard Devraux give instructions to the driver to take them via the side streets to the viewing stand outside the Nam Giao, and the moment the Renault accelerated away he began to sprint, veering diagonally across the wide boulevard towards the second Sûreté car.

The French driver of a Citroën traveling fast behind the rickshaw leaned on his horn immediately when he saw the rickshaw pull out into his path. He could have braked and avoided a collision without difficulty, but the seemingly idiotic change of direction by the *pousse-pousse* coolie irritated him. On hearing the horn, Dong glanced frantically over his shoulder, but he was too late to swing aside, and one of the Citroën's big chromium head-lamps caught the hood fabric of the rickshaw and knocked it over. The car's front wheels ground the frail wooden vehicle to match-wood in an instant and the force of the collision sent Dong sprawling. As he fell, the pistol tucked inside his shirt flew free and clattered noisily across the road in a sudden vacuum of silence. It came to rest by Devraux's feet, and picking it up, his driver held it towards him with an astonished expression on his face.

Dong, stunned in the collision, rose unsteadily to his feet; his shoulder had been gashed and blood was soaking through the tattered remains of his shirt. When Devraux gesticulated angrily in his direction and shouted to his driver to seize him, he turned and began to run back the way he'd come. A crowd of goggle-eyed Annamese gathered instantly to watch the aftermath of what they imagined was a simple road accident, and Ngo Van Loc forced himself to remain quietly in their midst as the driver caught up with the injured Dong and frogmarched him back to the remaining Renault. He was near enough to hear Jacques Devraux give the driver curt instructions to take Dong immediately to Sûreté headquarters for interrogation, and when the car had gone, he walked numbly away along the riverbank, blinking back bitter tears of anger and despair.

8

A thousand tiny lanterns set in the high ramparts of the Nam Giao glimmered like yellow stars in the midnight darkness. Inside the sacred enclosure a chorus of imperial heralds called for silence, and their shrill voices, carrying easily on the soft night air, were audible in the hushed streets of the city far beyond its walls. Above each of the four gates illuminated banners emblazoned with golden Chinese characters marked the four points of the compass; a black flag identified the north, white the west, blue the east, while a blood-red standard swung lazily in the breeze above the open south gate, which according to the cult's age-old doctrines, gave access to Heaven.

In the center of the compound flaming oil cressets set on tall poles bathed the stepped terraces of the Azure Temple with flickering orange light. On the highest level three altars dedicated to Heaven, Earth and the Imperial Ancestors had been set up beneath a dark blue tabernacle of dyed animal hides, which betrayed the origins of the ancient cult among the desert nomads of Central Asia; a single opening in this sacred marquee allowed a broad beam of white light to escape southwards into the night, and beneath it a massed throng of silent dancers and musicians spilled down the steps of the lowest terrace and out through the open south gate into the darkness beyond.

Joseph and Lan were standing together in the group of specially invited guests who had joined the governor general's suite on the first terrace below the yellow-draped Altar of Incense. Joseph had been among the last to arrive, but a moment before the heralds' voices rang out, he forced his way through the close-packed crowd to a place on the steps beside the Annamese girl and her brother. In the deep silence that followed, all eyes turned towards the House of Fasting where the emperor had secluded himself fourteen hours earlier, and as the crowd shifted, Joseph felt the softness of Lan's silk-clad shoulder move unconsciously against his arm. He looked down quickly at her; for the evening she had knotted a square of pale green silk around her hair, and in the flickering torchlight her cheeks seemed to glow like polished amber. Already the clouds of incense swirling into the hot night air from the nearby altar were making him feel dazed and light-headed, but this new glimpse of her shy beauty and the tantalizing softness of her body sensed in that fleeting moment of contact induced in him a passionate yearning.

"Ring the bells! Beat the drums! The Son of Heaven approaches!"

The falsetto voices of the heralds quavered again, then the instruments of the massed musicians jangled and throbbed in greeting as a line of flickering torches appeared winding through the trees of the Sacred Grove that ringed the House of Fasting. When the emperor's golden litter came into sight, Joseph heard Lan let out a little gasp of admiration, and he looked up to find Bao Dai arrayed magnificently in the elaborate antique court dress of the emperors of China. Over yellow robes he wore a wide-sleeved purple surcoat embossed with mythological symbols which only a

236

sovereign might display; around his waist was clipped a gem-encrusted belt hung with ornaments of jade and precious metals which tinkled as he moved to ward off evil spirits, and from the fringes of his bejeweled crown dangled another twenty-four auspicious pendants. The young emperor's thin face was pale and taut, but the grandeur of the moment transfixed the crowd, and Joseph seized the opportunity to take the jade bracelet from his pocket. Without anyone noticing, he slipped it into Lan's hand and closed her fingers carefully around it before she had realized what he was doing.

The bracelet was still wrapped in its envelope of silk and she glanced at him with a mystified expression, holding it out of sight at her side; then perhaps she guessed what it might be and turned anxiously to make sure that Tam hadn't noticed anything.

"Prepare to enter! Strike gongs and drums!"

The emperor was borne slowly aloft to the terraces above, where subsidiary shrines were set up, and Lan, her face suddenly animated, touched Joseph's arm to draw his attention to the booted and gowned figure of her father pacing up the temple steps with other senior courtiers who were to act as co-celebrants; they were dressed with equal ceremonial extravagance in state coats of blue, green and gray and wore about their waists clanking belts of metal pendants. The ritualistic chanting and musical responses continued until the emperor and his entourage entered the tabernacle of the Azure Temple, then silence descended abruptly on the sacred enclosure. The French officials around Joseph and Lan immediately began to shuffle and converse in low tones, and the Annamese girl turned to her brother.

"Before the final rites begin, Tam," she whispered, "I'd like to show Monsieur Sherman our family's tree in the Sacred Grove. May I?" Tam nodded, and Lan turned back to smile at Joseph. "It's the highest honor for a family to be given a tree in the Sacred Grove of the Nam Giao — like receiving a coat of arms from the king of France." She pointed in the direction of one of the burning pyres that had been used to prepare sacrificial buffalo meat: the flames were guttering now, but their glow still lit the dark screen of tall larches nearby. "It's over there — would you like me to show you?"

Joseph nodded eagerly and fell into step beside her as she led the way through the crowd of dancers and musicians towards the Sacred Grove. By the dark bole of one of the larches, Lan stopped and pointed. "This is the tree of the Tran family. My great-great-grandfather planted it at the invitation of the Emperor Dong Khanh. . . . But please wait a moment." She glanced over her shoulder to see if Tam was watching them, then hastily opened the silk envelope and looked at the bracelet. When she raised her eyes to his they were shining in the firelight. "It's exactly like mine, Joseph. Wherever did you buy it?"

"I didn't buy it, Lan — it *is* your own bracelet."

She held it towards the light of the sacrificial pyre, inspecting the fine golden flecks in the blue stone, then stared at him in disbelief. "But how did you get it back?"

"I took a sampan up the river before dawn this morning and slipped into the tomb before it was light. As soon as the sun came up I swam across the lake to the spot beneath the bridge where you dropped it." His smile broadened. "I was lucky — the bottom of the lake was not too muddy and I only had to dive four or five times before I put my hand on it."

She shook her head in wonder. "I can hardly believe, Joseph, that you've done such a kind thing."

Joseph took the bracelet from her and slipped it on her left wrist. "I'm glad I've been able to make you smile again."

She held it away from her, admiring it, her mouth curved in an unconscious smile of pleasure. "I'll never be able to thank you enough, Joseph. You always seem to come to my rescue. First at the governor's palace, then at the tennis match — now here in Hue."

Joseph felt the familiar breathless sensation constrict his throat, and he took hold of her hand suddenly and pressed it to his lips. "I did it because I love you, Lan! I love you very much. I knew the moment I saw you praying at the tomb — you're so pure and good, so beautiful. I want to be with you always — to protect you and take care of you. I never want to leave your side." The words tumbled from him in an impulsive torrent, and he was suddenly afraid that she might find his passion offensive. But to his surprise she said nothing; he thought he felt her body tremble once, then she detached her hand gently from his grasp and half turned away to steady herself with one hand against the larch tree.

"I feel a little dizzy, Joseph," she said softly, pressing her other wrist against her brow in a little gesture of distress. "Perhaps it's all that incense. . . ."

He took her by the arm, his brow crinkling with concern. "Why don't we get a breath of fresh air in the street outside?"

She nodded mutely and together they walked towards the south gate, which still stood open to allow the blessings of Heaven to flow in.

At the moment that Joseph and Lan stepped into the narrow, tree-lined avenue leading to the River of Perfumes, Jacques Devraux was descending for the second time that night into the dank cellar beneath the city's Sûreté headquarters half a mile away. Fingers of green mold reached up walls from which all whitewash had flaked long ago, and as Devraux entered, his nose wrinkled involuntarily with distaste at the strong smell of sweat and stale urine that hung in the air.

Because the cellar was close to the river, the cracked concrete floor never dried out entirely and puddles of condensation glimmered in the light of a single unshaded bulb. Close to the ceiling a thick wooden beam passed through the cellar, and Ngo Van Dong's ankles were lashed to it by coarse hempen ropes that had already chafed raw weals around the lower parts of his legs. His hands were manacled behind his back and the weight of his long, thin body was half supported on the damp floor by his shoulders, but every time the half-caste Indian guard slammed his heavy wooden baton against the swollen, bloodied soles of Dong's feet, the convulsion that racked his body lifted his head clear of the floor.

Devraux had left his jacket in his office upstairs but he still wore the pale trousers of the suit in which he had watched the emperor's procession leave the Citadel and he stopped two or three yards away from the prisoner because experience had taught him that at that distance blood would not splash on them. His ravaged features betrayed no sign of emotion as he watched the half-caste's baton rise and fall, but on the twelfth blow he stepped forward and tapped the Indian on the arm, motioning him to stop. Dong's loud cries of pain subsided immediately to a low, continuous moaning noise, and when Devraux walked round to stand beside him, the Annamese opened his eyes and twisted his head to look up into his face.

"Who are you?" The tip of one of Devraux's pointed shoes struck Dong a gratuitous blow in the ribs. "Who sent you? The Communists?"

The injury to Dong's shoulder sustained in the collision with the Citroën had been treated, but the wound had opened again since, and blood was soaking through the dressings. Devraux looked at him hanging upside down, without compassion, then kicked him sharply in the ribs again. "Who were your accomplices?"

Dong gritted his teeth and remained silent as he had done for the past fourteen hours, and the Frenchman, losing patience suddenly, stepped up close to him and repeated the questions in a more threatening tone. But instead of answering, the Annamese jerked his head sideways and spat a large gobbet of blood-flecked spittle onto the pale material of Devraux's trousers.

The Sûreté chief didn't speak or move. For a long time he just stood and looked at the Annamese as he twisted slowly at the end of the rope. Then he turned and spoke to the half-caste in a matter-of-fact voice. "Give him some water now."

The half-caste untied the end of the rope and tautened it, drawing Dong's ankles closer to the beam. When he had re-fastened it, he fetched a bowl of water and a soggy cloth from a table at the far end of the cellar. Dropping to his knees he soaked the cloth in the bowl, then pressed it hard against Dong's face so that it blocked his mouth and water streamed out of it into his upturned nostrils. He worked with quick, practiced movements, holding the back of Dong's head with his free hand as the Annamese choked and struggled on the rope. After two applications the half-caste repeated the questions, but still Dong remained silent.

"Give him some more water," said Devraux dispassionately.

"I don't think he's going to talk," said the torturer, glancing anxiously up at his superior. "I think he'd rather drown."

"They all talk," replied Devraux in a dull voice. "I've seen a hundred of them hold out until they get the water. Give him some more."

The Frenchman stood and watched for a moment longer, then glanced impatiently at his watch. "I've got to attend the governor general's champagne reception at the Nam Giao," he said in an irritable voice. "I'll interrogate him again afterwards. Just keep watering him."

As Devraux hurried away up the cellar steps he heard the half-caste dip the cloth into the bowl, and a moment later Dong began choking again.

Flickering lanterns suspended in the trees above little wayside shrines cast dancing shadows on the faces of Joseph and Lan as they strolled towards the river through the balmy night. Just short of the waterfront Lan stopped beside one of the shrines and traced the golden Chinese characters on a silk-fringed banner. "*Wan Sui*," she murmured. "If only the emperor could really live ten

240

thousand years in peace, Joseph. It's a beautiful thought, isn't it?"

"I feel tonight as if we're going to live ten thousand years, Lan," said Joseph, moving close to her in the scented darkness.

"Perhaps we are." Her eyes sparkled as she reached out and touched one of the pine trees surrounding the little shrine. "These pines are symbols of longevity."

Joseph touched the tree too. "Then I'll wish for a long, happy life for both of us — together."

Their eyes met and they smiled at one another; Joseph, to his delight, detected a new spark of excitement in her gaze, an intimacy of expression that told him beyond any doubt that she too was intensely aware of the enchantment of the night. As they stood there, the liquid chimes of tiny silver bells carried on the still air from the top terrace of the Azure Temple, and Joseph lifted his head to listen. "The ceremonies have begun again, Lan," he said gently. "Shall we return now?"

Lan listened for a moment, her head on one side; then she shuddered and pulled a face. "They're burying the blood and hair of the buffaloes. I'm happy to miss that. There are still quite a few duties of that kind to be performed before the Imperial Communion begins."

They crossed the wide road to the bank of the River of Perfumes and strolled on under the trees. Lan closed her eyes and lifted her face to let the faint breeze blowing off the water play on her cheeks. "It's cooler now, Joseph. And the river is so beautiful. There seems to be a magic in the air here, doesn't there?"

Joseph nodded happily. "The white tiger and the blue dragon are obviously at peace with one another tonight." He glanced down to find her smiling at him with unexpected warmth; unbidden, she drew closer to him, and he put his arm around her slender shoulders.

Clusters of empty sampans were drawn up by the bank, some with dim lanterns illuminating the cushioned, mahogany interiors of their little cabins; others were in darkness, and Joseph wrinkled his nose at the sweet, acrid fragrance floating under the trees. A coolie called something unintelligible in Annamese as they passed, and Lan laughed in embarrassment.

"What did he say?"

"He asks if monsieur would like to smoke a pipe or two of opium while he listens to the rites. You can hire his sampan, he says, for half a piastre. Very clean."

Joseph laughed too; then he stopped and ran back to talk to the coolie, and a note changed hands. When he returned to her, he was grinning broadly. "Would you like a cool ride on the river?" He spread his hands. "Strictly no opium, I promise."

Her face clouded with doubt. "It's not proper, Joseph, for me to go on the river alone with you. If Tam were with us, it would be different."

"Just for a few minutes." He took her hands in his and smiled into her eyes. "Perhaps the river breezes will blow the cobwebs of incense from your head before we return to the Nam Giao."

She laughed uncertainly. "All right, as you are a visitor to Hue I must be a good hostess. We'll go just for a short while."

She allowed him to help her aboard, and he settled her in the cabin before returning to the stern. The boatman's grin broadened with delight when Joseph thrust another ten-piastre note into his hands, and he helped push the sampan out into the stream. When Joseph didn't return to sit beside her in the cabin, Lan looked over her shoulder and, seeing him standing on the stern, her expression changed to one of alarm.

"What are you doing, Joseph? Have you ever rowed a sampan alone before?"

His happy laughter echoed across the water as he removed his jacket. "No — but don't look so frightened, I've been watching the coolies and I'm dying to try it for myself. It can't be that difficult." He turned the bows of the long boat southwards and got it moving. "You see!"

His confident smile reassured her, and she moved to the mouth of the cabin and sat down on cushions, facing him. Silhouetted above her against the starry sky, he worked the oar with an easy rhythm, and she watched him in silence, wondering at his grace and strength. For several minutes he rowed the sampan upstream, brushing beneath the willows that leaned out from the bank; as the river turned in a gentle curve to the southeast he pointed inland. "Look, Lan, you can see the southern light shining from the Azure Temple." He clutched excitedly at the tresses of a willow tree, halting the sampan.

Lan stood up beside him to look in the direction of the slender finger of light pointing down the southern sky. The faint beat of gongs reached their ears, mingled with the sound of trumpets and bells; then a joyful chorus of female voices rose thrillingly above the music.

"They're singing the Hymn of Happy Augury."

All around them the willow fronds rustled and whispered in the breeze. "I suppose it's time we turned back," he said hesitantly.

She didn't reply, and when he looked down, her lovely face,

barely visible in the faint light from the stars, seemed constantly to be dissolving and re-forming among the willow leaves. From the distant Nam Giao the choir of female voices began to sing a new and plaintive hymn.

"It's the Chant of the Exquisite," murmured Lan in a dreamy voice. "The offerings of silk and jade are being made."

The boat rocked gently against the current, and Joseph dropped his hand lightly on her shoulder to steady her. "We must go now if we are to see the climax to the ceremony," he whispered.

To his surprise she turned and put her hand on his among the leaves and tendrils of the tree. "We can follow the sacred rites from here, Joseph," she said softly. "The spirits of this beautiful river seem to have ordained it."

For a long time he just stood and stared at her shadowy face. Then he looped the sampan's mooring rope quickly over a bough of the willow. "All right, if you're sure that's what you want."

"We'll be able to hear the music and the singing quite clearly. I know every part of the ritual. I'll describe it to you."

When he lifted her hand to kiss her fingers, she didn't try to move away. The warmth of his lips against her skin made her feel as though her soul were suddenly melting within her; a sweet, trembling helplessness seized her and she longed to feel the strength of his arms around her, longed to bury her face against his chest.

"Lan, I love you, I love you," he murmured as he pressed her to himself. "Do you feel it too?"

He wondered the first time if the gentle motion of the sampan, the pale starlight and the shifting willow vines were conspiring to deceive him, but the second time he had no doubt; although she didn't speak she had moved her head quite definitely in a little ecstatic motion of assent.

Inside the sacred tabernacle on the highest terrace of the Azure Temple, the hot, scented air swam in the light of a thousand beeswax candles as the emperor advanced for the third and last time to the Altar of Heaven and flung himself down before it. In the same instant his mandarins, their assistants and all the servers attending the shrines on the other terraces prostrated themselves on their altar mats. When the heralds on the terrace outside cried "Receive the Blessed Nourishment!" the emperor straightened slowly and took the proffered platter of roasted buffalo flesh. Raising it to his forehead he held it there with closed eyes for several seconds before handing it on.

Then the heralds, drawing out their words with a sonorous finality, voiced their concluding chant: "Drink . . . now . . . the . . . Wine . . . of . . . Happiness."

The emperor received the goblet offered with utmost reverence by an assistant and raised it aloft; the hush that had fallen over the Azure Temple deepened, and beyond its walls the entire city seemed to hold its breath. In that magical fragment of time the emperor, in accordance with beliefs that had endured throughout recorded history, was drawn into solemn communion with the Divine Majesty of Heaven.

In the shadows of the sampan's little matting cabin on the nearby River of Perfumes, Lan trembled as Joseph took her gently in his arms. Her exquisite nakedness sent a flood of stark strength coursing through him but at the same time the fragility of her beauty excited a countervailing storm of tenderness that held his strength in thrall. In the glow of the tiny lamp their wondering eyes met again and again as they murmured incoherent words of love; then the tender agony became unendurable for them both and they clung blindly to one another, crying aloud in unison.

When his breath at last returned, Joseph lay watching a tiny red spider run slowly in a zigzag line across the roof of the little cabin. Lan lay still in his arms, her face turned away, her unpinned hair a living garment of silken black filaments that covered her slender body to the waist; the sampan continued to rock gently on the quiet river, the willow branches continued to caress the cocoa palm fiber above their heads, and eventually the tiny red spider climbed slowly around the bamboo frame and disappeared into the soft night.

In the tabernacle of the Azure Temple they were burning the prayer tablets and the offerings. The mysterious moment had passed; the Son of Heaven was already returning slowly to the House of Fasting.

9

Several times during his first week in Hanoi, Joseph had cause to wonder whether someone might be deliberately following him. On two or three different occasions he noticed the same languid French youth sauntering along the pavement at his back as he walked between his hotel and the archives of the École Française d'Extrême Orient; while strolling in the evening too through the cobbled streets of the northern capital's old craft quarter, he had spotted the youth, dressed in a pale tropical suit and trilby hat, apparently wandering aimlessly in the same area. But his suspicions remained vague and half-formed; it never occurred to him that his presence in the city could be of any interest to the French security authorities, and because his head was awhirl with excited thoughts of Lan and his new discoveries in the archives, he never focused his full attention on the possibility that he might be under surveillance.

Images of Lan had filled his thoughts, waking and sleeping, from the moment he left Hue. In his mind's eye he saw again and again her happy smile as she gazed at her recovered bracelet in the Sacred Grove; constantly he recalled the vision of her lying naked in his arms during those ecstatic moments on the River of Perfumes, saw her walking demurely beside him the next day in the garden of her father's official residence inside the red-walled Citadel and waving to him finally from the gateway when he reluctantly took leave of her. The close proximity of her family on that last day had made her reserved with him again, and she had insisted on his observing the proper Annamese formalities of courtship even when they were alone. Without saying so directly, she had indicated by her subdued manner that she had suffered some pangs of remorse because of her impetuous behavior the previous night, but this remorse had not entirely obscured her feelings for him. Once or twice her eyes had shone with that same inner excitement when she looked at him, and she had allowed him to hold her hand briefly, out of sight of the house beside the lotus pool. He had wanted to talk to her father there and then, but she had insisted that they allow some time for him to recover from Kim's defection. Eventually he had agreed reluctantly to her suggestion to wait until he returned to Saigon from Hanoi.

During that last meeting there had been a moment of anxiety for him when she announced in a grave voice that she had to ask him a very important question — the date of his birth. He had tried to make light of it, but her face had remained serious. When he told her the day and the year, she had counted on her fingers for a moment, then revealed that he had been born in the Year of the Dog.

"It's most important in my country to know in what lunar year you were born," she told him. "Before anybody considers marriage they must see if they are the children of harmonious moons."

245

"What year were you born, Lan?" he had asked anxiously.

"In 1915 — the Year of the Cat."

"The Year of the Cat?" he had repeated in alarm. "Can people born in the Year of the Cat and the Year of the Dog live in harmony?"

Her face had remained grave for a moment longer and his heart had stood still — then she had laughed at him outright. "When Buddha invited all the animals to appear before him to have the years named after them, only twelve came," she explained, still smiling. "But in our horoscopes the animals don't behave as they do in reality. Cat and dog may fight on earth — but the astrologers say that if the 'Cat' is female, she can bring peace and serenity to the life of a male 'Dog.' "

"Then our signs are favorable!" He had grasped her hands more tightly, feeling suddenly weak with love for her, and she smiled happily back at him.

"It seems they are, Joseph . . . but it's necessary to have detailed horoscopes cast by an expert to be really sure."

Her family had arranged to return to Saigon later that same day, and she and Joseph had taken leave of one another by the ornamental stone archway leading from the garden. He had kissed her hand tenderly again as he had done on the river, and for a moment her eyes had misted with tears of happiness.

"I'll write every day from Hanoi," he had promised fervently, and when he hurried off towards the railway station she waited, smiling and waving beneath the flag-draped archway until he disappeared from her sight.

As he journeyed north his love for her seemed to grow by the hour and by the time he reached Hanoi he was filled with an acute physical longing for her. He found the northern capital sweltering under unseasonably hot temperatures, and the heat made concentration by day difficult and sleep almost impossible by night — even under the breeze of an electric fan. Because his thoughts revolved entirely around Lan, he found his eyes drawn constantly to the sinuous Annamese girls moving gracefully among the city crowds, and their tantalizingly narrow haunches, the delicate tilt of their tiny breasts, the sensuous slap of their bare feet on the pavements all flashed the same messages of arousal to his brain. Often he groaned aloud in his throat as he walked: was he desperately seeking Lan in every Annamese girl, he wondered? Was he really honorably in love with her? Or were his senses, fevered by this exotic land, falling prey to impossible lustful desires? Sometimes in the fragrant dusk of evening in certain streets, a wire-wheeled *pousse-pousse* would pull silently to the pavement and a diminutive, amber-cheeked girl would whisper endearments in sibilant French to heighten his growing physical torment.

His obsessive love for Lan affected his work deeply too; instead of concentrating exclusively on Annam's historic kinship with Peking, he found himself driven to delve deeper each day into the dusty files of the archives in an effort to broaden his understanding of her country and its people. He spent many hours trying to discover the origins of her race and its language among the many tribes that had flooded southwards down the Indochina peninsula in the dawn of history, but discovered that after tracing vague links to the peoples of Indonesian stock who had settled the islands of the Pacific, French scholars had been unable to untangle the true roots of the Annamese and their culture. But wherever they came from, they had established their distinct nation — Nam Viet — in the northeastern coastal strip of the Indochina peninsula two thousand years before the French arrived, then throughout a long turbulent history struggled indefatigably to throw off China's tutelage. This struggle had lasted more than a thousand years, but during that time they had also expanded their own territory southwards in wars of conquest that exterminated a weaker peace-loving people known as the Cham. Joseph was surprised to find that even while the Annamese emperors were themselves paying tribute to Peking in later centuries, they established a supremacy in the peninsula which allowed them in turn to demand tribute themselves from the princes of Laos and Cambodia; when the French arrived from the other side of the world in the nineteenth century to colonize them, the tenacious people of Nam Viet were then poised to extend their own domains farther through armed invasion of the neighboring Cambodian and Lao peoples.

Joseph also found documents and papers that showed how the French government had been dragged into Indochina by merchant adventurers and soldiers who foraged for land and power for themselves before persuading Paris to support them. One vital memorandum written in 1790 by one of these soldiers of fortune urged France to seize Indochina because her great rival, Britain, already possessed India and Burma; if France wished to avoid humiliation and remain a contender for power and influence in the world, she must seize some territory in Asia, the memorandum insisted. No mention was made of the noble ideals of the *"mission civilisatrice,"* Joseph noted, until long after France was established in Indochina for much baser reasons of power. The archives also revealed that no consistent plan as to how the colony should be run had ever been conceived in Paris; policies had been chopped and changed haphazardly with the appointment of successive governors, and the picture that emerged from the hundreds of documents he scanned was one of accident and muddle which had led gradually by default to the crass exploitation of a people backward only in comparison with the advanced countries of Europe. He found studies by French scholars too, analyzing the brutal and bloodthirsty periods of Annamese history, and the files on this topic had been brought up to date with Sûreté Générale documentation of the Red Terror of 1931. Verbatim accounts of the Sûreté's own interrogations, bound in printed booklets, told in gory detail how Communists had murdered and tortured landlords, mandarins and even their own renegade supporters, and Joseph shuddered as he read the documents. Men and women, according to the interrogations, had been burned, butchered, buried alive and drowned in a sustained burst of medieval savagery, and somehow the horrors of which he read brought back to his mind the note of deep loathing in Ngo Van Loc's voice when he spoke in the market of how the French had murdered ten thousand of his countrymen during the uprisings of 1930–31. A conviction grew in him that the Annamese were an ill-starred people destined always to be haunted by violence and tragedy, and these thoughts oppressed him greatly. In an effort to lift his spirits he decided late one afternoon towards the end of his second week to immerse himself in the tranquillity of the Pagode des Corbeaux — the Pagoda of Ravens — a famous fifteenth-century Confucian temple dedicated to the study of literature.

The temple, built on the banks of the city's *Grand Lac*, was deserted when he arrived, and above its ancient grove of mango trees the flock of glossy-winged birds that had roosted there for centuries were wheeling in a last frenzy of activity before settling for the night. But even inside the ancient walls a sense of peace eluded him; as he paced slowly through the five connecting courts of the temple he realized that somebody had followed him there, and when he stopped to inspect stone tablets bearing the names of distinguished mandarin scholars of the glorious three-hundred-year Le dynasty, he clearly heard the sound of stealthy footsteps behind him. Turning abruptly he caught a glimpse of the same languid youth who had shadowed him earlier in his visit; for an instant their eyes met and the youth seemed almost to sneer at him before moving out of sight behind one of the lacquered pillars in the adjoining court.

Beyond the windows the dark shapes of ravens were whirling and shrieking in the luminous dusk and Joseph felt suddenly unnerved — both by the gloomy temple and by the youth who was so obviously following him now without making much effort to conceal himself. His reading of the Sûreté interrogations during the afternoon had left a strong impression in his mind of that organization's ruthless vigilance, and suddenly he was certain that for reasons he didn't understand he was being shadowed by one of its agents. Moving quietly on his toes, he walked back to the place where he had seen the youth conceal himself and stepped round the pillar.

"Why are you following me?" he demanded brusquely in French.

The youth showed no sign of surprise and made no attempt to answer or move away. Instead he gazed unblinkingly back at Joseph with a composed, insolent expression, and after a moment the American turned on his heel and strode out of the temple. Halfway along one of the tree-lined avenues leading to the pagoda he turned and looked back; the agent had come out of the pillared entrance and was standing gazing after him quite openly. A moment later a black official-looking Citroën slid into the temple forecourt from another direction, and the youth approached it deferentially. The rear window was wound down, and the youth leaned towards the rear seat. There was not sufficient light for Joseph to identify the car's occupant, but he saw the youth nod once in his direction as he talked; then he stepped back respectfully as the rear window was wound up again and the car came on slowly in his direction.

When it drew abreast of him and the rear door swung open across his path, Joseph was astonished to find himself looking into the gaunt, wasted face of Jacques Devraux.

"We can avoid unnecessary unpleasantness, Joseph, if you accept my offer to drive you back to your hotel." Devraux spoke in a flat impersonal voice and his clouded eyes gazed over the American's shoulder as he waited for his reply.

"I should have known you were responsible for having me followed," said Joseph, glowering angrily at the Sûreté chief. "Is this an official arrest?"

"I want to talk to you."

"To apologize for having me followed without reason?"

"That conclusion might be a trifle premature."

Joseph looked at him sharply. "What do you mean?"

"Please get in the car."

Reluctantly Joseph climbed into the rear seat and Devraux signaled the chauffeur to drive on. "I won't waste any time," said the Sûreté officer, sitting back in his seat and staring ahead. "I want to know why you met and spoke with the released prisoner Ngo Van Loc in Saigon."

Joseph turned and stared incredulously at the Frenchman's impassive face. "You were having me followed even then?"

"You met a known Communist who's already been involved in plots to overthrow our government here. What did you discuss with him?"

Joseph continued to stare. "That's my business. Why should it interest you?"

"Did you discuss political action?" Devraux's voice was cold and distant, as if he had no personal interest in the response.

"I refuse to answer your questions. It's none of your business."

Devraux sank back wearily against the leather upholstery and lit a cheroot, then opened the window to toss the match into the darkness. As he took the little cigar between his fingers, Joseph noticed that his hand shook slightly. "If I told you that an attempt was made on my life in Hue, would that make you think I had the right to ask you some questions?"

"An attempt on your life?" Joseph echoed the words in disbelief. "Do you know who it was?"

"Ngo Van Dong — Loc's son."

"But how does that involve me?"

"Under questioning, Dong claimed that he and his father were informed of my whereabouts by you. Is that true?"

The limousine was purring along the Quai Clemenceau, heading towards the Lake of the Restored Sword, and Joseph gazed out of the window into the gathering darkness in a horrified silence. "Yes, I suppose it's true," he said at last in a small voice. "But it was accidental — just an innocent remark."

"Our agents saw you waiting on the dockside for two hours. Do you expect us to believe that it was just a coincidence that you arrived in our colony as large numbers of Communist prisoners were being amnestied?"

Devraux drew deeply on his cheroot while he waited for an answer, and in its reflected glow he looked again for a fleeting moment more like the fierce-eyed hunting guide who had conducted their expedition eleven years earlier.

"Yes, it *was* just a coincidence. Paul told me he thought Loc had been in Paulo Condore — and I saw in the newspaper a ship was due in."

"But why did you want to see Loc?"

Joseph hesitated; the Frenchman was asking his questions in a toneless voice without turning his head to look at him. "I wanted to ask him about a personal matter," he said slowly.

Beside him the Frenchman seemed to be sitting very still. "You mean about the death of your brother?"

Joseph's throat suddenly went dry, and he was surprised to find himself nodding in agreement. "Yes — it was Loc who told me that Chuck had died trying to save my father."

Devraux shifted in his seat, then relaxed. "I think I understand now."

For a while they rode in silence; then Joseph leaned forward in his seat again. "But you really believed I was part of a murder conspiracy, didn't you? And I suppose your agents here expected to find me plotting in a pagoda somewhere to overthrow French rule."

"I didn't want to believe that," said Devraux, closing his eyes as though with fatigue. "But such ideas are not as fantastic as they appear. Undercover agents of the Comintern are working all over Asia — many of them are Europeans. So why not Americans too? Idealistic Marxists almost invariably come from wealthy, middle-class families. We can't afford to assume that every white-skinned visitor to Indochina is a devoted admirer of France."

"Perhaps if your government didn't exploit the people here so ruthlessly they wouldn't want to revolt against you," said Joseph grimly. "Maybe if your countrymen didn't milk the land of all the rubber, coal and rice they can lay their hands on, and didn't beat the *pousse-pousse* coolies in the streets, Loc and people like him wouldn't be trying to kill you."

Devraux opened his eyes again and drew reflectively on his cheroot. "You know from the files you've been reading in our archives, Joseph, that the history of the Annamese is full of bloodshed and brutality. There's a cruel streak in these people." He paused and exhaled smoke slowly towards the open window. "But they are also a deceptive race. They like to mislead with an outward show of passivity."

Joseph flinched inwardly, realizing that even the files he had been inspecting had been closely monitored by the Sûreté. A protest rose to his lips but he stifled it.

"Ngo Van Loc and his wife were spying on me for years before I found out. Their younger son, Hoc, murdered a rubber plantation director without reason — then they all turned up at Yen Bay and tried to do the same to Paul. They seem to be pursuing a pointless personal vendetta against us." He stopped speaking and turned his gaze on Joseph for the first time. "And Dong's arrest doesn't seem to have cooled them down. Since he was locked up, my men have detected one or two other furtive attempts to check my movements. My house servants have been threatened and pumped for information. . . ." He shrugged and turned away again, and his voice trailed off as though from lack of interest.

They had entered the Avenue Beauchamp, that ran beside the Lake of the Restored Sword, and glancing out of the window, Joseph saw that the moon was beginning to rise; a broad path of white light was flooding across the placid expanse of water, and he wanted suddenly above all else to be gone from the car. "If I'm not under arrest, Monsieur Devraux, I'd prefer to get out here," he said curtly. "I'd like to breathe some fresh air before dinner."

Devraux immediately signaled his driver to stop and opened the door. He allowed Joseph to climb out, but when the American turned to take his leave, he found that the Sûreté man had stepped out behind him. After giving instructions to the driver in rapid French, he fell into step beside Joseph. "You told me you spoke to Ngo Van Loc in all innocence," he said, lighting a fresh cheroot and glancing up at Joseph through a new flurry of smoke and flame. "Well, let me warn you that in Indochina innocence can be a very dangerous quality. The Annamese are not 'innocent'; they are an infinitely cunning people."

Joseph didn't feel like replying, and they strolled on beneath the gnarled trees at the water's edge in silence.

"Your concept of colonialism is a little 'innocent' too, if you'll forgive the term," said the Frenchman gently. "Perhaps the white man's dealings with the Orient have always been motivated by a basic, indefensible greed, and perhaps one day we'll have to pay a price for that. But there's never been any program of calculated evil mapped out by France here. Running colonies has always been a chaotic sort of business. But it's not all one-way traffic either. With the righteous part of their souls Frenchmen have always felt compelled to offer unselfish enlightenment and education to these people back in France. As a result, the best Annamese minds go off and soak up our knowledge — then come home and organize violent revolution against us."

"But why is it we never seem to learn anything here ourselves in return?" asked Joseph, feeling his interest aroused despite himself.

"You've been here twice already, haven't you? You've been in the jungles, the temples, walked in the crowded streets. You've felt the mysterious power of the East set your blood frothing like champagne, haven't you? Every European who ever comes here feels it. It's a land of great extremes, so vastly different from your own Virginia or my birthplace in Normandy that we really never learn to adjust. The mountains and jungles are hostile, the rice fields unending — and all the time the fierce sun and the wet heat force all growth to its limits and overexcite our nerves and emotions. The land teems with so much life that death doesn't seem to matter. Animals kill animals, men kill animals, and men kill one another too — it's all part of a brutalizing process. Violence is commonplace, an everyday occurrence, and our senses become permanently drunk with all this pulsating vitality. We respond to the heat like moths to a lamp. It's a land that fires the senses, not the intellect. That's why we don't learn anything. It's a land so elemental that sooner or later the brute climbs out of every man. Nobody's immune."

Devraux's voice had taken on a bitter, almost resentful, edge as though he were reliving his own past as he spoke. His hand was shaking more noticeably as he drew on the cheroot, and Joseph thought he sensed a growing tension in him.

"Then the people get under your skin. Because they're small and graceful, they seem to possess greater refinement than us. They seem so deft and subtle, don't they, and make us feel gross and clumsy beside them? Because they've been victimized by the elements for so long, they've cultivated the inner self to a high degree. The teachings of Buddha appear to have proved the futility of both ambition and remorse and the mystical rites they perform seem to give them access to secrets of the soul from which we're barred. All this devotion to tranquillity and spiritual harmony is very seductive to the restless souls newly arrived from Europe and America where physical activity is admired above all else. But perhaps most of all it's the fragile golden bodies of the women, isn't it? They're almost like toys, with their exquisite little hands and feet. Their passive beauty, too, rouses the blood like no other woman can." The Frenchman paused and raised a quizzical eyebrow in Joseph's direction. "Does what I'm saying strike a chord with you?"

Joseph stared at him, taken aback by the implication of the Frenchman's words. "So you had me followed all night in Hue too?" The Frenchman ignored the question, and Joseph felt his anger rise. "Perhaps, Monsieur Devraux, you should explain precisely why you're telling me all this."

"To give you a chance to think what you are doing. Bewitching first impressions aren't everything. Excessive love for the exotic can destroy the white European in the Orient. Many men think they go away from here with their souls intact — but then find in their own countries they've been profoundly changed by their experiences without knowing it. They become outcasts among their own people because everything at home seems insipid in comparison with the East. Then usually they're lured back again by the siren call of what has already ruined them. Try to see things as they really are. Stay as long as I have and you'll see that first enchantment turn to tropical languor and bad temper. All your restraint and self-discipline can dissolve here. The tropics too often drain away the energy and rot the moral fiber of good men. They come to despise that native finesse that they found so seductive in the beginning because they can't match it." Devraux paused and drew a long breath. "These lands are deeply inhospitable to men with white skins, Joseph — and too often that compels them to commit acts of which they can't be proud."

They had reached the waiting Citroën parked obediently by his driver at the roadside, and Devraux stopped beside it and crushed the stub of his cheroot against the bole of one of the lakeside trees. The glowing ashes fell to the ground in a bright shower, and after gazing at them for a second he squashed them out with his foot, twisting his sole with unnecessary force into the soft earth.

"You mean like that night of the storm in our jungle camp?" said Joseph in an emphatic undertone.

Devraux had opened the door of his car but he stopped and turned slowly back to face Joseph. In the direct light of the moon his face looked suddenly cadaverous.

"I couldn't sleep either," continued Joseph, watching the Frenchman closely. "And perhaps you ought to know that I've got a younger brother — who's ten years old now. At the end of that year my mother gave birth to a son."

Devraux stared at the American, a stricken expression slowly contorting his sallow features. "I'm sorry," he said in a half-whisper. "Tell her I'm sorry." Then he turned quickly away and got into the car without offering any parting salutation.

As the glow of the Citroën's taillights receded along the lakeside boulevard, the Sûreté chief was little more than an indistinct shadow in the rear seat, but Joseph could see that he sat with his shoulders hunched around his ears; something in his attitude seemed suddenly suggestive of hopelessness and despair, and the moment the car disappeared an urgent, indefinable anxiety seized Joseph. For a long time he stood without moving, staring

254

distractedly across the lake; on their twin islands, the old temples, symbols of an ancient and enigmatic Asia, were silhouetted sharply against the pale gold disc of the rising moon.

10

When the red-lacquered moon gate of the Imperial Delegate's residence in Saigon swung open for the second time in response to Joseph's impatient ringing of its little bronze bell, the same Annamese servant girl who had sent him away earlier in the day appeared again. She smiled shyly at him just as she had done that morning when she informed him that Mademoiselle Lan and her father were unable to receive visitors, and for an anxious moment he feared she was about to give him the same message. Then to his immense relief she stood back and motioned him inside.

The house, set at the end of an avenue of coconut palms and shaded by taller trees, was built in the traditional Annamese style; its pale, stuccoed walls were capped by ornamental crimson roofs, and the upper floors opened onto a curved verandah supported on red-lacquered pillars. As they approached the house, Joseph looked eagerly for some sign of Lan coming out to welcome him, but the steps beneath the verandah remained disappointingly deserted.

Inside, walking on polished teak floors, he was led past a succession of shaded rooms where French period ormolu and filigree blended discreetly with the hanging silks and sculpted wood of oriental furnishings. The ancestral altar visible in the austerely furnished principal room was decked with gold name tablets, framed photographs and incense burners, and Joseph saw a servant reverently setting out fresh bowls of fruit and flowers around them. He was conducted finally to a room where carved tables had already been set out for tea beside keg-shaped porcelain stools and he was left alone there for several minutes. A deep silence pervaded the house, and as he waited, his sense of foreboding grew.

The five-day rail journey from Hanoi had seemed agonizingly slow, and on his arrival in Saigon he had rushed straight to the house, unannounced. The servant girl's rebuff and her request that he return for an appointment later in the afternoon had immediately intensified the disquiet that had plagued him ever since his conversation with Jacques Devraux beside the Lake of the Restored Sword. Because of that unease he had rounded off his research hurriedly the following day and arranged to travel south again by the first available train. On the journey he had been unable to escape his ominous thoughts; although they defied rational analysis, the joy and happiness he'd glimpsed in Hue seemed irrevocably threatened, and his desire to marry Lan and spirit her away to safer, more familiar climes quickly became an obsession. Waiting alone in the quiet room to speak with her father, he realized that the moment of decision was near, and he felt the palms of his hands dampen with perspiration.

Because of his distracted state of mind he didn't notice them at first when Lan and Tran Van Hieu appeared soundlessly in the doorway. When he did look up, the Annamese mandarin, dressed in a simple black silk coat and cap, bowed low, and Joseph rose hurriedly to his feet to bow in return. Behind him Lan hesitated then smiled formally before seating herself on a stool set close at her father's side.

"I trust your visit to Hanoi has been crowned with success." Tran Van Hieu smiled courteously as he spoke his sibilant French, but Joseph saw immediately that his manner was strained.

"Two weeks was hardly enough. It's a fascinating city."

The Annamese nodded gravely, and Joseph shot a quick glance at Lan. He had considered saying that the interval had been too long an absence from his daughter, but if she had suffered the same agonies of separation, she gave no outward sign. She was dressed in a somber, unadorned *ao dai* of brown silk, and its very drabness served in Joseph's eyes to heighten the freshness of her beauty. But although he was sure she must have felt his eyes on her, she continued to gaze fixedly at her father as if the tender passion of their lovemaking on the River of Perfumes had occurred only in his fevered imagination.

"You must forgive me for not receiving you earlier, Monsieur Sherman," said the Annamese quietly, "but the tragic news from Hue concerning the father of Captain Paul Devraux has caused us all great personal distress — as I'm sure it has you."

"What news?" Joseph straightened suddenly in his seat.

Tran Van Hieu looked startled. "Forgive me, Monsieur Sherman, I assumed you'd heard. . . ."

"What happened?"

"Communist assassins last night murdered the father of Captain Devraux." The face of the mandarin colored faintly with embarrassment. "A terrible, senseless crime that makes all honorable Annamese feel deeply ashamed."

Lan was staring at the floor, and he saw that her face, too, was pale. The servant girl entered at that moment and placed steaming beakers of scented tea on each of the little tables beside them.

"How was he killed?" asked Joseph in a shocked whisper.

"He was shot many times in his bed. There were no signs of a struggle. His murderers must have entered his room while he was still asleep."

Joseph stared at the mandarin, aghast.

"My family and I are particularly saddened because only two or three days ago Captain Devraux made known to me his feelings for my daughter, Lan. But his father unfortunately died without knowing that our families were soon to be joined." Tran Van Hieu looked keenly at Joseph, then picked up his little porcelain beaker and sipped the steaming tea.

Beside her father Lan sat unmoving, her head bent, her eyes directed towards the floor. With the fingers of one hand she plucked distractedly at a loose thread in her dress, but otherwise she betrayed no emotion.

"I'm lost for words," said Joseph in a hollow voice. "It's a terrible shock to hear such news at a time when I should be offering my congratulations to Paul and Lan." He tried to sip the scalding tea, but his hand began to tremble and he had to put the tiny cup down.

"I shall be attending the funeral with members of my family of course, Monsieur Sherman," said Tran Van Hieu quietly. "That unfortunately will leave me no time to help you with your historical researches." He smiled formally in his daughter's direction. "Lan took the liberty of telling me that was the subject you wished to raise with me today."

Joseph glanced sharply at Lan, but found her staring fixedly into her lap. Inside he felt suddenly cold and sick and he was seized by an insane urge to kick over the little carved tables and rage wildly at the composed Annamese mandarin and his silent daughter. He wanted to shatter their composure by yelling that despite all the stifling Annamese codes of behavior he and Lan had pledged and fulfilled their profound love for one another on the river only two weeks before. They were still deeply in love and he insisted on taking her away to America to marry him! She didn't love Paul Devraux at all and he, Joseph Sherman, wouldn't allow her to marry a French officer out of misguided loyalty to her collaborationist father! He wanted to knock over the furniture, smash the teacups and drag her bodily from the house, but the implacable stillness of Tran Van Hieu's features as he sat looking silently at him from his seat only a few feet away seemed to paralyze Joseph's will to act.

"Is Captain Devraux still in Saigon?" he asked lamely at last. "I would like to express my condolences to him."

"Captain Devraux has already left for Hue to arrange his father's funeral," replied the mandarin in a flat voice. "But I would be more than happy to pass on any message you have to him."

Joseph looked distractedly back and forth from father to daughter, but still Lan studiously avoided his gaze. "Please tell Paul how deeply sorry I was to learn of his father's death," he said dully. "I saw Monsieur Devraux in Hanoi the day before I left. Tell Paul I'll write to him."

"Of course, it shall be done." Tran Van Hieu's voice was suddenly more brisk and businesslike. "I think my daughter might already have told you that her brother Kim has chosen to disgrace himself by associating publicly with the Bolshevik movement. Needless to say, he has caused us all great pain. Now with the murder of Monsieur Devraux by Communist assassins, the threat from that quarter to our country's stability has been accentuated. It is a time when all Annamese patriots should be taking pains to emphasize their loyalty and allegiance to our French protectors, and that is why, apart from personal considerations, I'm especially happy that our family is to be linked by marriage just now to an honorable family of France."

Tran Van Hieu's gaze had rested unwaveringly on Joseph as he spoke, and something in the deliberate manner of his speech made Joseph suspect that he knew the real reason for his visit to the house.

"Unfortunately, Monsieur Sherman," continued the mandarin in the same brisk tone, "this tragic assassination is causing me considerable extra work in my capacity as official representative of the Hue court. Therefore, I can't spare as much time as I would otherwise have liked, to converse with you. I hope you will pay my respects to your esteemed father and your family in America."

Tran Van Hieu stood up, obviously preparing to leave the room, and for a fleeting moment Joseph thought that Lan would remain to talk alone with him. But the Annamese touched his seated daughter's shoulder in an unmistakable signal, and she rose to stand obediently beside him. Joseph stood up too, looking desperately at Lan, feeling something close to panic rising in him at his inability to break through the invisible barriers that kept him from her.

"I expect I shall be leaving on the first ship tomorrow," he said, making up his mind suddenly, "so I will say my goodbyes now."

Tran Van Hieu inclined his head in a little bow of acknowledgment, then turned to his daughter, who raised her head just enough to direct a formal smile of farewell at Joseph. "Lan and I wish you a safe journey home, Monsieur Sherman. If you should visit our country again, please come to call on us." He stood aside, and as though by an unseen command, the servant girl who had shown Joseph in appeared to conduct him to the gate once more.

Joseph darted one last glance at Lan, but seeing the same expression of indifference in her eyes, he turned miserably away and followed the servant girl into the garden.

As the steamer taking him away from Saigon slipped down the winding river at dawn next day, Joseph stood on the deck and stared back at the twin spires of the cathedral for as long as they were visible. When their pointed pinnacles finally disappeared from sight beneath the spreading sea of vegetation, he went to his cabin and threw himself headlong on his bunk. Inside his head a dark curtain of desolation descended, and all his strength seemed to leave him. Outside, the shimmering green jungle, engorged by its daily diet of violent death, crawled closer about the river; gradually the light itself turned eerily green, and as the land which by turns had both fascinated and appalled him began to slip away, it seemed to Joseph that he was being borne deeper into a narrowing green tunnel that wound itself ever more tightly about the ship as it strove to force a passage to the open sea.

PART FOUR

War and Famine

1941–1945

In the spring of 1940 German forces overran Denmark, Norway, Holland and Belgium before forcing France to capitulate in June; as a result, twelve thousand miles away in Southeast Asia, the French governor general of Indochina, following the lead of the collaborationist Vichy government at home, surrendered control of the Annamese territories to the Japanese Imperial Army that was then matching the Nazi victories in Europe with its own expansionist conquests in China. Thereafter, for the duration of the war, the French authorities in Indochina collaborated peacefully with Japan, supplying her with rice, coal, rubber and other raw materials. This humiliation of France by an Asian nation destroyed completely the image of white colonial invincibility that had endured for almost a century and gave fresh encouragement to the native Communists and other anti-French groups in Cochin-China, Annam and Tongking. In June 1941 Hitler tore up the two-year-old Soviet-German Neutrality Treaty and invaded the Soviet Union, and this too proved to be a vital turning point for the Annamese Communists, because overnight along with the Russians they became allies of the Anglo-American forces in the fight against the Axis powers. In the closing months of 1941 the Japanese used Indochina to concentrate their land and sea strength for the massive onslaughts launched in the first week of December against Malaya, Hong Kong, Guam, the Philippines, the Dutch East Indies and other islands of the South Pacific; during the night of December 6, as Japanese aircraft carriers raced towards Hawaii to attack the American naval base at Pearl Harbor, Japanese land units surrounded all the compliant French garrisons in Indochina as a precaution — but the French troops offered no renewed resistance. Shortly after noon on the following day, Monday, December 8, 1941, President Franklin D. Roosevelt asked a joint session of Congress in Washington to declare war on Japan — an act which led to many Americans becoming involved in the affairs of Asia in the years that followed.

1

The hands of the gold-faced clock behind the chair of the vice-president of the United States stood at twelve forty-seven on the afternoon of Monday, December 8, 1941, as the eighty-two senators who had just heard Franklin D. Roosevelt call for a declaration of war against Japan filed grimly back from the hall of the House of Representatives into their own chamber in the north wing of the Capitol. Above their heads the public benches were filled to capacity with dismayed Americans who had flocked to Capitol Hill to watch the formal enactment of their country's entry into the spreading world conflict, and in the family gallery Joseph Sherman sat silently between his wife, Temperance, and his sixteen-year-old brother Guy, watching his father limp to his place close beside the vice-president's podium, supporting himself on a silver-topped malacca cane.

In his sixtieth year, Nathaniel Sherman's shock of hair and his mustache were a snowy white, but it wasn't for this reason alone that the senior Democratic senator from Virginia stood out among his fellow politicians; pale tentacles of scar still disfigured one side of his florid face, and the empty left sleeve of his jacket was tucked ostentatiously into his pocket. The shoulder from which an arm had been amputated in Saigon sixteen years earlier had been left badly misshapen, and he lowered himself with difficulty into the seat of his little mahogany desk. Despite his injuries, however, the senator still affected a flamboyant mode of dress, and for the solemn occasion had chosen to wear a cravat of dark silk and a stiff white collar with his Edwardian morning coat. While the roll was being called he leaned awkwardly on his writing box to scribble notes, and he didn't look up until the legislative clerk had finished reading for the second time the proposed House-Senate resolution declaring formally that a state of war existed between the United States and the Imperial Government of Japan.

"Is there any objection to the joint resolution being considered?" asked the vice-president of the United States, who was presiding.

When no voice responded the chairman of the Senate Foreign Relations Committee stood up. "Mr. President, because of the nature of the resolution, I would like to ask without further delay for the yeas and nays . . . ," he began, then paused when he saw Nathaniel Sherman rising awkwardly to his feet.

"If the distinguished senator from Texas will be gracious

263

enough to yield to me," he said slowly, "I wish to comment briefly on the joint resolution. . . ."

"Mr. President, on both sides of the chamber an understanding has been reached that all unnecessary remarks shall be withheld at this historic juncture," replied the Foreign Relations Committee chairman with ill-concealed irritation. "I was hoping there would be no comment."

"I appreciate the reasoning of the singularly able senator from Texas, Mr. President," continued Nathaniel Sherman, smiling deferentially towards the chair, "but if he will yield the floor further for just a moment or two, I'm sure I shall not interfere very greatly with what he has in mind."

In the family gallery, Guy Sherman grinned at his elder brother and leaned forward eagerly in his seat. On the other side of Joseph, Temperance too gazed down at her father-in-law with an awed expression. She had fallen under the spell of his mannered southern charm the very first time Joseph had invited her to meet his family at the Queen Anne plantation house on the James River five years before, and because of the unfailing courtesy he had shown her since, he had continued to grow in her estimation. The rich southern tones of his father's voice rising from the Senate floor produced in Joseph a different reaction, however; he rarely attended family political functions because he always had difficulty dismissing from his mind the impression that his father was motivated more by his desire to strike telling public postures than by deeply held political convictions. Occasionally he had wondered whether this attitude was uncharitable, but the suspicion nevertheless persisted, and as he scanned the rows of desks on the floor of the chamber below, he fancied he could detect similar expressions of irritation on both sides of the aisle. His father, however, remained stubbornly on his feet beside his desk, fully aware, Joseph was sure, that the mutilations of the old hunting accident made him a compelling, dramatic figure.

"Of course the senator has a right to speak if he insists," said the committee chairman distantly. "If he refuses to join the rest of the chamber in withholding comment, I have no alternative but to yield to him."

Nathaniel Sherman smiled warmly in response, then dipped his head graciously in acknowledgment towards the vice-president. "I'm grateful for the privilege accorded me to make these remarks, Mr. President. I happen to believe that the United States Senate is the greatest body of men to be found anywhere on earth — and as honest a body of men as ever assembled in any place in the world.

That's why in making this historic declaration today we should leave the world in no doubt as to our true feelings."

He paused, rocking back on his heels for effect, and let his gaze roam slowly around the chamber. "Out of peaceful Sunday skies, without a word of warning, Mr. President, Japan has launched the most infamous and cowardly attack in all history. She has violated our sovereignty and murdered our citizens, and this dastardly act lays bare a foul ambition that reeks of dishonor. To Japan, Mr. President, our reply should be this: 'You have unsheathed the sword, so by that same sword you shall die!' And to the president of the United States our reply should be: 'For the defense of everything that we hold sacred, we salute the colors and are ready to march!' "

He paused again, resting his one hand on the desk top, and his jaw jutted aggressively. "We are about to cast the most important vote we will ever be called upon to cast. We're about to do something no other branch of our government can do — declare war. The Constitution gives Congress this great power and this great responsibility, and our sentiments today must be expressed with the utmost clarity. Many times in recent weeks this chamber has echoed with damaging dissent. The voices of 'America First' isolationists have been raised all too frequently and such opinions have, I believe, been directly responsible for encouraging our enemies in their despicable acts. They have been allowed to hope that we might weaken from within — so today we must show them beyond any doubt that we are determined above all else to close this nation's ranks. We must demonstrate the strength of our will and our determination. Those are the twin foundation stones on which success must be built, and in this dark hour the whole round earth should be told that one hundred and thirty million Americans are united and resolved to fight. The world should know that America hates war, but America will always fight when she is violated . . ."

The senator's voice shook with emotion as he warmed to his theme, and in the gallery Temperance, visibly moved, shifted closer to Joseph and squeezed his hand. Her body, slender and athletic when they met, was now plumply voluptuous from the after-effects of her second pregnancy, and the soft waves of her chestnut hair framed cheeks that still shone with the unmistakable bloom of motherhood. When Joseph turned to look at her, he found that despite the concern she obviously felt, she wore the implacably serene expression of a contented childbearer on her unlined face, and feeling a surge of gentle affection wash through him, he squeezed her hand warmly in response.

They had met at a Baltimore exhibition of oriental art only a week or two after Joseph's return from Saigon and he had found her warm, uncomplicated American nature soothing after the emotional turmoil he had suffered in Asia. The daughter of a devout North Carolina lawyer, who had christened her two sisters Faith and Charity, she had been entranced by the Shermans' Queen Anne plantation home on her first visit to Charles County; she had sighed over the grandeur of the Great Hall and the sweeping staircase of carved walnut, claimed to be able to identify Joseph's ears and nose in the gilt-framed portraits of nine generations of Shermans on its paneled walls, and had charmed his father into allowing her to spend her first night in the creaking four-poster in which the family maintained General Robert E. Lee had slept during numerous visits as a young man.

Although Joseph had never admitted it, the simple charm of her enthusiasm for Virginia's golden age — which for him had paled rapidly as his fascination with the ancient Orient grew — had influenced him deeply in his decision to propose marriage to her. At a loose end after completing the manuscript of his book on the tributary states in June 1936, he had reluctantly taken over the running of the plantation estate at his father's suggestion — "just for a year or two" — so that the senator could devote himself more fully to political duties in Washington. Tempe, as his wife was affectionately known in the family, had just completed her law studies and had been thrilled at the prospect of becoming first lady in one of Virginia's most elegant and historic houses; they had been married in the late summer of that year in a lavish ceremony on the lawns overlooking a spectacular sweep of the James River and the senator, because of the warmth of his feelings for Tempe, had made the wedding the social event of the year, hiring two bands and inviting many leading political figures from Washington. Joseph had been uncomfortably aware at the time that the deep pangs of misery he suffered on his return from Indochina had influenced him to make a hasty marriage, but he had never spoken to her of the past and as the months and years slipped by, his painful memories had gradually faded from his mind.

Their first son, Gary, had been born a year later, the thirty-fifth Sherman of the male line to have begun life in the old plantation house, and while Joseph's energies were absorbed in mastering the unfamiliar day-to-day problems of managing the estate and its crops, Tempe threw herself with relish into the task of organizing the small army of black domestic servants who still ordered the social and domestic life of Virginians of their class. Although Joseph had felt a restlessness stir within him occasionally as their life settled into unchanging routines, the five years of marriage had been marked generally by a quiet contentment, and both he and Tempe had been delighted by the birth of their second son, Mark, in the early autumn of 1941.

The first reports of an ominous Japanese military buildup around Saigon that reached the United States in early November had made Joseph realize suddenly that a year or two had gone by without his giving any thought at all to his blighted love affair with the beautiful Annamese girl. Then mental images of Japan marching her modern military legions through the ancient lands where he had once felt so enraptured by the past made him wonder how Lan and her family might be faring. Had she married Paul Devraux after all? Had they continued to live in Saigon? And if they were still there, how was Paul himself faring, soldiering under the tutelage of the Japanese? Such thoughts drifted in and out of his mind throughout that autumn, but the passage of time seemed to have dulled his interest and he told himself that what he felt was no more than curiosity for people and events that could no longer affect his own life.

Like everybody else, however, he had been stunned by the momentous events of that first Sunday in December. News of the blazing, broken ships and dying sailors, coming over the radio just after he and his family had finished a leisurely lunch in their paneled dining room, had made him and all other Americans realize suddenly that the vast empty wastes of the Pacific could no longer protect them from the spreading turmoil of war in Asia. Throughout that Sunday he and Tempe had discussed their apprehensions in hushed tones so that their small son, Gary, shouldn't hear, but it wasn't until Joseph sat listening to his father talk pugnaciously on the floor of the Senate about retaliation that he became fully aware of what his true reaction had been all along — a subdued sense of elation!

The raid on Pearl Harbor would force America to carry the war deep into Asia, and instinctively he knew his own involvement would be inevitable. The war would almost certainly take him back to the continent whose history had fascinated him for so long, and the surge of pleasure he experienced at the prospect made him appreciate clearly for the first time just how unsatisfying his rural existence had become. This sudden awareness of his true feelings made him blush inwardly, and he glanced quickly at Tempe, fearing that something of these guilty thoughts might have

267

showed on his face. But his wife, to his relief, remained oblivious; she had already turned her attention back to his father, who still held the floor below them.

". . . For a long time Japan has been swaggering around Asia looking for war, but now, Mr. President, let Japan be in no doubt — she's got a real war on her hands! The United States is well on the way to securing a navy that will dominate two oceans, and an air corps that will command an all-skies airplane fleet. By attacking Hawaii, Japan probably hoped to keep us on the defense at home. But we can tell Japan loud and clear from this chamber today, Mr. President: 'We will not stay at home — and we will not stay on the defense!' "

Once more Nathaniel Sherman paused lengthily to heighten the impact of his words, and in the sudden silence it became clear that the entire Senate and the public gallery had fallen under the spell of his skillful oratory. For a moment he gazed around the chamber, nodding his head fiercely. "Let there be no mistake, Mr. President," he continued at last, speaking more quietly than before. "This war is our war now — and not only in Asia. We will have to fight in Europe too — and we'll win in both arenas. Today we announce: 'The American people are going to take hold, and when they're finished there'll be a new order. This order for the marauding nations will be: Keep the international law! Maintain the peace of the world! Dismiss your robber bands! Get back to the confines of your own country — and stay there!' "

He sat down abruptly as he finished speaking and stared belligerently towards the United States flag behind the vice-president. From the public gallery there was scattered applause, and even the senator from Texas, who had ceded the floor so reluctantly, nodded approvingly in Nathaniel Sherman's direction. Murmurs of support rose from all sides of the chamber until the vice-president politely ordered the resolution to be read again and put the formal question "Shall it pass?" Without further comment the roll was called, and after Senator Sherman had recorded his "yea" he was the first to rise from his desk. As he limped along the aisle towards the exit, silence fell briefly on the Senate, as though the sight of his disfigured body had a hypnotic effect on all those present. The swing door rocked back and forth on its hinges for a moment or two after he had gone, and the tap of his cane was clearly audible in the hushed chamber as his footsteps receded slowly along the tiled passageway outside.

2

The chill afternoon wind sweeping across the West Front terrace of the Capitol plucked fractiously at the flaps of their heavy winter topcoats as Tempe, Joseph and Guy waited for the senator. Against the leaden, overcast sky the cream stonework of the majestic rotunda seemed to glow with its own inner luminosity, and although there were several hours of winter daylight left, the black wrought-iron lamps on the stone balustrades facing the Mall were already beginning to flicker into life.

"Daddy certainly knows how to make a fine speech, doesn't he?" said Guy excitedly, hopping from foot to foot to keep warm.

"He not only knows how — he always knows where and when to do it to achieve the greatest impact for himself," replied Joseph acidly. "That one was more contrived than most."

Guy's sixteen-year-old face crinkled in puzzlement as he studied his elder brother's face. "Why is it, Joseph," he asked in a troubled voice, "that you always seem to go out of your way to put Daddy down?"

Joseph continued gazing along the Mall in the direction of the presidential memorials, his eyes narrowed against the stinging wind. "Let's just say, Guy, that I'm not so starry-eyed as you are in general about politics and politicians."

The young boy continued to stare at him in consternation for a moment, then hearing the unmistakable tap of a cane on the flagstones, shrugged and turned away.

"Did you enjoy that fighting speech from a winded old warhorse, young fella?" Nathaniel Sherman clapped Guy affectionately on the back and winked broadly at him. "Do you think we made the Sherman family viewpoint clear enough?"

"It was just wonderful, Daddy," replied the sixteen-year-old, falling into step beside him as they started down towards the broad greensward of the Mall.

The senator glanced more circumspectly at Joseph, aware that his silence implied a hint of criticism. "It was nice to see you in the gallery again, Joseph," he said quietly. "It's a few years since you've been up there, isn't it?"

Joseph nodded grimly without looking at his father. "I guess today's a special enough occasion to break old habits, whatever they may be."

"We all admired your address very much," broke in Tempe quickly, moving close to the senator and kissing him on the cheek. "It was quite uncanny — you seemed to say just what was on everybody's lips."

He stopped and patted her hand affectionately. "Thank you, my dear. You always manage to make my battered old heart feel young again."

As the four of them hurried on down the broad terrace of steps side by side, Joseph stole a quick glance at his father. His eyes still glittered brightly from the excitement generated by his speech in the Senate, and Joseph found himself wondering again at the eager, almost adolescent relish with which he still grasped every opportunity to steal the limelight. The terrible visible mutilation he had suffered in the hunting accident might have encouraged a different man to shun public life, he reflected, but his father, he was sure now, never had any compunction about exploiting for his own ends the sympathy his appearance invariably provoked.

On his return from Saigon five years before, Joseph had felt an angry compulsion to confront him over the accident that had caused Chuck's death; but somehow the sight of the disfiguring injuries themselves had always proved too daunting, and in the end he had never been able to bring himself to speak of what he had learned from Ngo Van Loc and Jacques Devraux. As they descended in silence toward Union Square, Joseph turned Guy's mystified question over in his mind and concluded uneasily that perhaps his own lack of courage had helped harden his hostile attitude towards his father and made him more inclined to avoid his company. His mother had been glad to move to Georgetown completely as soon as he and Tempe took over the running of the plantation house, and since then he had seen his parents on no more than two or three occasions each year.

". . . Do you think the Japanese will really invade California, Dad? I heard on the radio there was a rumor going around out there in the West that they already had."

Guy's voice broke into Joseph's thoughts, jerking him back to the present. They were passing the mounted statue of Ulysses S. Grant on Union Square, and all four of them were dwarfed by the life-sized bronze figures of Grant and a group of Civil War soldiers frozen in a moment of fear as they struggled with their plunging horses and a wheeled cannon. Nathaniel Sherman stopped suddenly beside the massive statues and turned back to look at the Capitol; the red, white and blue United States flag strained at its staff in the high wind, furling and unfurling spectacularly against the background of the pillared dome, and Joseph saw his father's mouth tighten with emotion.

270

"Nobody knows exactly what this war will bring, Guy," he said after a moment's thought. "It might change all our lives before it's finished. I hope it'll be all over before you're old enough to have to fight in it — but if it isn't, never forget that we're the inheritors of many great traditions." He turned to look westward along the Mall towards the slender stone needle of the Washington Monument. "We've been tested many times before and we've never been found wanting. But maybe our greatest test is coming now. All these symbols around us here in the heart of our capital, remember, should help to stir us to defend that proud heritage."

He was off immediately he had spoken, stumping along quickly with the aid of his cane beneath the flailing branches of the plane trees, his head forward, his shoulders hunched into the driving wind. Tempe and his two sons had to walk fast to keep up with him, and he didn't slacken his pace until they reached the Sherman Field Museum of Natural History standing in the shadow of the red sandstone towers of the Gothic castle which housed the head-quarters of the Smithsonian Institution. Built in the style of a Florentine Renaissance palace, the Sherman Field Museum's rounded arches and simple balustrades of rose-white Tennessee marble harmonized with the pink granite of the adjoining Freer Gallery of Art finished a year earlier in 1923, and on its western side gleaming new stonework indicated that a further wing had been added recently. Although separately financed by a Sherman family trust, the museum, like the others ranged along the Mall, had been placed under the Smithsonian's administrative control, and when the senator and his sons entered the building they found half-a-dozen prominent members of the institution's board of regents among the crowd of distinguished guests gathered inside. Nathaniel Sherman greeted them all by their first names, then acknowledged the chief justice, three or four other senators and half-a-dozen congressmen with quick handshakes as he passed through the throng. A tiny rostrum had been set up beside a broad ribbon strung across the entrance to the museum's new west wing, and beyond it the black bulk of a huge African bush elephant was visible, standing on a central pedestal with its trunk and forelegs raised in a posture of raging aggression. Above the entrance arch to the new galleries letters spelling out "The Charles Sherman Memorial Wing" had been inscribed in gilded Gothic script.

An attendant helped Nathaniel Sherman off with his coat, and a little ripple of applause greeted him when he stepped up onto the rostrum. "Ladies and gentlemen, when we set the date for the opening of this new wing of the Sherman Museum six months ago, none of us knew what a dark day it would turn out to be for America," he said, his expression grim and unsmiling. "But I saw no point in postponing our little ceremony, and I thank you all for attending in this time of deep national crisis. . . . Most of you know that when my father died in 1922 he made a bequest with which the Sherman Museum was founded. Since then it has proved itself a valuable adjunct to the bigger Smithsonian Museum of Natural History that faces us across the Mall. As a field museum we've always concentrated on the collection and exhibition of rare wild animals — and many of you will be aware that in making some of the early collections my family suffered a tragic loss in the jungles of Indochina. . . ."

He stopped speaking and dropped his eyes to the lectern for an instant, although he was speaking without notes. "That's why, ladies and gentlemen, these new galleries are dedicated to the memory of my late son, Charles. When he died on the threshold of life he showed great promise for the future and his untimely death was, I believe, a loss not only to his family but also to our country. He had high political ambitions and a strong desire to serve the nation, but first and foremost he was a young man of great courage and a fine huntsman and he was responsible for collecting many of the animals which visitors to the museum over the past sixteen years have enjoyed seeing."

He hesitated again, and when he looked up, those standing closest to the rostrum could see that his eyes had become suddenly damp. "Many of you present here today will know that I sustained my own injuries in the accident which cost Chuck his life. And, ladies and gentlemen, I've not missed him less as the years have gone by. It was this continuing sense of loss that decided me to pay an added tribute to his memory — in the shape of a composite tableau of the finest animals he shot in Indochina. The exhibits have been gathered together for the first time in the wing named for him, and they constitute a public memorial to his courage and skill."

He paused again and beamed at the family group where Joseph stood with Tempe, his mother, Guy and his sister, Susannah. "This, ladies and gentlemen, I should add, I've been keeping as a little surprise until now — even my family didn't know about the new tableau. But all of them were as fond and as proud of Chuck as I was — and will, I hope, share my pride that an appropriate permanent tribute has at last been set up to his memory." The senator picked up a pair of ceremonial scissors and stepped down from the rostrum. "So it gives me great pleasure to declare open the new Charles Sherman Memorial Wing of this museum."

Polite applause swelled from the gathering as the senator snipped through the tape, and uniformed waiters appeared immediately bearing trays of drinks and canapés. But Joseph brushed past them without accepting anything and hurried ahead of the crowd into the new gallery. In front of the memorial tableau he stopped and stared numbly at the huge black seladang bull which had killed his brother; its long murderous horns were lowered in an attitude of attack, its cloven hooves pawed the jungle floor, and two ferocious blue eyes glared out through the grass at his feet. The red banteng bull which Chuck had dropped from two hundred yards with a single shot the day before he died stood with its head raised in anger on one side of the seladang, and on its other flank the buffalo Joseph himself had spotted when he climbed a tree held its great scimitar-shaped horns belligerently low, ready to charge. A realistic riverside background of plain and jungle had been constructed around the animals, and in the grass by the seladang's feet a brass plaque announced: "Charles Sherman, at the age of twenty-one, courageously sacrificed his life to kill this prime example of a male seladang during a collecting expedition for the Sherman Field Museum of Natural History in the jungles of Cochin-China in 1925. The buffalo and banteng exhibited in this special memorial tableau, both fine bull animals in their prime, were also shot by the same hunter."

As Joseph stared down at the seladang, a terrible image of his brother thrashing in his death throes beneath its horns filled his mind, and he closed his eyes to blot out the sight of the animal. At that moment he felt a hand on his sleeve and he turned to find his mother standing pale-faced beside him.

"How could he do such a thing?" asked Joseph in an incredulous whisper.

For a moment Flavia Sherman didn't reply. In her mid-fifties, there was little trace left of the radiant beauty she had possessed at the time of her visit to Saigon; the birth of Guy in early middle age had taken a heavy physical toll on her, and her thickened figure had never regained its earlier grace. Her features too had slackened and bore the dull, withdrawn expression of one long since resigned to living in retreat inside her own thoughts and confidences. As she stared at the tableau, her mouth twisted with distaste and Joseph realized with alarm that she was on the point of tears.

"It's a shrine to masculine violence, Joseph," she said, speaking in a barely audible voice. "And to your father's foolish male pride — it's not a memorial to Chuck at all."

Joseph took her arm gently to comfort her and, glancing up, he saw his sister, Susannah, approaching quickly, carrying two glasses. Clear-skinned and as lovely in the flower of her womanhood as her mother had been in her own youth, she was already staring at the stuffed animals, and a worried frown clouded her face. From their expressions she realized instinctively how they felt about the tableau, and seeing tears in her mother's eyes, she turned her head anxiously in her father's direction; flanked by Guy and Susannah's politely attentive husband, Nathaniel Sherman was gesturing with his cane towards the African elephant on its central pedestal and smiling with pleasure as he headed in their direction.

"For glory's sake, Joseph, don't say anything to him here in public," pleaded Susannah quietly, handing her mother one of the glasses and taking her elbow to guide her away. "We must all bite our tongues for Daddy's sake. He doesn't mean badly."

Joseph took several paces backward across the gallery and pretended to scrutinize the tableau from a distance through half-closed eyes; he watched his father lead Guy and Susannah's husband to the glass and begin talking animatedly about the dead animals, gesticulating every now and again with his cane. Guy stood close to the senator, obviously hanging on his every word, and seeing them together like this against the vivid green jungle backdrop made Joseph stare. For a moment he didn't fully understand why; then he realized it was the tall, erect bearing of his younger brother. Beside the hunched figure of the senator, Guy seemed to stand ramrod straight, and Joseph suddenly saw again the square-shouldered figure of Paul Devraux striding away into the crowds of the Rue Catinat in his captain's uniform, saw too Jacques Devraux riding proudly upright at the head of their pony train as they trekked into the jungle. His younger brother's dark head contrasted vividly with the snowy white hair of the senator, and the smoldering resentment rose up suddenly within him with renewed force. Searching quickly among the crowd, Joseph found Tempe, seized her by the arm and without offering any explanation hurried her out of the museum into the windswept December afternoon.

3

In the chauffeur-driven limousine that took them to Union Station, Joseph sat apart from his wife in one corner of the back seat, staring out at the grandiose buildings of official Washington without really seeing them. Even after they were settled in their seats on the Richmond train he remained silent, and Tempe, sensing that he wished to be left alone with his thoughts, didn't venture to question him; instead she got on quietly with the woolen shawl she was crocheting for their baby son. Sometimes she caught him watching the little ivory crochet hook abstractedly as she worked the wool, and whenever their eyes met she smiled quietly at him. But these gestures of sympathy did nothing to soften his mood, and the train was approaching Richmond through the gathering darkness of the wintry afternoon before he finally spoke.

"I'm sorry, Tempe," he said, reaching out to take her hand in a conciliatory gesture, "I just couldn't stay in that gallery a moment longer."

"I know." She smiled fondly and put down her work. "You've never liked the museum, have you? It brings back too many unhappy memories, doesn't it?"

He stared at her, surprised by her intuitive understanding of his feelings. "How did you know that? We've never talked about it."

"We've only been there once before together. I made you take me soon after we met — the moment I discovered you were one of those famous museum Shermans, don't you remember? You explained everything very politely, but even then you looked uneasy — just as you did this afternoon when we went in."

"I suppose it brings back the memory of Chuck's death too vividly — but I didn't know I was that transparent."

"You're not transparent — you just underestimate the power of female intuition." She covered his hands with both her own. "I have a feeling it wasn't just the war and your father's insensitivity that made it worse today. . . ." She hesitated and dropped her eyes. "I think perhaps, Joseph, those animals help to remind you of something else too, don't they?"

"What do you mean?"

"When I first met you, you'd just come back from Indochina. You were tense and fretful for a long time — even for a while after we were married."

"The Frenchman who took us hunting on our first trip was killed while I was there," replied Joseph hastily. "I think it upset me more than I knew at the time. It probably helped open the old wound of Chuck's accident — that's all it was."

Tempe let go of his hand and took up her crochet-work once

more. "I sometimes wondered, Joseph, if you'd had an unhappy love affair."

For a second or two he gazed at her in astonishment. "How did you guess?"

She frowned and bent her head suddenly to unravel a snag in one of the loops of the shawl. "There's only one thing that makes a man behave the way you did, Joseph. I didn't ask you about it then because it wasn't any business of mine what had happened before we met. But I often used to feel your thoughts were far away. And since we left the museum this afternoon, it's been like that again — as if I'd lost you somehow."

Joseph stared at her, perplexed, aware that she had put her finger on a truth he'd previously refused to admit, even to himself.

"Do you mind talking about her?"

Joseph turned away quickly to look out of the window. "It was all such a long time ago."

"Who was she?"

"An Annamese girl — a mandarin's daughter in Saigon."

"Was she in love with you?"

Joseph shook his head uncertainly, still gazing blankly at his own reflection in the darkened window. "No, I don't think she was."

"But you loved her?"

"Perhaps I did — I don't really know anymore." He shook his head again and sighed loudly. "But I guess you're right, I did let her get under my skin for a while."

Tempe succeeded in righting the faulty stitch, and Joseph watched her hands resume their rhythmic movements in her lap.

"Did you make love with her?"

She half whispered the question, and for a moment he continued staring at her moving hands as though hypnotized. "No, I didn't," he said slowly. "Annamese mandarin families are very strict about those sort of things."

Tempe didn't look up, and Joseph felt the rocking motion of the train begin to change as they slowed on the approach to Richmond. "Let's just forget all about it, shall we?" he said, standing to put on his coat. "It's all in the past. We've got enough to worry about now with Pearl Harbor."

As they drove down the mile-long drive flanked by tall poplars, the lights of the tall Queen Anne plantation house were visible through the misty darkness. Inside the front hall the smiling black nursemaid for the children who greeted them assured them that their sons were peacefully asleep, but Tempe nevertheless ran up the great curved walnut staircase to look into the nursery. When

276

she came down again to join him in the paneled dining room her eyes were brimming with tears.

"The sweetest sound in the world, Joseph, is the whisper of a sleeping child's breath," she said softly. "I can't bear to think our happiness might be spoiled by the war."

He had switched on the radio in his study while she was upstairs and he nodded absently in reply as he listened to the voice of a newscaster reporting details of the new Japanese invasion of Hong Kong and Malaya. In Europe the Russians were claiming to have repulsed Hitler's forces around Rostock, but fifty German divisions were still reported to be pressing around Moscow. Not until her shoulders began to shake did he notice she was crying, and then he put a comforting arm around her. They stood listening to the news together for several minutes before he signaled for supper to be served, but when the food came neither of them was able to eat much.

"I shall have to go, of course," he said in a flat voice when the servants had removed the last of the dishes.

She nodded numbly from the other end of the table, realizing there was no choice. "What will you do?"

"The air corps, I think — if they'll have me."

Later, as he sat at the leather-topped desk in his study writing a letter applying to enlist in the air corps and undergo flight training, she came up behind his chair and put her arms around him. "Mark told me he would like to give you this to keep you safe wherever you go," she whispered, pressing something soft into the palm of his right hand.

Joseph smiled as he looked down at the lucky rabbit's foot mounted on a little gold chain that Tempe's father had given them as a christening gift for their second son; since the baptism six weeks before, the talisman had hung on the baby's cot.

"Is Mark sure he can spare it?" asked Joseph, smiling.

"He absolutely insists." Tempe blinked back her tears. "He says he feels lucky enough already having such a fine Daddy — and you might need it more than him."

Joseph slipped the rabbit's foot into his pocket. "All right — I know better than to argue with a two-month-old Sherman male who'll surely scream the house down if I make him sore."

After she'd left the room Joseph sat down beside the log fire that cracked in the hearth and looked over the letter he'd written. As he finished reading it he felt again a faint tremor of exhilaration pass through him; whatever the war held in store, it would take him away from the soporific daily round of Charles County, and for that he was at least grateful to the Japanese militarists. He folded the letter and was sealing it in its envelope when a sudden rushing noise in the chimney startled him, and the next moment a shower of soot cascaded into the grate, extinguishing the fire and filling the room with smoke. A series of muffled shrieks echoed from inside the old flue, and Joseph dashed outside to peer up at the roof.

Against the faint light of the night sky a dark wedge of shadow was visible on the rim of the chimney, and as he watched, it seemed to grow larger. Another series of shrieks echoed across the silent Virginian countryside, and Joseph's heart beat faster suddenly as he realized that one of the garden peacocks had flown onto the roof and was spreading its tail above the chimney stack. Frantically, he scooped up several handfuls of gravel and flung them at the tiles until the frightened bird flapped away screeching into the darkness.

After he had damped down his study fire he went upstairs and found Tempe seated in a nursing chair in the children's bedroom. Their baby son was drawing contentedly at one of her exposed breasts, but her own face was pale with anxiety. "I can smell burning, Joseph — and what was that terrible noise?"

"One of the peacocks got up onto the chimney," he said, trying to keep his voice casual. "It knocked some soot down into my study — that's all."

"But didn't you once tell me that's always been a bad omen in your family — when a peacock flies to the roof?" She started up in the chair, her eyes widening with alarm, and her movement plucked the nipple from the baby's mouth. Immediately the child began to scream, and Joseph dropped to his knees beside them.

"Relax, both of you," he whispered and stroked Tempe's hair as she settled the baby at her breast again. "I did mention it, I guess — but it's just a crazy old wives' tale. Don't worry."

Within a few minutes the baby fell asleep, and Joseph took him from her and lowered him gently into his cot. When he joined her in the canopied Robert E. Lee four-poster which she had renovated for their own use, she was still tearful and she clung to him fiercely in the darkness. Inside his head he could hear still the eerie wail of the peacock on the roof, but the heavy maternal ripeness of her body pressed against him gradually aroused him, and before they slept he made love to her, whispering all the time tender protestations of affection and devotion which he knew in his heart he didn't really feel.

4

The Curtiss P-40 Warhawk fighter-bomber of the Fourteenth
United States Army Air Force bucked and bounced in the strong
December winds driving down out of China as it climbed and
banked above the convoy of Japanese supply freighters plowing
doggedly across the Gulf of Tongking into Haiphong. Two of the
ships had already been hit and were burning, and other planes of
the Fourteenth's 308th Squadron were plunging through the
smoke to bomb and strafe the remainder. As Captain Joseph
Sherman leveled out at the top of his climb and brought the nose of
his P-40 around to dive for a second time, a third ship, obviously
carrying munitions, exploded, shooting a tumbling fountain of
orange fire high into the air. Flying level above the coast, Joseph
watched the flames consume the ship and saw clearly the antlike
figures of the Japanese seamen flinging themselves into the sea; for
an instant their tiny, helpless bodies were silhouetted against the
glare, then they were gone.

Without any feeling of compassion Joseph eased his stick forward to drop the nose of the P-40 once again into an attitude of
attack and held his hands steady as the aircraft rushed down
towards the vessels leading the frantic dash for the safety of the
harbor. Liquid tongues of flak from the Japanese shore batteries
were already licking up towards other Warhawks of the squadron
as they wheeled above the fleeing ships, but the closeness of
anti-aircraft fire had long since ceased to unnerve him. He watched
carefully for a second or two, then adjusted his controls fractionally to steepen his dive, confident that he would be able to
unload his two remaining hundred-pound wing bombs and climb
away to the east before the harbor guns could pick him up.

As the P-40 gathered speed, a stray shell exploded close in front
of its nose, rocking the whole aircraft, but it failed to deflect its
dive, and Joseph released his hundred-pounders onto a limping
freighter and pulled out in time to rake the bridge of the ship
ahead of it with six 12.7-millimeter Browning machine guns
mounted in the plane's wings. A new blaze of light lit his cockpit
from behind as he flew on, indicating that his bombs had found
their mark, and when he had put himself beyond the range of the
harbor guns, he turned and saw that the freighter was burning
furiously.

As usual he watched the flames with a detached feeling of
satisfaction; the burning vessel looked like so many others that he
had seen during nearly three years of combat flying. Now it was

just like watching magic lantern slides appear on the glass of his windshield; bullets and bombs exploded, ships, tanks, trucks caught fire, oily smoke and flame billowed ferociously for a moment or two, then as quickly as they had come they were gone, and the windshield of the swooping Warhawk was immediately redecorated with a fresh sheet of pale blue sky, darker blue sea, or perhaps the black cloak of the night blocking out all sight of the earth below.

Because of this feeling of detachment, it often seemed to Joseph that he had been fighting the war for much longer than three years. It was difficult to remember sometimes that he'd ever done anything else. He had been assigned to Midway Island to fly P-40s of 495th Squadron in late May 1942 on finishing his flight training; because of the emergency, the primary, basic and advanced stages of his training had been shortened from the normal seven months to less than six and he had difficulty identifying now with that dry-mouthed second lieutenant who had claimed his first "kill" in the famous rout of the Japanese fighter escort that came with their massive fleet to pound Midway in early June. He had surprised himself in the first place by volunteering for combat flying, and in the early days whenever he reached for the trigger of his wing cannon or the bomb release control, he had experienced the same deep repugnance of killing that he had felt when he held a hunting rifle in his hands earlier in his life. But in the end the fierce determination to overcome these instincts, born in him after Chuck's death, had helped make him one of the most successful combat pilots in the Pacific. The aerial mauling at Midway, which destroyed the myth of Japan's naval invincibility and turned the tide of the Pacific War in America's favor for the first time, had been a baptism of fire for Joseph, and when American Marines finally drove the enemy's land forces out of Guadalcanal early in 1943, his squadron had been moved there to help force the Japanese onto the defensive. It was the constant sorties flown from the Solomons that had inured him to the devastation he and his fellow pilots inflicted almost daily on ground and sea targets, and because of his growing reputation, when Japan launched its massive offensive in China in the summer of 1944, he had been promoted to captain and reassigned to the 308th Squadron of the Fourteenth, the force based in southern China that had been built around the nucleus of Major General Claire Lee Chennault's widely famed prewar group of volunteer aviators, "The Flying Tigers."

Japan had thrown two million men into her China offensive,

and the pilots of the "Flying Tiger" squadrons had for many months been operating around the clock countering land and air attacks and striking at vital Japanese supply routes into China and Indochina. Joseph had already flown several sorties over Tongking and Annam to attack bridges, railroads and supply depots being used by the Imperial Army, and the jungle-covered limestone crags of Tongking had become a familiar sight as he beat back and forth to his base at Kunming. But as he turned the nose of the P-40 northwest towards the Chinese border on that night in mid-December 1944, there was no moon, and darkness was descending swiftly over the two-hundred-mile stretch of mountainous jungle that separated the pilots of 308th Squadron from their home landing strip. The early winter monsoon was strengthening too, and because of the blustery wind the squadron reformed itself more slowly than usual as the glow of the burning ships outside Haiphong fell away behind them.

Joseph listened carefully as each pilot reported his presence to the squadron commander and when it became clear there had been no losses, little bursts of relieved banter began to crackle back and forth between the pilots. After a few minutes the engine-note of Joseph's Warhawk began to fluctuate, rising higher than normal then falling again, but at first he didn't worry unduly; several times in the past he had limped back to base with his engine misfiring, and he'd got used to finding his wings and fuselage riddled with holes on landing. But when the engine faltered and coughed suddenly, he felt instinctively for the furry rabbit's foot that he wore on a chain around his neck along with his dog tag; he had never once taken off without the good-luck charm, and over the three years had developed a deep superstitious attachment to it.

Touching it now made his thoughts turn for the first time in a long while to Tempe and his sons. He hadn't seen them for more than a year, and Gary and Mark, now seven and three years old respectively, knew little of their father. The long periods of separation and the exhaustion brought on by constant combat had seemed to dull his sensibilities, and there were times when he wondered whether he cared deeply for anybody, even himself. At thirty-four he was older than most of the other pilots in the squadron, but off-duty he drank as much as the younger ones, although without getting drunk in their presence. He had always made a point of avoiding their wild squadron sorties in search of sexual novelty, but the tensions of facing death and physical danger daily had sometimes led him to indulge in discreet bouts of sexual gratification from which he invariably emerged filled with self-disgust on account of his seeming lack of feeling and respect for his wife. During his rarer spells of home leave, his lovemaking with Tempe had become forced, without spontaneity, and although neither had left the marital bed, each of them had begun to retreat from the other. For that reason he hadn't returned home for his last leave but had spent ten anonymous days in Hawaii, drinking too much and waking to a succession of blurred, impersonal faces on the pillow beside him.

A moment or two after he pressed his fingers against the rabbit's foot, the Warhawk's engines settled to its normal steady drone again, and he smiled wryly in the darkness of the cockpit; at least that still retained its magic powers. Then almost immediately a little red light began to glow intermittently among the luminous green dials in front of him to indicate that the engine was overheating, and for the first time a cold shiver of fear crawled up his spine. He remembered then the stray shell that had burst ahead of him as he began his second dive and guessed that shrapnel fragments may have penetrated the cowling and possibly damaged the propeller blades. Over the next fifteen minutes the P-40's speed quickly fell to less than one hundred and fifty miles an hour and gradually the rest of the squadron drifted ahead of him, disappearing one by one into the black, wind-filled night.

He flicked the "transmit" switch of his radio and told the squadron commander tersely what was happening to him, then turned his full attention to trying to nurse the damaged plane home. Soon he was sweating profusely inside his flying suit from the effort of trying to hold the controls steady in the face of the rising wind. The red light that had been winking on and off became a bright, continuous glow only a second or two before he noticed the tiny tongues of flame licking around the engine's cowling. He considered feathering the propeller briefly in the hope that the fire might blow out and he could then restart the engine — but a renewed fit of mechanical coughing confirmed beyond any doubt that the P-40 had been fatally damaged by the close shellburst. He knew that if he lost power completely in the high winds he would plunge immediately into a downward spiral, and the plane would become a fiery coffin from which he would be unable to escape. In the few remaining moments that the afflicted engine would hold the plane in a level, head-up attitude, he knew if he was going to survive, he had to haul open the canopy and go over the side into the roaring, black void.

At the bottom of that void, his maps told him, lay only jagged, jungle-covered mountains slashed through with steep-sided tributary streams of the Li Chiang River. He calculated he was around twenty miles from the Chinese border, perhaps a hundred miles north of Hanoi where a million years before, it seemed, he had spent two weeks poring over ancient documents detailing the tribute paid by the ancient Annamese emperors to Peking. The prospect of pulling back the canopy that protected him from the hostile night outside filled him with dread, but the flames were spreading quickly, and the plane's progress had already slowed close to stalling speed. Feeling its nose begin to drop, Joseph grasped the canopy handle above his head and pulled sharply. When the release mechanism failed to operate, he sat staring at the white knuckles of his clenched fist in disbelief. He tried again with two hands, using all his strength, but it remained jammed, and in the next instant the P-40 rolled lazily onto its back.

It sank spinning slowly through the inky waters of the night like a dying fish, and the whirling of the aircraft whisked Joseph's senses into a froth of agonized perceptions. A cruel fate had obviously torn his P-40 from the sky over the Annamese lands with great deliberation! There his mother's betrayal had overnight changed the first elation of manhood to despair, and years later when he had at last surrendered himself to the joy of an over-whelming love, Lan too had in her turn betrayed him. With a blinding clarity he saw that the sense of emptiness and desolation that had always dogged him had sprung from the jungles and mountains below, and suddenly it seemed right and fitting that his life should end with those same jungles swallowing up him and his Warhawk. Sure that he was going to die, he was seized by a furious sense of regret that he would never see Lan again, and as the plane spiraled downward trailing flames from one wing, this feeling expanded until it seemed to fill his whole body.

But even though these thoughts dominated his conscious mind, his hands and feet still struggled instinctively with the controls, trying to correct the Warhawk's spin. He had auto-matically hauled the stick back as far as it would go and because the plane was spinning to the right, he kicked the right rudder all the way forward. He knew that he ought to hold the P-40 through at least four turns like this, but because he had no idea in the inky blackness how near the ground was, after only three, he snapped the stick away from him again and hit the opposite rudder as hard as he could with his left foot. As a result, the fighter-bomber righted itself as it plunged towards one of the highest mountains in the region and went into a glide for a few seconds before scything into the treetops at a shallow angle. One blazing wing was torn off immediately, and burning gasoline from the ruptured fuel tanks showered in all directions, setting a broad swathe of jungle alight. A hundred yards farther down the mountain the second wing broke away, and the bole of a tall tree shattered the jammed cockpit canopy. In that instant Joseph's conscious life exploded in a ringing burst of white light, and a few seconds later the remains of the P-40's fuselage came to rest on the lower slopes, with its nose buried in the moist earth and its tail snagged high in the branches of a creeper-choked tree.

5

The little group of squatly built Nung tribesmen peered fearfully up at the Warhawk wreckage by the light of their burning grass torches, then began backing away, jabbering excitedly among themselves. They could see the white pilot's body dangling from the smashed cockpit on its seat straps, and the gusting wind was making it twist slowly back and forth; as it turned, they saw that the pale face was hideously streaked with blood and one arm stuck out stiffly at an unnatural angle. Behind them, one of the tribal priests who had accompanied the group from their stilted village a mile away cut the air ritualistically above his head with a machete every few seconds to disperse the evil demons gathering around the crashed plane, and instinctively the group retreated to his side for protection.

"He has already joined the spirits of the mountains and the clouds," whispered one of the tribesmen, rolling his eyes towards the Warhawk. "We should go now."

The priest lowered his machete and stood listening for a moment; the noise made by the six-man Japanese border patrol that had also watched the Warhawk come down in flames was growing louder as they approached the crash site.

"Dead or alive, the thin man of Pac Bo who promises to make us free wants all white flying men returned to him," said the priest slowly. "Cut him down!"

The authoritative tone of the priest's voice reassured the frightened tribesmen, and they climbed quickly into the tree to sever the seat straps with their machetes. It took six of the stocky mountain men to bear the burden back to their little group of thatched huts, and as they staggered under the weight, the priest walked beside them, chanting imprecations to appease the powerful spirits of fire, sky and thunder which the tribe believed had created the earth. When they arrived at the village, a wide-eyed throng of tribespeople crowded into the smoke-filled hut of the priest and watched in silence as he prepared a little platter of betel leaves and a few rice grains to place in the mouth of the corpse in accordance with the tribe's traditional funeral rites. Before beginning the ritual, the priest signaled for water to be brought from the mountain spring outside, then cut away the blood-soaked cloth of the flying suit. In the act of swabbing blood from the exposed torso, the priest stopped suddenly and bent to press his head against the chest. When he straightened up, he beckoned quickly to one of his helpers.

"Prepare a bamboo litter at once — the white man is still alive! And send a runner to Pac Bo quickly to warn them to be ready at the river."

A gasp of excitement rose from the crowd of villagers, and they pressed closer around the priest as he began to bind leaves and jungle herbs tightly around the wounds that Joseph had suffered in the crash. One of Joseph's legs, as well as his left arm, was obviously broken, and when the priest had finished treating the wounds, he wrapped one of his own ceremonial robes about the American, then tied his legs together with twisted creepers and bound him firmly to a bamboo litter. The same six bearers who had carried him from the wreck hoisted him onto their shoulders again, and with an escort of a dozen villagers armed with machetes, they set off immediately down the mountainside.

The Japanese border patrol finally traced the blood trail to the village half an hour later, and when they found no sign of the pilot's body, they opened fire in their anger. The priest and two other tribesmen were killed instantly and ten other villagers were wounded. Before they left, the Nipponese soldiers set fire to all the huts and dragged half-a-dozen Nung girls screaming into the forest with them. A detachment of French troops riding short-legged mountain ponies from the border post of Soc Gian three miles away located the Warhawk wreckage an hour later; like all the French colonial forces in Indochina they were also under orders to seize and intern all American pilots shot down in the peninsula, but because of the resentment they felt at having to take orders from the Japanese, the Frenchmen simply shrugged their shoulders and turned their horses' heads towards their home base again when they found the cockpit empty. By that time, Joseph was drifting eastward along a steep-sided tributary of the Li Chiang

River on a flimsy bamboo raft piloted by Dao Van Lat and two other young Communist guerrillas.

The fervent revolutionary who had led the ill-fated march on Vinh in 1930 had poled the raft rapidly upstream from the Indochinese Communist Party's secret guerrilla base at Pac Bo on receiving the Nung message that an American pilot had been rescued alive. One of his two young companions knelt on the front of the frail craft holding a blazing torch aloft to guide them through the frothing rapids, while the second guerrilla crouched beside Joseph's litter at the rear, cradling an ancient flintlock rifle in his arms. The stream began to run more swiftly as it approached the main river, and it was the sound of rushing water that first penetrated Joseph's concussed brain; but only partial consciousness returned, and the blurred images of their rapid passage through the noisy, firelit darkness were terrifying to him. He began to shout incoherently and strain against his protective bonds, and Lat, fearing that he would capsize the craft, ordered the Annamese beside him to hit him with the butt of his flintlock.

Joseph immediately lapsed into unconsciousness once more, but the sound of his voice had reached a second Japanese patrol on the limestone bluff high above the river, and a moment later their opening shots were kicking up plumes of spray all around the raft. Lat drove his long pole frantically into the bed of the shallow river and sent the craft careering wildly through a long channel where the water boiled white between rocky reefs. He yelled frantic orders to the young guerrilla guarding Joseph to fire back at the Japanese, but in the act of raising his flintlock to his shoulder, the youth was hit in the chest and he toppled sideways into the water without a sound.

For a few brief moments the body of the Annamese rushed through the foaming water beside them, keeping pace with the raft; then abruptly it was sucked out of sight by the current and didn't reappear. When they sped out into the main river seconds later, Lat ordered the surviving guerrilla to extinguish his torch; immediately the shooting died away behind them, and the youth, white-faced with shock at the loss of his comrade, moved gingerly back to the litter to check that it was still secure. The raft slowed gradually in the gentler flow of the broader river, and with a long sigh of relief Lat lifted his pole clear of the water and rested on it, his chest heaving.

"Why do we take so many risks to rescue one foreign pilot?"

asked the young Annamese in a horrified whisper when Lat had regained his breath.

"Because America is powerful and her forces are going to win the war," said Lat patiently.

"But if America's so powerful, why does it need our help?" asked the youth in a puzzled voice. "There are so few of us and we're poorly armed."

"America doesn't need us at all," replied Lat quietly. "But if the Americans drive the Japanese out of our country, they'll be the conquering heroes to our people — and if we're seen fighting beside them, we'll be heroes too. When the Japanese are gone we will be able to get back to the real fight — against France. Helping American flyers escape from the Japanese or even rescuing their bodies will help us win the friendship of America — that's why we're risking our lives."

The youth nodded slowly as Lat stabbed his pole into the river again and steered the raft into a tiny inlet where another band of half-a-dozen crudely armed guerrillas was waiting. They took the litter willingly on their shoulders, and Lat led the way up through a series of steeply terraced rice fields into another high valley enclosed by sheer limestone crags. Fast-flowing streams had gouged deep caves from the limestone over the centuries, and in one of these deep fissures behind a waterfall, the bamboo litter was finally lowered to the sandy floor.

Noticing that Joseph had begun to shiver with fever, Lat ordered the other guerrillas to light a fire beside the litter while he made a pillow of folded garments and covered the American with two ragged blankets. As he was finishing these tasks a thin, aged-looking Annamese appeared silently on the edge of the circle of light cast by the fire: he appeared bent and feeble in the shadows, but when he stepped towards the litter his stride was brisk, and the firelight revealed that his gray goatee and his thinning hair were still streaked with black. His eyes shone with an unusual brilliance in an emaciated face, and there was a peculiar controlled stillness in his manner which caused the other men in the cave to fall respectfully silent and draw aside from him.

When Joseph opened his eyes for the first time he found the thin Annamese bending over him; because of the delirium brought on by fever and the agonizing pain of his injuries, the sunken face with its wispy goatee seemed unreal to him in the flickering orange glow of the fire, but when a tin mug of warm coconut milk was pressed to his lips, the American drank greedily from it. During the rest of that first long, cold night on the mountain, each time

Joseph swam up to the surface of consciousness the same hand invariably offered soothing liquid or mopped his streaming brow; the same startling face with its calm, knowing gaze also seemed to materialize and dissolve constantly before his feverish eyes, as though it belonged to a benign and paternal mountain spirit, and as he hovered on the brink of death, the sight of it became strangely comforting and reassuring to Joseph.

6

"I've personally always admired the United States of America, Captain Sherman," said the sibilant Annamese voice, speaking English confidently in a singsong accent. "It was the first colony in the modern world to win independence through a revolution, and I hope one day our little country will be able to emulate your great deeds of courage and endurance. All of us here have much to learn from the fortitude of Americans — that's why we have taken risks ourselves to save you from the Japanese." The face with the wispy goatee that for three days had appeared only hazily to Joseph through the mists of his delirium was clearly defined now, and it smiled at him for the first time; the expression lit up the gaunt features, and to Joseph, in his pain-racked state of exhaustion, it conveyed a rare feeling of warmth and concern.

"Perhaps you think our two countries have little in common — but maybe you weren't aware that the emperor of Annam begged for help from your government eighty years ago when the French first began to plunder us." He looked up again and smiled ironically. "Yes, believe it or not, a message was sent to Abraham Lincoln from Hue proposing a treaty of friendship — but I suppose Mister Lincoln can be excused for ignoring our little cry for help. He was quite busy at the time, I believe, dealing with the small matter of your own Civil War."

The Annamese was crouched barefoot by the fire, dressed in a shabby khaki tunic and baggy trousers; from time to time he stirred the embers thoughtfully with a twig, obviously not anticipating any response from Joseph who lay enfeebled and wasted with fever on a makeshift bed of palm leaves. While the fever had raged, Joseph had been dimly aware that other Annamese were moving in and out of the cave; Dao Van Lat had tended him constantly round the clock and a doctor whom the guerrillas had abducted and marched blindfolded to the hideout from the nearby town of Cao Bang had splinted his broken limbs and bandaged the most severe lacerations on his head and body. Using a burned forest root called *nua ao*, they had also made up herbal infusions which they forced past his burning lips every hour, and during the third night, the fever had finally reached its climax. At dawn the thin Annamese had hurried into the cave with a little dish of maize and mashed banana and dismissed the others while he fed him personally with a spoon; then he had squatted down by the fire and begun to talk.

"I visited your country myself many years ago," he said, gazing reflectively into the flames. "I left Indochina when I was twenty and sailed to Europe and America working as a ship's galley hand. I stoked furnaces and shoveled snow in London and worked for a time as a waiter in Harlem and Boston. It was sad for me to see the contrast between the lives of the rich clients in the hotels and the poor people who had to slave in the kitchens to feed them. I also saw how many Negroes were living in the direst poverty in Harlem." He sighed as he stared into the fire. "I admire very much the great democratic ideals of America, Captain Sherman, but unfortunately the light from the Statue of Liberty's torch doesn't shine equally on all Americans, does it?"

With difficulty Joseph raised himself onto one elbow. He still felt weak and light-headed in the aftermath of the fever, and the slightest effort made his senses swim. "Where am I?" he asked shakily. "How did I get here?"

Again the Annamese smiled his seraphic smile. "Don't worry, you're among friends, captain. I came myself to assure you of that. These are the caves of Pac Bo in northern Tongking. We're only one kilometer from the Chinese border. You were pulled from the wreckage of your plane by mountain men of the Nung tribe. They saved you from a Japanese patrol — and from the French who also have orders to take you prisoner. They contacted us and helped us bring you here. As soon as you're well enough to travel, we'll smuggle you past the Japanese border guards into China again and take you safely back to General Chennault and your famous 'Flying Tiger' friends." He smiled again when he saw Joseph's look of consternation. "I know your name, captain, because I read the 'dog tag' around your neck." He rolled the colloquial American phrase off his tongue with obvious pleasure. "And those ferocious teeth painted on the nose of your crashed Warhawk told us you were a 'Flying Tiger.'"

Joseph raised his head to stare at the Annamese in the flickering firelight, then sank back into his bed of palm leaves. "Who are you? And why are you helping me?"

"All of us here are nationalists of the Viet Minh. Like America, we're fighting against Japan. We're waging guerrilla warfare against the outposts in this region."

"What's the Viet Minh?"

"Viet Minh is the short way of saying the Viet Nam Doc Lap Dong Minh Hoi — the League for the Independence of Vietnam. It's an alliance of patriots fighting to liberate our country. First we'll drive out the Japanese — then someday the French too. Pac Bo is our temporary headquarters."

Joseph grimaced and closed his eyes. The mental effort of absorbing the simple information tired him, and changing his position even slightly on the palm-leaf bed filled his body with pain. Noticing this, the Annamese hurried across the cave and knelt solicitously beside him. Despite his seeming frailty, his grip on Joseph's shoulders was sure and strong as he helped him into a more comfortable posture.

"Rest now, captain," he said soothingly, pulling the blankets up around Joseph's shoulders. "I think we'll have plenty of time to enjoy talking together. I wanted only to assure you that you're in safe and friendly hands."

By the morning of the next day Joseph had recovered sufficiently to be carried out of the cave. He groaned loudly as Dao Van Lat and three companions lifted the litter, and outside, it took several minutes for him to accustom his eyes to the blinding glare of the morning sun. A thick growth of reeds hid the entrance to his cave beside a waterfall, and once he was settled on a broad ledge close by, he gazed in astonishment at the tall limestone cliffs towering above dense tracts of rain forest; in the distance across the border in China, other spectacular sugar-loaf mountain formations were materializing as the early mists cleared.

"So this is where I landed up," breathed Joseph. "You've sure chosen a beautiful spot to hide away from the Japanese."

Beside him Dao Van Lat stared too — but not at the spectacular scenery; on the sunny ledge, Joseph's face was more clearly visible to him than it had ever been inside the cave, and the Annamese was gazing down at him wide-eyed. "Have you ever been to our country before, captain?" he asked, speaking his halting English in a surprised voice.

Joseph turned to Lat with renewed interest. "Yes. I know Saigon and Hue — and I've been in Hanoi once. Why do you ask?"

"I met a young American in Hue many years ago," replied Lat excitedly. "He was very much like you."

As they looked at one another, recognition began to dawn on Joseph too. "I was at the emperor's palace for the Tet ceremony in 1925," said Joseph slowly. "And I returned in 1936 to visit Hue and Hanoi. Could we have met in one of those places?"

"We met in Hue in 1925," exclaimed Lat triumphantly. "You were with your mother."

Joseph nodded in amazement.

"My name is Lat — Dao Van Lat. I was the journalist you talked to after the *lam lay* ceremony."

Lat's features still bore signs of privation suffered during the years spent in Paulo Condore, and his earlier act of self-mutilation had also given his face a permanently strained, unnatural cast; but because of his high scholar's brow and the fiery glint in his eye, he was still recognizably the dedicated idealist who had spoken so heatedly to Joseph and his mother in the anteroom of Khai Dinh's palace.

"I remember you," said the American, screwing up his face with the effort of recollection. "You were angry about the hypocrisy of the Tet ritual, I think. And you told us you weren't allowed to write what you wanted."

Lat smiled ruefully. "You're probably right. Then I was young and impetuous." He bent over Joseph and shook him warmly by the hand. "I'm more glad than ever now that we've been able to help an old American friend."

Joseph smiled in his turn and shook his head in wonderment at the coincidence. "When did you stop being a journalist, Lat, and become a guerrilla fighter?"

"I decided to devote my life to freeing my country from the French on the eve of Tet in 1930," said the Annamese, his expression growing serious. "But I was captured in the uprisings in the north and spent five years in the dungeons of Paulo Condore. That didn't increase my love for the French, and after I was released I took up the struggle again." He drew a long, resigned breath. "They've been hard years. Although France surrendered Indochina to the Japanese at the start of the war, Tokyo has allowed the French to continue persecuting nationalists. They massacred six thousand of my countrymen in the worst operation in the south, and many villages were burned to the ground. While you and the rest of the world have been at war with Japan and Germany, our French colonial masters have gone on behaving here as they've done for the past eighty years. That's why the Viet Minh League was founded in 1941 to fight the Japanese *and* the French."

As Lat was speaking, Joseph saw the scrawny Annamese who'd visited him each evening emerge from another cave in the clearing below the ledge. He wore a battered cork sun helmet with his khaki drabs and carried a bamboo walking stick. As Joseph watched, he made his way to the bank of the little stream that ran through the encampment and began to undress.

"He bathes every morning in the icy cold water and does physical exercises for ten minutes before beginning work," said Lat, following Joseph's gaze. "Life is very hard in these mountains, so he sets us all an example by his self-discipline."

By the foot of the cliff the stream widened into a series of ponds and small lakes, and along its banks great slabs of rock hung with stalactites jutted out over the water. "That's his desk down there," said Lat, pointing to the flattest of the rocks. "He'll work there all day organizing our fight against the fascists of Japan and France. This morning he's writing articles for our little newspaper, *Viet Lap* — Independent Vietnam."

The Annamese raised his eyes to the ledge at that moment and waved his stick in greeting before descending with surprising vigor into the stream to dash cold water repeatedly over his frail body.

"Who is he?"

Lat stared in astonishment at the American. "I thought you already knew. He's our leader. For many years he called himself Nguyen Ai Quoc — Nguyen the Patriot — but now he has adopted a new *nom de guerre*, Ho Chi Minh. It means 'He who enlightens.' "

"Have you known him long?"

"I first met him in Hanoi in 1930. He was disguised then as a rickshaw coolie to fool the French Sûreté — and even I wasn't sure who he was. He's a brilliant man. His father was a mandarin, and he's traveled all over the world. He can speak French, English, Russian, German, Japanese, Czech — and three Chinese dialects. He was born in my home province, Nghe An, in central Annam." Lat paused and smiled proudly. "A local proverb says 'A man from Nghe An will oppose anything.' "

"And are you now a leader of the Viet Minh too, Lat?"

Dao Van Lat's face fell instantly into serious lines again. "I'm proud to say, Captain Sherman, that I'm one of Ho Chi Minh's closest comrades. Once I was foolhardy enough to think I knew better than he did how to lead our movement. Once I thought that anything could be achieved by a man if he had an iron will and the strength to sacrifice everything for his cause. He warned me that a political leader had to be sensitive to the people's moods and their needs, but I didn't have the sense to listen to him." Lat paused and turned away from Joseph. "Events proved him right and me wrong. I've never forgotten that lesson and since then I've learned many more. Often when we've been hurrying through a poor village, he's stopped and spent half an hour bathing a baby for a harassed mother — or collected a big heap of firewood for an old man who can't bend. His concern for people runs very deep — that's why all our supporters call him Pac Ho — Uncle Ho. They know he cares for them as if they were members of his own family."

"What age is he?" asked Joseph, feeling his curiosity aroused. "At first I thought he must be very old, but now . . ."

"No, he's not old, he's fifty-four," said Lat in a respectful voice. "But he's suffered greatly in Chinese jails recently — that has aged him beyond his years. He crossed the border in 1941 to offer Chiang Kai-shek an alliance with the Viet Minh to fight the Japanese — but the treacherous generalissimo threw him straight into prison. They clamped irons on his legs, put a wooden yoke around his neck and forced him to march hundreds of kilometers across China. He was held in thirty different jails in one year. He became so ill that sores covered his body and many of his teeth fell out. Many prisoners died beside him in the night in those freezing cells, and one terrible day we were informed that he'd died too. We held funeral ceremonies here at Pac Bo and mourned his death. Everyone was paralyzed with grief." A pained expression crossed Lat's face at the memory. "Then many months later we received a Chinese newspaper with a poem written in the margin. It was in his handwriting, and from the recent date on the paper we were able to deduce that he was alive. We all went wild with joy. To celebrate, Captain Sherman, everybody here learned that poem. Would you like to hear my translation of it?"

Joseph nodded absently, still watching the Annamese as he clambered out of the stream.

> ". . . . The clouds are making the mountains glow
> And in their turn the peaks embrace the clouds
> Beneath them the river gleams like a new mirror
> And on the western crests
> My heart swells within me as I wander
> Scanning the distant heavens to the south
> I am dreaming every day of old friends. . . ."

When Joseph glanced up at Lat, he saw that reciting the poem had caused his eyes to mist over momentarily. "To hear that he was still 'dreaming of old friends' was the best news we could've wished for," said Lat, his voice husky with emotion. "To help him survive during his long ordeal he wrote other poems too — always in Chinese, in the ancient classical style. I've translated all of them into English and French." He paused and tugged a sheaf of crumpled papers from the breast pocket of his tunic. "Here's another one he wrote about the horrors of long imprisonment. . . .

> *One day in jail is equal to a thousand years of freedom*
> *How right the ancients were to express it in those words. . . ."*

Joseph closed his eyes and lay back in the warm sunshine. The only sound, apart from Lat's voice reading the lilting poetry, was the soothing rush of the waterfall splashing down the rocks. Gradually the remote stillness of the high mountains, combined with the utter exhaustion brought on by the pain and fever, induced in him a profound feeling of peace and serenity; suddenly the frantic trafficking in death and destruction of the past three years seemed part of another, distant life. A strong sense of gratitude towards his rescuers was growing inside him, and he realized he felt drawn in particular to the frail, fatherly Annamese in the clearing below, who exuded a warmth and sincerity that obviously bound the little band of Viet Minh guerrillas to him with bonds as strong as those of family kinship. For a moment or two a vague feeling of regret that he had been unable to love his own father more intruded into his thoughts; but it didn't become strong enough to disturb the expanding sense of renewal and well-being that now pervaded his mind, and in the warm sunshine he drifted slowly into a peaceful, refreshing sleep.

He didn't begin to awaken until the sun was going down late in the afternoon, and at first he thought the rattle of machine gun fire was part of a dream of the past. Then he felt Lat shaking him gently by the shoulder and he realized that the flurry of single shots and the stuttering response of several machine guns were the sounds of a real battle coming from close by.

"The outer ring of guards has engaged a French patrol," said Lat urgently, signaling his helpers to gather around the litter. "We must move camp at once."

Looking down, Joseph saw the clearing come alive with scurrying Viet Minh guerrillas, and immediately the helmeted figure of Ho Chi Minh rose from the rock where he had been working. He rapped out a series of orders in a crisp voice, and within minutes the whole camp was on the move. Joseph was carried on his litter along a high ravine and over a succession of steep passes to the edge of the rain forest where the underbush grew thick and impenetrable. Half-a-dozen refuge huts had been built beneath a living canopy of skillfully interwoven rattan palms, and the guerrillas settled down immediately without fuss to resume their work.

Distant bursts of gunfire continued intermittently for half an hour, then eventually died away altogether. Later Lat told Joseph that two French soldiers had been killed by the guerrillas in a short, sharp skirmish fought to provide time for the cave base to be evacuated. When they'd done their job, the defenders had melted into the hills and didn't return to the new camp until after nightfall. Joseph was made comfortable for the night in one of the huts and when he awoke at dawn next day a bigger crowd of guerrillas than he'd seen before was already assembled for a formal parade in the middle of the clearing. They were armed with an odd assortment of weapons, and a dapper, quick-striding Annamese with an unruly shock of dark hair was moving energetically among them, correcting their posture and their dress.

"That's Comrade Vo Nguyen Giap, our military commander," said Lat quietly as he squatted beside Joseph. "He was an outstanding student of military history and law at the National School in Hue. He can draw the plans of all Napoleon's battles from memory — but his hatred of France is great because his sister-in-law was executed by the French and his wife died in a French jail."

Watching the little force being marshaled, Joseph counted thirty-four men; half of them clutched ancient flintlocks, and most of the others were armed with outdated bolt-action rifles. Two wore holstered revolvers at their belts, and just one held a light machine gun proudly across his chest. Their tunics and trousers, khaki or dark blue, were faded and frayed, and many among them were barefoot mountain tribesmen of the region. Behind them in the bright morning sun, a red standard emblazoned with a gold star fluttered from a flagstaff.

"That's our banner — the standard of the Viet Minh," said Lat, pointing. "We've decided that the time has come to begin building the army that will one day free our whole country. We've brought together the best fighters from groups scattered across the hills of Tongking. All those men you see out there, Captain Sherman, have been leaders of their own armed self-defense sections for some time — they're all valiant fighters who've proved themselves in action."

Joseph struggled, wincing, into a sitting position and scrutinized the gathering closely. All the thirty-four guerrillas held themselves proudly erect under the gaze of their little commander, but as a fighting force they looked insubstantial, and Joseph found himself wondering at the fierce spirit that obviously animated the raggle-taggle little band. As he watched, the scrawny figure of Ho Chi Minh appeared from one of the huts to review the force, wearing his now familiar battered cork helmet and carrying his bamboo cane. After walking gravely back and forth along the ranks, he stepped up to the flagpole to address them in a friendly tone, and Joseph listened attentively as Lat translated for him.

"We must all act resolutely and swiftly from the start," he said, looking into the face of each guerrilla in turn. "We must mobilize all the people of our nation and call on them to rise up with us — so most of our attention must at first be given to political activities and propaganda rather than military operations. But when you do attack the enemy, make sure your first strike is victorious! Appear unexpectedly — then disappear quickly without trace!" He paused and for a brief instant one of his brilliant smiles illuminated his haggard face. "All of you in this unit·are the senior members of a family that will grow and grow. One day its field of action will be the entire territory of Vietnam — from the far north to the deepest south. . . . Make sure that your deeds each day serve as an example to all who will follow!"

Without further ceremony Giap marched the unit briskly out of the clearing, and the man they called "Uncle Ho" stood watching them go; the moment they disappeared into the forest, he wandered over to Joseph's hut and sat down smiling on a tree stump by the door to share some coconut milk with the American and Lat.

"You've been greatly privileged, captain, to witness the birth of the 'Vietnam Armed Propaganda Unit for National Liberation,' " he said, smiling ironically. "A big name for a small force, perhaps — but we have high hopes it will grow rapidly from its humble beginnings. Our strategy now is to do propaganda work every-where and capture better weapons from the French and the Japanese. We need modern armaments, you see, very badly." He sipped the coconut milk reflectively for a moment without looking at Joseph. "We've already won the support of the mountain tribes. The Nung people are among our best fighters because the Viet Minh promises them autonomy when our country is free, and they've flocked to join our cause." He looked up at Joseph and smiled. "Lucky for you, Captain Sherman, that they did. It was the Nung who saved your life."

"I'm very grateful for your help — and theirs." Joseph smiled warmly at the older man. "I hope sometime I'll be able to repay you in some way."

Ho leaned towards the litter and patted Joseph's shoulder gently. "There's no need to think of repaying us, captain. To be able to help a brave American return to the fight against Japan is reward enough for us." He beamed toothily again. "And return you we shall — soon. Comrade Lat, who's told me you're old friends, thinks you're well enough to begin the journey into China this morning. I'd like to walk up to the border pass with you to wish you *bon voyage*, captain; would you mind?"

Joseph grinned and shook his head. "No — but I'm almost sorry to be leaving. I was beginning to like the peace and quiet of your mountain retreat."

"Then come back again, captain — but not so painfully next time." Ho chuckled and stood up. "I'll go myself and check the provisions that have been prepared to make sure you'll have enough nourishing food for your trek."

The Viet Minh leader climbed beside Joseph all the way to the pass, carrying a satchel of food himself and helping Lat and the other sweating bearers with the litter whenever they stumbled in the steep rock gulleys. All the time, to take Joseph's mind off the pain caused by the jolting of the litter, he talked — about his experiences in America, about the history of his own country and of the United States; he asked Joseph about his family, and listened intently as the American spoke through gritted teeth of his father's political career and of the study he himself had made of Asian history.

"It sounds to me, captain, as if you know this part of the world better than any of us here," he said admiringly as they arrived panting at the top of the pass and stopped to look down into China. "You're well aware how many setbacks we've suffered in our long bid for freedom — it's a pity you can't stay longer and help me teach some history to our young Viet Minh recruits."

"Maybe when the war's over." Joseph smiled as the bearers who'd hauled him up the mountainside handed the litter over to six other armed guerrillas who were waiting to take him down the valley into China. When Dao Van Lat offered his hand in farewell, Joseph shook it with both his own and thanked him effusively.

"I hope we might meet again one day in freedom, Captain Sherman," said Lat warmly.

"I hope so too." Joseph hesitated, still holding the hand of the Annamese in his. "Lat, when we met all those years ago you were

297

with the Imperial Delegate in Saigon, do you remember?"

Lat nodded. "Yes, of course. He married my older sister."

"How is Monsieur Tran Van Hieu and his family, do you know?" Joseph tried to keep his voice casual. "I met his sons and his daughter, Lan, on my last visit."

"Tran Van Kim is a prominent member of our Viet Minh League. He's working undercover near Phuoc Kiem to the south of here."

"And Tam and Lan?" prompted Joseph. "What of them?"

Lat shrugged and dropped his eyes in embarrassment. "I'm afraid, captain, I know nothing of them. I've had no contact with my sister or her children for many years — nor has Comrade Kim. These have been difficult times for all of us."

Joseph nodded quickly. "Of course, I understand."

"When you are safely back in Kunming, captain," said Ho, taking Joseph's hand in his turn, "please tell your senior officers that America has allies ready and waiting to help them in the mountains of Tongking. The Viet Minh will be honored to fight the Japanese alongside America. A lot can be achieved by sabotaging their supply routes and arms dumps."

"I'll tell them," promised Joseph, gripping the hand of the Annamese firmly. "They'll be grateful for what you've done for me."

"We'll help any pilot shot down in these jungles — you can depend on us. But as you've been our first American guest you'll always hold a special place in our hearts." A broad smile of genuine affection broke out on his face. "And don't be misled back in Kunming by the Free French or Chiang Kai-shek's people if they try to brand us as Communists. Tell them the Viet Minh is an alliance of patriots, and Vietnam today is like America must have been in 1775. Everybody who's willing to fight for independence and freedom is welcome to join us."

"Have you ever been a Communist yourself?" asked Joseph.

Ho's smile broadened. "If anybody inquires about my politics, captain, simply tell them this: 'His party is his country, his program is independence.' We'll keep fighting for that independence whatever happens — and our children will fight on after us if need be . . . *Bon voyage*."

Joseph closed his eyes and gritted his teeth as the guerrillas carrying him slipped and slithered on the steep, stony track leading down into China. They were hurrying to reach the shelter of the jungle on the lower slopes, and he couldn't help crying aloud with pain from time to time. As they approached the trees, he looked back and caught a last glimpse of the Annamese standing silhouetted against the bright morning sky. Joseph waved, and on the mountaintop the frail figure raised his cork helmet and lifted his cane above his head in a final gesture of farewell.

7

By the end of February 1945 the plaster cast that encased Joseph's right leg from hip to ankle was smothered with signatures and humorous obscenities. They had been scrawled on it by other wounded "Flying Tigers" recuperating with him in the Kunming base hospital, and prominent among the names was that of Major General Claire Lee Chennault, their famous, hawk-faced commander who had taken a break from directing the day and night air war against the Japanese to hear for himself how one of his best pilots had returned miraculously from the dead. Joseph had been missing for nearly three weeks when he was finally driven up to the gates of the Fourteenth Army Air Force headquarters on New Year's Eve in a rickety Chinese flatbed truck, and to make his return more mysterious, the two silent guerrillas who had accompanied him from the Tongking border had slipped away immediately to begin their long return journey.

It had been left to the astonished gate guards to carry him inside, and his surprise return had made the 308th Squadron's New Year's party more riotous than it might otherwise have been. Joseph, however, had taken no part in the merrymaking himself, because air force surgeons got busy straight away resetting his broken thigh and the previously undiscovered fracture in the lower part of his leg. When Claire Chennault strode into the hospital next morning wearing the twin silver stars of a major general on the shoulders of his battered leather flying jacket, the other disabled flyers had cheered Joseph to the echo, then launched into a raucously affectionate chorus of "Why Was He Born So Beautiful?"

The craggy features of the air force general who had become America's most renowned fighting man in Asia softened into a delighted smile as Joseph described how the Annamese guerrillas had spirited him away from the Japanese and nursed him back to health in their mountain hideaway before smuggling him safely into China. "We can sure use that kind of help," drawled

Chennault in a rich southern baritone that reflected his Louisiana upbringing. "Every Allied pilot's worth his weight in gold right now in the China-Burma-India theater. We're all mighty glad, Joseph, to see you back here in one piece — and we'll be even happier to see you back in the air again."

While Joseph recovered from his injuries, outside the windows of the sick bay the roar of heavy transports, bombers and fighters landing and taking off remained constant round the clock. The massive Japanese invasion army was still advancing westward across China, even threatening Kunming itself, and vital Allied supplies for the Chinese were still being ferried in nonstop from India over the "Hump" of the Himalayas to beat the enemy's blockade. In Europe British, American and Russian forces were sweeping inexorably into Germany from east and west, and it seemed almost certain that the global conflict was entering its climactic phase. But even though the noise of war was all around him in his hospital bed, Joseph still retained something of that curious sense of detachment that had come to him in the mountains of Tongking. To his surprise he no longer felt the same fierce compulsion to return to combat that he'd always felt before, and he found himself pondering the good fortune that had ensured his survival when he felt certain he would die. The images of his days with the Annamese guerrillas haunted his mind and drew his thoughts back to the past brushes with their country. He remembered too with a feeling of abiding affection the enigmatic guerrilla leader who had shown such concern for him at Pac Bo, but when a medical orderly brought him a brief handwritten message asking permission for its writer to visit him in the first week of March, he stared blankly at its signature.

"C. M. Hoo? I don't know anybody by that name." He studied the spidery scrawl on the sheet of green rice paper, then raised an inquiring eyebrow at the orderly. "Who gave you the note?"

The orderly shrugged. "An old Chinese guy. He looks like some kind of beggar. Says he'd like to wish you well and claims you once met someplace with a Chinese name I can't pronounce."

"You'd better send him in," said Joseph without enthusiasm, then sat up suddenly in his bed a minute later when he saw the familiar khaki-clad figure in the battered cork helmet hobbling down the ward, leaning on a bamboo cane.

"I'm glad to see you're getting better treatment here than at Pac Bo, Captain Sherman," said the Annamese humorously as he shook Joseph by the hand. "I hope you're almost recovered now."

"I didn't recognize the name you gave in your message," said Joseph, staring in disbelief.

"Ah yes, I wrote it the way most Americans like it — nice and simple with the family name last and an extra *o*. I'd forgotten you're a man used to the ways of the Orient."

"But what are you doing here in Kunming, Monsieur Ho?"

The Annamese continued to smile at Joseph's mystification. "I'm no stranger to Kunming, captain. Because it's close to the Tongking border, the 'City of Eternal Spring' has often served as a place of refuge over the years for nationalists from my country."

"And have you come here to seek refuge?"

"No." The Annamese shook his head, still smiling broadly. "I come here from time to time to find out what's happening in the rest of the world. I like to read back copies of your excellent *Time* magazine in the library of the U.S. Office of War Information — it keeps me up to date."

"And how did you get here?"

"I walked across the border to Ching Hsi."

Joseph gasped. "But that must be two hundred miles."

"Yes, maybe more," said the Annamese simply. "It took me two weeks. My feet are a little sore now, but I got used to walking when I was a prisoner in China."

"But you didn't walk all this way just to read old copies of *Time*," protested Joseph.

The dark intense eyes regarding the American twinkled suddenly and he nodded in assent. "You're right of course, captain. I came to offer the services of the Viet Minh League to General Chennault. I thought we could rescue more pilots if we had better arms and some radios — but your Office of Strategic Services shows no interest. They say no arms can be given to us in case we use them against the French, who are your allies in Europe. They won't even give me a single Colt .45 for myself — and they won't allow me to see your general."

"Didn't you tell them that you've already rescued one American pilot?"

The Annamese nodded. "Yes, but I don't think they believed me." He waved a self-deprecating hand at his dusty clothes and smiled ruefully. "Maybe you can't blame them. I don't really look capable of saving anyone — even myself."

When Joseph laughed, the Annamese joined in, and his

engaging honesty caused a new feeling of affection to well up inside the American.

"Your OSS officers are too preoccupied, you see, with the idea that we may be Communists," continued Ho, his eyes still twinkling. "They listen only to Chiang Kai-shek and the Free French intelligence people. I warned you about that, didn't I?"

"And what did you tell them?"

"I said that the French like to condemn as Communists all those who want independence in Indochina. And because Chiang Kai-shek has spent more energy fighting Mao Tse-tung than he has fighting the Japanese, he's anxious to condemn the Viet Minh as Communist too."

"I'll have a word with General Chennault myself," said Joseph impulsively. "I've already told him what your people did for me. Your request to see him has probably never got past his aides."

"Please don't go to any trouble on my behalf," said Ho, frowning and laying a restraining hand on Joseph's arm. "You must rest and recover from your injuries. I didn't come here to disturb you."

"It's no trouble after all you did for me," insisted Joseph, patting the hand of the Annamese and smiling.

"If a meeting proves impossible, I would be happy to have just a simple memento from the general," said Ho hastily. "I've heard that he keeps a supply of glossy photographs to give away to those who admire his leadership. If you could persuade him to sign one for me, I would be grateful."

Joseph laughed. "A glossy photograph is the very least you'll get, Monsieur Ho, I promise you that. And as a personal thank you from me, I'll see you get a few Colt .45s and a box or two of ammunition. But I think General Chennault will agree to see you when I tell him who you are and what you've done. How long will you be staying in Kunming?"

"A week or two. I've rented a little room above a candlemaker's shop."

"Then come back and see me again in a week."

The Annamese stood up suddenly, his face thoughtful. "Thank you, captain. . . . Those Colt .45s you mentioned would be most welcome — especially if you could let me have them unopened in their original sealed packages. . . . Now I must go before I tire you with too much talk." He shook Joseph's hand firmly and began to move away. Then he hesitated and turned back again, unbuttoning one of the pockets of his faded khaki tunic; for a moment a little smile of embarrassment played across his lined face. "Would you forgive a sentimental old man, Captain Sherman, if in return

for your kindness he offered you a humble poem he had written?"
Ho held a folded sheet of green rice paper towards the American.

"I'd be very glad to accept it," replied Joseph, touched by the gesture. "Lat read me some of your poetry at Pac Bo. I admired it then."

"I wrote this while I was walking here through the mountains. You came into my thoughts and I hoped you were making a good recovery. You had come close to death in your airplane and survived. It reminded me of my own escape from death — I almost died while I was in prison in China."

Joseph unfolded the paper to find a nine-line poem penned in the same spidery handwriting that he recognized from the earlier note. It was written in English, and had obviously been translated from the original Chinese. It read:

> *Everything evolves, that is how nature wills it*
> *After days of rain, fine weather returns*
> *Suddenly the whole world throws off its damp garments*
> *And carpets of green brocade sparkle on the mountains*
> *The sun is warm, the wind is clean, the flowers smile*
> *Rain has washed the trees and birds sing happily*
> *The heart of man is warmed, life reawakens*
> *At last sorrow gives way to happiness*
> *Because that is how nature wishes it to be*

Feeling himself moved by the poem's simple optimism, Joseph glanced up from the paper to thank its writer. But the Annamese was already stumping away down the ward, and although Joseph watched him all the way to the door, he went out without a backward glance.

8

The next visitor, who appeared at Joseph's hospital bedside five days later, was a stranger to him. A red-haired army colonel in his early forties, he made great play of placing screens securely round the bed before subjecting the graffiti on Joseph's leg cast to a long humorous scrutiny. When he'd finished he grinned owlishly and extended his hand. "That plaster should be preserved in a military museum when your leg mends, captain. It's good evidence for future generations of the average U.S. fighting man's sexual obsessions in the twentienth century. I'm Colonel John Trench. You don't know me, but I know a lot about you — mostly from an old Annamite buddy of yours who tells me he's practically crawled here from Tongking on his hands and knees."

Joseph grinned. "Where did you meet him?"

"Mister C. M. Hoo, as he likes to call himself, has been haunting the reading room of the Office of War Information off and on for months. Until General Chennault passed me your note about him last week we merely humored him — thought he must be some kind of Annamite oddball who got his kicks making up stories about saving Yankee pilots from the jungle. But when the Japanese suddenly closed off Indochina the day after we saw your note, we went running to look for that candlemaker's shop you mentioned and had a long talk with him." Colonel Trench paused and raised his eyebrows in an expression of inquiry. "You've been following the news, captain?"

Joseph nodded. All radio bulletins of the past three days had been carrying details of the surprise Japanese takeover in French Indochina. On March 9, a force sixty thousand strong had attacked the colonial garrisons that totaled only half that number, and all government buildings, radio stations, factories and banks had been seized. Some resistance had been offered by the French in Saigon, Hue and Hanoi, but it had been quickly overcome, and the troops, their officers and hundreds of prominent French civilians had been interned in barracks and special concentration camps. A few French units had escaped and, according to the news bulletins, were still fighting desperate rearguard actions as they retreated across the highlands towards Laos.

"What was it that made Tokyo turn on the French so suddenly, do you think?" asked Joseph.

"It was always in the cards, I guess, but the Japs seem to have got the idea that Uncle Sam's ready to launch an invasion any day now all along that fifteen-hundred-mile Indochina coastline. Maybe they reckoned the French were getting ready to hit them from the rear."

"And what gave them that idea?"

"After five years of close collaboration with the yellow dwarfs, the French were a bit hasty in trying to switch horses and prove they've been loyal Free French supporters of de Gaulle all along." The colonel grinned broadly again to indicate his skepticism. "Ever since Paris was liberated they've been sticking his picture on walls everywhere and daubing Free French slogans all over the streets."

"But are we planning to invade Indochina?"

The colonel peered out through the bed screens for a moment, then lowered his voice. "If we are, captain, nobody's bothered to tell me or anybody else in OSS Special Intelligence, Kunming."

He grinned at Joseph again as he watched the casual reference to the Office of Strategic Services sink in. As a pilot, Joseph knew little of the OSS role in China; he assumed that undercover agents had been organizing resistance groups wherever they could behind Japanese lines in accordance with normal OSS practice, but beyond that, the organization's activities were a closely guarded secret. "Monsieur Ho told me the OSS weren't much interested in him or Indochina," said Joseph, studying the face of the intelligence colonel closely. "He said you were too worried about possible Communist connections — and you wouldn't consider giving his group arms or equipment in case they used them against our French allies."

Trench nodded. "That's right, captain, that's just how it was — last week."

"So what's changed your mind?"

"The Japanese coup in Indochina! The flow of intelligence from the Free French underground has been turned off like a tap. Suddenly we're getting nothing on things like bombing targets, antiaircraft defenses, troop deployments. And with sixty thousand more Japanese rearing up on their hind legs down there, the spotlight's on that neck of the woods. Air attacks are being stepped up and the order of the day coming from OSS headquarters in Chungking is 'Get some kind of goddamned intelligence network down there — fast.' So we've recruited your friend Hoo into one of our little offshoot intelligence groups. His work name is 'Lucius' and we're flying him back to the border tonight with a two-way radio and a Chinese-American operator. If he's got a political organization several hundred strong spread across Tongking like you say, he should be able to deliver the intelligence goods we need if he's handled right." The colonel grinned and leaned across the bed suddenly, tapping Joseph's chest lightly with his forefinger. "And that's where Captain Joseph T. Sherman, late of the Fourteenth Army Air Force, comes in — to help do the handling. Nobody around these parts realized, until our old Annamite friend put us wise, that we were using somebody with a head full of Asian history and Chinese and French language capability to heave bombs and bullets at the Japs. And when I looked up your record and found you'd published a slim volume on the Annamites, I went hotfoot to Big Chief Flying Tiger to poach you

305

for OSS operations in Indochina. He'll yield to my powers of persuasion so long as you give the okay. What do you say, captain?"

Joseph felt a sudden throb of excitement somewhere deep inside him. "What sort of job are you offering me exactly, colonel?"

"Running the research and analysis backup in Kunming to start with. We're going to be parachuting people into Tongking soon." He nodded at Joseph's plaster. "When you finally dispense with your graffiti collection, maybe we'll send you in with a full team to swashbuckle around the jungle a little. Organize some training and some sabotage maybe. Your old Annamite pal speaks highly of you. You're Number One in his book. He says he'd be glad to make you welcome out there in the hills again real soon. Does that appeal to you?"

"Getting shot at on the ground might make a welcome change from getting shot at in the air, now that I think of it," replied Joseph, grinning suddenly.

Colonel Trench grinned too and patted him on the shoulder. "Okay. You can hobble on crutches already, can't you? I've arranged for you and Hoo to see the general together this afternoon before he leaves. I'll be there too."

"There's just one final condition," said Joseph quickly as the OSS colonel began drawing back the screens around the bed.

"What's that?"

"I need half-a-dozen Colt .45s, sealed and in their original packages, and a box or two of ammunition — and I need them today."

Trench's eyebrows shot up humorously. "The swashbuckling's supposed to come later, captain. What would a man in your condition want with stuff like that?"

"I want to give a present to our friend Monsieur Ho — a kind of personal thank you from 308 Squadron."

Trench pretended to consider the request with great gravity. "All right, captain, you win. But you'd better make damned sure you do six Colts'-worth of work for OSS before this war ends."

Outside General Chennault's office that afternoon, they were kept waiting for half an hour while grim-faced American and Chinese officers dashed in and out of hurried meetings with their commander. In the anteroom Joseph noticed that the Annamese, who greeted him with his usual warm handshake and brilliant smile, had pressed and darned his ragged khaki tunic for the occasion. Colonel Trench was carrying a zipped up canvas hold-all when he arrived, and he winked theatrically in Joseph's direction as he placed it beside his chair.

Although the walls had been soundproofed, the dull roar of aircraft arriving and departing was still faintly audible from outside, and when at last the three of them were ushered into the office they found Chennault working behind a big paper-strewn desk with the United States flag standing against the wall behind him. Three rows of bright medal ribbons gleamed above the left breast pocket of his uniform jacket, and he rose at once and offered his hand in greeting to the Annamese. "I'm glad to meet you, Mister Hoo," he said courteously. "It gives me the opportunity to say a personal thank you for rescuing one of my best pilots." A smile flitted briefly across the general's craggy face, but his manner remained distracted, as though with half his mind he was still considering how best to juggle the limited number of men, machines and supplies at his disposal to defeat the Japanese.

"The greatest privilege is mine, general," said the Annamese, inclining his head respectfully. "I never thought I should be fortunate enough to shake hands with such a famous American fighting man. I've admired you for many years, ever since you and your handful of volunteer Flying Tigers heroically drove Japan's bombers from the skies above China's big cities."

The unexpected fluency of his shabbily dressed visitor's English and the ardent sincerity of his words immediately brought a broad smile of pleasure to the American general's face, and he hastened to pull a chair into position for him beside his desk. "I thank you for your kind compliment, sir," replied Chennault chivalrously. "I'm surprised to find someone from your country knows about such things."

Ho Chi Minh glanced pointedly at the map of China and Southeast Asia on the wall behind the American, then smiled directly at him again. "There can hardly be anybody in Asia who hasn't heard of the man who's proved to be the greatest single obstacle to Japan's conquest of China, general. I can see, now that I've met you, why some of your own flyers talk of you as 'the nearest thing to God any guy will ever know.' "

All the Americans were moved to friendly laughter by Ho's deft use of American vernacular, and when a pretty secretary in khaki brought tea in Chinese-style cups with lids, they sat down and discussed with great good humor Joseph's rescue and his surprise return to Kunming. They talked too about possible future rescues, but in accordance with a briefing given him by Colonel Trench, the

Annamese studiously avoided introducing any discussion of politics, and as the OSS colonel saw Chennault glancing at his watch, he stood up to indicate they should leave.

"I thank you most humbly for sparing your time to receive me, general," said Ho, smiling ingratiatingly once more. "But before I go, may I ask one small favor?"

Chennault glanced impatiently towards a new sheaf of papers his secretary had just placed before him and nodded absently.

"It is nothing more than a schoolboy's request, general," added Ho hastily. "But I would like a memento of my meeting with you. When I tell people I've met the American who built the Flying Tigers into a mighty modern air force, I'd like to be able to show them your picture."

Chennault smiled with a mixture of relief and embarrassment and signaled for his secretary to bring a folder of glossy photographs. When she handed one to Ho, he stepped up to the desk and placed it on the blotter. "And if you could be kind enough to sign it for me, general, it would be more than I deserve."

Chennault uncapped his pen and scrawled *Yours sincerely — Claire L. Chennault* across the bottom of the picture, then handed it back to the Annamese. "Keep up the good work, Mister Hoo," he said with a note of finality, and before his visitors had filed from the room he had returned to his papers.

Outside in the waiting room Joseph handed over the canvas holdall containing the six Colt .45s and a thousand rounds of ammunition, and the face of the Annamese lit up with gratitude.

"You've more than repaid me for the little service I did you, Captain Sherman," he said, clasping Joseph's hand with both his own. "And Colonel Trench has told me that I may hope that we'll meet again when you are fully recovered. I shall look forward with great happiness to that day."

Two hours later a little L-5 "grasshopper," capable of landing in short jungle clearings, took off from Kunming and headed south over the city's ring of blue hills towards Ching Hsi carrying "C. M. Hoo," an OSS two-way radio and a trained Chinese-American operator. As soon as the plane landed the two men donned the garb of Nung mountain tribesmen to give themselves the appearance of border smugglers and struck out on foot through rain and darkness towards Tongking; the Chinese-American humped the radio equipment in big shoulder satchels and the frail Annamese himself carried the hold-all containing the precious, guilefully won symbols of American support — the new revolvers and the signed picture of Chennault. Because Tokyo had put its Indochina divisions on twenty-four-hour border alert following the coup, they were forced to walk by night and hide by day, and the journey to Pac Bo took them nearly two weeks. But once the radio was in place, accurate reliable intelligence about Japanese targets and troop movements began to flow steadily back to Kunming and was rapidly distributed to all America's allies. By the time Captain Joseph Sherman was sufficiently recovered two months later to transfer formally from the 308th Squadron to a desk in the Kunming headquarters of the OSS, radios, weapons and other supplies were being parachuted regularly into the Tongking jungle, and the Annamese agent, code-named "Lucius," who called himself Ho Chi Minh, had become the head of one of America's most successful wartime intelligence networks in Asia.

9

Lieutenant David Hawke watched intently through one of the side windows of the little single-engined "grasshopper" as eight other OSS men tumbled from the open door of the C-46 transport up ahead and plummeted down towards the terraced mountainside rice fields of Tongking seventy-five miles northwest of Hanoi. He held his breath until all their chutes had opened, then turned to peer out through the windshield over the pilot's shoulder as the L-5 went into a banked turn. Ahead lay another stretch of jagged karst hills and valleys smothered with jungle, and he scrutinized the wild landscape anxiously for signs of a level clearing.

"They told me when they lured me into this outfit, captain, that they wanted guys who were 'calculatingly reckless,' " he said, turning to grin wryly at Joseph Sherman. "But if you want my view, I think there's too much recklessness involved here and not enough calculation. Unless I see it with my own eyes I won't believe this flying matchbox can actually get down there in one god-damned piece and take off again."

Joseph smiled as he watched the crates of bazookas, machine guns, carbines and grenade launchers tumble earthwards from the door of a second C-46 behind them. "Don't worry, Dave, any man in the Fourteenth could stroll in and out of here with his eyes closed."

The young American pilot at the controls grinned at the

compliment as he eased the little plane towards the treetops, searching intently ahead for the first sight of the unmarked clearing hacked out of the jungle by the Viet Minh guerrillas. It was the last day of July 1945, and behind them the sun was already touching the western peaks of the mountains; somewhere in the dense rain forest below was the new secret headquarters of the Viet Minh League, the target of a ten-man OSS Special Operations team which Joseph was leading. Code-named the "Deer Mission," its task was to train and arm the Viet Minh for sabotage attacks against roads and railways linking Hanoi with Japanese bases in southern China. Since March the Allies had gradually forced the Imperial Army onto the defensive, but it had so far shown no signs of collapsing as Hitler's forces had finally done in Europe in early May. Consequently a long, hard Allied fight to subdue Japan was still in prospect, and a top-level order had gone out from the White House to "help anybody who will help us shoot at the Japanese."

Unexpectedly a little natural clearing that had been enlarged to a length of a hundred and fifty yards, opened up below the plane, and Lieutenant Hawke let out an exclamation of disbelief when he spotted a little group of guerrillas gathered at one end. "It's not much bigger than a goddamned football field," he gasped as the pilot waggled his wings and began turning to make a final approach. "I think I'd rather jump, captain — is there a chute on board?" The boyish features of the twenty-three-year-old Bostonian law graduate were flushed with excitement, and his easy grin belied his exaggerated expressions of alarm. He had completed a crash course in Annamese at the University of California only six months before and had been recruited into the OSS as an interpreter while still at Berkeley. "Did you spot 'Lucius' among the welcoming party, captain?" he asked, turning eagerly to Joseph again. "I'm sure looking forward to clapping eyes on him."

"I didn't see him. The last radio message said he's down with fever again. He drives himself hard and his health is poor."

"He's a real Chinese puzzle, that old guy, isn't he? Every American who's dropped in to work with him in the last few months raves about his 'gentleness' and his 'sweet nature.' But there wasn't anything gentle about the way he closed off Tongking to the Free French agents, was there? Marching the one Frenchman we sent in back to the border and threatening to snipe at any others who came in or starve them out didn't seem like the actions of a *gentle* old guy to me."

"The Annamese have good reason to hate the French, David," said Joseph quietly. "I don't think you'll find it too hard to sympathize with them when you've talked to 'Lucius' and some of the others."

As the L-5 passed over the treetops at the edge of the clearing, the pilot let it drop like an elevator, and it touched down and bumped to a standstill with twenty yards to spare. When Joseph climbed out, he recognized instantly the dapper little Annamese with the shock of dark hair who stepped smartly forward to greet him at the head of the small welcoming party of guerrillas.

"We're glad to welcome you back again, Captain Sherman," said Vo Nguyen Giap, speaking French, and smiling as he extended his hand. "I trust you've recovered from your injuries."

"I'm fine now, thank you, 'Monsieur Van,'" replied Joseph, using Giap's OSS code-name. "My leg's still a little stiff, but it's nice to be back with you standing on my own two feet. How's everything here?"

"All the Americans who parachuted in have landed safely. My men have gone down the valley to help them collect the supplies and guide them back to camp."

"And how is Monsieur Ho?"

Giap's face clouded with concern. "He's gravely ill, captain. Walking to and from Ching Hsi in the rains has badly sapped his strength. Have you brought a doctor with you?"

Joseph shook his head. "No — but one of the men who jumped in is a medical orderly and he's carrying drugs and medicines with him."

"Perhaps he could make an examination the moment he arrives," replied the Annamese, then turned and led the way quickly out of the clearing along a narrow jungle trail.

The guerrilla encampment, a huddle of crude stilted huts thatched with palm leaves, had been set up on the side of a hill in a dense bamboo forest close to the Kim Lung gorge, and as soon as the OSS parachutists arrived, Giap showed Joseph and the young medical orderly into one of them. They found Ho lying in a corner, trembling violently; he had become very thin, his skin had turned a sickly yellow color and he was moaning and crying aloud in a semiconscious state of delirium, obviously incapable of recognizing anyone.

"I spent all last night with him," whispered Giap to Joseph as the young OSS medic bent to examine the Annamese. "In between his comas he spoke with great urgency of what the Viet Minh League still must do. Every time he thought of something, he urged me not to forget it. I'm afraid that he believed they were his dying thoughts."

They watched grim-faced as the medic completed his examination. When he stood up his face was resigned.

"What's wrong with him, private?" asked Joseph tersely.

"Malaria and dysentery for sure. But he's probably suffering from half the tropical diseases in the book. I guess it's just a matter of time."

"Can't you do anything for him?"

"I can give him quinine and sulfur if he'll hold still long enough — but I don't promise any miracles."

"Okay," snapped Joseph, staring down at the skeletal figure. "Go ahead."

When the medic had prepared the syringe he knelt to inject the drugs into Ho's scrawny upper arm, but the Annamese suddenly began to struggle violently and the needle of the syringe snapped.

"Let me do it!" commanded Joseph impatiently, dropping to his knees. "Prepare a new syringe."

Taking the struggling Annamese by the shoulders, he leaned close to him. "Please listen carefully. I'm Joseph Sherman. I've brought American medicine from Kunming. You're not going to die." He spoke slowly in English, enunciating his words with great precision and keeping his own face in the center of the dying man's vision. "Please let me help you."

Almost immediately the rolling eyes grew still, and the Annamese ceased to writhe on the mat. Joseph signaled for the new syringe to be placed in his open hand, and he injected its contents into Ho's biceps at a spot indicated by the medic. For a minute or two he continued to kneel by the mat holding the clammy hands that gripped his own convulsively, then when they went limp, he stood up.

"Stay with him right through the night," he told the medic. "I'll look in from time to time."

Outside the hut Giap searched Joseph's face with anxious eyes. "Do you think there's any possibility he'll recover, Captain Sherman?"

"We can only hope and pray he'll respond to the drugs," said Joseph. "But my medic thinks you must be prepared for the worst."

All around them the Annamese guerrillas were dragging into camp the heavy crates of armaments and explosives that had been scattered across the rice paddies in the wake of the OSS parachutists, and Giap excused himself to give orders for storing the weapons. One of his lieutenants showed the OSS men to a separate group of new bamboo-floored huts in front of which a fire had already been lit, and after washing in a fast-flowing stream nearby, Joseph returned to his hut to find the appetizing smell of roasting meat wafting across the darkened clearing.

"We slaughtered a cow in honor of your arrival, Captain Sherman," said a friendly voice, speaking French, and Joseph looked up to find an Annamese standing in the doorway. "We thought our newly arrived American comrades-in-arms should enjoy their favorite dish — steak — on their first night with us."

Joseph stared at the face of the man, transfixed. Although he was in his early thirties, his delicate features were still, like many of his race, childlike, almost feminine, and in the gentle orange glow of the camp fire a fleeting hint of the beauty which Lan and her brothers had inherited from their mother stirred Joseph's emotional memory. For an instant the image of Lan's modestly lowered eyelids and the curve of her cheek glowing like warmed honey in the light of the Nam Giao sacrificial pyres flashed into his mind's eye, and he stepped forward impulsively and shook Tran Van Kim's hand with unwarranted warmth.

"It's been a long time, Kim, When I last saw you, you were whipping the French tennis champion in Saigon."

A wistful smile illuminated Kim's face. "That seems like part of another life now, captain. When my uncle, Dao Van Lat, told me he'd met you again at Pac Bo, I remembered with embarrassment I had not been very courteous to you at the Cercle Sportif."

"Don't worry about that," Joseph laughed and patted him on the shoulder. "I asked Lat how your family were, but he said you hadn't had any contact with them for many years."

Kim nodded his confirmation, his expression sad. "That's right. Unfortunately I fell out with my father. He believed our future lay with France — perhaps he still does. I've had to sacrifice my family ties to the struggle for freedom."

"And you haven't heard how Lan is? Or whether she married?"

"Distant friends told me she married a Frenchman."

"Was it Captain Devraux?"

Kim shook his head a little impatiently. "I'm sorry, I don't really know. I expect she made the marriage to please my father. . . . But perhaps we should talk of more important things, captain." He took Joseph's arm, beckoned to the other Americans and led them to a rough bamboo table near to the fire where the food had been set out. He ordered the meat to be served to the Americans, but took only bean sprouts and rice himself. "In the seven months since you first visited us, Captain Sherman, our forces have expanded greatly," he said as they ate. "We've got three thousand guerrilla fighters under arms now, and since the French were imprisoned we've won control of the six northernmost provinces of Tongking. All this region is our 'liberated zone,' and Hanoi is only seventy miles away. We've got better armaments too from abandoned French stores, but we're very eager to learn how to use the wonderful new weapons you've brought us. . . ."

At that moment Vo Nguyen Giap joined the circle and, with Lieutenant Hawke acting as interpreter, began to discuss the training program with the OSS weapons instructors. Towards the end of the meal, some captured Japanese beer was produced, and light-hearted toasts were drunk to victory over the country where it was brewed. As the group broke up to go to their huts, Joseph took Tran Van Kim by the arm and drew him to one side. "When you won your tennis final in Saigon, Kim, you were a convinced Communist, weren't you? Are you still?"

The Annamese shook his head vigorously. "Only the French and the Chinese spread propaganda that the Viet Minh League is Communist — because the French still dream of ruling us again one day and the Chinese are trying to set up their own puppet nationalist party here. Uncle Ho has said many times he no longer favors revolution. Once he believed in Communism, but he will tell you himself he's realized now that such ideals are impractical for our country. I share his new beliefs. Now it will be up to the people to decide the form of government they want. You can call us republican nationalists, if you like. If the people want to keep the emperor as a constitutional monarch without real power, we won't object."

"But what about the rest of the Viet Minh League? How many Communist members do you have?"

Kim grinned slowly. "How many different parties were there in America, captain, when you were fighting for independence from the British? Ninety percent of the people of Tongking support us, and most of them are uneducated peasants who understand nothing of politics. But they're all patriots who understand very well the words 'liberty' and 'independence' — and that's what all of us are fighting for."

Joseph nodded. "Sure, I can understand that. Thanks for killing the fatted calf for my men."

Inside his hut Joseph quickly wrote an arrival report for transmission to Kunming. It read: "Deer Mission down safely with all supplies. 'Lucius' found gravely ill but otherwise all is well. Weapons training begins tomorrow. Forget once and for all the Communist bogey. Viet Minh League stands for freedom and reforms from French harshness and is an amalgamation of all existing parties. It now claims three thousand men under its command and the support of ninety percent of Tongking's population. It is not — repeat not — Communist, or Communist-controlled or Communist-led. 'Lucius' is no rabid revolutionary but in my view a sincere, capable leader who wants autonomy for his people and speaks genuinely for them."

Just as he finished encoding the message with a one-time pad, Joseph heard a footfall outside his hut and looked up to find Kim smiling uncertainly and gesticulating across the clearing. When he stepped outside he saw two slender Annamese girls bending over the dying embers of the fire, stirring a cooking pot.

"We want you to be comfortable here, captain," said Kim awkwardly. "In case you should have difficulty sleeping in the jungle, I've arranged for you to try an ancient soothing drink of the hill tribes."

In the firelight Joseph could see that the girls were young, scarcely out of their teens. Both were dressed in the dark, high-necked *ao dai* of the north and wore their glossy black hair loose about their shoulders.

"They're entertainers in Hanoi," said Kim quietly. "We had them brought through the Japanese lines yesterday in time for your arrival."

On hearing Kim's voice, Lieutenant Hawke came out of the adjoining hut, grinning from ear to ear. "I don't believe it," he whispered incredulously, staring towards the fire, then began firing rapid questions at Kim in Annamese. When he turned to look at Joseph again his grin was broader than ever. "They're brewing up a potent jungle aphrodisiac made from cassava root and all kinds of things — maybe even dried tiger's penis. How about that?"

"Remember, lieutenant, we're here on U.S. Army business, fighting a war," grinned Joseph, taking Hawke firmly by the shoulders and propelling him towards the darkness of his bamboo shelter. "For that you need a clear head and lots of sleep — on your own." Turning back to Kim, he smiled apologetically. "Thanks for the kind thought — and please thank the girls too. But tell them we're all very tired."

After Kim had gone and he had dispatched the coded radio message to Kunming, Joseph lay awake listening to the night noises of the bamboo forest. Seeing the two young Annamese girls in the firelight had brought disturbing bittersweet memories of Lan flooding back into his mind; he remembered suddenly the silky feel of her long hair and saw again the soft, bright color of her golden body as she lay naked in his arms during that enchanted hour on the River of Perfumes. As the night wore on, he grew more restless, and twice he rose and crossed the silent clearing to Ho Chi Minh's hut; but each time he found him sleeping peacefully and stayed only long enough to supervise further injections of sulfur and quinine. Just before dawn he fell into an exhausted sleep and dreamed of Lan, more vividly than he had ever done before, and when the discordant cries of jungle birds broke this brief slumber, he felt strangely comforted and consoled by these fresh images of her lovely face. As he came fully awake, an indefinable sense of pleasure and contentment began to grow in him at the mere thought that he was back once more in the country where he had briefly known such intense happiness with her.

10

Every day during the first week of August 1945 Joseph and other team members of the Deer Mission rose at dawn and marched two hundred of the best Viet Minh guerrillas to a nearby jungle firing range. From five-thirty A.M. until five o'clock in the afternoon, without letup, they taught the ragged Annamese how to assemble and fire the carbines, light machine guns, antitank bazookas and grenade launchers they had brought from Kunming. The OSS men in their badgeless bush shirts, knee-length shorts, jungle boots and forage caps towered above the diminutive Asian guerrilla fighters, but without exception all the Americans quickly developed a strong, almost paternal affection for their charges.

As the training progressed, Joseph began to send out joint patrols to reconnoiter Japanese targets. From places of concealment they watched supply convoys roll down the nearby Colonial Route 3 and the major Hanoi–Lang Son highway farther to the east which led into China, and plans eventually were laid to make the first attacks the following week. In that remote and mountainous jungle terrain behind the Japanese lines, where they shared a common danger and a common diet of rice and bean sprouts, the high-spirited OSS men and their energetic Annamese allies soon developed a sense of close camaraderie rooted in a mutual respect. The Annamese were in awe of the big, good-natured Americans and their fine weapons, and in their turn the OSS soldiers found the guerrillas eager, unflagging pupils. At the end of the first week the chief OSS weapons instructor told Joseph that more progress had been made than he'd dared hope.

"The capacity of these little guys for learning is amazing," he said, shaking his head. "You've only got to show them once and they've got it. They're making the change from homemade knives and old muskets to antitank bazookas and grenade launchers without turning a hair."

During the first two days of training Joseph slipped back to camp from time to time to check on the condition of the sick leader of the Viet Minh, but these visits soon became unnecessary; with a speed that astonished the Americans and the Annamese alike, Ho threw off the fever and, only three days after receiving the first injections of American drugs, emerged unsteadily from his hut to walk around the camp. Although he was gaunt and hollow-cheeked, his eyes quickly regained their former brightness, and when he smiled, the warmth of the expression still transformed his ravaged face. By the end of the week he was back at work, and Joseph became aware that endless streams of Annamese strangers were slipping furtively into the camp day and night to talk with him in his hut.

During breaks in the training, however, Ho went out of his way to chat good-humoredly with each of the OSS men in turn, mixing polite inquiries about their families with earnest political discussion, as though he believed that each of them personally might carry his message to the White House. "All I ask is that you give news of Indochina to the rest of the world" was his most frequent smiling plea, and in the conversation he never failed to flatter and praise America for its "high political ideals." On the last day of the week, when he was obviously growing stronger, he invited Joseph to walk with him to the edge of the bamboo forest above the valley of terraced paddy fields onto which the Deer team's parachutes had floated a few days earlier. The sun was beginning to set behind the hills, bathing the spectacular landscape with golden light, and Ho sank down onto a tree stump, staring thoughtfully into the valley where peasants in wide straw hats were straggling home from fields, their hoes and plows slung across their shoulders.

"Life is strange, Captain Sherman, isn't it?" he said at last, turning a wistfully smiling face to Joseph. "Eight months ago I was able by chance to help save you from the Japanese — and now you've come back here to drag me out of death's jaws." His smile broadened and he held up a hand as Joseph made to protest. "Don't be modest, captain. My comrades told me how it was. They

317

were sure I was dying until you gave me that first injection."

"Your powers of recovery are remarkable," said Joseph. "You've obviously got a great determination to complete the task you've set yourself."

Ho smiled. "Perhaps. But I know I owe you and the United States of America a real debt of gratitude."

"The finest thing a man can do for another is give him his unselfish help," said Joseph quietly. "I'm glad I've been able to help someone with your remarkable gifts. I know something of what your country's suffered at the hands of France, and I admire you for what you're trying to do."

The Annamese sat staring down into the valley without turning his head. "Have you got a family, captain?" he asked at last in a quiet voice.

"I have two young sons."

"And what do you hope for them when this war's over?"

Joseph frowned, feeling a faint stab of remorse at the fact he had given so little thought to his family or the future for so long. "Only, I suppose, that they should be able to grow up in peace and freedom."

Ho Chi Minh nodded slowly in agreement. "I think in different ways we share the same hopes, captain."

"Have you any family?"

Ho continued gazing at the little knots of peasants wending their way homeward through the evening haze. "I've always devoted my life to my country," he said in an unemotional voice. "To me, all those men and women toiling down there are my family. I want the same peace and liberty for them as you want for your sons." He looked up at Joseph and smiled suddenly. "Can you by any chance recite those lines about liberty from your country's Declaration of Independence, captain?"

The American grinned affably. "I might be able to give you the essentials. We had to learn it by heart at my grade school." He closed his eyes to concentrate. " 'We hold these truths to be self-evident, that all men are created equal, that they are endowed by their Creator with certain unalienable Rights, that among these are Life, Liberty and the pursuit of Happiness. . . .' "

"Excellent! Please repeat that again slowly so that I can write it down."

Joseph opened his eyes to find the Annamese pulling a little sheaf of green rice paper from his tunic pocket, and he repeated the phrases again more slowly. "May I inquire why you're interested in the Declaration?" he asked when the older man had finished writing.

Ho smiled mysteriously as he tucked his pen and paper away. "I hope you won't have to wait very long, captain, to find out."

The sun was dipping behind the mountains, sending lengthening shadows creeping across the valley, and for a minute or two they watched the day fade together in silence. Then the Annamese drew a long breath. "Whenever I think about it, captain, I fear there's more chance of you getting your wish than there is of me getting mine."

"Why do you say that?"

"Because I'm sure France will try to return in force to rule us again. I know how the French mind works. They're proud people, the French, but insecure. There's only a small hope that they'll respect our rights and settle peacefully. And if they try to reimpose their rule by force, there will be great bloodshed." He nodded towards the valley. "Those people down there, like your sons, don't want revolution. That is why I'm determined to do everything in my power to negotiate peacefully with the French. But if this proves impossible, the people will fight — if necessary for ten or twenty years — for their own freedom and the freedom of future generations."

"Why are you worrying about this now?"

"Because we need the moral support of the freedom-loving American people. We know that they believe all nations should be free to choose their own form of government. They should be made aware of the true facts about the former French regime here. If Americans had this knowledge, I feel certain we would get their support. Couldn't you help us?"

Joseph shrugged apologetically. "Remember we're only soldiers, not diplomats. I can report what you say to my headquarters, but that's all. . . ."

Hearing the sound of running footsteps behind him, Joseph swung around to find one of his sergeant radio operators rushing towards them out of the forest.

"Captain Sherman, we've done it," he gasped as he skidded to a halt in front of them, his face flushed with excitement. "The Japs look like they're licked at last."

"What are you talking about, sergeant?" asked Joseph, mystified.

"We've hit them with a new secret weapon — something called an 'atom' bomb! We've just had a message from headquarters in Kunming. A whole damned city's been flattened. Place called

Hiroshima. . . ." The sergeant stumbled over the unfamiliar name. "They think it killed at least eighty thousand people. Eighty thousand, can you believe that? Kunming says a total Japanese surrender can only be a few days away."

When they had recovered from their initial surprise and the sergeant had gone, Joseph smiled ruefully at Ho. "If that message turns out to be true, I guess there won't be any Japanese lines to operate behind here much longer — and that makes the Deer Mission redundant."

"No, no, captain! You and your men must finish the training and march with us to Hanoi." Ho beamed and offered his hand. "And anyway, Hanoi is much nearer for you now than Kunming."

11

Ten days after Hiroshima was destroyed, Vo Nguyen Giap led the first excited detachment of Viet Minh guerrillas out of the camp to march on Hanoi. They carried their brand-new American carbines, bazookas and grenade launchers proudly on their shoulders, and beside them marched Captain Joseph Sherman and the other men of the OSS Deer Mission. As they descended through the forested valleys, they were greeted everywhere by crowds waving makeshift red flags emblazoned with the gold Viet Minh star. In the settlements of the hill tribes, native women in traditional blue costumes decked with silver thrust flowers into the arms of the tall Americans, and in the poor villages lower down the slopes, local guards clutching long knives and rusty rifles turned out to line their route. Modest gifts of eggs and bananas were pressed on them, and in some hamlets, groups of children gathered to sing songs about freedom and liberty as they passed. In this heady, festive atmosphere the guerrilla bands were feted like a conquering army, and Joseph and the other Americans, relieved above all else that at last the long war was over, whistled and sang their own marching songs as they swung along.

Sometimes the roads over which they passed were pitted with craters, and most of the bridges had been torn down; great tree trunks also blocked some vital road junctions, and Tran Van Kim, who marched beside Joseph, pointed out the obstructions with obvious pride. 'All this is the work of our own sabotage teams," he explained. "We dug these pits and smashed the bridges with our own hands to prevent the Japanese using the road."

Radio messages from undercover Viet Minh agents already in Hanoi reported that the Japanese forces there seemed stunned by the sudden surrender of their leaders. They had adopted a stance of passive neutrality, and as a result the capital was very quiet, the agents reported. No Japanese patrols were sighted by the guerrilla column during the first day, and it moved on openly at a crisp pace, crossing great flat expanses of flooded paddy fields where gold-starred Viet Minh flags fluttered from the roadside telegraph poles.

Occasionally the marchers passed through deserted, burned-out villages where the ruins still smoldered, but to Joseph's surprise, no order was ever given by Giap to stop and investigate. "What's happening to these places?" he asked at last as the column was led on yet another detour to avoid a devastated settlement where several bodies were visible lying among the smoking debris. "They look as if they've been attacked very recently."

"The Japanese razed them to the ground as they retreated," replied Tran Van Kim curtly, then hurried on ahead.

Lieutenant Hawke, who was marching beside Joseph, raised an inquiring eyebrow at him and jerked his head towards the village; when Joseph nodded, he chose a suitable moment to fall out of the line unnoticed and doubled quickly back to the jumble of smoldering huts. When he caught up to Joseph half an hour later, his face was grim.

"The Japanese haven't been near here for weeks, captain," he said in an undertone. "I found an old Annamese wandering in the ruins back there. An advance guard of our guerrilla friends came this way yesterday — and that village refused to cooperate. The old man told me it was burned and sacked to terrorize the rest of the region into supporting them. All his family were killed." Hawke paused and took a deep breath. "What's more, he didn't talk about the Viet Minh League. When I asked him who'd done it, he just cursed over and over again and said, 'Cong San Dang! Cong San Dang!' — the Communists!"

The information shocked Joseph, and when the guerrilla column halted outside the provincial capital of Thai Nguyen, he sought out Tran Van Kim and asked him where he could find Ho.

"I'm afraid he's very busy now, captain," said Kim apologetically. "He's got a great many things to organize — but I'll pass on your message that you wish to speak with him."

When Joseph hinted at his misgivings in a radio report to Kunming, OSS headquarters immediately ordered him to halt the

Deer Mission in Thai Nguyen and go no further. Because of the uncertain political situation in what was a relative backwater of the war, he was told, a new OSS team, code-named "Quail," was being sent to Hanoi from Kunming, headed by Colonel John Trench himself. Its primary mission was to locate and liberate Allied prisoners of war in Japanese hands and prepare for the arrival of the Allied Surrender Commission, but it would also gather intelligence; a similar OSS mission, Kunming said, was being sent to Saigon from Calcutta. Joseph asked if the Deer team could take the surrender of local Japanese forces but was told curtly: "Take no surrenders and stay where you are. The war's over as far as the Deer team's concerned."

After a brief rest, the guerrilla force split into two, and Joseph watched Giap lead a little spearhead force out of the town towards Hanoi, with their gleaming American weapons on their shoulders. The rest of the column laid a siege around the fortified barracks into which the local Japanese garrison had retreated, occasionally bombarding the defenders to test their new armaments. Joseph commandeered a big house on the outskirts of the town for himself and the OSS team, and while his men sunbathed in the garden he fumed with impatience as several days passed without any word from Ho Chi Minh.

At dusk on their third evening there, Tran Van Kim arrived at the house unexpectedly, his face alight with pleasure. "Today will certainly go down in our history as a great day for the people, Captain Sherman," he said excitedly. "We've just had a message from Vo Nguyen Giap saying that our advance party has seized control of the public buildings in Hanoi. The Japanese were astonished to see them arrive in the city with their powerful new weapons. They offered almost no resistance. We had to fire only a few volleys over their heads. Now the capital is ours, and the people are flooding into the streets waving Viet Minh banners!"

Joseph received the news in silence, the nagging suspicion that he and the Deer Mission had been exploited and misled growing into a certainty.

"The people of Hanoi are beside themselves with excitement," said Kim, still grinning. "They've been delivered from the Japanese and the French at one stroke. They've seen our fighters carrying American arms and are overjoyed that the might of America is on the side of their liberators."

"It's truly a great day for the Annamese people," said Joseph slowly, torn between the sympathy he felt for Ho and his followers and his anger at being deceived.

"You're right, captain," said Kim in a gently chiding voice, "except for one small important detail — it's a great day for the 'Vietnamese' people. We're not 'Annamese' or 'Annamites' any-more, and our country isn't divided into 'protectorates' any longer. Before the French came our land was called 'Viet Nam.' Now it will be 'Viet Nam' again. Eighty years of tyranny have ended at last! Our forces have already been renamed the 'Viet Nam Army of Liberation.' "

"I'm truly glad for you and all your people," said Joseph in a controlled voice, "but I would still like to talk with Ho Chi Minh as soon as possible."

"But of course, captain." Kim took the American's arm and led him towards the door. "That's why I've come — to take you to him. He's set up his secret headquarters in a jungle village not far away — he's always happiest in humble surroundings."

Half an hour later Kim showed Joseph into a bamboo and thatch hut in a village outside the town, and Ho rose from a paper-strewn table to greet him with a glowing smile. "I'm delighted to see you again, Captain Sherman," he said, gripping Joseph's arm in an affectionate gesture. "I expect you've already heard the good news from Hanoi?"

"You've pulled a very neat trick on us," said Joseph, his face unsmiling. "You've used our weapons and our presence with you behind the Japanese lines to make it look as though the United States backed your coup — that's abusing our goodwill in my book."

Ho's genial smile didn't falter. "Have some yellow tea, will you, captain? It's a soothing drink." Turning his back he kneeled and picked up a blackened kettle sizzling on an improvised hob of stones. "I've always had a strong admiration for your country, and getting to know you and your men has turned that admiration to affection. I would be saddened if you didn't understand that."

"Is that why you felt obliged to deceive us? My men and I couldn't help noticing that you entertained many strangers in the jungle camp during the last few days of training. Were you plotting this stratagem behind our backs all along?"

"I had no way of knowing Japan would surrender so quickly, captain. Like you, I knew nothing of the atom bomb. We were prepared to fight the Japanese with you for one year, two years — as long as was necessary." He stood up, holding two little beakers of tea, handed one to Joseph and sipped his own reflectively. "I once told you, didn't I, Captain Sherman, that my party is my country? Well, that was no deception. I came to admire Lenin when I went to live in Paris because I discovered he was a great patriot who liberated his countrymen. When I first read his 'Thesis on National and Colonial Questions,' I was so overjoyed I burst into tears. Although I read it alone in my attic in the Rue Bonaparte, I jumped up and shouted aloud, 'Dear martyrs, dear compatriots of Viet Nam! This is what we need, this is our path to liberation.' " He paused and smiled at the recollection. "I was one of the first members of the French Communist Party, and some years later I helped to found the Indochina Communist Party — but always my actions were motivated by the certainty that my weak country needed help from outside if we were ever to throw off the powerful rule of France. Your own George Washington accepted aid from the French to beat the British, didn't he? What you call 'Communism' teaches the oppressed to organize and discipline themselves against their oppressors — and those are valuable lessons. But in the end, the support of the United States has proved to be of the greatest importance to us. We appreciate the generous spirit in which it's been given, but during that time, captain, I haven't betrayed my cause — my party, you see, is truly my country."

"And what about the photograph of General Chennault and the side arms I gave you? What were they used for?"

The Annamese chuckled and hugged himself like a schoolboy caught out in a prank. "At the time, captain, there were others challenging for the leadership of the Viet Minh League. When I returned with the signed photograph and handed out the revolvers to my rivals, I did nothing to disturb the impression that I enjoyed the closest support of your famous general and that the guns were his personal favors. That little subterfuge allowed me to assume full unchallenged control of the Viet Minh movement at a crucial time."

His face lit up again so impishly that Joseph smiled despite himself.

"But I'm sorry that you feel your goodwill has been abused, captain." Ho tugged at his wispy goatee, his expression pained. "Things like this are perhaps difficult to say, but don't all of us use those we're fond of in one way or another? And does knowing that we do it prevent us from continuing to feel strong affection? I sense that you're drawn to my country and its people, and I hope nothing I've done will alter that. I want there to be lasting friendship between our two countries — but I also hope the friendship between the two of us will continue to grow."

"For friendship to grow, there must be mutual trust," said

Joseph firmly. "You could have taken me into your confidence earlier."

The Annamese leader gazed intently at Joseph for a moment; despite the ravages of his recent illness, which had left him pitifully thin, his face remained set in lines of calm determination, and Joseph saw more clearly than he'd ever done before the rare strength of character that sustained him. "There isn't always time to do all the things one would like, captain," said Ho quietly. "But because I value your friendship highly I will tell you exactly what happened in the jungle camp in those last few frantic days — we were very busy organizing our nation's future. The Viet Minh League is as yet little known among our people. We have only a few thousand trained activists. That means we have to work very quickly and not waste a second. The sudden surrender of the Japanese has created a vacuum, because our French masters are all still in prison. The Allies at Potsdam have decided that Indochina shall be jointly occupied by China and Britain — but their troops will not arrive for several weeks. In that time our tiny organization must perform a gigantic conjuring trick. The Viet Minh League must be made to appear to our own people and to the Allies as a vast and powerful organization of patriots capable of governing our country. It will be soon, but until that day comes we must create an illusion. Our few cadres have been dispatched to the four corners of our land to arouse the people, print banners, organize marches. It might have been difficult to explain all this to you before we began — but now you've already seen some results in the villages through which you've passed, haven't you?"

Joseph nodded. "So that was all faked up by your propaganda boys, was it?"

Ho smiled and shook his head slowly. "No, captain, not 'faked up.' Our people are responding spontaneously now to our leadership everywhere. There's nothing false about any of the demonstrations of support for the Viet Minh. To popularize a cause requires careful organization and much hard work — but it will come to nothing if the mass of the people don't respond from the heart."

"Weren't the people in those devastated villages we passed responding from the heart?" said Joseph stiffly. "My men discovered that you burned them down because the people refused to join you."

"Such instances are, fortunately, rare, captain," said Ho brusquely. "There's no profit in dwelling on them. If your countrymen had been slaves to a foreign tyranny for a hundred years and you were suddenly presented with the opportunity to make them free, how would you have responded? Would you have let a few doubters stand in your way? Would you have announced that you were weak and had no powerful friends? Would you have sat back and said, 'Our organization isn't yet big enough'? Or would you have acted as we did?"

Joseph gazed into the glowing embers of the fire for a moment. "I guess," he said slowly, "I would have done what you did."

A brilliant smile lit Ho's ravaged features, and he gripped Joseph's hands. "Thank you, captain. Let me give you another beaker of tea."

Still smiling broadly, he turned away and busied himself with the blackened kettle once more.

12

In the sumptuous throne room of the Palace of Perfect Concord, the Emperor Bao Dai watched uneasily as Tran Van Kim led the shabbily dressed Viet Minh delegation towards him. Wearing a golden turban and a brocade jacket, the emperor was standing in front of his throne instead of sitting on it, and at his side an apprehensive senior mandarin from the Ministry of Rites stood holding a velvet cushion on which were laid the ancient imperial symbols of power — the emperor's gold seal and a golden sword with a ruby-encrusted handle.

As Kim's eyes took in the tense figure of the emperor and his glittering sword, he felt his heart beat faster. This was the moment he had been savoring in his mind throughout the long dash south from Hanoi to Hue in a commandeered Japanese army truck. The man who symbolized the humiliation of his country's long collaboration with the French colonialists was about to surrender to him personally his right to rule! The people of Vietnam, in whose minds the emperor's "Mandate of Heaven" was a deeply rooted superstition, would know soon that he had ceded it to the Viet Minh League, and he himself would have the supreme satisfaction of knowing that the terrible quarrel with his father had been finally vindicated. He had been right and his father wrong! Events had proved it. If only his father could have been made to attend, to witness personally the emperor's capitulation to the son he'd ordered so contemptuously from his house nine years before!

Bao Dai's sudden decision to abdicate in the face of the public acclaim that had greeted the Viet Minh's seizure of power in Hanoi had taken Kim and the rest of the league's leadership by surprise. What had begun as a carefully engineered propaganda operation with small, organized demonstrations marching through streets decked with hastily manufactured Viet Minh flags and banners had quickly grown into a popular celebration of massive proportions in cities and villages the length of the land. The jubilant crowds, uninterested in the political complexion of the men who seemed to be freeing them simultaneously from the Japanese and the French, had turned out in their millions, and Bao Dai had announced his intention to give up the throne even before there had been time to form a provisional government in Hanoi. As a result, Kim had been hurriedly appointed to lead a delegation to Hue to accept the emperor's abdication at a private audience on August 25.

He had instructed his delegation members deliberately to arrive clad in the shorts, shirts and sandals that they had worn in the jungle, and as they crossed the gleaming tiled floor among the scarlet lime-wood pillars, their appearance contrasted sharply with the rich furnishings of the throne room that had enchanted the young eyes of Joseph Sherman twenty years before. Kim and the delegation, of whom more than half were Communists, walked jauntily with their heads held high, determined to show no servility to the emperor, but to Kim's surprise the sight of the magnificently ornate throne and its occupant reawakened in him instinctive, long-forgotten feelings of awe. He had grown up believing that the mystery of the "Mandate of Heaven" was made manifest in the person of the emperor who ruled from the palace where the white tiger dwelled in perfect harmony with the blue dragon, and he had seen the throne room for the first time as a small excited boy clutching his father's hand; later he had railed against the emperor as a *mannequin doré* — a gilded dummy — when he became convinced that only Communism could save his nation from the French, but as he stopped before Bao Dai his childhood instincts almost betrayed him and he had to make a conscious effort to prevent himself bowing to the sovereign. In the pocket of his shorts, he carried a small red Viet Minh emblem with a central gold star, which he intended to pin on the emperor's tunic as a final gesture of the Viet Minh's supremacy, and when he looked into Bao Dai's face he remained deliberately silent so as to cause him maximum discomfort.

For a tense moment or two the sovereign gazed blankly back at

Kim, then after a nervous glance at the gowned mandarin at his side, he cleared his throat diffidently. "In this decisive hour of our nation's history," he began quietly, "union means life and division means death. In view of the powerful democratic spirit growing in the north of our kingdom, we feared a conflict between north and south would be inevitable if we delayed our decision any longer. That conflict could have plunged our people into suffering, and although we feel a great melancholy when we think of how our glorious ancestors fought for four hundred years to make our country great, we decided to abdicate and transfer power at once to the new democratic republican government in Hanoi. . . ."

The emperor's voice shook slightly, but he managed to retain a quietly dignified composure as he spoke, and despite himself, Kim felt a twinge of sympathy for his humiliating predicament.

"During a reign of twenty years," continued Bao Dai, his voice gathering confidence, "we have known much bitterness, and it has been impossible for us to render any appreciable service to our country. From this day we shall be happy to be a free citizen in an independent country. Renouncing our reign name of 'Bao Dai,' we wish to be known now only as citizen Vinh Thuy, and in this capacity we offer ourself as a counsellor of state to the new democratic government in Hanoi. . . ."

Still without looking at Kim, the emperor took the cushion from the mandarin and, stepping forward, placed the ancient symbols of authority in the arms of the revolutionary. "Long live the independence of Vietnam," said Bao Dai, his voice cracking at last with strain. "Long live our democratic republic."

To Kim's consternation, his own hands began to tremble, and the jewel-encrusted sword almost slipped to the floor. He clutched at it frantically with one hand and passed the cushion hurriedly to the assistant leader of his delegation. "We accept your decision, Vinh Thuy, with a supreme sense of satisfaction," said Kim, employing an arrogant tone to hide the turmoil of his emotions. "Your abdication has freed the people of Vietnam from the bonds of slavery which have bound them to France for eighty long years and more recently to the fascists of Japan. It frees them, too, from a corrupt system of government which has too long defied the march of history! Long live independent and democratic Vietnam!"

Stepping close to the emperor, he plucked the little insignia from his pocket. Bao Dai stared straight ahead over his shoulder as Kim thrust the pin into the rich brocade tunic; but Kim's hands shook so violently that it took several attempts to secure it, and when he finally stepped back, the little red flag with its gold star stuck out crookedly from the emperor's breast.

To Kim's astonishment Bao Dai held out his hand towards him, and for a moment he stood staring at it nonplussed. The hand was clearly being offered to be shaken, but in all history Kim knew that no Annamese emperor had ever shaken hands with one of his subjects! Seeing his confusion, Bao Dai began to smile, and Kim, feeling a flush of embarrassment rise to his cheeks, quickly grasped the outstretched hand. As he shook it, the instincts of his childhood finally got the better of him, and to his horror he bent his head low towards the emperor in a gesture of loyalty and submission.

Half an hour later Kim stood beside the emperor on the ramparts of the Citadel while the imperial flag was lowered and the Viet Minh standard was run up the mast. A great crowd of people gathered below, cheering loudly, and Viet Minh agents among them began to lead them in chants of "Hail the democratic spirit of Vinh Thuy!" "Hail the delegates of the new Provisional Goverment."

Kim raised his arm high above his head in response and forced a smile to his face, but as he gazed up at the red flag fluttering on the masthead, despite the great satisfaction he felt, he couldn't rid himself of paradoxical feelings of sadness and disquiet at the thought that his father's familiar world and the world in which he had grown up had been destroyed forever.

13

Although news of what was happening in Hanoi and other cities had reached Joseph and the other OSS men by radio while they kicked their heels in Thai Nguyen, they were still taken aback by the tumultuous welcome they received when they finally entered the northern capital with the last of the guerrillas on the morning of September 2. After marching across the Kim Ma plain, they boarded open cars and trucks on the outskirts and rode into the city through wildly cheering crowds. Above their heads every street was festooned with Viet Minh flags and banners that proclaimed repeatedly in Annamese, English, Chinese and Russian: "Welcome Allies — Peace Is Here" . . . "Vietnam for the Vietnamese" . . . "Death Rather Than Slavery" . . .

"Independence or Death" . . . "Let's Bury French Imperialism!"

Tramcars and rickshaws trailed similar revolutionary banners, and hundreds of crudely painted likenesses of the goateed face that Joseph had first seen swimming before his eyes in the mists of his Pac Bo delirium were draped from the windows of houses and strung between the trees along the boulevards. The unbridled enthusiasm of the crowds and the sudden elevation to national heroes of the ragged guerrillas among whom they had lived in the jungle for a month astonished the American OSS men, and they shook their heads constantly in disbelief as they neared the center of the city.

"Maybe they should put your portrait up there alongside Uncle Ho's," said Lieutenant Hawke, grinning mischievously at Joseph. "They would, I guess, if they knew how you saved his ass with that timely injection."

Joseph smiled, but halfheartedly.

"I guess it all becomes clear now, captain, doesn't it?" Hawke gazed up wonderingly at the vehemently anti-French slogans. "Our 'Lucius' obviously wasn't going to allow any Free French patrols into Tongking when he was planning this little jamboree all along."

Joseph nodded abstractedly. As they moved slowly through the congested streets, with half his mind he was trying subconsciously to see the city again as he had last seen it during his ecstatically happy visit in 1936; but to his disappointment it was scarcely recognizable as the same place. The smart French shops on the main boulevards were boarded up, and the French street names glorifying heroes of the colonial conquest had been torn down and replaced with names of revolutionary heroes of Vietnam's own past; Boulevard Henri Rivière, he noticed, had become Dai lo Phan Boi Chau in memory of an early anti-French agitator, and Rue Mirabel had been renamed Duong Tran Nhan Ton to commemorate the Vietnamese sovereign who created the country's first popular assembly. In the old quarters the French translations had been obliterated from the blue-and-white street signs, and only the original Annamese names remained written in *quoc ngu*, the latinized national language that was meaningless to Joseph's eyes. Red Viet Minh flags fluttered proudly in the September breeze from the flagstaffs in the grounds of the governor general's palace, and Joseph noticed suddenly that none of the thousands of slogans strung across the streets was written in French.

"Changed a bit, has it, captain, since you were here last?" asked Hawke with a wry grin. "You look as if you wished you could turn the clock back. Or are you still wondering at the deviousness of that old scoundrel 'Lucius,' alias 'Uncle Ho'?"

"Maybe a bit of both, Dave," replied Joseph evasively. "But no matter how cunning he might have been, there's not much doubt now about his claim to speak for his people, is there? The French have given these folk a damned rough ride for a long time. I guess a little bit of chicanery along the way is forgivable."

The OSS "Quail" Mission, which had flown in from Kunming several days earlier, had already set itself up in the best suites in the Hotel Metropole. It had been their commander Colonel Trench who had at last given the Deer Mission the okay by radio to march into Hanoi, and when Joseph and Hawke knocked on his door, it was Trench himself who opened it. In high good humor, he was clutching a bottle of vintage Perrier-Jouet champagne in one hand and he waved them to seats around a low table where glasses were already set out; through an open doorway they could see that a radio operator had set up his equipment on an empty bed.

"Welcome to Hanoi, gentlemen," he said, filling three glasses with a flourish. "The eyes of the world may not be on this city right now — and maybe no American outside this hotel has ever heard of it. But the French champagne's good and there's plenty of it — so let's relax and drink a toast to the end of our war!"

"To the end of the war!"

Hawke and the colonel drained their glasses, but Joseph crossed to the window and sipped his wine thoughtfully, staring down into the street. From there he could see the little terrace where almost every evening during his last visit he had written a letter to Lan while idling over a glass of Pernod. The same wickerwork chairs and marble-topped tables were set out beneath the same striped sun awnings, and Joseph could even pick out the corner where he had sat. Some echo of the tense exhilaration that had possessed him constantly then returned, and for a moment or two the voices of the two other officers in the room blurred into inaudibility.

". . . I guess, lieutenant, he still can't get over the fact that agent 'Lucius' whom he found for us in a cave behind a waterfall has turned out to be the president. . . . Is that right, Joseph?"

Colonel Trench's boisterous laughter broke his train of thought, and Joseph turned to find the senior officer standing at his shoulder.

"I've talked to him a couple of times and he's still wearing the same old battered helmet and khaki drabs, you know. The Viet Minh's taken over the governor general's palace, but Ho's living in a little cottage in the grounds." Trench laughed again. "He's adamant now that he's no Commie, and to prove it he's promised to dress up a little for the big speech he's making in Ba Dinh Square this afternoon. We're all invited in best bib and tucker to stand on the rostrum with him. He's asked me a couple of times, Joe, if you're going to be there."

"Isn't anybody worrying about our giving America's blessing to a bit of political sharp practice?" asked Joseph with a puzzled frown.

Trench clapped him heartily on the shoulder. "Relax, Joe. Have the grace to behave like an honored guest, will you? Not everybody here's getting the red-carpet treatment. The Free French from Mission Five in Kunming were put under house arrest as soon as they arrived and they're still under guard in the old palace. Don't you remember President Roosevelt told the War Department before he died that he thought the French had milked Indochina for long enough? It's not our job to take a stand against a native government that's obviously got the support of the people. Look down there."

A chanting crowd of marchers bearing pictures of Ho and Viet Minh banners was filling the street on the way to Ba Dinh Square, while crowds cheered from the pavement; like all the other demonstrations Joseph had seen since arriving in the city, it seemed spontaneous and relaxed.

"Everything's hunky-dory here, Joe, so don't worry your head anymore. The Chinese occupying force is arriving within the week under the overall command of General Wedemeyer in Chungking. It's been decided that they'll respect the status quo. The Chinese will no doubt do a little gentle looting, as they've always done, but otherwise they'll get on with the job of disarming and repatriating the Japanese. If you want to do some worrying about your old Annamite chums, there's more fertile soil farther south in Saigon."

Joseph looked sharply at the colonel at the mention of Saigon. "What's happening there?"

"Sit down and have another glass of fizz and I'll tell you about the next assignment we've got in mind for you and Lieutenant Hawke."

Joseph waited impatiently while the glasses were refilled, leaning forward on the edge of his seat.

"Our OSS guys from Calcutta have just arrived in Saigon, and already they're sending up smoke signals saying 'help.' It's a little team called 'Detachment 404,' and they're doing fine locating Allied prisoners — but they're making heavy weather on the intelligence front. To quote their report, the political situation is 'a crock of shit' and their best bet is that a civil war is about to break."

Joseph sat straighter in his seat. "Why's that?"

"Well to start with, about fifteen hundred French soldiers of the Eleventh Regiment of the Infanterie Coloniale are still locked up like they are here, but the British occupying force is coming from the Burma-India theater so it won't be there for another couple of weeks. A Viet Minh Committee for the South has taken control in Saigon, but its members are busy quarreling among themselves. They organized a big parade through the streets a few days ago to celebrate the setting up of the Provisional Government — and it turned out to be more a show of force by half-a-dozen private armies than a celebration." Trench sighed and drank some more champagne. "There are some weird religious sects called the Cao Dai and the Hoa Hao tearing at each other's throats and a criminal secret society known as the Binh Xuyen is trying to run things too — all of them have got arms because the Japanese are deserting in droves and selling their weapons to the highest bidder. The 'yellow dwarfs' in general are refusing to do much about keeping law and order and most of them run off to the bars in the Chinese city of Cholon as soon as they're off duty and get drunk. To top it all, a Free French colonel has parachuted in and is trying to negotiate with the Viet Minh Committee to reestablish French control over the colony again. The mood's damned ugly according to Detachment 404. French statues are being dragged down all over the place and about twenty thousand French citizens spend most of their time barricaded in their own homes, praying the British will get there before they're butchered." Trench paused and grinned suddenly from ear to ear. "It's a goddamned powder keg waiting for a spark, and Detachment 404 hasn't got any Annamese speakers or anybody who knows Saigon. I thought you two guys might like to volunteer to help them out." Colonel Trench looked at Hawke. "What do you say, lieutenant?"

Hawke drained his glass, smacked his lips and held it out to be filled again. "Is the champagne as good down in Saigon as it is here, sir?"

The colonel nodded and poured more wine until it frothed over the rim.

"Then I'm ready to march," said the young Bostonian, grinning broadly and lifting the full glass to his lips.

"What about you, captain?" Trench held the bottle towards Joseph, raising one eyebrow in inquiry.

Joseph pushed his glass across the table without looking directly at the senior officer in case he betrayed something of the sudden surge of excitement he felt coursing through him. "I won't say no, either, sir," he said quietly.

Three hours later Joseph stood beside Colonel Trench and Lieutenant Hawke on a balcony above Ba Dinh Square, looking down on a sea of half-a-million Vietnamese faces gathered below. When the new, self-appointed president of the Democratic Republic of Vietnam appeared, a great roar of welcome rose from the crowd. He wore a dark high-necked tunic and his wispy goatee fluttered in the afternoon wind as he stepped up to the microphone; reading from notes he began to speak emphatically in his own language.

"All men are created equal. . . . They are endowed by their Creator with certain unalienable rights and among these are Life, Liberty and the pursuit of Happiness. . . ." He glanced up from his paper and for a fleeting moment caught Joseph's eye before looking back towards the crowd. "This immortal declaration was made in the United States in 1776. . . ."

"How do you like that?" gasped Hawke, who was translating quietly behind Joseph and the colonel. "He's even commandeering our Declaration of Independence for his own use."

". . . In 1791 in France," continued Ho, "the Declaration of the French Revolution on the Rights of Man stated: 'All men are born free and with equal rights and must always remain free with equal rights.' . . . Both these historic statements established undeniable truths, but for more than eighty years the French imperialists, abusing their own standards of liberty, equality and fraternity, have violated our fatherland and oppressed our citizens. . . ."

A roar of approval rose from the crowd, and Ho waited patiently until it lessened; then he resumed in a voice that quavered now and then with emotion. "The French deprived our people of every democratic liberty, they enforced inhuman laws, they set up different regimes in three parts of our country in order to shatter the unity of our people. . . . In the field of economics they fleeced us to the backbone, they brought poverty to our people and devastated our lands. They robbed us of our rice and our fields, our mines, our forests, our raw materials. They fettered public opinion, built more prisons than schools and murdered countless Vietnamese patriots without mercy. All our uprisings until today have been drowned by France in rivers of blood. . . ."

Ho's voice rose to a shout of indignation as he reached the end of his catalogue of French crimes, and the great crowd responded with another angry roar.

". . . In the autumn of 1940 the French imperialists reached a new low when they sank to their bended knees to hand our country to the Japanese fascists," he said, letting his voice fall dramatically. "From that day forward our people suffered the double yoke of French and Japanese oppression, and as a result more than two million citizens have died from starvation. . . ." For a moment Ho Chi Minh bowed his head before the microphone, and the crowd stared up at him in a stunned silence.

"Did he really say two million?" queried Joseph after Hawke had finished his translation.

"Yes — two million! There's been a famine for a year now in the provinces between here and the central highlands."

Joseph and the other OSS men on the balcony shook their heads in horror.

"One of his aides told me they've had a succession of bad harvests down there — but the Japs and the French still kept demanding their full quotas of rice," whispered Hawke grimly.

". . . But the truth is, citizens of Vietnam, we've wrested our independence finally not from France but from the Japanese," said Ho, raising his voice again to a shout. "The French have fled, the Japanese have capitulated, and the Emperor Bao Dai has abdicated! At long last we've broken the chains which have bound us for nearly a century, and we declare here and now that as from today all contacts of a colonial nature with France are at an end!"

Once again the dense throng of people acclaimed their new president's rousing words, and pandemonium reigned for a minute or two. When the square finally quietened again the faint drone of aircraft engines could be heard in the distance, and glancing up, Joseph spotted the familiar outlines of a squadron of reconnaissance P-38s of the Fourteenth U.S. Army Air Force winging north towards Kunming across the bright afternoon sky. As he watched, he saw the squadron wheel suddenly and begin dipping down to take a closer look at the massive crowd that was obviously visible to the pilots from a high altitude.

"We're confident now," continued Ho, glancing up at the approaching planes, "that the Allied nations will keep faith with their principles of self-determination and equality and will acknowledge the independence of Vietnam. We're sure they'll agree that people who have fought side by side with them against the Japanese must be free and independent. . . ." He stopped and looked up again; the blue roundels and silver stars on the wings and fuselages of the P-38s identified them beyond any doubt as American as they drew nearer, and the OSS men realized —

probably simultaneously with Ho — that yet another stroke of good fortune had delivered a U.S. reconnaissance patrol into his hands at the most opportune moment; for all the world the planes appeared to be staging an Allied fly-past in support of the new Viet Minh regime, and Ho raised his voice again to make it heard above the roar of their engines.

"So at this historic hour, fellow citizens, the Provisional Government of the Democratic Republic of Vietnam solemnly declares to the world that Vietnam has the right to be a free and independent country — and that it is indeed already free! We further declare that we are determined never to yield again to France! Our people will fight with all their strength and spirit, and if necessary they will lay down their lives and sacrifice all their property to safeguard this precious newfound liberty!"

As the cheering began Ho Chi Minh stepped back from the microphone and raised his clenched fist above his head in a dramatic salute; a moment later the fighter squadron swept in low over the city. To the surprise of the OSS men, a band struck up "The Star-Spangled Banner," and contingents of guerrillas began marching past in the square below with their new weapons. Seeing this, a smiling Colonel Trench threw up a smart salute and held it as cameras clicked to record the historic moment. Joseph and the other OSS soldiers followed suit, and the crowd applauded rapturously as President Ho Chi Minh smiled warmly in the direction of his powerful American benefactors who had unwittingly played a vital role in bringing him and his supporters to power.

14

Although the rest of Saigon was unrecognizable as the tranquil colonial capital he'd once known, the circular, red-lacquered moon gate in the wall surrounding the Imperial Delegate's residence looked just the same to Joseph as it had in 1936. The same bronze temple bell hung from the curved eaves of its little roof, and even from the driver's seat of his OSS jeep parked at the curb, he could smell the damp, heady fragrances of the fleshy-leaved tropical trees and flowers growing inside the walled garden. It was beginning to grow dark, and when he cut the jeep's engine, silence descended suddenly on the tree-lined street north of the cathedral square. For a moment the quiet unnerved him, then the stutter of distant gunfire broke the stillness again and curiously made him breathe more easily; the sounds of disorder and conflict, he realized, somehow helped him feel less guilty about making the visit.

Ever since accepting assignment to Saigon two weeks before, he had known he wouldn't be able to resist the temptation to try to see Lan again. Although he knew she had almost certainly married Paul Devraux and although he fully realized it was foolish and fruitless to try to turn back the clock, he'd been unable to stay away. He knew that the rational, sensible course would have been to forget the past — but that intense, all-engulfing sense of regret that had seized him when he thought he must die in his blazing Warhawk without ever seeing her again had overridden all his reasoned arguments. Countless times while waiting impatiently for the Chinese occupation forces to arrive in Hanoi and while under-going the ritual of formal briefings for the new Saigon post back in Kunming, he had savored in his mind the moment when he would step up to the red gate and ring the tiny bell. He had even sought out Kim before leaving Hanoi and asked him if he had any messages for his family, so as to give himself a valid excuse to visit the Tran household. Kim had flushed and tried to hide his embarrassment, then, avoiding Joseph's eyes, had said gruffly he had no message for his parents except that he was in good health and glad to be fighting at the side of President Ho Chi Minh for the cause of his country's freedom.

But as he made to climb out of his seat, Joseph hesitated, filled suddenly with doubt and apprehension. Although the red gates remained closed, he felt he could see the neat clusters of palms framing the curved roofs just as they'd done on his last visit; he saw again too, in his mind's eye, the shadowy room with its dark teak furniture and its hanging scrolls where he had been shocked to learn almost in the same moment of Jacques Devraux's death and Lan's rejection. Something of the youthful despair he had felt then surged back, and he remembered with renewed force just how greatly time had changed both their lives; now he had a wife and two young sons in Virginia, and Lan was also probably married.

But although these thoughts seethed inside his head, still he didn't restart the jeep. As he sat staring indecisively at the red gate, he knew that no matter what embarrassment and disappointment lay beyond it, he couldn't go away without trying to see her again, if only for a moment; he knew he couldn't live the rest of his life without attempting to find out whether it had all been a foolish dream, whether the restless sense of discontent from which he had

337

never been able to free himself since losing Lan was real or imagined.

For a minute or two after he jangled the bell there was no response; there appeared to be no movement in the house, and Joseph wondered suddenly why he had expected to find the Tran family still living there when so much else had changed in Saigon. The previous day he and Lieutenant Hawke had driven into the city from the airport, beneath banners proclaiming "Welcome to the British and the Americans — but we have no room for the French." Along the roadsides, sullen, narrow-eyed Japanese soldiers of the Imperial Nipponese Army stood guard dressed in their distinctive crumpled forage caps and puttees; on the pavements behind them jubilant crowds of Vietnamese cheered the small advance contingents of the British Army's Twentieth Indian Division who were arriving daily from Rangoon by air to disarm and repatriate the defeated forces. Until a sufficiently large Allied force was assembled to take over from them, the forty thousand Japanese soldiers were having to help patrol the uneasy city, but they were performing their duties listlessly and without enthusiasm.

Among the flags of Britain, America, China and Russia draped across the streets, there was no sign of the French tricolor, and outside the Hôtel de Ville at the top of the Boulevard Charner where the Viet Minh Committee for the South had set up its headquarters, Joseph had seen armed Vietnamese guerrillas standing defiantly on guard. The French colonial troops were still prisoners behind the wires of the concentration camps into which the Japanese had forced them at gunpoint in March, and on the Rue Catinat, which had been renamed the "Street of the Paris Commune," the once-fashionable French shops were shuttered and begrimed. Looting of isolated French properties had begun, and few of the twenty thousand French civilians who remained at liberty were visible in streets where there were no white troops to protect them. The small number of Indians and Gurkhas who had already arrived were fully occupied guarding the airfield, the power station, banks and police stations, and the main bulk of the British force was not expected to arrive by sea until early October. When Joseph and Lieutenant Hawke drove through the city on their first patrol after reporting to the OSS unit commander, they found the central markets standing silent and deserted because the Viet Minh had ordered a strike to protest against the British commanding officer's refusal to hold talks with them. A dawn-to-dusk curfew had been ordered, but there were not enough British

338

troops to enforce it properly, and skirmishes between the various Vietnamese armed groups had become commonplace.

A prolonged exchange of fire from the direction of the cathedral made Joseph turn his head to listen, and he didn't notice when one semicircular segment of the moon gate swung open silently behind him. When he turned back he found himself looking into the unsmiling face of Lan's brother Tam, and for a moment they stared at one another in surprise; then Joseph tore off his forage cap.

"Tam! C'est moi, Joseph Sherman! Vous vous souvenez?"

Tam gazed quizzically at the American's grinning face and his captain's shoulder bars, but made no attempt to widen the gap in the gate. "Yes, Captain Sherman, I remember you," replied the Vietnamese uncertainly in French. "But why have you come back to Saigon?"

"I've been assigned here with the American mission. I flew in yesterday. I've been in Hanoi and I met your brother Kim up there. I thought you and your parents might like to know that he's in good health."

Tam's eyes narrowed at the mention of his brother's name, but otherwise his face remained expressionless and he made no reply.

"Your mother and father are well, I hope, Tam," said Joseph haltingly. "And your sister, Lan?"

"Nobody is very well in Saigon today," said Tam in a dull voice. "As you must know already, it's a city filled with fear."

"Forgive me, Tam, if I'm intruding, but I thought perhaps your mother would be glad to have some news of Kim. He told me he'd had no contact with you for many years."

After another moment's hesitation Tam swung the gate open. "Come and wait inside. I will ask my mother if she wishes to speak with you."

The Vietnamese closed and barred the gate carefully, then walked ahead of Joseph towards the house. In the twilight the American saw that the garden had become wild and overgrown and the lotus pool was choked with weeds. By the time he reached the house Tam had disappeared inside, and he waited uncertainly on the steps.

Several minutes passed before Lan's mother appeared in the doorway with her son at her shoulder. "I'm surprised you have the audacity to return here, Captain Sherman, after what happened between you and my daughter," she said quietly in French without looking at him directly. "I've come out to talk with you only because Tam tells me you have news of my son Kim."

To Joseph's eyes, in the fading light the slender Vietnamese woman bore a striking resemblance to her daughter. Still beautiful in middle age, she was dressed in a dark, high-necked embroidered tunic and trousers, and she stood with her eyes downcast, her hands clasped tightly in front of her. Behind her, through the open door, Joseph could see candles flickering on the family's ancestral altar as if he had disturbed her at prayer. "I'm sorry, Madame Hieu," he began hesitantly. "I don't understand . . ."

She raised her head to look directly into his eyes, and he saw then that her face was stiff with unconcealed hostility. "What news have you, please, of my son Kim?"

"I spent a week working with him in northern Tongking," said Joseph quickly. "He's a leading aide of Ho Chi Minh and he's very highly thought of. Now he's working with the new government in Hanoi."

A pained expression came into the eyes of the Vietnamese woman, and she turned her head away without responding.

"I hope Monsieur Trant Van Hieu is well," said Joseph, an edge of desperation creeping into his voice. "And Lan, how is she? Did she marry my good friend Paul Devraux?"

When she turned to look at Joseph again, she was fighting to control the tears that had started to her eyes. "Yes, captain, she did. And they have a young son."

Joseph forced himself to smile. "That's wonderful news. And did they stay in Saigon?"

Madame Hieu lost her struggle to hold back her tears and she turned away again to bury her face in her son's shoulder. "We've all been living under great strain, captain," said Tam, putting a protective arm around his mother. "After their marriage Lan and her husband remained in Saigon, but Major Devraux, along with all the other French soldiers, was imprisoned by the Japanese six months ago. He's still a prisoner. After he was taken away, Lan and her son came to live here with my parents and my own family for safety."

"May I see her, please?" asked Joseph, fighting down the agitation inside him.

"She's not here anymore, captain. She and my father got caught up in the violence of the independence day riots."

Joseph stared at the Vietnamese in alarm. "What happened?"

"The Viet Minh organized a great parade to celebrate the declaration of independence in Hanoi, and my father and Lan went to watch. But trouble broke out around the cathedral. A

French priest was shot on the front steps, and my father and Lan were knocked to the ground and trampled on when the crowd stampeded."

"And where are they now?"

"My father is resting here at home, but Lan is still in hospital. She suffered concussion and was unconscious for a time."

"Which hospital is she in?" asked Joseph anxiously.

"I forbid you to try and see her!" Madame Hieu raised her tear-stained face from her son's shoulder. "She wouldn't wish it. You've caused her enough unhappiness already. She's to be released from the hospital soon, and we'll all be leaving the city then."

Joseph, taken aback by the vehemence of her words, stared at the Vietnamese woman helplessly. "I don't know what you mean, madam. . . ."

"My sister doesn't wish to see you, captain," said Tam firmly. "I think that must be clear to you."

"I'm very sorry," stammered Joseph. "If there's anything I can do to help . . ." His voice trailed off and he turned away in bafflement. He was halfway down the steps when he heard Madame Hieu call his name again.

"Did my son Kim send any message, captain?" she asked tearfully.

Joseph hesitated. "He asked me to tell you that he was happy to be helping bring freedom and independence to your country," he said slowly.

"Nothing else?" She searched Joseph's face anxiously as she waited for his response.

"He said he was very sad that he had not seen you all for so long," said Joseph, lying without knowing why. "He said he thinks of you often."

Madame Hieu lifted both hands to her face and turned away into the house, weeping uncontrollably.

"You had better leave now, captain," said Tam, motioning Joseph towards the gate. "And please, for my mother's sake, don't ever come here again."

15

Lieutenant David Hawke hauled the back-pack radio from the jeep and carried it wearily up the front steps of the mansion that Detachment 404 of the OSS had commandeered for its headquarters on the northwestern outskirts of Saigon. The former home of the French chief executive of the Bank of Indochina, the house stood on the edge of a golf course in its own grounds, and on the orders of General Douglas Gracey, commanding officer of the British occupation force, it was guarded by a detachment of Japanese troops. Both Hawke and Joseph, who followed him up the steps, returned the resentful salutes of the Japanese sentries without looking at them, and once inside the front hall, Hawke dumped the radio pack angrily on the table.

"Why in hell's name did we have to agree at Potsdam to let the British take Indochina south of the sixteenth parallel? If it had been left in General Wedemeyer's South China Command, we'd have had a massive Chinese presence and a bigger American outfit down here long ago." Hawke patted the tunic and trousers of his battle-dress distastefully, raising clouds of dust that had been absorbed during a long afternoon and evening patrol. "Instead we've got a few thousand Indians and their British *sahibs* running around the place using the enemy as policemen — and we're all teetering on the edge of a precipice."

A door of one of the downstairs offices opened unexpectedly, and the bespectacled major commanding the detachment emerged, grinning. A brilliant Wall Street investment analyst in civilian life, he tried to apply the same careful methods of logic and detailed research to his military intelligence work but had already confessed himself baffled by the confused political scene in Saigon.

"Has nobody told you, lieutenant, that Admiral Lord Louis Mountbatten changed the name of his outfit at the end of the war? 'SEAC' doesn't stand for 'South East Asia Command' anymore. It stands for 'Save England's Asian Colonies.' That's why the British were so keen to grab part of the Indochina action at Potsdam. With Burma and India next door they couldn't let the natives here get too restless —or the humble folk in their own colonies might start getting the wrong ideas."

Lieutenant Hawke expressed an obscene personal opinion about the British under his breath and began to unfasten his tunic, but the major lifted a warning hand. "Hold it right there, lieutenant; your day's not over yet. I'm sure Captain Sherman's going to want you to accompany him on a little trip to Saigon Cathedral."

Joseph looked inquiringly at the major. "Why should I want to go to the cathedral, sir?"

The major unfastened the breast pocket of his shirt and pulled out a crumpled envelope. "A mysterious Vietnamese delivered this note an hour ago. He said it was urgent. It says. 'Please ask

342

Captain Sherman to be in the cathedral at the rear of the south aisle at nine P.M.' " The major handed Joseph the note scrawled on ruled paper in badly spelled English. "It's signed 'Ngo Van Loc.' Do you know anyone of that name?"

Joseph read the note himself, then looked up at the senior officer with a surprised expression on his face. "Yes, I do. Loc is somebody I met here a long time ago."

"And was he mixed up in the politics of the place?"

"I think I could say yes to that," said Joseph grimly.

"Fine; then go and meet him. Maybe we'll find out something we don't know already about what's going on around here. Lieutenant Hawke will come along to ride shotgun in case they've got any ideas about kidnapping a token American."

When Joseph and Hawke approached the Basilica de Notre Dame half an hour later, the curfew hour was close and the streets were already empty. As they parked the jeep, they heard the crackle of gunfire from the direction of the docks, and a few seconds later a truckload of Gurkhas roared across the deserted Place Pigneau de Behaine, heading towards the sound of fighting. Inside the cathedral, the gloom was relieved only by a bank of votive candles and the little sanctuary light above the high altar. The pews at the rear of the south aisle were in deep shadow and apparently deserted, but Joseph stationed Hawke behind a nearby pillar with his hand on his revolver butt as a precaution before sitting down to wait. When Ngo Van Loc appeared silently at his side a few minutes later, Joseph didn't recognize him immediately. The peasant he had first encountered as a ragged camp "boy" in 1925 now wore the long dark coat and black turban of a middle-class Vietnamese and had grown a goatee that substantiated his disguise; but then Joseph noticed that his paralyzed left arm, shattered by the French dive-bombers at Vinh, still hung limp at his side, and when Loc glanced in his direction, his dark eyes were as watchful and suspicious as Joseph remembered from their previous encounter nine years before in the covered market.

In keeping with the disguise he wore, Loc knelt for a moment as though in prayer, then sat back and picked up a missal from the bench in front of him and began turning its pages. "So you've returned to Saigon as a military intelligence man, Captain Sherman," he said softly in French, pretending to read the prayerbook. "The city has changed greatly since your last visit, hasn't it?"

"How did you know I was here?" asked Joseph in a surprised undertone.

"Word was sent to us from Hanoi. President Ho Chi Minh

himself told us you and the other OSS Americans were sympathetic to our cause."

"Are you an official of the Viet Minh League?"

Loc nodded, still keeping his eyes fixed on the missal. "I'm a member of our Committee for the South."

"And why do you want to talk to the OSS? We've got no real standing here."

"Gracey, the British general, is too arrogant to negotiate with us, and the French colonel, Cédile, who jumped in by parachute and now calls himself 'High Commissioner,' is a pigheaded man. He pretended to hold discussions with us for a few days, but in reality he was trying to force us to capitulate." Loc spat his words out in a fierce whisper, and Joseph had to lean closer to make out clearly what he said. "Neither of them realizes the dangers they face. You've been in the north and seen how the people have risen to support our national revolution. Here in the south we've set up revolutionary committees everywhere to replace the corrupt councils of notables and mandarins. But the British don't understand that and refuse to listen to us. They're preparing to restore the rule of France — we know French troopships are already on their way here from Marseilles and Calcutta. . . ."

Loc stopped speaking as the dark-clad figure of a French priest passed in front of the altar, and he followed him with his eyes until he disappeared into the sacristy.

"But why are you telling *me* this?" insisted Joseph.

"Because we need the support of America," replied Loc vehemently. "You must tell your government about us! Your political leaders must bring pressure on Britain and France to recognize the Viet Minh as the lawful government of our country."

"It doesn't matter how much I sympathize personally with the cause of the Viet Minh," said Joseph quietly. "The OSS mission here in Saigon can't take sides in your internal politics."

"The Viet Minh helped the Allies fight the Japanese while the French collaborated with them," said Loc heatedly, turning to look at Joseph. "Doesn't that count for anything? Do the French deserve your support?"

Joseph shrugged helplessly. "France and Britain are our allies. There are many conflicting interests for the United States government to consider — especially in Europe."

"You mean that Vietnam isn't important enough — nobody will care if there's war in such a small and insignificant country." Loc studied Joseph's face for a moment, then nodded quickly to himself in confirmation of his suspicions.

"One of the problems," said Joseph slowly, "is that nobody really knows whether the Viet Minh is secretly a Communist front organization. How many of your committee are Communists?"

Loc turned the pages of the missal with rapid, agitated movements. "You, more than anyone, captain, should know that you don't have to be a Communist to hate what the French have done here. Our committee has fourteen members and no more than three or four are what you would call 'Communists.' But that's not important. What *is* important is that the Viet Minh wants to negotiate with France. Our leaders in Hanoi told you that. We know we are a poor country and we need French commercial interests to help us develop. It's the other nationalist groups outside the Viet Minh who are urging the committee to fight the French. And by refusing to negotiate with us, the British and the French are making a war certain. We want negotiations, captain, but if the French try to return without negotiating much blood will be spilled — we will never surrender the independence we've just won."

"Maybe your fears are exaggerated, Loc. In the north, the Chinese occupation force is respecting the Viet Minh government. The British have come to Indochina only to organize the evacuation of the Japanese forces and their formal surrender — those are their orders."

Loc snorted angrily and closed the missal with a snap. "Already the British have shut down our newspapers, and hour by hour they're cooperating more openly with France. Our agents have discovered today that General Gracey has ordered posters to be printed proclaiming martial law. Within a day or two all political freedom is to be denied us in our own country! The next step will be an outright attempt to restore French rule!"

Joseph studied the profile of the Vietnamese beside him; his bony face was gaunt and wasted by imprisonment and physical suffering, and his dark eyes gleamed ferociously whenever France was mentioned. "Just after we met the last time, Loc, your son was arrested in Hue for trying to murder Monsieur Jacques Devraux," he said evenly. "Then Monsieur Devraux *was* murdered in his bed a week or two later. Were you responsible for his death?"

The Vietnamese looked steadily at Joseph for a long time. "That's a personal matter, captain. I haven't come here to discuss such things. But I asked to speak to you because, better than anybody else, you know how much hatred there is for the French in the hearts of my countrymen. They robbed me of my wife and son, and there are many many thousands like me who have lost

345

their loved ones because of the cruelty of France. That is why we will fight to the death to be free." Without warning the Vietnamese stood up. "Tell your allies that — before it is too late."

Loc disappeared into the shadows as silently as he had come, and Joseph sat staring at the stumps of the many hopeful candles that had been lit throughout the day by frightened *colons* and their families. One by one they were going out, and the light they provided in the gloomy cathedral was growing dimmer. When he sensed a presence at his side, Joseph turned and found David Hawke standing beside him, buttoning his revolver back into its holster.

"Did he tell us anything interesting, captain?" asked the young Bostonian in a quiet voice.

Joseph nodded slowly and stood up. "Yes. I'd better head back to headquarters right away and get a report across to the British. I don't suppose it will do any good, but the Viet Minh say that if the French don't negotiate, they won't be able to stop the other hotheads from starting a war."

As they left by the west door, the last of the votive candles guttered and went out, leaving the cathedral in almost total darkness behind them. Outside, the stars shone brilliantly in the night sky, but an unnatural hush had already fallen over the streets, as though the whole city was holding its breath in expectation of unwelcome news.

16

In the late afternoon of the next day, September 22, as he was driving along the old Rue Catinat, Joseph saw a Japanese trooper pasting a series of printed posters on the walls of the Continental Palace Hotel. Stopping his jeep at the curb, he hurried across the sidewalk to peer over the soldier's shoulder. Printed in Vietnamese, French and English, the notice was headed "Proclamation Number One" in heavy black type, and after scanning its contents Joseph felt his spirits sink; as Ngo Van Loc had predicted, it amounted to a declaration of martial law.

It proclaimed that General Douglas Gracey, acting on behalf of the Supreme Allied Commander, South East Asia, was in sole charge of all military forces, armed groups and police units in

French Indochina south of the sixteenth parallel. The population were warned that in future, looters, saboteurs and other wrongdoers would be summarily shot, and that all demonstrations, processions and public meetings were banned henceforth. From the time of the posting of the edict, the carrying of arms, even sticks, staves and bamboo spears, was forbidden to all except British and Allied troops.

As Joseph returned to his jeep, he glanced along the boulevard. The shady pavements beneath the tamarinds, normally aswarm with people at that hour, were almost deserted; sensing that trouble was coming, the Vietnamese population of the city had been fleeing to the countryside in increasing numbers, and few French *colons* dared any longer venture from their homes. During frequent reconnaissance tours with Lieutenant Hawke that day Joseph had seen only isolated Japanese foot patrols and an occasional truckload of British Gurkhas moving in the streets; in the daylight hours the armed gangs of the Cao Dai, the Hoa Hao and the Binh Xuyen were keeping out of sight. The Viet Minh strike had now succeeded in shutting down the markets completely, and the British had already begun to airlift some essential supplies into the city.

During the past two days as the streets had grown noticeably more tense, Joseph had been wrestling hour by hour with his conscience. To know that Lan was somewhere in the city but didn't want him to contact her had sometimes seemed an unendurable agony. He had been unable to put from his mind the accusing expression on her mother's face as she spoke to him from the steps of her house, and he had been tortured by the knowledge that the wife of a French officer would almost certainly be treated at the central Hôpital Militaire in the Rue de la Grandière. Once or twice, while driving past the sprawling complex of two-storied, verandahed buildings, he had been tempted to stop and go in, but the presence of David Hawke beside him had always restrained him. In the late afternoon, however, he had driven out alone from the OSS headquarters, his own private sense of unease increasing with the heightening tension in the streets, and after reading the British proclamation he sat behind the wheel of the jeep for only a moment before finally making up his mind. With all political rights suddenly denied to the newly free Vietnamese, some kind of explosion seemed unavoidable, and the anxiety he felt for Lan's safety finally broke down his earlier resolve to comply with her mother's wishes. When he drove past the Hôtel de Ville and saw the Viet Minh sentries still standing guard with their weapons in defiance of the martial-law edict, he pressed more urgently on the accelerator, and at the Hôpital Militaire the apprehensive French doctors took one look at his American officer's insignia and deferred without hesitation to his request for information.

When they located Lan they agreed immediately that he might visit her. The nurse supervising the ward in which she was being treated explained that Lan had almost recovered from her concussion and would be able to leave the hospital in two or three days. Lan was sleeping just then, the nurse said, but remembering the meaningful look the senior doctor had given her, she invited Joseph to wait at her bedside until she awoke.

Outside the door of Lan's room he hesitated again, wondering if he should at the last moment try to resist that irrational compulsion that had driven him there. He thought of Paul languishing in some dark cell not far away and wondered how he would explain his actions to him when they met. He decided he would say only that he had come to see if he could help the wife of his old friend, but this intended deceit only increased his feeling of disquiet. His final agony of indecision, however, lasted little more than a second or two, and when he stepped through the doorway, his eyes fell upon her immediately. Her long hair was spread across the white pillow like wreaths of dark smoke, and in repose the delicate beauty of her oval face was also voluptuous. He stood transfixed at the sight of her, and his heart seemed to swell suddenly inside his chest; the finely arched brows, the closed, heavy-lidded eyes and gently smiling mouth gave her the appearance of an Asian Madonna, acknowledging with shyly lowered gaze an adoration beyond her understanding. One hand, small and narrow like a schoolgirl's, lay on the top of the coverlet, and he had to check a sudden impulse to cover it tenderly with his own. She showed no signs of waking, and eventually he removed his cap and seated himself quietly on a chair by the foot of the bed.

For a quarter of an hour he just sat and looked at her; she slept propped high on her pillows, her head turned slightly to one side, and he could see a tiny pulse beating strongly in the base of her throat. She is just as beautiful as I remember her, he thought wonderingly — more beautiful perhaps. Listening to the gentle sigh of her breath, he felt a new stirring of the giddy passion they had once shared, and suddenly he knew that however unjust it was, he had never loved Tempe — and never would — with the same intensity. A feeling of anxiety gripped him as she began to waken, but when at last she opened her eyes and turned her head in his direction, she showed no sign of surprise.

348

"You shouldn't have come," she said softly in French.

"Lan, I know," said Joseph leaning towards her in his anxiety. "I'm sorry I didn't respect your mother's wishes. I had to see you again. Are you really recovered from your injuries?"

She nodded vaguely, her eyes still hazy with sleep. "There's nothing for us to say, Joseph. We must let past things remain in the past."

"But your mother said I'd caused you unhappiness. I didn't know what she meant."

With the gradual return of full awareness, her eyes began to widen in alarm. "She told me yesterday you'd come back to Saigon. I knew she'd forbidden you to visit me, but before I woke, I dreamed that you would come. . . ."

"But what did she mean? How could I have made you unhappy, Lan?"

"She thought that you knew. She thought I had told you in a letter after you left."

Joseph stared at her in puzzlement. "Told me what?"

She dropped her gaze and began twisting the coverlet abstractedly between her fingers. After a moment he noticed that the corners of her mouth were trembling.

"Told me what, Lan?" he prompted gently.

"That I had borne your child."

For a whole minute he sat and stared numbly at her, unable to speak. Then he reached out and gently touched the back of her hand with his fingertips. "Lan, if only you *had* written to me. . . ."

She shook her head quickly without looking at him. "It would have made things worse then if you had known."

Joseph closed his eyes for a moment. "Was it a girl or a boy?"

"She was a beautiful little girl. I called her Tuyet — the name means 'snow.'" When at last she raised her gaze to his, her eyes were brimming with tears. "Nobody knew of her birth. I went away. A year later I married Paul Devraux to please my father. We have a son of our own."

"But where's Tuyet now?"

"She was brought up as the daughter of one of our house servants — the girl who showed you to the gate the day you left."

"Then she's here in Saigon?" asked Joseph eagerly.

Lan shook her head quickly and looked out of the window. "No. My mother insisted that they be sent away. They went to live in the village in northern Annam where my mother was born. The servant girl married there later and had other children of her own."

Joseph stood up and paced back and forth agitatedly in the confined space of the small room, struggling to come to terms with the enormity of the news. Then he stopped and sat down again. "Have you seen Tuyet since her birth?"

Lan bit her lip and nodded. "Yes, I persuaded my mother to make a journey to the north once a year with me, at first under the pretext of visiting the birthplace of her ancestors. She went reluctantly — it was my idea, you see, that Tuyet should be sent there so that I might know something of her upbringing. But we saw her for only a day or two each time."

"Is she still living there?"

Lan looked distressed. "I'm not sure. For the past five years, since the Japanese came, it's been impossible to travel."

"Tuyet . . ." Joseph repeated the name to himself in an awed whisper, looking wonderingly at Lan. Then a wave of tenderness swept over him and he reached out and took her hand. "I'm truly sorry, Lan. If I'd known, I would have come back. You know I wanted to marry you. I never dreamed anything like this had happened."

Her hand tightened in his for an instant, and tears trickled down her cheeks. "If I hadn't dreamed of you I would have said nothing."

"But, Lan, what can we do?"

"There's nothing to be done, Joseph," she said quietly. "And there's nothing more to say." She freed her hand from his and brushed the tears from her cheeks. "You must go now. Please don't try to visit me again."

"But Lan," he began desperately, "we can't just pretend it never happened. . . ."

He broke off and drew away from her on hearing a commotion of hurrying footsteps in the corridor, and a moment later a tall, shabbily dressed European burst into the room. It was a second or two before Joseph recognized Paul Devraux; all badges of rank and other insignia had been ripped from the ragged battle-dress he'd been forced to wear during his six months as a prisoner of the Japanese, and his face was gray and haggard. Joseph stood up immediately and moved away from the bed, and with scarcely a glance in his direction the French officer knelt and seized his wife's hand.

"Lan, are you all right?" His eyes searched her face as he pressed her hand fervently to his lips. "I've been to your parents' house. They told me you were hurt in the riots."

"I'm almost recovered. It wasn't serious." She spoke in a scarcely audible whisper, her demeanor obviously restrained, and Paul reached out to touch her cheek in a tender gesture of affection.

"I'm so glad." His haggard features relaxed into a broad smile and he remained on his knees looking fondly at her. "I was very worried about you."

Pained by the sight of their reunion and seeing that his presence was acutely embarrassing to Lan, Joseph began to move quietly out of the room, but Paul stood up suddenly and whirled round, grinning from ear to ear.

"Joseph, my old friend, don't go! Lan's mother told me the 'Amorous American' had come back to Saigon as an OSS captain." He gripped Joseph's hand fiercely, then flung both arms around him in an emotional greeting. "But she didn't tell me you were trying to steal my wife while I was in prison."

Joseph looked back at him uncertainly, but the Frenchman, exhilarated by his return to freedom, laughed uproariously at what was to him clearly an outrageous jest. "I came to see if I could be of any help," he said, avoiding Paul's gaze. "Things look pretty bad in Saigon."

"Don't worry, Joseph. Everything's going to be all right now!" Paul slapped the American delightedly on the shoulder again. "The British have just released my regiment. Between us, we'll have things under control again in no time at all, you'll see."

Joseph stared into the grinning face and felt a genuine surge of affection and sympathy for the courageous French officer, who had obviously suffered at the hands of his Japanese captors. In his mind he was still struggling to come to grips with Lan's momentous revelation, and the significance of what Paul had said sank in only slowly. "Do you mean that you and the British are going to break up the Viet Minh government by force of arms?"

Paul nodded. "It's putting it a bit high, Joseph, to call it a government."

"But the people are behind the Viet Minh," said the American earnestly. "I've been in the north with their leaders. If you'd seen what I've seen, you'd feel differently. They want to negotiate — but they'll fight back with everything they've got if you attack them."

Paul seated himself on the bed beside Lan and took her hand again. "This is no time for a political debate, Joseph. I think you know how I feel about this country. I've spent more of my life here than I have in France. The Viet Minh Committee for the South are mostly Communists loyal to Moscow as far as I can see. I want the people here to get their independence one day as much as you do — but not this way."

"I'm sorry, Paul, forgive me ! I'm intruding here. I'm damned glad your ordeal is over and you've come through in such good spirits." Joseph shook the French officer warmly by the hand once more and smiled quickly at Lan. "Let's hope we can all get together sometime when things improve."

Back behind the wheel of his jeep, Joseph drove in a daze, and at first he didn't register the groups of newly released French prisoners of the Eleventh Infanterie Coloniale roaming the shuttered streets. Seeing Lan again after so long and discovering that she'd borne his child had filled him at first with a wild exhilaration, but the sudden entry of Paul in his prison garb had come as a shock; the obvious privation the French officer had suffered in prison heightened Joseph's feeling of wretchedness at having to conceal the truth from him, and for a time these conflicting emotions filled his mind to the exclusion of all else.

He'd been driving through the streets of the city center for two or three minutes without thought for where he was going before he began to focus his attention properly on the freed French prisoners. Like Paul, they were dressed in the same worn and badgeless uniforms that had become their prison clothes, and when the noise of a scuffle drew his attention to a particular group, he noticed that they were carrying new British .303 rifles. At first sight the troops appeared to be sparring high-spiritedly among themselves, then with a shock Joseph saw a Vietnamese in their midst and realized they were attacking passersby at random. Suddenly he remembered that for the past month since the Japanese surrender, most of the French prisoners had been under the guard of Viet Minh jailers, and now in the first heady moments of freedom they were lashing out at anyone who resembled their most recent tormentors. In the Rue Catinat he saw half-a-dozen French soldiers tear down the "Paris Commune" sign, then use it to bludgeon a startled Vietnamese youth to the ground; by the time he arrived back at OSS headquarters he had seen a dozen or more Vietnamese civilians being brutalized by the newly freed troops with their rifle butts. As darkness fell on the city, French civilians began coming cautiously into the streets again and they, too, released from weeks of fear, began to join the troops in abusing any Vietnamese unfortunate enough to cross their paths.

17

Just before daybreak on Sunday, September 23, 1945, Major Paul Devraux whispered an urgent command to the troops in his detachment to follow him, then set off at a run eastward beneath the camphor laurels bordering the Boulevard Luro. His men were in full battle order, and their faces, like his, were blackened with camouflage paint. In his right hand he clutched a loaded service revolver at the ready and he moved stealthily in a running crouch, taking advantage of the deeper shadows beneath the trees. He was heading towards the Hôtel de Ville, the headquarters of the Viet Minh Committee for the South, and simultaneously, all over Saigon, other detachments of a hastily assembled French force of fifteen hundred men were beginning to converge in the predawn darkness on police stations, the post office, the treasury and the former Sûreté Générale headquarters.

The force was under the overall command of Colonel Jean Cédile, General de Gaulle's "High Commissioner" who had parachuted into the paddy fields outside Saigon at the end of August, and their objective was to seize back control of southern Vietnam from the Viet Minh in a lightning coup d'état. Among the men loping silently behind Paul in rubber-soled combat boots were a hundred battle-toughened paratroopers who had jumped in with Cédile; all of them had been promptly interned by the Japanese on landing, but they had finally been freed twelve hours earlier by the British along with the fourteen hundred men of the Eleventh Regiment Infanterie Coloniale. Because they had been caged like animals for six months, first by the Japanese and then by the Vietnamese, all the French soldiers, Paul knew, were keyed up and spoiling for a fight. For that reason, at their assembly point under the walls of the city's old Vauban fortress, he had lectured his group severely against any vengeful bloodletting; like Joseph he had been horrified the previous evening by the sight of French soldiers and civilians attacking innocent Vietnamese on the streets, but although he had threatened his unit with courts martial if they disobeyed his orders, he had sensed that they listened unwillingly and still felt keenly the humiliation of their long imprisonment.

At the junction where the Boulevard Luro joined Rue de la Grandière, Paul halted his force in the shelter of a high wall while he checked to make sure that the route ahead was clear. He glanced briefly towards the Hôpital Militaire, and the sight of the complex of verandahed medical buildings made him wonder briefly if his wife was still asleep in her room there. Then he waved his men quickly across the wide street and ran on, aware suddenly just how precariously his own personal emotions were balanced in the conflict that had so unexpectedly ensnared him.

Now that the moment of confrontation with the Viet Minh was near, the assurance he had felt the day before was hedged around with twinges of doubt; he remembered Joseph's earnest expression when speaking of the massive popular demonstrations of support for the Viet Minh he'd seen in the north, and he wondered if perhaps he might now be betraying all his earlier instincts. Seeing how his father's generation had embittered contacts between his country and the Annamese had made him determined above all else not to repeat those mistakes; right up until his father's violent death at the hands of Annamese assassins, these feelings had made their relationship strained. Perhaps his anxiety to compensate for the insensitivity of his father's generation towards the Annamese had even played a subconscious part in his decision to marry Lan; he couldn't be sure. Although he was effusive in his love for her and their son, he was aware that there had always been a hint of reserve on her side, and occasionally he'd wondered in the back of his mind whether he had made an impossible choice. Now, in the aftermath of the war, the people of her country had out of the blue taken control of their own destiny for the first time in a century, and he was about to help break their fragile grip on freedom and return them once more to a state of colonial bondage. Didn't that make nonsense of everything he'd believed in the past?

In the distance the pillared façade of the Hôtel de Ville came into view at the end of the Boulevard Charner, and when he caught sight of the ragged Viet Minh guerrillas on sentry duty outside its lighted windows, he braced himself inwardly. Surely this wasn't the way it should happen! For the sake of the many Annamese who were loyal to France, wasn't it the duty of all honorable Frenchmen to give their backward country a better start than this, to guide them more slowly towards a truly democratic freedom? With the Viet Minh in control, wouldn't French tutelage be replaced by something much worse — domination by Moscow through the Comintern? Suddenly the confidence in the rightness of his choice returned with a rush and, waving his men into a narrow side-turning that led to the rear of the Viet Minh headquarters, he concentrated his mind again on the task of leading them unseen towards their target.

Unknown to the French attacking force, almost all the members of the Viet Minh Committee for the South had already fled from the Hôtel de Ville. They had been virtually living in the former city hall since General Gracey ordered them out of the palace of the governor of Cochin-China where they had set up their original administration; but the previous evening their alert intelligence network had learned of the intended French attack, and all but one of the committee's members had slipped away quietly into the night with their families. Only Ngo Van Loc, who had no close relatives in Saigon, volunteered to remain, to forestall any French claim that their administration had deserted and abdicated its rule, and as dawn approached, he lay dozing on a camp bed in an empty attic beneath the clock-tower belfry that crowned the ornate, turn-of-the-century building. On the floor beside the bed lay a stolen Japanese machine pistol, and a young Viet Minh guard cradled a similar weapon in his arms as he dozed in a chair by the door.

Both of them woke with a start when the street outside was filled suddenly with the roar of gunfire; the Viet Minh sentries before the doors were scythed down without warning by a sustained burst from the paratroopers' automatic weapons, and moments later they heard the sound of shots and running feet coming from the lower floors. Ngo Van Loc listened for a moment, then ordered the young guard to conceal himself in a cupboard at the back of the room. When he'd closed the door, Loc stationed himself with his back against it, holding his own machine pistol in front of him. Slowly the noise made by the French troops grew louder as they mounted the stairs to the upper floors, and he could clearly hear their shouts of anger as they discovered that the building was virtually empty. The crash of filing cabinets being overturned and ransacked reached his ears, then he heard the rush of feet in the corridor leading to the attic.

He had locked the flimsy door, but the paratroopers kicked it down and even before they caught sight of him, two of them opened fire simultaneously. Loc threw himself to the floor to avoid the haphazard fusilade, dropping his own weapon in the process, and the paratroopers forced the door back on its hinges before stepping into the room with the muzzles of their guns trained on him. Like the major who followed them in, their faces looked grotesque in the half-light, smeared with black face paint, and he tried in vain to move aside as the first paratrooper aimed a vicious kick at his face. The toe of the French soldier's boot caught his temple, stunning him, and only hazily did he hear Paul Devraux's angry shout as he ordered his men to stand back.

When he dropped to his knees beside Loc, Paul recognized his father's old hunting camp "boy" at once. "Loc, it's me — Paul!" he

355

said quickly. Bending over him, he slipped an arm beneath Loc's narrow shoulders and lifted him into a sitting position. He called loudly for a medical orderly, and when the medic panted up the stairs, he took his satchel from him and pressed a gauze pad soaked in surgical spirit against the bloody gash that the paratrooper's boot had opened up across Loc's cheek. When he had staunched the blood, he laid the gauze aside with a muffled sigh. "I'm sorry, Loc, that it's come to this."

Loc glowered at him, saying nothing, his face a mask of loathing. He took a deep breath and seemed to gather himself to speak, but without warning, he changed his mind and spat deliberately in Paul's face.

The French officer sat back on his heels and wiped his cheek slowly with his sleeve. "You shouldn't blame all Frenchmen for the actions of a few, Loc," he said wearily. "You'll be granted independence one day — but it'll take time."

Loc glared ferociously round at the two paratroopers who still held their automatic weapons pointing at his head; then he swung back to face Paul. "Our hatred for France knows no bounds. We'll fight for our freedom with our last drop of blood."

Appalled by the depth of hatred in the eyes of the Vietnamese, Paul hauled himself slowly to his feet; inside he felt a growing sense of despair, and he had begun to turn away when he heard Loc scream a frantic order from the floor in his own language.

"Giet! Giet! — Kill the officer!"

Glancing over his shoulder, Paul saw the door of the cupboard at the back of the room fly open, and an instant later the young guard's machine pistol spat flame. He felt the bullets strike him high in the back and their impact spun him around and flung him across the room. Halfway through the burst the guns of the paratroopers opened up and riddled the scrawny body of the young Vietnamese with more than a dozen bullets. Then they turned their weapons on Loc, and shot him again and again in the chest and head until his limbs finally stopped twitching and he lay still in a spreading pool of his own blood.

18

Lieutenant David Hawke spun the wheel of the OSS jeep right, then left, and slammed the accelerator pedal flat against the floorboards to send the little vehicle careering through a broken roadblock on the Avenue Gallieni. The crash of mortars and the sudden stutter of heavy machine-gun fire only fifty yards from where they had emerged onto the boulevard told Hawke and Joseph they had almost fallen into another running fight between a platoon of the First Gurkha Rifles and a large force of Viet Minh guerrillas. The swarthy little Nepalese soldiers were trying to clear and hold the Avenue Gallieni that ran south beyond the railway station towards Cholon, but as fast as they drove the guerrillas out of one section, they were reappearing at another point and throwing up new barricades. In the distance Joseph could hear the deep boom of twenty-five-pounders, and from time to time single-engined Spitfires and Mosquitoes bearing the red, white and blue roundels of the British Royal Air Force roared low overhead to strafe a Viet Minh strongpoint.

It was September 27, and for the fourth day running the Vietnamese were making frenzied attacks on the center of Saigon from all directions, infiltrating sabotage squads towards the city's vital installations and trying to mount lightning raids on the British and French headquarters. The three thousand British troops were hard pressed to contain the attacks, and although Japanese units had been thrown into the battle, the guerrillas were already proving themselves a resourceful and elusive enemy.

When a new volley of shots rang out from an unseen group of guerrillas, pitting the wall of a building ten yards ahead of them, Joseph tugged his helmet low over his eyes and ducked, cursing, below the level of the dashboard.

"May the devil take Gracey's balls for shish-kebabs," muttered Hawke angrily as he swung the bucking vehicle out of the line of fire and headed across the square in front of the railway station. "Who does he think he is? 'Only the British commanding officer's limousine will fly a flag of any kind'! If we could fly the Stars and Stripes from this damned jeep, the trigger-happy natives might stop shooting at us. Shall I get us a flag?"

"Better not, David," replied Joseph, keeping a wary eye on the road ahead. "The British are crazy enough right now to court-martial all of us for insubordination if we don't stick to orders."

Hawke nodded in reluctant agreement. During the four days that had passed since the French coup, they had watched with a growing sense of anger and frustration as fighting engulfed the city. After being woken by the sound of continuous gunfire early on Sunday morning, they had driven into the center of the city to find the French tricolor already fluttering from flagstaffs on the

Hôtel de Ville, the governor general's palace and all other public buildings. As the day wore on they had witnessed the same kind of ugly scenes they'd first seen on a small scale the night before; finding the Hôtel de Ville deserted, the French troops had begun to make house-to-house searches, and countless Vietnamese were beaten in the streets or marched off to prison with their hands tied as the long-pent-up emotions of the soldiers and the French civilians exploded in an hysterical lust for revenge.

Within twenty-four hours the outraged Vietnamese struck back, declaring a general strike and launching successful attacks on the power station and the water works; the central markets had been set ablaze, and roadblocks were erected all around the city so that during the night Saigon became a burning, barricaded enclave without water or electricity. In those nightmarish conditions the Binh Xuyen had carried out a terrible massacre of French civilian officials and their families in a quarter of Saigon that should have been guarded by Japanese troops; nearly two hundred men, women and children had been hacked to death and tortured in their beds during a night of barbaric atrocities, and two hundred more had been carried off as hostages. The next day Joseph and Hawke had watched thousands of French civilians flock to the Continental Palace Hotel, which was turned into a fortified strongpoint, and there the *colons* and their families huddled on the floors of the corridors and public rooms as the fighting raged all around them in the city outside.

Horrified by the turn of events, General Gracey had confined the French troops to their barracks again, only twenty-four hours after freeing them, and he had arrested the Japanese commander, Field Marshal Count Terauchi; after threatening to charge him with war crimes, the British general had ordered the Japanese officer to send his men immediately into the battle lines against the Vietnamese, and Joseph and Hawke had quickly become accustomed to the sight of fully armed Japanese soldiers rushing into action alongside the British Gurkhas. The Japanese had helped kill more than a hundred Vietnamese in the first few days of fighting, and Joseph had listened in dismay to British officers praising the discipline and the spirit of the Japanese troops who had borne the brunt of the casualties.

Outside the railway station a company of the Imperial Nipponese Army was mounting up into trucks under the direction of a British officer, and on catching sight of them Joseph let out an exclamation of disgust. "Goddamnit! How can they live with themselves when they're using enemies to fight our friends? How must those brave little Gurkha tribesmen who fought the Japanese to a standstill in Burma feel rushing around with men who two months ago were killing their closest buddies?"

"Maybe you'll have the chance to ask them tonight," replied Hawke with a grim smile. "We're invited to dine with the British officers — you, me and the major."

Joseph shook his head in disbelief.

"Takes more than a little colonial war, don't you know, to stop the British observing the niceties of mess rules and dining-in nights," added the Bostonian, aping a British accent. "We'll have to sit and hold our tongues with both hands instead of eating."

Joseph nodded, feeling a new surge of anger rising in him at their helplessness. Watching ineffectually from the sidelines as the city descended into chaos had been a harrowing experience — not least because his own emotions were so inextricably bound up in the turmoil. For several nights he'd slept only in snatches in his uniform, and watching the brutal and shameful behavior of the French had saddened him deeply. At the same time his feelings for Lan had intensified after seeing her again, and the shock of learning that they had an eight-year-old daughter living in an obscure northern village had continued to haunt his mind day and night. He longed desperately to visit Lan again to hear more about little Tuyet, but the prospect of deceiving Paul further filled him with renewed feelings of guilt. As he watched the fighting spread, he felt a deepening sympathy too for the French officer who had committed so much of his life to the Annamese for unselfish reasons. He had been distraught to discover on visiting Colonel Cédile's headquarters early in the week that Paul had been wounded during the early hours of the coup and had been airlifted for treatment to a military hospital at Dalat. Knowing how deeply grieved Paul must have been by the fighting and the destruction had served to heighten Joseph's own feelings of distress and resentment at the way the British had mishandled the crisis, and these thoughts were uppermost in his mind when he sat down to dinner that evening with the senior British officers at a table agleam with regimental silver, polished glass and linen napkins.

Over a glass of sherry in the mess there had been some jocular discussion of the difficulty of pursuing the guerrillas when they melted into their jungle villages beyond the city borders, and as the soup arrived in plates bearing the crest of the Twentieth Indian Division, a portly major with a booming voice took up the subject again.

"I've told my men that when they find it difficult to distinguish

359

friend from foe, they must always use the maximum force available to make sure all hostiles are wiped out — *maximum force!*" He rolled the phrase off his tongue with obvious relish. "If one uses too little, one might not live to tell the tale — but if one uses too much, no great harm is done. That's what I say — am I right?" He chuckled and sipped his glass of claret appreciatively, then looked around for approval.

Little murmurs of agreement rose from all round the table. "Quite so, I've even written it into my daily orders," said a ruddy-faced colonel with obvious pride, touching the corners of his drooping blond mustache with his linen napkin. "I tell my chaps it's perfectly legitimate to treat all locals found anywhere near the scene of shooting as hostiles — and damned treacherous ones at that. It seems to be getting the required results too, I must say."

The officer on Joseph's right hand, Colonel Sir Harold Boyce-Lewis, his intelligence counterpart, raised an amused eyebrow in Joseph's direction. "Seems your Viet Minh chums are getting more than they bargained for, captain, doesn't it?" he said dryly. "In that report you sent us they made a lot of noise about wanting to negotiate, but the way I read it they really wanted to trigger off a good old-fashioned shooting war to make their tin-pot revolution look a bit more realistic. Cédile assures me the vast majority of the Vietnamese support the French and want to see orderly French rule restored."

Joseph stared at Boyce-Lewis in disbelief. "You couldn't be more wrong, colonel. All but a tiny minority of the Vietnamese loathe the French — and with good cause. They're deeply outraged that Britain has helped take away the first taste of freedom they've had for a hundred years. But the Viet Minh are realists — I know because I've talked to Ho Chi Minh in the north. He's a hard-headed political leader and he knows they still need France. The Viet Minh were desperate for some negotiated return of the French that would recognize their sovereignty."

"My dear fellow, recognition of a Vietnamese government would be a political act. We're only soldiers, remember." Boyce-Lewis smiled pityingly. "The manual of military law, as you should know, lays down that the commander of an occupying army must try to observe the existing laws of the country. We're here to maintain order. Their little revolution is disturbing good order. I think we're following the book pretty closely; France is the sovereign power, the laws are French, nothing could be simpler. Returning power to the French is restoring the status quo. Your Viet Minh haven't been elected by anybody."

"Did the people of this country elect the French to govern them?" asked Joseph, his voice growing loud with indignation. "France hasn't been the sovereign power here by any stretch of the imagination since 1941. If the British are going to go around the world restoring *that* status quo, they'll have their hands full."

Boyce-Lewis bent his head towards his soup spoon and waved his free hand dismissively at Joseph. "Down here at least the Viet Minh's just a lunatic fringe — and the other nationalists have been goaded into action by the Japs who just want to make things sticky for us. That's why they gave their arms away to the likes of the Cao Dai and the Hoa Hao."

Suddenly the disdainful tone of the British officer brought all the pent-up emotion inside Joseph to the boil and he stood up abruptly, knocking his chair over with a crash. "Listening to what's been said here tonight makes me wonder what we fought the war for," he said hotly, glaring down at Boyce-Lewis. "Remember the Atlantic Charter of 1941? Didn't Churchill and Roosevelt agree we'd respect the rights of all people to choose their own form of government? You were sent here to disarm and repatriate the defeated Japanese — but instead you're keeping their troops under arms to crush a little nation whose only sin is it wants to be free." A shocked hush had fallen over the table, and several of the British officers were gazing at Joseph open-mouthed. "Have you seen their hand grenades made out of old food tins — their poisoned arrows and bamboo spears? Crude weapons, aren't they? But it shows how deeply they feel about getting rid of their foreign masters. We're supposed to have fought this war to defend freedom and democracy — but all you've done here is put the slave-driver's whip back in the hands of the French. That's not something you should be proud of — in fact it's a goddamned betrayal of everything Western democracy is supposed to stand for!"

Joseph turned and strode white-faced to the door without looking back, leaving Lieutenant Hawke and the OSS major embarrassed and uneasy in their seats among the British staff officers. There was silence in the room for a moment or two, then Boyce-Lewis glanced towards the ranking officer present, a thin, sour-faced brigadier.

"Best way to deal with that angry young captain, I suggest, sir, might be to declare him *persona non grata* and have him shipped back to Calcutta pronto, don't you think?"

The brigadier nodded slowly, then picked up his wineglass

and twisted it reflectively between his thumb and forefinger. "Indeed I do, colonel. Indeed I do."

19

As they approached the central Saigon market next morning, Hawke and Joseph saw that thick smoke was pouring out through the blackened dome above the covered halls again. The market had been set ablaze for the first time four days earlier, and the sporadic fighting in the surrounding streets had prevented any attempt to extinguish the fire. In a narrow street running alongside the burning building, Hawke slowed the jeep to a crawl, shaking his head in dismay. "If these markets stay closed and the guerrillas keep their food blockade intact around the city, I guess we'll start to see famine conditions down here in the south, too, before long."

While he was speaking, a ragged little Vietnamese boy toddled unexpectedly into their path from the mouth of a narrow alleyway, gazing awestruck at the pall of smoke, and Hawke had to stamp hurriedly on the brake. Springing from behind the wheel, the lieutenant swept the startled boy up in his arms; he was no more that three or four years old, and Joseph sat up in his seat suddenly, staring at the child. Within seconds the boy's distraught mother rushed from a house in the alleyway and snatched him from the arms of the amused Bostonian, but when Hawke returned grinning to the jeep, he found Joseph staring at him strangely, his face contorted as though with pain.

"What is it, captain?" he asked anxiously.

"The famine!" said Joseph in an anguished whisper. "How in God's name could I forget the famine?" His face had drained of color and he was staring through Hawke as though he wasn't there.

"What are you talking about?" asked the lieutenant in a puzzled voice.

"The famine in the north!" Joseph closed his eyes for a moment. In all the confusion of the last few days his thoughts had returned constantly to the imaginary face of the eight-year-old daughter he had never seen; but until that moment he had not associated the anonymous northern village where she had been sent to live with the terrible famine zone of lower Tongking and northern Annam.

"I don't follow you, captain," said Hawke, grinning in his bafflement.

"Just get in the jeep — fast." Joseph shifted quickly behind the steering wheel, his face set in resolute lines. Before Hawke was properly seated, he accelerated furiously away and drove at breakneck speed to the Hôpital Militaire. In the front courtyard he brought the jeep to a screeching halt and tore past the startled sentries, leaving Hawke to deal with identification procedures. He ran all the way through the echoing corridors to Lan's room, and when he arrived panting at the door, he brushed the duty nurse aside without offering any explanation for his presence. To his intense disappointment, however, the bed was empty and the room's impersonal cleanness no longer betrayed any sign that Lan had ever been there.

"She was discharged three days ago, captain," said the nurse sharply from the doorway. "She said she would be leaving Saigon immediately with her family."

Joseph ran all the way back to the jeep, took the wheel once more and drove with the same frantic urgency to the Imperial Delegate's residence. There he found the red-lacquered moon gate had been smashed from its hinges, and he clambered over it with a sinking heart. Even before he reached the front door, the scattered belongings on the steps told him the house had been looted. Inside, the family altar lay toppled on its side, and its gilded incense burners and statues were gone. The Louis XIV furniture lay smashed like matchwood, the Chinese and Annamese scroll paintings had been ripped from the walls, and in the room where the traditional teak mandarin's bed stood, an unsuccessful attempt had been made to start a fire. In another bedroom he found some of Lan's silken *ao dai* hanging untouched in a lacquered cabinet and he was seized suddenly with a feeling of black despair; the filmy garments still smelled faintly of her perfume, and taking one of them in his hands, he buried his face in it. It was several minutes before he could bring himself to leave the room and then he walked slowly and dejectedly back to the street.

"Just what in hell's name's going on, captain?" A mystified smile creased Hawke's face, and Joseph noticed he was sitting pointedly behind the wheel of the jeep. When Joseph made to move to the driver's side, the young lieutenant held up both hands in mock horror. "I'll take us back to base if you like. My nerves are in shreds and I'd like us to get there in one piece."

Joseph, nodding absently, slumped into the seat beside him and they traveled in silence for several minutes, heading towards OSS headquarters along the Rue Paul Blanchy. Hawke drove with ostentatious care, and when they approached the first of the log-pile road blocks which the Vietnamese had put up around the city to enforce their food blockade, he slowed to less than ten miles an hour. Since the day of the coup, the OSS men had become accustomed to zigzagging their vehicles at walking speed through the staggered barricades close to their headquarters; usually they were manned by half-a-dozen unarmed men, and the Vietnamese always waved them through, apparently acknowledging that they were Americans. As they approached the last barricade a quarter of a mile from the OSS mansion, Hawke's curiosity finally got the better of him.

"Since you risked my neck as well as your own getting us there, captain," he said with a smile, "do you mind if I ask what it was you were looking for at the hospital and in the looted house?"

Joseph let out a long breath. "There was somebody here in Saigon, David, who once meant a great deal to me. . . ."

He paused as Hawke slowed the vehicle to begin negotiating the first section of the roadblock that was constructed of tree limbs and brush. Unlike the others, it appeared to be unmanned, and without taking his eyes off the road, Hawke nodded and smiled understandingly as comprehension dawned. "It all becomes clear now — an affair of the heart, eh?"

"I found her again for the first time last Saturday— in the hospital. . . ." As he spoke, Joseph's eye was drawn to a pile of loose brush heaped in the roadside ditch; it was the same kind of brush of which the roadblock itself was constructed, and he realized suddenly that he had seen it shift.

In the same instant Hawke noticed the movement too, and turned his head to look more closely. The jeep was halfway through its maneuver, moving at walking pace, and too late, both men realized they were a sitting target.

"*Nous sommes américains! Nous sommes américains!*" screamed Hawke desperately as the brush was flung aside, but his shout was too late to prevent the concealed machine gun opening up on them from point-blank range.

The entire first burst from the gun struck Hawke in the head, blowing away part of his lower jaw and shattering his skull. His blood flew in all directions from the terrible wounds, spattering the windshield, and after ramming into the barricade the jeep toppled slowly into the opposite ditch. Joseph fell face down in the moist earth and lay paralyzed with horror, listening to the machine gun raking its chassis. When he turned over he saw Hawke's body suspended above him on the steering wheel; his face was unrecognizable and he had obviously died the moment the bullets struck him. Lifting his head above the rim of the ditch, Joseph saw three Vietnamese emerge from their hiding place and start in his direction; they carried their rifles loosely in their hands, and he guessed they had assumed he was dead too.

Each two-man OSS patrol carried a pair of Colt .45s and two M-1 rifles as a matter of routine, and Joseph grabbed a rifle and a pistol from their clips before scrambling out from beneath the jeep and flinging himself through the bamboo hedge bordering the golf course. The three Vietnamese crossing the road opened fire immediately, and he felt their bullets crash through the foliage close to his head. On the other side of the hedge he dived into a depression in the ground and turned to fire back in the direction of his pursuers. To his surprise, he heard one of them scream as he fell to the ground, and the other two dashed back towards the concealed machine-gun nest. Joseph took aim more carefully as they ran, but the rifle had jammed and he flung it from him with a curse.

In the lull that followed he found that he had three clips of ammunition for the Colt .45 — twenty-one rounds in all — and he hurriedly loaded it. A minute later to his horror he saw a dozen other armed Vietnamese emerge cautiously from concealed positions around the barricade and begin crawling in his direction. Glancing to the west he saw that about five hundred yards separated him from the safety of the OSS mansion. The hedge provided some cover for half that distance, but he realized that if he remained where he was, he had no chance of survival. Taking a deep breath he rose to his feet and set off at a fast run along the edge of the golf course. When they caught sight of him, the whole force of Vietnamese guerrillas rose out of the grass to give chase, firing as they ran.

As he neared the end of the protective hedge Joseph stopped. He could see that he would almost certainly be caught and killed by the guerrillas in the open unless he slowed them down, and after looking around frantically, he leaped into the ditch again. When the leading group of Vietnamese was only fifteen yards away, he lifted his head and, using both hands on the gun, emptied the Colt .45 into the running group. Two more guerrillas staggered and went down, and the rest immediately flung themselves flat on the ground. Using the fire-and-movement tactics he had been taught during his brief OSS training in Kunming, Joseph reached the end of the hedge safely, then sprinted hard across the open ground.

The guerrillas fired volley after volley at his back from a range of seventy yards, but he weaved and bobbed as he ran and reached the gates of the OSS house a minute later with only two bullets of his twenty-one left.

"Hawke's been killed," Joseph gasped when the major commanding Detachment 404 rushed down the front steps to help him in. "I think they mistook us for the French."

The major quickly posted guards on the roof and ordered out extra Japanese sentries from their nearby blockhouse. When Joseph had regained his breath, the senior officer laid a hand gently on his shoulder. "This may not be the best time to tell you, captain, but British headquarters have just informed me that you've been declared *persona non grata*. They don't like your views — or how you expressed them last night. You've got to fly out to Calcutta within twenty-four hours."

Still deeply shocked by Hawke's death and the battle for his own life in which he had probably killed three Vietnamese, Joseph stared back at his superior without really taking in what he'd said.

"And there's another thing," said the major, drawing Joseph towards the waiting room inside the front door. "There's a Vietnamese here to see you. He's been here a couple of hours. He insists on speaking to you personally and won't tell anybody else what he wants."

When Joseph entered the waiting room Tran Van Tam rose unsteadily from his seat; a bloodstained bandage was bound around his head, his clothes were torn and dirty and there was no sign in his manner of the hostility he'd shown Joseph at his parents' house a week before.

"Captain Sherman, I've brought a message from my sister, Lan," he said hesitantly. "She wishes to see you urgently. I'll take you to her, if you'll come now."

20

The winding, thousand-mile coast road from Saigon to Hanoi, first trodden by imperial courtiers before the Christian era dawned, has always given travelers the uneasy feeling that they are passing under sufferance through hostile, threatening terrain. For most of its length, the Mandarin Way is intimidated not only by the dense jungle that so often borders it, but also by two other great natural enemies: from the west the Annamite Cordillera occasionally thrusts down great spurs of rock to block its way, while from the east, the South China Sea seeps repeatedly across its path through the many crevices in Vietnam's winding coastline. At the beginning of October 1945 it was still little more than a narrow, single-lane track and Allied bombers had scarred and pitted its surface during intensive raids in the closing months of the war. But the craters had been largely patched and filled, and the ancient route of Annam's mandarins bore Captain Joseph Sherman's OSS jeep steadily northward over the roots of the mountains and through the clutching fingers of the sea as it had carried peasant carts and imperial palanquins during earlier centuries.

On the third day of his journey it led him red-eyed and weary into the provinces of Quang Tri and Quang Binh, where the highway's intangible air of threat had long since been replaced by a real and horrifying devastation. There the rain poured down from a low, leaden sky onto a desolate expanse of paddy fields that had been flooded by the repeated August typhoons. The wheels of the jeep churned through an unending sea of gray mud, and the damp chill in the air caused Lan to wrap her hooded cloak more tightly around herself in the jeep's passenger seat.

They had been puzzled when they saw the first ruined village; charred corner timbers and smoke-blackened earth walls were all that was left of a cluster of houses that Lan remembered as a once thriving village. Farther on, an emaciated peasant squatting listlessly at the roadside told them the villagers had pulled down their houses piece by piece and made fires with the wood to keep themselves warm; long before, they'd sold all their belongings to buy rice gruel. Many people had already died, he said, and those who were strong enough had moved on to seek food elsewhere. As he spoke the rolled mat lying in the mud at his side, apparently containing a bundle of his belongings, had shifted. Joseph heard a faint whimpering and assumed a dog had made the noise. But when Lan questioned him he admitted without taking his eyes from the flooded field beside the road that his two-year-old son was wrapped in the mat. He was waiting for him to die, he said tonelessly, so that he might bury him.

Joseph had leaped from the jeep, broken open a package of C rations and tried to force some nourishment into the coolie's hands. But he refused doggedly even to look at the food; instead he waved Joseph away from his bundle with threatening gestures. "We've already known great suffering. My wife and three other children are already dead," he said defiantly. "It is better now that we should die." When they drove away, the starving peasant had remained crouched by the rolled mat at the roadside, staring unseeing into the rain. The open packs of food which Joseph had insisted on leaving lay untouched before him on the flooded ground. After the faint whimper they had heard no further sound from the rolled mat.

The sight of the first ox cart piled high with a dozen tangled bodies had left them both numb with shock. Flopping, fleshless arms and legs stuck out in disarray as the plodding animal dragged its obscene load towards them through the muddy street of another ruined village. The shrunken beast, starving itself, moved slowly at the urging of an exhausted coolie who beat its bony rump feebly from time to time with a bamboo rod. The cart halted to allow them to pass, and to his horror Joseph saw one of the heads, its long hair matted with mud and rain, jerk convulsively. He looked sharply at Lan, but found she had closed her eyes and turned away.

Joseph stopped and ran back through the rain. He shook the coolie by the shoulder and pointed frantically to the body that had moved. Gesticulating and using a mixture of French and the few words of Vietnamese he had picked up from Hawke, he tried to make him understand that one of the "corpses" was still living. But like the dying peasant at the roadside, the man quickly became angry. He shouted and screamed abusively and pointed to the figure, now motionless like the rest. Then he turned away towards the nearby burial ground, and Joseph went slowly back to the jeep, fighting down a feeling of nausea.

They soon became accustomed to the sight of charred houses littering the gray, devastated landscapes through which they passed. Sometimes families were still living in the shells of their homes, crouched like docile animals in the one corner still left standing. They saw other ox carts too, removing the dead, some piled with twenty or thirty corpses. Once Joseph saw the wasted body of a young peasant woman slumped in death beneath a gaunt, blackened tree that looked as if it had been struck by lightning; her half-naked body and the tatters of her clothes were streaked with gray slime, and she was scarcely distinguishable from the muddy ground on which she lay. It was the twitching at her breast of a scrawny baby, only months old, that drew his eye to her; the dying infant was mewling faintly in the dead woman's arms and gnawing in vain at her shriveled teats. As he watched, another shrunken woman appeared, plucked the baby away and vanished into the blurred curtain of rain. They saw other corpses on the roadside, lying like twisted bundles of rags, from which the living, moving like sleepwalkers, kept their eyes averted.

Joseph had stopped imagining he could do anything to help after he tried to distribute another packet of C rations to a group of stick-limbed children begging at the roadside. Their despairing eyes and outstretched hands made him stop, but the sight of the jeep immediately brought other swollen-bellied youngsters limping from the winding paths leading out through the thick bamboo groves that concealed their village. When he handed out two little packets of the food, the children had begun to fight among themselves with a terrible ferocity, tearing at each other's faces and scattering the contents of the precious packages in the mud. A crowd of hollow-eyed adults, attracted by their screams, came running from the thicket, and Lan called frantically to Joseph to get back behind the wheel before the desperate villagers were tempted to attack them and loot the jeep. The children and the older Vietnamese, although obviously weakened by their hunger, chased after the vehicle, screaming pitifully as they ran, and the cries rang in Joseph's head long after they were out of earshot.

Even when they were back on the empty road, the smell of the wretched, starving people they had mingled with didn't leave them; famine seemed to produce a sickly sweet smell of smoky putrefaction, as though hunger itself were burning and rotting the flesh on the living bones of the people, and although Joseph couldn't be sure he wasn't imagining it, the odor seemed to cling to the jeep as they drove on. It seemed to penetrate even into his mind, and he felt his own personal sense of despair deepening; what chance could there be amid all the casual horror they had already seen, of finding alive the frail daughter Lan had borne him without his knowledge nearly nine years before?

Lan's previous visits with her mother had always been made by train, and approaching by road, she had been unable to find the way because all signboards had been torn down and burned. As a result, they had to make a tortured search through village after village in the coastal area north of Dong Hoi.

"These fields have always been green or gold when I came before," she said suddenly in a haunted voice, gazing out through the windshield at the wasted land onto which the cold gray rain was still falling. "The people should be working now planting for the *chiem* harvest of the fifth month next year. Not only will there be no crop for this year's tenth month harvest, but next year will be barren too."

Joseph noticed that she had begun to hold herself rigid in her seat, and he feared that hysteria might not be far away. The lowering skies were growing blacker, and he realized that it was more important for them to find shelter for the night than to continue searching the devastated villages as darkness fell. During most of the long journey from Saigon she had been subdued and distant; they had talked hardly at all as they headed northeast out of the city past Bien Hoa and into the vast region of regimented rubber plantations. He too had been abstracted; he found his own thoughts returning to his first melancholy journeys on that road with his mother in 1925, first traveling north to Hue in a state of youthful distress, then returning later, shocked and stunned at the news of Chuck's death. As they passed through the rubber groves and on into the tropical forests where he had so long ago hunted with his father and brother, he was haunted too by memories of Ngo Van Loc's tragic family.

They had begun their journey before dawn, and by driving hard through the day and into the darkness they had covered over two hundred miles to reach Nha Trang. There they had slept a few hours in rooms they were able to take in the old French-run inn that used to serve the railway when the northbound line ended there. They had risen at four A.M. and driven hard again all the next day before snatching a few hours of sleep in a similar inn at Tourane, the port that would later be renamed Da Nang. As they passed the road running up into the highlands at Dalat and drove on above the massive natural harbor at Cam Ranh Bay, Lan's mood had lightened abruptly. She had begun to talk animatedly of her idyllic schooldays at the Couvent des Oiseaux at Dalat; wistfully she described the mists that had shrouded the lake every day, the fragrant pines, the heady mountain air and the timeless beauty of the sun shining on the sparkling waters.

"I would wander with my friends every day through the woods around the lake reading aloud . . . Lamartine . . . Baudelaire . . . Chateaubriand. . . . We would pick orchids and sing. We sang 'Les feuilles sont mortes' in the still air on the shore of the lake every morning, and our voices could be heard right across the other side. It was so lovely, so very romantic, Joseph." Her eyes shone with the pleasure of the memory. "I was sure then my life would be filled always with romance."

Joseph had been deeply moved by the simple beauty of her words, spoken innocently without any trace of sadness. He felt suddenly that they were on the verge of entering some new and intimate realm of understanding, but then she had withdrawn quickly into an inexplicable silence again, her manner as enigmatic and uncertain as it had been when Tam had taken him to her on the day of Hawke's death. When he arrived at the house in which she had lived since her marriage to Paul, she looked anxious and ill at ease. She told him that her parents had already left for the fortified country house with her young son. Tam had been injured by drunken Frenchmen, she told him angrily, in the wild hours following the coup. In his fury he had let himself be drawn into one of the non-Communist "national resistance" movements like most other moderate pro-French Vietnamese in those days. She admitted she was frightened; with Paul wounded and in the hospital, her whole world appeared to be collapsing around her with no safe avenue of retreat. Her conscience had troubled her, she had explained, without looking at him. She felt he had the right to know, if he wished, to which village his daughter had been taken to grow up. In an instant he had made up his mind. "We'll go together and find Tuyet," he said, seizing her by the hands. "You must show me where she is. I'll look after you, protect you!"

She hesitated and didn't agree immediately, but he had persuaded her to wait until he returned early next morning. He had promised her he would take her then wherever she decided to go, and at OSS headquarters, he had secretly loaded up a jeep with as many jerricans of gasoline as it would hold and thrown in four crates of C rations. Risking action later for desertion, he had returned to her house at dawn on the day he should have been deported to Calcutta, and found to his delight she was mutely willing to go with him. The fake orders he had given himself with the aid of an OSS typewriter, claiming that he was journeying to inspect American missionary properties in Dalat and Hue, appeared convincing enough for the few British and Viet Minh patrols he met on the road outside Saigon, and he passed off Lan in her hooded cloak as a sister of the order returning to the mission. Although there had been rumors that peasants outside Saigon were murdering rich landlords and corrupt village officials in a wave of revolutionary terror, during the drive through Cochin-China and southern Annam little seemed to have changed outwardly since Joseph's previous visits; the tropical sun shone brightly, the fields were green with growing crops and the roads had been filled with the familiar jogging lines of straw-hatted peasants hauling food and livestock to crowded country markets. Although the railway track beside the road lay smashed in many places by Allied bombs, the ancient road ferries were all in action on the rivers and inlets, and their owners helped the jeep on its way without question; the invisible ferrymen were summoned still as they had been for centuries, by a blast of a buffalo horn hung from a riverside tree.

But gradually as they drove northwards the weather worsened, and it was dawn on the third day as they headed on up the coast past Hue that they drove into the cold northern rain belt. The soldiers at the Chinese guardpost at the sixteenth parallel had shown a healthy respect for the little American flag fluttering from the jeep's aerial, and they had displayed no curiosity at Joseph's verbal claim that he was traveling north to Hanoi with his wife to rejoin his old unit under General Wedemeyer's command. As they drove on into Quang Tri province where the towering mountain chain thrust its bulk to within a few miles of the sea, they began to notice the first manifestations of famine; terraced fields on the mountainside lay bare and uncultivated, and from the few remaining aged peasants they learned that the population had already departed southward. The signs of devastation had increased as they continued northward until the landscape was at last transformed into a wasteland.

As the darkness deepened on the third night, Joseph found himself peering with growing anxiety through the rain-spattered windshield. There had been no sign of an inn for many miles, and he felt a quiver of revulsion pass through him at the thought of sleeping in one of the partly ruined houses in those dying villages. A few miles south of the town of Rao Nay, the headlights of the jeep fell onto the rain-lashed waters of a narrow river as they rolled downhill towards a ferry point. When he got out, he found the riverbank was deserted and the ferry had ceased operating; clearly they could go no farther until the next morning. An uncomfortable night in the cramped jeep seemed the only alternative, then Joseph noticed the dim outline of a building that turned out to be a European bungalow that had perhaps once been a modest auberge for travelers. Its windows and doors were padlocked, its paintwork peeling, and its French owner had obviously long since departed. Joseph inspected it with a flashlight, then using a tire iron from the jeep, broke into the building by forcing the window shutters. Inside it was bare and musty from lack of habitation, but he found some wood and built a fire in the stone fireplace of its echoing kitchen, which still smelled faintly of wine, stale cheese and dust; then he led Lan shivering from the jeep and sat her gently on a chair beside the flames.

He brought in a kerosene lamp and a small spirit stove from the jeep and boiled some water before the hearth. A half-empty bottle of cognac had been left abandoned in a cupboard, and in his service mug Joseph mixed a measure of the brandy with some boiling water and handed it to Lan. While she sipped the steaming drink he spread out the contents of two C ration packs on a wooden stool by the fire — some sausages, fruit and a square of cheese. But when he urged her to eat, she shook her head and looked away into the fire. They sat mutely by the flickering flames in the dusty kitchen without moving for perhaps an hour. The horrors of the day seemed to have deadened their senses, rendered them speechless, and although the cold and the damp evaporated slowly, the awful numbness induced by the harrowing sights their eyes had witnessed seemed destined then to remain with them forever.

Neither of them knew how they arrived at the moment when they were clutching each other with the convulsive hands of drowning swimmers. They held one another blindly, aware only that the other was reassuringly alive and whole, and their two bodies trembled as one with the despairing fear of having come close many times to death at its most grotesque. Recoiling from the unbearable images of slack and ravaged corpses, unable even to eat what little food they had, they were nourished, each of them, by the closeness of the other. Stark dread of the death they had seen spilling slowly across the cold, drowned countryside had frozen their tears inside them too, so they couldn't weep. Instead they clung to one another in a long shuddering silence, their lovemaking an act of helpless reverence before a dreadful, uncaring fate. The frantic joining of their bodies at last was a flight from inexpressible grief and sorrow which had seemed profound enough to destroy them while they sat apart, contemplating the awful tragedy all around them in which a daughter of their love was lost.

Later they slept deeply in each other's arms, wrapped in blankets on the floor of the abandoned house, the meager ration of food still uneaten upon the stool before the embers of the fire. They didn't touch it until the following morning when they rose wordlessly in the blurred light of dawn to continue their agonizing quest. Then they ate mechanically, without pleasure, before hurrying out again into the freezing rain.

21

They found the ancestral village of Lan's mother, close to the sea, soon after dawn. Like most northern settlements, it was surrounded by dense groves of bamboo, first planted centuries before when marauding pirates and hostile clans had posed a constant threat to its safety. Coconut palms and areca-nut palms hung with betel vines grew along the nearby shore, and once, Lan told Joseph before they arrived, the village had been prosperous for the area. Large three-roomed houses had been built around a beautiful lotus pool, guava and fig trees abounded, and during childhood visits she had played hide and seek along the sun-dappled pathways that wound through the whispering bamboo thickets.

When they finally came in sight of the village, however, it bore little resemblance to Lan's description; a freezing wind was blowing off the sea and rain squalls blotted out the frowning mountain peaks to the west. They had seen no living soul on the road or in the fields that morning, and the approaches to the village were silent and deserted; only the constant hiss of the rain broke the eerie silence, and even before they entered the dripping bamboo thickets, Joseph knew what they would find.

In the lotus pond in the center of the village, the bloated body of a man was lolling half in and half out of the water; his bloodless face, the same gray color as the mud, had swollen and burst, and as they walked by, Lan stifled a sob. Half the thatched houses were derelict skeletons of charred wood, and sodden piles of ashes were all that was left of other dwellings; the walled house of the village council chairman, the office her maternal grandfather had once filled, was locked and barred. Unable to speak, Lan lifted a trembling hand to point to one of the few thatched houses still standing on stilts on the far side of the pond; part of it had been burned, but one end remained intact, and Joseph motioned her to stay where she was while he looked inside. As he slithered through the slime beneath the withered trees, his heart lurched within him; the sickly stench of putrefying flesh hung heavy in the air, and he was certain he would find nobody alive.

The gray light filtering through the driving rain left the interior of the house in shadow, but as he peered in through the door, Joseph caught a glimpse of a familiar face — that of the Annamese servant girl he had last seen in 1936 opening the red moon gate to him in Saigon. She lay propped in a hammock slung from the roof beams, and her lifeless head was level with his own. Her lips were drawn back hideously from her teeth as though in a silent scream, and at the moment of his arrival there was a sudden commotion in the gloom. He heard rather than saw the engorged bodies of the rats flop to the floor and scuttle away into the darkness, and when he finally switched on his flashlight and swung its beam around the room, a wave of nausea swept over him. Alongside the far wall, a man of her own age, presumably her husband, lay dead on a straw plank bed, and like hers, his body had been horribly preyed upon by the rats.

Joseph stumbled outside and leaned weakly against a dead tree; standing bareheaded, he lifted his face and let the cold rain fall on his cheeks until the feeling of nausea left him. When he returned to Lan's side, she searched his face with distraught eyes for a moment, then bit her lip fiercely and turned away without speaking. A minute or two later the bent figure of an old bearded Vietnamese, hobbling beneath an umbrella of oiled paper, emerged from the mist and approached them. His sodden, frayed gown marked him unmistakably as the village chairman, but beneath his mandarin's cap his face was gaunt from starvation. He bowed once gravely towards Lan before speaking.

"The family you seek are all dead like the rest of the population of Ben Thoung. Neither our village nor our country has ever known such a terrible calamity in all our history." He spoke French, but his voice was a dry rattle in his throat, and he kept his head half bowed as though he was deeply ashamed of what he had to say. "Many flocked here to the countryside to avoid the bombing. We distributed our stocks with great strictness, and when the rice ran out they ate the husks. We distributed edible roots for them to grow and they swallowed the bulbs and planted only the stems. Then they tore up the stems and ate them also. They ate the roots and vines of their potatoes and they ate the seeds of next year's crops. They ate the roots of banana trees — even pennywort from the marshes. When they had nothing else they bought clay in the markets to staunch the pain of hunger in their empty bellies."

The old man swayed on his feet, supporting his thin body on a bamboo cane which he clutched tightly in a clawlike hand. He had spoken to Lan as if he recognized her, although he made no open acknowledgment. When he looked up at Joseph, the American saw his rheumy eyes were brimming with tears. "There has been much suffering, monsieur. Parents had to decide whether to starve themselves to let their children survive — or keep the food from them and watch their little ones die before their eyes. Some tied their offspring to the hut timbers to keep them from stealing food in the house." He shrugged hopelessly. "They hoped to live long enough to begin new families. . . . Now I am the only living person in the village, and soon I will die too."

Lan pointed to the house by the pond again. "Did all the children of Nguyen Thi Thao die?"

375

The old man turned unsteadily to look at the house, "The three children died two weeks ago," he said quietly over his shoulder. "Last week the parents died. They were the last surviving family in the village. He lost his mind at the end and tore out his own eyes. There was nobody left to bury them."

Lan swayed, and Joseph circled her shoulder quickly with his arm. "But they had *four* children," she whispered when she had regained her composure.

The old man nodded slowly. "The fourth, the girl with the pale skin, they sent away six months ago to her sister's village — Dong Sanh, four miles to the south. They thought the prospects would be better there."

"And are they?" asked Joseph in an agonized voice. "Are people still surviving there?"

The old man didn't answer immediately, but closed his eyes for a long moment as though gathering his strength. "People are dying everywhere. Nobody knows or cares any longer what happens in the next village."

Joseph offered the old man food from the jeep, but he refused to accept anything at all from them. When they left the village, he was still standing in the rain at the spot where they'd spoken to him, and before they went out of sight he waved his umbrella once in a final pathetic salute.

It took them an hour to reach Dong Sanh because the road was badly flooded, and neither of them spoke during the journey. To express any hope at all amidst such horrifying scenes of desolation seemed to be tempting fate, but when they arrived, to their relief, they found people still struggling to stay alive. Shortly after they reached the village the rain stopped for the first time in days and small ragged crowds of spindly-legged Vietnamese came out to throng a makeshift market where a few food sellers were setting out shallow dishes of rice gruel. Those without money crowded round watching with yearning eyes as others with the few necessary coins poured the steaming liquid into their throats. Gangs of begging children, wearing mats or bundles of hay tied with banana ropes, wandered lethargically among desperate vendors who were offering for sale their ancestral altars, half-burned house timbers and even the ragged clothes from their own backs to get money to buy food. Sometimes at the roadside Joseph and Lan saw a motionless figure wrapped in a rolled mat, dying or already dead, and the obviously lifeless corpses they noticed were being covered quickly with big banana leaves on the orders of a patrolman who moved among the crowds wielding a bamboo cane.

They quickly found the half-wrecked house where the sister of Nguyen Thi Thao had lived, but it turned out to be deserted, and Lan was told by a woman too weak to rise from her plank bed in the next house, that the parents of the family living there had died ten days before. The woman scarcely had strength to speak herself, but when Joseph prompted Lan to question her further, she admitted that some of the children might still be alive. They could be running wild with the other orphans of the famine in the village, she said, and together Lan and Joseph hurried back to the market square. There the gangs of starving children were still milling aimlessly among the displays of tawdry goods spread out on sodden mats, and Joseph watched Lan's face with a fast-pounding heart every time they drew near to a small girl. But each time she shook her head, and after an hour, feeling sick at heart, they reluctantly turned away and headed back towards the jeep.

It was Joseph who noticed the tiny figure kneeling alone by the steps of the muddy village pond as they prepared to drive away; hardly daring to hope, he touched Lan's arm and they got out of the vehicle again and walked quietly back towards the pond. When they drew near, they saw that the long hair of the girl was matted and tangled in muddied skeins down her back; she was pitifully thin, and the only garment covering her body was a torn mat tied about her waist with twisted banana leaves. Her head was bowed, and as they approached, they saw that she was staring listlessly into the slimy water.

Lan stopped a few feet away and peered intently at the girl, but when she looked up at Joseph again she was biting her lip and he could see that the interval of four years and the ravages of the famine left her uncertain. The little girl had not turned her head, and Joseph on an impulse stepped towards her and dropped to his knees. "Tuyet," he called softly, "Tuyet . . . *con dung so!* — don't be afraid."

At the sound of the name, the little wasted figure tensed, and the instant she turned towards him, Joseph knew their search was over. Although she was pitifully thin and her overlarge eyes burned luminously in a haunted face, he saw in her features an unmistakable inheritance of Lan's beauty. Close to her, he could see that beneath the grime her skin was paler than the other children's, and the less-pronounced tilt of her eyes showed him too that his blood and Lan's were mingled in her. Suddenly his temples throbbed at his release from agony and he reached out his arms to her in an imploring gesture.

The girl, obviously terrified by the sight of his white face, backed

377

away and almost slipped down the bank into the pond. But he made gentle, reassuring noises and advanced slowly and patiently until, trapped with her back to the water and too feeble to resist further, she dropped her head and allowed him to pick her up in his arms. Beneath the sodden mat her sticklike body was shivering with cold, and she seemed in his big hands to weigh nothing. He pressed her wildly against his face and the earthy smell of the wet rotting mat and that same sickly sweet odor of famine that permeated every village of the region engulfed his senses. When at last he held her out at arm's length, her big burning eyes looked blankly back at him. She stared with the same uncomprehending expression, too, at the tears that had begun flowing unashamedly down his cheeks.

PART FIVE

Dien Bien Phu

1954

By the time Britain handed over its responsibility for southern Vietnam to France in early 1946, more than two thousand Vietnamese had been killed by British forces. In the north the Chinese army of occupation finally withdrew in March 1946 under an agreement with France that allowed a limited number of French troops to enter the north in return for France's giving up all claims to its concession territories in China. Ho Chi Minh's government, which had remained peacefully intact in Hanoi during that time, gave a wary welcome to the returning French forces, and Paris recognized the new Democratic Republic as a state within the French Union. Negotiations between Ho and the French leadership continued until the autumn, with France stubbornly refusing to grant the Vietnamese full independence, and it became obvious that both sides were preparing for open conflict. Vietnam, however, remained an unnoticed backwater in world affairs, and during this time, with the Soviet Army straddling central and eastern Europe, President Harry Truman swung the United States firmly behind France because of that country's importance in the crucial Cold War arena of Europe. Several times Ho Chi Minh wrote to President Truman seeking his backing, but the letters went unanswered. Support for France in fact had never wavered in the American State Department, and the intimacy that had developed between the OSS and the Viet Minh in the closing days of the war was frowned on by American diplomats. Eventually Washington formally announced its intention to respect French sovereignty in Indochina and the OSS mission was abruptly withdrawn from Hanoi in October 1945. Not until much later would American leaders wonder whether a golden opportunity had been missed to turn Ho Chi Minh into an Asian Tito, friendly to the West. During his year in power, however, Ho Chi Minh had gained an unshakable grip on the minds of his countrymen, and when full-scale war with France broke out throughout Vietnam on December 19, 1946, he retreated confidently once more to those same limestone caves in Tongking from which he had descended in triumph sixteen months earlier. During its brief period of office, his Viet Minh government had overcome the famine in the north by mobilizing the people to plant quick-growing crops on every spare inch of land, and it had also won fairly held elections in Annam and Tongking. The dominant Communists in the Viet Minh League, however, did not hesitate to employ terror tactics against those nationalists opposed to them, and they murdered most of their prominent opponents during those turbulent early days. But it was clear that the vast majority of the Vietnamese nevertheless approved of the Viet Minh, and as a result, after the war began, the French found that even with 150,000 troops in Vietnam they could control only the centers of the cities and the lines of communication between them, while the Viet Minh held sway over the rural villages, the rice paddies and the jungles. After a few early French victories, a military stalemate was reached and this lasted until October 1949, when the victory of Mao Tse-tung's Communists in China's civil war produced a major change in the tide of world history. Overnight China became a safe sanctuary across the northern borders of Tongking where Ho's guerrilla forces could retreat for prolonged training under Vo Nguyen Giap. In a matter of months they were transformed into full field formations armed with modern American artillery weapons salvaged from the arsenals of the defeated Chiang Kai-shek, and a French military victory became impossible. In late 1950, forty-three of these new Viet Minh battalions burst across the Chinese border and smashed through the frail line of French defense forts to inflict the most humiliating colonial defeat on France since General Montcalm was defeated and killed at Quebec by the British in 1759. Six thousand French troops were killed, and enormous quantities of weapons and transports were captured. Openly dominated at last by its Communist leaders and allied firmly with Moscow and Peking, the Viet Minh controlled Vietnam thenceforth from the Chinese border to within a hundred miles of Saigon, with the exception of the fortified perimeter held by the French around the Red River delta and Hanoi. More importantly for the world at large, Mao Tse-tung's victory had deepened the West's fear of a monolithic, expansionist Communism, and this brought the Indochina war out of the obscurity under which it had, until then, been fought. China and the Soviet Union recognized Ho Chi Minh's government in its mountain stronghold in January 1950, and this prompted the United States to recognize an alternative French-sponsored Vietnamese government headed by chief of state Bao Dai. Moscow and Peking's blessing "removed the last illusions about the nationalist character of Ho Chi Minh's aims and revealed him as a mortal enemy of native independence," said American Secretary of State Dean Acheson and Washington began pouring military and economic aid into Vietnam and the other countries of Indochina to help France block further Communist gains; at a stroke, France's colonial war had been turned into a crusade to stop Communism spreading across Asia. Western apprehensions about Indochina were intensified further in June 1950, when North Korea invaded its southern neighbor and Western forces under the United Nations flag were drawn into conflict with the Communist armies of North Korea and China. As a result, President Truman sent a military mission from Washington to Saigon that summer to liaise closely with the French, and this act marked the beginning of a fateful United States involvement in Vietnam. Support in the form of aid snowballed, and by 1954 three billion American dollars had been poured into France's military coffers in Indochina. In 1953, a cease-fire in Korea allowed the Communists to concentrate all their military efforts on Indochina, and Russian and Chinese supplies to Giap's forces increased dramatically. In response, the nineteenth government to hold office in Paris in nine crisis-wracked years made a last desperate effort to extricate France honorably from what had become a muddled, hopeless cause. It approved a plan by military leaders to lure the core of General Giap's regular forces into a decisive set-piece confrontation behind Viet Minh lines in the remote northern valley of Dien Bien Phu, where it was thought French air superiority and greater firepower could easily destroy an enemy which possessed no aircraft, no tanks and only limited means of transport. Once before, the French had pulled off the bold stroke of dropping a fortress from the air into a narrow limestone valley behind Viet Minh lines at Na San; when General Giap attacked there without sufficient preparation, he had lost a whole battalion amidst the wires and mines of the fortifications, and the French high command hoped this success could be repeated more decisively. But instead of yielding a quick, easy victory, Dien Bien Phu in the event became the setting for one of the most fateful and historic clashes ever between East and West.

1

The tangled mantle of green-black jungle vegetation which centuries of moist heat had woven into the dragon-backed mountainsides of Tongking showed only patchily through the banks of low
cloud as the French Air Force Dakota lumbered through the gray
dawn of an early February morning in 1954, heading for Dien
Bien Phu. Its two-hundred-mile journey from Hanoi to the
remote, northwest corner of Vietnam close to the Laotian border
had taken an hour and a half, and during that time Joseph
Sherman had crouched uncomfortably on a tip-up metal seat
amidst a cargo of coffin planks, blood plasma, tinned food and a
dozen illicit crates of French beer. On his knee he held an air
reconnaissance map which showed the valley of Dien Bien Phu as a
tiny, isolated island of green ink amidst the unending gray sea of
Tongking's sprawling limestone massif; ten miles long and four
miles wide, the valley had sheltered a score of thatched villages
before French paratroopers seized it at the end of November 1953
to turn it into a fortified camp with a defense perimeter of over
thirty miles. Since then its garrison had been built up to a strength
of thirteen thousand men, and heavy artillery, trucks and even
tanks had been dropped in by parachute.

"Hold tight to your seat, monsieur," said the French pilot grimly
over his shoulder. "To get down into this pisspot we have to make a
high approach to clear the Viet Minh antiaircraft units, then dive
steeply through the clouds, using the ground radio beam."

Joseph tightened his seat belt a notch and smiled at the pilot's
black humor. He had used the term *pot de chambre*, the vulgar
nickname given to the mountain-ringed basin of Dien Bien Phu by
the French aircrews who for the past two months had been
valiantly landing or parachuting eighty tons of supplies into the
camp every day through thick mists and drizzle. In private conversation few flyers made any secret of their contempt for the
strategic plans of the French army high command, and as the
Dakota broke through the bottom cloud layer, the pilot let out a
little snort of derision.

"There's your first sight, monsieur, of what our senior officers in
their wisdom conceived as 'an offensive base from which to strike
against enemy rear areas.' " He motioned sarcastically through the
windshield with his head. "It may have looked good once on
General Navarre's wall map in Saigon, but from up here you can

see it for what it really is — a self-made prison."

Joseph peered down anxiously at the patchwork of yellow clay rice fields scarred with sandbagged machine gun nests and trenches; a shallow river wound across the valley bottom, its banks wreathed with endless entanglements of barbed wire, and he could see big gangs of soldiers still digging busily with their trenching tools on the slopes of the low hills that formed natural defense points within the perimeter. "You're right," breathed Joseph, scanning the high peaks which towered over the valley on all sides. "One of the oldest rules of war is 'never let your enemy get up above you,' and the peaks have all been left to the Viet Minh."

The pilot nodded. "Now you see why we call it *un pot de chambre*? From those mountaintops the 'yellows' can urinate all over us. General Navarre and his staff must be living in a dream world. They think the enemy is going to rush down from the hills again like he did at Na San and impale himself obligingly on our barbed wire so that we can pulverize him with air attacks and our artillery — but I for one will be surprised if General Giap falls for that trick twice."

"It doesn't seem possible that anyone could have been so foolish," said Joseph incredulously.

The pilot snorted again. "It's all based on military classroom theory. They've worked it out carefully on their little sand tables at headquarters and nobody believes the 'yellows' can move enough weapons and supplies through three hundred miles of mountain jungle to sustain a real siege here." He shrugged and glanced down again at the forested hillsides beneath the descending plane. "But if they're wrong, it'll make Custer's Last Stand look like a picnic."

Joseph continued to scan the fortifications with a professional eye, and as the Dakota lost height his frown deepened. "They seem to be putting a lot of faith in those fortified hillocks inside the perimeter," he said at last. "But if the Vietnamese get that far, there's going to be some nasty close fighting."

The pilot nodded and gestured through the windshield again. "Those three hills at the northern end of the valley are called Gabrielle, Beatrice and Anne-Marie. That one to the south is Isabelle, and the little group clustered round the command center in the middle are Dominique, Elaine, Françoise, Claudine and Huguette." The pilot glanced quickly around at Joseph, his face set in unsmiling lines. "In case you hadn't heard, I should tell you that the officer commanding, Colonel de Castries, has a wide reputation as a lady's man and his troops believe the hills are named after his current mistresses — but they're not very amused by the idea."

Through the windshield Joseph noticed white puffs of smoke breaking out along the rim of the valley nearest to the landing strip, and above the roar of the Dakota's engines he recognized the distinctive bark of light 75-millimeter mountain guns. "It looks like we're going to get a warm reception from the Vietnamese People's Army," said Joseph, leaning close to the pilot's ear.

The Frenchman nodded grimly once more without turning. "They'll mortar the runway too as we go down. It's practically routine now. As soon as we stop rolling, you must make a dash for the headquarters jeep they'll be sending out to meet you."

As the Dakota swooped in to land, Joseph watched the mortar bursts kicking up fountains of yellow earth alongside the gridded airstrip that had been laid down by the Japanese during the Second World War. Through a side window he could see a command jeep zigzagging among the exploding mortar shells, and even at a distance of a hundred yards he recognized the tall, straight-backed figure seated beside the driver, wearing camouflage battle dress and the crimson beret of the Second Battalion, Colonial Paratroops. On the ground the dull thud of the shells detonating was much louder, but unlike the jeep's driver, the officer sitting beside him disdained to wear a helmet, and the vague pangs of remorse and guilt that had been growing in Joseph over the past two or three years were suddenly intensified by this display of calm courage,

As soon as the Dakota halted, Joseph flung himself through the hatch and ran bent double towards the jeep. Its driver slowed the vehicle to walking pace to allow him to clamber aboard, then turned and raced back towards the fortified bunkers of the command post that had been constructed six feet below ground level.

"I thought this valley was supposed to be an impregnable fortress," yelled Joseph boisterously as he seized the hand of the French lieutenant-colonel in both his own.

"It is, *mon vieux*, I assure you," replied Paul Devraux, grinning hugely and shouting at the top of his voice to make himself heard above the roar of the exploding shells. "Don't worry! The 'Amorous American' won't get his precious balls shot off here — they can't really lay down an effective barrage with those little 75-millimeter peashooters."

As the jeep screeched to a halt at the mouth of the sap leading down into Paul's fortified bunker, a squadron of M-24 tanks emerged from the swirling dust and rumbled past them. "They're off to deal with the mountain guns in those foothills over there," said Paul, pointing towards the northeast. "It won't take long to silence them. We can stay here and watch if you like."

For two or three minutes they listened to the deep boom of the tank cannons echoing across the valley, then abruptly the Viet Minh shelling of the airstrip ceased.

"You see," said Paul delightedly, flinging an arm affectionately around Joseph's shoulders. "Wasn't I right? Isn't this the safest place in all Indochina?"

Joseph grinned back but couldn't prevent himself from casting an occasional dubious glance in the direction of the mountain peaks above the valley.

"If you don't believe me, I'll arrange for you to talk to our artillery commander, Colonel Piroth. He'll set your mind at rest." The French officer laughed and motioned Joseph courteously into the bunker ahead of himself. "But most important of all, I have a bottle of good cognac to toast our reunion and welcome you to Dien Bien Phu." He clapped the American warmly on the shoulder once more. "It's just wonderful to see you again, Joseph, after all these years."

2

On a forested mountainside three miles from Lieutenant-Colonel Paul Devraux's fortified bunker, Ngo Van Dong, the eldest son of his father's one-time hunting camp "boy," was at that moment straining against a long rope of plaited jungle vines that was cutting bloody weals into his bare shoulders. Groaning and bathed in sweat, he was helping a hundred of his men drag a massive Chinese 105-millimeter howitzer up the side of a sheer ravine under the austere gaze of Dao Van Lat, who wore a neatly pressed khaki tunic without rank insignia, which along with his prematurely gray hair marked him as the senior political commissar at General Vo Nguyen Giap's headquarters. Each time the long-barreled weapon was shifted even an inch or two up the precipitous slope, the group of artillerymen clustered around it forced massive wooden chocks under its rubber-tired wheels to stop it slipping back again, and each time Lat nodded his approval.

"*The ravines are deep — but none of them are deeper than our hatred of the French!*" chanted Lat rhythmically whenever the company paused for breath, and all down the perspiring line of men the chant was repeated in a ragged chorus before a new effort was made.

"Heave now and heave hard!" yelled Dong intermittently, and each time his orders won an immediate response from his men; their feet slipped and slithered on the rocky sides of the ravine as they strained at the ropes, but always the ponderous artillery piece was jerked another foot or two upward.

For three days Dong's company had been dragging the heavily camouflaged gun up the mountain, moving it no more than a yard a minute, half a mile in a whole day. To ease its passage, a long trench had been hacked out of the limestone by hand, and a camouflage of thick foliage had been woven into wide nests strung across the gully above their heads. The gun was the last of twenty-four 105-millimeter howitzers which General Giap's 351st Heavy Division had dragged undetected through the five hundred miles of mountainous jungle between Dien Bien Phu and the Chinese border; the other twenty-three were already concealed on the other mountain peaks, and Dong's company had been accorded the honor of siting the last one in recognition of his brave leadership in many earlier battles. But he and his men had already been toiling that morning for several hours, having risen long before dawn, and their strength and their spirits were beginning to flag; all of them knew it would take another whole day to haul the long-range weapon up to the camouflaged casemate which sappers had hewn from the summit of the rockface high above them, and Dong, after seeking Lat's approval with an inquiring look, ordered a halt.

Many of the company were no more than boys in their middle teens, and as soon as he gave the order to rest and eat, they collapsed in heaps on the mountainside. Several minutes passed before they were able to drag themselves upright again, and then they gobbled down their fist-sized rations of cold boiled rice like hungry wolves. As he watched them, Dong's thoughts raced back to the wretched year and a half he had spent on the Vi An rubber plantation. Just like the youths before him, he and his brother, Hoc, had often sunk down weak with hunger among the rubber trees to bolt their meager rations of rice, but their only concern had been to survive the bestial conditions in which the foreign plantation owners made them live and work; the new generation had at least been given the chance to fight to free itself from the hated French colonialists who had oppressed their nation for so long. How fortunate they were compared to poor, dead Hoc!

Although they too were close to exhaustion, they had the pride and dignity of soldiers!

Moved by these thoughts, Dong began sauntering quietly among his troops, offering a few words of encouragement to each of them in turn as they rested; all listened respectfully and nodded as he moved on — to them he was already a heroic figure. They knew that the stoop of his narrow shoulders had been made more pronounced by the long years he had spent crouching in the cells of Paulo Condore after his arrest in Hue in 1936, and he had never lost the gaunt, undernourished look with which he had emerged from prison in 1945. When he learned of his father's death in the course of the French coup d'état, he had volunteered immediately to fight with the Viet Minh, and on account of his courage and his bitter hatred of the French, he had been recruited into General Giap's regular battalions in the north soon after the outbreak of war in December 1946. During the next eight years his tall, round-shouldered figure had become a familiar rallying point in the thick of battles fought by the 59th Regiment of the 312th Division, and he had risen to the command of first a platoon, then a company. During those eight years of bloody warfare, he had been wounded many times, and he still carried irremovable shrapnel splinters embedded in his shoulders from a grenade blast that had almost killed him in 1951.

As Dong moved solicitously among the men under his command, Lat watched him carefully, noting with approval the respect which they instinctively showed him, and when he finally came over to sit by him, Lat patted the company commander lightly on the shoulder. "You handle your men well, comrade," he said quietly. "You're wise enough to know that's the way to get the best out of them."

Dong nodded his thanks, but his face remained furrowed in a frown of concern. "A lot of them are out on their feet, Comrade Commissar. And I was just thinking they remind me of my own young days on the rubber plantations. Our French bosses often drove us until we dropped then — but we'd have given our right arms for the chance to shoot back at the bastards with a gun like this!"

Lat stared thoughtfully at the rough-voiced peasant for a moment. "Then why don't you tell them about it, Dong?" he said quietly. "Perhaps it will help them forget their weariness — inspire them to greater efforts."

Dong nodded obediently and, snatching off his palm leaf helmet, he leaped to his feet and waved it above his head to attract attention. His voice shook with emotion as he gave a stumbling account of his life on the plantation, describing the leaking huts, the frequent deaths from fever, the dawn burials of dead friends in the gray jungle. His face grew dark with anger as he spoke of the beatings administered by the Corsican plantation director, and when he arrived at the point where his young brother was dragged screaming from the hut during a night of torrential rain, his voice died away altogether. On the ground around him the exhausted soldiers stopped eating and looked up expectantly.

"My brother, Hoc, was raped by the labor recruiter," said Dong at last in a fierce whisper. "But he got his own back the next day by splitting open the Corsican's head with his *coupe-coupe* — and when they saw this, the other coolies attacked the rest of the French pigs. But because we were ignorant and badly organized, the revolt was crushed, and a year later Hoc was butchered by the French with their stinking guillotine. My mother died too in one of their filthy prisons, and my father was badly wounded in 1931 when French planes bombed ten thousand peaceful marchers at Vinh. . . . Although one of his arms was left paralyzed, my father still helped the Viet Minh take over Saigon in 1945. Then just as I was being released from Paulo Condore, the French murdered him too and smashed our new government. . . ." Dong's words had poured out in an emotional torrent and he paused with heaving chest to regain his breath. When he glanced around uncertainly at Lat to seek his reaction, the commissar inclined his head slightly in a little gesture of encouragement. "But my story, comrades, isn't unusual," continued Dong, turning back to his men. "Most of you have got mothers, fathers, uncles or friends who've suffered like this too. I've got a wife and children of my own, and when my children were born I vowed they'd never suffer like this. Now at Dien Bien Phu we can show the French swine what we've been storing up for them all these years, can't we?"

Dong's impassioned outburst had stunned the men to silence, but although they were obviously moved, they gazed at him uncertainly. Seeing this, Dao Van Lat moved quietly to Dong's side and placed an arm about his shoulders.

"Comrades, I can verify part of your brave commander's story," he said in a calculatedly quiet tone. "I was marching at Vinh beside his father and saw the French bombs drop into our midst. Hundreds of innocent men, women and children were killed — and among them was someone who was very dear to me." Lat paused and scanned the faces of the young soldiers around him again; their expressions were rapt, and he saw to his satisfaction that his skillful intervention had won their interest immediately.

"She was a girl, comrades, who was not only young and beautiful but also brave and patriotic," he went on. "I loved her and she loved me, and she was marching beside me that day because she was as dedicated as I was to freeing her country from foreign tyranny. Her death caused me the greatest agony, and since then I have had to live with that agony every day of my life, because I organized that march." Lat lowered his head for a moment, overcome at the memory, and when he looked up again his face bore a strained expression as though he was reliving an intense physical pain. "It was especially hard to bear, comrades, because even before that day of horror, we had made a special pact — to deny ourselves the pleasures of physical love for the sake of our country! I feared that often I wasted my energies pursuing the gratifications of the flesh. Therefore, to devote myself completely to the cause of our revolution, I took a knife and removed from my living body the means of such wasteful gratification!"

Dao Van Lat stopped speaking and remained silent for almost a minute, gazing up towards the mountain peak in a theatrical attitude that at the same time expressed the real pain he still felt at the memory. Until that moment he had inspired in the young soldiers the kind of respect customarily accorded to remote scholar figures, and this unexpected display of emotion astounded them; as the full significance of what he was saying sank in, they stared back at him in an awestruck silence.

"That was twenty-four years ago," he said at last in a low voice. "During that time I've never regretted the great sacrifice I made. Nor have I ever wavered in my determination to make our nation free one day. For most of that time I've worked willingly at the side of Uncle Ho and Comrade Giap, and now here at Dien Bien Phu we're at last on the brink of achieving the success of which I first dreamed all those years ago. All of us here have been chosen by history to fulfill the hopes of those millions of Vietnamese patriots who've died in chains. And we mustn't fail them! Thousands of our countrymen are at this moment trudging secretly through three hundred miles of jungle, pushing bicycles loaded down with the rice and ammunition we need to win this battle. The French are convinced it's impossible for us to supply an army of fifty thousand men in this remote corner of Tongking. They also believe it's impossible to lift guns to the tops of mountains. But I know — and you know — that already we've made too many sacrifices to think of failure!" Lat paused dramatically, then ripped open the buttons on the front of his tunic. Dropping it on the ground beside him, he stood stripped to the waist before the troops, and they stared in surprise at his pale, wasted torso. "We shall not fail those who've put faith in us, comrades — and most important of all we shall not fail ourselves and the promises we all made long ago. Comrade Dong and I have suffered greatly at the hands of the French, and we're ready to give the last ounce of our strength to lift this gun to the peak of the mountain. You must do the same — now and at all times during the coming battle. Then we can drive the French out of our country and achieve the great final victory that our ancestors began dreaming about a hundred years ago!"

Turning aside, Lat bent to pick up one of the ropes attached to the long-barreled howitzer and, looping it over his bare shoulder, he started up the mountain at a run. When Dong shouted an order for the company to join him, they rose up as one man, cheering wildly. Within moments they were arching their backs and chanting in unison as they took the strain again, and slowly the heavy gun began to shift and jerk upwards once more towards the rock chamber from which it would be able to pour lethal shells directly into the midst of the detested French enemy in the long valley below.

3

"You can tell the readers of the *Washington Gazette*, Monsieur Sherman, that we have a very strong battery of 155-millimeter guns," said Colonel Charles Piroth, the one-armed artillery commander of Dien Bien Phu. "We also have twenty-four 105-millimeter guns and sixteen heavy mortars. That's more than enough artillery to do the job we have on hand here."

Joseph was riding in a jeep beside the lugubrious, bearlike French officer responsible for the deployment of the major defense weapons in the fortified camp. Beetle-browed and swarthy, Colonel Piroth wore the empty sleeve of the left arm shot away in the Second World War tucked tidily into a pocket of his uniform jacket, and although his manner was formally polite, he was answering the American's questions with barely concealed impatience.

"In Korea," said Joseph, scanning the gun emplacements they were touring, "the United States had to concentrate artillery in massive batteries in the end to hold the Chinese and the North Koreans. I'm amazed you have so few guns here."

Piroth shrugged and pursed his lips in a little gesture of dismissal. "I've been offered more guns from Hanoi — but there's no need for them. I'm quite satisfied that my fireplan will be effective."

Now that the dust of the Viet Minh barrage had settled, trucks were beginning to move back and forth along the valley floor, the garrison's little force of fighters and B-26 bombers were taking off again to strafe and fire the hills with napalm wherever it was thought the enemy might be gathering, and other Dakotas, ferrying supplies and groups of reluctant soldiers returning from leave in Hanoi, were continuing to swoop down onto the dusty landing strip.

"But doesn't it worry you that the camp is surrounded by those high mountains on every side?" asked Joseph, taken aback by the artillery officer's complacency. "Can you still sleep soundly at night knowing those peaks are in the hands of the enemy?"

A ghost of a smile flitted across Piroth's heavy features. "I should have thought that a correspondent of your experience, Monsieur Sherman, would have at least some slight grasp of military strategy by now. Colonel Devraux told me you'd covered the civil war in China as well as Korea, isn't that right?"

Joseph nodded. He had joined the *Gazette* in 1947 after two restless years as professor of Asian studies at the University of Virginia in Charlottesville, and when appointed as the paper's Far East correspondent late in 1948 he had moved with Tempe and his two young sons to Hong Kong. He had arrived in time to cover some of the climactic battles between Mao Tse-tung's Communist divisions and the demoralized forces of Chiang Kai-shek, and when the Korean war broke out in 1950, he had reported with distinction on the fierce fighting and mass slaughter he'd witnessed amid the bleak, treeless hills of the East Asian peninsula that was so different from Indochina. "What I know about war is based on experience, colonel, rather than textbook knowledge," replied Joseph evenly. "And giving the enemy the heights above you has never seemed like a good idea to me."

"Let me explain in more detail," replied Piroth, speaking slowly and deliberately as though addressing a dull child. "Those mountains which worry you so much are very steep, and they lie two or three miles from the center of the basin here. The classic artilleryman's strategy would be to site 105-millimeter cannon safely out of sight on the far side and lob shells in a high arc over the top onto our camp. But I've inspected the mountains very carefully from the air, and I assure you they're so steep that if guns were sited on the far slopes, the 'yellows' wouldn't be able to fire them anywhere — except straight up into the air! If they move them back far enough to fire over the top at us, they won't be able to reach the camp at all — but in any event our own 155s will be able to drop shells easily onto the other side of the crests and smash any batteries they set up there."

"But what if they site some guns *inside* the ring of mountains or even on the top?" asked Joseph in an incredulous voice. "What then?"

"My dear sir," retorted Piroth, "I suggest when you fly out you have a close look at those mountains. And if you still think that human beings can haul guns up those rockfaces and through all that jungle, I shall be very surprised. However, if the 'yellows' proved themselves capable of working miracles, don't you think we should spot them? And as they struggled to carry the guns up there on their backs, do you think we wouldn't blast them to kingdom come before they got them in place?"

Joseph looked up at the crests again. "Those damned jungles are so thick, colonel, it's not inconceivable that the enemy might get weapons up there without anyone seeing them."

"A feat like that would put Hannibal's elephant march over the Alps firmly in the shade, Monsieur Sherman. But if your fantasy were to become reality, as soon as they opened up and revealed their positions we would neutralize them with our superior counterbattery fire." The French officer turned his heavy-jowled face towards Joseph and raised his bushy eyebrows. "Have you and your American newspaper readers forgotten we're dealing with an army of peasant foot soldiers? They've got only a handful of Russian trucks, no air power, no tanks. Their depots are three hundred miles away at Yen Bay, and to supply several divisions with rice, let alone ammunition, would require a sophisticated logistics operation with a massive fleet of trucks — if there was a modern road network leading to this valley, which there isn't. Our air force is also flying constant reconnaissance missions and is ready to bomb any concentration of troops or supplies as soon as they're discovered. The enemy has no answer to our modern artillery and air power."

"But what about the March monsoon?" asked Joseph slowly. "Won't that hamper your flyers and favor those peasant foot soldiers up in the hills?"

"Our plans have been laid with the greatest care," replied Piroth with a shrug. "When the 'yellows' come down from the hills, you will see why our men are already calling this 'Operation Meatgrinder.' "

The French officer raised his head and gazed absently into the heavens; white and khaki parachutes, guided through the low clouds by a moored meteorological balloon, were blossoming from the leaden sky. Crated foodstuffs, ammunition, bolts of barbed wire, trenching tools, mosquito nets, boots and all the paraphernalia of a military camp under siege were continuing to flutter down like ragged snowflakes onto the yellow plain, and as the jeep drove on from one artillery battery to the next, little squads of Legionnaires, dark-skinned Moroccans of the Infanterie Coloniale, Algerians and even little Vietnamese soldiers loyal to the Bao Dai government scurried quickly from the trenches to retrieve the supplies.

"Are all your big guns set up like that, colonel?" asked Joseph as the jeep passed the sixth or seventh circular pit he'd seen in which an artillery piece was mounted unprotected on its swivel base. "Doesn't that make them a little vulnerable to a direct hit?"

"The guns are deployed in that manner to allow them an unrestricted field of fire. This way they can be brought quickly to bear in all directions without difficulty. Fortifying them would reduce their effectiveness." The French officer glanced down at his watch. "Now, if you'll excuse me, Monsieur Sherman, I have other inspections to carry out. If there are still aspects of our artillery arrangements which puzzle you, speak to your own American colleagues at your military mission in Saigon. They've all made inspection tours of Dien Bien Phu — even General O'Daniel. And all of them agree that our defenses for the camp and airstrip are sound."

Without addressing Joseph further, the colonel ordered his driver to halt the jeep close to another gun emplacement and climbed out. He gave a crisp order for Joseph to be taken back to the central command post, then turned and strode rapidly away to talk to the waiting gun crew.

4

The drone of the duty Dakota taking off to drop guidance flares over the darkening hills reached faintly into the log and sandbag bunker of Colonel de Castries' chief of staff as Paul and Joseph settled themselves on facing army cots. The ground shook as the plane passed along the nearby airstrip, and Paul covered his own tin mug and dropped a hand over Joseph's an instant before a shower of fine red powdered earth drifted down onto them from the low ceiling.

"If you choose to live like a mole, Joseph, you must learn a few of the mole's tricks to make life bearable." The French officer laughed affably and raised his drink to toast the American. "Courvoisier *fine champagne* isn't at its best drunk out of an enamel service mug, but it tastes worse mixed with the red dust of subterranean Dien Bien Phu — *Salut!*"

"*Salut.*" Joseph lifted his mug smilingly in response, drank, then leaned back wearily on one elbow. He had spent the day touring the hills and installations of the fortified camp with different escorts, and the green war correspondent's fatigues in which he had trudged through China and Korea were streaked with dust. The notebook in his breast pocket was crammed with details of conversations he'd had with a dozen different officers and NCOs, and the camera he invariably carried slung around his neck had consumed several rolls of film in the course of the day. Paul had set up a sleeping cot for him, beside his own in the bunker, and during the previous half-hour, Joseph had watched the French lieutenant-colonel wading conscientiously through his chief-of-staff duties with the help of a junior officer. The leather-bound field telephones on the makeshift desks whirred constantly, piles of supply papers came and went, and Paul rose frequently from his chair to update cellophane-covered maps and stores charts with colored chalks. Every time a shell landed in the vicinity of the camp, clouds of fine red earth showered down from the low roof, and the straw mats covering the walls did little to restrain the damp, sour smell of the earth that permeated everything in the dugout.

"Needless to say, Joseph, this isn't my idea of what soldiering should be," said Paul, ruefully waving a hand around the bunker when his aide had gone. "I'd take a day patrolling in the mountains any time for every hour I have to spend here." He paused and sipped his drink again. "But I'm glad you've turned up because it's reminded me how long it's been since I went out. And to put that right I've persuaded Colonel de Castries to let me go with the patrol that's taking you into the hills in the morning."

"That's great news," said Joseph, grinning.

"Yes, I'll be able to keep an eye on you — make sure you don't stray into any smoky native huts." Paul smiled back at him with real pleasure. In his late forties, the Frenchman had lost none of that infectious warmth which had helped make them firm friends the moment they met nearly thirty years before. His close-cropped hair was now steel gray above his temples, but his body was still spare and fit-looking, although there was a new gauntness in his features that made him look more like his father than he had done in his youth.

"Can we expect any help then from the local tribes in these parts?" asked Joseph, grinning facetiously.

"No." Paul sighed exaggeratedly and shook his head. "There aren't any friendly Moi chieftains offering us *ternum* anymore. Those days are gone forever."

Despite Paul's cheerfulness, Joseph thought he detected a note of sadness and resignation in his voice, and this filled him with fresh feelings of guilt and remorse. He had been to Indochina perhaps a dozen times in the past few years to cover the war, and during his early visits Paul had always been away from Saigon on duty with the French Expeditionary Corps. What had begun as tentative visits to his home in the hope of finding him there had developed as time went by into carefully calculated efforts to arrive when Paul was away. Almost without their realizing it, both he and Lan had begun to go back on the firm decision they'd taken in 1945 to go their separate ways. After the brief euphoria of finding Tuyet together, they had been forced to face up to the stark reality that with the ending of the war, their paths must diverge once more; with young families and partners dependent upon them in countries on opposite sides of the world, there had seemed in the end to be only one choice. Joseph had insisted on making arrangements to help support Tuyet financially while she was brought up, at Lan's suggestion, in her brother Tam's household, but beyond that they had agreed there should be no further contact between them.

When he first returned to Saigon with the *Gazette* five years later, however, Joseph had become aware within moments of seeing her again that Lan, like himself, was still torn between loyalty to her marriage vows and her feelings for him. She had said enough to make it clear that she and Paul were not close, and during his subsequent visits, although she had insisted on stopping short of any outright act of disloyalty, she had given in to her emotions sufficiently to continue meeting him secretly. That alone had induced in Joseph intense feelings of guilt, and each time he'd seen her he'd anxiously sought reassurance that Paul knew nothing of their meetings or Tuyet's existence. A few days before his first visit to Dien Bien Phu, he had learned that Paul had been appointed chief of staff to the camp's commander, and realizing that a meeting between them was at last unavoidable in the beleaguered camp, he had promised himself that he would try to tell Paul the truth; but now that they were face to face in the bunker, Joseph found he couldn't keep that promise; seeing the French officer smiling cheerfully despite the obvious dangers and disappointments he faced caused his resolve to desert him completely.

"Do you still suffer any ill-effects, Paul, from the wound you got in Saigon?" he asked lamely instead.

Paul shook his head. "They don't keep cripples on in the 'paras.' The shots were high, and two of the bullets went straight through me. I was lucky." He looked at Joseph for a moment with the same mischievous twinkle in his eyes that the American remembered from the reception in the *grand palais* of the governor of Cochin-China — then his gaunt features fell into serious lines again. "But there are more kinds of ill-effects than just physical ones. I've never forgotten the look on Loc's face as he screamed for his guard to kill me. From that day I knew that there was nothing I could do to wipe out the memory of what my father's generation did here. The agony runs too deep."

"And how have you managed to keep going, knowing that?"

"By trying to be a good soldier and not thinking too much, perhaps. A soldier, remember, isn't supposed to reason why — just to do and die."

"But that can't have been easy in your position. Not many officers in the Expeditionary Corps have your long connections with the country."

"No, it hasn't been easy. And it hasn't been possible to keep the poison from creeping into my family life."

Joseph looked sharply at his companion; Lan had always loyally refused to discuss her relationship with Paul in any detail, and this sudden frank admission that all was not well between them made Joseph's pulse quicken. "How do you mean?" he asked casually.

"It took me a long time to realize that I probably married Lan to prove that all Frenchmen weren't colonial rapists and galley-masters. I think I was more idealistic than I knew at the time. Unconsciously I saw my marriage as living proof of my commitment to the Vietnamese — my determination to change things, if you like." Paul shrugged and picked up the bottle of cognac to replenish their mugs. "But because of that, there was probably always something missing. We love our son deeply, but what I first thought was love on my part was shot through with a lot of wishful thinking. And with Lan, I know now there was always something lacking."

A rumble of distant explosions shook the bunker, bringing down a new flurry of red dust from the ceiling, and on his cot Joseph stared fixedly into his drink, trying not to betray the new sense of hope surging through him.

"In a funny way the marital bed has been divided down the middle by politics for a long time." Paul tried to make the remark lightly, but he couldn't keep a note of regret from his voice: "It all has a terrible logic, somehow." For a minute or two they sat without speaking, listening to the distant sounds of the garrison's B-26s attacking the heights around the valley with napalm. When Joseph finally looked up he found the Frenchman smiling at him with an expression of undisguised affection on his face. "It's good to be able to tell someone, you know, Joseph," he said quietly. "Those aren't the kind of things I can say lightly to my brother officers."

"I guess not." To his dismay, Joseph found he couldn't look his friend in the eye, and raised his mug hurriedly to his lips to hide his discomfort.

"What about you, Joseph? How is that side of your life?"

"All right, I guess. I have two fine sons who're growing up fast. My wife and I get along well enough." Joseph looked up to find Paul watching him closely, and he smiled with an effort. "I suppose no marriage is all fun."

Paul didn't reply, but continued to look quizzically at him. "Are you sure you're keeping to our old rules of total honesty with one another, Joseph? You seem a little on edge — that's not like you."

"I'm fine, Paul — just fine." Joseph took another nervous pull at his cognac. "It's you I'm worried about. Have you ever thought of resigning your commission and getting out before it's too late? Couldn't you take Lan and your son back to France where you belong?"

As he watched for Paul's response, Joseph wondered if in his anxiety to change the subject he'd just destroyed his last chance of persuading Lan to make her future with him; but to his relief the French officer shook his head slowly from side to side.

"It may seem strange, *mon ami*, but I find it hard to think of France as my country now. Perhaps I'm a bit like some of those Legionnaires out there in the trenches — perhaps I don't have a country to call my own anymore. I'd feel like a fish out of water in France. I've spent more of my life in Vietnam than anywhere else. I've never considered doing anything except seeing it through."

"But for what? For the sake of all those colonial shareholders in

Paris who are still skimming off profits from the rubber trade, the mines and their shipping and banking interests?"

"No." Paul shook his head more emphatically this time. "For the same reason that your own country has poured three billion dollars into our Indochina war chest already — to stop Moscow and Peking from taking over. We're fighting Chinese weapons and training now — but if we can hold the Communists off until the other Vietnamese nationalists have set up a strong government, maybe they will still be able to build themselves the kind of future I've always hoped for."

Joseph stood up suddenly and began pacing agitatedly back and forth. "I've never believed we should think of Vietnam as another Korea, Paul — they're two different kinds of problems. We had a chance to make a friend of Ho Chi Minh nine years ago and we botched it. But from what I've see here today, if Dien Bien Phu is going to be a model for defeating world Communism, the West's lost already." He stopped and turned an apologetic face towards his friend. "I'm sorry, I don't mean to seem unsympathetic. But damn it, this camp looks like the nearest thing to a site for mass military suicide I've ever seen in my life."

Paul shrugged. "I've got some private reservations of my own, of course, but every day you'll hear officers here telling one another that we're only frightened of one thing — the Communists deciding not to come down and attack us. Until now we've never been able to maneuver their main force into a position where it's become a concentrated target. It's always been like chasing a will-o'-the-wisp — you know that. General Navarre is confident, Colonel de Castries is confident, Colonel Piroth is sure our defenses are sound." Paul shrugged again. "There's no choice left now. We've got to put our shoulders to the wheel and push."

"But your pilots aren't confident," retorted Joseph. "And they're your lifeline. The monsoon season's coming on fast, and if your air support goes down . . ." The American hesitated, his expression indicating that the prospect was too gruesome to express in words.

Paul got up from the cot, holding the bottle of cognac loosely by its neck, and led Joseph by the arm towards the sack-covered doorway. "Let's go up and get some air, *mon vieux,* before we turn in, shall we? It's stifling in here."

Outside, at the top of the sap, they watched the duty Dakota circling above the mountains, dropping flares. From time to time one of Colonel Piroth's artillery batteries opened up, and the exploding shells set patches of jungle alight high on the distant

399

mountain slopes; beside Joseph, Paul sucked the cool night air noisily into his lungs.

"You know, Joseph," he said at last with a sigh, "the French are no longer the only people doing crazy things in Vietnam. If the 'Amorous American' went in search of his dusky princess in her Moi village today, do you know what he'd find?"

Joseph shook his head.

"He'd find she no longer displayed her naked bosom proudly to the world. Such sights have offended the eyes of your newly arrived American missionaries and some of your Economic Aid Mission's funds are being spent on free brassieres for the Moi women. A new *'mission civilisatrice'* is under way — the uplifting American way of life is beginning to penetrate into Vietnam."

Joseph chuckled quietly. "You're not serious, Paul."

"But I am, *mon vieux*. And that's not all. Your countrymen are trying to teach the Moi and the Vietnamese peasants Western food hygiene — they distribute cheese wrapped in cellophane to the villages, and the peasants don't know what it is. They try all kinds of things and even wash themselves with it, thinking it might be soap. So you see, your Moi princess, when you find her, will be sobbing bitterly in the corner of her hut, that beautiful bosom once so proud and free pinched tight inside a wired American brassiere. What's more, her whole body will reek of Wisconsin cheese as well because she's mistakenly washed herself with it."

The guns ceased suddenly, and the flares dropped by the Dakota were swallowed up one by one in the black jungle; slowly the stars above Dien Bien Phu became visible again, and Joseph and Paul's laughter was for a moment the only sound in the sudden stillness of the night.

"But none of these things are important," said the Frenchman, resting a hand affectionately on Joseph's shoulder and offering him the corkless cognac bottle again. "What matters most is that I feel so much better for seeing you."

5

The battalion-strength sortie moved stealthily out of the camp before dawn next day, the French paratroopers gliding like silent wraiths through the clammy fog that cloaked the foothills. Beyond Beatrice, the northeastern strongpoint, the undergrowth was so thick that the wiry pathfinders from the Third Thai Battalion had to hack their way through the vines and creepers with their long-bladed *coupe-coupes*, and initial progress was slow. Near the front of the column Joseph marched watchfully behind the erect figure of Paul Devraux, his hands, unlike those of the armed and fully equipped troops around him, swinging free and empty. He had deliberately refused Paul's offer of a service revolver before they set out; in China and Korea he had decided a war correspondent should always go unarmed, and he had clung stubbornly to the decision through several close brushes with death under fire. He wore a canvas-peaked cap with his olive-green drabs and around his neck he carried his only "weapons" — a small pair of French binoculars and his camera.

There had been no barrage by the French 105-millimeter or 155-millimeter howitzers to soften up the ground ahead, no tanks had rolled in front of them to the edge of the valley with guns roaring as they often had done in the past before a sortie was mounted; the patrol was going out unannounced this time, Paul had told him, to try to silence the battery of light mountain guns which had shelled the airstrip during his arrival.

On waking Joseph had found Paul already dressed, moving briskly round the bunker, whistling softly to himself. He wore his red beret at a rakish angle and his manner was lighthearted, almost carefree, as if he felt a heavy burden had been lifted from him, at least temporarily. From time to time as they trudged up the narrow mountain track, he turned to grin encouragingly at Joseph and in the pale light of the approaching dawn his lean, leathery face looked suddenly more youthful, less careworn.

"These mountains are home to several different hill tribes that would interest a man of your tendencies," said the French officer playfully when they halted to catch their breath. "The Meos grow opium up there on the crests to make a harsh life bearable — but watch out for the Xas who live down here in the foothills! They're an ancient, backward people still living in the Stone Age. They look more like jungle animals than humans. The women particularly have sloping foreheads and long apelike arms — much more your type than mine." He punched Joseph lightly on the arm and moved off again, laughing quietly to himself, and Joseph followed, trying to smile to hide the turmoil growing inside him.

His failure the previous evening to give Paul any hint of his guilty attachment to Lan had left him deeply troubled. He had slept badly, listening often to the sound of the French officer's steady peaceful breathing in the quiet bunker, and the realization that his visit had cheered and relaxed Paul had only served to make Joseph more acutely aware of the grossness of the betrayal he would have to commit if he and Lan were to join their lives at last. As he climbed the mountain path in the growing light, he turned over in his mind the reasons for his failure to speak out, and he remembered suddenly with a stab of shame a conversation he'd had with a Legion corporal during his tour of the camp the previous afternoon. When he had mentioned that he was going out on a patrol next morning, the German corporal had laughed cynically and said that the only patrols sent out were minor ones for the purpose of deceiving visiting journalists. "The enemy knows very well we can't maneuver successfully from here because of the dense jungle and their tight encirclement," the corporal had said with a resigned shrug. "It's simply a matter of waiting until they choose to attack now." Had it been that casual admission, Joseph wondered, that had really convinced him that Dien Bien Phu was doomed? Was he remaining silent because he hoped that when the dust of battle had settled, there would no longer be any need to ask a dead man if he minded him stealing his wife?

The shock of this possibility made Joseph stop abruptly in his tracks, and for a moment he stared at the receding back of the French officer, gripped by a feeling of profound self-disgust. Then the paratrooper behind him stumbled into him with a muffled oath and Joseph apologized hastily before hurrying on again.

A fresh breeze that had risen with the coming of dawn stirred the waist-high grass as the patrol continued to make its way up the mountain ravine, and slowly the wind's gentle force began to tear jagged holes in the dense curtain of morning fog. Through one of these sudden gaps the men of Ngo Van Dong's company caught their first glimpse of the French paratroopers. Along with half-a-dozen other companies of the 59th Regiment, they were manning one of the valley's many carefully prepared ambush points at the top of the ravine, and from their trenched and fortified positions amid trees and tall grass, the five hundred Viet Minh soldiers were able to follow the patrol's progress a quarter of a mile below without risk of discovery.

Dong and his men had been granted only six hours' rest after hauling the last howitzer into its mountaintop casemate, but they had been issued with special extra rations of lump sugar to help restore their energies. The many ambush points that ringed the French camp had been manned round the clock for weeks, and

Dong's company had been moved into position the previous evening during a routine rotation of units. For several hours they had watched the French camp fires flickering in the darkness below them and had been able to hear clearly the sounds of troops splashing in the Nam Youm River; they had even been able to make out the words of the ribald songs sung by the Legionnaires before they settled down to sleep. Throughout the long night Dong had ordered his men to rest in carefully organized relays, and during his hours on watch he talked quietly to those around him to ensure their morale remained at the same high pitch that had enabled them to hoist the heavy artillery piece up the mountain in record time.

Because all patrolling of any consequence had virtually ceased two or three weeks before, Dong and the other ambush commanders were surprised by the strength of the force climbing towards them in single file. Through a captured pair of French field glasses Dong studied the line of troops carefully as they crossed a stretch of rocky open ground only two hundred yards beneath his hiding place. He could identify clearly the little Thai guides at the front; they were of the same Highland stock as the village people of the valley who were only just beginning to shuffle sleepily from their huts in the early dawn light, and they moved quickly and nervously ahead of the first group of French paratroopers. He swung the powerful lenses from man to man, passing over the tall upright figure in the red beret and camouflaged battle dress and the civilian in plain green drabs without being able to recognize either of the men who long ago had gamboled with him and his brother in a jungle hunting camp. Dong's company had been detailed to man the forward positions on the steep bluffs that overhung the top of the ravine, and he was searching intently for the spearhead radio operator so that he could detail his sharpest marksmen to pick him off in the opening onslaught. When at last he pinpointed him, Dong muttered a quick command to the sharpshooters at his side and the rest of the company lifted their rifles to their shoulders too; hardly daring to breathe, they peered intently into the swirling mists waiting for the white-skinned men to come into range.

As Paul Devraux breasted the tall grass and brushed aside the tangled creepers hanging from the trees, he scanned the hills and surrounding scrub constantly with the instinctive, narrow-eyed gaze of a trained hunter. But although as he approached it, he looked directly several times towards the bluff where Ngo Van

Dong's company lay concealed, he saw no hint of their presence amidst the gently waving grass. When a quick movement did eventually catch his eye a hundred yards away on an adjoining hillside, he turned smiling to Joseph and pointed. "Look quickly — there! Do you see the Xas?"

Joseph lifted his binoculars and studied the little group of naked Xa women who had broken out of the scrub and were scampering across a bare rockface. They moved like animals, as swift on all fours as on their legs, and the strangeness of their movement riveted his attention. From the length of the patrol there came the sound of coarse laughter, and some derisive shouts sounded across the ravine when one of the terrified women slipped and tumbled shrieking down a steep scarp. None of the paratroopers about to move into the jaws of the ambush suspected the truth: that little groups of the Stone Age tribespeople were held captive all over the valley by the Viet Minh to be released as a diversion whenever it suited their purpose. In this case the ruse worked perfectly; the Xas distracted the unsuspecting patrol successfully for a few seconds, and at the precise moment when they finally scurried out of sight into the mouth of a cave, the first withering fusillade of shots rang out from the ambush positions above the patrol, scything down a dozen men. The rest dived frantically into the cover of the long grass, and immediately most of Dong's company rose up stiff-armed on the bluff above to send a thick shower of grenades arcing down among them.

Joseph and Paul rolled together into a shallow gully alongside the radio operator, whose face had been mashed to a bloody pulp by the accurate opening shots of the Viet Minh marksmen. As they crouched stunned against one rocky wall, a young lieutenant scrambled down beside them, tugged the radio from the dead operator's grasp and began calling for Red Cross helicopters to evacuate casualties. The mountains quickly came alive with the rattle of rifle and automatic weapons fire as the French troops began to shoot back, and all around them groans and screams from the wounded and dying rose above the hubbub of the battle. Joseph gasped with horror when he turned and saw the body of the paratrooper who had cursed him a few minutes earlier slumped over the rim of the gully; his chest had been torn open by the simultaneous impact of several bullets, and one arm had been blown away by a grenade. The fingers of his remaining hand were visible hanging over the gully edge and they were twitching spasmodically, keeping time with the soft murmurs of agony that escaped from his bloodied mouth as he died.

Beside Joseph, Paul was barking orders to the young lieutenant to begin pulling men back down the narrow track, and when the American turned to look at his friend, he saw that blood was trickling into his eyes from a wound on his forehead.

"You've been hit, Paul," he gasped.

"It's just a shrapnel graze," retorted the Frenchmen sharply, motioning down the hill with one hand. "Start working your way back along this gully — and keep your head down!" He brushed the sleeve of his combat jacket quickly across his brow to clear the blood, then seized the radio and began calling urgently for B-26s to strafe and napalm the heights above them.

Joseph ducked away and began slithering down the gully, but something made him stop and look back. Paul was still huddled against the rock wall, yelling into the radio, and he hadn't noticed the Viet Minh trooper arrive on the lip of the gully above him. The enemy soldier had already fixed a bayonet to his rifle and for a moment was silhouetted against the dawn sky, holding the weapon pointing downward like a long, obscene dagger; with his feet apart and his back curved in an ungainly crouch, he was preparing to throw all his weight into the bayonet thrust, but before he moved, Joseph lunged back up the gully, yelling a warning as he went. Bunching his knees beneath him, Joseph flung himself bodily at the Vietnamese soldier as he leaped downward, and they fell grappling blindly with one another beside Paul. The Vietnamese hit the ground heavily and the rifle flew from his grasp, but he soon recovered and began jerking and struggling frantically in an effort to break free. By the time he extricated himself from Joseph's grip two paratroopers were rushing up the hillside to the aid of their senior officer, and he scrambled out of the gully and disappeared.

After the Vietnamese had gone, Paul lay staring white-faced at Joseph, aware suddenly how close he had come to dying on the bayonet. Then he grinned lopsidedly. "You move quickly for a veteran campaigner, *mon vieux*. I'm glad you came."

Joseph didn't reply; he had already begun to tremble with delayed shock, and when one of the paratroopers took him by the arm and began to rush him back down the slope, he went without protest. His impulse to help Paul, he knew, had been a reflex action; he had acted instinctively, without conscious thought, and as his rational mind took over again, he realized with a sickening clarity that he had risked his own life so recklessly for only one reason: although he despised himself for it, deep in his heart he wished Paul Devraux dead.

6

"Are you really my father? I can hardly believe it sometimes." Tuyet's gaze was bright, a smile almost. To anyone glancing casually at their table on the terrace of the Café Chez Maria in the Boulevard Barbet, her expression might have seemed warm and sincere: but Joseph had come to recognize of late the hard edge of mockery in her tone. The first of her moods, at fourteen, had been an innocent bewilderment; then her silences had changed in their quality from shyness to a dull, resentful sullenness. She was seventeen now, her pale gold complexion shining with a youthful radiance, and she had adopted during his last two or three visits to Saigon a light, mocking manner, as though she had realized instinctively that this would prove most wounding to him.

She had appeared suddenly from nowhere at the last moment and seated herself at his table as he was paying his bill and preparing to leave. Straight and slender as a pencil, she perched on the edge of the chair and rested her chin delicately on the back of one hand while she looked at him. Her face held little of that chalky whiteness which often characterized mixed race girls, although her skin was noticeably paler than normal and her eyes were wider than her mother's; but her beauty was no less striking than Lan's, as the number of male heads that turned in her direction from the surrounding tables confirmed. She wore a high-collared primrose yellow *ao dai* tailored tightly around her slender wrists and waist, and her natural gracefulness was heightened by an air of self-possession unusual in a Vietnamese girl.

"I often find it very hard to believe too, Tuyet." He spoke quietly, trying not to let the choking emotion he always felt on seeing her show in his voice. "Until one of these rare occasions comes around and your lovely face is in front of me, that is. You're growing up to be as beautiful as your mother."

"If you thought she was lovely, why didn't you stay here and marry her?" She tossed her head and the question came out gaily as though she had been practicing it for hours in her English class at the Lycée Marie-Curie. Joseph wondered fleetingly whether he detected a faint hint of hysteria in her voice; had she been screwing up her courage to ask these uncharacteristically pointed questions that she had never dared venture before? A waiter approached, but she dismissed him with an angry little shake of her head.

When the waiter had moved away again Joseph placed his hands palms downward on the table and studied them in silence for a moment. "I wanted very much, Tuyet, to marry your mother," he said huskily. "But her feelings of loyalty to her father and her country made it impossible for her to say yes."

His daughter's reaction was impossible to gauge from her expression. It was as blank as it had been half an hour earlier when she had looked across the boulevard in his direction on emerging through the school gates with a laughing group of friends. He had stepped out from the shade of the tamarind tree where he had been waiting and waved to her, and he was sure that she had seen him. But she had turned away in the opposite direction without acknowledgment and continued walking arm-in-arm, chattering animatedly, with the other raven-haired girls of her class. Their excited giggling drifted back to him as he followed them slowly on his side of the street, but she hadn't looked back.

The first time he had come to the school gates one blazing Saigon forenoon in 1951, he had needed the photograph Lan had given him. With its help he had recognized her easily and hurried quickly across the boulevard among the swarm of *cyclo-pousses* which had by then replaced the old rickshaws of the city. Her fourteen-year-old face had contracted into a grimace of genuine alarm when he approached and touched her arm, and the expression had reminded him for a fleeting instant of the terror he had seen in her burning eyes on the edge of that muddy pond in northern Annam six years earlier. But otherwise there had been nothing to remind him of the desperate, starving child he had clutched to himself then with such a wildly beating heart.

After that he had always stayed on the opposite side of the boulevard and waved and waited where he stood. The first few times he went to meet her, she had detached herself reluctantly from her friends and come across to greet him. Sometimes they had walked to the Jardin Botanique or strolled through the public park around the old governor general's palace where he had first met Lan when she was only ten years old. When Tuyet ignored him completely for the first time outside the school gates, he had been astonished and hurried after her; but she had deliberately led him a dance back and forth through the dazzling blooms of the flower market in the Boulevard Charner and had eventually disappeared from sight with her wildly giggling friends. From that time onwards he had made a habit of following her for only a short distance if she chose not to acknowledge his presence outside the school; then he fell into the habit of taking a seat on the terrace of the nearby Café Chez Maria to give her the opportunity of returning to speak with him if she wished. Sometimes she came, sometimes she didn't; there had been perhaps seven or eight meetings in the three years before that day, and they had invariably been stilted and uncomfortable, with Joseph always trying desperately to overcome the innate hostility she had shown him from their first meeting. He had begun learning Vietnamese in an effort to get closer to her, but if he tried to converse in that language she invariably ignored him and insisted on speaking English.

Whenever he had asked her about her life she had always spoken with enormous affection of "Uncle Tam" and his wife, enumerating their acts of kindness repeatedly as though to emphasize the obviously deep resentment she felt that he and her mother had not brought her up. Whenever she spoke of Lan, her manner had been cool and reserved, although she had never expressed any open animosity towards her. Joseph had told her a hundred times how much he regretted the way things had turned out, but she had always listened to his protestations in an unresponsive silence. Yet although her demeanor had invariably been distant, he was certain that not far beneath the surface she was struggling to conceal deep feeling of hurt and betrayal.

"Do you still love my mother then, despite all that?"

Joseph looked up sharply, taken aback by the directness of her question. For a moment her eyes held his, then she turned her head away, embarrassed suddenly by her own boldness. As he gazed at her delicate profile, her likeness to Lan made his breath catch suddenly in his throat.

"Yes, Tuyet, I do," he said at last, his voice cracking slightly. "I love her very much. I've never stopped loving her, and I haven't given up hope that one day we'll still be married."

She glanced at him quickly, with a startled expression in her dark eyes, but said nothing.

"And I carry this with me wherever I go too." He drew out his wallet and took from it the photograph of Tuyet at fourteen, now a little creased, which he had carried with him the first time to the school gates. In the photograph, her expression was apprehensive, even a little sad. "I've seen your face looking like that too often, Tuyet," he said, pushing the photograph across the table. "I'd like to help make you laugh and smile more. If Lan and I marry, I'd like to take you both away from Vietnam. I want us all to be together as a family."

"Isn't it a little late for that?" She tossed her head disdainfully, scarcely glancing at the picture in front of her, and turned to look absently out into the street through one of the metal bomb-protection grilles that had first been bolted across the city's café terraces eight years before when Viet Minh bicycle guerrillas had begun bowling grenades among their tables.

"I hope not. The war's definitely going the Communists' way now and things look worse and worse at Dien Bien Phu — but I don't think it's too late. If the Communists do win, many things might never be the same again here in Saigon ... that's why I wanted to talk to you." He leaned forward earnestly to engage her attention again, but she appeared not to be listening, and her gaze remained fixed on the street.

Beyond the metal grilles through which Tuyet stared, Saigon had already become a vastly different city from the one Joseph had encountered for the first time thirty years before. Although the French still thronged the fortified café terraces at midday and seven o'clock for their ritual aperitifs, a thousand or more of Joseph's fellow Americans now walked the boulevards of the "Paris of the East" every day. The star-spangled banner had become a familiar sight in many streets in the city center as the five-hundred-strong staff of the United States Embassy was gradually augmented by the Economic Aid Mission and a dozen other government agencies that had begun arriving in the wake of President Truman's crucial decision to take a stand against Communism in Asia. To house them, modern concrete apartment blocks were shooting up to tower above the pastel-shaded stucco of the French villas, stamping a distinctive American imprint on the city, and shops in the Rue Catinat had begun to stock nylon shirts with button-down collars, spearmint-flavored toothpaste, Coca-Cola and other goods Americans habitually favored. This small army of American government civilians, Joseph knew, had begun intriguing among the Vietnamese religious sects and other native power groups in an effort to groom an anti-Communist force that could, with American help, save Vietnam from Marxism when the French finally departed, and he had already written articles for the *Gazette* warning his countrymen to tread cautiously in a strange and complex country they had scarcely started to understand. To cover the war successfully, like other visiting journalists he'd cultivated clandestine contacts with wary-eyed Viet Minh agents who were ever eager to explain their cause at secret meetings in jungle villages outside the city or in flyblown cafés in the poorer quarters of Saigon. He'd learned enough to make him fear that whatever the outcome of the war, Vietnam was approaching a turning point in its affairs, and that much danger and uncertainty lay ahead.

"Tuyet, I'm worried about what might happen to you if the

Communists did win the war," said Joseph more insistently when at last she turned to look at him again. "Perhaps you aren't very interested in politics, but the Viet Minh want to change the way everybody lives here, including you."

"I've managed very well until now in the country where I was born," replied Tuyet, smiling with a brittle sweetness that she knew must be wounding. "It's very nice of you to be concerned, but I think I shall be able to survive without your assistance."

"Please, Tuyet, let me explain what I've got in mind." He reached tentatively across the table to take her hand. "It doesn't cost anything to listen, does it?"

She pulled her hands quickly into her lap and smiled again. "No, it doesn't cost anything to listen. But unfortunately I don't have the time just now. My friends are waiting for me." She stood up and offered him her hand in a little show of mock formality. "*Au revoir*, Monsieur Sherman, and thank you."

To avoid embarrassing her, he rose reluctantly, and in the brief instant their hands touched, she smiled sweetly at him again. Still standing, he watched her walk away across the crowded terrace, then when she'd gone he lowered himself slowly into his seat once more. On the table-top the sad-faced photograph of her still lay untouched before her empty chair.

7

When dawn broke over the hill resort of Dalat on Saturday, March 13, 1954, the pine-clad peaks that border the Lang-Biang plateau were still shrouded in mist. No breeze stirred the cool mountain air, and not even the calling of a bird broke the calm of the early day. Slowly, as the sun's rays strengthened, the mother-of-pearl sky became suffused with warmer tints of gold, and the high, somber crags emerged darkly from the haze like vague Chinese watercolor shapes daubed on a scroll of gray silk. From the shore of Dalat's highland lake Joseph gazed spellbound at the mountains; beside him as they walked Lan was singing softly, her voice as wistful as the plaintive words of "*Les feuilles sont mortes*," and the haunting beauty of the moment made him wonder if he might be dreaming.

Beneath the dripping pines they seemed to be alone in the world; the strange little sailing craft with brightly colored sails, which visitors to the hill station maneuvered noisily across the lake by day, hadn't yet appeared, and the woods, too, were deserted at that hour. Here and there in the shadows beneath the trees the sudden glow of a yellow or white orchid caught his eye, and words of wonder started to his lips; but always he checked them, not wanting to break the spell of the early morning which Lan had invited him to share with her.

Listening to her sing made it easy for him to imagine her strolling there as a girl with her friends from the Couvent des Oiseaux, all of them wide-eyed and eager for the life that was, for them, just beginning. He had never forgotten that poignant description of her happy schooldays in Dalat which Lan had given him during their drive north nine years before, and when after flying out of Dien Bien Phu he discovered that she was taking a villa there for a month to be near her son at the Dalat Military College, he had immediately hurried north from Saigon. He had taken a room at the Lang-Biang Palace Hotel where he had first stayed with his mother in 1925, but the sad thoughts that returning there invoked had been quickly dispelled by Lan's obvious pleasure when he arrived unannounced at her rented villa. She had insisted that next day they should watch the dawn break over the mountain lake as she'd often done in her schooldays, and back in his hotel he had scarcely slept at all before rising while it was still dark. They had met in the half-light beside the placid expanse of water and begun to walk hand in hand without speaking.

"I went back to the convent last night, Joseph, and slipped into the chapel to listen to the nuns sing Compline." She had stopped singing suddenly, but she spoke in the same subdued and wistful tone. "I stole in quietly and kneeled on the floor among the other schoolgirls just like I used to. Nobody noticed."

He smiled and squeezed her hand, unable to speak. There was an innocence in her expression which made her look little more than a girl in the blurred dawn light, and a lump had come into his throat when he thought how alike she and Tuyet were; both of them in their different ways remained elusive to him, seeming always to remain tantalizingly outside the grasp of his real life, and this realization filled him with a deep sadness. Suddenly these thoughts changed the complexion of the morning for him, and looking down at her pensive face he wondered fleetingly whether her nostalgia for the past had blinded her to the present. Was she unaware how faded and tawdry in reality the grandeur of the hill station had become? Built in the heyday of French colonial dominance, the once-magnificent Lang-Biang Palace was now a shabby ghost of a great hotel; the air of opulence and luxury was gone, replaced by frayed carpets and peeling paint, taps that didn't produce water, and Vietnamese servants who tended the guests' needs in the overlarge rooms with cigarettes poking insolently from their mouths. The Catholic convents on the hill crests and the spire of the church still materialized romantically from the mist each morning, and the former emperor, Bao Dai, still inhabited one of the villas with the finest mountain views; but the town that had been built so grandly around the lake now had a tired and bedraggled air, as though like the French colonizers who had created it and enjoyed its reinvigorating pleasures, it was fast approaching the end of its useful life. Even the banks of the small lake had been worn and trampled by too many feet, and only the sparkling air and the distant panorama of hills remained as Joseph remembered them.

"Lan," he began gently. "I don't want to spoil the charm of Dalat for you, but I can't help feeling that time is running out fast for France in Vietnam. Maybe the whole way of life that your family long ago chose to follow is coming to an end too. . . ." He took her elbow to try and make her stop but she smiled up at him briefly then continued walking through the trees, looking out towards the lake from which the mists were beginning to lift.

"From that moment at your bedside in the hospital, I knew," he said more insistently as he caught her up. "After seeing your beautiful face again I knew I would never be able to rest until we'd joined our lives. Back home I tried to forget — but in my heart I always knew it would be impossible."

She smiled tolerantly towards the ground as she walked. "There's more to life than beautiful faces, Joseph. Are all Americans so incurably romantic?"

"If being strongly drawn towards beauty and love is romantic, then I am," said Joseph quietly. "Those are the only things that make life truly worthwhile. Back home after the war, every time I closed my eyes the memory of you came back to me. I knew I still loved you and I wanted you to be my wife. I knew then that I hadn't stopped loving you during the nine years that we'd been apart. That's why in the end I became a foreign correspondent, I think — so I could have a reason to come back to Saigon and look for you again." He banged his right fist loudly into the palm of his other hand as they walked, and the sudden noise echoed across the mirrorlike surface of the lake. "Why on earth were we so foolish, Lan? We should have thrown caution to the winds long ago!"

"We've been through all this before, Joseph. What's the use of going over it again?" She smiled sadly at him. "When you first arrived, you said you wanted to talk about Tuyet."

"Yes, I did — but I want to talk about us too." This time he took her firmly by the shoulders and turned her to face him. Because of the damp she was wearing the same dark cloak that she'd worn during their drive north in 1945 to search for their daughter. The hood was thrown back, and for the early morning walk she had dressed her hair loosely about her shoulders. In her late thirties, he realized, her beauty had acquired something indefinable — an extra dimension of sensuality perhaps; her lips seemed fuller, her lustrous eyes more knowing, as though the full bloom of woman-hood had revealed to her some calming secret about herself she hadn't known before. Looking at her more intimately than he'd done for many years, he wondered anew at the strength of his attraction to her; she seemed lovelier in the pale light of that dawn than ever before, and it was difficult for him to believe that the reason for her presence in Dalat was a prolonged visit to a son who was already a cadet in the French military academy, almost a grown man.

"Have you *seen* Tuyet recently, Joseph?" she prompted gently, seeing that his mind was becoming distracted.

"Yes, two days ago — but she behaved very strangely. She asked if I was really her father and why we hadn't married. She asked me too, quite openly, if I still loved you."

Lan's smooth brow crinkled in a puzzled frown. "Normally she's so distant and withdrawn."

"Yes, exactly. But this time it was uncanny — almost as if she'd read my thoughts. You see, I'd already made up my mind. I don't know why — perhaps it's a feeling that the war here is reaching a crucial stage. Everything is going into the melting pot now. . . ." He gripped her more tightly, and a new intensity came into his expression. "Lan, we've thrown away two golden chances already. I should've made you agree to marry me that day in your garden in Hue. And when we found each other again at the end of the war, we both behaved as if we were insane. . . ."

She began to interrupt, but he held up a hand to silence her. "I know what you want to say. 'But, Joseph, that war had caused such a terrible upheaval in all our lives.' Yes, it's true. We were like two drowning swimmers then — we had to find our way back to shore to make sure we were still alive. We both had young families who needed us." He stopped and smiled tenderly into her eyes. "That was all true. We both knew what obstacles there were, and we chose deliberately not to face up to them. But what was it that drew me back to Asia? Why, when we met again, was it as if nothing had happened in between — as if time had stood still?"

She dropped her eyes suddenly, as though shamed by his recalling the intensity of the passion that had survived two long separations to flower again so powerfully in both of them. "Because we feel this way, Joseph, it doesn't mean we can just turn our backs on our responsibilities."

"But, Lan, now things are different! We've both made our sacrifices. We've done our duty! Neither of us can go on with these guilty secret meetings behind Paul's back. And I'm deceiving Tempe by pretending all's well. We've had two chances and wasted them — now I want to make up for all the mistakes of the past before it's too late. And soon it will be too late. The world's changing, Lan! Vietnam's changing — much faster than we realize. If the Communists win, nobody knows what might happen in Saigon. I want to take you *and* Tuyet away from here. I want to take you some place where we can always be together. Singapore perhaps, I don't know — any place where I can try to make Tuyet understand. Here I can't get near her. She's always so suspicious — so hurt and resentful." His face clouded suddenly, as though with pain. "Sometimes I'm sure she hates me for what I've done. And that's very hard for me to bear."

He searched her eyes for some sign that she might be wavering but saw only the same doubt and indecision that had always been there before, the same stubborn determination to stand by a conscious decision taken long ago, no matter how badly it had turned out.

"It's not a good time now Joseph," she whispered, looking away from him, "with Paul at Dien Bien Phu."

Joseph looked at her undecidedly for a moment, then leaned closer. "Please listen carefully, Lan. At Dien Bien Phu, Paul and I talked about you. He told me that things hadn't been right for a long time. You've always been wonderfully loyal in not speaking to me of that side of your life — but now that I know things haven't really worked out, I don't feel so badly about us. . . ."

"Did you tell him the truth?" Her eyes had widened in alarm. "Did you tell him we'd been meeting?"

Joseph shook his head and looked away. "No. I wanted to — but somehow I couldn't bring myself to do it."

"Then why did he talk of our marriage?"

"We were discussing his hopes for Vietnam — and it just came out."

Her eyes searched his face anxiously. "Does he suspect there's anything between us?"

"No — I almost wish he did. It might have made it easier to speak out." Joseph shook his head in a little motion of distress. "I can't bear deceiving him, Lan. He thinks of me as his most loyal friend. I have to fly into Dien Bien Phu again soon to do another story, and I'll hardly know how to face him. However things turn out, I've got to tell him everything when all this is over."

"But why, Joseph?" A hand flew to her mouth and she stared at him in horror.

"I can't go on living these lies any longer. I want you and Tuyet with me all the time — somewhere safe." Joseph's voice shook with emotion, and he felt tears start to his eyes. "Don't you understand, Lan? I want this more than anything else in the world."

"But what about your own wife and your sons?"

"I've decided to tell Tempe everything. She ought to know the truth, too. My boys are growing up now and I'm going to ask her for a divorce. I want to do that to show you and Tuyet how much you mean to me."

For a long time Lan stared unseeing across the brightening lake, saying nothing.

"What's your answer, Lan?" he asked at last, lifting her chin gently so that she had to look up into his face. "Will you leave Paul and marry me?"

"Paul's my husband, Joseph." She spoke in an almost inaudible whisper, and he had to bend his head to catch what she said. "I don't know what the future has in store — for me or my country. I'm afraid, I suppose. But I'm more afraid of what life would be if I made the wrong choice and left Vietnam."

Joseph gazed back at her, perplexed. "But, Lan, you're not being fair to yourself!" He looked around, desperately searching for words to persuade her. "Don't you remember how you once dreamed by this lake that your life would always be filled with poetry and romance? Well there's no reason to let that hope die! Marry me, Lan, and I'll make you happier than you've ever been before."

She looked back at him with troubled eyes. "I can't decide now, Joseph, at a time like this."

Joseph sighed and let his hands fall to his sides. "I suppose not."

"And please, Joseph, you must promise me one thing."

"What's that?"

"That you will say nothing of this to Paul when you go back to Dien Bien Phu. Say nothing at all until I've seen him again."

Joseph searched her worried face for a moment, then smiled. "All right, Lan, I promise. I'll wait till it's over."

They walked until the sun was high above the plateau, threading their way without speaking through the green meadows and gardens where the succulent strawberries and lettuces so highly prized in Saigon were grown. They parted for lunch but met again in the afternoon and drove down a river valley to the neighboring plateau of Djiring, passing tumbling waterfalls and many neatly marshaled plantations of tea and pineapple. The car disturbed great yellow clouds of butterflies on the isolated roads, and flocks of bright-colored birds swooped among the tall jungle trees at the roadside. The area was still a no-man's-land ignored by the Viet Minh and French troops alike, and it was the butterfly clouds that triggered his memory first; then when he saw Rhade men and women trudging along the sides of the road wearing only breech-clouts about their naked haunches he fell into a reverie, thinking of that fateful family hunting trip in the nearby jungle twenty-nine years before. Because they couldn't talk of what was uppermost in their minds, they seemed to reach a mute agreement not to talk at all, and the exhilaration Joseph normally felt in Lan's presence was tempered this time by the gnawing fear that this might be the last day they would share together.

That night, perhaps sensing intuitively what he was thinking, she agreed to dine with him in the restaurant of the Lang-Biang Palace where Bao Dai still frequently entertained. In contrast to the rest of the crumbling hotel, its cuisine was still fit for an ex-emperor, and beneath the high, gilded ceilings they lingered at their candlelit table until the other diners had departed; both were subdued, conscious of the bittersweet sadness of what might be their last meeting, and afterwards they sat on the terrace under piercingly bright stars, sipping Vietnamese liqueurs with their coffee.

"I was sitting here with my mother when we heard the news that my brother Chuck had been killed," said Joseph quietly, toying with his liqueur glass. "It all seems so long ago now — as if it happened in another life."

"Were you very fond of him?"

"Yes, I think I was probably fonder of Chuck than anyone else then." Joseph's face grew pensive. "I was only fifteen, and about that time the world seemed to be collapsing around my ears."

"Why?" She looked at him with new interest, her expression softening. "What happened?"

"It's not worth talking about — I was oversensitive as a boy, I guess. It all seems very silly now." He fell silent again and gazed up at the stars that were clustered like clouds of luminous dust in the purple heavens overhead.

"Please go on, Joseph. You've never talked much about yourself before."

An embarrassed look passed across his face, and he stared into the darkness that had fallen over the lake. "My brother always outshone me, you see, Lan. He was a brilliant athlete, a good scholar — and very popular. I lived in his shadow, and my father made no secret of his preference for Chuck. That used to upset me, and I suppose I turned more to my mother because of it."

"And was she fond of you?"

"Oh yes — but something happened while we were here that shocked me deeply. And it took me a long time to get over it." He turned to smile sadly at her and found her staring at him with a strange intensity.

"It happened on the second night in our hunting camp in the jungle. There was a storm, and I couldn't sleep. I got up and stood watching the lightning — and it was then that I saw her."

"Your mother?"

"Yes." His voice sank to a whisper and he looked away again, his expression pained. "She was running across the camp through the storm, and because I thought she might need my help I ran after her. . . ." He stopped talking to sip his drink, and Lan noticed that his hand was trembling slightly. "She went to the tent of Paul's father, and I couldn't help hearing what happened between them. I didn't understand too well about those things then, but it seemed such a dreadful betrayal — not just of my father but of all three of us. . . ."

Lan stared at him aghast. "How awful for you."

Joseph started guiltily, as if in his self-absorption he'd almost forgotten she was listening. "I'm sorry, Lan, I've never spoken of this before. . . ."

Moved by his vulnerable expression, she reached out and touched his hand. "There's no need to apologize."

"I think it made me suspicious and distrustful of every woman I ever met after that — until I saw you again. You seemed so pure, so perfectly lovely. I'd never known anyone like you. When I saw you kneeling in the shrine at the emperor's tomb, I felt something I'd never felt before."

For a long time they sat without speaking and when Lan finally broke the silence, she spoke in a whisper. "Did your father ever find out?"

"I don't think so. I think he was very drunk that night. My mother didn't know that I was awake either. . . ." Joseph's voice faltered again. "My younger brother Guy was born at the end of 1925. My

417

mother's never said anything, but I'm sure he's Paul's half brother."

Around them on the shadowy terrace the desultory murmur of French voices had gradually died away, and seeing that they were left alone, she took his hand in both her own. "I don't know what to say, Joseph."

"It's all water under the bridge now." He managed a faint smile, but saw that her face had become tense.

"I know I've always held my feelings back from you, Joseph," she whispered. "I've never been able to bring myself to tell you how painful it was for me to part with Tuyet after we found her together. I know she was never very far away, with Tam — but it always hurt me very deeply, and I know now it was wrong."

Her lower lip trembled, and he could see she was on the verge of tears. To console her he held her hands more tightly, and they lapsed once more into silence. When at last he rose to drive her back to her villa, to his surprise she took his arm and turned him gently in the direction of the French windows leading into the hotel. When he glanced down at her, she was studying the tips of her sandals intently as she walked.

In his room she flung back the heavy damask curtains from the long windows so that they could catch sight of the stars, and looking down over the tops of the pine trees they found they could also see their pinpoint reflections sparkling like gems in the black-lacquered surface of the lake. For a long time they stood close together in a reverent silence, then she undressed herself without any sign of shyness and let her hair fall loose down her back before walking into his arms. Barefooted, she seemed suddenly small, and despite the roundness of her purple-tipped breasts and the gentle swell of her hips, she could have passed easily in the shadows of the room for one of the schoolgirls at the Couvent des Oiseaux who were at that hour gathering in the chapel to hear the nuns chant the rituals of the seventh service of the day. As she came to him, he felt the huge emotional dam he'd built inside himself half a lifetime ago begin to crack; her nakedness and the glowing look in her eyes moved him deeply, and he folded his arms about her trembling body at last with great tenderness.

In his log and sandbag bunker seven hundred miles to the north-west, Lieutenant Colonel Paul Devraux at that moment lay dozing fitfully on his army cot. He was fully dressed in his camouflage battle dress and he still wore a surgical dressing on the scalp wound that was proving slow to heal; close to the cot a steel helmet hung on the back of a chair within easy reach. The jumble of paperwork heaped around the leather-bound field telephones on his work-table was, like his wall charts and everything else in the under-ground bunker, covered with a fine film of red dust, but for the moment the showers of powdered earth that fell regularly from the low ceiling had ceased. Outside the night was unusually still; the sporadic Viet Minh mortar attacks, which had become almost routine in recent weeks, had gradually died away, and several of Paul's fellow officers had smilingly predicted that the Communists, realizing there was no alternative, must be preparing at last to gamble on an all-out infantry assault against the valley fortress.

There had, however, been many such hopeful predictions as the days and weeks passed, and Paul had become accustomed to preparing repeatedly for an attack that never came. He had taken to making and renewing the command dispositions ordered by Colonel de Castries with his usual methodical thoroughness, then snatching sleep in brief bouts while the endless minutes and hours of waiting ticked by. He had grown tired of trying to guess against which quarter of the thirty-mile perimeter the first enemy thrust might be made, and after six weeks of living underground the tension of waiting had become so familiar to him that it seemed little more than a minor irritant. Because he had been effectively shackled in the valley for so long, his mind too had become confined and blinkered, and since Joseph's visit he had given little thought to the wider implications of the war. Messages from General Henri Navarre's headquarters in Saigon frequently emphasized that the French Expeditionary Corps was still holding firm in the Red River delta and that the new operation being mounted against the Viet Minh in the central highlands was going well; success at Dien Bien Phu would augment the less spectacular achievements in these other areas, but if the strategy did not work out as planned, it would not be a major failure — that seemed to be the view of the French high command and Paul had come to share it. The fact that the enemy at hand remained tantalizingly invisible in the surrounding mountains and had so far failed to mount any significant attack had lulled him, like most of the other senior officers at Dien Bien Phu, into fearing only that General Giap and the Communist leadership might at the last moment decide not to attack in strength and so deprive France of the spectacular victory it had planned.

On waking after fifteen minutes' sleep, Paul heard in the bunker only the quick tick of the watch on his wrist. The silence was so complete that he sat on the edge of his cot for a moment listening intently for some sound. But he heard nothing; even the garrison's little force of aircraft, he realized, must have temporarily ceased operating. Rising stiffly to his feet, he filled a saucepan with water and set it to boil on his spirit stove. He was in the act of spooning powdered coffee into his tin mug as he did a dozen times each day when the bunker was shaken suddenly by what sounded like a deafening roll of thunder directly overhead. Because of the silence that had preceded it, the noise shocked Paul into immobility. Quiet returned for a second or two, and he found himself listening hopefully for the pounding of rain at the head of the sap. But then the stillness was shattered by further explosions that shook the earth all around him, and he recognized then the unmistakable roar of heavy artillery. The terrible detonations quickly became continuous, and through the sack-covered doorway he heard the high-pitched whine of flying shells begin punctuating the din.

Paul stood rooted to the spot, listening in an agony of suspense for the louder roar of the nearer French guns to open up in reply. It was probably no more than a matter of seconds before the first salvos of counterbattery fire boomed across the valley, but to him it seemed an age and even when it came, the response seemed ragged and badly coordinated. His instinct was to fling himself to the field telephones to begin preparing a report for Colonel de Castries on the readiness of the various unit commanders around the fortress — but he held himself in check. They had prepared so many times for this moment that it would be insulting to them to intrude in the first chaotic moments of the attack. Like himself, the other officers must have been shocked by the weight and density of the artillery bombardment, which Colonel Piroth had insisted could be mounted only from outside the ring of mountains. As Paul listened, he wondered for the first time if Piroth could have been mistaken; if the enemy's howitzers had been placed on the outer slopes of the mountain basin they would have been at least five or six miles from the command center, but to his ears the guns seemed much closer. After a moment's pause he put on his steel helmet, then called the artillery commander on one of his field telephones.

"Charles," he yelled at the top of his voice to make himself heard above the noise of the barrage, "the enemy seems to be doing better than we thought with his artillery, am I right?"

At the other end of the crackling line Piroth's answer was not intelligible.

"Could they have got some 105s onto this side of the mountains?" shouted Paul, drawing his words out slowly. "They seem nearer than we expected."

"Yes. . . I think somehow against all the odds they have." This time Piroth's reply was audible, and Paul could hear that the familiar note of confidence was missing from his voice.

"Just a few, do you think, *mon vieux?*"

There was a long pause at the other end of the line. "No," replied Piroth at last with obvious reluctance. "They seem to have more than a few 105s. And they've sited them very high too, I think."

"But you're marking them now, yes?" prompted Paul. "They won't be coughing and spitting at us for too long, will they?"

"We're doing everything we can to neutralize them!"

The line went dead abruptly, but the dismay in Piroth's voice was unmistakable, even over the field telephone. Feeling a knot of alarm tightening inside him, Paul snatched up a clipboard and dashed through the connecting tunnel to the central headquarters bunker. When he entered, he found the commanding officer of Dien Bien Phu standing gray-faced beside his map table; with his head cocked on one side he was listening to the unceasing torrent of noise that was filling the darkened heavens above the valley.

"Their firepower is much greater than we thought, isn't it?" asked De Castries in a strangled whisper.

Paul saluted and nodded grimly. "Colonel Piroth says somehow they've managed to get 105-millimeter howitzers up high on this side of the mountains."

De Castries turned away distractedly and began fiddling with a wooden ruler. "But our counterbattery fire will deal with them in due course. And all units are fully prepared to resist the ground assault when it comes, yes?"

"Of course, sir!"

"We've nothing to worry about then, have we? Contact the commander of each strongpoint for an assessment and report back to me again as soon as you can."

Back in his own bunker the incessant roar of French and enemy guns made it impossible for Paul to get together a clear picture by field telephone of the destruction caused by the surprise opening barrage. Although some units reported that their troops were welcoming the attack jubilantly after the nerve-wracking weeks of waiting, most of the officers commanding the Legionnaires and paratroopers could not make themselves heard. A worrying number of his calls also went unanswered, and when he heard a rolling explosion blot out all other sounds outside, Paul raced up the sap to the bunker entrance and stared out into the night.

The sight that met his eyes brought an involuntary gasp of horror to his lips. One of the enemy's mountaintop salvos had scored a direct hit on the garrison's napalm and gasoline store, and a spiraling tower of orange flame was climbing into the black sky above the valley. By its light Paul could see the charred hulks of several aircraft caught and destroyed beside the little airstrip, but what made him catch his breath was the sight of the mountainsides at the northern head of the valley. As he watched, the lower slopes were coming alive with wave after wave of Communist infantrymen; swarming like countless ants in the glare of the blazing fuel dump, several thousand green-uniformed soldiers wearing flat bamboo helmets were pouring out of their jungle trenches and heading towards Beatrice and Gabrielle. The two vital hills were defended by crack units of the Foreign Legion, but neither commander had responded to Paul's persistent efforts to contact them, and it became clear suddenly that the main weight of the first bombardment had fallen there.

As he watched, Paul's attention was distracted by the arrival of a jeep outside an adjoining bunker. In the orange glare from the flames he recognized the tall, bulky figure of Colonel Piroth; to his astonishment he noticed that the artillery commander had driven himself back from his gunnery headquarters without a helmet, and although Paul called out to him, he climbed down from the jeep and headed unsteadily towards his own bunker without acknowledging him. Sensing something was wrong, Paul dashed across the open ground and caught Piroth by the shoulder.

"Charles, you should take more care of yourself. Where's your helmet?"

When the one-armed artillery officer turned his head, Paul was shocked by the sudden change in his appearance; the long-jowled face, composed when he'd last seen him in its habitually haughty lines, was suddenly haggard, the face of a man haunted by guilty knowledge. His eyes too were distant, glazed almost, and he made no attempt to answer.

"Come to my bunker and I'll make us some coffee," said Paul

insistently. "I need you to give me an estimate of the enemy's artillery strength."

"They've done the impossible! Their guns must be embedded in the rock on the very peaks of the mountains — we can't knock them out. Three of our 155s have been destroyed already." Piroth stared over Paul's shoulder. "It'll be a terrible massacre. There's nothing we can do to stop them — and it's all my fault."

"Pull yourself together, Charles," said Paul sharply. "We're all responsible. Come to my bunker and calm down." He tried to tighten his grip on Piroth's remaining arm, but the distraught officer tore himself free.

"I've got something urgent I must do first," said Piroth sharply. "I'll come in a few minutes."

Paul stood and watched him as he hunched his shoulder to duck through the sack-covered entrance to his bunker. Then as he disappeared from view Paul looked back to where the attacking force was beginning to mount the lower slopes of the two northern strongpoints. The artillery bombardment was gradually petering out as the Communist troops neared their main objectives, and Paul heard clearly the roar of the single explosion that came from inside Piroth's bunker.

As he raced down the entry tunnel he recognized the acrid smell of the explosion fumes. Inside the bunker itself he found the artillery commander of Dien Bien Phu sprawled on the earth beneath his own cot. When he turned him over his face was no longer recognizable, and he saw that the grenade which he had pressed against his own heart in the depths of his despair had blown off his remaining hand as it killed him.

9

The white-painted Red Cross Dakota carrying Joseph back to Dien Bien Phu skimmed in fast and low through a break in the mountains, banking and turning sharply to avoid flying across areas where the Viet Minh had burst through the defense perimeter in strength. Through a side window Joseph caught his first glimpse of the endless trenches which had been dug rapidly across all the hillsides, like contour lines, as the Communists had moved inexorably down on the camp. At some points he saw that they had already advanced to within a mile of the command center, and inside the perimeter itself, the wreckage of burned-out aircraft, trucks and devastated gun emplacements bore tragic witness to the great toll that the enemy's daily artillery barrages had already taken on French resources.

"Those two hills to the north, Gabrielle and Beatrice, were overrun in the first few hours of the attack," said a grim-faced French medical orderly who was flying in with blood and plasma supplies to help evacuate wounded from the overflowing field hospital. "Since then the Communists have pulverized the camp with their guns nonstop for fifteen nights." He leaned closer to Joseph and pointed to the heart of the fortified camp where a swarm of troops and vehicles was coming and going. "That's the field hospital. It was built underground to deal with only forty wounded at a time because our masters in their wisdom thought all casualties could be flown out to Hanoi. Now the Communist guns keep the airstrip closed for all but an hour or two a day, and hundreds of injured men are lying around in tunnels leading into the hospital. Every night the monsoon rain floods the tunnels, and gangrene has become as common down there as salt in the sea."

The medic's voice was bitter and resentful, and Joseph could only nod wordlessly; although in Hanoi the French high command had admitted the battle wasn't going well, the visible deterioration in the camp since his last visit shocked Joseph deeply. In the early morning light he could see that the overnight storms had left the area awash with gray and ocher slime, and the entire valley floor was littered with muddied parachute silks. It was obvious from the air that a high proportion of the food and ammunition packages being dropped to the garrison were now falling among the enemy outside the shrinking perimeter, and Joseph wondered how Paul had been faring in all the mud and chaos of the past two weeks. Battles had raged constantly day and night during that time, and he knew from the press conferences he had attended in Hanoi that several officers on the staff of Colonel de Castries had been wounded or had collapsed under the strain.

As the plane turned its nose towards the battered airstrip, anxieties that he'd been holding at bay during the long flight from Hanoi crowded back into his mind once more. With the military situation deteriorating rapidly in the Viet Minh's favor, his desire to spirit Lan and Tuyet away to some safer place in Asia had become an obsession that haunted his thoughts day and night. He had been sleeping badly and had spent much more time than was necessary chasing battle reports and badgering military contacts in Hanoi for information. Each new admission of Viet Minh success had heightened his feeling that time was running out, and seeing how fast the defenses of Dien Bien Phu were crumbling, he was filled with new fears that all would be lost if he didn't act quickly.

The growing signs of devastation in the French camp below him by some strange association also made him feel more acutely than ever the wretchedness of his betrayal of Paul. Struggling courageously against the odds in his fetid bunker, the French officer suspected nothing of his long deceitful liaison with Lan and was utterly unaware of Tuyet's existence. The thought of confessing to years of deliberate deception, although he ached to do it, filled Joseph with horror, and as he watched the trenches and barbed-wire entanglements rise towards the plane, he suddenly found that with part of his mind he was almost hoping he might find Paul already dead; the chances that he wouldn't survive the terrible siege had to be high, and despite the ignoble nature of the thought, Joseph found himself wondering if that wouldn't be the kindest trick that fate could play. Already deeply disillusioned about Vietnam's future and his own attempts to make amends for the past, how would Paul be able to endure defeat *and* the news that his wife had betrayed him over many years with a man he had always trusted as a loyal friend? The truth about that, thought Joseph miserably, would almost certainly prove the last straw. Or would it? he wondered, with a sudden wild surge of hope.

Perhaps the bond of friendship they shared might even be strengthened by his forthright confession. Might not Paul respect him the more for his honesty? He might even welcome the news once he got over the shock. After all, it had been Paul himself who had admitted that his marriage had long been a failure. Freed of the burden of a hopeless future with Lan, wouldn't Paul be able to see the war and his own role in it in a clearer perspective? He might realize then he must at long last tear himself away from the hopelessly lost cause Vietnam had become for him and look again to France for his future. . . .

The sudden mortar barrage that greeted the Dakota's arrival on the airstrip broke into these muddled thoughts, and Joseph clutched the sides of his seat as the plane's wheels made contact with the pitted surface. It braked rapidly to a standstill, and while groaning French soldiers on stretchers were hurried aboard amid the din of exploding shells, Joseph crouched beneath the aircraft's fuselage; when its hatches were slammed closed he rode back to the command center in one of the makeshift ambulances and got the driver to drop him at the chief of staff's dugout. He hadn't tried to give advance warning of his arrival this time, and when he knocked on the side-post and pulled back the sacking covering the entrance, Paul looked up from his paper-strewn table in astonishment.

"*Mon Dieu*, I don't believe it! I must be suffering hallucinations." The French officer rose from his seat and gripped Joseph's outstretched hand fiercely. "You're either very brave or very foolish, Joseph, to come back. Not even French journalists are venturing out here anymore."

"The *Gazette* decided they had to have one more worm's eye view report from Dien Bien Phu, and I jumped at the chance to come and drink some more of your cognac." Joseph grinned, but inwardly he was taken aback by Paul's appearance. Part of the head bandage visible beneath his steel helmet was grimy and discolored, his eyes were bloodshot, and his face was gray with fatigue. His movements too were stiff and slow, signalling clearly the strain he'd undergone in the past two weeks.

"You'd better put this on." Paul handed Joseph a steel helmet and waved him to a chair. "Even the worms are wearing them in the valley now." He sank back into his seat with a weary smile, and from outside, the sudden stutter of small arms fire became audible, interspersed with deeper-throated artillery salvos.

"Things look much worse than when I was here last," said Joseph tentatively. "And you look about all in, Paul."

The French officer shrugged. "There's not much point in trying to tell you otherwise, *mon vieux* — the situation's grim. From the moment we lost Gabrielle and Beatrice we knew Dien Bien Phu wasn't going to produce any magic victory for us. They lay down a heavy bombardment on us every night, then follow up with massive 'human wave' attacks. Our own artillery's been virtually knocked out, and it's only a matter of time before the runway's destroyed. Then we'll really be at their mercy." He paused and lifted a warning finger in Joseph's direction. "I don't advise you to stay here very long. Not many more planes are going to get out."

Joseph shook his head in dismay. "What does Colonel de Castries plan to do?"

"I'm afraid de Castries has taken it all very badly," replied Paul with a troubled look. "He's hardly been out of his bunker since the attack began. He doesn't chair the daily command meetings either. Colonel Pierre Langlais, a Breton paratroop officer, has virtually taken command. He's planned what counterassaults have been made on Elaine, Dominique, Françoise and Huguette — those are the hills closest to the command center." Paul broke off and pointed to the map on the wall behind him where the shrinking perimeter had been re-marked daily in red. "But as you can see, the enemy are squeezing us into a smaller area all the time. As soon as we succeed in putting the flag of France back on one hill, the Viet Minh run theirs up on another."

"How many men have you lost?"

Paul's face darkened. "Maybe a thousand dead all told and twice that number wounded. We estimate that we've killed five times as many of the enemy, but Giap is making a calculated sacrifice, and he can replenish his forces indefinitely. With the airstrip almost unusable, only paratroops can replace our casualties. Most of the Algerians and the Thais have deserted already and gone to live in holes in the riverbank." Paul's shoulders sagged and he slumped lower in his chair; outside the noise of a new action on one of the group of hills close to the command center was growing, but Paul ignored it. "If I were you, Joseph, I'd get out on the next plane that comes in. I'll get my adjutant to give you a quick tour in a jeep for your story — then get back to Hanoi as fast as you can." He picked up a field telephone, ordered the vehicle, then grinned wearily at the American. "Things may be bad but that's no reason to let a good friend get caught here like a rat in a trap."

For several seconds Joseph sat listening indecisively to the sounds of the battle raging outside; then he drew a long breath. "Thanks, Paul. I appreciate your help very much — but I hate the thought of you having to stay on in this hellhole."

The Frenchman shrugged and said nothing. He shuffled some paperwork abstractly on the desk, then glanced up at Joseph again. "And how's everything in the outside world, old friend? What have you been up to since you were here last?"

"I've divided my time between Saigon and Hanoi mostly, trying not very successfully to keep tabs on this mystifying war of yours." Joseph hesitated, wondering with a feeling of panic whether Lan might have mentioned in a letter meeting him in Dalat. "I managed to snatch a couple of days off at the Lang-Biang Palace. It's all changed there now — but the scenery's still magnificent."

"Lan's at Dalat too right now, I think," said Paul, sorting idly through his papers again. "Did you see anything of her?"

"Yes. When I heard she was there I paid her a visit to tell her I'd seen you." Joseph found himself hard-pressed to keep his voice casual. "I told her you were well despite the circumstances."

Paul nodded without looking up. "And how was she?"

Joseph hesitated, feeling his heart begin to beat faster. "As lovely as ever, Paul. She seemed very concerned about you."

Paul raised his eyes and stared at Joseph, but at that moment the

427

door curtain was pulled aside and his adjutant entered. Paul cocked his head on one side, listening for sounds of gunfire, but the valley had gone quiet. "You'd better get your reconnaissance trip over while this lull lasts," he said with a sudden briskness. "We'll drink some cognac when you get back."

Joseph followed the adjutant up the sap with a profound feeling of relief and clambered into the jeep beside him. During the next hour he was glad that he had to concentrate on the junior officer's briefing as the little vehicle raced around the remaining strongpoints. When he returned to the chief of staff's dugout, Paul had already opened a new bottle of cognac, and he rose and poured generous measures into two mugs.

"And what are your impressions of our gallant fortress now, Joseph?" His voice was heavy with irony, and he pushed a mug towards the American with a resigned smile. "You see some changes have occurred since your last inspection, yes?"

Joseph nodded unhappily. "It all fits with what you told me before I went out, Paul. It doesn't look very promising."

"Then let's drink to better times in the future, *mon vieux*. It's better not to dwell too much on the present." Paul lowered himself wearily into his seat once more. "There's another ambulance plane on its way in. My adjutant will drive you out to meet it — there may not be another one in today."

Joseph nodded his thanks, and they drank in an uneasy silence.

"Joseph, my friend, I can't help feeling that something's worrying you besides this nasty business." Paul gazed at him intently over the rim of his mug. "In the past we've always been open with one another, but now somehow you've become a different man. You never look me in the eye anymore — you have a furtive air about you."

"It's just the damned war, Paul," said Joseph quickly. "Correspondents may not do any fighting — but they suffer from battle fatigue, too."

"Are you sure that's all it is?"

Joseph avoided his eyes. "Sure I'm sure."

Paul continued staring at him, and Joseph shuffled his feet uncomfortably under his gaze. "Maybe life in this damned rabbit warren is warping my senses, *mon ami*," he said speaking very quietly, "but to my eyes you looked shiftier than ever when I asked you about Lan. Is she doing something I don't know about? Is she having an affair with somebody?"

Joseph had been standing beside the desk looking down at Paul, but the question struck him like a whiplash, and he turned away.

He searched his mind frantically for some suitable evasion, then realizing that he had already betrayed his feelings, he turned slowly back to face Paul again. "The last thing I wanted to do was to speak of this here," he began hesitantly, his voice barely under control. "In fact, Lan made me promise I'd say nothing to you until it was all over. But now that you've said what you have, Paul, maybe it's better for all of us that you know the truth. It's been agony for me keeping it from you."

The Frenchman went very still in his seat, and all the color drained from his face. "What are you talking about?"

"It's me, Paul — I'm in love with Lan. I have been ever since I first met her all those years ago."

Paul's only reaction was a slight narrowing of his eyes; otherwise he remained motionless in his chair.

"I've been meeting her secretly off and on for a year or two now in Saigon. I'm desperately sorry this has happened, you must know that."

Paul removed his helmet and placed one hand gingerly against the soiled dressing covering his head wound as though it suddenly pained him — but still he said nothing.

"It isn't something that's just begun recently," continued Joseph in a desperate voice. "Lan and I were lovers once, long before you married her. It all began before she agreed to become your wife. I asked her to marry me first — but she refused."

"Where did you become lovers?"

"In Hue at the time of the last Nam Giao ceremony. . . ." Joseph hesitated and drew another long breath. "Lan begged me not to tell you this, but I think you should know the whole story. A baby girl was born to her before she married you — my daughter. I knew nothing of her existence until I came back to Saigon at the end of the war. She was eight then and she'd been brought up secretly by one of the family servants in a village in the north."

Paul straightened slowly behind his desk. "Does she still live there?"

Joseph shook his head. "While you were recovering from your wounds, Lan and I drove north to look for her. We found her just in time. She almost died of starvation. We took her back to Saigon and she was brought up secretly in the household of Lan's brother, Tam."

There was a long silence and outside they heard the noise of gunfire start up again. As he stared at Joseph, Paul's face darkened with anger. "So you've been meeting secretly behind my back all this time in Saigon."

Joseph nodded miserably. "I hated deceiving you, Paul, but I couldn't help myself. Lan and I didn't become lovers again until we met at Dalat ten days ago — that was the first time since 1945. She always insisted on remaining loyal to you before. But now I'm sure we can be happy together. I want to make amends for the past. I've asked her to marry me — and I'm going to offer Tuyet a home with us too."

On the table Paul's knuckles whitened abruptly as he clenched his fists. "Has she agreed to go with you?"

"She's refused to give me any decision until . . ." Joseph's voice died away and he shifted guiltily under Paul's gaze. "Until she's seen you again."

"You mean until she knows whether I come out of here dead or alive!" Paul rose slowly from his chair, his features contracting into a grimace of cold fury. "You're both waiting, aren't you, to see whether the Communists clear the way for you!"

"Paul, you told me yourself your marriage hadn't been right for a long time." Joseph's voice took on an imploring note. "Don't you see, knowing that changed everything for me."

"Lan's been my wife for nearly twenty years!" Paul spoke through his gritted teeth. "We've got a grown son — or had you forgotten that?"

"No, I hadn't forgotten." Seeing the Frenchman's expression harden, Joseph drew back in alarm.

"Does Lan love you?"

"She's always stopped short of saying so, out of loyalty to you. But I'm sure she does — I think she did from the start."

"Then why did she marry *me*?"

"Because her father wished it! He wanted to demonstrate his loyalty to France through her, don't you see? She was just obeying his wishes."

The moment the words were out, Joseph regretted saying them. Paul started back, glaring at Joseph with a new expression of loathing in his eyes. For a long time neither of them spoke, and outside the bunker the intensity of the firing increased. Without taking his eyes from Joseph's face, Paul dropped his hand to the flap of his revolver holster and lifted it to free the grip of the weapon. "You wouldn't believe me, Joseph, would you, if I told you that after your last visit I felt your friendship was one of the few worthwhile things left in my life?"

Joseph felt his heart lurch sickeningly inside him, and he took an instinctive pace towards the Frenchman. "I'm sorry, Paul, I'm deeply sorry. I've been such a goddamned fool. . . ."

"Keep away from me!" Paul drew the gun and took a pace backwards, pointing its muzzle at Joseph's chest. "Nobody's going to ask how a crazy American journalist got himself killed at a time like this."

Joseph stared transfixed at the gun. "Paul, let me stay. Let me see it through with you — there's plenty here for me to write about."

Paul's chest rose and fell erratically, and his voice took on a note of incredulity. "You still think you can square your conscience even now, don't you? You still think there's a noble way out."

The roar of an aircraft passing low over the bunker momentarily drowned out the sound of the guns outside, and on hearing it, Paul extended his arm stiffly in front of him. With calm deliberation he leveled the revolver at Joseph's head, and his finger began to whiten inside the trigger-guard. Then the sacking covering the doorway was wrenched aside, and Paul's adjutant burst in; he gazed openmouthed at his superior for a moment before recovering himself.

"The hospital plane's just landing, sir — if Monsieur Sherman is to take it, we must go now."

"Monsieur Sherman is refusing to obey my order to board the plane," snapped Paul, without shifting his gaze from Joseph's face. "You will escort him to the airstrip and embark him at gunpoint."

The young lieutenant quickly drew his own pistol and motioned Joseph ahead of him up the sap. Five minutes later, as the Red Cross Dakota, laden with wounded, lifted ponderously off the pitted runway, Joseph looked back towards the command bunkers; as he watched, the sack covering the entrance to the chief of staff's dugout was moved aside and Paul emerged blinking into the daylight. He was helmetless and although he held himself characteristically upright, the grimy bandage around his head gave him a bedraggled, crestfallen air. His revolver dangled limply in his right hand, and as the Dakota climbed away through a light mortar barrage he gazed blankly up into the leaden sky; a moment later the aircraft was swallowed up in the low cloud hanging over the valley and the last image of Dien Bien Phu that Joseph carried away with him was of the forlorn, diminishing figure of Paul standing alone in the heart of the doomed fortress.

10

An hour before midnight on May 6, 1954, Ngo Van Dong pulled his flimsy helmet of plaited bamboo low over his eyes and raised his head cautiously above the edge of one of the forward trenches facing the Elaine group of hills. His mouth was dry, and he hugged his carbine tight against his chest with its bayonet fixed, ready to clamber out of the slimy ditch as soon as the signal to advance was given. Like all the other men of the 59th Regiment of the 312th Division of the Vietnamese People's Army, he now wore a gauze mask over the lower half of his face because of the risk of disease in the oozing, mud-filled trenches where they trod constantly on the putrefying bodies of their own and French dead. The dugouts and blockhouses through which the battle had swirled for fifty-five days reeked of excrement and vomit too, and in the heat of the day, flies and maggots infested the bloated corpses.

Beneath the glare of parachute flares dropped by French transports which still flew in relays from Hanoi, Dong could see other Viet Minh units swarming through the outer defenses of the smaller strongpoints in the Elaine group. On their crests dwindling bands of French and Foreign Legion paratroopers were pouring desperate bursts of machine gun and mortar fire into their ranks, but sensing that victory was near, the Asian soldiers were advancing endlessly now over the corpses of their dead comrades and overwhelming the Europeans by sheer weight of numbers. Elaine Two, the hill in front of Dong's company, was the group's key bastion; it was manned by the remnants of the First Battalion, Parachute Chasseurs who had set up their command post in the house of the former French governor of Dien Bien Phu on its summit, and because the hill was the last major stronghold in the valley in French hands, Viet Minh sappers had spent several days tunneling deep into the hillside and wiring together thousands of kilos of explosives to make a massive underground mine. The blast had been scheduled for 2300 hours that night, and Dong had led his company stealthily into position through the maze of trenches half an hour before.

Few of the troops waiting around him had taken part in the fierce fighting that had gone on all through April; while capturing the cluster of Huguette hills to the west of the French command center, General Giap had seen the strength of his four divisions reduced from fifty thousand to thirty thousand men, and many of the soldiers in Dong's company were sixteen-year-old boys who had arrived only a week before. But in daily indoctrination sessions their political commissars were constantly reminding them now that the French garrison of thirteen thousand men had been reduced effectively to less than a third of that number and that the survivors were close to exhaustion. Final victory was at hand, they had been told repeatedly during the last few days, and as they crouched in the trenches around him waiting for the giant mine to be detonated, Dong could sense the fear and tension in them.

But he, too, was unusually keyed up and on edge. The bitter hand-to-hand conflict that had gone on for nearly two months had taken a terrible toll of Dien Bien Phu's attackers as well as its beleaguered defenders, and Dong, like the rest of the Viet Minh forces, was, without fully realizing it, nearing the limits of his endurance; he had subsisted since early February on little more than a few daily handfuls of rice supplemented by a meager issue of a dozen peanuts once a week; he had also lived constantly with the fear that even a minor wound might eventually kill him, since the field medical facilities — half-a-dozen doctors and surgeons working in hastily erected palm-thatch huts in the mountains — were even more rudimentary than the underground hospital on the valley bottom which overflowed daily with the French dead and dying. With the exception of some new shell splinters in his bandaged left shoulder, however, Dong had come through the fighting unscathed, and the knowledge that the climax to the long siege was approaching had helped him forget his weariness. Waiting impatiently for the underground explosion to signal the charge, his thoughts returned involuntarily to the first time he had waited like this in the darkness to attack the French — at Yen Bay. Then, he reflected grimly, his father and little Hoc had been at his side, and as he gazed up the flare-lit hillside, he made a silent promise to his dead family that he would fight bravely and unselfishly that night to help avenge them once and for all.

When at last the massive subterranean mine exploded a few minutes after eleven o'clock, it shook the hillside like an earthquake, and Dong saw an enormous fountain of black earth and smoke soar upward; then the night was filled with a delayed roar, and mud and debris began to cascade down over the Viet Minh lines. The moment the deluge ceased, Dong rose up out of the trench yelling, "*Tien buoc! Tien buoc!* — forward!" then flung himself up the hill.

As he ran, he let out a full-throated scream, and hearing thousands of his countrymen giving simultaneous voice to their hatred of the enemy filled him with a murderous ecstasy. Stumbling and leaping through the smashed trenches, he felt he was being borne irresistibly upwards by an unstoppable wave, and with a wild cry of triumph he bayoneted to death two terrified French paratroopers who had been trapped and wounded by the blast in an abandoned dugout. One by one the remaining machine guns of the defenders either grew too hot to touch and seized up, or fell silent when they ran out of ammunition, and Dong and his men found those few French troops who had survived the massive explosion crouching stunned and shocked behind walls of French corpses killed in earlier assaults.

While he was skirting the great black chasm gouged from the hillside by the mine, however, half-a-dozen youths new to his company were caught in a hail of machine-gun fire coming from the old governor's house, and Dong watched helplessly as they toppled, shrieking, into the pit. Looking towards the incongruous European mansion on the hilltop, his anger boiled up afresh; the building seemed suddenly to symbolize all the hatred he felt for France, and without stopping to think whether it was wise, he rushed up through the remaining trenches alone, and crawled swiftly across the open ground around the command post. Drawing a grenade, he plunged down a flight of outside steps towards a lighted cellar window, then stopped and crouched down beneath the sill when he heard the sound of a French radio operator's voice calling a frantic message to command headquarters.

"Tell Colonel Devraux that Elaine Two can't hold out much longer without reinforcements," yelled the radio operator, repeating the message emphatically over and over again to make himself heard above the din. "Tell Colonel Devraux we must have reinforcements — now!"

Dong's eyes narrowed as he registered the name; then he sprang to his feet, kicked open the door and fired three shots into the radio transmitter, shattering it beyond repair. When the young French radio operator turned, still wearing his headphones, he found Dong's bayonet tip pressed against his chest.

"Who is this 'Colonel Devraux' you were contacting?' snarled Dong in French. "Which unit is he commanding?"

When the terrified radio operator didn't reply, Dong jabbed the bayonet harder against his chest. "If you don't tell me, I'll kill you. What is Devraux's other name? Who is he?"

"He's Colonel *Paul* Devraux," whispered the radio man. "He's chief of staff to Colonel de Castries, I think he knows Vietnam well — he's lived here a long time."

Dong's eyes glittered suddenly in his grime-streaked face, and with a convulsive movement of his whole body he plunged his bayonet into the Frenchman's chest.

11

As dawn brightened the lead-colored skies above Dien Bien Phu next morning, Dao Van Lat accompanied the stocky, quick-striding figure of General Vo Nguyen Giap to the parapet of a fortified observation platform high in the mountains. As usual the fastidious Viet Minh commander in chief was determined to double-check all his facts, and Lat waited patiently while Giap swung his powerful field glasses repeatedly back and forth across the devastated French camp.

Even with the naked eye Lat could see that the massive artillery bombardments and infantry attacks, which had continued through the night, had brought the French garrison close to the point of collapse. Disorder was rife and there were signs of destruction everywhere; the pre-dawn monsoon downpour had inundated their broken defense trenches and dugouts to a depth of several feet and half-filled the great crater created by the mine planted in tunnels beneath Elaine Two; on the hill's summit a red Viet Minh flag bearing a gold star fluttered from the ruined walls of the old governor's house, and the French were obviously no longer capable of mounting a counterattack on the crucial strongpoint that overlooked their command post. The shallow Nam Youm River, Lat could see, was choked now with dead bodies from both sides, no vehicles moved along its banks, and although Dakotas from Hanoi were already dropping fresh supply parachutes, none of the exhausted, half-starved troops were venturing from the protection of their muddy holes to retrieve them. Outside the French command headquarters, the last surviving jeep lay burned out in a water-filled crater, and behind the Viet Minh lines, crowds of French prisoners taken during the night were already being marched away towards the forest, their hands tied behind them with jungle creepers.

"We shall be able after all to present our delegates at the Geneva Conference with just the bargaining card they need, won't we, comrade general?" Lat's eyes gleamed with an excitement he could no longer conceal as he gazed down into the valley. "There's surely no way out for France now!"

Giap lowered his field glasses and nodded his head. "Yes, the right moment's arrived. There are obvious signs of confusion in their ranks."

As he spoke, Giap glanced up again at the scudding clouds through which an occasional French Navy Privateer was diving to bomb the Viet Minh trenches, and Lat guessed he was calculating whether bigger American warplanes might still make some eleventh-hour effort to save the French garrison. Western newspaper reports had revealed several weeks before that France had sought help from the United States, but neither President Eisenhower nor the leaders of Congress in Washington had been willing to go ahead with heavy bombing raids from the Philippines without the full support of Britain and her leading Commonwealth allies. The British prime minister, Winston Churchill, however, had since declared himself implacably opposed to intervening since such action might spark off a new worldwide conflict, and the foreign ministers of the United States, Britain, France, China and Russia had already begun a meeting in Geneva to discuss peace in Asia. For the past two weeks they had devoted themselves to the topic of Korea, where an armistice had been signed in June 1953, but they had concluded no agreements on that bitterly divided country, and the talks were scheduled to turn to the subject of Indochina the very next day, May 8.

"If the Americans were going to send their fleet of B-29s to bomb our positions, comrade general, I'm sure they would have done so by now," said Lat in a reassuring tone. "It would make no sense to do it after they've sat down with the Russians and the Chinese in Geneva."

Giap's austere features broke into a smile to acknowledge that his chief political commissar had accurately read his thoughts; then he lifted the glasses to his eyes once more. "Without outside help there'll be no alternative but surrender for most of the garrison," he said softly, as though speaking his thoughts aloud, "but the fittest units might still try to break out." Again he scrutinized the entire valley minutely, his brow furrowed deeply with thought. Then he dropped the glasses back into their case and turned his back on it abruptly, his mind finally made up. "My orders will be: 'Stick closely to the enemy!' Transmit that to all the unit commissars. Tell them that the encirclement must remain impregnable as we close in to finish them off. Not even one soldier must be allowed to escape."

"It will be a pleasure to convey such a final battle order!" Lat's face lit up with a smile of delight as they turned back towards the commander in chief's headquarters concealed in caves close to a nearby waterfall. "I've been waiting twenty-four years, comrade general, for this day to dawn — since the terror bombing of Vinh. Whenever I've felt my resolve weaken over the years I've closed my eyes and summoned up those terrible pictures of French bombs falling among our helpless marchers. I'll never forget their faces and the screams of the dying as long as I live."

Giap stopped and patted Lat on the shoulder. "At a time like this every man in our entire army is probably dreaming of settling old scores — and reliving old regrets. My wife died in a French jail, remember?"

Lat stared hard at his commander in chief, wondering whether intuitively he'd grasped the deeper, more intimate feelings he hadn't expressed. "Perhaps terrible sacrifices are unavoidable if a man decides to devote himself to a cause like ours," said Lat in a resigned voice. "I made a wrong choice as a young man — President Ho was the first one to make me realize that. But all those years of suffering since have become worthwhile here at Dien Bien Phu."

Giap nodded his approval of Lat's sentiments but offered no comment.

"But in the end even a wrong choice can be useful in helping us reach a better understanding of ourselves and others around us. It taught me the importance of subtlety." Lat smiled ruefully and held up a paper-wrapped package that he'd been carrying in his hand. "I have to apologize for commandeering one of our precious bicycles to transport this and a gramophone from Hanoi — but I'm hoping you'll agree it was worth it."

Giap's face crinkled in an impatient frown. "What exactly is it, Comrade Lat?"

"It's a recording of the '*Chant des Partisans.*' I thought we should play it on the enemy's command wavelength before the final attack begins."

A slow smile of admiration spread across Giap's face.

"It tells of the bestial foreign army — the black crows — flying all over the land and calls on the people to rise up and drive them out — do you remember?"

Giap nodded; the "*Chant des Partisans*" had passed into the folklore of France in the closing months of the Second World War and was universally known as the anti-Nazi anthem of the French Resistance. Glancing at the watch on his left wrist, the Viet Minh commander in chief made a quick mental calculation. "Begin broadcasting it into the valley in half an hour from now — it will coincide with the start of the final advance."

Thirty minutes later Lat seated himself before a radio set and watched its operator tune it to the French command wavelength. Then he set the wind-up gramophone going and spoke gently into the transmitter in French. "Don't destroy your radios yet, *mes enfants.* President Ho Chi Minh offers you a rendering of the 'Song of the Partisans.'"

In their dripping bunkers and dugouts all over the shrunken camp, French paratroopers and Legionnaires were startled to hear a haunting, urgent female voice issue forth suddenly from their communications sets, accompanied by the stirring throb of a guitar. *"Companions,"* she sang, *"freedom is listening to us now . . ."*

As the old scratched record spun slowly in the high mountain cave, Lat smiled at the radio operator and patted him on the shoulder. "Just keep playing it over and over again on that frequency, comrade — until the very end." He stood up and made to leave but stopped when a call for him came through on one of a bank of field telephones. When he pressed the receiver to his ear, he recognized the voice of the political commissar of the 59th Regiment, one of the dozen men to whom he'd conveyed General Giap's final battle order a few minutes earlier.

"Comrade Lat, I've been asked to pass you a request from one of my company commanders," said the voice. "He wishes to volunteer for the task of planting our flag on the French command bunker if you are forming a special assault squad."

"Yes," replied Lat tersely. "We're assembling a party of volunteers. What's the name of your company commander?"

"You know of him I think," said the 59th Regiment's commissar. "He and his men dragged the last howitzer up the mountain. His name is Ngo Van Dong."

"Yes of course," said Lat without hesitation. "Comrade Dong is a renowned and courageous fighter. He deserves the honor."

12

In his bunker under the earth of the valley floor Colonel Paul Devraux sat staring blankly at the mat-covered wall in front of his worktable. Despite his efforts to ignore it, the thrilling French female voice singing the "Song of the Partisans" over the command radio system was making it impossible for him to concentrate properly on his morning report of the enemy's battle order. His sweating face was gaunt and deeply lined with fatigue, and every minute or two he rubbed his hand agitatedly across his bandaged brow.

". . . Soon now, the enemy will know the price of our blood and tears! Rise up friends, from our desolated cities, rise up from the hills. . . . Freedom is listening to us tonight!"

From contacts he'd already had with the commanders of the surviving strongpoints, Paul knew that the emotive song was having a mesmerizing effect on the garrison's troops. In their holes in the ground, dazed French parachutists and Legionnaires had even begun to sing along distractedly with the recording. On the low hills of the Elaine group the song was ringing in the ears of the last French defenders while new waves of Viet Minh were advancing through their trenches and dugouts in monsoon squalls. One by one even the minor redoubts were falling despite heroic last-ditch resistance, and the main camp had shrunk to little more than the size of a football stadium.

As he listened to the song, the whirring of a field telephone at his elbow made Paul start, and glancing at his watch he realized it was almost ten o'clock. Without stopping to lift the receiver, he picked up his papers and hurried through the communicating tunnel to the commanding officer's bunker. A new nameplate on the doorpost described de Castries now as a brigadier-general; along with all his troop commanders he had been promoted a few days before by the otherwise helpless French staff officers in Hanoi, but the new shoulder boards and a bottle of vintage champagne dropped by parachute for them to celebrate their new ranks had fallen with a tragic irony among the enemy trenches. Inside the bunker Paul, who had been made a full colonel, found de Castries seated listlessly at his table with a cigarette hanging from his lips. With his tan uniform he wore the red forage cap of the Moroccan regiment he had once commanded, and he greeted his chief of staff with an abstracted nod.

"The enemy's now massing his 312th and 316th Divisions on our eastern flank along with two extra regiments from the 308th Division," said Paul launching straight into his battle order report. "Only one regiment is being held back opposite our western flank. In all he seems to have about thirty-five thousand troops at his disposal. His artillery is still surviving the attentions of our air force, and we've got definite proof now that new Russian multi-tube Katuysha rockets are being deployed and used against us."

"And what's our own strength?" De Castries' voice was as resigned as his expression. "If 'strength' is the right word to use, that is."

"A maximum of four thousand men fit to fight." Paul paused and rubbed the back of his hand slowly across his sweating face; his head ached blindingly, and his vision was blurring from time to time. "But even the toughest paras and Legionnaires can't go on much longer without sleep and food. The three last companies of

439

Moroccan Rifles probably won't fight anymore, nor will the Thai tribesmen. Our Vietnamese parachute units are still holding up well, but there's only two companies left of the First and Second Foreign Legion Parachute Battalions, two of the Eighth Parachute Assault . . ."

De Castries waved Paul to silence and indicated he should drop his notes on the table for him to read later. "We must fight tooth and claw with what we've got to hold on to the western riverbank, otherwise we'll be without water as well as food. Those units capable of making it should start preparing for the breakout tonight."

"I don't think many of the men are strong enough, sir, to fight their way through the jungle — even if we can hold out until dark . . ." Paul felt a wave of dizziness sweep over him, and he reached out a hand to support himself on the table. "Three more hills in the Elaine group, you see, have fallen in the last hour. . . ."

De Castries looked up sharply at his chief of staff. "Are you feeling unwell yourself?"

Before his eyes the face of his superior seemed to dissolve, and Paul shook his head to clear his vision. "Like everyone else, sir, I suppose I badly need some sleep, that's all."

"It might be more than that," said de Castries quietly. "You look as though you may be getting a fever. Go and try to sleep for an hour. I'll send someone to wake you if the crisis comes."

Back in his bunker Paul sank down on his cot and lay shivering beneath a blanket; almost immediately he fell into a troubled doze, and as he slipped back and forth between sleep and a dazed state of wakefulness, thoughts he'd been struggling to subdue since Joseph's departure flooded back into his mind. Released for the first time in eight weeks from the nerve-wracking tension of helping direct the desperate defense of the valley, he experienced again with great intensity the pain of the murderous rage that had first seized him as the full meaning of Joseph's confession sank in. Although he and Lan had long before grown cool towards one another, her uncharacteristic betrayal of their marriage vows with someone for whom he'd always felt a strong affection had shocked him deeply, and his initial fury had given way later to a mood of black melancholy. Unbearable images of their secret meetings had haunted him day and night, and in his fevered dreams he saw them together repeatedly, writhing naked and ecstatic in one another's arms. Weighed down by deep feelings of futility and loss, he had rapidly become indifferent to his own safety; as casualties had mounted among the officers of the garrison, he'd volunteered to lead counterattacks himself on the Huguette group of hills, and his reckless bravery had brought the units a series of surprising successes against the tide of battle. This return to action had in the end restored his faith in his ability to shape his own life again, and gradually a new, stubborn resolve had begun to grow in him: somehow, he would survive the debacle of Dien Bien Phu and return to Saigon. There he would confront Lan and Joseph and make Lan see that there was still a future for them together, even if it were in France. If he could salvage his marriage from the wreckage of the war, that at least, he came to feel, would prove his instincts hadn't been irretrievably wrong from the beginning.

He'd suffered no new wounds in the fierce fighting, but his old head injury had plagued him increasingly, and the camp surgeon had finally discovered a peppering of previously overlooked grenade splinters still embedded in his skull. Even after they'd been removed he'd continued to suffer blinding headaches, but his determination to survive and carry through his new plans had led him to conceal the pain he suffered from those around him. Since the underground field hospital and its communicating tunnels were now crowded with hundreds of wounded, and the handful of exhausted surgeons were operating amidst horrifying heaps of amputated arms and legs, there had been no alternative but to carry on with his chief-of-staff duties. The fever had begun to make itself felt two or three days earlier, and he'd flung himself into his daily tasks with a new desperation, hoping to shake it off, but as he lay shuddering beneath the blanket he knew that he was losing the struggle. As the French singer's voice told repeatedly of "black crows darkening the plains" and the homeland "groaning beneath its chains," he began to imagine that he could hear the bunker filling with the ominous flap of wings and the clank of shackling irons, and when he felt a hand grip his shoulder suddenly he cried out involuntarily and sat up in alarm.

"It's after fifteen hundred hours, *mon colonel*," murmured his adjutant. "The Viets are beginning to cross the river, and General de Castries is calling an emergency meeting of senior troop commanders."

Paul thanked the junior officer and hastily dashed some water on his face before making his way unsteadily through the communication saps to the command meeting. The shriek of artillery shells overhead and the constant earthshaking roar of the resulting explosions above the command post made discussion difficult, but the sight of the drawn and haggard faces of the other troop commanders in the dugout was enough to tell him as soon as he entered that the situation had deteriorated beyond recovery while he'd slept.

"We have no choices left," said Colonel Langlais grimly. "The main position here won't hold until nightfall. That means there can be no organized attempt at breaking out. The wounded and the units who've already run out of ammunition will be massacred if we don't tell the enemy that we intend to cease resistance soon."

Paul mopped his face with the sleeve of his battle dress tunic, listening hazily to the uncomfortable discussion of how the bitter prospect of defeat was to be faced, and when the meeting broke up General de Castries motioned for him to wait behind. "Are you well enough to handle the final general order?" he asked in a subdued voice, and Paul nodded. "Good — then pass this message to all units at once. 'By order of the commanding general, the ceasefire will be effective as of seventeen hundred hours today, 7 May 1954. All equipment and supplies will be destroyed before that hour so that nothing of use falls into enemy hands!' That is all."

Paul started to raise his hand in a final formal salute, but de Castries, already white-faced behind the dark glasses he had chosen to wear for the meeting, turned away quickly without acknowledging it. Then as Paul was in the act of ducking out through the curtained doorway, he spoke quietly over his shoulder.

"Don't forget to burn your red beret before they get here, *mon vieux,* will you? The others are going to, and it might save your life. The enemy have good reason not to love *les paras.*"

For a moment Paul gazed at his commanding officer's back in surprise; but still de Castries didn't turn to face him, and he hurried out without responding. On waking from his disturbed sleep his fever seemed to have lessened, but after returning to his dugout and passing the cease-fire order to those few units still holding out, he began shaking and sweating uncontrollably once more. He tried to focus his eyes on the grit-covered papers on his table, and found himself re-reading the citation that had been sent from Hanoi when the entire garrison had been awarded the Croix de Guerre ten days before. It read: "Their courage shall remain an example forever," but as he peered at it, the words began to swim before his eyes, and he snatched up the paper and crumpled it into a ball with a muffled curse.

The "Song of the Partisans" that was still playing softly over the communications radio receiver was being interrupted regularly now by the desperate voices of paratroopers and Legionnaires announcing that they were destroying their weapons and radios as the enemy approached; infantry weapons were being jammed into the earth and fired to burst their barrels and phosphorus grenades were being tossed into the muzzles of the remaining tank guns and artillery pieces to render them unusable. Messages from other vantage points reported that Viet Minh troops were beginning to swarm across the shallow Nam Youm River in strength and that the Algerians and Moroccans who'd deserted to live in caves in the riverbank were already hoisting their own flags of surrender made from discarded parachute silks.

As he listened to the reports, Paul clenched and unclenched his fists slowly at his sides. Then he rummaged quickly among his papers and charts until he unearthed a small silk map of northwestern Tongking. The map showed clearly the narrow mountain trails leading into Laos, and after removing his left combat boot, he wrapped the map carefully around the lower part of his leg, pulled his sock over it and slipped a miniature compass into his other boot.

The effort brought on another wave of dizziness, and he sank down in his chair until it passed. Still shivering, he burned his own personal notebooks in a mess tin and added a small sheaf of letters from Lan to the flames, sheet by sheet. As the little tongues of fire consumed the pages his features remained determinedly expressionless, and even when he came to a smiling photograph of his wife, his feverish gaze rested on the image of her beautiful face for only a moment before he set fire to that too. Just before the flames died away his eye fell on his red beret lying on the table beside the tin; he started to reach for it, remembering his commander's last exhortation, then he checked himself. Standing up, he set the beret carefully on his head, cocking it instinctively over one eye in the rakish fashion in which he'd always worn it.

From outside he heard a babble of confused shouts, then a few scattered French cries of "Here they come!" A ragged volley of shots rang out, followed by the rush of sandaled feet crossing the bunker top. Drawing his revolver, Paul stepped towards the radio set and fired all his bullets into it at point-blank range before turning the weapon around and smashing the wreckage with its butt.

Above his head at that moment Ngo Van Dong was running among a jubilant group of green-uniformed troops, carrying the furled Viet Minh standard tucked under his left arm. A Russian-made submachine gun with a curved magazine clipped to it was slung round his neck on its strap, and he held it at the ready in front of him with his right hand. Leaping onto the roof of corrugated steel and punctured sandbags, Dong drove the pole of the Viet Minh flag into the sand and held it there while his comrades banked stones and ballast around its base to hold it upright. When it was firmly in place, three of the Viet Minh soldiers remained on guard while the captain in command of the special squad led Dong and the remaining men into the mouth of the sap leading down to the command bunker beneath. When they burst in, Brigadier-General Christian Marie Ferdinand de la Croix de Castries was standing waiting for them in a clean uniform, complete with its row of medal ribbons, and when he saw them pointing their submachine guns at his chest he said quickly, "Don't shoot!"

A moment later he was being dragged up the sap into the daylight by the jostling crowd of enemy troops, but Ngo Van Dong didn't go with them. Seizing a young French lieutenant by the shoulder, he made him wait at gunpoint until the other members of the special assault squad were out of earshot.

"Where is Chief of Staff Devraux?" he snapped. "Which are his quarters?"

The apprehensive lieutenant pointed wordlessly along the communications sap, and immediately Dong drew a grenade from a pouch on his belt and dashed away.

Inside his bunker Paul was standing unsteadily by the smashed radio, fighting another wave of dizziness, when he heard a noise in the doorway behind him. Turning slowly he found he could see only a blurred, indistinct outline of an Asian face and a flat bamboo helmet bearing a red star emblem. In his turn, Dong stared uncertainly for a moment at the obviously sick and exhausted French officer who wore a filthy bandage round his head; then he stepped closer, still holding the grenade in his left hand, and recognized him. Despite the two-day growth of stubble on his chin, Paul bore a strong resemblance in maturity to his father, and Dong drew in his breath sharply.

"Devraux, you're a captive of the Democratic People's Army of Vietnam," he breathed. "You must obey my orders now."

Paul screwed up his eyes and with an effort brought the Viet Minh soldier's face into focus. When recognition dawned on him, he shook his head slowly in confusion. "Who sent you here, Dong?"

The features of the Vietnamese tightened convulsively. "My dead mother, my dead father — and my dead brother, Hoc. Get down on your knees! I'm going to kill you!"

Outside the bunker silence had fallen suddenly over Dien Bien Phu for the first time in more than two months, and Paul wondered through his haze of pain if what he was seeing was a hallucination. He felt himself begin to sway again, and he had to clutch at one of the wooden roof supports to prevent himself from falling. "You've won the battle, Dong. You deserve your victory. Isn't that enough for you?"

"It isn't enough for my dead family. Get down on your knees!"

Paul shifted away from the post and began to move unsteadily towards the Vietnamese, holding his empty hands loose at his sides. "The killing's finished, Dong. Now we've all got to start picking up the pieces. I'm your prisoner — but I'm going to join the other prisoners."

Although Dong's face began to work nervously, at the last moment he stepped aside, and Paul continued walking slowly past him towards the door of the dugout. As he reached out a hand to push the sacking aside, the Vietnamese called desperately once more for him to stop; but still Paul ignored the command, and Dong opened fire. With his face contorted in an agonized expression, the Vietnamese held his finger curled tight round the trigger of the submachine gun for several seconds, and the French officer, after collapsing against the wall, fell face down in the mud without a sound and didn't move again.

13

On the morning of the first Friday in July, Joseph sat down to breakfast in the paved inner courtyard of the Continental Palace Hotel in Saigon, trying hard not to look at his wristwatch. Normally he found the fragrant flowering shrubs and the elegant statues amidst which the tables were set soothing and refreshing, but after a restless night in one of the high-ceilinged Continental bedrooms, he had fallen asleep properly for the first time only at dawn, and as a result had woken unaccustomedly late, feeling anxious and on edge. When the waiter approached his table, he ordered strawberries with his rolls and coffee as usual, but as soon as the little dish of crimson Dalat fruit was set before him, a mental picture of the neatly tilled terraces of the Lang-Biang plateau, where the berries had been grown, flashed in his mind, and he found he couldn't eat even one of them.

Suddenly it seemed much longer than three months since he and Lan had spent those few poignant hours together in Dalat, and because the agonizing weeks of waiting were almost over, he wondered for the first time, with a stab of alarm, how he would come to terms with life without her if, against all his expectations, she decided not to marry him. By mutual agreement they had decided to avoid meeting again while the battle raged at Dien Bien Phu, and Joseph had let a whole month go by before contacting her after the news came out that Paul had been killed on the day that Dien Bien Phu had fallen. He knew that she would have to observe the proper Vietnamese interval of mourning if she were to marry again, but she had told him that she would give him her decision at least at the beginning of July. He had flown into Tan Son Nhut from Hong Kong the previous evening, leaving Tempe white-faced but determinedly calm, making preparations to pack her belongings and return to Baltimore; although visibly shaken by his abrupt request that she give him a divorce, Tempe had won the battle to retain her self-control, and her very calmness, instead of making it easier to leave, had somehow heightened the feelings of guilt and anguish that had haunted him constantly since his last departure from Dien Bien Phu. During the many sleepless nights that followed his last visit to the crumbling valley fortress, he had been unable to dismiss from his mind the memory of Paul standing outside his bunker as the last Red Cross Dakota lifted him into the monsoon clouds, and when, a few days after the garrison fell, Paul's name appeared on the Red Cross list of those who had died, the intensity of the grief Joseph felt had made him physically ill for a day or two. During the next few weeks he drank frequently and with unaccustomed heaviness and didn't allow himself to think of the future. But when his grief began to lessen, the conviction that perhaps fate all along had determined that he should marry Lan had revived in him. Somehow at last it all seemed to have been destined and he became convinced that taking Lan and Tuyet away from Saigon was the only way of putting the terrible tragedies of the past behind them. On his arrival at the Continental Palace the night before, he'd found a note from Lan awaiting him, promising that she would meet him on the hotel terrace next morning at eleven o'clock, and as soon as he awoke he'd begun peering impatiently at the hands of his watch every few minutes.

As a result time hung heavy on him, and in an effort to calm himself Joseph picked up from beside his plate the French-language *Journal de Saigon*, which every visiting foreign correspondent turned to on arrival to catch up on events in Vietnam. The main story on its front page purported to give details of the sweeping land redistribution program being carried out all over the northern half of Vietnam by the Communist cadres of President Ho Chi Minh's renamed Lao Dong Party — the Workers' Party; according to the newspaper, assassination and terror tactics were already being employed on a massive scale against members of the landowning classes, and tens of thousands of deaths had already been reported. Although the Geneva Conference of world leaders on Indochina had still not produced any formal agreement after two months of discussions, General Giap's victory at Dien Bien Phu had virtually forced France to begin seeking an armistice the day after its garrison was defeated, and in the north particularly, unashamedly Communist policies were rapidly being put into force in the vast areas under Viet Minh control. A separate story on the *Journal*'s front page also related how even in the Mekong delta in the south, the Viet Minh were becoming daily more confident of their strength; a clandestine radio broadcast the previous night had announced that a stage-by-stage campaign was being launched immediately to eradicate big landholders there too, although the Geneva Conference seemed likely to end with Vietnam being divided into two zones, with the Communists holding the north and non-Communists the south.

Joseph ran his eye over all these news items, but found himself unable to concentrate on the details; he'd come to Saigon ostensibly to prepare a dispatch on the mood of the colonists in the wake of the humiliation suffered at Dien Bien Phu, but because of his inner preoccupations, he rose distractedly from his breakfast table after a few minutes' scrutiny of the newspaper and strolled out into the Rue Catinat, promising himself that he'd get down to work properly that afternoon.

For half an hour he wandered aimlessly, lost most of that time in his own thoughts, but even in his abstracted mood he couldn't help noticing how palpably the city he'd known for nearly thirty years was changing before his eyes. During the long eight-year war the thirty thousand French *colons* who had reestablished themselves in the city after the Second World War had affected a pose of studied unconcern; it came to be regarded as "bad form" to peer about nervously searching for bombs or grenades while sipping an *apéritif* on a café terrace, and discussion of the Viet Minh had always to be light, dismissive and *dégagé*, as though the anti-French movement were a trifling irrelevance to life in the city. But with the advent of Dien Bien Phu, all that had changed. Some ten thousand *colons* had already left the city, and now the usually genial and flamboyant proprietor of the Continental Palace no longer greeted coffee hour guests on his *terrasse* with his customary flourishes; instead Joseph saw him frowning deeply as he bent close to a grim-faced French financier Joseph knew by sight. In the Pagoda Tea Room, the Café de la Paix, where the veteran *colons* gathered, and in the Bodega, patrons and waiters who were normally expansive and relaxed conversed now in small anxious groups, their eyes furtive and alert. Usually the Sûreté Générale headquarters with its heavily barred windows at the top of the Rue Catinat was aswarm with activity, but as Joseph passed, it seemed to stand unnaturally quiet; few French or Vietnamese were entering, and this uncharacteristic calm gave Joseph the impression that the dark and secret struggles it had for so long conducted were on the point of being abandoned. In the bearing of every Frenchman he passed there was at least a hint of apprehension, and Joseph realized that the increasingly visible groups of Americans from the U.S. Embassy and other government agencies walked by contrast with an easy, free-swinging confidence; without being aware of it, by their relaxed laughter and their self-assured smiles they betrayed their smug belief that the French had only themselves to blame for their failure in a backward country like Vietnam. If they, the Americans, had been fighting the war, their attitudes seemed to say, the result would have been vastly different.

As he strolled on through the growing heat of the day, Joseph began to wonder how far this dangerously simple line of reasoning might be taken by his own country. Although the French Union Forces were still holding in place in the Red River delta, the central highlands and the south while the Geneva Conference dragged on, it was clear that the will of France to continue the war had been broken psychologically at Dien Bien Phu. Not only had more than five thousand men been killed or wounded there, but the Russian news film of ten thousand more mud-covered skeletons being marched off to prison camps by their Viet Minh guards had shocked France and the world. The French people at home had always been indifferent to the faraway war in Indochina, and popular revulsion at the outcome of the battle in the valley in northwestern Tongking had ensured that France would at long last be forced to give up the remnants of its colonial rule there. But although the foreign ministers of the Soviet Union, Britain, China and France were discussing Indochina's future at Geneva, the fervently anti-Communist American secretary of state, John Foster Dulles, had pointedly absented himself from the proceedings early on, leaving a deputy holding a watching brief; by this gesture he had given notice that the United States would not willingly acquiesce in the concession of territory to the Communists in Indochina and by means of a growing presence of Americans in Saigon, Joseph realized, he was already signaling Washington's intention to continue the battle where France left off.

Often while the French defenders were battling heroically at Dien Bien Phu to hold off the massed Viet Minh divisions, Joseph had recalled how he and a handful of OSS men had trained the nucleus of ragged guerrillas from which that massive force had sprung. He had often wondered, too, how differently things might have turned out if the American government had responded to the seemingly sincere overtures made by Ho Chi Minh then; perhaps the goodwill won by the OSS could have been expanded and built upon. What if President Truman had replied to any of the half dozen or so letters Ho had written seeking support against French attempts to destroy his revolution — wouldn't some kind of friendship have been possible? And when China fell to Communism in 1949, might it not have been possible to woo Ho Chi Minh and his followers away from the Russians and the Chinese as Tito had been in Europe? Conjecture was obviously futile because now there was a strong chance that Joseph's own government was about to compound these earlier mistakes by seeking a more direct confrontation with Ho Chi Minh. President Ho had convinced Joseph during their brief friendship that he and the people he led were determined to right the very real injustices they'd suffered under the French; he had understood very clearly that their deep sense of historical grievance was the powerful engine of their strength, and to plunge heedlessly into such a complex political whirlpool in order to confront Russia and China, as the American secretary of state seemed determined to do, seemed to Joseph a venture doomed to failure. These gloomy memories that swirled through his mind as he walked only served to reaffirm his conviction that he must remove Lan and Tuyet as quickly as possible from the evident dangers that lay ahead, and oppressed suddenly by these reflections, he stopped in mid-stride and turned back towards the Continental.

But when he got there, although it was already eleven o'clock, there was still no sign of Lan on the terrace, and after waiting impatiently for a quarter of an hour, he slipped into the hotel foyer and persuaded the concierge to let him use the telephone behind her *guichet*. He listened anxiously to the ringing tone for more than a minute before the receiver at Lan's home was lifted; but to his intense disappointment, one of her house servants answered.

Speaking sibilant, heavily accented French, the servant explained that Madame Devraux had left some time before to pay an urgent visit to her father; she offered her apologies but had said that if he called, he was to be told she hoped to arrive at the Continental within half an hour.

Unable to face another long wait on the terrace, Joseph stepped out into the Rue Catinat and began walking once more, this time towards the docks and the Saigon River. At the foot of the boulevard he hurried past the garish little Corsican-run bars where loud music spilled out onto the pavements and crossed to the concrete quays beside the river. Hoping the activity of the waterfront would soothe him, he leaned against a bollard and watched the crowds of sampans working back and forth among the oceangoing freighters. But the seething bustle of the waterborne craft, instead of relaxing him, reminded him of Hong Kong, and against his will the image of Tempe's strained, white face staring back at him against the backdrop of the harbor forced itself once more into his thoughts.

She had been standing with her back to the window in their house on the Peak when he had dropped his bombshell. For a long time she had said absolutely nothing, but had let him stumble on until he had exhausted every flimsy justification he could think of for what he knew in his heart was shoddy recompense for the loyalty and love she had always shown him. When at last she spoke there had been more pity in her voice than anger.

"So the wide-eyed boy in Khai Dinh's throne room is still searching for another jeweled bonnet, is he, Joseph?" The words had come out in a tremulous whisper, and for a moment her face had threatened to crumple; then she had regained her composure. "You've always been dissatisfied with me, haven't you? I'm too ordinary, aren't I? You've always yearned for the exotic, for the unattainable. Perhaps you can't help it. Perhaps it's in your nature. Most boys give up trying to live out fairy tales long before they become grown men — but maybe your mother forgot to teach you that!"

Because she was close to tears she had laughed then, making a strangled sound in her throat that by a strange coincidence reminded him of the curious noise that she invariably made at the climax of lovemaking; he had always, without fully realizing it, found the sound faintly irritating, and to counter the irrational surge of anger which it suddenly provoked in him he had turned away from her and stared down into the harbor, concentrating hard on the distant turmoil of junks and sampans.

"You lied to me thirteen years ago, didn't you, Joseph?" she said softly, moving up behind him. "On the train coming back from the ceremony in the new wing of the museum, do you remember? I asked if you had made love with your mandarin's daughter, and you said in an outraged tone, 'Oh no, Vietnamese families are very strict about that!' And already she had borne your child, hadn't she? Ever since, you've been living a lie. Maybe if you'd told me the truth then, it might have helped me to understand."

At his shoulder he heard her breathing become ragged as she fought to hold back her tears. "It was nine years before I knew," said Joseph desperately, swinging around to face her. "Can't you understand? I had asked her to marry me; she only decided against it later because of her father!"

Tempe nodded quickly, biting her lip. "And you came home looking for a comforting haven — I suppose I knew that deep in my heart. But I gave you what you wanted and needed, Joseph — two fine sons! A stronger man might have put his past behind him then for the reality of the present." She shook her head pityingly. "But not you. You've always gone on yearning for the magic mysteries of the East that captivated you at fifteen. Now you're middle-aged, but still you can't bear to think that you're not going to find another jeweled palace, can you — even if it's between a Saigon woman's thighs!"

He had closed his eyes then to blot out the unbearable sight of the hurt in her face. "It was just an accident," he had whispered. "Don't you understand? If I hadn't gone back to Saigon quite by chance at the end of the war and discovered Tuyet, I don't suppose anything more would have come of it."

"I don't think you went back entirely by chance, Joseph."

He had opened his eyes wide then in amazement. "What do you mean?"

She shook her head in bewilderment. "I don't know. But there's something inevitable about all this. I suppose I've always known you would do something of the kind. If it hadn't been Saigon and the French officer's wife, it would have been someone else, somewhere different."

She had been holding a glass of French wine in her hand as she spoke, and for an instant he'd thought that she might dash its contents in his face; then she put the glass down quietly on a table and walked from the room, bending forward slightly and hugging herself in her anguish; at that moment she looked old and vulnerable, and he had wanted desperately to comfort her. By the time he left for the airport an hour later, she had made her face up carefully and she watched him go, tight-lipped and pale but in full possession of herself. Above all else she had been determined not to shed any tears in front of him, and the recollection of her courage shamed him so that he could stand still no longer on the quayside.

When he turned his back on the river he found he was looking again at the first view he'd ever had of Saigon when the *Avignon* sailed up the river thirty years before. The same trees that had given shelter to the betel-chewing coolies then were still casting their shade on the burning streets, and the twin spires of the cathedral were still visible jutting above the rooftops. Suddenly a wave of terrible compassion for himself and all humankind swept over him; how could that innocent fifteen-year-old boy who had mistaken exhausted men for massacre victims have been expected to know how to deal with all the impossible complexities of life that were to follow? How could anyone prepare a child for all the terrible pitfalls that lay in its path? Wasn't there any way of preventing grown men and women from injuring and wounding one another grievously generation after generation? Using their own sad weaknesses and failings as blunt instruments, they battered away at one another until all that was left was emotional pulp.

He turned these somber thoughts over endlessly in his mind as he walked back to the Continental, and he had almost reached the hotel again when he saw Lan coming towards him beneath the tamarind trees. She wore a pink flowered silken *ao dai* over billowing white trousers, and as she walked she was talking animatedly to someone at her side — but it was a moment or two before Joseph recognized her father. Portly from years of good living, Tran Van Hieu wore a Western business suit of a pale expensive linen now instead of his mandarin's gown, and the hair above his moonlike face was stiff and white. His expression remained as shrewd and watchful as ever, but because he was concentrating on what his daughter was saying he hadn't noticed Joseph approaching among the crowds thronging the pavement. The sight of Lan holding her father's arm startled Joseph; he remembered all too clearly how she had sat silently beside him in an attitude of rejection on his return from Hanoi, and seeing them together for the first time since then caused his spirits to sink.

But then he noticed that they were smiling happily at one another and he decided that Lan must after all have made up her mind in his favor. Unable to contain his impatience, Joseph stepped down from the hotel terrace to greet them in the street and almost knocked over a gangling Vietnamese peasant boy running fast along the inside of the sidewalk. The boy stumbled, then recovered himself and the reporter's eye in Joseph automatically registered the loose calico tunic, the dirty white trousers and the scuffed sandals that the youth wore. But then something odd about the way he was running compelled Joseph's full attention; the natural outline of his clothes was broken by the bulge of a lumpy package below the waist, and as he ran, he was supporting it awkwardly with one hand. Remembering the *Journal de Saigon*'s front-page story of that morning, Joseph yelled a frantic warning and began to run, but the crowds outside the hotel did not recognize immediately, as he had done, a trained member of Battalion 905, the Viet Minh suicide squad. The youth was running faster now to carry out the first symbolic assassination under the new land reform decree, and Tran Van Hieu, long-time collaborationist, absentee landlord and owner of vast tracts of rice land in the Mekong delta, looked up at him for the first time at the moment he flung a fatal arm around his neck.

For a fleeting moment Joseph allowed himself to hope he had been wrong — the boy was merely expressing his gratitude for some favor Tran Van Hieu had done his family in the rice fields. Then Lan shied away from him, and he saw the smile freeze on her face as the peasant began jerking obscenely at his clothing below the waist with his free hand. Making an incongruous pair, the ragged peasant and one of Vietnam's wealthiest aristocrats swung crazily in the middle of the pavement for a moment in a macabre dance, their arms tight about one another's necks. Then the terrified crowd began scattering, and Joseph saw Lan trying to pull the youth off her father. But he held Tran Van Hieu fast in the crook of his arm as he must have held many practice "victims" in his jungle training camp and the old man's eyes began to bulge with fear. Joseph tried to lunge towards them, but a Vietnamese woman, fleeing in panic, cannoned into him, sending him sprawling in the gutter. When the fragmentation grenade strapped to the youth's thigh exploded, it lifted Tran Van Hieu and the youth bodily off the ground, and they fell back together in a tangled heap. Several other passersby collapsed around them under the horrified eyes of the *colons* taking coffee on the Continental terrace, and their blood mingled with that of the assassin and his victim in a spreading pool on the pavement. Because he was lying prone on the ground when the grenade detonated, Joseph escaped injury, but when he rose and walked unsteadily towards the carnage he could see that Lan's body, lying a few feet from her father's, was twisted and broken. He wasn't able to see her face because it was pressed against the pavement, but the pink silks of her dress were quickly turning crimson in the bright sunlight, and there was no sign of movement in her slender limbs.

14

"I suppose you think I must be cold and unfeeling because you haven't seen me weeping," said Tuyet quietly as she walked beside Joseph through the dappled shadows of the tamarinds lining the Rue Catinat. "You probably think I don't care at all, don't you?"

"No, I don't think that," replied Joseph, uncomfortable under her challenging stare. "I can think of lots of reasons why you might want to keep your feelings to yourself." He glanced down to find her watching him unblinkingly and found he couldn't hold her gaze. She was wearing a plain, unhemmed mourning *ao dai* of white silk, and a long white scarf trailed down her back, but although the traditional Vietnamese costume of the bereaved was designed to convey that all thought of adornment was deliberately neglected in a time of grief, he found the natural beauty of her face almost painful to look on. During the funeral ceremonies for Lan and her father he had not dared look in her direction, but afterwards he had asked her to meet him later outside his hotel, and she had arrived promptly at the arranged time.

"Perhaps you ought to remember that I've had a lot of practice at not crying when I'm unhappy. It's something that can become a habit."

"I do realize that," said Joseph miserably. "And of course it'd be quite natural if you didn't feel the same deep sense of shock about your mother's death that I do. But the last time I talked with her alone, she told me how unhappy she was that you'd had to grow up without knowing her very well." Instead of replying, Tuyet tossed her head and looked away quickly across the boulevard, but not before he'd noticed the hurt look in her eyes. "But I didn't ask you here to talk about the past and the unhappiness we've all suffered," he continued gently. "I wanted to talk about the future."

"I'm surprised to hear that. I thought after what happened yesterday you'd never want to come back to Saigon again."

"As long as you're here I'll never stay away!" Joseph spoke with such vehemence that she glanced up at him in surprise. "That's what I wanted to discuss with you. Don't you remember the last time we met I tried to ask you something — but you were in too much of a hurry to listen?"

She shook her head stubbornly. "No, I don't remember."

"Well I did try." He stopped and took a deep breath. "I was going to ask you if you'd like to leave Saigon and make your home with me."

He watched anxiously for her reaction, but she kept her gaze fixed on the ground and didn't reply.

"I don't mean in the United States," he added hastily. "We could live in Asia — Singapore perhaps, Hong Kong or even Tokyo. I could persuade my newspaper to base me in any of those places. I want it to be somewhere where you'll be happy."

"Why do you want to help me now when you've never troubled yourself before? Has that awful explosion left you with a guilty conscience?" Because she asked the question without noticeable rancor, the implication of her words shocked Joseph more deeply than if she'd screamed at him.

"Tuyet. I've always cared — from the very moment I knew of your existence. I've always sent money for you ever since. I thought you knew that."

"Money! Do Americans think everything can be solved by money? A child that doesn't know its real parents can't love money in a bank account!"

Joseph gazed at the swarms of passing *cyclo-pousses*, feeling a sense of desperation rising within him. "Tuyet, I'm terribly sorry about all the things that went wrong in the past. I've made a lot of bad decisions in my life, but now I want to try to make the right one with you."

"Did you discuss this with my mother before she died?" She asked the question hesitantly, but watched his face with a peculiar intensity as she waited for him to reply.

"Yes I did. We talked about it at Dalat. I wanted both of you to come away with me — both of you, don't you understand? I wanted all of us to be together as we should have been from the start. I wanted us to travel together, really get to know one another properly . . ."

"And what did she say?"

Joseph looked away. "She said we ought to wait . . . until we knew what was going to happen at Dien Bien Phu."

"But that was all over two months ago."

"I know. But her husband was fighting there, remember."

"And she never gave you an answer?"

Seeing from her expression how important the question was to her made his heart begin to sink. "I think she might have agreed."

"But she never told you — you're not really sure what she wanted to do?"

Joseph shook his head helplessly. "No. She had promised to tell me yesterday — but she never got the chance."

They walked in silence for a minute or two, and Joseph searched his mind desperately for new arguments that might help sway her; beside him he could see she was biting her lower lip in agitation.

"I don't want to leave Vietnam," she said suddenly, blurting the words out in a defiant tone. "I don't know even now whether I can trust you. I know nothing of the way you live. Besides there's someone here who really loves me."

Joseph stared at her in dismay. "I know your uncle Tam's been very kind, but you don't seem to understand. . . ."

Her dark eyes flashed suddenly. "I don't mean Uncle Tam!"

Joseph stopped and looked at her with a puzzled expression. "What do you mean, then?"

For a moment she fiddled with the sun hat she'd been carrying, then placed it carefully on her head and took her time tying the silk ribbons beneath her chin. When she looked up at him, her face in the shadow of its brim reminded him more than ever before of Lan. "I have a friend," she said in a voice that broke a little. "He doesn't love the French or America — but he does love me. Perhaps he's the first person who ever has."

She turned away suddenly, and he gazed down helplessly at her, realizing she was close to tears.

"I'm going now. Don't try to contact me anymore. Goodbye . . . Father!"

She turned and ran quickly away along the boulevard, holding her hat in place with one hand, and she didn't slow to a walk until she was almost out of sight. He stood watching her slender figure until it was finally swallowed up by the late afternoon crowds moving across the Place du Théâtre, but she didn't stop or turn her head again to look back at him.

PART SIX

Pax Americana

1963

The Geneva Conference that finally ended the first
Indochina war divided Vietnam at the seventeenth parallel
to allow the French Union forces to regroup in the south while
the Communists moved their forces to the north. The delegates
agreed that the division should be temporary and that elections
to unify the country should be held within two years — but
because the United States was determined not to concede
further ground to Communism in the wake of the Korean war, no
American signature was ever placed on the final Geneva
agreements, and Washington encouraged President Ngo Dinh
Diem of South Vietnam to dissociate himself from the decisions
too. Because it suited their purposes at the time, neither China
nor the Soviet Union objected very strongly. As a result, the
Saigon government turned the provisional demarcation line at
the seventeenth parallel into a national border and refused to
cooperate with Hanoi in the holding of elections that would
certainly have swept Ho Chi Minh to power after his spectacular
defeat of the French. When Ho descended in triumph from the
hills of Tongking at the close of the Geneva Conference to set up
his government in Hanoi, nearly a million frightened
Vietnamese Catholics born in the north followed the French
forces south; some ninety thousand southern supporters of Ho

meanwhile trekked northward, and these two internal migrations helped polarize the country into opposing Communist and anti-Communist camps. During the next five years the Communists, exhausted after their long war, were content to consolidate their rule in the north, while President Diem did the same in the south. But although the United States poured massive amounts of military and economic aid into Saigon, the government of South Vietnam became increasingly oppressive and never won the support of the largely peasant population of the region. Ngo Dinh Diem, an austere Catholic bachelor born of a Hue mandarin family, had been appointed prime minister by Bao Dai before the former emperor abdicated for the last time, and after proclaiming himself president following a dubious referendum, Diem succeeded in restoring order to the chaotic southern areas of Vietnam by breaking the power of the religious sects and dispersing their private armies. But as time passed, he resorted increasingly to undemocratic methods to sustain his government; nepotism and corruption became commonplace, and under the influence of his megalomaniac brother, Ngo Dinh Nhu, the government security apparatus terrorized their serious opponents and herded even the mildest critics into prison camps. It was in this atmosphere of strife and discontent that Ho Chi Minh turned his attention once more to the task of completing the revolution he had embarked on nearly half a century earlier. In 1959 he began infiltrating the ninety thousand southerners who had gone north in 1954 back to their homelands, and within a year these Communist cadres had fused a dozen disparate political groups and religious sects into a new organization called the Mat Tran Dan Toc Giai Phong — the National Liberation Front of South Vietnam. Dedicated to overthrowing "the camouflaged colonial regime of Diem and the United States," the Front armed itself with American weapons captured from the Army of the Republic of Vietnam — popularly known as "ARVN" — and by 1962 it commanded support in four-fifths of all the villages in the south. President Diem's propaganda ministry inaccurately dubbed all members of the Liberation Front Viet Cong — Vietnamese Communists — although the movement was led, like the Viet Minh before it, by only a small core of convinced Communists who employed the same propaganda-and-terror tactics that had proved so effective in converting uneducated peasants to the anti-French cause. In the United States, the real hardships that the historically downtrodden peasants of South Vietnam were continuing to suffer under President Diem were not seen in their true perspective; to the peasants, Ngo Dinh Diem and his government seemed no different from the corrupt mandarins who had battened on them for a hundred years, except that the white colonial overlords behind them were now Americans, not French. In Washington, however, the new Liberation Front was seen only as an artificial cover organization for Communist aggression, directed from Moscow and Peking, and when President John F. Kennedy took office in 1961, determined that his country should "pay any price and bear any burden to ensure the survival of liberty," South Vietnam seemed to be just the place where such lofty idealism should be put into practice. At that time there were only seven hundred Americans attached to the military advisory team that had first been established in Saigon in 1950, but over the next few years President Kennedy constantly increased their strength. By 1963 a million and a half dollars were being spent on the jungle and paddy field war every day, some sixteen thousand American "advisory" troops were involved in the fighting, and the casualty toll was mounting — in 1961 fourteen Americans had died, by the end of 1962 more than a hundred. On the political front American funds were being used to build "Strategic Hamlets" — villages fortified by barbed-wire barricades and palisades of spiked bamboo — and by 1963 ten million of South Vietnam's fifteen million peasants had been herded into these stockades to separate the guerrillas from their main base of support, the people. But although American involvement was increasing in all areas, considerable tension plagued key battlefield relationships between the American military men and the little Asian soldiers they were trying to advise. President Diem developed an obsession with keeping losses among his own troops to a minimum, and because he demoted officers who allowed their units to suffer more than minimal casualties, the Americans often found themselves going into action with soldiers whose first thought was to avoid contact with the enemy. Despite this drawback, however, the introduction of American helicopters and armed river craft gave the South Vietnamese a dramatic new mobility, and towards the end of 1962 for the first time the Viet Cong began to suffer sizable casualties in swiftly mounted search-and-destroy missions. To counteract these battle successes and the effects of the Strategic

Hamlets program, the Communist leadership in Hanoi began sending to the south high-level North Vietnamese party cadres who had fought at Dien Bien Phu; this was done secretly to maintain the deception that the insurrection in the south was a purely local affair, but it stiffened the Liberation Front, and in the early months of 1963 the conflict in and around the vital Mekong delta intensified rapidly as the better-organized guerrillas and the American-equipped forces of President Diem threw themselves into a new struggle for supremacy.

1

Down-drafts from the rotor blades of a dozen United States Army H-21 helicopters churned a swath of the Mekong delta's muddy surface waters into a trembling wake as the aircraft charged across the rice paddies in formation at treetop height. Like the wings of dragonflies in flight, the whirling twin rotors were almost invisible in the burning air, and the flooded fields beneath them reflected only the swift-moving images of their banana-shaped fuselages. Inside the lead helicopter, a dozen wiry little South Vietnamese soldiers dressed in green combat uniforms gazed out through the open hatches with blank, indifferent expressions on their faces; although they wore field packs and steel helmets and clutched American M-2 automatic carbines in their hands, they squatted listlessly on the studded metal floor of the aircraft like bored bus passengers enduring the tedium of an unwanted journey, and only occasionally did they exchange a few desultory words with one another about what they were seeing.

In contrast, the two white American officers crouching among them, wearing steel helmets and mottled combat fatigues, scanned the fast-changing panorama of fields and dikes with intent eyes; giants in comparison with the slightly built Asian troops, they subjected each belt of jungle to the closest scrutiny and paid special attention to the tree clumps that invariably ringed the delta villages. In the front and rear doorways, the eyes of the two American sergeant gunners also roved restlessly back and forth across the paddies, followed by the silent muzzles of their swivel-mounted machine guns as they covered every potential hiding place that might be used by Viet Cong snipers. Occasionally the white Americans and the little Asians, too, turned their attention back inside the aircraft to shoot a quick glance at the pale-skinned English television reporter who sat apart on a webbing seat, her long blond hair tucked out of sight beneath a badgeless combat cap. Sometimes they saw her talking quietly with the two white civilians hunched beside her amid the satchels, bags and cases that contained equipment for recording television film pictures and sound, but otherwise her wide gray eyes remained fixed in the shimmering distance beyond the open doors. Her expression betrayed no hint of fear, only a total absorption with the harsh landscape of the Mekong delta that had remained unchanged

461

since biblical times, and if she was aware that her unflattering green fatigues did not entirely blunt the impact of her sexuality on the crowd of men around her, she gave no sign.

Like everyone else riding inside the racing helicopter, she knew that the timeless serenity of the paddies flashing past beneath the aircraft was deceptive. The rich delta silts of the Mekong might have been tilled since the dawn of civilization with the same horned animals and crude wooden plows that the peasants of South Vietnam were still using; those peasants might still be living, too, in the same kind of crude bamboo and palm-thatch huts as their ancient ancestors — but now beneath the seemingly tranquil surface much had changed. Although they could see nothing, all the helicopter occupants were aware that guerrilla fighters loyal to Ho Chi Minh and his modern Marxist creeds might easily be hiding under the muddy waters below them, breathing through hollow bamboo tubes; they might also be concealed in tunnels dug beneath the delta villages, and they would remain hidden all that day if they wished to avoid contact with the soldiers who came to "search and destroy" in the name of freedom, democracy and the West.

If on the other hand they had already decided that they would give battle, they might be waiting in strength among the trees encircling Moc Linh, their target village — and the Americans and the South Vietnamese would only find that out when they jumped from the helicopters into the flooded paddy fields to begin their final advance. The aircraft were being flown fast ten feet above the ground for that very reason — to cloak the dangerous moment of their arrival with surprise. During the journey from My Tho, headquarters of the ARVN Seventh Division situated forty miles south of Saigon, they had flown at three thousand feet, using height as a protection against any Viet Cong guns that might be concealed in the trees and brush; then as the flotilla neared its landing zone close to Moc Linh, the pilots had swooped down to hug the ground contours and use the hostile tree belts as cover.

The nearness of the ground heightened the sense of speed for all those inside the H-21s, and as they closed on their objective the helicopters began leapfrogging dizzily over groves of coconut palms and wild banana trees surrounding neighboring villages. When the English journalist touched her cameraman's shoulder, he began filming their furious approach through the open hatch, and groups of thatched huts appeared abruptly in his viewfinder;

startled faces of women and children stared up out of dark doorways, chickens and pigs fled squealing from the din of their passage — then on a broad dike two hundred yards short of the first hamlet of Moc Linh, the headlong dash ended abruptly. The H-21s fluttered to the ground and immediately the ARVN troops and their towering American advisers heaved themselves into the murky water of the rice paddy and began wading fast towards the tree line.

As soon as the leading aircraft began to disgorge its troops, the English journalist and her film crew went swiftly into action; she jumped down onto the dike and dropped to one knee twenty yards from the H-21 so that its steel bulk framed the background on one side. Behind her the little South Vietnamese troopers in their overlarge American helmets were trudging away through the flooded field, holding their weapons above their heads, and she waited patiently while her cameraman squinted past her to check that the unfolding drama was contained within the frame of his lens. When he was satisfied, he set a reel of film spinning and at the same moment the soundman thrust a microphone into her hand and stepped aside to switch on a tape machine.

"These sweltering paddy fields that you're looking at in an obscure corner of Southeast Asia have suddenly become the front line in a new hot war between the West and the Communist world," she said, raising her carefully modulated English public school voice to make herself heard above the noise of the other helicopter engines. "But it's not the sort of front line that anybody who fought in the Second World War or in Korea would recognize. These South Vietnamese troops and their American advisers are hoping to catch a concentration of Viet Cong guerrillas unawares in Moc Linh, the village you see behind me — Moc Linh is only one of five thousand such settlements in the region, and because the guerrillas can hide themselves easily in the jungle or among the villagers, on many missions like this no trace of them is ever found. Even if this dash into the heart of the Mekong delta succeeds in taking the Viet Cong by surprise, we still probably won't know just how successful it's been — because the guerrillas invariably melt away into the jungle again after each action, carrying their dead with them. . . ."

A brief burst of gunfire from the direction of the tree line augmented the roar of the helicopter engines suddenly, and the television reporter quickly ducked aside while the H-21 rose into the air again to allow its door gunners to join the action. The leading ARVN soldiers, wading quickly, had almost reached the trees, and the cameraman filmed them on telephoto for a few seconds before turning his lens back towards the reporter.

"That could be a nervous South Vietnamese trooper setting off his trigger-happy companions," she said, speaking calmly towards the camera once more. "That often happens when you're searching for guerrillas who seem to be able to appear and disappear at will. The key question in this trying situation is: Can America with its vastly superior military resources help the South Vietnamese destroy their elusive enemy quickly without getting more deeply involved? Or could this frustrating little war be the beginning of something bigger? That's what we've come here to try and find out. . . ."

As she fininished speaking she stepped down the bank into the muddy water of the paddy field and began wading towards the distant tree line. The cameraman continued filming her receding figure for a full minute more until the little grinning Vietnamese sergeant assigned to protect them finally motioned for him to follow. Holding their equipment clear of the water, the cameraman and the soundman slithered into the paddy with looks of extreme distaste on their faces and trudged after her.

2

The first hamlet was deserted when the troops reached it. A few scrawny chickens were scratching in the shade of one of the huts, but otherwise there was no sound or sign of movement. At a signal from Captain Hoang, their Vietnamese commander, the ARVN soldiers advanced cautiously beyond the trees and began moving slowly from door to door, searching the dwellings. After several minutes they had assembled in the middle of the clearing only three sullen-looking peasant women dressed in shapeless black trousers and tunics, and Captain Lionel Staudt, the senior American adviser, turned away, cursing softly beneath his breath.

"You see now, lieutenant, no matter how good ARVN intelligence is, Viet Cong intelligence is always better." He loosened his helmet strap and scowled at the fresh-faced young West Point officer standing beside him. "Maybe a battalion of main force guerrillas was here recently — but it sure as hell isn't within five miles of Moc Linh now."

"Aren't we jumping to conclusions too quickly?" asked Lieutenant Gary Sherman earnestly. "There are half-a-dozen hamlets strung out along the canal according to the map."

"There always are, son, there always are. And you won't find no main force VC in any of them. After a year here you get to know their style." The lean, sharp-featured infantry captain, who had seen action in the ranks in Europe and Korea, turned his back on the hamlet and wandered through the trees to the edge of the rice paddy once more to wait for the British television crew; for a moment his eyes lingered on the slender figure of Naomi Boyce-Lewis as she waded towards them, the muddy water lapping halfway up her long thighs. "And if our little friends shooting at shadows and warning off the enemy isn't enough to try our patience today," he said quietly, "we've got ourselves saddled with a spoiled English debutant who wants to play Hemingway games in the rice fields of Asia."

"I don't think she's come here to play any games," said Gary Sherman seriously, following his gaze. "She's been out on a couple of long foot patrols from My Tho — and walked all the way both times. She's a real tough cookie. There's nothing she won't do to get a good story."

"Nothing?" Staudt's features relaxed into a lecherous grin. "Are you sure about that?"

The young officer ignored the innuendo. "I meant, captain, she's very professional and very ambitious. The story going around the mess is that she comes from a wealthy family. Her father was a baronet — until he got himself killed out here at the end of the Second World War. But apparently she's very determined to prove she's got what it takes — without his money."

The captain let out a low whistle. "So there's a whole bunch of money riding on that classy English ass too? We'd better make sure the 'friendlies' take good care of her." He raised his arm and waved to the little sergeant escorting the film crew, indicating that he should hurry up, but the Vietnamese NCO continued trotting obliviously through the water beside the taller Europeans, grinning and chattering animatedly in pidgin English, his rifle hanging loose on his shoulder. When the English reporter reached the bank, Staudt jumped down into the water and offered his hand to steady her as she climbed out, but with a little dismissive shake of her head she declined his help and clambered nimbly out of the water on her own. By the time he caught up with her she was entering the hamlet, and they both saw that some idle ARVN soldiers had begun chasing the villagers' chickens, hoping to snare one for lunch. Staudt took in the scene at a glance and nodded towards the cameraman who was preparing to film the apprehensive-looking village women.

"I'd sure appreciate it if you decided not to record the hen-hunt for posterity, Miss Boyce-Lewis," he said in a mock-beseeching voice. "We try to teach the 'friendlies' that nobody loves a looting army — but they just giggle and tell us they're underfed and underpaid." He paused and rolled his eyes. "And maybe they are — their generals pay them only fifteen dollars a month each because they stash most of our military aid into their private bank accounts."

"We're after something a little more telling than frightened chickens, captain, thank you." The English reporter smiled perfunctorily and turned to watch Gary Sherman hurrying towards them across the clearing.

In his hands he carried a crumpled cotton banner, half red, half blue, with a gold star emblazoned in its center, and his eager young face was alight with excitement. "Look, captain, the intelligence was right. They have been here."

"Sure — you've captured the flag of the People's Liberation Front, lieutenant," said Staudt sarcastically. "But this isn't the kind of war where you get a Purple Heart for that. We need to find the bodies of one or two brave Asian boys who fight under it to make it count."

"But there's a whole VC propaganda kiosk set up in the hut where I found this," protested the lieutenant. "And there are lots of those big earthenware jars that they use as personal air-raid shelters buried in the floors of most of the huts." He broke off and gestured eagerly towards his Vietnamese counterpart, a young ARVN lieutenant who was beginning to interrogate the three silent women. "Lieutenant Trang tells me that he thinks one of his men has found a tunnel entrance under one of the stoves — it looks like we've hit a fortified VC hamlet this time for sure."

Staudt rubbed his sleeve across his brow and glanced slowly about him. Although it was only nine-thirty, the morning was already hot; sunlight shimmered on the roofs of the thatched huts, and the heavy air was still and hushed. "Surprise, surprise," he said softly. "Out of five thousand hamlets in the whole

Mekong delta we know four thousand have already gotten to be fortified VC hamlets of one kind or another. If we can stumble into just one of them from time to time against all those odds and find it empty, I guess the war's as good as won."

A flush of embarrassment reddened the young lieutenant's cheeks, and he turned away suddenly so the English reporter would not notice.

"I'm just glad, Gary, that we're finding this kind of crowning success at the end of my year in Vietnam — and at the beginning of yours." Staudt favored the television reporter with a brilliant smile. "Lieutenant Sherman's been here just two weeks, you see, miss. Ten days from now I wind up a twelve-month tour and twenty years of service in the U.S. Army that began on the Normandy beaches. I guess capturing an empty VC hamlet, a muddy flag and a propaganda kiosk alongside fine Asian soldiers like these is as good a way to cap all that as any, isn't it?"

"Does this mean you intend to abort the mission, captain?" asked the English reporter coolly.

Staudt shook his head with exaggerated slowness. "No, ma'am. Not at all. There's nothing the 'friendlies' would like better than to call back the choppers and haul their little asses out of here right away. They're too fond of using good intelligence about Viet Cong movements to make sure they arrive too late. That's how they keep their casualty rate down. But I'm going to teach 'em a lesson today. They're gonna search all six goddamned hamlets and work up a sweat at least before we head for home — or my name isn't Lionel Staudt." Turning irritably on his heel, the captain strode over to where the young ARVN lieutenant was questioning the last of the three women, and Gary Sherman and the British news crew followed. "What are these old crones telling us about the VC, Lieutenant Trang?" demanded the American officer brusquely.

The pale, obviously Eurasian features of the ARVN lieutenant, who had been assigned to the unit only the day before, registered instantly the offensive note in Staudt's voice, and although he'd clearly understood what had been said, he waited deliberately until the sergeant interpreter beside him translated the question into Vietnamese. When he'd finished, Trang answered in his own language so that Staudt had to wait again for the sergeant to translate. "The women are lying as usual. They say only what they have been told to say — that several hundred Viet Cong troops passed through the village yesterday. Because they were

467

frightened, all the men and boys of the hamlet ran off to hide in the jungle."

The American officer listened with ill-concealed impatience to the explanation, then his face hardened. "It couldn't be, Lieutenant Trang, could it, that you're not trying hard enough? All our lives could depend on your interrogation of these hags, remember?"

The ARVN lieutenant's eyes glittered suddenly, and he answered this time in English. "Maybe you've already guessed, captain, that my father was French. He fought against the Communists in the north before Dien Bien Phu. He was captured on a patrol one night after he got separated from his unit. When they found him next day he'd been tortured to death — but that wasn't all. To show how deep their hatred was they'd cut off his testicles and forced them down his throat before he died. So if you think you've got more reason to despise the Communists than I have, captain, you're welcome to your delusions!"

For the moment the American officer looked startled; then a smile spread slowly across his weather-beaten face. "It's good to know, lieutenant, you've got good reason to be one hundred percent on the team. It makes a real nice change."

3

Directly beneath the feet of the quarreling American and Vietnamese officers, Tuyet Luong was at that moment moving rapidly through a narrow tunnel on her stomach. Wearing the regional black blouse and trousers that had become the Viet Cong's battle dress, she propelled herself with quick, practiced movements, digging her knees and elbows rhythmically into the dry earth like paddles. Tied tight to her right thigh so that it didn't impede her progress, she wore a captured U.S. Army Colt .45 pistol in its holster, and a twisted garter of jungle creepers was knotted about her left thigh to make it easier, as she'd often told the men of her special assault platoon, to drag her dead body from the battlefield.

Through a spy port hidden among the roots of a clump of bamboo twenty yards from the edge of the clearing, she had just seen and heard the American captain and the young ARVN lieutenant talking — and although she hadn't been able to make out what they'd said, she had been close enough to register the unmistakable hostility in their voices. She had also counted the troops she had seen entering the hamlet, and as she crawled through the dark earth, she went over again in her mind the list of their weapons that she'd memorized; a dozen World War Two M-1s, nineteen M-2 automatic carbines, one BAR, and two of the formidable new M-79 grenade-launching shotguns that could fire a grenade shell accurately over two hundred yards. The American officers as usual were carrying AR-15 Armalites, and if the planned ambush succeeded, there would be a rich haul of weapons for the Liberation Army's crack 514th Battalion.

When she came to a larger tunnel, Tuyet Luong scrambled to her feet and began moving faster in a crouching run, anxious to report her information as soon as possible to the underground command center half a mile away. She knew her way through the fifteen-mile maze of tunnels that radiated in all directions beneath Moc Linh almost as well as she knew her way above ground because she had helped the peasants of the village with the long, back-breaking work of digging them during the previous six months. Like similar networks that had already been dug in thousands of villages north and south of Saigon, the tunnel system was of far greater sophistication than the Americans or their ARVN allies had so far dreamed. Built in accordance with the well-trained techniques of underground guerrilla warfare first developed by Mao Tse-tung's Communists in China and refined later in Korea, the network consisted of escape tunnels leading into the surrounding jungle, storage cellars, observation shafts studded with camouflaged lookout ports, and in the banks of the canal and along the dikes of the rice paddies, firing embrasures had been hollowed out at regular intervals.If the firing positions which covered all approaches to the village had been manned that morning, many of the ARVN troops could have been cut down easily before they had waded halfway across the open field; but the plan was to lure them deep into the heart of Moc Linh and engage them only when the troop carriers and the escort helicopters armed with rockets and machine guns had lifted off — that way the Liberation Army would risk fewer casualties and capture more weapons.

As she ran, Tuyet Luong was careful to avoid the numbered entrances to the special decoy tunnels that had been planted with mines and poisoned *punji* traps — sharpened bamboo spikes smeared with buffalo or human excrement. These passages had been prepared with special care so that if enemy troops discovered and entered the tunnels, they could be ambushed easily in the darkness. So far, she knew, the ARVN soldiers had shown little inclination to enter any of the few tunnels they'd found in other villages; the smoke bombs, flame-throwers and grenades they used had often failed to dislodge the guerrillas hiding in them, and the government forces, unaware of the extent of the networks, had usually been content to blow up the odd entrance they found without looking farther. The command post at Moc Linh had been set up in a "Dien Bien Phu" kitchen, an underground chamber from which sloping shafts radiating outwards like wheel spokes dispersed cooking smoke invisibly from dozens of ovens into thick jungle hundred of yards away, and when Tuyet Luong entered she was surprised to find the gangling figure of Ngo Van Dong, the 514th Battalion commander, engrossed in conversation with an authoritative-looking stranger.

"At Outlet Seventeen, Comrade Dong, I counted thirty-four Diemist soldiers with two officers and two Americans," she said breathlessly, without waiting for an invitation to speak. "They're carrying a dozen M-1 Garands, nineteen M-2 automatic carbines, one Browning automatic rifle, two Armalites — and two of the new M-79 grenade weapons. The Diemist lieutenant interrogated the three women we left in the huts — but afterwards he and the Americans argued and they seemed indecisive."

Ngo Van Dong, as gaunt and gangling in his early fifties as he had been in his youth, turned with a faint look of irritation on his face, but his expression relaxed when he saw who had spoken. "Are there only thirty-four troops in all, comrade?" he asked, moving quickly to the map of Moc Linh and its tunnels that was tacked to the mat-covered wall of the cellar.

"No, I said I *saw* only thirty-four myself," replied Tuyet tersely. "But the lookouts at the forward ports around Field Thirteen told me a full-strength company of over one hundred men landed from the helicopters." She pointed to the map. "They're grouping together here in the first hamlet."

Dong stared thoughtfully at the point she had indicated on the map. "Good — then we'll stick to the plan we've made." Smiling suddenly he turned to the gray-haired man at his side. "I'm sure you've already heard something about our famous platoon leader Tuyet Luong. She's as fearless and resourceful as all the stories about her suggest." He turned back to Tuyet. "Our visitor is a

470

senior officer of our movement who's come to observe today's operation. He's an old comrade-in-arms of my father — and I fought under him at Dien Bien Phu. For reasons of security he's known as 'Comrade Pham.' "

Dao Van Lat's lined face creased into a gentle smile as he studied Tuyet's appearance. Her combat clothes and her cheeks were smudged with earth from the tunnels, and she wore her hair scraped back severely from her face, but her proud bearing, her slender figure and the pistol on her thigh nevertheless made her a compelling figure. "Your reputation as a courageous fighter is well known," said Lat without taking his eyes from her. "But your beauty which is also widely spoken of still has the power to take a stranger's breath away."

"The latter is of little importance compared with the former," replied Tuyet, her face stiff and unsmiling. "Compliments about my appearance are of no interest to me."

Lat's gaze flickered briefly over the drab black tunic, which didn't entirely conceal the soft outline of her breasts, and for a fleeting moment somewhere deep inside him he felt a muted tremor of the agony that had continued to assail him intermittently over the years at moments like this; something indefinable in Tuyet's expression — perhaps it was a rare fusion of beauty and a fierce pride — made him think of Lien for the first time in many years, and suddenly it was as if a ghostly hand was forcing the honed edge of that glittering knife against his flesh once again. "For a patriotic woman of such great courage perhaps it's not important, Tuyet Luong," he said softly. "But for the impressionable young fighters you lead, I'm sure it helps inspire them to even greater deeds of bravery."

Tuyet stared straight in front of her and said nothing. Since joining the guerrilla forces she had deliberately kept her relationships with the men around her cold and impersonal, and she had never made any exceptions to this rule, even with high-ranking cadres. She was astute enough, however, to guess that "Comrade Pham" must have come south recently from Hanoi to help strengthen the Liberation Front's organization, and knowing that Communist purists saw her as an unreliable adventurist acting on emotional impulses, she decided it would serve no useful purpose to alienate his sympathy. "No doubt you yourself have come here to Long An province to perform special tasks of much greater importance, Comrade Pham," she said formally. "In which case, I wish you success."

"I've come to contribute my modest talents to the struggle which we all know will one day be crowned with a general uprising in the South," said Lat, his eyes twinkling as he served up the official Liberation Front line with elaborate courtesy. "I hope you and I will be able to work side by side towards that goal!".

"I'm ready to do whatever is required," replied Tuyet in a tight voice. "But for now I must return to my observation duties."

For several seconds Lat continued staring at the tunnel exit through which Tuyet Luong had left, then he walked thoughtfully over to where Dong was standing by the wall map. During their conversation a steady stream of messengers had been arriving with little envelopes containing slips of paper two or three inches square; most of the messengers were spindly-legged boys of not more than eight years of age, bare-chested and dressed only in ragged shorts, and Dong praised each one quietly before scrutinizing the information they'd brought. Their young faces mirrored their inner excitement as they waited impatiently for Dong's scribbled response, and he sent them all on their way with an encouraging pat on the head. A table beneath the wall map was already piled high with used slips, and pointing to them, Dong smiled.

"It's going to plan, Comrade Pham. All observers report that the Diemists and the Americans are advancing straight into our trap. They're in the second hamlet now, searching the huts and interrogating the old women again. It shouldn't take more than ten or fifteen minutes to get them where we want them."

Lat nodded his approval and accepted a little beaker of bitter yellow tea from one of Dong's aides. Sitting down beside the map, he sipped the steaming liquid thoughtfully. "Comrade Tuyet Luong is obviously a remarkable young woman. I seem to remember hearing that her husband was killed by Diemist torturers in Saigon — am I right?"

"Yes, two years ago. She swore then to avenge his death. He was Dang Dinh Luong — he joined the Viet Minh while he was a student."

"But she has mixed blood, doesn't she? Could that be what makes her so aloof?"

Dong shook his head. "I don't think so. In battle she's merciless — she fights just like a man, and she has killed many times. Perhaps the coldness is her way of keeping the strong emotions inside her under control."

472

Lat stared at the battalion commander with a pensive expression. "But there's just a hint of hysteria in her manner now. The hardness is becoming brittle."

Dong shrugged and smiled. "Your eyes are sharper than mine, Comrade Pham. I hadn't noticed anything."

"What's her family background, Dong?"

"Her mother came from a rich mandarin family, but she was born before her mother married and had to be raised in secret by relatives. She grew up very bitter and ran away to marry Luong when she was seventeen. They had two children, and people in the village say she was happy then for the first time in her life. When Diem's thugs murdered Luong, she had to go and identify his body — but she didn't weep. She just vowed there and then to avenge him."

"And did she?"

"Yes. She planted a bomb under a café table and killed his Vietnamese interrogators. She threw a grenade at two American CIA agents who'd questioned him too — but they weren't seriously hurt."

"How did she get into your battalion?"

"She had to flee from Saigon when another tortured prisoner gave her identity away. She brought her children to her husband's village near here, but she couldn't settle, and the local Liberation Front cadres persuaded her to join a special activities cell. She adopted her husband's name as a *nom de guerre* — Tuyet Luong — and without much persuasion she carried out several assassinations of corrupt village officials."

"Is that how you got to hear of her?"

Dong nodded. "Yes. About a year ago I put her in charge of a special assault platoon. Twenty or thirty percent of our fighters are females down here — but Tuyet Luong is by far the most fearless in all the main force units."

Lat drained his teacup and stood up. "And what have you assigned her to do today?"

"I've put her in command of two platoons — forty fighters. They'll advance through this field to kill any survivors of the ambush and drag away their weapons." He pointed to the map. "Between the third and fourth hamlets there's a dike half a mile long which the enemy will have to cross in single file. The canal runs along one side and we've set up a machine gun on the far side of the canal halfway along the dike. The Diemist troops will be strung out, so our gunner will make sure he doesn't hit too

473

many of them with his opening burst — just enough to make them all jump off the dike into the paddy field to take cover." He paused and smiled slowly. "We've lined the bottom of the bank with mines and *punji* traps and set up two other machine guns in a camouflaged tunnel opening in the top corner of the paddy so that they'll be firing along the bottom of the bank from close range at those who survive the mines and the traps. Tuyet Luong will take her men through the tunnels to the other side of the field and lead the charge to finish off the remnants."

"It sounds like an excellent plan, comrade — worthy of a *chien si Dien Bien*." Lat patted Dong warmly on the shoulder and nodded towards the Dien Bien Phu campaign insignia which the battalion commander still wore proudly on the left breast of his tunic. "How did you lay your trap? Enemy forces haven't penetrated into this region before, have they?"

"No, we moved five companies of the 514th Battalion through Moc Linh yesterday as bait. We made sure a known government informer saw them, and we ordered them to remain here until just before dawn. Then I marched them away into the jungle — they're ten miles from here now, hiding underground. Our agents tell us a whole battalion of Diemist troops is standing by to fly in when contact is made — that's why I'm putting only a small number of our fighters at risk. They can disappear quickly into the tunnels you see before an air strike is launched or any new troops are landed." He smiled again. "It's a simple operation."

A thin, tousled-headed boy dressed only in a pair of shorts rushed in with a message envelope at that moment and thrust it into Dong's hands. While he waited, he watched the older man's face intently, hopping excitedly from foot to foot.

"Good Little Slug, well run," said Dong softly when he had read the message. "Now race as fast as your legs will carry you through Tunnel Route Eleven — and stay and guard your mother and sister in the jungle for the rest of the day."

As the boy dashed out, grinning delightedly, Dong turned to Lat, his face serious again. "The enemy's now entered Hamlet Three. I'm ordering Tuyet Luong to take up position with the two assault platoons."

While the battalion commander scribbled another note, Lat called for more tea for them both and handed Dong a cup when he had finished. "That last messenger boy was your younger son, if I'm not mistaken," he said smiling. "The physical resemblance was very strong."

474

Dong's face softened as he drank his tea. "Yes, he's called Kiet — but as you heard he's known affectionately in the family as 'Little Slug.'"

"And don't you have an older boy too?"

"That's right — Minh is sixteen now. He's acting as a sniper for the first time today. I've ordered him to hide in a tree at the far end of the field and help attract enemy fire if we need to lure the company across the dike."

"But why do you give him such a hazardous task for his first battle?" asked Lat in a surprised voice.

Dong's face stiffened a little. "I don't want anyone to think I'm giving him special treatment because he's my son. I want his training to be hard like ours was. But anyway, Minh lives only for the liberation struggle — that's how I've brought him up. You should see his old Garand rifle — it's shinier than any weapon I've ever seen in my life!"

"But it wouldn't hurt to nurse him along a little, my old friend," said Lat gently. "Because your family suffered at Yen Bay and Vinh, there's no need to be quite so hard on Minh."

Dong sat staring at the map for a long moment. "It was here in Moc Linh that my father had the only plot of rice land he ever owned," he said at last in an emotional voice. "My brother, Hoc, and I were born in the village — only a mile from here. The land was confiscated when we couldn't keep up with our taxes and loan repayments, and it was then that my mother and father had to go and find work as domestic servants. Perhaps you can understand now why I jumped at the chance to come back here from the North. Here I can at least try to settle some of the old debts owed to my father — and Minh wants to do everything he can to help."

Lat nodded slowly and sighed. "Yes, Dong, I understand — life is so ironic, isn't it? Once your father and mother were forced to act as hired slaves for a French hunter and his rich American clients who came to our jungles for sport. If only they could've known that your sons and all our sons would one day become hunters in these jungles — and that the French *and* the Americans would become the quarry."

Dong glanced at his watch, nodding absently, and Lat saw for the first time the tension in his abstracted expression.

"Our snipers should just be taking up their positions now," said the battalion commander in a tight voice.

4

"How in hell's name can you fight a goddamned war if you can't find it?" muttered Captain Lionel Staudt through his clenched teeth as he stood, feet astride, in the center of Hamlet Three. It was ten thirty A.M., and the South Vietnamese soldiers were listlessly regrouping after completing another unproductive search of the huts. The usual knot of old women and small children had been assembled and questioned without result, and most of the troops now had dead ducks or chickens hanging from their packs, their minds obviously on the long noon break when they habitually cooked their main meal of the day; overhead the April sun was now producing a fierce, strength-sapping heat, and this was helping to heighten the tension between the Vietnamese officers and their perspiring American advisers.

"If we spent as much energy fighting it as we've done looking for it, this flyblown war would have been over a year ago!" Staudt moved into the shade of a clump of coconut palms, mopping his brow, and stood watching Lieutenant Trang conferring with Captain Hoang outside the last hut. "Or maybe I mean *not* looking for it. The only thing that's being 'sought and destroyed' around these parts so far today are three dozen Vietnamese barnyard fowl."

The British camera crew to whom the remarks had been addressed dumped their gear in the shade of the trees and sat down to rest, grinning broadly, but Naomi Boyce-Lewis, still looking cool and composed despite the heat, glanced out along the dike they would have to use to cross the shimmering expanse of rice fields to the next hamlet. "How much farther is this operation going, captain, could you tell me please?"

Staudt unslung his Armalite AR-15, leaned it against the trunk of a palm tree and took a long pull at his water canteen. "You're well aware by now, Miss Boyce-Lewis, that I don't have operational control here. If Americans had direct command in this theater, you'd see us whip the VC pretty damned quick. I gave my advice that we should search right through Moc Linh half an hour ago — but we have to wait while our little allies make up their minds whether to accept all of that advice, some of it — or none of it at all."

"Are you so very sure, captain, that the South Vietnamese don't want to beat the Communists just as much as you do?"

The well-bred English voice seemed suddenly incongruous to

the American amidst the torrid heat and rank animal odors of the Mekong delta hamlet; it conjured images in his mind of delicate traceries of lace, fine bone china, an obsequious butler with a tray entering from a dark panelled hall, and he looked at her quizzically for a moment. "Maybe one or two of them do — but President Diem's never really changed the old French colonial way of running this part of the world, you know. All forty-five provinces are still run by a bunch of majors and colonels — mandarins in military uniform."

"But that doesn't necessarily affect the quality of the army, does it?"

"If you're running a province or a district, you collect taxes, call all the shots and get plenty of kickbacks — especially if you can misappropriate a few million dollars' worth of American aid and supplies along the way. It makes more sense, doesn't it, to get rich as an army bureaucrat than to get yourself killed fighting the Viet Cong? So most of the ARVN officer corps want more than anything else to be fat cats behind a desk — and Captain Hoang's no exception."

The reporter glanced across the clearing to where the two ARVN officers were engaged in what appeared to be a heated conversation, and she saw Captain Hoang summon his radio operator and take the handset from him to speak into it.

"When I ship out of here in ten days time, Captain Hoang's supposed to have absorbed everything I learned in Normandy and Korea — that's the theory," muttered Staudt. "But Hoang's mind, if you ask me, is fixed on some quiet little provincial administrator's office where he can start feathering his own nest. . . ."

Lieutenant Gary Sherman returned to the group at that moment and nodded meaningfully at Staudt; on his instructions the young American had been using their radio quietly out of earshot to pass on their own recommendation to the American major at Seventh Division headquarters that the sortie be pressed rapidly into the three remaining hamlets. The U.S. major, they knew, was sitting side by side with the ARVN commander of the operation and could help override any reluctance of the Vietnamese officers on the spot to continue. Gary Sherman's confidential nod told Staudt that their message had been received and understood at headquarters, and he patted the lieutenant approvingly on the shoulder and moved away towards Captain Hoang.

When he'd gone, Gary Sherman grinned ruefully at the English reporter, removed his helmet and ran a hand over his close-cropped blond hair, which was dark with perspiration. "I guess to an outsider Captain Staudt can seem a little hard-boiled, Miss Boyce-Lewis," he said quietly after glancing circumspectly over his shoulder to check that he wasn't being overheard. "But that's just his way. He'd be the first to admit he's a soldier not a diplomat — but under all that tough talk he believes as much as any American officer out here in the job we're trying to do."

The English reporter nodded and smiled, touched by the earnestness of the young American officer who was several years her junior. "I quite understand, lieutenant. I can see your job isn't an easy one."

"I guess the captain tends to be a little hard on the ARVN troops — and their officers too. They're not really all as black as he paints them. A lot of them, like Lieutenant Trang, have good reason not to love the VC. And they can fight just as well as the VC do — they're the same people, after all. Families have been split down the middle since the time of the French war, and what it really boils down to is how well they're led. . . ."

Naomi Boyce-Lewis smiled again, more playfully this time. "For someone who's been out here only two weeks, lieutenant, you've obviously got a good grasp of the situation already."

Gary Sherman's youthfully handsome face crinkled suddenly into an embarrassed smile. "I'm sorry — I didn't mean to try to come on too strong, Miss Boyce-Lewis. I've still got a lot to learn, I realize that. But my father spent some time out here as a correspondent in the 'fifties." He paused and mopped his brow again, and a faintly shamefaced expression crossed his features fleetingly. "I haven't seen him in quite a while, but I guess I soaked up stuff like that from him without realizing it."

"Then perhaps I can try and pick your brains sometime if the two of us ever get the chance to have a quiet talk." She favored him with the kind of practiced, intimate smile that had long since become second nature to her when talking to men who might help her with information for her news stories, and the young American, flattered as she'd intended he should be, grinned with pleasure.

"I'd be glad to help you any time I can, ma'am."

Over his shoulder she saw Hoang call his interpreter to his side and begin speaking to Captain Staudt in excited high-pitched Vietnamese. "It looks as if we might be about to get some kind of decision now," she murmured, signaling to her crew to pick up their equipment, and all of them trooped across to listen.

"I had decided that we should curtail this operation and withdraw," the little interpreter was saying on Hoang's behalf while the Vietnamese captain stared angrily at his American counterpart. "But when I reported my intention to headquarters, to my astonishment my superiors countermanded my decision. They say the reserves are still standing by and can be here within minutes."

"So what are your orders, captain?" asked Staudt with scarcely concealed satisfaction.

Hoang's expression showed clearly that he knew he'd been out-maneuvered, and his pinched features darkened as he turned and pointed to the next hamlet. "We'll proceed to Hamlet Four at once! I've already told my men to move briskly across the dike in single file and not bunch together."

"You've what?" Staudt's voice was shrill with incredulity, and he stared aghast at the Vietnamese. "Have you taken a look at the terrain, Captain Hoang? That's the most exposed stretch of ground we've faced all morning — ideal for an ambush. If I wanted to set one myself, that is where I'd do it. Your men must go through the goddamned paddy. Spread 'em right across on a broad front. . . ."

The face of the Vietnamese remained as stiff as a mask, and although the American officer knew he must have understood him, Hoang insisted that his sergeant translate the reply. Then he rattled off another volley of Vietnamese, which the NCO conveyed haltingly into English. "The men are tiring. It's very hot. To make them wade through the mud and water again would be foolish. I've already given my orders, captain, and they won't be changed."

Staudt stared at him thunderstruck — then relaxed and drew a long exasperated breath. "Okay — so who's going point?"

The Vietnamese officer's jaw flexed several times as he struggled to conceal his anger at being questioned further. "Does it really matter who goes point approaching an obviously deserted village, Captain Staudt?"

"Yes, it sure as hell does matter! It has to be the best man you have! With a hundred soldiers moving forward one behind the other, they could all be killed with the same goddamned bullet if it keeps going long enough. The only two men who can return fire if there's a head-on attack are the point and his companion.

All your other men will be shooting each other up the ass if they open up!"

"Then Lieutenant Trang will go point!" The ARVN captain spat the words out rudely, then turned and strode away towards the rear of the column, motioning the waiting troops past him.

Lieutenant Trang, his handsome face expressionless, picked to accompany him a muscular little sergeant carrying one of the M-79 grenade launchers, and Captain Staudt, coming to a sudden decision, nodded towards Gary Sherman. The West Pointer immediately unslung his PRC-10 radio pack, and half a minute later the two young lieutenants led the column out onto the dike under the hot glare of the delta sun.

5

The Viet Cong machine gunner, concealed in a clump of palm trees about a hundred yards from the canal, curled a forefinger around his trigger as soon as he saw the ARVN column emerging from the shade of Hamlet Three. Spacing themselves carefully ten yards apart in accordance with their commander's orders, the government troops began to spread steadily across his field of fire like pop-up targets on a fairground rifle range. They were little more than silhouettes under the fierce flood of sunlight, but he could distinguish easily the bigger Americans among the smaller Asian troops; the taller, long-striding one near the front, the other, bulkier man humping a radio pack halfway down the line.

The guerrilla's captured Thompson machine gun, oiled and cared for more carefully than any other possession in his young life, was set up at right angles to the marching column halfway along the dike, and he had to curb his impatience to begin firing at once. He was under strict orders to wait until the last man was well clear of Hamlet Three; then the whole column would have to take cover down the far side of the bank where the fifty improvised mines were buried at two-yard intervals. They had been made from captured 105-millimeter shells, and the fuses in their tips had been replaced with percussion caps linked by wire to a detonator hidden in undergrowth at the edge of Hamlet Three; there, another guerrilla waited to activate all of them simultaneously thirty seconds after the machine gun opened up.

Before he left the cover of the trees, Captain Staudt, acting on an impulse, had called up the American major at headquarters and asked him to divert two armed HU 1-Bs to the area immediately; hairs that had sometimes prickled on the back of his neck in France in 1944 and amidst the bare hills of Korea nearly a decade later, hadn't felt quite comfortable suddenly. The major had promised he would get the choppers over as soon as he could, but they were supporting another skirmish at the moment. As he walked on across the dike, Staudt scanned the fields on either side ceaselessly for suspicious signs; an unnatural hush seemed to have fallen over the paddies, and he was certain now that his scalp had begun to tingle. He turned to look back at Captain Hoang, but the Vietnamese officer was walking near the back of the column, ignoring him, his lips still pursed in an expression of petulance and affront.

Staudt, cursing under his breath, turned to peer forward again, and he happened by chance to be looking directly at the clump of trees where the machine gun was concealed at the moment it opened up. He saw the first muzzle flashes spurt from the weapon as it began to hose the column from front to rear with a long unbroken burst of fire, and for a moment he stared at it stupefied. Then with the shrieks of half-a-dozen dying men ringing in his ears, he flung himself to the ground and swiveled to face the attack. Keeping his head low, he peered out under the rim of his helmet and began yelling for those around him to return fire on the tree clump. But there was no response, and when the machine gun began raking the column again in the opposite direction, he heaved himself reluctantly backwards off the dike into the paddy.

Fifty yards behind him Captain Hoang had gone over the edge the moment the machine gun started firing, screeching orders for his men to do the same. He fell straight into a small pit filled with three-foot-long bamboo spikes, and at least half of his men tumbled cursing into similar traps. But their oaths were drowned seconds later by the roar of the fifty howitzer "mines" exploding as one. Geysers of earth, flames and muddy water rose among the tumbling, shrieking bodies, and into this inferno the two other machine guns concealed in a gun port at the base of the bank poured long new bursts of withering fire.

One of the mines blew off both Lieutenant Trang's legs and hurled his broken body high into the air above the head of the horrified Gary Sherman; dazed with shock, the American stood up, looking wildly around for cover, but despite this foolish mistake — or perhaps because of it — he miraculously survived the first bursts of the twin machine guns. The squat Vietnamese sergeant with the M-79, in the eye of the storm with him, also escaped unscathed, and he remained crouching on the ground by his feet, his face frozen in an inane grin of fear.

His commanding officer, Captain Hoang, however, was less fortunate; as he twisted and flapped like a speared fish at the rear of the column, trying to free his feet and legs from the *punji* trap, he caught the eye of Ngo Van Minh, the eager young son of the Viet Cong's battalion commander. Settled comfortably in a sniper's nest in a tree bordering Hamlet Four, Minh watched Hoang intently, squinting through the sights of his gleaming World War Two Garand rifle, and when the company commander finally extricated his legs and flung himself gasping with pain on the bank, the boy squeezed off one careful shot. It missed by several feet, but taking his time, he fired carefully again, and this bullet hit Hoang low down in the back. His third shot, entering between Hoang's shoulder blades, killed him, and the elated boy, seeing the ARVN commander stop moving suddenly, defied all his orders and began scrambling down from his hideout.

In the opening barrage from the enfilading machine guns, Captain Staudt had been wounded in the chest. Wincing with pain and cursing the goddamned soldiers and officers he was fighting with and the goddamned country he was fighting in, he lay three-quarters submerged in the mud of the paddy, radioing the coordinates of their position for the helicopters and the T-28s which he was calling in to make a napalm attack on Hamlet Four. When he had replaced the handset, he glanced over his shoulder and saw that the British television crew had managed to scramble up the dike onto the path and against all the odds had almost reached the cover of the trees. One of them, the cameraman, was hobbling badly with a leg injury, and he saw that Naomi Boyce-Lewis was helping to support him, her arm about his shoulders. Not far away his camera lay shattered by a mine, and tangled skeins of film were spread around among the writhing bodies of wounded and dying Vietnamese. No more than two dozen of the troops, as far as he could judge, had escaped injury altogether.

Staudt began shouting fresh orders for fire to be directed along the bank at the machine gun nest, but nobody responded; those terrified Vietnamese who hadn't already been killed were obviously pretending they had, hoping they could escape that way, and he fished his own Armalite out from under the water where it had fallen. But even before he tried to fire it, he saw that mud and slime had clogged the moving parts, and cursing the weapon as well as the soldiers around him, he flung it away.

The Thompson that had first raked the column from across the canal had strewn half-a-dozen dead or dying bodies along the dike path before unaccountably falling silent; the mines and traps together had killed and maimed perhaps another thirty or forty men, and most of the two dozen or so ARVN troops who had survived these onslaughts had dived into depressions in the shallow paddy field to avoid the heavy-caliber machine-gun fire. A few, like Gary Sherman, after getting over their astonishment at finding themselves alive, had scrambled back up the bank to get clear of the deadly hail of frontal fire, and as he went, Gary had grabbed the petrified sergeant with the M-79 and hauled him bodily across the dike into the waters of the canal; crouching chest-deep to gain protection of the banks on both sides, he ordered the Vietnamese in sign language to load the grenade launcher. Christened "the elephant gun" by its users, the M-79 was a new weapon just introduced to the war. It looked like an enormous single-barreled shotgun, and its shell-shaped grenades sprayed enough hot metal in all directions on impact to kill everything within a twenty-yard radius. When the Vietnamese had loaded the weapon, to give him cover Gary straightened up suddenly and fired a long burst from his Armalite in the direction of the machine gun nest in the foot of the dike. The Vietnamese at his side grinned toothily, whether through relief or fear, Gary couldn't tell, and lifted the unfamiliar weapon to his shoulder. Because it was designed for ranges up to several hundred yards, the little sergeant had to adjust its sights repeatedly, and it took him several trial shots to get his aim; but with the American officer firing covering bursts and urging him on, he worked fast, slapping shells into the breech in quick succession, slamming it closed and firing. His fifth grenade turned out to be right, and it rose in a gentle arc to drop accurately into the corner of the paddy below their direct line of fire. Immediately both machine guns fell silent, and the Vietnamese turned his gap-toothed grin on Gary again, this time undoubtedly beaming with delight. But as the American patted him on the shoulder in congratulation, he realized suddenly why the Thompson across the canal behind them had stopped firing; from the corner of his eye he saw two platoons of black-garbed main force Viet Cong rising from their camouflaged foxholes on the opposite side of the field to begin charging through the muddy water towards them.

To Captain Staudt, lying prostrate in the muck of the paddy field, the skirmish line of Viet Cong seemed to be walking on water. He could see Captain Hoang slumped motionless on the bank of the dike, and since there were no commands coming from the point, he assumed Lieutenant Trang must be out of action too. At last, he realized, he had what he'd wanted so desperately for the past year — operational control! But the line of guerrillas was only twenty yards away now, close enough for him to see their narrow-eyed faces contorting with hatred as they splashed towards him with bayonets fixed, and he knew then that for him operational control was going to last about five seconds more. Hauling his pistol from its holster he took careful aim at the guerrilla racing ahead of the line — then with a palpable sense of shock he realized it was a woman and his finger faltered on the trigger; a second later several bullets from her revolver slammed into his head and chest, killing him instantly.

In the canal Lieutenant Gary Sherman brought his Armalite to bear on the advancing enemy, but it jammed without firing another shot, and he watched helplessly as the Viet Cong closed with the remnants of the company, some shooting and stabbing with their rifles, others wielding crude, village-smelted knives. Methodically amid the butchery, the front rank of the guerrillas began wresting rifles, ammunition and radio packs from the dead troops, and on his orders the sergeant at Gary's side fired his last two grenades at the second wave of attackers. But the speed of their advance made them a difficult target, and although one or two crumpled into the mud, the majority ran on and the last gaggle of ARVN survivors began flinging themselves into the canal in a desperate effort to escape the final act of the carnage in the paddy field.

Almost all of them had already tossed their weapons aside and they ignored Gary's desperate attempts to rally them. When he spotted one man still clutching his M-2, he rushed through the water to wrench it from him, and resting his elbows on the canal bank he sighted on the nearest Viet Cong, a dark-clad figure racing towards the head of the column where Lieutenant Trang lay dying. Like Captain Staudt before him, Gary Sherman experienced a moment of shock when Tuyet Luong turned her head in his direction; she hadn't noticed him until that moment, and he saw the expression of alarm spread across her unexpectedly beautiful face as she caught sight of his leveled rifle. For the briefest instant their eyes locked, and the startled American delayed his shot; then Tuyet ducked out of sight below the bank and was gone.

A moment later the two HU 1-Bs called in by Staudt as a precaution burst into view above the trees, their rotors thumping and stirring the quivering air above the battlefield. Immediately a whistle shrilled and the guerrillas broke off from their grisly task to begin racing back towards the camouflaged tunnel entrances in the far bank. In the few seconds it took for the heavily armed helicopters to swing around and start their attack, most of the guerrillas disappeared, dragging their war booty behind them, but out on the field the lone figure of young Minh was left struggling through the mud. From his sniper's nest in the tree he'd had to run twice as far as the rest of the two platoons to get in at the kill, and he had arrived among the prostrate government troops only moments before the helicopters appeared. He had seen the American captain toss away his Armalite, and after Tuyet Luong had shot the captain dead, Minh had been forced to grub around beneath the muddy water to find it. In his anxiety to catch up with his comrades he had fallen twice, and now as he panted across the field, weighed down by his Garand and the prized trophy of the new Armalite, he looked up and saw the first American helicopter sliding down through the air above him, bringing its guns to bear.

Because he was long-limbed like his father and a fast runner, he was sure he could dodge and sprint to outwit the unwieldly aircraft, despite the weight of the weapons he carried, and as he quickened his pace he gloried in the unexpected excitement; for as long as he could remember he had ached with impatience to grow up to be the kind of hero his father was, and now he'd be able to boast a little of how he had killed the Diemist captain with his third shot and then outwitted the American gunners in their iron skybirds. Perhaps he had disobeyed orders, but as soon as his father saw the new Armalite he would be proud of him, he was sure!

When the fiery red tracers from the HU 1-B's six-barreled machine guns punched into the muddy water just ahead of him, Minh turned abruptly aside and set off in a fast zigzag towards another set of tunnel entrances fifty yards away. The other helicopter, seeing this, swerved to cut him off, pumping its

7.62-millimeter bullets into the paddy at the ferocious rate of six thousand a minute — but again Minh swerved from its firepath and doubled back on himself, throwing them off his track.

Inside the first helicopter, the American gunner seated beside the pilot bent intently over his mirror gunsight, and a little grin of satisfaction began to spread across his face. "Okay, buddy boy," he said quietly, "I think you've had all your fun for today."

The pilot slid the Huey down a slow, slanting track, dropping almost to the ground behind the tiring Vietnamese boy, and the gunner rapidly traversed the four big Gatling-style machine guns mounted on either side of the landing skids. The controls were finger-light, and the ammunition belts linked to the storage holds in the rear of the aircraft jumped and quivered like living serpents as the four guns began roaring again. Minh, twisting and turning with increasing desperation, looked around fearfully as the helicopter swooped down at his heels, and to his horror he saw that this time he wasn't going to be able to avoid the great torrent of bullets kicking up a wake of spray behind him. A second later he felt himself lifted bodily from the ground and then he fell limp in the muddy water, cut almost in two at the waist. As he lay there, vaguely conscious that parts of his bleeding body littered the ground all around him, he experienced through the burning pain an even deeper agony. Could his life really be ending? Could it really be over before he'd even started to become a hero of the liberation struggle like his father?

As Tuyet Luong slid down into the moist darkness of her escape tunnel she was astonished to find Ngo Van Dong himself waiting at the foot of the shaft. His face was tense and pale, and she stared at him, at a loss for words: such a senior commander, she well knew, normally stayed in a secure area far away from the action, and his presence there could only mean that something had gone badly wrong.

"Where is Minh?" He shouted the question loudly, his face disfigured by his anger and anxiety.

"Wasn't he supposed to stay hidden in the tree?"

"He joined the assault against my orders. One of the messengers saw him go. He must still be in the field."

"I didn't see him," said Tuyet Luong slowly. "But I think there was somebody who was cut off by the helicopters. . . ."

Dong pushed past her up the exit shaft before she had finished speaking, and when he crawled out into the bright sunlight of the field, all was ominously quiet. For a second or two he crouched motionless in the tunnel mouth, his head cocked towards the sky — then he ran out into the paddy, scanning the few black-garbed bodies that lay half-submerged in the muddy water.

Only thirty yards from the edge of the field, he found Minh, his face and body reduced to little more than shapeless offal by the 7.62-millimeter rounds. He recognized him chiefly by the lovingly polished Garand rifle that was lying beside him, but it too, like the captured Armalite and everything else within a radius of several yards, was now stained with Minh's blood. As he stooped to pick up his son's mangled corpse, Dong heard the sudden beat of another HU 1-B's rotor beyond the trees of Hamlet Three; it had let down there in response to Staudt's last radio order to lift out the British television crew, and he saw it rising into view above the trees as he began stumbling back towards the tunnels bearing his wretched burden.

Inside the Huey, the co-pilot manning the attack weapons saw only an anonymous Vietnamese peasant in black pajamas hauling one of the dead bodies away towards a hole in the ground, and Naomi and her camera crew felt a fierce surge of heat as the twin rockets burst from the pods slung beneath the helicopter's skids. The gunner had targeted the weapons with unerring accuracy, and all those inside the Huey watched them explode with a hollow roar in the bank of the rice paddy. Ngo Van Dong was in the act of dragging his dead son into the mouth of a tunnel when he was hit, and the rockets blasted both their bodies to fragments in an instant. A great geyser of white smoke and black earth spiraled upwards, obscuring the point of impact, and the tunnel that collapsed around them became their tomb.

6

"The pride of a man can sometimes be his greatest asset, Comrade Tuyet — but too often it's his worst enemy!" Dao Van Lat muttered the words fiercely in the quiet of the deserted command post, but there was a break in his voice, and before he turned away from her, Tuyet Luong saw that his eyes were misting with tears. "If Comrade Dong hadn't been so determined to make his son a hero before he was ready, they might still both be with us here now!"

Tuyet sat white-faced at the table beneath the map, watching Lat pacing agitatedly back and forth across the beaten earth floor of the cellar; the ground above their heads shook occasionally with the impact of bombs that American T-28s, called in by the dying Captain Staudt, were still dropping, and the acrid gasoline stench of the blazing napalm was already seeping deep into the tunnel network. The two Liberation Army platoons that had taken part in the ambush had already dispersed safely through the subterranean escape shafts into the jungle, but Lat and Tuyet both knew that the dozen or so women and children who had been ordered to remain above ground in Hamlet Four could not have survived the saturation bombing.

"When I take the news to his family I know exactly what I'll find," said Lat, stopping before Tuyet and gazing down at her with a helpless expression in his eyes. "His younger son, 'Little Slug,' will be doing his duty 'looking after' his mother and sister and waiting happily for news of the battle — until now it's all been like a game to him. But then he'll see his mother begin weeping inconsolably and the rest of his life will be warped by what happened here today. His heart will grow heavy with hatred and the poison will have been passed to another generation." He stopped and raised his head to listen as the distant rumble of the air attack began to die away; then he began pacing again. "I worked with Dong's father in the early days of the revolution and spent many years in prison with him. They're a courageous family who've suffered greatly, and it pains me to see their suffering continue." His voice rose in exasperation and he punched his right fist angrily into the palm of his other hand. "Especially as it all could have been avoided if I'd been more alert."

"But what could you have done, Comrade Pham?" asked Tuyet in surprise. "You couldn't have foreseen what would happen to Minh."

"I ignored a danger signal. I should have overruled Dong when I found out that he was letting pride cloud his judgment about his own son." Lat swung around and came to stand in front of her again. "It's vital that we dedicate ourselves to our cause — but we shouldn't let it blind us to our own human needs. If we do, we could lose something more important than this war."

"But there's nothing more important than the war," protested Tuyet in an incredulous voice. "How can you say the war isn't important?"

"Of course the war's important — but we should always try to strike a balance with the other things in our lives." Lat fell silent and walked distractedly back and forth in front of her. Then he stopped and spoke again in a gentler voice. "A long while ago, Comrade Tuyet, I did something very foolish because I was too vain and too proud. I thought there was nothing more important to me than our cause, and I was foolish enough to think I could put myself beyond all normal feeling. As a result, I hurt somebody like you very deeply. . . ."

He let his right hand fall until it rested on her shoulder; at his touch she stiffened in her seat, holding herself rigid, and she didn't relax even when he began speaking again.

"I've rarely spoken of this, Comrade Tuyet, but I'm telling you because something about you reminds me of her. . . . She was beautiful and brave in just the way that you are." His voice broke with emotion and sank to a whisper. "I thought my love for her was distracting me from the revolution, you see, and I mutilated myself with a knife to put an end to what I thought of as my wasteful desires. But ever since then my dreams have been haunted by the faces of sons and daughters who might have been ours. Having no children, no offspring, I realize now, was too great a sacrifice to make. I regret what I did with all my heart and I always will."

Tuyet felt his hand tighten convulsively on her shoulder, and turned to find him gazing down at her with a look of deep compassion in his eyes. "But why do you speak to me of these things at a time like this?" she asked in a mystified voice.

"Because, comrade, I sense that you are making the same kind of mistake as I made. You have lost a beloved husband and your pain has been great. But without realizing it you are destroying yourself. In trying to stifle the pain, you've stifled all human feeling. If you continue to do that, you'll forget how to feel love and kindness. Hatred can devour you from within. Soon your life will become as arid as mine."

"Since my husband, Luong, was murdered I haven't dared allow myself to feel love for any living creature," said Tuyet savagely. "If I let myself weaken, somehow I know I'll only suffer some terrible new loss."

"Don't your children deserve your love, Comrade Tuyet?" he said carefully. "Don't they need you?"

"They are well cared for by their grandmother," she said fiercely. "If I let myself think of them I wouldn't be able to do

489

what I have vowed to do — avenge Luong's death." Her eyes flashed and her voice rasped in her throat. "And I wouldn't be able to do what I did today!"

"What was that?" He moved around to face her again. "Tell me about it."

"I killed the Diemist lieutenant in cold blood — but if I'd let my feelings get in the way I might not have been able to do it."

"Why?"

Suddenly her lower lip was trembling. "Both his legs had been blown off at the waist by one of our mines. He was still conscious and as I bent over him to take his pistol he tried to speak. But no words came out — he could only make a gurgling noise. He was like me, Comrade Pham — a *métis*. I took his pistol and turned away, but then I heard the gurgling sound again. I looked around and saw him pointing to the pistol. I'll never forget the awful pleading look in his eyes. In battle you expect to find only hatred in the face of the enemy — but he really wanted me to help him die." She closed her eyes, and Lat saw tears squeeze from beneath her lids. A moment later her shoulders began shaking silently. "I shot him in the head with his own pistol just before the helicopters came. He didn't make any sound at all — he just rolled over on his side."

She choked on her last words and buried her face in her hands, wracked by a fit of sobbing. Lat watched her for a moment, then reached out his hand and patted her shoulder consolingly. "Comrade Tuyet, this war will see many more tragedies yet before it's won — but you've done enough here. Let your agony pass now — today's horror may have been a blessing in disguise. With your education you could serve the Front better doing intelligence work. Take your children with you and go away from this region. I'll arrange a new post. Put the past behind you and try to look to the future."

She looked up at him, nodding mutely, then without warning she seized his hand in both of her own and pressed it against her tearstained cheek. "This is the first time I've wept since the day Luong died," she whispered. "The very first time."

7

The early morning sun of Tuesday, June 11, 1963, flooded the streets of Saigon with dazzling yellow light. Without discrimination it illuminated the elegant, tree-shaded French boulevards, which were old, the high-rise, air-conditioned American apartment buildings that were brash, new and still rising, and the crowded shack and shanty slums huddled in the timeless habit of Asia along the city's narrow canals and waterways. It shone, too, on yet another marching column of Buddhist demonstrators, and its radiance turned the saffron robes of the priests to shimmering mantles of gold. It was barely nine o'clock, and in the early glare, the bowed, shaven heads of the monks and nuns were indistinguishable as they shuffled along, pressing their palms together in the traditional pose that reflected the passive, contemplative roots of their ancient faith.

Because most of them were barefooted, the four hundred demonstrators padded noiselessly out of the dusty lane that led from their pagoda onto Phan Dinh Phung, the central, north-south boulevard known under the French as the Rue Richaud. Marching four abreast and carrying cloth banners attacking the Catholic government of President Diem, they headed for the heart of the city, but although they passed through streets filled with rush-hour traffic, their demonstration did not excite special attention. Such demonstrations had become almost commonplace following an incident in Hue in early May; then, government troops had killed several Buddhists protesting against a government ban on the flying of their flag, and the sense of outrage among the normally quiescent Buddhist monks had sparked off a wave of protests throughout South Vietnam. Only one thing distinguished the demonstration of June 11 from hundreds of others like it — half-a-dozen senior Buddhists were not marching on foot like the others but rode at the head of the column in a battered green Austin saloon car. Among them on the rear seat sat Thich Quang Duc, an unassuming monk in his early seventies whose pinched, bony features reflected the austere, ascetic life he had always led; straight-backed and unmoving, he stared fixedly ahead through the windshield, his face composed in an expression of blank concentration, and to the few onlookers who stopped to watch the marchers go by, he appeared no different from the other bonzes seated beside him. But in the privacy of his thoughts Thich Quang Duc was preparing to endure voluntarily several minutes of the fiercest physical agony a man can suffer — an agony that he knew would be relieved only by his death.

As the procession moved slowly along Phan Dinh Phung, to calm his rising panic he reminded himself that he had spent his whole life practicing *Thien*, a philosophy and mode of living which gave a man the power to master his inner self and make his will implacable. Without being conditioned by any set of dogmatic beliefs, *Thien* demanded of its adherents rigorous techniques of diet, breathing, meditation and concentration, and because he had always been a devoted priest and practitioner, Thich Quang Duc knew that at that moment he was closer than ever before to attaining *Satori*, the cosmic awareness that was the goal of his religion. Hadn't all his deeds and thoughts since childhood been aimed at achieving this elusive state of perfection? Hadn't every act of devotion taken him another step along the path towards the ultimate moment of fulfillment that was now at hand? Mustering all his considerable powers of concentration, he willed his mind to dwell only on this thought to the exclusion of all else, and gradually his apprehension began to diminish. Fingering a string of fifty-four holly oak seeds, he repeated over and over again the whispered mantra "*Nam Mo Amita Buddha*" — Return to Eternal Buddha — and as his lips formed and reformed the sacred phrase, a sense of peace and joy began flooding through him and eventually became so profound that he ceased to be aware of his surroundings.

To the bystanders at the curbside that morning, however, Thich Quang Duc remained anonymous and unremarked in the shadowy interior of the car — and even the car itself attracted little attention. The Scottish television cameraman working with Naomi Boyce-Lewis at first didn't bother to film the vehicle at all. Walking backwards at the head of the parade, still limping slightly from his Moc Linh *punji* wound, he concentrated instead on holding the brightly garbed figures of the marching monks in tight focus as they moved towards him, and at the junction where Phan Dinh Phung met Le Van Duyet, he dropped the camera from his shoulder briefly to rest. As he hand-cranked its clockwork mechanism, Naomi Boyce-Lewis moved up close beside him and spoke quietly in his ear.

"Be sure, Jock, won't you, to get a good shot of the car driving over the crossroads."

The Scot turned his perspiring face towards the reporter and rolled his eyes in exasperation. "The car? I've been doing my damnedest to keep it out of shot up to now. A broken-down British jalopy like that doesn't exactly conjure up the timeless rituals of Buddhism, does it? In fact it beats me why we're filming this parade at all. It looks just like a hundred other Buddhist demos we've seen."

The reporter sighed and shook her head. "Jock, a Buddhist bonze doesn't come to my room in the Continental at six A.M. every day to tell me 'something very important is about to happen.' Let's just take him at his word and film everything carefully, shall we? There are monks in the car too."

"Okay, Naomi, as long as it's understood I'm not paying for wasted footage." The Scot glanced at the soundman, who was busy picking up street noises on his directional microphone, and raised his eyebrows in a good-natured expression of complaint. Then he turned and began filming the march again, taking care this time to include the car.

The small crowd that gathered to watch the demonstration cross the busy intersection was mainly Vietnamese, but here and there among them, Naomi recognized some of the American wire service and newspaper journalists then resident in Saigon; it was obvious that hers had not been the only name on the Buddhist visiting list that morning, but she noted with a little surge of satisfaction that no other television crew had shown up, so whatever the promised sensation turned out to be, her coverage would be exclusive. Inwardly she congratulated herself on the time she had spent cultivating the English-speaking monks at Xa Loi, the main Saigon pagoda, and to encourage Jock to greater efforts she moved to his side again to point out that his would be the only television news camera present. As she stepped back onto the pavement, she felt a hand on her elbow and turned to find herself looking into the face of a smiling, dark-haired American who was holding out his hand in greeting.

"I'm Guy Sherman, foreign service officer, American Embassy — you must be Naomi Boyce-Lewis, the famous survivor of Moc Linh."

She studied the face intently for a moment; lean, tanned, with a hard, determined mouth, it belonged to a man in his late thirties who made no secret of his high degree of physical self-assurance, and because she sensed instinctively that such a man must hold a responsible post at the embassy which gave him access to high-level political information, she smiled warmly in response and allowed him to take her hand. "I'm surprised the safety of a mere

English television journalist should even have come to the notice of someone like you, Mr. Sherman," she said lightly. "I thought you had your hands full trying to run a war and prop up your friend President Diem."

"You're right — the workload's killing lesser men. But perhaps you remember Lieutenant Gary Sherman? He's my nephew, and he talked a lot about 'this devastating English blonde' who kept her cool when all around her were losing theirs." He smiled directly into her eyes as he spoke, letting her see that she had aroused an immediate sexual interest in him. "And let me say for the record that I go along with every word of young Gary's description of you."

Holding his gaze coolly, she inclined her head an inch in acknowledgment of the compliment. "Gary never spoke of his uncles — there wasn't time. But if he had I would have imagined them as older men."

"I was only twelve when Gary was born — I was a late twinkle in my father's eye, I guess." Guy Sherman's lean face creased in another grin. "But let's save my family history for another time, shall we? I happened to overhear you talking with your cameraman about how the bonzes gave you newspeople the nod today on this march. I'd like to have the opportunity to buy you a drink and hear some more about that sometime."

"Why does that interest you?"

Still smiling, Guy Sherman made a little dismissive gesture with his hands. "Would you believe that we're having a helluva job at the embassy making any contact at all with the Buddhists? We can't do it openly because President Diem and his family see it as consorting with the enemy." He paused and glanced around quickly to see if they were overheard, then laid a hand on her arm. "It won't be a one-way trade, Miss Boyce-Lewis. Maybe I can give you one or two pointers in return to ease the chores of news gathering."

The lips of the English journalist parted in a little conspiratorial smile. "That sounds like a reasonable deal."

"Okay, how about eight o'clock this evening, then? On the terrace at the Continental? And please call me Guy. . . ."

At that moment her soundman touched her arm and interrupted them. "Look, Naomi — something odd's happening."

She turned to find that the car carrying the Buddhist bronzes had halted unexpectedly in the middle of the intersection. The marchers were moving past it, walking suddenly with greater purpose, and they quickly formed themselves into a ring that effectively cordoned off the junction. At the same time the monks alighted gravely from the green Austin and one of them raised its hood. Leaning inside he lifted into view a five-gallon plastic container filled with a dark liquid, then walked slowly towards the center of the intersection beside Thich Quang Duc. Another monk carried a cushion, and when they reached their chosen spot he placed it reverently on the asphalt surface of the road.

Thich Quang Duc lowered himself slowly onto the cushion in the yogic lotus posture, and when he had composed himself with his legs folded beneath him, he placed his hands, one on top of the other, in his lap. For several seconds he remained immobile, lost in the depths of meditation, then he opened his eyes and nodded once towards his helpers. The monk holding the plastic container immediately began splashing its contents onto Thich Quang Duc's head, and the liquid coursed down his neck and shoulders, darkening his saffron robe and spreading out in a puddle all around him on the roadway. The faint morning breeze wafted the pungent fumes of the gasoline swiftly towards the crowd of onlookers on the pavements, and when they realized what they were about to witness, little muffled gasps of horror broke from several throats.

"May the saints preserve us," breathed the Scottish cameraman as he continued filming beside Naomi. "This time they really mean business."

In an electric silence Thich Quang Duc's helpers placed the empty plastic container on the ground a few feet away from him and retreated to join the circle of onlookers. For several seconds Thich Quang Duc himself remained perfectly still, sitting stiffly upright, then the crowd saw his lips move to frame one final mantra before his hands fluttered briefly in his lap.

The flames that spurted from his body as he struck the match smote the morning air with a hollow thump; twisting and fluttering in the breeze, they seemed at first to be dancing on the head and shoulders of the impassive monk without harming him, and only gradually did his face and robes begin to char and blacken inside the pillar of fire. But even then no utterance escaped his lips, and he remained unmoving in his cross-legged posture on the ground.

All around the circle, the other monks and nuns pressed their hands together in prayer and stared transfixed at the blazing figure; from time to time moans of anguish rose from their ranks, and when the sickly sweet smell of burning flesh became recognizable amidst the reek of gasoline, there were sounds of weeping among the Vietnamese crowds behind them. Some white-uniformed Saigon policemen with tears streaming down their faces tried to break through the cordon of monks to put out the flames but they were held back.

"Do you want to try voicing a piece to camera, Naomi, with the flames behind you?" asked the cameraman in a strangled whisper as he stopped to put in a fresh magazine of film. "These pictures are probably going to go right around the world."

For a second or two she stared at him aghast; the awful spectacle of the fiery suicide had left her dry-mouthed with horror, and the odor of roasting human flesh was beginning to bring on a feeling of nausea. "I can't, Jock — it's too damned awful. Just film it straight and I'll do a 'voice-over' commentary later."

"But we may never get a better story than this in our whole lives, Naomi," he hissed, refocusing the camera with shaking hands. "This could make your face famous in five continents."

She turned round to stare with anguished eyes towards the blazing figure of Thich Quang Duc; the puddle of gasoline on the ground all around him that had ignited at the outset to produce a broad pyramid of fire had almost burned out, and the flames were now concentrating all their fury on the body of their victim. In their midst, the monk's blackened head made him look more like some primeval, mummified totem than a man, but still the rigorous self-control exercised by his living mind held his agonized body erect.

"Don't worry about what you'll look like or sound like, Naomi," persisted the cameraman in an undertone. "It won't hurt to be a bit emotional — the main thing is to be seen here."

"You're right, Jock!" She nodded towards the soundman, and when he handed her a microphone she moved swiftly to a position where the blazing body of the monk could be seen over her shoulder. Closing her eyes to compose her thoughts, she waited until she heard the whir of the camera, then opened them again and gazed steadily into the lens.

"Watching a man burn himself to death in public is an experience too awful to describe accurately in words," she said in a voice that trembled. "So I won't try — but the Buddhists of South Vietnam couldn't have chosen a more dramatic way of expressing the growing opposition to the government of President Diem, which they see as oppressive and corrupt. The monk has chosen to take his own life in a fountain of flame in Saigon because the Buddhists are convinced now that their country would be better served by a different government. And this horrifying scene should make America and the rest of the Western world think too — because the United States is now lending massive military and economic support to the government here in a spreading war against Communism."

Naomi Boyce-Lewis paused and glanced around at Thich Quang Duc; in the extremes of agony his blackening body was beginning to twitch involuntarily from time to time, but still his fierce resolve held him upright in the lotus posture, and with the aid of a megaphone, one of the watching monks had begun to chant repeatedly in English and Vietnamese: "A Buddhist priest burns himself to death — a Buddhist priest becomes a martyr!" Cloth banners bearing the same slogans in Vietnamese and English were also now being unfurled by other monks, and Naomi read them quickly before turning back to the camera.

"Death by burning may seem to us to be a particularly barbaric and savage way to make a political protest — but it shouldn't be thought that South Vietnam's Buddhists don't know how to put their message across in the modern world. They were careful to ensure that a few selected Western journalists would be present here, myself among them — and those English banners and slogans make it clear their protest is as much directed at the ears and eyes of Washington as at their own government. But when all that's been said, standing here today still leaves me with one overwhelming feeling — a deep sense of revulsion and horror. . . ."

The moment she finished speaking, she turned with professional deliberation to look again towards the dying monk, and the cameraman used his telephoto lens to move into a new close-up of the fiery figure. Almost ten minutes had passed since Thich Quang Duc struck the match that had set his body ablaze, and at last he had begun to sway from side to side. New shrieks and moans of anguish rose from the watching crowd, then suddenly the monk's body toppled over backwards in the pool of flame. For several seconds his arms and legs jerked spasmodically and his fingers clutched vainly at the air beyond the shroud of fire enveloping him; then he flung his arms wide, as though in one last act of supplication, and his whole body shuddered convulsively before he finally lay still.

By the time the last of the flames had died away, a truck drew up carrying a simple coffin, but the rigidity of Thich Quang Duc's limbs, outstretched in his death agonies, made it impossible for his corpse to be placed inside. After a hurried consultation, half-a-dozen monks removed their orange robes, bound them about the body and set off to carry their burden to the Xa Loi pagoda, a quarter of a mile away. The circle of demonstrators opened to let them pass, then they regrouped into a column and fell into step behind. As the procession wound its way through the heavy morning traffic, a bell in the pagoda began to toll a solemn death knell, and the crowds that had gathered at the intersection began drifting away, speaking in uneasy whispers of what they'd witnessed. As he moved off towards his embassy car, Guy Sherman stopped to touch Naomi lightly on the shoulder.

"That was a very impressive performance indeed," he said quietly.

She glanced around at him in puzzlement, uncertain of his meaning. "Are you talking about the Buddhist monk — or me?"

"Both of you," he said raising one eyebrow slightly. "And I'm looking forward more than ever now to talking to you tonight."

8

By eight-fifteen that evening the terrace of the Continental Palace Hotel was filling up with its regular nightly crowd of Americans from the embassy, the aid agencies and the U.S. Military Assistance Command. Most of the soldiers, still under orders not to flaunt their uniforms in public more than necessary, were dressed in civilian clothes, and here and there a few sleek middle-class Vietnamese with government connections were talking earnestly with their white-skinned benefactors. Guy Sherman had arrived early to make sure of the table in the corner of the terrace where he could sit with his back to the wall and scan the sidewalks of Duong Tu Do — Freedom Street — as the old Rue Catinat had been renamed on the departure of the French; from that vantage point, too, he was able to watch the exits from the hotel without shifting in his seat, and he spotted the English television reporter the moment she stepped out onto the terrace. Her pale blond hair, normally pinned back tidily from her face, fell in soft waves to her shoulders, and as she came towards him he saw that she had forsaken her workday safari jacket and trousers for a fashionable suit of natural cream shantung that looked as if it might have been tailored in Paris. She moved with an easy assurance, obviously aware that many male eyes were turning to follow her, and she paused only once to talk to a waiter. By the time she reached Guy's table he was on his feet holding one of the deep wickerwork chairs for her, and he smilingly waved aside her murmured apology for lateness.

"Don't worry about it — those fifteen minutes gave me the chance to work out why you choose to stay here in this crumbling French hotel when you could have a nice modern air-conditioned room at the Caravelle on the other side of the square. I've decided that it has to be the faded red damask and the cracked chandeliers — they must bring back happy memories of imperial grandeur for all you dyed-in-the-wool European colonialists, don't they?"

He smiled teasingly as he spoke, but to his surprise she sat down without responding; for a moment she glanced around the crowded terrace, acknowledging the friendly waves she received from the huddle of resident American foreign correspondents seated at a distant table. But when she turned to look at Guy, her face was serious again.

"The last letter I ever received from my father was written on Continental Palace notepaper," she explained, her tone distant. "He wrote to me from here the day before he was killed in the autumn of 1945. I was nine at the time, and I'd been waiting for five years for him to come home — I suppose that's the main reason why I stay here."

The smile faded instantly from the American's face. "Naomi, I'm sorry, I didn't know. I hope you'll forgive my undiplomatic gaffe."

A waiter arrived at the moment with a chilled *vin blanc cassis* that she had obviously ordered herself on the way to the table and she sipped it for a moment in silence. Then she sighed and smiled wearily at him. "I'm sorry too — I didn't mean to sound quite so offensive." She closed her eyes and pressed her fist against the space between her eyebrows. "Today's events haven't left me with much in the way of emotional reserves, I'm afraid."

"There's no need to apologize at all," said Guy hastily. "You must have had a helluva time. Did you get your film out okay?"

She nodded. "I went to the expense of sending my sound recordist out to Hong Kong with the spools hidden under his shirt — I couldn't risk the film being confiscated at the airport. But ever since the story broke, my London newsroom's been clamoring for more explanatory commentary by telephone."

"They're not the only ones. The stills taken by one of the wire service men here have already hit the front pages of the late editions back home — and every damned office in the White House, the State Department and the Pentagon is screaming frantically for authoritative explanations."

Naomi continued to sip her drink without taking her eyes from his face. "And what's your embassy telling them?"

He glanced about him with studied casualness for a second or two, then peered intently into his glass of bourbon. "I wish there was a clear and simple answer to that question — but there isn't."

"I thought you said this morning, Guy, that this was to be a two-way trade." In using his Christian name for the first time, she seemed to inject a subtle hint of intimacy into her voice, and he looked up to find her smiling archly at him.

"That's right, Naomi, I did," he said slowly. "But this may be one instance where your guess is as good as mine. Our so-called experts on oriental religions in the embassy don't even seem to be able to agree among themselves on such simple damned things as exactly how many Buddhists there are in this country. You can take your pick on any number between twenty and eighty percent of the population — then every figure will be qualified by talk of Confucianism, Taoism and the worship of spirits. The one thing they seem to be sure about is that there are only a million and a half Vietnamese Catholics — and most of them are either in the government or the officer corps of the army." He sighed loudly in his exasperation. "What are you telling your viewers in England?"

"I spent hours haunting Xa Loi and one or two other smaller pagodas and talked to several venerable old monks who weren't seeking out Western journalists. One of them told me that ritual suicide has never been seen as an act of despair in Vietnam — it's traditionally been an honorable and unanswerable means of proving virtue and demonstrating the guilt of a more powerful opponent. He reminded me too that a great river doesn't rise in flood because it's pulled from the front — it's the massive weight of water pushing from behind that unleashes the torrent. When I asked him exactly what he meant by that, he just gave me a toothy smile and said Buddhist priests would never try to lead the people unless they were absolutely certain that their feelings had already reached a flashpoint."

"And did you build your piece around that information?"

Naomi nodded. "Yes, I think President Diem's trigger-happy brother probably did the government a great disservice when he rolled his tanks over those few Buddhist marchers complaining about the banning of their flag in Hue. It seems to have sent apathetic Buddhists flooding back into the pagodas in their thousands and brought to a head all the resentment that has been building up against Diem for years. Some of the bonzes told us privately weeks ago they were planning a public suicide. Of course we could all be wrong, even now — the Viet Cong might somehow have stage-managed the whole business. But I suppose we'd need a friendly CIA man to tell us the score on that."

She smiled mischievously, shrugging her shoulders out of her jacket at the same time, and Guy saw that she wore a sheer silk blouse beneath it; in the act of turning to hang the jacket on her chairback, the thin stuff of the blouse stretched tight across the points of her breasts, and the filmy lace and shoulder straps of her brassiere gleamed tantalizingly white suddenly against her suntanned skin. In that moment he was seized by a powerful urge to see her beautiful, disdainful face clenched tight in the extremes of sexual abandon, to hear her well-bred English voice moaning and gasping with pleasure beneath him, and he drew in a long, slow breath as he waited for her to turn and face him again. When she did, he looked directly into her eyes and lowered his voice.

"So far, Naomi, there's no evidence of Viet Cong involvement at all — although it's sure as hell the kind of trick they'd like to pull." He paused and let the corners of his mouth relax in a confidential smile. "But if we get anything on it, let me assure you you'll be the first to know — unattributably, of course."

"Of course." She held his gaze as she drained her glass and allowed him to take it from her hand when it was empty. While he summoned the waiter, she stared thoughtfully out into the traffic-filled plaza surrounding the old Opera House which had been converted to house the National Assembly. The nightly swarm of cars and motor scooters that had flooded into Saigon under the American economic aid programs were filling the humid night air with their acrid exhaust fumes; many of the scooters were being ridden by slender Vietnamese girls, and the split skirts of their gossamer-light *ao dai* fluttered in their wake like the wings of butterflies. All along Tu Do she could see more evidence of change; gaudy neon signs in English pointed the way to countless dimly lit bars with names like "The Shack," "The

Capitol," "Fifth Avenue" and through their open doors the raucous jangle of Western pop music could be heard day and night. In their gloomy interiors she knew that painted Vietnamese bar girls waited to welcome the growing population of American GIs whenever they took time off from fighting the Viet Cong, and she found herself wondering how different her father would have found the French colonial capital he'd last known in 1945. Would he even recognize the tawdry, honky-tonk hybrid city that was now part Asian, part Western but becoming increasingly corrupted, it seemed to her, by American aid and spending power. . . .

"Here's to Anglo-American cooperation, Naomi!" Guy's voice broke into her thoughts, and she turned back to the table to find him holding a new drink in his hand. Picking up the *vin blanc cassis* that a waiter had just placed in front of her, she clinked her glass against his.

"Long may it thrive." She returned his smile and fumbled in her handbag until she found a small sheet of Continental Palace notepaper on which she'd written the name of the Buddhist monk who'd alerted her that morning to the suicide. She placed it face-down on the table, still smiling, and pushed it towards Guy but didn't release it. "Here's the first installment from England — but before I part with it I'd like to ask you one or two questions."

"Fire away. As many as you like."

"Why do you need my sources so badly? You must have your own at the embassy."

"Sure we have some — but this situation is so damned volatile and not a little unfathomable. So every lead we can get our hands on could be vital."

"But doesn't the confusion make you and your colleagues a little uneasy sometimes? Don't events like today's make you worry about the wisdom of America's role here?"

"Naomi, we don't set policy at the embassy. We just try to supply a clear picture of what's happening here. It's for others in Washington to make the decisions — you know that."

"But that doesn't mean you don't have opinions."

"Of course not. But believe me, everybody in the embassy is one hundred percent behind the military effort we're making here — especially me. I'm sure deep in my bones what we're doing is right." He put down his drink and leaned earnestly towards her across the table. "What's happening here, Naomi, is part of a worldwide Communist offensive. They call it a 'war of liberation' in their doublespeak — but they're using the same kind of subversion and infiltration techniques here as they're using all over the world. This way the Communists in Moscow and Peking can chip away at the West's security country by country without risking a major confrontation. Unless we make a firm stand in South Vietnam and anywhere else they choose to fight, the West could go under without a single missile being fired or a single border being crossed. Communism's got to be stopped — don't make the mistake, Naomi, of thinking this isn't an important war. It might even be more important than World War Two."

"I don't think anyone in Whitehall would disagree with any of that, Guy — they wouldn't work up as much enthusiasm and conviction as you do, of course, but they would go along with the general philosophy." She smiled and implied admiration of his energy by her tone of voice. "But what I was really wondering is whether a war like this can be won — especially after my experience at Moc Linh."

"Moc Linh wasn't typical," said Guy quickly. "The war's being fought on two fronts and being won on both — that's an inside view, believe me, from someone with access to all the important data. We're keeping the Viet Cong on the move now with fast deployment of the ARVN troops in helicopters and armored rivercraft. You've seen the Hueys with their 7.62-millimeter miniguns and rockets, you saw the T-28s and the effectiveness of our artillery and napalm attacks — we're smoking them out fast now with our superior technology. And on the political front we've got ten million people safely walled up now inside the same kind of fortified hamlets that you British used to win your ten-year war against Communism in Malaya. You've seen the bamboo palisades, haven't you? Don't they look a little like the old cavalry stockades out West? Well take it from me, Naomi, we're winning out here in the East as surely as we won in the old West."

"But the French fought here for eight years and killed possibly a million Viet Minh — and still they lost. Doesn't that ever give you sleepless nights?"

"The French didn't fight the right way, Naomi. And they didn't have our technology. What's more they were colonials. We Americans, remember, were the first nation to throw off the colonial yoke. We're not tainted with a colonial past." He rolled his eyes humorously. "Funny how easily you English forget that."

"Perhaps none of us think enough about history."

503

Guy shook his head emphatically. "I don't think that's true. I believe worrying too much about history impedes action. Determination and the will to act are the vital ingredients in a situation like this. Those two qualities are what sets America apart. I guess that's the chief thing my father taught me. He's represented Virginia in the United States Senate for over forty years now living by those principles."

"But 'determination and the will to act' aren't bringing home the bacon, are they, according to those gentlemen over there?" She nodded in the direction of the resident American correspondents. "They've been out on a lot more patrols than I have, and they're not sending glowing reports back home to their editors, are they?"

Guy glanced briefly towards the youthful group of American journalists and his expression hardened. "There's more than one war going on in Saigon, Naomi, unfortunately. Our press corps and the embassy are barely on speaking terms."

"Why's that?"

"They're probably friends of yours, so I'd better choose my words carefully. Let's just say we suspect they look for bad news — sensational news — all the time because that's the stuff that they think's more likely to win them a Pulitzer Prize. They love nothing better than to write slanted stories about how badly the war's going and how tyrannical the Diem government is."

"Is that why you're so set on cultivating my friendship, Guy?" She smiled faintly as she spoke to take the sting out of the remark. "Do you hope I at least will tell it the way your embassy wants it told?"

He paused in the act of lifting his drink to his lips and looked at her thoughtfully; then his rugged face softened in a half smile. "You're not only a very beautiful and determined woman, Naomi — you're obviously a very perceptive one too. Sure, the embassy's got an interest in seeing the news look right — seeing it told the way it really is. But I promised you, didn't I, that if you help me, I'll help you. That's the way I want it to be — and if along the way we become good friends, I won't object to that."

She brushed a lock of hair from her eyes with one hand and smiled enigmatically. "Neither will I."

Without taking his eyes from hers, he placed his middle finger on the slip of paper on which her hand still rested and drew it across the table. She watched him for a moment, but before he could turn it over she reached out and covered his hand with her own.

"Just one more thing, Guy," she said softly. "The information you give me will be unattributable — but the same thing must always go for anything coming from me to you. That name and address are given in the strictest confidence."

"That goes without saying." When she leaned back in her seat he folded the paper without looking at it and slipped it into an inside pocket of his jacket. Then he drained his glass and stood up. "I've enjoyed our talk, Naomi. I hope we'll get to see a lot of one another."

He let his gaze linger on her for a moment longer, then walked quickly away down the terrace steps into the evening crowds thronging Tu Do. Before she'd finished her drink the little knot of American reporters broke up and began to depart. They smiled at her as they passed her table and the last one, the young correspondent of a major wire service, stopped beside her and pulled his sunglasses from his pocket. Turning up his jacket collar around his ears, he put on the glasses and glanced exaggeratedly about the terrace before bending to speak to her in an undertone.

"Be most careful, Miss Boyce-Lewis," he hissed in a comic foreign accent. "We all suspect Mr. Sherman is a spook. We thought you ought to know — for your own safety!"

She smiled broadly at the pantomime act of secrecy. "A spook?"

The journalist hunched his shoulders higher around his ears and leaned closer. "Counterinsurgency specialist, Special Forces liaison — all that nasty, shadowy stuff the CIA gets up to out here. You've been warned, Miss Boyce-Lewis."

"There's no need to worry," she whispered. "I'd already worked that out for myself."

The American removed the glasses and raised his eyebrows high in feigned astonishment. Then he grinned again and hurried away to catch up his colleagues, walking bent double across the crowded terrace in a Groucho Marx crouch.

9

The high-ceilinged, marble halls of the Gia Long Palace were cool and shadowy in contrast to the throbbing midday heat of central

Saigon, but when he stepped in through the portaled front entrance, Guy Sherman removed his dark glasses only long enough for his U.S. Embassy pass to be inspected. As soon as it was returned to him by a narrow-eyed soldier of the American-trained Vietnamese Special Forces unit that served as the presidential bodyguard, he replaced the glasses again immediately and trotted briskly up the wide marble staircase to the second floor. President Ngo Dinh Diem's office, he knew, was situated one staircase higher, on the third floor; furnished simply in the austere tradition of the Annamese mandarinate with a desk, a hard teak bed, bookshelves and a document table, it served as a bedroom, dining room, and office for the withdrawn bachelor who had been South Vietnam's head of state for nine years. There he received all his official Vietnamese visitors, but only those few selected foreigners, including Central Intelligence Agency officers like Guy Sherman, whom he wished to meet privately. The grandeur of the state reception room on the ground floor over which the French governor of Cochin-China had originally presided, he reserved for formal foreign guests.

But on this occasion the CIA man went no farther than the second floor, where the Supreme Counsellor to the President, his brother Ngo Dinh Nhu, had his office, and outside its door he was subjected to a careful body search by a white-uniformed Vietnamese Special Forces major. Nhu, a ruthless Machiavellian intriguer by instinct, suspected everybody else spent as much time as he did embroiled in secret political plots and counterplots, and only when the unsmiling soldier was satisfied that the American carried no concealed weapon did he show him into a room that was several times larger than the president's. It was decorated with the stuffed heads of tiger, buffalo and deer shot, Guy presumed, around Dalat, the favorite hunting grounds of the president's brother, and on one wall hung an imposing life-sized portrait in oils of a proud Vietnamese beauty dressed in a sheathlike *ao dai*; to Guy, the painter seemed to have exaggerated the essential characteristics of his subject, making her petite figure dramatically full-breasted and oversensual, and she had been given also the imperious, flashing eyes of a stylized Peking opera villainess. Nhu himself, who was seated behind an enormous black lacquer desk, wore tight-fitting black trousers and a pale short-sleeved shirt of yellow silk, and he didn't trouble to look up as Guy approached. Standing before the desk, the American saw that he was reading from a buff-colored file bearing the printed title "*So Nghien Cuu Xa Hoi Chinh Tri*," and he knew enough Vietnamese to recognize the euphemistic name of the "Social and Political Research Service" — South Vietnam's notorious secret police organization of which Nhu was the head. Looking more closely, Guy was able to make out his own name typewritten beneath the red "Top Secret" classification stamp in the right-hand corner, and when Ngo Dinh Nhu finally glanced up, his thin smile indicated that the revelation had not been accidental.

"So, Mr. Sherman, your father brought the family here to hunt in our jungles in the 'twenties — and your eldest brother was tragically killed. How unfortunate — or was it carelessness?" He spoke French in a low, rasping voice, but the question was obviously not posed in any expectation of receiving an answer and Guy remained silent while the Vietnamese lit a cigarette. "Another brother of yours has also had cause to return here on a number of occasions, I believe, and is the author of an obscure historical work on our country. No doubt you've benefited from his scholarly insights — is that why the CIA chose you, Mr. Sherman, to inquire into how we're intending to react to the Buddhist outrage?"

Guy, still standing, since he had not been invited to sit, studied Nhu's pale, venomous features as he considered his reply; once he must have been sharply handsome in the manner of an Asian matinee idol, but now, at fifty-two, the skin of his face, stretched unnaturally tight across prominent cheekbones, had become sallow and prematurely wrinkled as a result of his opium-smoking habits. His expression remained fixed in an icy smile, his eyes glittering with an unnatural brightness, and Guy decided that rumors that he also used heroin were probably true as well.

"My brother Joseph confines himself exclusively to academic studies on Vietnam's past these days, monsieur counsellor," said Guy, choosing his words in French with care. "Like any other foreign service officer I'm concerned only with the present. We try to provide policymakers at home with reliable information — I don't imagine you've forgotten the war in your country is judged to be of vital strategic interest to the United States."

"I've sometimes thought it might be better for us Vietnamese if it weren't," replied Nhu, his smile frozen and unchanging. "I've just been informed an hour ago that your military commanders have ordered all U.S. advisers to be withdrawn from units sent to control the Buddhists. You don't seem to realize that dying for a cause does not make it just — you don't seem to be able to grasp that the Buddhists are merely dupes of the Communists!"

"If you have reliable evidence to support that contention, I'd be glad to pass it to the U.S. ambassador immediately. Meanwhile we've got to assume the problems are unrelated. The ambassador's already told your brother, I believe, how concerned Washington is that the Buddhist trouble might destabilize your country to such an extent that the military effort is undermined. At the end of that road, American troops here could be endangered."

Nhu stubbed his cigarette out in an ashtray with a languid movement of his hand, then selected another one immediately from a tortoiseshell box on the desk. When he'd lit it, the mirthless smile reappeared on his face once more. "Mr. Sherman, I'm glad you've come here today. An informal meeting of this kind with a man like you allows me to air my intimate thoughts in a relaxed way. With your ambassador there is so much reliance on formality. Please sit down and make yourself comfortable." He waved with mock affability towards a chair beside the desk, and Guy lowered himself into it. The Vietnamese gazed at him intently for a moment, then his false smile deepened. "You see, Mr. Sherman, I've been seriously wondering whether I ought to persuade my brother to dispense with American military help altogether. Strictly between ourselves I can tell you that the French are offering now to facilitate contacts for us with Hanoi — no doubt to further their own selfish economic interests in our country. But just as Washington talks to Moscow, I suddenly thought: 'Why should Saigon not talk to Hanoi?' We shouldn't forget, should we, that alternatives to American solutions exist?"

Guy drew in his breath slowly. The threat in the slyly veiled remark was unmistakable; if the intention to negotiate with Hanoi had been declared openly to the American government, it would, as Nhu obviously appreciated, have had the effect of a diplomatic bombshell and would greatly embarrass the United States. "We talk to Moscow because we're not at war with them," replied Guy expressionlessly. "Our troops are here because Saigon is at war with Hanoi. It might be worth reflecting on that difference before you make up your mind."

Nhu gazed steadily at the American, still smiling, but didn't reply, and at that moment on the other side of the door behind him there was the sudden sound of fast-moving, female footsteps. The angry click of heels on a marble floor grew rapidly louder, then suddenly the door flew back on its hinges and a tiny figure swept into the room; glancing up, Guy noticed with a start that the woman in the portrait on the wall had come dramatically to life. Dressed in a dazzling *ao dai* of primrose yellow silk splashed with brilliant green fronds of weeping willow, Madame Nhu radiated an electric vitality. The dress clung to the dramatic curves of her body like a second skin, and her face had been artfully made up to emphasize her dark upswept brows, the high hollows of her Asiatic cheeks. As he stared at her, Guy modified his opinion of the portrait painter's work; he had not caricatured his subject at all but had conveyed a faithful likeness. Madame Nhu had begun pouring out a shrill torrent of words in French as soon as she entered the room, and she waved a sheaf of American and foreign newspapers furiously at her husband as she reached his side.

"Look at these! The American photographers must have bribed that monk to barbecue himself for their cameras." She flung the papers violently on the desk in front of her husband. "It could only have been a Communist-inspired plot!" While Nhu leafed quickly through the newspapers, his wife glared furiously over his head at Guy, and he noticed then that her costume differed from the traditional *ao dai* in one respect: instead of a high collar that fitted demurely under the chin, it had been designed with a scooped décolleté neckline that drew added attention to her full breasts, and her expression showed that she was fully conscious of the impact of her provocative appearance. "Or perhaps, Monsieur Sherman," she said in the same angry tone, "the CIA itself is plotting to provoke a coup d'état through the Buddhists."

Guy shifted uneasily in his seat; he had heard many secondhand accounts of Madame Nhu's rages and her highly charged sexuality and had tended to dismiss them as exaggerations of the truth, but seeing her in the flesh for the first time he realized that she more than lived up to her reputation. She continued to glare challengingly at him as she waited for his answer, but before he could frame a reply Nhu raised his head from the papers to smile at him again. "If the CIA should try to do that, our response would be simple. To protect ourselves we should have to withdraw our forces on a large scale from the Mekong delta to garrison Saigon."

"That sounds to me as though you're threatening the United States with your own defeat in the war," said Guy in an incredulous voice. "Does that make any sense?"

Nhu's raddled features hardened, and the smile disappeared altogether for the first time. "The prestige of the United States is irrevocably committed here, Monsieur Sherman. I can't speak for my brother, but my wife and I understand the American mentality better than you think. If you lose here, if you desert the country you've aided since 1954, what will American support be worth elsewhere in the world? Wouldn't there be a universal crisis of confidence among your allies? Americans love to be winners; they're simple people who admire above all else mindless physical vitality and winning — whether in games or in war. The French are subtler, they have much greater intellect — that's why I prefer France to the United States."

"Americans are certainly simple in one respect," said Guy calmly. "We know what we stand for — we don't shift our ground easily. Here we support whatever helps the war effort — and whatever interferes with it, we oppose. We're not in business to see wars lost to Communism."

"But you'd like to see us give in and lose the war against the Buddhists!" Madame Nhu planted her hands on her hips and set her feet apart in a defiant stance; although she wore three-inch stiletto-heeled shoes of emerald green leather from Paris, she was still not much more than five feet tall, and she spat her words out with the ferocity of an angry cat. "The only way for our family and our government to regain the support of the population is to smash the Buddhists! If you've come here to find out what our attitude to the Buddhists is, monsieur, let me tell you this: if another bonze wishes to burn himself to death, we'll gladly supply the gasoline and a match."

"By alienating the Buddhists aren't you effectively turning the whole country against you? Wouldn't it be easier, as our ambassador has suggested to your brother-in-law, to admit the Hue shootings were not ordered from Saigon — and offer the victims some compensation?"

"The Americans are all Ivanhoes! You always favor the underdog — even when you're not sure who the underdog is! If we appease them there'll be no end to the Buddhists' demands! Appeasement would be interpreted as a sign of weakness, and we don't intend to commit suicide just to appease them." The eyes of the Vietnamese woman flashed, and she tossed her head contemptuously. "If they wish to barbecue another monk, I personally will clap my hands!"

"In the democratic countries of the world you'll lose all

sympathy if you always crush your opponents by force." Guy looked down at the man behind the desk as he spoke. "Have you thought of that?"

"The Communists are enough opposition right now," rasped Nhu. "When we've won the war — that will be the time to consider whether we can play the game of democracy with legal opposition groups. Perhaps we might do better to eliminate from our ranks all those trained by sentimental Americans — this would make our forces stronger!"

"I don't know what your informers are telling you," said Sherman quietly. "But the self-sacrifice of Thich Quang Duc hasn't horrified only the American public. It's affected a lot of ordinary Vietnamese deeply too. More than one houseboy has told his American employer in Saigon that this proves the government of President Diem is bad."

"You'd be better advised not to listen to the prattle of houseboys," said Nhu, watching the American thoughtfully through the smoke of his cigarette. "But I don't really think I have to tell you that. You've wisely come to my office to seek enlightenment and not gone to the third floor." He raised his eyes significantly to the ceiling and the office of the president, above them. "At least the CIA understands now where real power resides. My brother, you see, is unfortunately afflicted by your disease — the desire to conciliate and appease. He wishes, as the French like to say, to have 'a circle with corners.' He wants everyone shaking hands, no bloodshed." He paused and spoke more slowly for emphasis. "But we'll make sure he doesn't carry through such a foolish policy. And if necessary we wouldn't hesitate to mount a coup against him if he disagrees with our advice."

Madame Nhu leaned forward suddenly and brought a tiny fist crashing down onto the lacquered desk top. "Yes! We'll smash the Buddhists! Smash them, make no mistake about that." She gazed at the American, her eyes blazing, her tiny frame shaking with the ardor of her words. "No matter what the rest of the world thinks of us."

For a moment there was a silence in the room. Then Nhu shifted impatiently in his chair. "So, Monsieur Sherman, I think you have some idea of our position now, yes? But about the CIA's attitude we're not so sure. Is it turning against us — becoming a Buddhist sympathizer?"

Guy sighed wearily. "I get a little tired of reminding people the

CIA doesn't have a policy, monsieur counsellor. The Agency serves the U.S. government by gathering information. I'm here because we wish to understand your thinking. We know your influence and the influence of Madame Nhu on the president are of vital importance. We want to keep our lines of communication to you open."

"But sometimes to keep channels of communication functioning smoothly, Monsieur Sherman, a demonstration of goodwill is vital," said Nhu sourly. "Otherwise we might find it impossible to push unwelcome thoughts about you from our heads."

"I'd anticipated something like that. Americans can be good at reading character, too." Guy smiled suddenly and reached into an inside pocket of his jacket. Taking out a folded sheet of paper, he placed it on the desk in front of Nhu, then rose and walked to the door. He paused with one hand on the doorknob and looked back to find Madame Nhu peering over her husband's shoulder at the sheet of Continental Palace notepaper. "That's the name of the monk who tipped off the British television crew — and probably the rest of the foreign press corps as well. I thought you might be interested to have it."

As he turned to close the door behind him, Guy saw Madame Nhu take the sheet of paper eagerly from her husband, and Nhu began smiling his cold humorless smile once more.

10

In the fading light of a soft August evening the hewn granite stonework of the Cornell University buildings at Ithaca, New York, had taken on a hallowed, ancient air; the high, neo-Gothic gables were casting chasms of dark shadow across the tree-lined lawns, and the muted trills of birds preparing to roost for the night deepened the mellow tranquillity of the deserted, vacation-time campus. Only Joseph Sherman's long-striding figure disturbed the stillness when he emerged from the main entrance of Uris Hall, which since 1950 had housed the Department of Far Eastern Studies' Southeast Asia Program; he had been conducting a vacation seminar, and as he headed across the dappled grass towards one of the faculty houses, there was a certain restless agitation in his step that suggested he had never been able to reconcile himself fully to the reflective, unhurried ways of the academic world. Although he was in his early fifties, his fair hair was flecked only lightly with gray; lean, broad-shouldered and upright, he had retained the bearing of the athlete he had been in his youth, but the habitual frown he wore and his tightly drawn mouth hinted at tensions beneath the surface that were other than physical. In front of his door, his frown deepened suddenly as his eye fell on the latest edition of the *New York Times;* set in the kind of heavy type reserved for stories of major importance and spread across four columns of the front page, its main headline proclaimed: "South Vietnam's Crisis Deepens — Diem's Forces Raid Pagodas" and he picked up the newspaper quickly and began scanning the story while opening the door.

Inside, his attention was diverted momentarily by an envelope lying on the hall table where his cleaner had left it; it was edged with red and blue airmail stripes, and the handwriting and the Saigon postmark told him immediately that it was a letter from his son Gary. He stopped reading the news story long enough to tuck it into his jacket pocket, then wandered distractedly into a sitting room decorated exclusively with oriental furnishings. Chinese rugs covered the floors, inlaid lacquer paintings and calligraphy scrolls from the Imperial City of Hue hung on the walls, and several screens bearing Annamese dragon motifs were crowded among tasseled brocade divans that once had graced the homes of mandarin courtiers in Peking. Every table and sideboard bore clusters of Vietnamese porcelain, jade figurines, gilded bodhisattvas or incense burners, and several sloe-eyed porcelain figures of life size were draped with collections of brilliant-hued court robes from Indochina and Thailand. But standing in the center of the room, holding the newspaper, Joseph seemed for once oblivious to the art objects he had collected so fastidiously during his years in the Far East. According to the news agency dispatch from Saigon datelined August 21, hundreds of armed soldiers and police had stormed into the Xa Loi pagoda and other Buddhist temples during the night, and Joseph shook his head in disbelief as he read through the details: several monks were believed to have been killed, hundreds had been dragged off to prison, and President Diem had declared martial law. Tanks and armored cars had taken up position at major intersections in Saigon, the wire service reported, and troops were patrolling the streets everywhere. In an official statement, the president's brother Ngo Dinh Nhu had described the

Buddhists as "Reds in yellow robes" and accused their leaders of plotting to organize a coup d'état.

When he had finished reading, Joseph flung the newspaper aside with a muffled curse and because the room was beginning to grow dark he switched on a silk-shaded lamp before tugging the airmail letter from Gary out of his pocket. The handwriting on the envelope, like Gary himself, was neat, precise, military, and the letter inside had been penned on the headed, airmail-weight notepaper of the Caravelle Hotel. To read it Joseph sat down by the lamp, and he scanned each line with unconcealed anxiety as though he feared the pages might contain information he desperately hoped not to find..

"*Dear Dad,*" the letter began,

> I guess I was pretty surprised to get your letter after all these years of silence between us. My reactions at first were "mixed," I must admit — for reasons which are maybe still too painful to go into in detail. For a day or two I swore to myself I wouldn't answer you at all but after I'd read it a few times I think I started to realize that maybe I ought to be glad you cared enough to write at all after the things I said to you during our last painful meeting at the museum. I also started to realize as well that it would be brainless to turn my back on someone with as deep a knowledge of this country as you have — especially when it's becoming impossible to understand what the hell's going on around here.
>
> So when I got a much-delayed weekend pass to Saigon, I brought your letter with me so that I could do my bit to help along the thaw. I also decided that for the time being at least I'd let sleeping dogs lie as you wisely did in your letter and keep off the ticklish subject of you, Mom and the past. Let me just say that with the passage of time I've come to regret a little the ferocity of some of the things I said at the museum. As I grow older I guess I'm beginning to realize that nobody's all bad or all good and that there are almost always two sides to every question. Now that I've got that off my chest I'm going to stick to asking you a few dumb questions and telling you just how goddamned hard the soldier's life is out here. As a precaution I'm also dropping this into an anonymous mailbox down the street rather than submit it to the normal censorship channels. Having the chance to do that of course is something akin to being in heaven right now. The civilized delights of this exotic city are very welcome after another six weeks slogging through the paddies chasing the goddamned Viet Cong. I was beginning to think my feet and legs would stay permanently black from the mud but now the odd glass of iced beer is doing wonders for restoring my morale — to say nothing of the gorgeous Vietnamese girls in their flimsy, figure-hugging outfits. . . .

And while we're on that subject don't be too surprised, will you, if I come home some day with a slant-eyed maiden on my arm? The girls here as you must know are a sight for sore eyes although I can assure you of one thing — it won't be anyone like the president's so-called first lady, Madame Nhu. She's maybe one hell of a looker but she's known around here now as the "Dragon Lady" because she's just banned taxi dancing, the "twist," prostitution, divorce, contraception, abortion, cockfighting — in fact every damned thing that makes life worth living for the average Vietnamese man. Rumor has it that a foreign ambassador who was her lover threw her over in favor of a taxi dancer and in accordance with the "hell-hath-no-fury-like-a-woman-scorned" principle, she shut down all the dancing shops as an act of revenge. I wouldn't go on about all this, Dad, if it didn't lead me to my first dumb question: why in heaven's name did we decide to go to bat in the first place for a government headed by people like the "Dragon Lady," her husband and her brother-in-law? The way they're handling the Buddhists, for instance, has got us all baffled. While we spend weeks on end up to our asses in mud in the delta trying to win the war, they seem hellbent on losing it for us in Saigon and the other cities. The South Vietnamese troops in my unit have taken to wearing little patches of yellow cloth supposedly cut from the robes used to carry the body of that Buddhist monk who burned himself to death. This, they tell me, demonstrates their support for the Buddhists who're trying to overthrow the government they're fighting for! What's more, Buddhist and Catholic officers are refusing to eat together — can you make sense of that? I'm damned if I can. A South Vietnamese officer I respect told me the other day that Buddhists are very susceptible to Communist influence — but hell, almost everybody in South Vietnam except the Diem family seems to be Buddhist, so what in God's name are we doing here? (That's the last dumb question this time round, I promise.)

There's some bad feeling among our guys out here that Americans are dying now for a government more concerned with hanging on to power than beating the Viet Cong. We're sacrificing massive amounts of dollars and American lives but the Viets show no sign of gratitude — quite the reverse. Our ARVN opposite numbers most of the time are downright arrogant with us. A lot of them give the impression they don't want us here at all. I don't understand why we don't get off our butts and get tougher with them. I tried to tackle Uncle Guy on this subject when I met him for a drink at the Continental yesterday but he was very vague. He more or less implied that it was all too complicated to explain to a mere army lieutenant. He hardly stayed five minutes then rushed off on some mysterious political errand which he implied was highly secret and very important. The air here, as you've no doubt read, is thick right now with rumors of coups and countercoups.

But, despite all the confusion and the dissatisfaction, it's surprising how some U.S. officers here are developing a really strong sense of commitment, of mission, almost. The jungles, the endless rice fields and the inscrutable natives seem to cast a strange kind of spell on some of us. Volunteering for a second tour isn't uncommon at all anymore and I'm not sure the paddies aren't beginning to get to me a little, as the saying goes. Perhaps not being able to fathom it all out is part of the peculiar fascination of Vietnam. But more than anything else any American who comes to this stricken little country these days is invariably horrified by the tragedy he can run into every day — it seems never-ending. Every officer I've talked to has his own version, some experience or other of terrible suffering, almost always accepted passively. With me it was something that happened at Moc Linh, the ambush you probably read about in the papers. My ARVN opposite number seemed a really nice guy for a change — just before the VC hit us he was saying how much he hated the Communists because they'd tortured and killed his father during the French war. A few minutes later both his legs were blown off by a mine and later I found they'd put a bullet neatly through his left temple just for good measure. Maybe it was because he was my age and rank but somehow it's personalized the war for me, made me a little more determined to make the Communists pay in some way the next time we catch up with them.

I guess I'm sorry to end this letter on such a downbeat note but I don't want to leave you with the impression that this war isn't a pretty grim business. I guess that's another thing that made me want to write — thinking that if I left it any longer I might not be able to. So let me say, Dad, I appreciated your letter and I'll try to respond, God willing, if you want to write again. Now a chilled beer or two in a shady sidewalk café calls so I'll wrap it up there.

Yours ever,
Gary

Joseph let the hand holding the letter fall into his lap, and he stared unseeing into the darkness beyond the circle of light. The muscles of his face tightened for a moment as though he were enduring physical pain; then his expression relaxed again and he leaned back on the divan with his eyes closed. The sound of the front door opening and closing reached him, followed by soft footsteps in the hall, but he didn't turn or rise. A moment later the shadowy figure of a young Asian girl with long, straight black hair reaching almost to her waist appeared in the doorway. Because of the hot night she wore brief shorts, a sleeveless T-shirt and thong sandals on her bare feet.

"Are you all right, Joseph?"

516

The anxiety in her tone made him open his eyes, and as she hurried across the room towards him, her bare thighs shone like polished amber in the dull glow of the lamp. She stopped beside the divan and laid a tentative hand upon his shoulder, a frown of concern crinkling her smooth forehead. "You were so still, honey, and the house so quiet. . . ." Her voice trailed off and she glanced down at the letter he still held in his hand. "Has the mailman brought bad news?"

He shook his head, laying the letter aside, and stood up. "No, Emerald, I'm okay — it's just a letter from my son Gary in Vietnam."

Beside him she seemed tiny, the top of her dark head reaching only halfway up his chest. "Then I haven't come here in vain," she said, cocking her head on one side and smiling up at him as she held out a sheaf of manuscript paper she had been holding behind her back. "This is chapter eleven of what I hope Professor Sherman will decide eventually is a brilliant doctoral dissertation on the Taiping Rebellion — presented for critical comment." Her West Coast accent bore not the slightest trace of her Chinese ancestry, but her manner, like her voice, was soft and delicate, obviously Asiatic, and Joseph forced a smile to his lips as he took the papers from her.

"You should smile more often, Joseph," she said, pressing her face gently against his shirt front and slipping her bare arms around his waist. "You look so stern and forbidding — as though you'd never once been happy in your whole life."

He glanced at the manuscript she had given him for a moment or two, then dropped it onto a red-lacquered coffee table with an apologetic smile. "I'm sorry, Emerald. I'll look at it later. I can't concentrate right now. That letter's the first word I've had from my older son in seven years — I guess it's making it hard for me to turn my mind to anything else."

She unwound herself from him and, taking his hand, motioned for him to sit down beside her on the divan. "Has it upset you badly? Do you want to talk about it?"

Joseph sat staring indecisively at the letter.

"You've never talked about Gary or your other son," she prompted gently. "Are they very like you?"

"I've never talked about Gary because he's twenty-five — your age." Joseph's voice was heavy with resignation, and he spoke without looking at her.

"But that doesn't matter," she whispered. "Your age makes no

517

difference to the way I feel. Please tell me about Gary if it's important to you."

"I guess I find it difficult to talk about my sons because I realize I'm mostly responsible for the bad blood that exists between us," said Joseph, speaking very quietly. "Even while they were growing up I didn't spend as much time with them as I should have, because I was always on the move traveling all over Asia. They went to school back home here, and my mind always seemed to be more on my job than on my family. Then I left my wife and disappeared from their lives completely when Gary and Mark were in their teens — when they were just beginning to think about what they were going to do with their futures. It took me a year or two to realize just how badly I'd neglected them. Then one day I got a letter from my wife in which she mentioned Gary had made up his mind to go to West Point and Mark was beginning to think about a career as an air force pilot — and I got a rush of blood to the head."

"Why?"

Joseph rubbed a hand agitatedly across his face. "Because that was the last thing I wanted for my sons. My own father tried to persuade me to take up a military career when I was their age, and I had to fight tooth and claw to go my own way. My wife got married again quickly after I left her — to a full colonel in the Pentagon — and I suddenly realized that his influence or maybe even that of my own father had replaced mine."

"And what did you do?"

"I wrote to Gary and Mark asking to see them both urgently. Mark turned me down flat. Both of them took my leaving their mother pretty badly, but Mark was totally uncompromising. Gary at least agreed to talk, and I flew down to Washington one weekend to see him."

"And did that do anything to help heal the breach?"

Joseph shook his head emphatically. "On the contrary — we were at daggers drawn. In the end, during a visit to our family museum, Gary let rip with a few home truths that still hurt whenever I think about them."

"And is the letter that arrived today very hurtful too?"

Joseph sighed again. "Not exactly. I took the plunge and wrote to him first a couple of months ago — after the Buddhists in South Vietnam began to complicate things. He was sent out there earlier this year, and I couldn't stop thinking how damned confusing it must be for him. I just offered a few insights that I hoped might help him feel less at sea — and if I'm going to be really honest I suppose I hoped it might be a lever to help me get on better terms with him too. I thought for a while he wasn't going to answer at all. . . ."

"But he has, so things are better between you now?"

"Maybe a little — but his reservations are still fairly pronounced."

"I'll fix us a drink, Joseph — you need to relax." She squeezed his hand, slipped off her sandals and ran barefoot into the kitchen. He listened for a moment to the rattle of the cocktail mixer, then his glance fell on the headline about the pagoda raids and he picked up the newspaper once more. When Emerald returned with two martinis, he sipped his distractedly while reading accounts of the stunned reaction in Washington, and gave no sign that he'd noticed when she unfastened the top two buttons of his shirt and began stroking his chest.

"Sitting here worrying in Cornell won't change anything on the other side of the world, Joseph," she whispered, brushing the lobe of his ear with her parted lips. "Please forget it all for a little while. I've been looking forward so much all day to seeing you — let's go to bed now."

Reluctantly he put the newspaper down and finished his drink. She helped him off with his jacket, then he let her lead him by the hand into the bedroom. When they had undressed, he stretched out on his back on the quilted teak bed and lay staring at the ceiling while she continued to caress his bare chest. Slowly her movements gained urgency and she began to stroke his thighs with the tips of her fingers.

"You've got the body of a much younger man, Joseph," she murmured, nuzzling closer to him. "I can't think why you should have worried that Gary was my age." Taking his hand she drew it between her thighs and her breathing quickened. "Ching Ping Mei would tell us now we shouldn't worry about the sinister flight of the crows, isn't that right? When the Pillar of the Heavenly Dragon is ready to enter the Jade Pavilion, doesn't the wise book say that we should think of nothing else?" She gasped and shifted her body onto his, and when he finally tightened his arms around her, she closed her eyes and responded avidly to his movements. But before he was fully aroused his passion subsided abruptly and she opened her eyes to find him gazing at her with a remote faraway expression in his eyes.

"Emerald, I can't — I'm sorry." He made his apology abruptly and rolled away from her, pulling the sheet over the lower part of his body.

"Joseph, what's the matter?" Her voice was suddenly tearful and indignant. "When you look at me like that I sometimes think you're looking through me. It's as if I weren't there — as if you weren't really seeing me at all."

She continued to gaze uncomprehendingly at his naked shoulders, but Joseph neither turned back to face her nor offered any answer.

11

It had been one of those stifling Washington summer days with the temperature hovering around the hundred mark and low gray clouds as dank as wet rags oppressing the city; lying restlessly awake on the teak bed beside the sleeping Emerald, Joseph found he could still remember the clammy feel of his shirt sticking to his back, although seven years had passed. He recalled too with a surprising clarity that even the pinnacle of the Washington Monument had been shrouded by cloud when the taxi that brought him from the airport drew up outside the Sherman Field Museum of Natural History in the Mall. He had agreed to go there at Gary's suggestion so as to avoid both the home in Maryland where Gary and Mark lived with Tempe and her new husband, and the complications that would inevitably intrude in the presence of the senator and Joseph's mother at the family mansion in Georgetown.

The museum had been closed temporarily for redecoration at the time, and Gary had greeted him politely inside the front entrance; their feet, he remembered, had echoed hollowly in the empty, sheet-draped galleries, and Gary's face had begun to betray something of the embarrassment he obviously felt at having to talk alone with him after so many years of noncommunication. Over coffee in the public cafeteria which had been kept open for the decorators, they had exchanged small talk, then Gary had offered to show him around the refurbished displays. It was as they strolled together into the memorial wing dedicated to his brother Chuck, Joseph realized later, that any slender chance that their meeting might turn out well had been fatally undermined by an unthinking remark he had made.

"I haven't been through here, Gary, for about fifteen years," he had said conversationally — then immediately regretted his words.

"Why not?"

He hesitated, realizing the true explanation was unlikely to help his cause. "I disagreed strongly with my father about the wisdom of setting up some of the exhibits here. . . ."

"You mean the animals shot by Uncle Chuck?"

Gary's tone was distant, disinterested, and Joseph wondered then whether it might be wiser not to try to explain further. They were passing the glass-fronted tableau of the big game animals killed in Cochin-China over thirty years before, and he had been startled to find that due to the meticulous care with which they'd been preserved, the baleful banteng and buffalo looked as lifelike and glossy-coated as they had when they were roaming the plains beside the La Nga River. The newly painted frames and surrounds also gave the tableau a shocking freshness, and he had felt a renewed sense of horror as he stared at the murderous horns of the massive, hump-necked seladang that had gored Chuck to death. Glancing up he had found Gary watching him intently.

"Why did you think it was wrong to show these exhibits?" he had asked quietly, as though suddenly sensing his father's embarrassment.

"I wasn't fond of shooting at that age, Gary. I thought this tableau would always be seen as a memorial to the misplaced pride of the Sherman family. We're all likely enough to fall prey to the worst sides of our natures, God knows. Too often we get carried away by the idea of wanting to win at all costs — worrying about our goddamned virility being doubted drives us to all kinds of excesses. This tableau is just a painful reminder of all those things as far as I'm concerned."

Gary listened in silence, a puzzled frown crinkling his brow. "And you said all that to my grandfather — to his face?"

"Maybe I didn't say it all to his face, no. You're probably aware that I've never been that close to him."

Gary had turned his head away then, and an awkward silence had expanded between them; something, however, kept them rooted to the spot before the tableau and he realized suddenly what Gary must have been thinking. There was no way of preventing him from seeing the parallel between their feud and his own quarrel with the senator, and in desperation he had decided to try to make a virtue of it. "We both know why I asked to talk to you, Gary," he had said quietly. "When I heard you'd decided to go to West Point I couldn't help remembering that your grandfather tried to push me into a military career at your age. I resisted because I was damned sure it wouldn't be right for me — and I guess because I haven't been around for a couple of years I've got to worrying you might have been influenced unduly by the senator — or your stepfather. Have you really thought it over carefully, Gary? I think you're worthy of something better — the military's not what I want for you in peacetime."

He had been unable to keep an imploring note out of his voice, and he watched with a growing sense of hopelessness as an expression of distaste spread across Gary's normally cheerful, boyish features.

"Unlike you, Dad, I don't hide my feelings, so let me ask you one thing — what right do you think you've got to come here interfering? You went off, remember, for your own selfish reasons, leaving Mom and us to make our way as best we could. You were too busy then with your oriental concubines to bother with me or Mark — so why the sudden interest now?"

"How much did your mother tell you about that?"

"Not much at all — but enough to make Mark and me not think very highly of you for what you did to her. She said you never really had your feet on the ground — and she was right. I'd like to have had a father whose eyes didn't get a kind of glazed look whenever I talked to him. Somehow you always managed to make Mark and me feel we weren't really worth wasting your precious time on!"

"Haven't you ever considered that I might have changed — that I might have regretted doing what I did?"

Gary had laughed then, and the sound of his laughter had echoed hollowly through the deserted gallery. "That's incredible, really incredible! You haven't changed at all — you're still so selfish you can't see that what's important is what *I* want to do with my life — not what *you* want me to do."

"You're making this all the harder for me, talking that way. Maybe some day you'll live to wish you'd done something differently."

"If you've decided now you made the wrong choice, that's just too bad," replied Gary coldly. "But don't expect any sympathy from us. Mark was right — you're not worth the trouble it takes to talk to you."

He had turned on his heel then and walked out of the museum, leaving Joseph standing alone before the tableau, and glancing down at the wickedly curved horns of the seladang, he had shuddered; the ferocious, glassy-eyed animal made the empty museum feel like a haunted tomb, and he had wandered out into the stifling heat of the Mall again, feeling depressed and sick at heart.

The memory of that desolate moment, brought vividly to mind again by Gary's letter, produced such a feeling of agitation in Joseph that he found it impossible to lie still any longer, and rising from the teak bed with care so as not to disturb the girl, he put on a silk kimono-style dressing gown and slippers and tiptoed out of the bedroom. One end of the long, overfurnished sitting room served as a study, and collecting Gary's letter from the table where he had dropped it earlier, he went to his lacquered Chinese desk and sat down. When he switched on the desk light a small clock beneath it showed three A.M., and he rubbed his eyes wearily and ran a hand through his tousled hair before taking the letter from the envelope. After reading it through quickly once more, he picked up a sheaf of paper and a pen and started to write.

"*My dear Gary*," he began,

I can't tell you how delighted I was to get your letter today. I've been feeling worse and worse about being estranged from you and Mark as the years have passed, and more than anything else in the world I guess I'd like to get back to some kind of understanding with you both. I've had a lot of time for regret and remorse to do their job, but as you say, I guess letters aren't the right place to unburden ourselves on that score. Let me just say that my thoughts are constantly with you — even more so since your letter arrived here simultaneously with a copy of the *New York Times* announcing the storming of the Buddhist pagodas. I was so shocked by that and so moved by some of the things you said about your growing attachment to Vietnam that I've not been able to sleep or think of anything else since. I've just got up now in the middle of the night in fact to write you. . . .

His hand flew across the page, and because he kept his head bent intently over his task he didn't notice the naked figure of Emerald appear silently in the bedroom doorway behind him. She stood watching him sleepily for a moment, then began wandering through the deep shadows of the room, stopping now and then to caress a piece of jade or porcelain or run her fingers over the finely worked silken embroidery of a mandarin's sleeve.

I guess I'm at a bit of a loss to know what to say to you now, but let's begin with something impersonal — the answer to your query about why we decided "to go to bat," as you put it, for the Ngo family. The story's a sad and sorry one — and I know because I was closely involved for a time. Several things, you see, happened all at once about the time I left your mother. Maybe I'll say more one day, but as a result I decided rather hastily to give up my career as a newspaperman that same year and returned home to bury myself away as far as possible from Asia — in the quieter realms of the academic world. But it was harder to shake off that part of my life than I thought and I couldn't settle at first at Cornell. When Michigan State invited me to participate in a government-financed program in 1956 to create a modern government structure for Diem I went back to Saigon very much in the spirit of trying to contribute something. But it was not long before disenchantment set in. . . .

Joseph stopped writing and sat back in his chair, lost in thought. Some of his deep personal disillusionment, he knew, had been directly attributable to the fact he had been unable to find any trace of his daughter Tuyet in those six months he had spent in Saigon. From Gary's remarks at the museum he was almost certain Tempe had never told his sons of her existence, but he had always been aware that his desire to find her again had contributed to his decision to return to Vietnam. To his dismay when he arrived there he discovered Tuyet had disappeared overnight without trace in 1954; she had gone "underground" after informing Tam and his family she was marrying a member of the Viet Minh and to all intents and purposes she had ceased to exist. After that discovery Joseph had found that the painful memories the city held for him had weighed on him increasingly; above all else he had never been able to pass the Continental Palace without a feeling of horror when he reached the spot on the sidewalk where Lan and her father had died so bloodily before his eyes, and gradually the desire to leave and never return had grown in him.

A rustling sound interrupted his train of thought, and he swung around to find Emerald in the act of removing a sea-green court gown from one of the life-sized porcelain statues. Knowing she had attracted his attention, she smiled wanly and wrapped it slowly about herself, hugging the silken material to her naked body with both arms.

"Sometimes I can't help thinking, Joseph, that I'm just another object in your oriental collection." She spoke plaintively, without any note of accusation in her voice, but her lips trembled as though she might be on the brink of tears. In the shimmering mandarin's robe, her face seemed more classically Asian, the slant of her cheeks more pronounced, and Joseph stared at her transfixed for a moment; then he gathered himself again.

"Please go back to bed," he said quietly. "I've got to finish what I'm writing."

"I can't sleep without you."

"Please go and try." Joseph turned back to his desk, and after watching him for a minute or two she wandered away sulkily into the shadows once more.

"*I found that the Michigan State Group wasn't all it seemed to be,*" Joseph wrote, his pen gathering speed once again.

There were about fifty professors, some doing legitimate work on the constitution and the civil service, but a big part of it was a cover for intelligence operatives who were channeling guns, ammunition, grenades, and tear gas to the secret police outfit they were training for Ngo Dinh Nhu in the likeness of the FBI. They were also building up a paramilitary police force, and political repression seemed to become the focus of the group's efforts. Soon this overshadowed all the attempts we were making to install democratic institutions, so I resigned after six months. I'd never been enthusiastic about Diem. He's not the sinister character that his brother Nhu is — he's never been interested for example in getting rich himself, but he's always turned a blind eye to corruption to keep himself in power. He's a strangely remote, inflexible man, with fixed ideas of Confucian loyalty to family which have always stopped him dispensing with the assistance of his corrupt brothers and his sister-in-law who've poisoned his relations with the people. Perhaps the best construction to put on President Diem is that he's a victim to a large extent of his ruthless, power-hungry family — but that's maybe being too kind.

Closer to home for you, the arrogance of some of your ARVN officers doesn't surprise me. Southerners in Vietnam, you see, have traditionally enjoyed an easy life in the fertile delta region and as a result they're a different breed to the tougher Vietnamese from the harsher lands in the center and the north. The southerners were also colonized more thoroughly and they collaborated more closely with the French, so they developed an intense desire to emulate their colonial masters. The officer corps in South Vietnam for instance practices a more rigorous form of class distinction than any other similar country in Southeast Asia — but at the same time they feel a kind of schizophrenic compulsion to show their contempt for their foreign lords — once the French, now the Americans — who brought them wealth, privilege, and the very idea of superiority. I don't know whether this will help you get on any better with your next ARVN lieutenant when the bullets are flying across the paddies, but it's offered in the hope that it might.

Joseph stopped writing, picked up Gary's letter and scanned it again until he came to the passage describing the death of the ARVN lieutenant. He reread it slowly with a pained expression on his face, then sat and stared blankly at the wall in front of him. After a minute or two he picked up his pen, but it hovered indecisively over the page for a long time before he finally began writing again.

Your account of the death of the Vietnamese officer was very moving, and thinking back on similar experiences in my own life, I can guess how you must feel. Coupled with that I want to say how well I understand and sympathize with what comes through your letter between the lines as a growing fascination with Vietnam and its people. I'm choosing my words very carefully now and know how sensitive you would be to my "interfering" again. (I've learned my lesson on that by the way; it goes without saying that I admire your courage in choosing the career you wanted and I'm damned impressed by the way you're getting ahead.) But I find I can't close this letter without a cautionary word not to let your heart run away with your head. I did, you see, and now I'm going to break another rule — one we've only just made — about unburdening myself and maybe I should add that my hand's shaking a little as I write this.

What led me to break up the family I now so dearly miss, you see, was an *affaire de coeur* in Vietnam when I was roughly the age you are now. I fell in love with the daughter of a mandarin. Her name was Lan — which means "orchid" — and in a rash moment I asked her to marry me. She accepted — then changed her mind later because of her father. I managed after a struggle to put her out of my mind and later met and married your mother — but when I found myself in Saigon at the end of the Pacific War I met her again.

Joseph paused and wiped the sleeve of his kimono across his brow; he found the palms of his hands were damp too and he pressed them against his sides for a moment.

I never thought I'd be able to say this to you, Gary, and maybe I still couldn't face to face, but I discovered then to my amazement that I had a daughter I'd never met — your half sister. Her name is Tuyet; she was eight then but she'd been brought up secretly by another Vietnamese family in harrowing circumstances. From then on

526

somehow I could never entirely push from my mind the feeling that I'd failed that little girl very badly indeed. Maybe that accounts for what you once called that "glazed look" in my eyes — my preoccupation if you like. I hasten to add I don't expect to make you feel less wronged by telling you this — but when I decided to part from your mother I hoped to marry Lan and offer your half sister a home too. In the event Lan died and Tuyet refused the offer I made and I've never seen her since. I tried to find her when I was in Saigon the last time but I had no luck.

All this is very painful to confess to you, Gary, and of course I do it with no pride. My reason is to try to show you how very badly I need to set the record straight between you and me. I hope I'll get the chance sometime to get on terms with Mark too. You may have felt that the love of a father like me was never worth very much but it exists nevertheless — stronger now perhaps than ever before. So I hope you'll accept this baring of my heart in the spirit it's given. The effort of writing this I should say has left me feeling wrung out and I think I need a good stiff drink now — although it's four A.M. So until I hear from you again, make sure you take damned good care of yourself.

Joseph thought for a moment before signing off, then added simply: "With love — Dad."

Pushing the paper away from him, he pressed his knuckles hard against his eyes, then stood up and headed for the kitchen. As he did so the girl emerged from the shadows again at the side of his desk. For a second or two she stood staring at him with a hurt expression in her eyes, holding a framed photograph clasped against the front of the embroidered court gown; then she stepped deliberately in front of him, barring his way. "I used to think when I first started coming here, Joseph, that I was happier in this room than I'd ever been in my whole life. But now I know I was wrong to feel like that." She turned the photograph around suddenly and held it towards him. "Is this who you think about when that strange look comes into your eyes?"

He stared at the photograph of Tuyet for a moment in silence.

"If it isn't, why keep a framed picture face-down in a drawer?"

"This is my daughter," he said, taking the picture from her. "I last saw her nine years ago and I find it too painful to see her likeness every day now." He walked slowly across the room to replace the photograph in the drawer, and when he turned around he found the girl standing with her head bowed. Suddenly her shoulders began to shake and her hands flew to cover her face; but he watched her, pale-faced and impassive, from where he stood, leaning against the closed drawer, and he didn't move until she had dressed and left the house. When the sound of her car finally died away he returned to his desk, and in the deep stillness of the night he glanced through the letter he had written to Gary; but suddenly the shaming emotionalism of the final paragraph was too painful to read, and he closed his eyes tight. He remained standing like this for a long time, then he opened his eyes again, picked up all the pages, tore them through and let them fall piece by piece into the wastepaper basket.

12

"I must know what the American government's attitude would be if there was a change of government in Vietnam in the very near future," said the tall, burly Vietnamese major general, addressing Guy Sherman slowly and deliberately in French. "My fellow generals and I are more aware than anybody just how rapidly the situation is deteriorating. The Strategic Hamlet program is collapsing in the delta, the government no longer has the support of the people, and unless action's taken soon, the war will be lost to the Viet Cong."

Despite the seriousness of his words General Duong Van Minh's face broke into his famous cavernous grin; all of his teeth except one in front had been ripped out by a Japanese torturer during the Second World War and he had never made any attempt to disguise the fact; his rawboned figure and his height — he was close to six feet tall — also made him an unusually imposing figure for a Vietnamese and had earned him the nickname "Big Minh." He was a graduate of both the French École Militare and the Fort Leavenworth General Staff School in the United States, and Guy Sherman knew that this big, affable man also responded jovially to his Vietnamese nickname "Beo," which meant "fat boy."

As he looked at him, Guy wondered whether in view of his appearance the general might be grinning at the irony of their secret meeting taking place in a deserted dentist's office in the heart of Saigon. They had entered surreptitiously by separate doors, and Guy had found Big Minh already seated in the dentist's chair. "You understand, don't you, general, that I'm here simply to listen to what you have to say and pass it on," said the American guardedly. "But before I say anything at all I'd need to know a lot more about your plans. Which other generals, for instance, support you? And how exactly do you plan to 'change' the government of President Diem?"

For several seconds the Vietnamese sat gazing speculatively at the CIA man, who remained standing; then he smiled wryly again. "We have three possible plans, Monsieur Sherman. First, we can assassinate his brothers Ngo Dinh Nhu and Ngo Dinh Canh simultaneously, leaving Diem alone in power. That's the easiest to accomplish. Second, we could throw a ring of steel around Saigon with various units under our command and move in that way. Or, third, we could bring about a direct confrontation in Saigon between our forces and units loyal to the government. Under this plan we would divide the city up into pockets and clean them out one by one." Big Minh shrugged his bull-like shoulders. "Nhu could count on perhaps five thousand troops remaining loyal to him and his brother — no more." Still smiling, he studied Guy Sherman's face intently as though trying to gauge his reaction.

"If you're waiting for me to state a preference for one of those plans," said Guy Sherman quietly, "we shall both be here a very long time."

Big Minh waved a dismissive hand. "My chief concern is to get an assurance from you that the United States government will not try to thwart our plans. That will be sufficient. We do not expect or need specific active involvement from your side."

"But you still haven't told me who's with you."

"Major General Tran Van Don, the chairman of the Joint General Staff, Brigadier General Than Thien Khiem, the executive officer of the Joint General Staff, Major General Kim . . . need I continue?"

Guy Sherman pulled a notebook from his pocket and jotted down the names with slow deliberation before looking up at the general again. "May I ask why you speak again now of a great urgency? Why do you need to know Washington's reaction so quickly? At the end of August we expected a definite move from you — but for five weeks nothing has happened."

Again Big Minh shrugged his ample body in the depths of the dentist's chair. "There were difficulties. I, for one, was under close surveillance — some junior officers were arrested suddenly. But in these few weeks things have changed. Not only regimental

529

commanders but even battalion and company commanders are now so angry with the regime that they are all working on coup plans of their own. Such rash plots by inexperienced officers could of course be a danger to our own plans — that's why we must act fast now."

"And if your plot's successful and both Nhu and Diem are overthrown, what then?" asked the American carefully.

"I've got no political ambitions for myself," replied Minh in a matter-of-fact tone. "Nor have any of the other staff officers. Immediately after the coup there'll be a two-tiered government structure. I will head a Military Committee as interim president. We'll oversee a cabinet composed mainly of civilians. My only purpose is to win the war — but to do this, a continuation of American military and economic aid at the present level is essential." His eyes glittered and he sat up in the chair, gripping its arms tightly with both hands. "At the present rate of one and a half million dollars a day, that is, Monsieur Sherman. Now do you understand the importance of my question to you?"

The CIA officer studied the face of the Vietnamese intently; laughter lines were etched deep into the round cheeks of the forty-seven-year-old general, but a certain coldness in his gaze gave him an air that was at once cherubic and ruthless. Big Minh, he knew, had made his reputation by crushing the private armies of the Binh Xuyen and the Hoa Hao sect for President Diem soon after he took office; he was known to be brave to the point of foolhardiness, a genuinely inspirational officer, and face to face with him alone for the first time, Guy Sherman could feel how that curious mixture of geniality and harshness might bind the men under him to his command. He understood too, suddenly why President Diem, ever conscious of the threat from his subordinates, had ten months earlier appointed Minh as "Military Adviser to the President," a meaningless desk job in the palace that had effectively separated the charismatic general from a power base of loyal regiments.

"Since I didn't know what you would say before I came here today you'll appreciate I'm not authorized to give specific answers about noninterference in your plans by the United States government," said Guy Sherman at last, choosing his words with meticulous care. "I'll report everything you've said to my superiors, of course. And you can rest assured this will go right back to the White House."

"Will it also go right back to that office filled with stuffed animal heads on the second floor of Gia Long Palace too?" Minh spoke in a deceptively mild voice, but his manner had suddenly changed and his eyes had become narrow slits of suspicion in his round face. "It's well enough known that your CIA chief of station is a close confidant of Ngo Dinh Nhu and his 'first lady.' " Minh paused significantly. "And other agents have been seen to visit his office frequently too. My fellow generals and myself have even wondered sometimes whether Nhu and Madame Nhu might be on the CIA payroll."

"Our present station chief, as you must know, has just been relieved of his post," said Guy Sherman shortly. "He left Saigon today."

"But that doesn't fully answer my question."

"You're reputed to have an exceptional grasp of politics for a soldier, General Minh. Ambassador Nolting, who was a close confidant of President Diem, has recently been recalled — President Kennedy replaced him with Henry Cabot Lodge the day after the pagoda raids, remember? You surely have noticed that Ambassador Lodge has deliberately kept his distance from President Diem since his arrival. The CIA station chief you refer to who knew Ngo Dinh Nhu well was removed at Mr Lodge's specific request — those facts point clearly in a certain direction, don't they?"

"You're still avoiding answering my question, Monsieur Sherman."

"Sometimes," said the American, his face expressionless, "you just have to trust the United States."

Minh leaned backwards suddenly in the dentists's chair and stared at the ceiling, his big hands flexing from time to time on its leather arms. "If we decide to take that risk, we shall obviously have to meet again," he said without looking at the CIA man. "I quite understand, Monsieur Sherman, that for now you are unable to comment on behalf of your government on what I've said — but what is your private opinion?"

"I'm not paid to have private opinions, general," said Guy flatly.

"Yes, yes," said the general, grinning broadly again. "I'm well aware of that — but nevertheless, if you were, what would your view be?"

Guy moved closer to the chair and picked up one of the dentist's drills; he studied the control panel for a second or two, then touched a button which set the drill in motion. Its high-pitched whine filled the office and Big Minh watched him suspiciously as the American leaned towards him. "To help you, general, I'm going to give you some highly confidential information. I'm going to read you two top-secret telegrams." He fished in his inside pocket with his free hand and pulled out two folded sheets of paper. "The first one was sent to Washington by the ambassador here on August 29. It reads: 'We're launched on a course from which there is no respectable turning back — the overthrow of the Diem government. The chance of bringing off a generals' coup depends to some extent on the Vietnamese officers concerned — but we should proceed to make an all-out effort to get the generals to move promptly.' . . . " Guy raised his head to look at Big Minh. "Is that clear enough?"

Minh nodded slowly, then arched a skeptical eyebrow. "That might have been the stand of the United States on August 29. But since then President Diem has sent Madame Nhu abroad, his brother the archbishop of Hue has left the country — and there are signs of confusion in the White House."

By way of reply Guy showed the other sheet of paper to the Vietnamese general. "The second telegram bears today's date, October 5," he said slowly. "It was sent here to Saigon from the White House only a few hours ago. It reads: 'The President today approved a recommendation that there should be an urgent covert effort under the broad guidance of the ambassador to identify and build contacts with a possible alternative leadership. But this effort should be totally secure and fully deniable.' " Guy switched off the dental drill and replaced it on its hook; folding the telegrams, he returned them to his pocket. "Does that give you a better idea of the attitude in Washington?"

Minh's smile broadened. "Thank you, Monsieur Sherman — but at our next meeting I'd appreciate it if you could give me more concrete assurances on the questions of aid and non-interference. Then perhaps we can also discuss our plans and how we intend to carry them out."

"I'll report everything you've said in great detail," said Guy politely, "and I'll return with replies as soon as I can."

"Then I look forward to another meeting with you soon."

General Minh made no attempt to rise from his chair, and the American left the room quietly, unlocked a door in the passage outside with his own key, and let himself out into an alleyway leading to the central market. As he hurried into the square he heard a sudden flurry of screams, and above the heads of a small crowd he saw black smoke belching upwards. When he drew nearer, the charred head and shoulders of a man seated on the pavement became visible, and he realized another Buddhist monk, the fifth since Thich Quang Duc, was burning himself to death in the center of Saigon.

13

The leaves of the tamarind trees along Saigon's deserted lunchtime boulevards hung limp in the fierce, saturated heat of Friday, November 1, as the tanks, armored personnel carriers and artillery pieces of the forces in revolt roared through their shade towards the Gia Long Palace. The unsuspecting population of the city heard their rumble only dimly at first through a haze of sleep; it was one-thirty P.M., midpoint of the daily three-hour siesta, and Big Minh and the other insurgent generals had chosen the date carefully — All Saints' Day, a Catholic holiday — so as to catch the president and his defenders off guard. The fitfully slumbering city came abruptly awake at that unfamiliar hour, however, when Marine units spearheading the rebel battalions ran into a fierce barrage of gunfire from the palace defenders, that reverberated through the enclosed canyons of the capital's streets like spring thunder.

On the deserted roof of the Caravelle Hotel, Naomi Boyce-Lewis stood beside her Scottish cameraman, biting her lower lip in suppressed excitement as he panned his lens slowly across the wide panorama of tree-lined boulevards radiating from the Gia Long Palace. From that high vantage point, the attacking forces moving into the city down the three northern highways from Tay Ninh, Ben Cat and Bien Hoa looked like slow-crawling columns of predatory insects converging by communal instinct to destroy some threat to their existence, and as he filmed them, Jock whistled softly in appreciation.

"I've got to hand it to you, Naomi — whoever tipped you off about this knew his stuff all right. I don't know how you do it — or maybe I do, but I'm not saying." As he shifted to cover a new angle of the advance, he winked at the soundman, who was leaning over the parapet holding his long microphone towards the roar of the advancing armor.

The English journalist delivered a mock punch to the side of his jaw with a small fist and smiled affectionately. "You've got a monorail mind, Jock — just concentrate on getting our exclusive coverage in the can, will you, please. The competition are going to come stumbling out from under their mosquito nets any minute now to start trying to catch up."

"Was it that rugged American diplomat with the come-to-bed eyes who wants to spite the American press corps? Have you been working your siren spell on him, Naomi?"

"No comment, Jock — just keep filming."

In fact Guy Sherman had surprised her by appearing unannounced at the door of her room in the Continental Palace before breakfast that morning. Although he had affected a casual air, she'd noticed that his manner was tense beneath a surface calm, and he had insisted on entering the room and turning on the bedside radio before he spoke. Then he had explained in little more than a whisper that what he was about to tell her would be in the strictest confidence, and when she had given him her word that she would never reveal the source of her information to anyone, he said: "Today's the day, Naomi! Get your camera team up on the Caravelle roof for one-fifteen. Then you'll have a fine view of the cavalry coming over the hill."

It had been the first time she had seen Guy for a week. They had met on the Continental terrace for drinks on a number of occasions in the days following Thich Quang Duc's suicide and eventually had begun to dine together regularly. As the conflict deepened following the raids on the Buddhist pagodas, student riots had broken out, several Buddhist leaders had sought asylum inside the American Embassy, and Ngo Dihn Nhu was reported to be suffering Hitler-style brainstorms as the situation deteriorated. With Saigon drowning in a sea of intrigue and plots and counterplots proliferating daily, Guy had become an invaluable source of information to her; with a wink or a nod he had smilingly confirmed or denied any rumors she had discussed with him, and largely because of his help she had provided consistently accurate and well-informed coverage of the growing crisis, which had won her praise and acclaim in both England and the United States. In the course of their frequent meetings, a teasing bond of intimacy had also grown up between them; they both made frequent lighthearted allusions to the selfish motives that drew them to one another, but at the same time she had sensed that the strong attraction Guy had flippantly confessed to at their first meeting was growing into a deeper infatuation.

534

She herself was no longer sure that the desire to cultivate a highly knowledgeable source of information was her sole reason for meeting Guy so regularly; as time passed and the crisis grew more confused she had come to have a genuine regard for his seemingly unshakable confidence in the American mission in Vietnam, and whenever she was with him his dark good looks and his air of vigorous masculinity always gave her a comforting sense of security in a city which seemed to become more dangerous with each passing day. On more than one occasion after dining together late at night they had strolled through the darkness of the tense city, acutely aware that their senses were mutely in tune, that they were drawn physically to one another. But always she had called a halt at the brink; always she had subordinated her emotions to her hard-headed determination to stay on top of the story and she had deliberately parted from him on these occasions with a murmured endearment and a smiling hint of promise for the future. This calculated ploy had produced precisely the effect she had desired, and Guy, seemingly accepting that she was holding herself in check till the story had run its course, began to take her increasingly into his confidence. For this reason she had been puzzled that he had stopped contacting her during the last days of October, but when he had appeared unexpectedly at the door of her room that morning she had known by his expression and the barely suppressed excitement in his voice that nothing had changed.

After delivering his message he had made to leave, but then he turned back and took her hand impulsively in his. "Stay tuned to me, Naomi," he'd said with deliberate emphasis. "If you do, I'll make sure you keep ahead of the opposition on the inside story too. Okay?"

"Okay, Guy, thanks — and good luck." Feeling her own excitement rising in response, she had returned the pressure of his hand, and he had dashed from the room. She had begun immediately to make her preparations, renting several different cars and stationing them secretly at various selected locations around the center of Saigon to ensure that she and her camera team remained mobile during the inevitable dislocation that would catch the other film and newsprint journalists off guard. She had alerted Jock and their soundman to steer clear of the rest of the press corps and had sought out two or three Western visitors who were due to leave the city later that day and arranged for them to try to carry out her undeveloped film to Hong Kong.

One of the rented cars with its Vietnamese driver at the wheel was waiting in a side street close to the Caravelle Hotel, and as soon as she was satisfied that Jock had enough general rooftop shots of the initial rebel advance into the city, she led the way down the stairs to the street at a run.

But the unfolding coup d'état that from the high vantage point had seemed simple and dramatic was at street level confusing and incoherent. During a quick tour of the city center, they heard distant scattered flurries of small arms fire, but by the time they had tracked down the shooting they found that the crack Marine spearhead units had already seized their primary objectives; the main police headquarters, the two radio stations and the central telephone exchange had obviously been occupied by the rebels without much trouble, but there was little to film except small groups of steel-helmeted Vietnamese troops in leopard camouflage leaning casually against the walls. Armored cars were guarding the approach boulevards to the palace, standing still and silent in the roadway, their guns leveled and their hatches closed despite the stifling midday heat, but otherwise Naomi had to be content with pictures of anonymous infantry columns or truckloads of helmeted troops who rushed by without giving any indication of whether they were being deployed by the rebels or by the president.

Here and there the ominous, dun-colored bulk of a tank was visible squatting astride a road junction; in the peaceful, civilized streets of the city the sight of these war machines was, as the plotting generals had obviously intended, frightening and intimidating, and Naomi repeatedly ordered their driver to turn around and seek another route. From time to time a T-28 wheeled across the burning, cloudless sky to release a burst of rockets on the Gia Long Palace, and this always drew a rattle of heavy machine-gun fire from its defenders — but no concerted bombing attack or artillery barrage was mounted. By filming at the limit of his telephoto lens along some of the approach boulevards, Jock got pictures of the Presidential Guard preparing for a last-ditch stand; batteries of mortars, antiaircraft guns and even tanks were being dug in among the shrubs and tamarinds of the formal gardens, while on the roof heavy machine gun posts had already been set up around the glass and wrought-iron cupola. Dense barbed-wire entanglements had been strung around the palace railings in preparation for the siege, and it was obvious that the stubborn president and his brother were determined to resist to the bitter end their own army's efforts to unseat them.

The people of Saigon, startled from their siestas, eventually began emerging from their homes. Few vehicles ventured onto the boulevards that had become a battleground, but pedestrians thronged the sidewalks, peering fearfully at the stationary tanks and watching the passing troops with anxious eyes. They scattered and dived for cover whenever the boom of a tank's cannon, deafening in the confined streets, or the stutter of a heavy machine gun sent shells and bullets crashing through the branches of the tamarinds, but in the intervals of calm, small children rushed squealing from their hiding places to scoop up the empty brass cartridge cases. Gradually the sound of small arms fire and the crump of mortars were heard with greater frequency as the rebels attacked the Ministries of the Interior and National Defense; more planes dived down, their cannon pounding streams of shells into the pro-Diem navy frigates moored in the Saigon River and when her frightened driver bolted unexpectedly, Naomi herself drove the car to the Majestic at the foot of the old Rue Catinat so that Jock could cover this fierce battle between the Vietnamese navy and air force from the hotel roof. While it was in progress she did a brief filmed commentary standing by the parapet, pointing out that although it was not apparent in the confusion, the insurgent generals were slowly tightening their ring of steel around the Ngo Dinh brothers trapped in their palace.

As soon as the brief river battle ended, Naomi called Guy Sherman's number at the embassy to try to check on what was really happening behind the scenes — but a brusque American voice told her that Mr. Sherman was "not available." When she asked at what time she would be able to contact him, the voice told her even more brusquely that Mr. Sherman would be taking no calls at all for the rest of that day.

At that moment, Guy himself was reporting in by telephone to the CIA acting chief of station, who was seated in an adjoining office in the embassy. Over a secure line from the headquarters of the ARVN Joint General Staff close to Tan Son Nhut airport, he was giving details of the rebel battle order that had just been handed to him on a typewritten sheet of paper by Major General Duong Van Minh.

"Two Marine battalions, two battalions of Airborne troops and two battalions of the Fifth Division are all now deployed downtown under the command of junior officers," said Guy, speaking in a calm voice. "They started moving into the city three-quarters of an hour ago behind forty tanks and armored cars. The airport was secured before the armor began rolling, and additional units have been deployed to block and defend against any counterattack by forces loyal to Diem from outside Saigon. First reports from the unit commanders indicate all objectives are being seized against minimal resistance. . . ." Feeling a tap on his shoulder, Guy covered the mouthpiece and turned to find one of Big Minh's aides beside him.

"Come quickly, Monsieur Sherman," whispered the Vietnamese officer in French. "The staff meeting is assembling."

Guy nodded and turned back to the telephone, lowering his voice. "The launching of the coup was timed to coincide with the regular Friday luncheon meeting of all senior staff officers here," he said quietly. "Those officers not involved in the planning are about to be told what's happening — I'll report again in half an hour."

Guy replaced the receiver and hurried in the wake of the aide to the crowded conference room. Big Minh was already on his feet on a dais at one end, and as Guy entered he saw him set the spools of a big tape recorder spinning. Many of the officers present looked tense and pale, and their uneasy expressions deepened at the sight of an American civilian. The moment Guy seated himself unobtrusively at the back of the room Minh began speaking.

"The day the people have been waiting for has come," he announced in a ringing voice. "For eight years the people of Vietnam have suffered under the rotten, nepotic Diem regime but now the armed forces have come to their rescue. While we were taking luncheon today Marine and Airborne battalions have moved into Saigon to surround the palace. All police stations, the radio stations, the Ministry of the Interior and other strongpoints are already in the hands of our forces. . . ."

As he was speaking, doors at either end of the conference room opened to admit two dozen armed troops in full battle order, carrying American M-16 automatic rifles. They ranged themselves quietly around the walls, and many of the senior staff officers blanched visibly at the sight of them.

"The aim of myself and those officers who have planned this coup with me," continued Minh, "is to depose Ngo Dinh Diem

538

and his brothers and set up a military council which will govern in their place until democratic civilian rule can be restored. I shall act as interim president. Some of you have already sworn your allegiance to us, but others among you have yet to make up your mind. To those I would say that we have made this move today because, to cap the long catalogue of crimes committed by the Diem government, Supreme Counsellor Nhu has recently begun secret negotiations with Hanoi. This crass betrayal of everything we're fighting for was the final straw which goaded us into action. And we trust all of you here will have the good sense to join with us. . . ." He paused and let his gaze roam meaningfully around his audience. "Perhaps I should inform you, gentlemen, at the outset that the commander of the navy was told about this coup while on his way here today under armed escort. But he refused to forswear his allegiance to Ngo Dinh Diem, and was promptly executed by his escort on my orders. Other officers whose loyalty we are doubtful about are at this moment under close arrest in the basement of this building. They include the commanders of the air force, the Airborne Brigade, the Marines and . . ." Minh paused once more to heighten the impact of his words. ". . . and Colonel Le Quang Tung, the commanding officer of the Special Forces."

A ripple of astonishment greeted the mention of Colonel Tung's name; the Special Forces, financed and trained directly by the United States, had been withdrawn from the war against the Viet Cong six months earlier by an increasingly jittery President Diem; since then the elite troops had been deployed purely as a presidential bodyguard, and the news that their own commander was already in the hands of the coup leaders seemed to seal the fate of the president and his brother. Before the commotion among the staff officers died away, Minh held up his hand and pointed towards the silently spinning spools of the tape recorder.

"Now all of you here are to be offered the opportunity to declare your support publicly for our cause. I want every officer present to step up to this microphone, announce his name, rank and command and pledge his loyalty in his own words. We shall begin broadcasting this recording over the captured radio networks later this afternoon." He stopped speaking and his round face broke into a smile. "Who will be first?"

Without hesitation General Tran Van Don, chairman of the Joint General Staff, came forward and spoke his name into the microphone. "I swear to dedicate myself to the overthrow of the corrupt Diem regime," he said slowly, "and pledge my most loyal support to the Military Council headed by Major General Duong Van Minh. . . ." He turned and sat down as quickly as he had risen, and one by one the other tense-faced generals, brigadiers and colonels stepped up onto the platform and made similar declarations. Guy Sherman jotted down each name carefully in his notebook, and after they had finished he hurried from the room to the secure telephone that had been set up in the adjoining office; when the acting chief of the Saigon CIA station came on the line again, Guy read him the complete list of names. Half an hour later radio sets all over the capital began broadcasting this same dramatic roll call, which for better or for worse publicly committed the majority of South Vietnam's senior military officers to the overthrow of their government; a long monotonous tally of individual voices that were clearly recognizable to the listening Vietnamese population, it was broadcast over and over again, sounding through the embattled city like a mournful dirge composed specially in preparation for the passing of Ngo Dinh Diem's regime.

14

In his ornately furnished office on the second floor of the Gia Long Palace, Ngo Dinh Nhu, Supreme Counsellor and brother to President Diem, smiled patiently as he listened to the excited jabberings of a Vietnamese voice coming through the earpiece of his telephone. Leaning back in his chair he put his feet up on his black lacquer desk and blew a fine stream of cigarette smoke towards the ceiling.

"Yes, yes, of course I understand clearly, my dear captain," he rasped, his smile broadening. "Armored cars and men of the Marine Corps are surrounding your police station — that's quite natural. They're doing that because I planned that they should. Try to calm down and don't worry. Pretend you're surprised when they come in and just let them take over."

Nhu dropped the telephone back onto its cradle, still smiling, and flicked a tiny speck of ash from one leg of his immaculately creased black trousers. For a moment he sat listening to the intermittent sound of gunfire coming from outside the palace windows, then he opened the tortoiseshell box on his desk and lit a fresh cigarette from the glowing stub of the old one. As he did so the door of the office burst open and the short, rotund figure of President Diem appeared; he was dressed in one of his favorite suits of dark blue sharkskin, but the comic eccentricity of his rolling gait was exaggerated by his haste, and his brother's brittle smile returned as he watched him waddle across the broad expanse of carpet dotted with stuffed hunting trophies. But Diem did not return the smile; he was panting for breath when he stopped in front of the wide desk, and his chubby face was perspiring freely in his anxiety.

"What exactly is going on out there, Nhu? What have you done this time? Please explain yourself."

"Nothing's changed since we spoke on the telephone fifteen minutes ago," replied Nhu with an amused shrug. "There was no need to upset yourself and come rushing downstairs like this. You've said often enough you don't wish to concern yourself with what methods I use to achieve our ends. Everything happening out there in the street is part of my plan."

The roar of one of the palace tanks firing rattled the window frames suddenly, and Diem turned and peered anxiously into the ornamental gardens through each of the windows in turn. The dark outlines of rebel tanks and armored cars squatting in the shade of the boulevard trees were distantly visible through the palace railings, and as the president watched, a slow-moving Air Force C-47 lumbered across the distant rooftops, showering leaflets into the streets.

"If this really is part of some harebrained scheme of yours, I don't approve of it," said Diem turning angrily on his brother once more. "Where precisely is it leading?"

"To the defeat of all our enemies at one fell swoop!" Nhu flourished his cigarette in a theatrical fashion as if to indicate he found explaining his ingenious maneuvers tiresome. "Because it was obvious some kind of coup would be mounted against us sooner or later, I decided to get in first — that's all there is to it."

Diem stared at his inanely grinning brother. "What do you mean 'get in first'?"

"With our own 'coup' of course." Nhu laughed abruptly. "It even has a code name — Bravo Two. At the end of it the likes of 'Fat Boy' Minh and the treacherous Tran Van Don will find themselves shackled in irons."

Diem drew a long breath, fighting to control his anger. "Those tanks out there with their gun barrels pointing at us look very real to me."

"Of course they do, my dear brother, of course they do. That's the whole point. It's got to look like a real coup against us. Those troops out there are from General Dinh's Fifth Division. I ordered him to move four battalions against the palace to make it look as if they are genuinely trying to overthrow us. I even ordered four of our Special Forces battalions out of Saigon to make it look more convincing. . . ."

Diem's face turned pale. "You've sent four battalions of the Presidential Guard out of the city? That means we have only one battalion protecting the palace!"

"Please relax," said Nhu in a chiding voice. "General Dinh is awaiting my orders to drive off the attackers with other units of the Fifth Division. But we've got to let them appear to succeed for a time — then you and I will reemerge victorious from the beleaguered palace. If we're seen by the world to put down a rebellion and identify Minh and Tran Van Don as the chief culprits, our position will be strengthened and our enemies will be in disarray, don't you see?"

Diem's anxious expression relaxed slightly. "But how do you know that General Dinh can be trusted to come to our rescue?"

"You know as well as I how conceited and ambitious the military governor of Saigon is. I promised him promotion and a post in the government as a reward — he'll do anything I say."

Diem took a folded white handkerchief from his breast pocket and mopped his brow distractedly.

"You should have learned by now to trust me," continued Nhu reproachfully. "I got us out of trouble when they dive-bombed Doc Lap Palace in 'fifty-nine, didn't I? And didn't I find a way of blocking the paratroopers' coup a year later? Each new attempt to unseat us, don't you see, requires a different response — a different brand of genius." A telephone began ringing on his desk, but the grinning Nhu ignored it. "We must let them lay siege to the palace for a few hours to allow time for the attention of the country and the outside world to focus on us — then we'll move to crush the rebellion with great speed!"

Diem gazed dubiously into his brother's raddled face, then turned and walked slowly back towards the door. Nhu picked up the phone and listened without speaking; then he cupped

542

his hand over the mouthpiece. "It's for you," he called to his brother. "Fat Boy Minh has something important to say that he won't impart to me."

The president's face registered his disquiet as he returned to take the telephone, and as soon as he identified himself, Big Minh launched into a prepared speech.

"As commander in chief of all the military forces besieging the Gia Long Palace, I call on you and your brother to surrender to us," he said in a belligerent tone. "The people of Vietnam have suffered long enough — now, under the leadership of the Joint General Staff, the armed forces have come to their rescue."

The president drew a sharp breath. "You are bluffing. I order you, General Minh, and all senior officers to report to the palace at once."

"You must surrender — or we cannot guarantee your safety," retorted Minh coolly. "The time has passed when you can give me or anybody else orders."

"You will be shown no mercy when this is over, general," said the president in an icy voice. "General Dinh and the Fifth Division are at this moment preparing to counterattack the forces around the palace. When they've been driven off, you and your co-conspirators will be dealt with most severely."

"General Dinh is here with us at the headquarters of the Joint General Staff," said Minh's voice smoothly. "We offered him the post of minister of the interior in a new government, and he has come over to our side. The great majority of the staff officers have also sworn a joint oath to drive you from power."

"You lie!" Diem's voice rose angrily. "I don't believe you."

"Even Colonel Tung is with us — the commander of the Special Forces that protect you and your evil brother."

"Colonel Tung would never betray us!"

"Perhaps not," said Minh in a matter-of-fact voice. "But we aren't giving him any choice. As proof that he's here, I shall allow him to speak to you briefly — after that he will be dealt with as we see fit. Hold the line, please."

Diem turned an anguished face to his brother. "They say Dinh has joined them and they've taken Colonel Tung prisoner."

Nhu's raddled features flexed suddenly into an angry grimace, and he snatched the telephone receiver from his brother. "Allow me to speak to Colonel Tung," he demanded in an imperious voice.

A moment later the nasal tones of the widely feared Special

543

Forces commander who'd led the raids on the Buddhist pagodas, echoed in the earpiece of the telephone. "I'm being held here against my will, supreme counsellor," he said, speaking with difficulty. "I was tricked into coming and have taken no part in the proceedings. They held a gun at my head and forced me to order all Special Forces troops at our headquarters to surrender. . . ."

"Rest assured the uprising will soon be crushed," yelled Nhu suddenly, his voice high-pitched and hysterical. "You'll be freed unharmed, Colonel Tung, never fear."

"I repeat my demand that you and your brother surrender immediately!" The voice of Big Minh cut in again, as calm and controlled as before. "And if you don't believe the whole army is against you, I suggest you turn on your radio."

The line went dead abruptly, and after staring wild-eyed at his brother for a second or two, Nhu hurried across to switch on a radio standing on a side table; he gazed unseeing at the voluptuous life-sized portrait of his wife on the wall before him as the sound of the staff officers declaring allegiance to the rebel cause filled the room. Both men listened intently for several minutes, then when General Ton That Dinh's voice finally denounced them, Nhu switched off the set with a muffled curse. "We'd better go down to the communications center," he said, his voice unnaturally calm again. "Once we contact My Tho, it won't take long for the Seventh Division to enter Saigon and rout the Fat Boy's treacherous lackeys!"

In a corridor at the Tan Son Nhut headquarters of the Joint General Staff, Guy Sherman watched impassively as armed troops hustled Colonel Tung away from the telephone which had been used to call the Gia Long Palace. Still wearing camouflage battle dress, his hands were already manacled behind his back and his ankles were hobbled with ropes. He struggled and dragged his feet as the troops forced him along the corridor towards stairs that led down to a walled courtyard, and Guy stepped aside to let the group pass. As the Special Forces colonel drew abreast of him, his eyes met Guy's and his narrow features twisted into a sneer.

"I should have known you filthy American motherfuckers were behind these cowardly traitors," he screamed in English and loosed a stream of spittle that splashed across the CIA man's cheek before he could turn aside. One of the soldiers clubbed Tung with the butt of his M-16 and he stumbled and almost fell;

half carrying him they bundled him down the stairs, and Guy moved to a window, wiping his face with a handkerchief, and saw the escort drag him into the courtyard below. There Tung stood looking dazedly around the yard, trying to watch a number of exits at once, but he didn't notice the grim-faced ARVN captain who suddenly hurried from a corner door, drawing his revolver as he came. At the last moment the Special Forces commander turned his head and caught sight of him, but the captain placed the gun against Tung's temple without difficulty; the instant the trigger was pulled he fell limp in the arms of his captors, and they quickly dragged his lifeless body away through an open archway.

In the underground communications center beneath the palace the president and his brother worked frantically in their shirtsleeves for the next hour, operating the telephones and radio transmitters themselves behind bolted steel doors. They made repeated efforts to contact those provincial leaders and unit commanders who were based within reach of Saigon, but each time they found they were able to raise only low-ranking aides. After a dozen unsuccessful attempts, Ngo Dinh Nhu made contact with the headquarters of the Seventh Division at My Tho, forty miles south of Saigon, and the president stood by anxiously as his brother listened to the voice crackling into his headphones; but although Nhu screamed and ranted, threatening and cajoling by turns, he finally broke the radio link without issuing any coherent order and slumped back listlessly in his seat.

"What is it?" demanded Diem in frightened voice. "What's happened there?"

"The top commanders have been made prisoners," he said dully. "Our enemies have withdrawn all the river-crossing craft to the opposite bank of the Mekong — the Seventh Division's out of action."

A minute later there was a flurry of knocking on the steel door, and when the president opened it, a flustered aide entered. "The rebels are surrounding the barracks of the Presidential Guard," he gasped. "They're moving up artillery and mortars — they obviously intend to begin a sustained bombardment soon."

The nervous aide's hands shook as he handed a typewritten version of the message to the president, but Diem's face became thoughtful as he locked the door again. "There's only one last avenue left open to us now," he said quietly and seated himself beside a telephone once more. Glancing at his wristwatch he noticed that it was four-thirty P.M., and taking out a small private address book, he looked up the home telephone number of the United States ambassador, Henry Cabot Lodge. As soon as he'd dialed, a Vietnamese servant answered, and both men waited tensely until the clipped American voice of the ambassador came on the line.

"This is the president speaking," said Diem in English, struggling to disguise the rising anxiety he felt. "Some units of the army and the air force have made a rebellion, and I want to know what is the attitude of the United States."

The ambassador didn't answer immediately, but when he spoke his patrician voice was haughty and formal. "I don't feel well enough informed to be able to tell you. I've heard the shooting, but I'm not acquainted with all the facts. Also it's four-thirty A.M. in Washington, and the U.S. government cannot possibly have a view."

"But you must have some general ideas!" The voice of the president took on an incredulous, plaintive tone. "After all, I *am* a chief of state. I've tried to do my duty and I want to do now what duty and good sense require." He hesitated, summoning a note of pride. "I believed in duty above all."

There was an even longer pause at the ambassador's end of the line. "You've certainly done your duty — I admire your courage and your great contribution to your country. No one can take from you the credit for what you've done. Now I'm worried about your physical safety. I have a report that those in charge of the current activity offer you and your brother safe conduct out of the country if you resign. Had you heard this?"

The president absorbed the shock slowly: the ambassador's use of the term "current activity" made it clear beyond all doubt that the backs of his chief sponsors were now turned finally against him. "No," he said at last, drawing out the word in dismay, "I hadn't heard that." Another long pause followed, then he added lamely: "You have my telephone number?"

"Yes," replied the ambassador, and a further embarrassing silence ensued. Then, in case he had not made it clear enough, Henry Cabot Lodge labored his point once again. "If I can do anything for your *physical safety*, please call me."

The Vietnamese felt his anger rise as he contemplated the humiliating offer that was being made to him — shelter in the very embassy where, he realized now, his overthrow must certainly have been connived at. Suddenly all the stubborn, defiant pride for which he was renowned, and even a trace of scorn, flashed back into his voice: "I shall continue my efforts to restore order," he said fiercely — and as soon as he'd spoken, President Ngo Dinh Diem broke off his last contact with the United States of America.

15

Like all the other foreign journalists covering the coup, Naomi Boyce-Lewis spent the tense afternoon and early evening hours trying desperately to penetrate the confusion that cloaked Saigon like a dense fog; attempts to count up and codify units loyal to the palace or the plotters always came out inconclusive because of insufficient information, and there was no sure way of testing the repeated claims of the rebels that their uprising had already succeeded. About six o'clock in the evening they unleashed a massive artillery and mortar barrage against the Presidental Guard encampment a few blocks from the Gia Long Palace, and the buildings were reduced rapidly to ruins; but although the sound and fury of the destruction provided dramatic pictures and copy for Naomi and the rest of the press corps, its effect was minimal, since most of the troops billeted there were already deployed inside the palace grounds. Over the radio, General Minh's tape-recorded voice continued to proclaim that the armed forces had rescued the people from eight years of misrule, and crowds of cheering Vietnamese emerged to cluster around the rebel tanks and armored cars whenever there was a pause in the action. There was even some celebratory looting of shops, but with the palace and its defenders still holding out defiantly, an atmosphere of nervous uncertainty spread through the city as the evening wore on.

Naomi and her camera crew positioned themselves in a deep doorway within sight of the palace gates, but long hours of waiting produced little reward; occasionally they saw one of the loyalist tanks rumble into the palace forecourt and lurch through the soft flower beds to fire its cannon at the ring of attackers entrenched in the surrounding streets; machine-gun fire spurted sporadically from the windows between the ornate pillars of the palace's cream-colored stone façade and from time to time a voice that sounded like President's Diem's attempted to rally the troops over a public-address system with vague promises that loyal units were racing to the rescue. But gradually it became clear that a lull was developing, and as the dusk deepened a fine, warm drizzle of rain began to drift down onto the city. A seven P.M. curfew was declared over the radio, and rumors began to spread that the coup leaders had got cold feet and were divided on whether they should launch an all-out attack on the palace or not.

Naomi returned twice to her hotel room to try to contact Guy at the embassy, but each time she received the same curt response — he was "not available." As she replaced the telephone the second time, she heard a soft footfall in the corridor outside her room and looked up to see a white envelope slide beneath the door. When she opened it, she found a note inside written in spidery letters which said simply: "Relax and get some sleep until three-thirty A.M. Guy."

The note was obviously not in Guy's handwriting, and she tore open the door to see a Vietnamese waiter disappearing silently along the corridor. When she called him back, he explained that he had taken down the message by telephone from "an American gentleman" who had not given his name. Naomi thanked the waiter and gave him five hundred piastres then hurried back to the street to tell her camera crew to get some rest. She drank a large whisky herself before climbing into bed for a few hours, and when she awoke with the ringing of her alarm clock at three A.M., she roused her crew and they hurried into the streets again to find that an unnatural hush had fallen over the city.

The moist air was stifling at that hour, but the pre-dawn darkness was relieved by the glare from several burning tanks and an occasional building that had suffered a direct hit. They dashed across Lam Son Square to the Caravelle Hotel, and when they reached the roof they found it crowded with a dense throng of people who had been trapped there by the curfew. In the light of the fires they saw then that Saigon's other rooftops and balconies were crowded too, and thousands of silent faces were watching and waiting like spectators in a giant grandstand for the climax of the drama. From time to time a magnesium parachute flare blossomed in the dark sky above them, and whenever a plane appeared, red globular tracers arced upwards from the Gia Long Palace.

On the Caravelle roof terrace, white-jacketed waiters still moved among the crowd, serving refreshments, and Naomi noticed that some of those present — diplomats, correspondents, visiting businessmen and hotel workers — were somewhat the worse for drink. They had been watching the grim spectacle for many hours on end, and to some it seemed to have become an entertainment. Somewhere a radio was playing twist and cha-cha music; the rebels had begun to intersperse their repeated communiqués with this music during the night because it had been previously banned by Madame Nhu, and a group of junior American Embassy staffers and female secretaries were dancing exaggeratedly to the radio, bursting into noisy laughter at frequent intervals. But at three-thirty A.M. precisely, their sounds of hilarity were suddenly drowned by an ear-numbing torrent of noise. The deep boom of 75-millimeter tank guns, the thud of mortar and artillery shells and the stutter of 50-millimeter machine guns all combined to produce an unbroken roar that obviously signaled the beginning of the final assault on the palace. Shot and shell poured down every boulevard leading to Gia Long, and the building's already-pitted façade splintered and cracked under the onslaught. Soon the few loyalist tanks, the heavy machine guns behind the rooftop balustrades and the mortar batteries dug in around the grounds were adding to the din, and from the Caravelle terrace the night seemed to be alive with a million muzzle flashes. As Naomi watched, the interior of the glass cupola on the palace roof was lit suddenly from inside by dancing flames, and she guessed that the upper floors had caught fire inside.

"Beautiful, just beautiful," breathed Jock as he squinted at the scene through the eye of his camera. "I've never seen anything to match it."

The barrage lasted for an incredible two hours, and when it finally died away pale streaks of morning light illuminated the final rebel advance into the palace. Under lowering skies from which drizzling rain still fell, tanks, armored cars and armored personnel carriers, followed by running, crouching men, inched slowly towards the wrought-iron railings, and finally at about six-thirty A.M. Naomi saw a solitary white flag of surrender flutter out of one of the palace's high windows.

The Vietnamese Marines were wearing scarlet scarves about their necks by this time to distinguish them from the defenders, and on spotting the white flag they rose up into the open, screaming their battle cries in unison, and raced across the pitted lawn towards the smoking ruins. Naomi and her crew were among the handful of journalists courageous enough to follow them, and a few stray shots were still whistling across the formal gardens as they dashed for the shattered main door; because Marines were scuffling with fleeing Special Forces troops and blocking the steps, Jock led the way through a gaping hole blown in the wall, and inside they found the marble floor littered with the glass of smashed chandeliers and fallen masonry. Groaning Special Forces troops, their bodies shattered by shell fragments, lay on the broad staircases alongside men already dead, plaster from the high ceilings covered the brocade chairs and potted palms, and the air was filled with choking smoke and the reek of cordite. The attack had severed the power supplies, and the jubilant rebel soldiers, not to be denied the spoils of victory, lit candles and began carrying away books and ornaments in an hysterical mood of celebration.

Guy had long ago explained the palace layout to her, and Naomi led the crew up the wide staircase towards the offices of the president and his Supreme Counsellor, but before they reached the top a Marine colonel leaned over a balustrade and begun yelling wildly to a brigadier and a group of senior officers waiting below. "They're not here — their rooms are empty!"

The little brigadier nodded grimly. "The communications shelter is deserted too! Come down!"

Naomi ran back down the stairs to the brigadier and took him by the arm. "Where could they be?"

"We've found three tunnels under the palace," he said, shaking his head. "They all lead into the sewers — they've escaped."

Naomi nodded her thanks and led the way up the stairs once more towards the office of President Diem on the third floor. All around them the air rang with the sound of rebel soldiers sacking the palace: one group of Marines rushed by carrying armfuls of whisky and brandy bottles from Ngo Dinh Nhu's cellar, others bludgeoned gold filigree fittings from the walls and stuffed them in their pockets, while some simply fired their weapons, shrieking with laughter, into the antique French mirrors covering the walls. When Jock and Naomi reached Diem's office, they found the drab room musty and in disarray. The president's double-breasted sharkskin jacket hung from the back of a rickety rocking chair, and a French book with a curiously prophetic title lay on the cluttered desk. Naomi glanced around the room, screwing up her face with distaste, and silently held the book to Jock's camera so that its title showed; it was called ironically *Ils Arrivent* — They Are Coming.

In Ngo Dinh Nhu's larger office on the floor below, they found the looters had already finished their work. Sawdust was spilled everywhere from the stuffed hunting trophies that had been slashed open and torn from the walls; the sensuous portrait of Nhu's wife above his desk had been lewdly defaced with a bayonet that had been left jutting from her lower abdomen, and in her own suite some of the long rails of filmy, silken *ao dai* had been ripped apart and strewn around the room. Others remained hanging neatly in their closet above line after line of stiletto-heeled shoes, and Naomi guided Jock in filming these and the smashed bottled of Vent Vert perfume that lay scattered around the bathroom with its big pink sunken bath and wash-basin of black Venetian marble.

As they passed through Ngo Dinh Nhu's office again on their way back to the ground floor, Naomi had to wade through a litter of files that the looters had scattered across the carpet. On a whim she stopped and bent to look at some of them and discovered that their buff-colored covers were stamped with the title of Nhu's notorious Social and Political Research Service. Under the glow of the camera light which Jock held for her, she flicked idly through one or two of them; they appeared to consist mainly of informers' reports on Saigon politicians and army officers, written in French or Vietnamese, but her attention was arrested abruptly when she turned the cover of one file and saw Guy Sherman's name printed on its front. She opened it and was startled to find herself looking at a piece of Continental Palace notepaper on top of the file, which bore her own handwriting. The name and address of the Buddhist priest who had alerted her to Thich Quang Duc's suicide seemed to leap off the page at her, and she knelt there on the floor staring numbly at the note for perhaps half a minute, no longer hearing the crash of breaking glass nor the shrill, crazed laughter of the troops plundering the palace all around her.

16

Four hours later, just after eleven o'clock on that morning of November 2, there was a brisk knock on the door of Naomi's suite in the Continental, and she opened it to find Guy Sherman smiling broadly at her. He wore no jacket and his clothes looked crumpled as if he hadn't changed them for a long time, but he had a frosted bottle of Laurent Perrier tucked under his arm and two long-stemmed champagne glasses dangled from the fingers of his right hand.

"What are we celebrating?" she asked with a weary smile, standing aside to let him enter.

"Just the overthrow of the dreaded Ngo Dinh brothers," he replied, shrugging exaggeratedly. "Nothing more — the whole thing went like a dream. Maybe we'll drink a toast to your outstanding exclusive coverage of that subject, too." Instead of entering he leaned forward, took her by the hand and led her down the corridor into the adjoining suite. "I rented this specially just to be near you today, Naomi. And nobody knows I'm here. So we can both hide away from the damned telephone for an hour or two, right?" He grinned again, knocked the door shut with his heel and walked confidently across the room to put the champagne and glasses on a low table in front of a sofa.

"Thanks to your timely tip we certainly got off to a flying start while everyone else was enjoying their siesta." Naomi smiled as she sank onto the sofa. "And thanks for your note too. It allowed us all to grab some much-needed sleep last night while the opposition went red-eyed. We've certainly got some marvelous footage — enough to make an hour-long documentary. But even so, my coverage is still just a tiny bit inconclusive at present."

She relaxed against the sofa back with a long sigh and closed her eyes. The tension of the last few hours had left her feeling drained; while her crew were trying to ship their film out to Hong Kong and onward to London, she had forced her way through the jubilant crowds to the central post office to telephone a voice report for the news bulletins. On the way she found that the fact that the president and his brother were still missing had not in any way dampened the frenzied celebrations that were being mounted in the streets. Joy mixed with vengeful violence had been evident everywhere; the offices of the regime's English-language newspaper, the *Times of Vietnam*, were burning fiercely when she passed, and gangs of students chanting "Long Live the Junta" were rampaging along many of the boulevards. She saw a mob hauling down the massive statue of Vietnam's legendary heroines, the Trung sisters, because one of them had been fashioned in the likeness of Madame Nhu, and homes of pro-Nhu ministers and officials were being ransacked all over the city.

She had watched the crowds leaping onto tanks and hugging the soldiers, who were clearly startled by such warm expressions of affection from the ordinary people, and soon everywhere girls were throwing bouquets of flowers and gifts to the delighted troops. But she had found herself most deeply moved by scenes she had witnessed outside the pagodas; army trucks had arrived every few minutes bringing groups of haggard Buddhist prisoners newly released from jail. They were embraced deliriously by their fellows and many, because they were weak from torture and privation, had to be carried into the temples. After she'd finished her call to London she had made a special detour to inquire about the monk who had been her informant in June, but amidst the near-pandemonium at his pagoda, a nun had told her there was no trace of him; he had disappeared suddenly even before the raids on the pagodas, she said tearfully, and he was believed to have been secretly murdered by the security forces.

Naomi, stunned by the news, had passed close to the ruined Gia Long Palace as she made her way back to the hotel, and here and there she had seen the crumpled body of a soldier or a civilian still lying huddled in the gutter. The sight of these corpses and the sense of shock she had experienced on learning about the disappearance of the Buddhist monk were still preying on her mind as she watched Guy's fingers rip the gold foil from the champagne bottle, and she started involuntarily when the cork exploded from its neck. Guy smiled, never taking his eyes from hers, and filled the two glasses frothing to the brim. Then he came to sit down beside her on the sofa and handed her one, but before he drank he withdrew from his trouser pocket a circular tin of sixteen-millimeter film and laid it on the table between them. "Your coverage isn't inconclusive anymore, Naomi," he said softly. "Shall we drink to it?"

She looked questioningly at the tin lying on the table. "What's that?"

"Film of the bodies."

Because she was still half thinking of what she had seen so recently in the gutters outside the palace, she gazed back at him blankly. "Whose bodies?"

"Diem and Nhu."

She sat upright suddenly, spilling some of her champagne. "They're dead?"

He nodded. "Yes — and this is the only film in existence of their demise."

"Who killed them?"

"A police major sent to bring them from Cholon where they were hiding. They loaded both of them into the back of an M-113 armored personnel carrier with the major and closed the hatch. Diem was shot in the head and Nhu was bayoneted to death en route. They were both dead by the time they got back to the headquarters of the Joint General Staff."

She stared at the little film, her eyes suddenly bright with interest.

"And you, Naomi," he said, raising his glass in her direction with an ironic little smile, "have some exclusive footage of the view into the APC when they opened the hatch."

"Who filmed it?" she said when she found her voice.

"None other than yours truly." His smile broadened. "Although of course only you and I will ever know that."

"May I look?"

He nodded, and she put down her champagne untouched to open the tin. Holding it carefully by its edges, she pulled the strip of film off the reel and lifted it eagerly towards the light of the window.

"It isn't very distinct — I'm not the world's greatest cameraman and I had no special lights. But it's usable." He leaned towards her and squinted through the back of the film, pointing with his finger. "The bodies are lying face forward on the seats. Most of what you can see is their backs and the backs of their heads. The bigger, roly-poly body on the right is Diem of course, and the smaller one with several bayonet wounds is brother Nhu: I've screened it once for myself in our little photo lab — you can see it's them okay."

"It's incredible film, Guy," breathed the English journalist. "How were they caught?"

Guy's pleasure in her reaction showed plainly in his face, and letting his hand fall casually onto her knee, he began to stroke her trouser-clad thigh slowly as he talked. "They were betrayed early today by one of their palace aides. They slipped away last night about nine o'clock using one of their secret underground tunnels. They'd got a Red Cross Land Rover waiting for them at the tunnel exit and it whisked them off to Cholon, where they'd already set up a direct communications link with the palace in the home of a friendly Chinese merchant. They kept up their contacts through the night with their supporters in the palace and even intermittently with the coup headquarters. General Minh offered them safe conduct several times if they surrendered — but they turned him down. So Minh had to plan a careful general assault. Nobody except a couple of their closest aides knew Diem and Nhu had gone until Gia Long was finally stormed. It was Diem himself who gave the order to show the white flag in the end — but by telephone from Cholon."

"Did they give themselves up after that?"

"Diem called Minh about six-thirty A.M. and offered to surrender in return for a guarantee of safe conduct to the airport and a flight abroad. Minh agreed, but Diem, devious to the end, didn't reveal where they were — or perhaps in this treacherous little country he knew what to expect anyway. After the aide betrayed their hideout, they fled to the St. Francis Xavier Catholic Church in Cholon to take communion. They were still on their knees when the arrest party found them there. They bundled them both into the M-113, and shots were heard inside as soon as they moved off."

Naomi's face registered her distaste. "But why were they murdered so callously?"

Guy shrugged. "I guess it was inevitable from the start. The junta would never have felt safe with the Ngo Dinhs alive and kicking — wherever they were."

"So they were killed on General Minh's orders?"

Guy nodded wordlessly, still stroking her thigh, but without warning Naomi stood up and walked over to the window. She folded her arms and stood looking down at the excited crowds thronging Lam Son Square, a frown creasing her brow. "How is it you're so well informed?" she asked quietly without turning around. "Were you on the inside of the coup? I tried to call you several times yesterday, but they always said you were unavailable."

Guy sipped his champagne and smiled. "Let's just say I was keeping a close watching brief at the coup headquarters. By the time the bodies came back in the M-113, nobody protested when I stepped up and produced my little home movie camera — is that what you mean?"

Instead of replying she pulled a folded slip of paper from a pocket in her blouse and walked back to the sofa where he sat. "I think you must have dropped this sometime, Guy," she said tonelessly, holding towards him the note about the Buddhist monk she had given him five months before.

He glanced at the paper then back into her face, still smiling easily. "Where did you find it?"

"On the floor of Ngo Dinh Nhu's office at six-thirty this morning. Isn't that where you dropped it?"

He continued to smile at her unabashed. "Sometimes in my job, Naomi, you have to play along with both sides to make sure you know what everyone's thinking. Quite often you have to deal with people you don't particularly like." He took the slip of paper from her and looked at it for a second before letting it drop onto the table. "Intelligence work is like any other business — for a deal to work well, both sides have to be seen to get something out of it."

Naomi's voice trembled slightly. "But giving that monk's name to Nhu probably led to his murder."

"Lot's of people die when there's a war on, Naomi. If you really believe in what you're doing, you can't worry about every little sacrifice that has to be made along the way."

"But doesn't the monk's death bother you at all?"

Guy drained his glass and refilled it, nodding towards the paper on the table. "Naomi, you benefited from what I did. That little *quid pro quo* kept my lines of communication open to Nhu and his dragon lady. They kept right on talking to me — and you willingly used what I gave you in your dispatches. You wanted good reliable information as badly as I did, didn't you?"

Naomi stared down at him wide-eyed; then reluctantly she nodded.

"So let's stop worrying our heads about all that stuff, shall we?" He took her hand, and she let him pull her down onto the sofa beside him. Gazing at her with a new intensity, he raised her hand to his lips and kissed her fingers, nodding at the same time towards the little tin of film on the table. "In there, Naomi, you've got another world exclusive — I've delivered the goods. So it's time now for grown-up girls to stop hiding behind hints and promises, isn't it?"

She looked at him undecidedly for a moment, then nodded once more in agreement.

"I'm really glad things have worked out for us at last, Naomi. I'm not accustomed to waiting this long, you know. It's only because you're so damned special. . . ." He began unfastening her blouse as he talked, and when he leaned close and began to kiss her bare shoulders, she closed her eyes. She let him unbutton her trousers and remove them, but her expression remained strangely blank as she watched him take off his own clothes. Even when he was naked and leaned down to kiss her again on the lips, she still didn't respond, and he pulled back from her with a puzzled smile.

"I didn't figure you for an English ice maiden, Naomi," he said slowly. "You're not really one of those girls who can't get started until they're taken roughly, are you?" His smile broadened when she didn't reply, and he dropped his gaze pointedly to the filmy lace of her brassiere. The dark whorls of her nipples were clearly visible through the flimsy garment, and with both hands he seized it suddenly and ripped it in two at its narrowest part, fully exposing her breasts.

"God, Naomi, you're beautiful," he said in a faltering voice as he caressed her. "I've never wanted any woman as much."

She felt her nipples tauten beneath his fingers and her own breathing quickened involuntarily as he forced her silken underpants down over her hips with quick, clumsy movements; but even when he rose above her, fully aroused himself, she still stared back at him with the same frozen expression on his face.

"It's going to feel like I'm raping you, Naomi, if you lie there much longer like that with your knees pressed together," he gasped. "Relax! The teasing game's over."

He tried to slip one hand between her knees to prise them apart, massaging the pale gold haze of hair at the base of her belly feverishly with his other hand — but she squirmed away from him suddenly.

"Please stop, Guy," she said sharply. "I don't want this to go any further." She sat up and turned away from him, covering her face with her hands, and he stared at her nonplussed.

"What in hell's name is going on?" His voice was thick, and his chest rose and fell rapidly with his erratic breathing. "I don't get any of this!"

She took her hands from her face and stared across the room, dry-eyed. "I'm sorry, Guy. *You* may be able to shrug off the death of that young Buddhist quite easily, but I can't. It's made me realize suddenly what I'm doing."

"What *are* you doing?" he asked in an astounded voice.

"Trading other people's lives for my own selfish ends!"

"Look, maybe you'll feel better later — have some more champagne." He touched her bare shoulder and made to get up and refill her glass, but she shook her head.

"No, Guy — I don't want any more. I'm going." She rose and pulled on her trousers.

"Naomi, what's gotten into you?" He stood up quickly and tried

557

to take her by the shoulders, but she pulled away from him. He glanced down at the table, snatched up the tin of film and held it towards her. "Don't you even want this?"

"Five minutes ago I wanted it very badly," she said in an urgent undertone. "But now I'm not going to take it from you."

"Why in heaven's name not?" He moved towards her and forced it into her hands. "I want you to have the damned film. I went to a hell of a lot of trouble to get it for you."

Avoiding his eyes she took the film and hurled it savagely towards a wastepaper basket. It struck the side of the metal container and sprang open, and the film uncoiled in snakelike loops across the carpet. Without stopping to finish dressing she walked quickly towards the door, carrying her blouse, and with one hand on the doorknob she stopped and spoke over her shoulder.

"Guy, I don't want you to think I'm passing judgment on you because I'm not — that's for you to do yourself. It's my own actions that I'm suddenly disgusted with."

Without turning around again she opened the door and stepped out into the corridor; Guy called her name more urgently, but she ignored him and walked quickly away towards her own room, the shreds of her torn brassiere still hanging loose about her naked breasts.

PART SEVEN

We Have Fought
a Thousand Years!

1968–1969

President Kennedy's decision to encourage and support the overthrow of Ngo Dinh Diem proved to be a fateful turning point in the United States' involvement in Vietnam. The American president was himself assassinated three weeks after the anti-Diem coup, but General Duong Van Minh's administration in which he had invested so much hope lasted only three months before it was overthrown in its turn by another military junta. A bewildering succession of ineffectual "revolving door" governments emerged from the flurry of coups and countercoups that followed, and relations between them and the mass of the people in South Vietnam remained as poor as they had been under Diem. The Buddhists, elated and strengthened by the success of their campaign to bring Diem down, expanded into a formidable antigovernment, anti-American force in the cities, and public strife became a familiar, everyday occurrence. Buddhists and Catholics died in street fighting, student unrest compounded the troubles, and because the new governments in Saigon wished above all else to avoid the crude, police-state methods of Ngo Dinh Nhu, these disturbances were dealt with only tentatively. Against this background of growing chaos, the Strategic Hamlet program collapsed in the countryside, and the Viet Cong went from strength to strength. Ho Chi Minh and the rest of the Communist leadership in Hanoi were not slow to exploit this deteriorating situation, and they began for the first time to infiltrate large tactical units of the North Vietnamese Army into South Vietnam through Laos and Cambodia. Under these circumstances a hoped-for withdrawal became impossible for the United States, but although President Lyndon Johnson increased the number of military advisers in Vietnam to thirty thousand, by early 1965 the Communists were standing clearly on the brink of total victory, and it was then that he decided to change radically the nature of America's commitment. He first ordered U.S. warplanes to begin regular bombing raids against targets in both North and South Vietnam in February, and in July of that same year he sent the first batch of fifty thousand ground combat troops into Vietnam to fight independently of the South Vietnamese. With aircraft carriers and destroyers of the Seventh Fleet already cruising off the coast of the war zone, the might of the United States Army, Navy and Air Force was from that time firmly committed to the war, although the commitment was termed "limited" and it had been made by political stealth, without any formal declaration of war. Such a commitment had been made possible by mystery-shrouded events that had occurred off North Vietnam's coast in the Gulf of Tongking in August 1964; according to an announcement made by the president himself, North Vietnamese patrol boats had attacked two U.S. destroyers without provocation, and in response to "Communist aggression" he had ordered air strikes against the patrol boat bases and oil storage depots in North Vietnam. This dramatic revelation was made to reporters at midnight on August 4, and in an emotional atmosphere three days later, the U.S. Congress passed almost unanimously a resolution drafted in the White House giving blanket approval to any measures the president might take to prevent "further aggression." Known as the Gulf of Tonkin Resolution, the legislation also stated that the United States regarded Vietnam as vital to both its national interest and world peace, and it allowed President Johnson a few months later to start the bombing and begin dispatching a force of ultimately half a million men to Vietnam without further reference to Congress or the people. Later it became clear that the U.S. Navy ships had not been innocent victims of aggression at all, but the controversial Tonkin Resolution nevertheless remained in force for six years, until antiwar sentiment eventually forced its repeal. The million or more GIs sent to fight in Vietnam under its provisions, however, found themselves no more able to find and defeat their elusive enemy than the French or the ARVN forces had before them. Even though they were aided by North Vietnamese regular battalions, the Viet Cong still rarely fought anything but guerrilla-style actions and a third of all American combat casualties throughout the war were victims of booby traps and mines. As the number of troops committed by President Johnson rose, the U.S. aid bill to Vietnam also grew for what was variously termed "rural development," "pacification" or "the other war" — but these efforts to woo South Vietnam's peasants away from allegiance to the Viet Cong did not meet with much success either. In fact, far from improving living conditions, the policies of the Johnson administration had a disastrous impact on the life of many people in the South; by early 1968 the combined effects of the American search-and-destroy operations, the chemical defoliation of the jungles and the bombing in the South had produced millions of new homeless refugees who flocked to the already overcrowded cities to live in shanty zones. There they faced a new struggle for survival because the presence of so many Americans and their generous aid programs produced a massive economic inflation. Meanwhile the political leadership of South Vietnam became more stable, first under the premiership of Air Marshal Nguyen Cao Ky and then under General Nguyen Van Thieu's presidency, but these administrations remained as fundamentally unpopular and corrupt as that of President Diem, and they never won the support and trust of the people at large. As the war continued inconclusively through the mid-sixties, the United States resorted increasingly to air attacks against the North in an effort to convince the Communist leaders in Hanoi that there was a firm resolve to defeat them; but in practice, the privations of the bombing served to unite the people of North Vietnam and make them more determined than ever to resist the "foreign enemy" that had haunted them throughout their history. During these years a growing number of American air force and navy pilots shot down over the North were made prisoners of war in Hanoi, and as their numbers grew, rumors began to filter out that they were being subjected to brutal, medieval tortures in the course of "brainwashing," and as a result, this small group of Americans became a focus of intense emotional interest in the United States.

1

The heart óf Hanoi was blacked out, and the broad, deep waters of the Lake of the Restored Sword reflected only a dull glimmer of light from the thinly clouded night sky as a rattling, twenty-year-old government Tatra nosed cautiously along its northern bank in the last week of January 1968. As usual the streets were clogged with mule carts, hand barrows and bicycles piled high with farm produce, and the Tongking peasants hurrying to resupply the capital under the cover of darkness refused doggedly to yield to the honking motor car. Already they could hear the distant drone of American B-52s and F-105s, and this familiar sound that they had heard almost every night for the past week was causing them to quicken their pace and lean their shoulders against their loads with a greater urgency.

Because the weather was still oppressively hot, the windows of the ancient Czechoslovakian-built vehicle were wound right down in their rusty runnels and the noise of the aircraft engines was clearly audible to Lieutenant Mark Sherman, who sat hunched between two armed Vietnamese guards on the rear seat. But if he heard them, he gave no sign to his captors; his wrists were manacled, traveling irons had been locked around his ankles, and he stared out listlessly at the dim outline of the lake's pagodas and the swarm of passing peasants without registering them. He still wore the olive drabs which he had donned with his flying gear the night he took off from Da Nang for the last time early in 1966; these flying overalls had long since grown threadbare, and his appearance now bore little resemblance to that of the spruce, young air force pilot who had climbed so eagerly into his F105D Thunderchief two years before. His skull had been shaved and the pallid skin of his gaunt face was stretched taut across his bones, leaving his eyes darkly ringed in their hollow sockets; his shoulders sagged, his gaze was lifeless, without light, and his shackled hands dangled limp in an attitude of hopelessness between his splayed thighs. Occasionally the gastric stench of the Tatra's poorly refined Soviet benzene caused his features to twitch into a grimace of distaste, but his face otherwise remained devoid of expression.

From time to time, Tran Van Kim half turned in the front passenger seat to look at him, but the American showed no curiosity. In his early fifties, the round face of the Vietnamese above his high-necked cadre's tunic was still curiously youthful, effeminate almost, and if Mark Sherman could have seen the high-ranking aide to Ho Chi Minh with his father's eyes, he would have detected instantly in the regular cast of his features a hint of that quality that had produced a face of such great beauty in his sister, Lan. But Mark remained oblivious to his presence and continued to peer listlessly out into the night as he had done throughout the entire, hour-long journey from the Son Tay prisoner-of-war camp northwest of Hanoi.

"Have you no wish to know where you are being taken, Lieutenant Sherman?' asked Kim speaking English in a sibilant undertone. But although both his guards jabbed him sharply with the muzzles of their machine pistols, the question still drew no response from the American, and after warning the guards with a little hand gesture not to repeat their actions, Kim turned away and relaxed in his seat again.

The Tatra, with its bizarre tailfin jutting through the camouflage covering of palm leaves and jungle vegetation, chugged on around the lake and skirted the old craft quarter of the city before heading towards one of the outlying suburbs on its southern borders. Once, the density of the crowds thronging the streets brought it to a standstill, and the army driver stuck his head out of the window to listen to the sound of the aircraft for a moment.

"Haiphong — the harbor again would you say, Comrade Kim?" he asked over his shoulder.

Instead of replying Kim listened intently to the drone of the aircraft above the clouds; the roar of their approach was growing louder as twin missions converged from U.S. bases in northern Thailand and Seventh Fleet carriers in the South China Sea, and it became clear from the sudden added noise that some anti-aircraft and missile batteries ringing the city were beginning to open up. "It sounds to me as if they might be coming our way tonight," said Kim quietly, signaling for the driver to press forward again. "The sooner we get to our destination, the better."

The driver restarted the engine and moved off, peering intently through the windshield as he eased the car through the shadowy crowds by the inadequate light filtering through the blackout grilles on the headlamps. On display boards at the roadsides every few yards, giant head-and-shoulder portraits of Ho Chi Minh gazed down between posters showing Vietnamese peasant girls destroying American warplanes with a single rifle shot, and seeing these, Kim turned towards the back seat again.

"Since you show no curiosity, Lieutenant Sherman, about the purpose of your visit to our capital, I shall tell you why you've been brought here — you are to be accorded the honor of being received by the beloved leader of the Vietnamese people. The president of the Democratic Republic of Vietnam, whose portrait you see all about you here, wishes to talk with you in person."

Kim watched his prisoner closely, but no flicker of interest disturbed the blankness of Mark's expression, and in the silence that ensued, the distant crump of falling bombs became audible.

"Perhaps you don't believe me, lieutenant. Perhaps you find it impossible to believe that such an important national leader would remain in the heart of the city at a time when there's great danger from your imperialist bombers." Another brittle smile flashed across his face. "But you Americans don't understand the true nature of his greatness. He insists on sharing all the dangers that his people and his comrades face. . ."

A brilliant orange glare lit the interior of the car suddenly as a bomb exploded with a great burst of light on an oil storage depot a mile or two ahead of them, and the driver stopped the car instantly in the middle of the street and dived out of the door. Kim watched the flames for a moment then rapped out instructions to the guards on the rear seat before flinging himself out of the door on his side. All around the car the peasants were abandoning their produce carts and dashing towards the sidewalks to clamber into rows of barrel-sized, one-man bomb shelters that had been excavated from the street and lined with concrete; once inside they pulled lids, like manhole covers, into place above their heads, and within a minute the area appeared deserted.

The two guards dragged Mark clumsily from the car and forced his tall, angular frame into one of the tiny shelters. But he refused to crouch down and remained limp in their grasp, doing nothing to cooperate in getting himself under cover; in their frustration they began to shout and scream at him, clubbing him repeatedly with the butts of their weapons and when another stick of bombs exploded much nearer, showering the road around them with earth and rubble, they let go of him and flung themselves into nearby shelters on their own. As they pulled the protective covers into position, the flash and roar of exploding bombs became continuous, and debris rattled down on the abandoned car close by. The light from the blazing oil storage complex gradually filled

565

the whole sky with an orange incandescence, and gazing upwards, Mark Sherman's face tightened into a mask of fury. Standing upright suddenly in the inadequate shelter that had been designed for slighter Asian men, he flung the cover from him; it cartwheeled away across the street until it came to rest with a clatter in the opposite gutter, and stretching his clenched fists towards the darkened heavens, he screamed incoherently at the invisible American planes.

His words were garbled and unintelligible, little more than animal sounds gushing uncontrollably from his throat in the hysterical cadences of abuse; sometimes they were drowned in the elemental roar of the attack, at others his screaming rang piercingly through sudden intervals of silence. Once, the cover of the shelter beside him shifted slightly, and Tran Van Kim looked out through the narrow slit with startled eyes. Then another heavy deluge of rubble made him clamp the cover shut again, and a moment later a fist-sized chunk of masonry struck Mark on the forehead, stunning him, and he pitched forward, half in and half out of the shelter. He lay there without moving while the roar of the attacking planes faded gradually into the darkness. When quiet eventually returned to the street, the faint sounds of his sobbing were for a few brief moments the only human sound in the stillness of the night.

2

Ten minutes after the bombing raid ended, the Tatra halted for inspection at a heavily guarded gate in a high wall, then pulled into a fortified courtyard behind a featureless modern building that owed its austere lines to the influence of the bleak Stalinist architectural styles of the 1940s. On the Tatra's rear seat, Mark Sherman was fully conscious again; his forehead was discolored and swollen where the fragment of falling masonry had struck him, but he still sat slumped against the seat back as before, his features robbed of all expression. Unresisting, Mark allowed himself to be led down several flights of steps into a deep basement, and at a succession of checkpoints in its corridors, wary groups of soldiers of the North Vietnamese People's Army armed with Russian AK-47 assault rifles glared at him with unconcealed hostility while inspecting Kim's credentials.

The leg-irons and the makeshift prison sandals made from old auto tires that he wore forced Mark to shuffle along the dimly lit passageways in an ungainly fashion, and his two guards prodded him with their weapons whenever he faltered. Before a plain, unadorned door flanked by four more soldiers, they ordered him to halt, and Kim knocked once before entering alone. While Mark waited, all the guards glared at him with hate-filled eyes as though scarcely able to restrain themselves from attacking him bare-handed there and then, but the American remained oblivious, standing with his head bowed and his manacled hands hanging loose in front of him. Even after he had been led inside and the door closed behind him, he still didn't raise his head, but continued staring sightlessly at the floor.

At the far end of the basement room the figure of a wizened Vietnamese was hunched over a clutter of paperwork strewn across the polished conference table. The empty blotters that had not yet been removed and the disarranged chairs suggested that a meeting of the Politburo of the Lao Dong had recently ended, and on the wall behind the old man, a black-and-white portrait of Vladimir Ilyich Lenin gazed sternly down on the room, the eyes ablaze with revolutionary fervor, the goatee jutting aggressively beneath a square, determined mouth.

"Advance!" One of his guards urged the American forward with his rifle, then ordered him to halt a few yards short of the table. The old man went on writing for fully a minute without looking up, but when at last he put down his pen, he waved the guard's gun aside with an impatient gesture.

Mark raised his eyes then for the first time but gave no sign that he recognized the shriveled yellow features and straggling beard as belonging to a man whose name had become a greater inspirational totem to would-be revolutionaries around the world than the portrait of Lenin on the wall behind him. Against the backdrop of Lenin's commanding visage, the aged Vietnamese Communist leader looked frail and insignificant: his skin was cracked like ancient parchment, his concave chest left his cotton jacket sagging scarecrowlike from his bony shoulders and only his eyes seemed to retain any spark of vitality. Piercingly bright and possessed of an extraordinary, calm strength, they seemed to gather and concentrate all the light and energy of the room into their unwavering gaze, and when his lips parted, the forbidding face was transformed unexpectedly by a warm, avuncular smile.

He continued smiling as he lit a cigarette, then tapped a sheet of paper on the table with a bony finger.

"Your father has written a letter to me, Lieutenant Sherman," he said in clear confident English. "Please sit down."

The guard with the gun moved forward warily as the American shuffled towards the indicated chair, but again the old man motioned the soldier away and he retired a pace or two.

"Your father also sent me this photograph of us together." Ho Chi Minh pushed a small, sepia-tinted snapshot across the polished table, still smiling. "When that was taken he was not much older than you are now. We were friends then, and I can see that the family likeness is strong."

Tran Van Kim, who had been standing quietly beside the president's chair, moved around behind him to study the young American's face as he looked at the snapshot. It showed a smiling, fifty-five-year-old Ho Chi Minh relaxing with a group of OSS officers in a jungle clearing in August 1945. The Americans were dressed in forage caps, shorts and jungle boots, and Joseph Sherman stood grinning at Ho's left shoulder.

"Those were memorable days for us," said Ho, letting out a long, resigned sigh. "I helped your father get home after he was shot down by the Japanese and he rendered valuable assistance to us too — but sadly such close cooperation between our two countries didn't last long."

Mark Sherman looked up slowly from the photograph of his father to stare at Ho. Among the more courageous American prisoners, the North Vietnamese leader was referred to as "Horse Shit Man"; they distorted the pronunciation of his name deliberately in this way in front of their torturers, and for this willful insult they were invariably punished with great severity. But it had become a matter of honor among them not to say the name any other way, and for a moment a troubled expression crossed Mark's face; once or twice his lips moved as though he was about to speak, but then his features collapsed suddenly once more into their familiar blank expression.

Ho studied him intently for a second or two, then smiled warmly again and opened one of several bottles of beer standing on a tray at his elbow. He poured the amber liquid frothing into a glass and pushed the drink towards Mark before pouring another for himself. "It's a tragedy of history that the American nation should have withdrawn the hand of friendship so gladly given in 1945. Instead it offers us now only the sword of war. So we should drink to your country's past wisdom, lieutenant — not your present folly. Perhaps one day your leaders will again become wise." He raised a bony hand, signaling the American to drink, but Mark stared back at him impassively, leaving the beer untouched on the table.

The old man drank noisily from his own glass and pointed towards the swelling on Mark's forehead. "The bombs of your countrymen almost killed you on your way here tonight, didn't they? How ironic that would have been. I invited you, you see, only to reassure myself of your safety for an old-time comrade."

Behind the chair Tran Van Kim made a surreptitious hand signal in the direction of the second guard at the far end of the room, and he turned and went out quietly.

"You've had two years to think over the foolishness of your country's actions, haven't you?" Ho smiled at Mark again, but this time his expression was sardonic and without humor. "By now you've learned enough about us to know that our cause is just. We've fought a thousand years for our independence, after all, and we must have convinced you that we'll never rest until we're victorious." He paused for a long moment, his eyes burning into Mark's face. "The realization is growing even among your own countrymen at home that the United States must give up its neo-colonialist war of aggression. They've become aware since you've been our prisoner that the people of Vietnam are certain in the end to win total victory. You could help speed up that process and limit the suffering of yourself and others like you if you were to denounce publicly your country's folly."

Mark's only response was to slouch lower in his chair, but at that moment the door behind him opened and the scuff of the second guard's sandaled feet advancing quickly towards them broke the silence. When he reached the table he placed a little cloth bundle in the pool of light between the two men and returned dutifully to his place. Tran Van Kim stepped forward to unknot the bundle and spread its contents carefully on the table-top; when he retreated again an unposted airmail letter in a blank envelope lay beside a few crumpled piastres, some keys, a hand-kerchief, and the fur-covered foot of a small animal mounted on a fine gold chain.

"These items were found in Lieutenant Sherman's possession when he was captured, comrade president," said Kim quietly.

The long wisps of white beard brushed the table-top as Ho leaned forward to pick up the letter. He opened it, read it, then looked across at Mark again. "For reasons of compassion and in response to your father's inquiry about you, we shall allow this letter you wrote to your mother before you took off on your last flight, to be mailed now. This at least will provide evidence for your family of your continued well-being. I trust you'll appreciate that this is a concession made out of deference to your father's past services to us."

Ho tapped the envelope to emphasize his words, but Mark wasn't listening. The glassy expression had disappeared from his eyes and he was staring intently at the little collection of articles on the table. Sensing that his mood had changed, Kim motioned the guard forward, but before he reached Mark's side, the American without any warning catapulted forward out of his chair. His manacled hands scrabbled frantically across the table-top until they closed round the little furry object, but before he could draw it to himself, the guard unbuttoned his revolver from its leather holster and brought it crashing down on his knuckles. In the same movement he clamped a rough stranglehold around Mark's neck from behind, but although the American gagged and choked, and his eyes bulged wildly under the pressure of the lock, he still didn't release his grip on the talisman.

"What is this thing?" The parchment of the old man's face wrinkled in inquiry as he addressed Kim impatiently in their own language.

"I think it's the foot of a rabbit, comrade president. Under interrogation Lieutenant Sherman in the end admitted he always carried it in his flying overalls during operations. In the West such objects are believed to bring the bearer good fortune."

The guard, who had been listening, reached down suddenly with his free hand, forced Mark's fingers apart and wrenched the rabbit's foot from his grasp. With a little grin of triumph he tossed it back onto the table, but although his hands were still firmly manacled, Mark struggled frenziedly once more and tore himself free. He lunged towards the table in a new attempt to grab the rabbit's foot, but the other guard, who had raced forward from his position by the door, flung himself on the American too. With considerable difficulty the Vietnamese soldiers wrestled Mark to the floor and pinned him there, breathing noisily.

The president watched the three thrashing bodies for a moment, then turned again to Kim. "Under what conditions has Lieutenant Sherman been held captive?"

Kim leaned forward close to his ear. "He's been the most stubborn of all the American captives. For nine months he successfully resisted all persuasive techniques. Consequently he's been in solitary confinement since his capture. For the past three months since the arrival of his father's letter he's been under special twenty-four-hour surveillance to prevent suicide attempts."

"And what exactly do you propose to do with him? So far you've told me only that you think he could be used in a special way."

"I think it might be wise to grant compassionate clemency for propaganda purposes." On the floor Mark was still moaning between the two guards, and Kim paused and lowered his voice again. "At the right moment, that is. We might release him six months from now — but allow me personally to supervise his detention during that time. I've studied his case closely, and I believe if he's handled correctly he could prove to be a great asset to those Americans campaigning for an end to the war."

The older Vietnamese nodded his agreement and sighed. "Your genius in these matters is too well known for me to argue with you, Comrade Kim. Go ahead and do as you please."

Kim smiled his thanks and motioned the two guards to pull Mark to his feet; then he leaned over the old man's shoulder again to whisper in his ear. The president nodded and turned back to the table to pick up the rabbit's foot; his piercing eyes subjected Mark's clenched face to a careful scrutiny for several seconds before he signaled with his head for the guards to release him. When they stepped back, he held the talisman towards the American in an outstretched hand.

Mark stared at it for a long time, his face working nervously, then he took an uncertain step forward. After one last suspicious look at the wrinkled face, he snatched it away and concealed it between his manacled palms. The old Vietnamese continued smiling at him for a moment like a fond uncle regarding a favored child. Then abruptly the smile evaporated and with a dismissive gesture he resumed his seat, busying himself immediately with his papers as though he was already alone in the room.

All the way back to his new cell in the former French Sûreté jail in the heart of Hanoi, Mark squeezed the rabbit's paw convulsively in his hands in the darkness of the Tatra's back seat, his face flexing and unflexing in time with his fingers; sometimes he dug the paw so fiercely into the heel of his hand that its tiny claws drew blood, and when at last he was left alone in the total blackness of a solitary punishment cell, he squatted on the stone floor in a fetal crouch sucking the furry tip of the paw as if it were a baby's pacifier. Ignoring the scuttling rats which the guards had deliberately allowed in through a small hole in the floor, he rocked back and forth like this for a long time, moaning quietly to himself, until eventually he fell into the release of an exhausted sleep.

3

While his youngest son slumbered fitfully in a wretched prison cell in Hanoi, Joseph Sherman was pacing uneasily through the darkened streets of Saigon, one thousand miles to the south, trying not to see the ghosts of the past which threatened to haunt him at every turning. He was back in the southern capital for the first time in twelve years, but although it had been changed almost beyond recognition by the unceasing roar and confusion of the massive American war effort, the emotional intensity of the memories evoked by his return after such a long interval frequently blotted out the reality of the present for him.

Strolling along Cong Ly with the silent, diminutive figure of Tran Van Tam at his side, he scarcely saw the stark modern outline of Presiden Nguyen Van Thieu's Doc Lap Palace behind its sinister-looking rocket screens. Instead, as he glanced through the railings at the shadowy parkland that colonial landscape gardeners had laid out around the French governor general's original *grand palais*, he saw only a blushing fifteen-year-old boy in his first white tuxedo dashing madly across a marble terrace to save a priceless Chinese vase from the clutches of a baby gibbon. He saw too in his mind's eye the proud, uncertain mandarin who was the father of the man at his side, standing apprehensively on the steps as he emerged from Saigon's other palace with the struggling animal trapped inside his torn tuxedo. The expression of innocent mystification on the enchanting ten-year-old face of the mandarin's daughter as she eyed the strange foreign savior of her pet also rose unbidden from the recesses of his memory, and he glanced quickly down at Tam, wondering if the Vietnamese had sensed the intensity of the nostalgia that filled his mind. But

Tam's features, which were still those of an Oriental cherub, even in late middle age, were set in their usual watchful expression; his eyes were following the passage of a noisy convoy of U.S. Army trucks, and his girlish mouth puckered with distaste as the vehicles passed, their air horns blaring, their exhaust pipes engulfing the boulevard in clouds of thick blue smoke.

Without speaking they turned off the old Rue Taberd towards the Cercle Sportif where, Joseph had already discovered, disdainful French planters, noisy official Americans and diffident Vietnamese and Cholon-Chinese merchants gathered now in uneasy social disharmony; all trace of its former aura of colonial exclusivity had disappeared, but as the gates of the Cercle came in sight, the romantic image of that tiny, horse-drawn *malabar*, in which he had escorted Lan home from the tennis final nevertheless forced itself into his mind, and his mood of aching sadness deepened. He had been in Saigon only three days, and the past had started to come vividly alive even before his plane had touched down at Tan Son Nhut. He had hardly slept at all on the twenty-hour flight from Washington, and as the Pan Am Boeing began its long, flat glide across the silver veins of the Mekong's tributaries, he had caught a distant glimpse of the twin towers of the cathedral and was reminded immediately of how that mysterious landmark had seemed to dart around the jungle like the ears of a hidden jackrabbit as the *Avignon* made its way slowly up the twisting Saigon river over forty years before; once down on the ground, however, he found that only occasional vestiges of the old Saigon remained.

The city's familiar swamp-fever humidity hadn't altered, but now choking gasoline fumes which never seemed to clear clogged his throat and the journey from Tan Son Nhut to the Continental Palace had turned into a nightmare drive through snarled traffic jams. The *cyclo-pousses*, operated by the same kind of scrawny Vietnamese who had run the rickshaws in colonial days, still existed, as did the little blue Renault taxis and a few battered Citroëns and Peugeots belonging to latter-day French *colons*, but they were swamped now by the unending flow of U.S. military juggernauts and the more numerous Chevrolets, Pontiacs and Mercuries of American officialdom. Vietnamese youths and girls threaded their way in and out of the melee on sputtering Lambrettas and Hondas, and Joseph was delighted to see that many of the girls still wore the captivating *ao dai*; some even wrapped flowing silk scarves around their faces to counteract the choking engine fumes and floated through the motorized chaos with the same fragile gracefulness that had first entranced him so many years before.

The rush and bustle of war had, however, destroyed the Saigon siesta, he soon found, and even the four-hour curfew that began at midnight was rent by the unending roar of military convoys rushing through the cleared streets. Some store owners still lowered their steel shutters for an hour or two in the middle of the day, but the garish neon-lit bars and tawdry souvenir stands that had sprung up along Tu Do, Le Loi and Nguyen Hue remained open to serve the swarms of off-duty GIs who crowded the traffic-choked streets. Shoddily built new apartment blocks that had shot up everywhere to cater to the ever-increasing American demand for living space had to his dismay obliterated almost completely the fading elegance of French colonial Saigon, but he had been relieved to find on his arrival that the government post he had accepted after much thought — senior adviser at the Joint United States Public Affairs Office — entitled him to one of the old colonial villas on Cong Ly. It was there that he had just entertained Tam to a dinner prepared by the aged Vietnamese *bep* who went with the villa, but despite the length and occasional intimacy of Joseph's acquaintance with Tam and his family, the Vietnamese had for most of the evening remained guarded and evasive in what he said.

He had giggled with embarrassment when asked about his big inherited landholdings in the delta and Joseph had realized then that the fact that he still enjoyed a big landowner's privileges after years of American pressure for some kind of major land reform had added a new dimension of defensiveness to his manner. He was currently a deputy minister of information in President Thieu's government, and it was a position, Joseph reflected, with minimal public exposure and therefore low political risk, which would automatically give him inside knowledge of all exploitable business opportunities in the booming, corruption-ridden wartime economy of South Vietnam; under prompting he had admitted with another embarrassed giggle that he had many other business interests now "in such things as property, construction and import agencies" but despite these revelations, his demeanor still remained wary, as though he were certain that the most uncomfortable question of all would be asked of him sooner or later.

Joseph in the end managed to contain himself until they were sipping French liqueurs on the terrace of his villa and breathing the heavy night scents of the darkened garden; he had by then exhausted his questions on the new government, the recently promulgated constitution and Tam's views of the pacification program, and in his turn the Vietnamese had complimented Joseph effusively on the *cha gio* of his chef and the delicacy of the French wines he had served. But at the very mention of Tuyet's name Tam had fallen silent for such a long time that Joseph felt certain he was going to ignore the question altogether. When he did finally answer he peered intently into the darkness of the garden so that he didn't have to look at Joseph, but even so his voice still betrayed a trace of embarrassment.

"I know nothing more concrete than what I told you in 1956," he said softly. "Your daughter simply disappeared — virtually without trace."

"You say 'virtually,'" said Joseph, unable to conceal the tremor of hope in his voice. "Does that mean you've had some news of her since then?"

The Vietnamese lapsed into a reflective silence again and Joseph fancied that his expression hardened. "They were only rumors that were never substantiated. And since Tuyet decided to give her loyalty to the Communist side, nobody in our family, you understand, has ever pressed inquiries. We heard stories that she married a guerrilla fighter by the name of Dang Dinh Luong who died in custody here in Saigon. His wife's name at any rate was Tuyet, and she's supposed to have sworn to avenge his death. She joined a Viet Cong assassination squad that killed some members of our security services and the same girl later became a notorious main force platoon leader in the delta. She called herself 'Tuyet Luong' in memory of her husband."

Joseph sat forward in his chair, staring at the Vietnamese in horror. "I can't believe it."

"As I said, there's no real evidence that 'Tuyet Luong' is your daughter," added Tam hastily. "It's only hearsay. 'Tuyet,' after all, isn't an uncommon name in Vietnam. But the rumors did suggest she was of mixed race."

Joseph sank back in his seat and absorbed in a stunned silence the implications of what Tam had said. Then he rose and began pacing agitatedly back and forth along the terrace. "When did you hear these rumors, Tam?"

"In the early sixties."

"And has anything been heard of 'Tuyet Luong' since then?"

Tam shook his head. "She seemed to disappear suddenly from the scene in the delta around about 1963."

"So she could have been killed!" Joseph stared at the Vietnamese in dismay.

"It is possible of course," replied Tam, avoiding Joseph's eyes. "But as I said, our family has not been anxious to inquire too closely. It's possible the Liberation Front leadership ordered her to undertake some less glamorous task. The Communists demand conformity and discipline above all else. A beautiful young woman roaming around wearing American pistols on her hips like a western gunslinger hardly fits that mold. Perhaps, she was becoming too famous."

Joseph stopped pacing and refilled their glasses, and for a long time the two men sipped their drinks without speaking; then Joseph turned towards Tam once more, his expression thoughtful. "Is it possible, do you think, that 'Tuyet Luong' might have been assigned to Da Nang in some kind of intelligence role?"

"To spy on the American flyers when they go out on the town, you mean?'

Joseph nodded eagerly, "Exactly!"

"It's possible. Why do you ask?"

"Because my youngest son, Mark, joined the air force and flew from Da Nang until he went missing on a mission over the North two years ago. We don't know whether he survived the crash, but one of his last letters to his mother contained a mysterious reference to a Vietnamese girl in the town who he thought called herself 'Tuyet.' It was all very unclear in the letter, but it seems 'Tuyet,' whoever she was, had learned his name and passed a vague message to him through another girl about 'her father in America.' Mark wrote about this very casually and obviously didn't understand what it was about."

"Didn't he know he had a half sister?"

Joseph shook his head quickly and looked away. "No. Neither of my sons has been told about Tuyet. To my deep regret I've had very little to do with either of them since they've grown up."

"And have you been to Da Nang yet?"

Joseph nodded. "I flew up there almost as soon as I arrived."

"And what did you discover?"

Joseph let out his breath slowly. "Nothing — nothing at all. I couldn't find any trace of her. But then I had so little to go on."

A sad little smile of sympathy appeared suddenly on Tam's face. "If 'Tuyet Luong' is your daughter, it must be very painful for you, Joseph, to think that she has sided with the enemy. But perhaps it helps you to understand our unfortunate country a little better. We have something in common now — we both have people of our own flesh and blood fighting against us on the other side in this terrible war."

"I'm sorry Tam," said Joseph quietly. "I was thinking only of myself. I'd forgotten your brother, Kim."

"Don't apologize. It's very rare for an American to find himself in this situation — but for a Vietnamese it isn't at all uncommon."

"We had our own civil war not so long ago," said Joseph dully, "so I suppose we should understand better. What contact have you had with Kim over the years?"

Tam shrugged and turned his face away once more. "What contact could a leading member of the Hanoi Politburo have with a minor government minister in Saigon?"

"But it's not unknown, is it, for Viet Cong guerrillas to sneak home to their families to celebrate Tet even though they're in the opposing camp."

"That's possible only for minor functionaries. For my brother nothing less than leading the revolution was ever good enough, and the day he dishonored my father I swore never to speak with him again until he begged forgiveness on his bended knees." He let out a bitter, mirthless laugh. "Can you imagine Kim coming to kneel before me in Saigon now after all the blood that's been spilled? My mother concealed her broken heart for many years before she died — but she never knew happiness again after Kim insulted my father and all our ancestors so deeply." He shrugged his shoulders once more in a gesture of helplessness. "But even though so much divides us, even though Kim is a Communist above all else, he's still my brother."

"Yes, and Tuyet, wherever she is and whatever she's doing, is still my daughter," said Joseph resignedly.

They had lapsed into silence again after that, and to break the melancholy of their mood, Joseph had eventually suggested a stroll through the nighttime streets of the capital. They walked side by side but separately, wrapped in their own thoughts, and slowly the intimacy that had grown up between them in the garden had evaporated. Struck by a sudden thought, Joseph had asked Tam what had become of Lan's son; shaking his head sadly, the Vietnamese told him that the boy had been killed in battle only a few months after graduating from the Dalat military academy. This news served to depress their mood further, and

577

conversation between them ceased altogether.

In the heart of the city, noisy crowds of GIs were still lurching in and out of the bars, and in Quach Thi Trang Square around the central market some of the homeless refugees who had swollen Saigon's population to around three million people were already settling down for another night in doorways and on the pavements. Instinctively Joseph and Tam quickened their pace to put behind them sights which reminded them all too forcibly of what the war was doing to the Saigon they had both known in more tranquil, dignified days, and when they reached the cathedral square they shook hands, bade one another good night and went their separate ways.

Joseph turned towards his villa on Cong Ly, then halted uncertainly after a few paces; although saddened by his evening with Tam and appalled by what Saigon was becoming, something of the fascination which the city and its people had once held for him still lingered indefinably in the streets. In the clammy heat he was aware suddenly that he still felt a strange, almost pleasurable, sense of disquiet, a kind of restless unease which tautened his senses to the verge of breathlessness, and after a moment's hesitation he turned back towards the Rue Catinat, which still clung unofficially to its original French name rather than "Tu Do." Crossing deliberately to the other side of the boulevard to avoid the sidewalk in front of the Continental terrace, he strolled into Le Loi Square. Beneath the massive black statue of Vietnamese Marines in action a small crowd had gathered, and as he drew nearer he saw the bright glare of television camera lights above the heads of the watchers. One of the duties he was preparing to take over at JUSPAO was supervision of the daily press conference in the air-conditioned auditorium on Nguyen Hue Street; the increasingly skeptical crowd of American and foreign correspondents who appeared for the late afternoon briefings on the progress of the war already irreverently termed the sessions "The Five O'Clock Follies," and one of his major tasks was to find a way to lend more conviction to the proceedings. Expecting to find a correspondent of one of the major American television networks recording a commentary, he moved closer out of professional curiosity to hear what was being said, but the sound of a female voice delivering a report to camera in what some Americans called "Mayfair English" surprised him.

Craning his neck above the heads of the Vietnamese onlookers, he was able to see in the glow of the lights a tall, striking girl in

578

combat boots and a crumpled safari suit of pale linen that suggested she and her camera team had just spent several days in the field filming the war. Her soundman was holding up prompt cards with brief script headings for her behind the camera, and Joseph guessed she was recording a final summary for a film already shot in the war zones. Once or twice as he listened, she fluffed a word because of tiredness and had to repeat the commentary, but the cadences of her voice indicated she had almost finished, and Joseph moved closer when she paused to allow the cameraman to zoom in for a final close-up.

"I first began reporting this war five years ago when only a few thousand American advisers were involved," she said, speaking with slow deliberation. "Now there are more than half a million American fighting men in Vietnam. But although official U.S. spokesmen constantly tell us that 'every quantitative measurement' shows that the Communists are being beaten, victory, like smoke between the fingers, remains elusive and difficult to grasp." She paused for a moment to give emphasis to her concluding words, then she added formally: "This is Naomi Boyce-Lewis reporting from Saigon."

Joseph stared hard at the brightly lit face of the English reporter as her cameraman held the shot to provide some end-footage for their film editors in London, and for a few seconds his memory grappled unsuccessfully with the half-familiar name. Then in the instant that the camera was cut and the lights were switched off, he remembered. The silent crowd of Vietnamese who had been watching the recording being made drifted away with reluctance, and by the time he pushed through to the foot of the statue she was bending to help the crew pack their gear.

"I couldn't help hearing your pay-off line, Miss Boyce-Lewis," he said quietly. "Would you by any chance be related to a Colonel Sir Harold Boyce-Lewis who was with the British Army out here at the end of the Second World War?"

She turned at the sound of his voice and looked at him with a startled expression. "Do you mean my father . . .?"

The American's smile broadened and he held out his hand. "I suppose I do. I'm Joseph Sherman. How is Sir Harold?

"My father was killed here in 1945, Mr. Sherman," she said in a small voice. Then she looked at him more intently, her eyes brightening with interest. "But if you knew him at all I would love to talk to you some time."

4

The baying of the Hanoi crowd reverberated in Mark Sherman's ears like the shrieks of tormented souls in hell. They closed all around him, men, women and children, showering him with their spittle, striking him with their fists and feet, ripping handfuls of living hair from his head. Time and time again they drove him to the ground, kicking his face, trampling him against the tarmac road, tripping, stumbling and falling about him like stampeding cattle in their frenzy. Above the heads of the seething mob, the ominous black lenses of television cameras recording the public agony of the fifty shambling United States Air Force and Navy pilots seemed to stretch and elongate themselves until they too were abusing the officers, stabbing at them, knocking them viciously to the ground. The cameramen, Slavic Caucasians from Russia and Eastern Europe and narrow-eyed Chinese and Vietnamese, leered and grinned gleefully from behind their lenses as they worked, the features of their faces stretching and distorting until, with mouths open wide, they too joined in the hysterical howling of the mob.

"Bow, Sherman! Bend your head in shame, you filthy Yankee motherfucker!"

The voices of their prison guards loping beside them rang out deafeningly through megaphones that they held clamped against their mouths; the American slang they used was distorted by their accents, but every time an American's name was called, the crowd immediately took up the chant in shrill imitation. The shrieking rose quickly to a crescendo, then Mark felt the sharp point of a bayonet slash his back and the rifle butt of another guard thudded simultaneously into his solar plexus, forcing him to bend double in agonized response to the rising chants.

"Kowtow, Sherman! Kowtow! Bow your head! Kill the imperialist air pirates! Hang them for their inhuman crimes against the Vietnamese people!"

A flame of pain seared his groin as he went down again under a flurry of flying feet. He dragged himself upright only because his partner urged him on; otherwise he would have been content to lie on the ground until they kicked him insensible. At first the vast crowd watching from specially constructed grandstands on either side of the street had stared open-mouthed and in silence as the apprehensive Americans were unloaded from the truck that had brought them from their prisons to the center of Hanoi. They were handcuffed in pairs, and it wasn't until their blindfolds were removed that the muttering began, and then the crowd had started to spill out of their seats. With the aid of their megaphones, the guards had whipped the mob into a calculated frenzy before pushing the manacled prisoners into their clutches, and the demented screaming had begun almost at once.

"Johnson is a murderer! Rusk is a murderer! McNamara is a butcherer of women and children!"

With the hate-filled shrieks reverberating in his ears, Mark felt himself lifted and carried on the surge of the crowd as though he was awash in heavy seas; his clothes were in tatters and blood poured down his face from wounds in his head. He tried to roll over and dig his arms and legs into the mass of bodies to swim free, but he was jerked back violently by the handcuff which chained him by his left wrist to a young navy pilot. The navy man, unconscious now and covered in blood, had already sunk beneath the surface, and Mark felt himself being dragged inexorably downward, felt himself begin to drown in the squirming, seething mass of slippery Asian bodies. He twisted and turned, gasping for air, but the harder he fought, the more closely they pressed about him, and their flesh seemed to liquefy and flow suffocatingly into his mouth and nostrils like water.

Then the ground beneath him opened without warning, and the feeling that he was drowning gave way to a greater terror: he was tumbling downward out of a high, bright sky toward distant land below, rolling helplessly in the free air watching his empty F-105D Thunderchief spinning away beneath him, belching smoke. It exploded on a jungle-covered hillside beside the Red River in a bright orange geyser of fire, and angry tongues of flame leaped hundreds of feet into the air, reaching out to his falling body, setting his flying suit and parachute afire, roasting his flesh and accelerating his downward plunge. But as always he somehow fell lightly to earth, landing nimbly on his feet, and he was surrounded in an instant by the same yelling crowd of Vietnamese peasants who always ran screaming from beneath the same clump of lac trees at the foot of the hill on which an old French fort still stood. They beat his body with machetes, cutting him deeply with their crude blades until his own free-flowing blood extinguished the agonizing flames. He drew his .38 pistol, screaming at them to retreat, but as usual they didn't hear him, and he thrust its muzzle towards the face of the Vietnamese nearest to him. Always, as had happened in reality, the first shot

581

was a red tracer round and it tore a jagged hole in the middle of the peasant's face. As always the peasant collapsed on top of him, pinning him to the ground, but no matter how hard he struggled, he could never free himself of the scrawny corpse, and its unexpected weight bore him rapidly downward into the soft earth, heavier on top of him, it seemed, than a forty-story building.

A sea of Vietnamese faces peered curiously over the retreating rim of what had become an ever-deepening grave, and he spotted his mother, the gray-haired Pentagon colonel who had become his stepfather and his brother, Gary, among them; they watched blankly, shaking their heads from time to time in silent bewilderment, and although he tried to cry out to them, they faded quickly from his sight and immediately he was writhing again in that black, fetid cell where they had first locked his feet into the rusting ankle stocks built by the early French colonizers. Invisible hands shackled his wrists behind him in "hell cuffs," ratcheting them tightly through flesh and sinew until their jagged jaws bit on the bones of his wrists; in an instant his arms turned black, swelling to twice their normal size, and the open wounds around his wrists turned yellow and festered before his eyes. Bloated green scorpions and black rats scuttled back and forth over him, suppurating boils and sores sprouted like fungus from his limbs again, and bowls of food and liquid floated tantalizingly beyond his reach like disembodied ghosts. Taunting laughter rang crazily in his ears as the starvation and dehydration pains intensified, then the leering face of his Vietnamese torturer whom he had on that first day dubbed "The Swineherd" started to inflate in the tiny confined space of his cell; grew bigger and bigger, like a child's balloon, forcing him to retreat whimpering into a corner, and the jailer's slack, drooling maw opened and closed slowly like a fish's mouth as he repeated over and over again "*Bao cao! Bao cao! Bao cao!* — Inform! Inform!"

Although he pressed himself frantically against the wall to try to avoid the ropes that drifted towards him like fronds of dark seaweed, they tightened by themselves around his arms again with an agonizing suddenness; his shoulder blades were forced together in the middle of his back, his breastbone threatened to burst from his chest, and when the familiar fear that his whole body would split open from crotch to gizzard returned, a voice began screaming hideously, providing a high descant to the torturer's repeated yells of "*Bao cao! Bao cao!*" This demented shrieking rose quickly to a crescendo like a steam whistle, and

Mark eventually realized that he was no longer trapped in the toils of his nightmare but was lying awake on the concrete floor of the punishment cell listening to his own crazed voice. The face of "The Swineherd" close before his eyes too was no longer the suffocating "balloon" of his nightmare but the flesh-and-blood reality of his sadistic jailer. He was shaking him by the shoulder to rouse him, and as his vision cleared, he saw too in the gray light of dawn that the immaculately attired North Vietnamese cadre who had escorted him in the car the night before was standing behind "The Swineherd." The same faint smile seemed to be fixed upon the cadre's face, and the moment the screaming died away, he began talking in a soothing voice.

"You've been having bad dreams, Lieutenant Sherman — but you can relax now. I've come to take you somewhere we can talk quietly." Kim stooped and picked up the rabbit's foot which lay beside the American on the floor and placed it gently in his hand. "Don't worry anymore — everything will be all right now."

He opened the cell door and stood aside to let Mark pass in front of him, then motioned to "The Swineherd" to follow. Kim directed him into the rear seat of the same Tatra outside in the prison yard and got in beside him; the jailer traveled in the front passenger seat, and only minutes later the car deposited them all in the courtyard of the Ministry of Justice building that stood close to the jail. In an empty interrogation room, a small table had been laid with a simple breakfast of toast, cereal and orange juice, and Kim waved the American towards it while he sat down on a nearby stool and took a buff folder from the document case he carried. The jailer remained on guard by the door, and after eyeing the table suspiciously, Mark sat down and began to eat; crouching in the chair like an animal, he devoured the food noisily, darting suspicious glances at Kim and "The Swineherd" from time to time, as though afraid they might change their minds and try to take it from him.

"From your file I see on your arrival you chose to undergo extended punishment for three months rather than reveal even your name, service number and date of birth," said Kim quietly without looking up. "That obviously requires courage of a high order."

Mark gazed dully at the Vietnamese for a second, still chewing, then hunched lower over the table to finish the food.

"It was a great pity you chose to demonstrate your courage in that way. If we'd known who you were from the start, we could have given you special consideration." When Mark made no response, Kim resumed his reading of the file. After two or three minutes' silence he glanced up again. "I shouldn't tell you this, lieutenant, but you are one of the very few prisoners who have refused to condemn your government's misguided involvement in Vietnam. Almost every one of your fellows has recorded or written denunciations that have been published or broadcast abroad. And why not? Some senators and other important public figures in Washington are now beginning to describe your country's role here as 'the gravest treason.' "

The Vietnamese drew a small tape recorder from his document case and set it up on a small table beside the stool. When he switched it on, the strained voices of other captured American pilots filled the room one after the other, condemning their participation in the war. The adjectives "vile," "illegal," and "immoral" were used repeatedly and the pilots frequently described themselves as the "the blackest criminals" who had carried out "inhuman air raids." But if Mark registered the content of the recordings, he gave no sign, and Kim leaned over and switched the machine off.

"Reading your file is very interesting, lieutenant, you know, because in your determination not to say those things we would like you to say, you've talked about everything else under the sun with your interrogator." He tapped the file on his lap with his forefinger. "I was very saddened for instance to learn that you fell out with your father when you were sixteen and have never seen him since. I knew your father too, you see. He's a remarkable man — he was responsible for saving the life of President Ho Chi Minh in 1945. So we have cause to admire him. And good cause to do something to return his kindness — such as sending home the son he believes might already be dead."

Mark raised his head slowly to look at the Vietnamese, and although his gaze still didn't seem to focus properly, Kim noticed he was frowning as though disconcerted for the first time.

"Perhaps you've forgotten now, but you once told your interrogator you swore never to speak to your father again after he deserted your mother. The file says you were delirious one night and told the whole story of your quarrel with your father."

Mark appeared to make a renewed effort to concentrate on what Kim was saying and leaned forward on the table. Seeing this, Kim rose and walked slowly across the room until he was standing beside the American.

"You know that you hurt your father deeply by your behavior because your brother has talked with him, hasn't he? You were glad to hear he was suffering for his past indiscretions, weren't you? But it didn't make you any more inclined to meet him and talk to him. You wanted to hurt him as much as possible by your silence, didn't you? You wanted to get back at him at all costs." Kim paused to study the effect his words were having, and seeing Mark's frown deepen, he smiled. "But it's obvious that your father still cares for you despite all that, isn't it? Otherwise he wouldn't have taken the trouble to write a letter to our president pleading on your behalf. Despite your harshness towards him he's obviously still very concerned about you. That's perhaps more than you deserve, isn't it?"

As Kim watched, Mark's features tautened again as though he was confused by his thoughts; then he looked up at the Vietnamese cadre with a bemused expression in his eyes.

"Sometimes we go too far in our feuds with those closest to us. We long to take revenge for imagined hurts we've suffered, not realizing how cruel we are. I know myself what pain can be caused by strife between father and son, because I quarreled violently with my own father when I was young. Like you, I swore never to have anything more to do with him. He was killed fourteen years ago at the end of the French war, and although nothing has altered to change what divided us then, I've always felt a deep sadness that I never did anything to tell him of my feelings before he died. Perhaps the same thing will happen to you. Perhaps you will stay here for many years because of your stubbornness and by the time you are released, your father and your mother may be dead. Have you thought of that possibility?"

The muscles in Mark's jaw tightened and he stared hard at Kim; seeing that he was beginning to get the response he'd been seeking, the Vietnamese turned away casually and walked back towards the stool on which his document case lay.

"But perhaps I'm misjudging you. Perhaps, unlike me, you're not a man to feel regret or worry about what others are feeling. Perhaps you're able to seal yourself up in your own selfish world, pleasing only yourself. Why should you, after all, concern yourself with bringing relief to your worried father — and your mother? The pleasure your homecoming would give them is no concern of yours, you tell yourself, I expect. Am I right? I don't suppose it's ever occurred to you, has it, that in a different way while you choose to go on suffering here, they must suffer

585

agonies of a different kind back home in America because of your stubbornness."

Kim turned again to look at the American and found him staring distractedly in front of him; an anguished look had come into his eyes, and he was beginning to breathe unevenly.

"If it were left to me alone," continued Kim in a consoling voice, "I would have you released immediately, lieutenant — for your father's sake. But unfortunately there are other leading comrades who must be consulted who don't know your father. They would have to be convinced that your release won't harm our cause. That's why if you wanted to go home I would have to ask you to make a statement. It's just a precaution — and it's no more than all your fellow prisoners have done. But of course I don't really know whether you want to be released, do I? Since you continue to refuse to talk to me, I can't judge whether you really would like to return to the comfort of your home in America. Maybe you are strong enough to withstand prison life here indefinitely . . ."

Kim drew a single sheet of typescript from his document case and studied it intently for a minute or more. From the corner of his eye he noticed Mark turn in his chair to look at him.

"Of course if you turn down the opportunity I'm offering you today," continued Kim in a regretful tone, "it can't be offered to you again. If you decide you don't want to read what's written on this paper, I'll have no choice but to hand you back to the care of your jailer. You'll have to be returned to the punishment cells." He raised his head and glanced briefly towards "The Swineherd," who stood impassively by the door; then he turned back to Mark again. "But I hope you won't force me to do it. If you decide you *can* read for us, I'll make sure you're put in line for an early release — and you can go home and thank your father who cared enough to help you!" Kim picked up the tape recorder and walked over to Mark's table. He signaled for the jailer to clear the food tray away, then placed the sheet of paper and the tape recorder in front of Mark. "It will only take a minute or two to read," he said gently. "And there's no hurry — you can take as long as you like over it."

When Mark lifted his head to stare at the Vietnamese, he found him smiling sympathetically; suddenly a look of utter bewilderment came into the American's eyes and his head sank down on his arms. A moment later, his shoulders began to shake, and the sound of his sobbing, quiet at first, gradually grew louder until it filled the room. He wept for nearly a quarter of an hour, and during that time Kim waited patiently beside him; when finally he fell silent, Kim patted him encouragingly on the shoulder and switched on the tape recorder.

"Just read it, lieutenant, in a normal voice," he said soothingly. "That's all you need to do."

For a long time Mark didn't move, then he straightened slowly in the chair and picked up the sheet of typescript. His face worked convulsively from time to time as he read it through, then he turned to face towards the tape recorder.

"I'm First Lieutenant Mark Sherman, of the United States Air Force," he said reading aloud in a hollow, halting voice. "My grandfather is Senator Nathaniel Sherman, who has served as Democratic senator from Virginia for more than forty years, and I wish it to be known that, contrary to his views, I see the cruel war of aggression being waged against the heroic Vietnamese people by the United States as a crime against all humanity. I was shot down while carrying out inhuman air raids against churches, hospitals and schools in the Democratic Republic of Vietnam and I regard my role in the war as evil and shameful . . ."

Here and there he stumbled over a word, and whenever he did so Kim patiently told him to go back and reread the sentence again. Each time he stopped and looked up, he found "The Swineherd" staring fixedly at him from his place by the door and he reluctantly resumed his reading.

". . . The barbaric and immoral policies of the United States government stand condemned by all the decent peoples of the world," he continued as the spools of the tape recorder spun silently on the table beside him. "And my conscience will not rest easy until the last of the American imperialist aggressors has been driven from Vietnamese soil . . ."

5

"I always felt cheated by Vietnam," said Naomi Boyce-Lewis with a rueful little smile. "Even before I knew what or where it was. All the other girls in my class at school had their fathers back, we'd had the celebrations and the war was obviously over — but I was still told I had to be patient and wait. I'd been getting occasional letters from this strange place called 'Saigon' that nobody had ever heard of, then suddenly they stopped and I was told he wasn't *ever* coming back. I took it pretty hard, I suppose, and quite illogically when I came here for the first item in 1963 I was still nursing the grudge deep down. I think without fully realizing it I felt Vietnam owed me something."

She picked up a spoon and toyed for a moment with the little French sorbet ice that the white-jacketed Vietnamese waiter had brought to their table on the verandah of the Cercle Sportif, and watching her, Joseph felt himself deeply moved. Although twenty-three years had passed, it had come as a shock to hear in Le Loi Square the previous night that the British intelligence colonel with whom he'd worked had been killed in action only a day or two after his own departure from Saigon in 1945; in his memory Colonel Boyce-Lewis had been an aloof, faintly conde-scending figure who had dismissed American sympathy for the native Vietnamese with some disdain, but the mental picture of a distressed nine-year-old girl waiting fretfully for her father's return from the war aroused an intense feeling of compassion in him. The news had also carried his own thoughts vividly back to those moments in late 1945 that had been so poignant in his life — his reunion with Lan and their rescue of Tuyet from the famine-stricken North — and this too colored his response.

"How was he killed exactly?"

"He was shot through the neck with a poisoned arrow in montagnard country north of here. He died within a few hours." Naomi spoke in a flat, unemotional voice without looking up from her plate, but Joseph closed his eyes for a moment.

"I'm sorry, I shouldn't have asked." An awkward little silence developed, and they ate for a while without speaking. "Sir Harold as I remember him was the kind of Englishman all Americans admire greatly despite themselves," he said at last, resorting to a white lie about his recollection of her father in an effort to break the ice again. "That unfailing courtesy and dignified bearing no matter what the provocation is something your crass, ex-colonial subjects born on the other side of the Atlantic just aren't capable of. It can be infuriating sometimes — but it's a much-envied quality. I remember the dinner in the British staff officers' mess that last time I met him was a tribute to the British sense of style in difficult circumstances, too. Regimental silver, linen napkins and a great sense of decorum was observed by all — even though a civil war raged in the streets outside. For me it was a memorable return to civilization after those weeks in the jungle in the North. I was ungracious enough to blow my top that night, on the subject of British policy, but your father, who was sitting beside me, merely smiled politely and pointed out what he saw as the error of my ways in a tolerant voice."

"That sounds just like Daddy!" She looked up at him, her warm smile reflecting the inner pleasure that his reminiscences had invoked. "I've never met anybody who knew exactly what he was doing out here before he died and it's so strange for me to hear you talk about those times. He was such a misty figure in my own life, you see, because he was away most of the time. Listening to you talk like this about him helps somehow to lay the ghost of his memory for me." She continued smiling at him for a moment, then looked away quickly as if embarrassed by the inadvertent intimacy of her confession.

"I'm delighted that what little I've been able to say has been some help," said Joseph quietly. "I wish there was more I could tell you."

"Hearing what it was really like here in 'forty-five from somebody who lived through it is rare enough." She smiled at him again a little wistfully; she wore a crisp white shirtwaist dress and her hair, freshly coiffed, fell in soft waves to her shoulders. In the candlelight she looked rested again, almost radiant, but the sadness which the conversation obviously induced in her tugged down the corners of her mouth from time to time, giving her beauty a touchingly vulnerable quality. During most of the dinner she had sat motionless in her seat, her chin resting on her fingertips, as Joseph described in detail the events in which he and her father had been caught up during the autumn of 1945. She had barely touched her food or her wine and had spoken little herself until he reached the end of his account. "I suppose because of my father I'd have been drawn here some time or other to see what it was like, even if I hadn't become a journalist," she said, a faraway look coming into her eyes. "But as soon as I arrived in Saigon for the first time, I think I knew I was going to have a kind of love-hate relationship with the place. I stumbled across the most dramatic stories of my life almost immediately with the pictures we salvaged from the ambush at Moc Linh and the burning of Thich Quang Duc. I can still dine out on either of those in London whenever I like, even five years later . . ."

"It's strange you should feel that way too." Joseph's voice suddenly had an emotional edge. "I've had something of a love-hate relationship with Vietnam all my life too — and even now I can't make up my mind which feeling is the strongest."

"Why do you say that?"

"I first came here on a shooting expedition when I was fifteen — to help collect animals for a natural history museum founded by my grandfather. I was just bowled over by the exotic people, the jungles, the palaces in Hue — but on the last day of the hunting my elder brother was killed. So I was entranced and horrified by the country at one and the same time. But it was that trip that made me decide to major in Asian history and like a moth drawn to a flame, I came back to do research here ten years later. That's when my love affair with Vietnam started to go deeper than yours, I fancy . . ." He broke off abruptly, a faint look of embarrassment showing on his face. "Damn it, Naomi, I can see why you make such an outstanding journalist. I've hardly known you two minutes and you've got me pouring out my heart in a way I've never done to anyone before."

"But I've barely asked you a single question," she protested with an amused smile.

"Maybe that's the secret of it!"

His exasperation was so genuine that for the first time that evening they both laughed, but when their laughter died away he continued without any further urging to recount the story of his unhappy love affair with Lan, his marriage to Tempe and his later discovery of Tuyet's existence. In her turn Naomi was moved to see the handsome, confident man opposite her grow hesitant and embarrassed at his own words, and her eyes softened as she watched him fiddling with the stem of his wineglass. Most of the time he kept his gaze averted from her, speaking slowly and haltingly of emotions that she could see had lain buried away inside him for many years, and he passed quickly over Lan's death, Tuyet's later disappearance and his retreat to Cornell before finally falling silent.

"But after staying away for twelve whole years," she prompted gently, "what was it that made you decide suddenly to risk reopening all those old wounds and come back again?"

Joseph shook his head slowly from side to side and sighed. "I was afraid you were going to ask me that. When I left my wife, you see, Naomi, she married a career army man who I think in my absence made military life look very glamorous to my sons. Gary, whom you met at Moc Linh, chose the army and my younger son, Mark, went for the air force. They both took my leaving very hard — Mark has refused to have anything at all to do with me since, and although I've had some contact with Gary he's still cool towards me. He's been back here a few months now on his second tour and we had lunch the other day — but it was hard going. Mark was shot down over the north flying from Da Nang two years ago. I live in hope that he's survived the crash, but I've had no news of him at all. When Gary came out here again I was still sitting on the fence in Cornell watching my country tearing itself apart. I found I couldn't line up with the peace marchers or the draft dodgers, I didn't fit comfortably among the doves or the so-called silent majority, and it suddenly dawned on me that both my sons were out here doing their duty in this godawful war mainly because of my own stupidity. If I hadn't turned my back at the wrong moment maybe neither of them would have chosen the careers they did. And even my brother Guy's back here now for a second tour at the embassy — so I suddenly felt like a backslider, and first off I decided to write a personal letter to Ho Chi Minh about Mark. I was with an OSS unit that dropped into Tongking at the end of the war and I met Ho then and got to know him well. I went to see my former wife about the idea, and by chance she showed me one of Mark's old letters. He'd passed on a garbled message without understanding it from a girl in Da Nang who he thought called herself 'Tuyet' . . ."

Naomi's eyes widened suddenly. "And you thought you could find your missing daughter! That's what really brought you back?"

Joseph pursed his lips as though he wasn't proud to own up to the motive and nodded reluctantly. "I guess if I'm going to be honest I have to admit I suddenly wanted to try to salvage something from the wreckage of my life. There's not much chance that Gary will ever see things my way, and God knows whether I'll ever see Mark again. But I always sensed that deep down Tuyet might be hiding her real feelings . . ." He sighed again and finished his wine. "Several government agencies had tried to persuade me to take posts out here over the past year or two because of my background, and I'd always turned them down. But the JUSPAO offer dropped out of the sky two months ago, just after I'd heard about Mark's letter and I decided there and then to put my moral objections on ice."

"You're right, Joseph, it's very strange." Naomi spoke slowly, as though thinking aloud, and there was a note of wonderment in her voice. "We don't just seem to have a love-hate relationship with Vietnam in common. In different ways I think perhaps both of us have come here time and again, almost against our will, looking for something important — something we don't have much hope of finding."

He raised his head to look at her in surprise, and their eyes met and held; in that instant they both sensed instinctively that a new intimacy was being born, and he smiled at her. "When you're looking for something you never dared hope to find, Naomi, it's especially nice to find something you never dared dream of looking for."

She smiled playfully back at him. "That sounds as if it might have been translated from the mysterious works of some Chinese sage — or is that pure Joseph Sherman-style wisdom?"

"The Chinese have a nice unsentimental proverb to describe those who get lucky against all the odds. They say, 'Even a blind cat sometimes trips over a dead rat.' "

They laughed together, and looking up he saw for the first time that the rest of the diners had gradually drifted away, leaving them alone on the verandah; several waiters were watching impatiently for signs that they were ready to leave, and Joseph signaled apologetically for his bill, then led the way out into the tree-lined boulevard running alongside Doc Lap Palace. In the warm darkness beneath the trees they strolled side by side for several minutes without speaking, content to enjoy the pleasurable ease they suddenly felt in each other's presence, and it was Naomi who broke the silence at last.

"I don't think any European who's ever had anything to do with Vietnam goes away entirely unchanged," she said in a pensive voice. "Perhaps we're not so different from all the others in that respect. There's some hypnotic quality I can never put my finger on that casts a spell over all our minds when we're here. And whatever it is, it seems to have the power to bring out the best or the worst in us — sometimes even both."

"I think I know what you mean."

"I felt it on my very first day in Saigon in 1963. And in the beginning I think it brought out the worst in me."

"It sounds like you're working up to some juicy true-life confession," said Joseph humorously. "This could be interesting."

"I suppose I am — but this isn't a joke. I told you earlier that I'd met Gary and your brother Guy briefly when they were here before — well I wasn't being really honest then. It's true I met

592

Gary only once, but I got to know Guy quite well because we found we had a mutual interest in comparing notes during the Buddhist troubles. We had a faintly flirtatious friendship, that never really came to anything and I wanted to tell you that, in case I ever meet you together." She stopped walking and he saw that her face in the shadow of the trees was serious. "I'm saying this, Joseph, because I have a strong intuition that your friendship's going to be important to me — do you understand?"

Her eyes searched his face anxiously and he nodded. "Yes, I understand."

"There was something else too that happened then, about the time of the Diem coup. It involved Guy, but I don't think I can tell you about it now. Perhaps when I know you better it will be easier. But it made me see myself with a sudden clarity — made me realize that I was in danger of becoming something I didn't admire."

"What was that?"

She looked at him uncertainly, then turned and began walking again. "I've always been very ambitious, Joseph. Perhaps it's something to do with being the daughter of someone rich and titled who was a stranger to me. Perhaps your psychoanalysts back home would tell you I'm trying desperately to prove myself to my dead father, or show that I can succeed at something where my privileged background's no help — or some such mumbo jumbo. Well I don't know what the reason was in the first place, but I certainly did set out to convince myself and the world I could do my job as a television correspondent as well as anyone else — or even better. And I haven't really changed my mind about that. But the incident I'm talking about made me realize I was so anxious to succeed that I didn't care who suffered in the process — that's what I meant when I said Vietnam at first brought out the worst in me."

"You can't be as bad as you paint yourself," said Joseph quietly, "if you've listened to your conscience."

"I'm going to borrow your phrase now — I've never talked to anyone like this before. But listening to you tonight made me suddenly want to confide in you — I can't tell you why. And since the Diem coup I've tried consciously to see my stories with a more compassionate eye, tried to think of the story first, not myself. I don't know whether I've always succeeded, but I'm trying at least."

"I haven't known you long, Naomi," said Joseph, smiling again.

"But it's been long enough for me to know that you're a rare spirit."

They crossed Le Loi Square, heading in the direction of the Continental Palace Hotel, and Naomi moved closer to Joseph to slip her arm companionably through his. "You Americans are very quick on the draw with a compliment. I'd hoped to get in first with something like that about you . . ."

As he came down the steps of the Continental Palace with another officer of the 301st Infantry Division with whom he had been dining, Captain Gary Sherman glanced casually across the street in front of the hotel and noticed a broad-shouldered man in a pale, tropical-weight suit escorting a strikingly elegant woman with blond hair. The man, graying at the temples, was laughing, and Gary watched the couple idly for a moment or two before he realized with a start that the man was his father; a moment later he saw that he also knew his companion. They were walking close together arm in arm, and as soon as he recognized them, he stopped where he was and watched them approach the hotel. Because they were engrossed in their conversation, Joseph and Naomi didn't see Gary until they began climbing the steps, and then they looked up to find him blocking their way.

"Gary! What a surprise!" Joseph's face broke into a broad smile of pleasure. "I thought you weren't going to be able to get away from your unit again for another week at least. You know Miss Boyce-Lewis already, I believe."

"Sure, Dad, we met once." Gary's voice was deliberately cool and he greeted the English journalist with a curt nod.

"We've just been dining at the Cercle," said Joseph, still smiling. "It's a pity we didn't know you were in town. You and your friend could have joined us." He glanced at the other officer, but Gary made no move to introduce him.

"I was watching you both cross the street — I don't think somehow that would have been a good idea."

The smile on Joseph's face faded a little but he patted his son's shoulder warmly. "Nonsense. But what I'd really like to do, Gary, when you get into Saigon again is to have you come to dinner at my villa. I'm settled in now. You'll get to meet some of the American correspondents who write about the war."

"That will be just great — but you'd better send me your printed invitation well in advance so I can fix it with the VC for a night they're not working. So long." Gary grinned as he spoke but there was an unmistakable note of sarcasm in his voice, and he nodded formally at Naomi again before moving off briskly down the steps.

Joseph watched him go for a moment then turned apologetically to Naomi. "I'm sorry about that."

"Don't apologize," said Naomi quickly. "I sensed it was partly my fault for taking your arm."

"I don't want any apologies on that score," said Joseph firmly. "I wouldn't have missed that for anything."

In her third-floor suite Naomi waited until the Vietnamese waiter had delivered a tray of Scotch, ice and Perrier water then sat down beside Joseph on the sofa. After a moment's hesitation, she took hold of one of his hands. "I can't tell you how much this evening has meant to me, Joseph. Thank you for indulging me with so much talk about 1945 and my father — and for everything else."

"I've talked at least as much about myself, it seems to me," replied Joseph, smiling; then on an impulse he lifted her hand and pressed his lips gently against her fingers.

She watched him in silence, her face expressionless, but she made no effort to remove her hand. "I really ought to get some sleep now, Joseph. I've got an early flight to Hong Kong tomorrow."

Joseph nodded understandingly. "I only wish you were staying longer."

"I'll be back again before very long." She rose to pour a drink and placed it on the low table in front of him. For a moment she stood indecisively beside the sofa — then she smiled at him again. "I'm going to get ready for bed now. You may take five minutes to drink your whisky, and after that you're free to leave." Still smiling at him she removed her shoes and walked to the bedroom door in her stockinged feet; but before opening it she looked around at him and smiled again. "Or you can stay, if you like."

Joseph looked up in astonishment. "I thought you said you had to get some beauty sleep."

"You didn't listen carefully, Joseph. I said I *ought* to."

After she'd left the room, Joseph took off his jacket and tie, and spent ten minutes over his whisky. When he finally opened the bedroom door he found the room in shadow; only one lamp was lit, and Naomi was sitting on the far side of the bed with her back to him. She wore a white lace nightdress which left her shoulders bare and she was brushing her hair in a distracted fashion.

"I began to think you weren't coming." She spoke in a whisper but didn't turn round.

"I felt I ought to wait — in case you wanted to change your mind."

She shook her head quickly and put the brush down. After a moment he began to undress, then she felt the bed take his weight. "I ought to tell you, Joseph, I'm not awfully good at it," she said softly. "I hope you won't be disappointed."

She laughed a little muffled laugh but the tension in her body was unmistakable, and when he brushed his lips across her shoulders he felt her quiver.

"Neither am I," he said smiling at her back. "It's surprising how deceptive appearances can be."

When she finally turned to him, her eyes were open wide as though she was startled by her own actions, and he kissed her gently on the forehead before taking her in his arms. Their lovemaking was tentative, almost reverent, without high passion, but each sensed wordlessly in those moments that the separate obsessions that had drawn them back to Saigon again and again had led at last to an unexpected solace for them both.

6

Joseph's personal telephone began ringing while he was still unlocking the door to his office at eight-thirty A.M. the next morning, and when he lifted the receiver the note of urgency in his brother Guy's voice was immediately evident.

"Can you get over to the embassy right away, Joseph, please? Something special's come up."

"What's it about?"

"I can't say over the telephone. I've been calling you at your villa all night. I gave up finally at four A.M. when your *bep* told me you still weren't in. You didn't leave a contact number."

Joseph's eyes narrowed as he registered the note of reproof in his brother's voice. "Something unexpected turned up, Guy. Do you mind giving me some idea why I should run over there right away?"

"I'd rather tell you when you get here," replied Guy with slow deliberation. "But let me assure you it's in your own interest to get here fast."

"Okay, I'll be there right away."

As he hurried towards the new fortified embassy that had been built on the site of the old French Bureaux de l'Infanterie north of the cathedral square, Joseph puzzled over his brother's urgent summons. Guy had come back to Saigon for the second time nearly a year before as a counterintelligence case officer, and normally the staff of the Joint United States Public Affairs Office had little or no direct contact with the CIA Saigon station that now occupied the top three floors of the ultramodern Chancery block. At a personal level, the antipathy which Joseph had felt from the start for the brother who was sixteen years younger than himself had not lessened with the passage of time, and by habit and mutual consent, relations between them had always remained cool and distant. Joseph therefore concluded that the reasons for Guy's call must be professional, and searching his memory he recalled hearing some behind-the-hand talk at a cocktail party that intelligence reports suggested a new Viet Cong offensive was being planned to coincide with the annual Tet holiday, due to begin in two days time. The expert reaction, he already knew, had been that if plans of a major offensive had leaked out so easily, they must be part of a new propaganda ploy, and not much credence was being given to the threat. Perhaps, thought Joseph, some new evidence had come in and Guy wanted to brief him personally, but he gave up speculating as he came in view of the embassy, struck suddenly by its ugliness. It had taken two years to build and only four months before, in September 1967, had it finally replaced the former French bank premises overlooking the Saigon River which until then had served as the United States diplomatic headquarters in the city. Like President Thieu's Doc Lap Palace, the entire facade of the Chancery was protected by a rocket and artillery shield, a concrete carapace that gave the building a sinister, fortresslike aspect. A ten-foot wall also surrounded the compound, and a raised helicopter pad had been built on its flat roof; inside, a Marine force of sixty men patrolled the grounds day and night, and as one of the Marine corporals on gate duty checked his pass at the main entrance on Thong Nhut Boulevard, Joseph reflected ruefully that the rocket screens on the embassy and the palace had turned them into grim monuments to the indefatigable Viet Cong; these essential defenses were an ever-visible public acknowledgment that the guerrilla forces would always be strong enough to strike unimpeded at the twin headquarters of their enemies in the heart of their own capital.

In his room on the fifth floor of the Chancery, Guy wasted no time on preliminaries. As soon as Joseph stepped through the door, he waved him to a chair and pressed a button on the tape recorder on his desk. Because the quality of the voice reproduction was poor, Joseph couldn't make out the opening words, but he sat bolt upright in his seat the moment his ears attuned to what was obviously a recording of a short-wave broadcast.

". . . *My grandfather is Senator Nathaniel Sherman, who has served as Democratic senator from Virginia for more than forty years, and I wish it to be known that, contrary to his views, I see the cruel war of aggression being waged against the heroic Vietnamese people by the United States as a crime against all humanity. . . .*"

Joseph's knuckles whitened on the arms of his chair and he stared at the tape recorder with an anguished expression. "Thank God! At least he's alive."

Guy nodded grimly but lifted a finger indicating they should hear the recording through.

". . . *I was shot down while carrying out inhuman air raids against churches, hospitals and schools in the Democratic Republic of Vietnam and I regard my role in the war as evil and shameful. . . .*"

Joseph listened to the rest of Mark's confession in a shocked silence, and the moment Guy switched off the recording machine, he buried his head in his hands. When at last he looked up again his face was pale, and he spoke through gritted teeth. "He's alive, Guy — but what in hell's name have they done to him to make him say that?"

"They've tortured him just like they've tortured all the other poor bastards who've fallen into their hands," said Guy in a voice that shook with emotion. "Mark's so damned gutsy they've probably had to work harder on him than most — that's maybe why it's taken them all this time to squeeze that obscene bullshit out of him."

"Where did that come from?" Joseph nodded towards the tape machine.

"Havana Radio put it out last night."

Joseph cursed softly and closed his eyes again.

"Even if Mark wasn't my nephew, that would turn my goddamned stomach," said Guy fiercely. "But knowing what a brave, decent guy he is makes it ten times worse." He rose from his seat,

598

paced angrily across the office and stood staring out through the window. "It must simplify things a little in your mind too, Joseph, doesn't it? Doesn't it make you care less about those deep historical complexities you've always warned me about? Doesn't it make you wonder whether all the trouble really stems from the 'monstrous exploitation' these people suffered under the French?" Guy labored his quotation in an exasperated tone. "Couldn't it just be that these people have got a sadistic streak a mile wide that makes them want to kill and maim other human beings for the sheer hell of it?"

Joseph sighed wearily and stood up. "Perhaps we could debate that old theme some other time, Guy," he said quietly. "Meantime I'd like to borrow that tape if I may and listen to it again on my own."

"Sit down please, Joseph. You're right — maybe this isn't the moment for airing our differences." The younger man's tone was conciliatory suddenly and he returned to his desk and sat down again. "I didn't ask you to come over just to listen to the tape — there's more to it than that."

"What do you mean?" Joseph resumed his seat, lines of anxiety furrowing his brow.

"All that follows is classified, okay — for your ears only."

Joseph nodded his agreement.

"In the last few months, the Viet Cong have begun putting out subtle feelers about talks on prisoner exchanges and what they tantalizingly call 'other political issues'. . . ."

Joseph's eyes widened in surprise. "Do you mean the Viet Cong want peace talks? That's way out of character, isn't it?"

"It's downright unprecedented. It may be a cover for something else — we can't rule that out. But anyway, over the last two or three years we've been steadily picking up some important prisoners here in the South — leading cadres in the Liberation Front. Their cover is so deep even our friendly Vietnamese interrogators here in Saigon can't get the real names out of some of them. They all usually have at least six aliases. You know as well as anyone the military and political leadership down here has been sent in from Hanoi — but proving it is something else."

"But now you've had some approaches about those prisoners, is that what you're saying?"

Guy nodded. "Right. The first contact through third parties three months ago threw up a list of half-a-dozen prisoners the Front wanted released right off. They suggested American pilots in Hanoi might be freed in exchange. We've heard nothing at all for several weeks but there was a new contact last night — just a few hours after Mark's confession went out on Havana Radio."

"Do you think that was deliberate?" asked Joseph quickly.

"Almost certainly. They seem to see Mark as a trump card because he's the grandson of the famous Senator Sherman. The Front last night offered a list of a dozen Americans, naming names for the first time — and Mark's name was among them."

"But that's marvelous news, Guy!"

"Well, let's try and keep this in perspective — it's early days yet. And the plot gets thicker."

"What do you mean?"

"In the list of the Saigon prisoners the Front want released in exchange, there's one new demand — for a very special prisoner indeed. He was captured in the delta a year ago and he's been held in solitary confinement ever since in a whitewashed, refrigerated cell in the old Sûreté cellars at the top of Catinat. He's so goddamned tough he hasn't even revealed his name yet. He's known only as 'the man in the white room' — that's the way the Front listed him. We're sure he's on the Central Committee of the Lao Dong at least — maybe even a member of the Politburo. We're beginning to think he might be the object of the whole exercise and they've probably waited until now to ask for him in an effort to play down his importance. He hasn't said a single word in twelve months, but we're as sure as hell he's the highest-ranking North Vietnamese we've ever had in our hands."

"So why are you telling me all this?"

"Because it struck me suddenly last night after Mark's name came up — you may know something no other American in Saigon knows."

"What's that?"

"You ran around the Tongking jungles for several weeks with half the present Hanoi Politburo in your cloak-and-dagger days with the OSS, right?"

Joseph nodded guardedly.

"I thought maybe you might just know 'the man in the white room' by sight. He might just be an old buddy of yours. If we could pin him down, it would help us evaluate the swap deal." Guy rose abruptly from behind his desk. "I thought we might go and take a look at him."

7

Joseph shivered as the white door of the special cell in the old
Sûreté cellar clanged shut behind them, and he had to screw up
his eyes against the glare of the bright overhead lights that reflected off the floor, the walls and the ceiling which were all painted a
dazzling uniform white. Through rows of grilles set high in the
walls the faint hum of invisible high-intensity air-conditioning
units was audible, and the sharp chill inside the cell testified to
their efficiency. At least twenty-five feet square, the room was
furnished with a chair, a table and a plank bed, all painted a
gleaming white, and there was a simple, unadorned hole for a
toilet in one corner. Its lone occupant was seated on the chair
with his back to them — a shrunken, aging figure dressed only in
a ragged pair of white shorts. He was bent almost double with his
shoulders hunched around his ears, and he had clasped his arms
about his own waist in an attempt to provide his shuddering body
with a vestige of warmth.

"We built this cell especially for him," said Guy in a normal
voice. "A Special Forces patrol stumbled on his headquarters by
accident in an old Dien Bien Phu kitchen near Moc Linh. He had
an entourage of six personal guards and two cooks so we knew
we'd netted a big fish." As they walked towards the prisoner, the
CIA man pointed to the row of vents set high in the walls. "Not all
those grilles are air ducts. We installed high-fidelity microphones
and television cameras to record every move and every sound he
makes twenty-four hours a day, whether he's awake or asleep. So
far he's given away nothing — but then until now he's never come
face to face with an OSS officer who helped train that romantic
little Viet Minh guerrilla band in 1945."

Guy raised his voice so that it carried clear across the cell, but
the scrawny Vietnamese did not move or turn as they
approached; even when the two Americans walked around in
front of him, he continued to lean forward in a crouch, hugging
his wasted body with his bony arms and only the top of his bowed
head remained visible to them.

"I've brought an old friend of Uncle Ho's to see you, comrade,"
said Guy quietly in French. "Let him get a good look at you."

For a long time the prisoner kept his head bowed, but when he
raised his eyes at last to look at them, Joseph tensed suddenly.
Although his cheeks were hollow and sunken, and his gray hair
was cropped close to his head, the high scholar's brow and the

brightness of his gaze made the Vietnamese instantly recognizable, and Joseph's memory sped back nearly twenty-five years to those few days he'd spent on the ledge outside the Pac Bo cave while he was being nursed back to health after the crash of his Warhawk. Dao Van Lat's eyes widened for a fleeting instant too in a moment of mutual recognition, then his expression became blank once more.

Guy was watching both men intently and he spotted the involuntary signals. "You recognize him, Joseph, I can tell!" He spoke sharply, unable to keep a note of triumph from his voice. "Who is he?"

Joseph continued staring at Lat, his mind awhirl with contradictory impulses. How could he reconcile his memory of the idealistic young Annamese who had read Ho's poems to him on a Tongking mountainside and the ravaged guerrilla leader who had obviously been helping direct Viet Cong operations in the South? And if he identified him as one of Ho's close aides, would that encourage the U.S. government to exchange him for a group of captured pilots that might include Mark? Or would knowledge of who he really was make them more anxious to hold him? For several seconds Joseph agonized over which course would be most likely to bring about Mark's release — then unable to decide, he turned his back suddenly on Lat.

"I don't know for sure," he said slowly. "I think maybe I do recognize his face — but I'm not certain."

A shadow of relief passed across Lat's features and he bent his head once more to stare at the floor.

"But he *was* one of the group with Ho in Tongking, wasn't he?" Guy's voice was angrily insistent, and Joseph turned back, frowning, to face him.

"I've spent a lot of time in Vietnam over the years, Guy, and met a lot of people. I think I recall his face from somewhere — but it may have been twenty or thirty years ago. And he hadn't been through the hell of a year in solitary then. I don't really remember where it might have been."

"We've got pictures going back forty years at the embassy," said Guy quickly. "We inherited the old Sûreté photo-archives. Maybe you can identify one with a name on it." The CIA man glanced down at Lat, who sat staring vacantly in front of him, behaving as though they had already departed. "But there's something else, Joseph, that might help jog your memory — it's entered on his file under 'scars and distinguishing physical characteristics.' "

Taking hold of one of Lat's manacled arms, Guy lifted him to his feet and with a quick movement of his free hand, pushed his loose shorts down his legs to the floor. He retained his grip on the arm of the Vietnamese so that he could not bend to retrieve the garment and turned him towards Joseph in a way that exposed his groin. "You see now what I mean — he's got no goddamned balls!"

Lat, helpless in the American's grip, tried without success to straighten his pathetically thin body but managed to keep his head up and stared at the far wall, striving to achieve a posture that would have some dignity, at least in his own mind.

"How do you account for that, Joseph? Could he have been some kind of court eunuch in Hue in the old days? Was that where you might have met?"

Lat was struggling to keep his balance, and Joseph turned away and walked towards the door so that he didn't have to look at the shrunken, mutilated body of the sixty-five-year-old Vietnamese. "It's no help, Guy — let him get dressed. We'll go and look at the pictures." He knocked loudly on the door to indicate to the guard outside that they wished to leave and didn't turn round again, but out of the corner of his eye as he waited he could still see Lat, crouched shivering on the white stool, struggling with his manacled hands to pull the tattered shorts up around his waist again.

8

Because the CIA photo-archive of terrorist suspects stored on the top floor of the Chancery was classified "secret," Guy had to escort Joseph past several security checks and remain with him while the search was made. Outside, the rhythmic clatter of a helicopter landing or taking off from the top of the building became audible from time to time, and the steady hum of rooftop shredders destroying classified waste provided a monotonous drone of background noise as Joseph began the laborious task of scrutinizing the hundreds of old photographs filed in pull-out drawers. Guy watched over his shoulder, turning away occasionally to gaze impatiently out of the plastic windows at the restricted view of the street visible through gaps in the rocket screens, but Joseph found it difficult to concentrate. He worked mechanically, peering at the succession of anonymous Vietnamese faces pictured beneath 1930s protest banners without really seeing them; in his mind's eye he could see only the haggard face of Dao Van Lat, trapped in that bare, shimmering dungeon that seemed more suited to the realms of science fiction than a police headquarters, and after several minutes he stopped and turned round to look at his brother.

"Whose idea was it to build that nightmare cell, Guy?" he asked in a puzzled voice.

"That was dreamed up here by the Agency."

"But why's it painted white? And why the near-freezing temperature and the spy cameras?"

"You know the Vietnamese rush to put on sweaters whenever the thermometer·falls below seventy, don't you? Like all his compatriots the prisoner imagines his veins will contract in cold temperatures — it's disorientation technique. It's been painted white for the same reason."

"A place like that's more likely to drive a man out of his mind than make him talk."

"That's a surprising sentiment," said Guy quietly, "coming from someone who's just learned his son's being tortured witless in Hanoi."

"That's no goddamned reason for us to do it, too!"

Guy placed his hands deliberately on the table and leaned towards Joseph. "Listen, our little allies here in Saigon know as much about the gentle art of persuasion as their cousins in Hanoi and we can't stop that — this is their country, remember. *We* insisted on putting our friend in that special cell to get him out of their clutches — to protect him. Those Vietnamese manning the doors and the cameras are on *our* payroll — they're Agency employees. We insisted on that. If he'd been left to the South Vietnamese, he'd have been dead long ago."

Joseph snorted with exasperation. "Congratulations! You've discovered the world's first humane form of torture."

"If you're so concerned about our friend, just find his picture and give us his name," snapped Guy. "Then maybe he'll talk and we'll give him an overcoat and you'll feel a whole lot better about it. Don't you understand? We've got a golden opportunity to do a major deal that will get Mark released — if you can just come up with a name for him."

Because Guy's face was so close to his, Joseph was suddenly more intensely aware than ever before of the Gallic cast to his features; the dark hair, the narrow face and the eager expression reminded him suddenly of someone he'd known well, and he started inwardly when he realized he was seeing another version of the boyish face of Paul Devraux. Guy's eyes were alight with the same kind of fervid idealism that had in the end proved fatal for the Frenchman, and in that moment Joseph made up his mind to pass over any likeness he might find of Lat in the archive. Without replying he turned back to the table and began going through the motions of inspecting the photographs once more.

For almost a quarter of an hour he sorted through drawer after drawer, consciously trying to give the impression he was examining each envelope with care, pretending to subject some to closer scrutiny and passing over others more quickly; Guy grew more restless as the minutes ticked by and he began pacing slowly back and forth while he waited. By chance, Joseph decided to peer closely at what seemed to be another anonymous portrait and found himself looking at a female face that made his heart leap into his throat. Although he hadn't been concentrating fully, the curve of her cheeks and the distinctive lustrous eyes that had mocked or condemned him by turns whenever they met flashed a message directly to some part of his brain that might always have been waiting unsleeping to receive it. The photograph looked like an enlargement of a shot taken at long range with a telephoto lens; hatless and obviously unaware of the camera, his daughter was pictured with her long hair dressed in a thick practical braid that hung in front of her left shoulder. Behind her there was a background of thatched huts and palm trees that suggested she was in a village of the Mekong delta. With shaking hands Joseph turned the print over and read the inscription on the back: "Tuyet Luong, Long An province, January 1963."

After staring at it transfixed for some time, he realized Guy had stopped his pacing, and glancing up, he found his brother watching him intently from the far end of the room. Their eyes met for an instant then Guy began moving back towards him, but before he reached his side, Joseph calmly replaced the photograph in its brown paper envelope and slipped it back among the others.

"Did you find someone who looked like him?" asked Guy sharply.

"No — nothing interesting." Joseph didn't look up again and he went on inspecting the files for another five minutes before standing up and rubbing his eyes. "Do you mind, Guy, if we call a break there and finish this some other time? I'd like to take time out to listen to Mark's tape again — and maybe contact Gary too with the news."

Guy nodded reluctantly. "Okay — but let's try to get back to it real soon."

He escorted Joseph to the embassy entrance, then returned immediately to the photo-archive. He went straight to the last drawer Joseph had worked on and examined the dog-eared folders covering the pictures. While walking towards the table he had taken a careful look at the folder in which Joseph was replacing the picture that had so obviously startled him; one corner, he had noticed, was slightly torn, and he had memorized its position towards the front of the drawer while Joseph was replacing it. Pulling it out again, he extracted the photograph and stared at the face of a beautiful Vietnamese girl who looked as though she might have been of mixed parentage. Turning it over, he read the caption and made a note of the name and reference number on a slip of paper. In response to a phone call, an assistant came to the room, and Guy asked him to run a computer check on the name. Guy remained in the archive, glancing occasionally at the picture, and five minutes later the assistant returned.

"Several unconfirmed trace reports on Tuyet Luong have gone on file over the past three years, but none has been followed up," he said, glancing down at the printout in his hand. "Routine sightings have been reported from Qui Nhon, Da Nang — and the latest one two months ago came from Hue. Her original sin was suspected murder of two members of the South Vietnamese security police in 1961 — and she's believed to have thrown a grenade at two of our operatives a month later. They escaped with minor injuries. The first two trace reports were routine and they weren't acted on when received because other more urgent cases currently had priority. The last one's been lying on the file because nobody was interested enough to follow it up. Tuyet Luong's a back number these days, you might say."

Guy nodded and took the printout from the assistant. "Have the Hue trace checked and let me know the result as soon as it comes in."

"Okay, sir," said the assistant briskly. "I'll get on to it right away."

9

Joseph sat alone at his own dining table that evening, staring absently into the shadows beyond the candles his *bep* had lit. A bowl of *canh chua* soup stood before him but it was untouched and growing cold, and every minute or two the *bep* peered anxiously around the kitchen door to see if he was ready for his next course. A bottle of Vietnamese *ruou de* stood beside a slender-stemmed glass at his elbow, and from time to time he sipped the rice wine but made no attempt to touch his food.

When the *bep* appeared noiselessly beside him, he started in surprise, then made an apologetic gesture as he saw the Vietnamese gazing accusingly at his full soup bowl. "I'm sorry, Chinh — I'm not very hungry this evening."

"But Mister Sherman, *canh chua* is my best soup," complained the cook with a beseeching smile. "Is my speciality — shrimp, bean sprouts, pineapple, celery — I put all good things in for you. And your *bo nuong la* is ready now."

"Okay Chinh, bring in the *bo nuong la*. I'll try to eat a little."

The Vietnamese removed the soup and hurried back to the kitchen. Before he appeared again with the main dish the telephone rang, and Joseph heard him answer it with a sibilant flurry of broken English. When he reappeared with the food – finely chopped tender beef wrapped in grape leaves — he was smiling delightedly. "That was your brother, Mister Sherman. He asked if you here and when I tell him you alone, he say he coming right over. Shall I bring *bo nuong la* for your brother too, Mister Sherman?"

Joseph's face clouded for a moment, then he nodded. "All right — if he hasn't already dined."

Guy arrived a quarter of an hour later, and the *bep's* smile broadened as he conducted him into the dining room; before another minute had passed, a dish of food had been placed before him.

"I didn't mean to invite myself to dinner," said Guy apologetically. "I just wanted to talk to you."

"My *bep* likes people to enjoy his food and I'm letting him down tonight." Joseph's expression was guarded as he poured *ruou de* for them both. "Has there been any reaction from Washington yet on the prisoner exchange?"

"No — but we've had an urgent request from the State Department to try to find out who 'the man in the white room'

607

really is. Nobody in D.C. is fond of the idea of letting a nameless man go free." Guy sipped his wine and began to eat, using his chopsticks with quick, deft movements. "That's why I'm here — to try to persuade you to come back to the embassy this evening to finish the photo search."

Instead of replying, Joseph drained his glass and refilled it again; he neither looked at his brother nor touched his beef, and Guy ate in silence for a few minutes, then pushed his plate away and sat back.

"You know, Joseph, I've never been able to read what goes on inside your head," he said in an impatient tone. "You've always been damned cool with me for reasons best known to yourself and I've come to accept that as the norm as far as you and me are concerned. But hell, I'm beginning to think you must be some kind of cold-blooded animal all through. Don't you have any human feelings at all? After two years you discover your younger son's alive when he might've been dead, and instead of doing everything you can to help, you closet yourself here in your villa taking dinner on your own and doing nothing! I just don't get it."

Joseph put down his glass and glanced across the table at his brother. "Hasn't it occurred to you, Guy, that if your prisoner in the white room turned out to be someone of the top rank from Hanoi, it might jeopardize the whole deal involving Mark? Hasn't it occurred to you that if I could identify him positively, that fact in itself might condemn Mark to several more years of torture and suffering — maybe even worse."

"I guess I hadn't looked at it from that angle." Guy gazed at Joseph thoughtfully for a moment, and when he spoke again his voice was suddenly more sympathetic. "Does that mean you already know who he is — but aren't saying?"

Joseph got up abruptly from the table and went to the kitchen. When he returned he was carrying a new bottle of *ruou de*, and he filled both their glasses without speaking.

"Okay, I can see you don't want to answer that question and I won't press it right now." Guy picked up his glass. "But maybe we've made some progress. For the first time in your life you've actually shared a confidence with your kid brother. Maybe we should drink to that."

Guy smiled lopsidedly as he raised his glass to his lips, but despite his faintly sarcastic tone his manner had softened noticeably, and Joseph felt a sudden stab of remorse for always having kept him at arm's length.

"Perhaps there's something I should tell you too, Guy," he said hesitantly. "I didn't just get one shock today. Hearing Mark's confession would have been enough on its own — but while I was going through those photographs, I got another one."

"When you saw the picture of the Vietnamese girl, you mean?" Guy paused significantly. "Tuyet Luong?"

Joseph's eyes widened in astonishment. "How did you know?"

"I saw the expression on your face and I made a mental note of the file's position as you pushed it back into the drawer. I checked it out after you'd gone and I guessed she must have been someone you met sometime — someone you didn't think was a Communist then maybe. Is that it?"

"No, that's not it." Joseph bowed his head and spoke towards the table. "Tuyet Luong is my daughter."

"Your daughter?" Guy's mouth fell open in disbelief, and for a long time he sat and stared at Joseph; then he nodded his head several times. "I think I understand now why you're sitting here in the dark not eating dinner."

"I haven't seen Tuyet since 1954 — she was seventeen then. Since I got back I've heard rumors that someone with a name like hers had got on the 'wanted' list — but I never really believed them until I saw that picture this morning."

"But who's her mother? And what the hell was it that made her go over to the VC?"

"It's a long story, Guy," said Joseph resignedly. "But if you have time to listen, I'd like to tell you."

"Sure, go ahead," said Guy quickly. "If it'll help."

In a voice that sometimes cracked with emotion Joseph told his brother of his long involvement with Lan and Tuyet, leaving nothing out, and when he'd finished Guy let out a low whistle. "I'd heard bits and pieces through the family grapevine over the years, but I never dreamed you'd been living with all of that." Guy picked up the wine bottle and filled Joseph's glass and his own again, and they lapsed into a companionable silence.

"That's the first time in your life, you know, Joseph, that you've ever let your guard down with me," said Guy at last in a wondering voice. "And I appreciate that more than you might think. When I was a kid I spent a lot of time worrying about why you seemed to have your knife in me. You made me feel for a long time like I wasn't good enough to be a brother of yours or Chuck's. Do you remember?"

"I know," said Joseph quietly. "I knew I was doing it and I'm not proud of it — it really wasn't your fault."

"How do you mean?" Guy smiled in mystification.

"Quite illogically I blamed you for something that had nothing to do with you."

"What was that?"

As Joseph considered how to phrase his answer, he realized to his dismay that without meaning to, he'd arrived on the brink of telling Guy the one thing he'd sworn always to stay silent about. He glanced at the second bottle of *ruou de* on the table between them, saw that it was three quarters empty and regretted that his tongue had begun to run away with him. "Forget it, Guy," he said hastily, rubbing a hand across his eyes. "It's just the rice wine talking."

"Oh no, you don't slip out of it that easy." Guy laughed and emptied the entire contents of the bottle into their two glasses. "Now that the wine's started talking, let it finish."

Joseph smiled in return, and they raised their glasses to drink in the same moment. "I'm not too sure how I ought to go about this, Guy — but I guess you're right — it's something you really should have known all along. . . ."

"Come on, quit the softening-up process," said Guy with a smile. "I'm a big boy now."

"Well, didn't you ever wonder how it was that mother and father lived all those years in that big house in Georgetown on separate floors? Didn't you ever wonder why mother drank so much in her last years? Didn't you ever wonder how long that had been going on?"

Guy's smile waned a little. "No, I guess I didn't ever really think about it. I suppose I always kind of assumed that the rambunctious senator from Virginia always needed a lot of space for his larger-than-life political activities and our wise mother liked to give him a wide berth."

Joseph stared into his drink, seeing again suddenly his mother on that day a month before she died welcoming him to her sumptuously furnished apartments on the upper floors of the big Georgian mansion in Dumbarton Street. There had been separate bottles of wine at either end of the long table for luncheon, and she had finished one of them on her own. Afterwards she had dropped her balloon glass of brandy in the hearth and sobbed uncontrollably in his arms while blurting out what she had called the "terrible secret" of Guy's birth; she had stared at him in horror when he told her that he already knew, that he had seen her by chance that night in the jungle storm and had recognized Guy's unmistakable likeness to his natural father as he'd grown up. Before he left, she had made him promise never to reveal her secret to his father or Guy, and the memory of the vow he'd made then haunted him fleetingly as Guy waited for him to continue.

"The fact is, you see, Guy, they hadn't just been living on separate floors for the last twenty-five years as you remember — they were living on 'separate floors' for quite a few years before you were born."

"Is that why the old man likes to make those sly references to me being 'bred' in the jungle on that hunting trip?"

"In a way — but what he's never known is just how true that was."

"You'd better say now what you mean, Joseph — so we both know what you're getting at."

"I'm trying to tell you, Guy, that the man you've always thought of as your father *isn't* your real father."

The smile faded instantly from Guy's face, and his features turned to stone. The enormity of the revelation rendered him speechless, and Joseph felt a sudden tide of alarm rise inside him.

"No other living soul except me knows this, Guy," Joseph went on hurriedly. "I swore never to tell him — or you — but I think you have a right to know."

"And why in hell's name were you let into the dreadful secret?" asked Guy, speaking fiercely between his teeth.

"Mother blurted it out to me a few weeks before she died. It had preyed on her mind, and she had to tell someone to ease the pain."

"But why did it have to be you?"

"Perhaps she sensed that I knew already that the story about the hunting camp was true. The great senator from Virginia, you see, was as high as a kite on the night in question. I saw him staggering as he went back to their hut. Then a while later the flap opened and I saw Mother run out into the storm. . . ."

"So you played Peeping Tom! That's how you knew the identity of my real father!"

Guy's voice rose accusingly, and Joseph nodded.

"So who was he?"

"Our French hunting guide — an ex-French army officer. He became an inspector in the Sûreté Générale here in the 'thirties."

"Is he still alive?"

Joseph shook his head quickly. "He was assassinated by Vietnamese nationalists in Hue — in 1936."

Guy's chair fell over backwards with a crash as he rose to his feet; his face was white and his breathing became ragged. "So sanctimonious little mother's boy Joseph decided thereafter to spend the rest of his life looking down his nose at his kid brother because he considered him a semi-bastard — is that right?"

"I guess I've always known deep down it was wrong, Guy — but somehow I could never shake myself out of it." Joseph looked up miserably into his brother's face. "I'm sorry."

"Don't waste your breath apologizing!" A look of cold fury had come into Guy's eyes, and Joseph thought for a moment he was going to lash out at him; but Guy controlled himself with an effort. "If you're hoarding any more nasty family secrets, keep them to yourself — I don't want to hear them!" Guy spun around and strode towards the side door of the villa, but before he reached it Joseph got up and hurried after him.

"Guy, wait! For God's sake, if I'd though you'd take it like this I would never have told you. . . ." Before he reached the door it was slammed in his face, and a moment later he heard a car start up in the street outside; its motor was revved furiously for a second or two, then there was a crash of gears and the car accelerated away and was soon traveling at high speed.

Joseph didn't go to bed but sat up all night; the sound of firecrackers exploding in the street at midnight startled him at first, then he remembered that it was the eve of Tet. The explosions continued for several hours, and he made frequent cups of coffee and paced sleeplessly back and forth through the house listening to them; occasionally he dozed fitfully in a chair, but when the dawn came, he went out into the garden and walked there. Several times his tortured thoughts went back to the agonizing confrontation he'd had with Paul Devraux at Dien Bien Phu. Then as now his rash belief that the truth would conquer all had been the cause of deep emotional anguish, and he cursed himself repeatedly for his stupidity. He tried to think of some means of making amends to Guy, but realized with a feeling of despair that there was no way back.

By the time his Vietnamese *bep* arrived to begin his duties, Joseph was already showered and shaved, and he asked him to serve breakfast on the verandah. Halfway through the meal, the bell outside the courtyard gate rang, and when the cook opened it, to Joseph's astonishment Guy was standing on the sidewalk holding a briefcase. The smiling Vietnamese led him to the breakfast table, and the two brothers sat in silence until fresh coffee and croissants had been brought. For a long time Guy toyed with his knife, obviously ill at ease, and when at last he spoke he kept his eyes fixed on his plate. "I guess I'd like to hear something from you about my real father, Joseph. What was he like?"

Joseph was seized by a strong feeling of compassion for his brother and he felt a lump come into his throat. "His name was Jacques Devraux," he said quietly when he had recovered his composure. "I was fifteen at the time of that hunting trip and I was deeply impressed by him. He was a crack shot, knew everything there was to know about the jungle and wild animals and seemed totally fearless. He was a man of few words and he held himself very straight — he reminded me of one of the old Greek warrior heroes in my history books. . . ."

They talked for half an hour, and throughout the conversation Guy's manner remained subdued and free of hostility. He asked questions in an embarrassed voice but Joseph answered them patiently, trying always to emphasize the positive aspects of Jacques Devraux's character. He spoke too of Paul and their long friendship and told Guy that he had noticed in him the same kind of eagerness and a tendency to strong enthusiasms which he had admired so much in Paul. When the subject seemed to have been exhausted they lapsed into an uneasy silence; then as Joseph rose from the table and began preparing to leave for his office, Guy pulled a manila envelope from his briefcase and placed it on the table.

"I think you'll be interested in that, Joseph," he said quietly.

"What is it?"

"A confirmed trace that came in late last night. I checked the computer and followed up an old lead. Tuyet Luong's living in Hue."

Joseph snatched up the envelope and began opening it with shaking hands. "Have you got an address for her?"

Guy nodded. "It's all in there. There's an Air Vietnam flight from Tan Son Nhut at four o'clock. I've already booked a seat on it in your name. You'll find a ticket in there too."

"Guy, I'm more grateful to you than I can say. After last night I hardly expected any help from you."

Guy waved an impatient hand to silence him. "Maybe we can just move onwards and upwards now — let's discuss it some other time." He hesitated, looking searchingly at his elder brother. "But there's one more important thing I have to tell you. As soon as we ask for confirmation on a trace report, an operation is put in hand automatically by our South Vietnamese security friends. And they always bring the suspect in without further instructions if the trace turns out to be positive."

"So Tuyet's going to be arrested?"

Guy shrugged. "That depends on you. I can't stop it — but I do have authority to stall the order for twenty-four hours. That's standard procedure to give us a chance to coordinate any necessary movements of our own agents. I've just issued the hold order. They won't move against her until this time tomorrow. If you get there before they do . . ." Guy shrugged again and let his voice trail off.

Joseph finished opening the envelope and read the notes inside then looked quizzically at his brother again. "Guy, what brought about this sudden change of heart?"

"There must be a reason — but don't ask me for it now." The CIA man turned away, and they walked side by side to the gate. On the way Joseph checked his watch; it was eight-fifteen on the morning of Tuesday, January 30, the first full day of the Tet holiday — the dawning of the Year of the Monkey. Normally at that time on a Tuesday, Saigon's early rush hour was in full swing, filling the city with a torrent of noise, but because of the holiday and the traditional Tet truce, the street outside the villa still lay eerily quiet when Joseph opened the gate. He walked to the curbside with Guy and at the car offered him his hand. Guy shook it wordlessly, then slipped behind the wheel. Before he started the engine he leaned out of the window and gestured towards the envelope Joseph was holding. "Just in case it should come as a shock when you get there, I ought to warn you: the address I've given isn't a private house — it's Hue's biggest brothel."

Without another word Guy started the motor and eased the car away from the curb, and Joseph stood watching it until it had disappeared from view along the deserted boulevard.

10

The light was beginning to fade as Joseph crossed one of the little humpbacked bridges of ornamental stone spanning the moat of the Hue Citadel. An evening breeze was blowing gently from the south, stirring the cream and crimson lotus flowers clustered on its stagnant surface, and looking down over the parapet, Joseph saw the image of the Imperial City's ramparts reflected in the waters change color suddenly; a bright, fiery red in the glow of the setting sun, the high walls had in an instant become burgundy, the color of blood. He turned in time to see the rim of the sun dip behind the purple peaks of the Annamite Cordillera to the west, and its dying rays illuminated for him the broad, shadowy sweep of the Huong Giang, the River of Perfumes, lying tranquil and empty of movement in the softening light. He could hear the bankside willows and reeds rustling in the wind, and he stood for a long moment drinking in the sight, lost in a reverie of his last visit; then he gathered himself and hurried on into the Citadel.

It was the first time he had been in Hue since 1936, and although he knew well enough that the old, fortified city of the Emperor Gia Long had become the headquarters of the First Division of the Army of the Republic of Vietnam, he was still taken aback by the incongruous sight of a modern fighting force encamped within its historic walls. Jeeps made in America and diminutive, green-clad South Vietnamese infantrymen carrying American arms were scurrying among the gold-roofed palaces where he had last seen silk-robed courtiers and wizened, bearded mandarins; at key points, the ugly bulk of camouflaged tanks had taken guard where once patient elephants decked in dazzling cloths of imperial yellow had stood as sentinels, but even the presence of the South Vietnamese army in the old Citadel had not destroyed the city's unique atmosphere.

Despite the ravages of war in the rest of the country, along the banks of the serenely flowing River of Perfumes, the history and traditions of the Vietnamese nation still appeared to Joseph to be preserved in harmony with the gentle beauty of the landscape. He gazed up with a tangible sense of pleasure at the snarling porcelain dragons on the curved roofs of the palaces, and as he walked among the shrubs and miniature trees of the formal gardens, he detected the beguiling scent of jasmine; in the distance he could hear the gentle cadences of a pagoda bell tolling, and he found himself hoping fervently that all these symbols of a peaceful past might turn out to be omens of good luck for him in his quest to find his daughter.

As soon as his taxi pulled away from Phu Bai airport after the five-hundred-mile flight from Saigon, he had felt himself transported into the past. Phu Bai was ten miles south of the old Annamese capital, and the rough, narrow road wound through low green hills that appeared untouched by the war. Smiling children dressed in their bright new Tet clothes had rushed from the bamboo thickets surrounding their villages to wave delightedly at the car, several times the taxi had been forced to halt at the narrow wooden bridges to allow a slow, plodding buffalo to cross ahead of them, and frequently during the half-hour drive he had caught glimpses of ornate temples hidden amidst groves of banyan or tamarind. All this and the timeless peace of the open rice fields and the scattered hamlets of thatch and bamboo had reminded him forcibly of how his country had corrupted and Americanized Saigon and the other major cities in the course of the effort to save the country from Communism, and he had felt a fierce nostalgia for his youth when Vietnam had still seemed undisturbed by the present.

His first glimpse of Hue's broad boulevards and the placid river flowing quietly beneath the walls of the Citadel had brought to his mind again one of the first remarks that Lan had ever made to him. "If you listen carefully, Joseph," she had said, those many years before, "you can hear the heart of Annam beating in Hue." But, as the taxi headed along Le Loi Boulevard on the river's southern bank, the only heartbeat he had heard was his own. The address Guy had provided, his Vietnamese taxi driver had told him, was situated in Gia Hoi, an old, densely populated quarter of the city outside the walls of the Citadel on the north bank; its narrow streets converged on a sprawling marketplace not far from the end of the Clemenceau Bridge, since renamed Truong Tien, and Joseph, his anxiety rising, had directed the taxi to take him straight across the bridge to the address without stopping to check in at the Imperial Hotel where he had reserved a room.

The houses bordering the narrow streets of the old quarter, when they reached it, were decked with blood-red paper streamers bearing felicitous Tet slogans in Chinese characters, and before the doors Joseph noticed the same kind of bamboo poles tufted with leaves and charms to ward off evil spirits that had stood outside the throne room of the Emperor Khai Dinh during his first visit to Hue as a boy of fifteen. The solemn ceremonies to mark the annual visitation of the spirits of their ancestors had already been celebrated in Hue and elsewhere during the previous night, and relaxed and laughing crowds now thronged the streets; new detonations of celebratory firecrackers to mark the New Year's Day itself were also beginning to break out again with the approach of dusk, and through the open doors of the tiny houses as the taxi passed, Joseph could see candles flickering on altars still decked high with fruit and flowers. Crowds of excited men and boys squatted on the pavements outside, giggling and arguing over dice and other gambling games, and because they were unused to seeing Americans in that part of the city, the strolling Vietnamese often stopped in groups to peer in through the windows of the taxi at him.

As a result of these festivities, their progress through the crowds was unusually slow, and this heightened the feeling of tension that was growing in Joseph. The prospect of seeing Tuyet again would have filled him with unease under any circumstances, but her imminent arrest and a possible later charge of murder had added a new dimension to his agitation. Because he'd dreamed in vain for so long of seeing her again, he had begun to fear that something must go wrong at the last moment. Perhaps Guy's delaying order would not be observed, perhaps it would turn out to be a case of mistaken identity and she wouldn't be there at all, perhaps the address had been wrongly given; these and many other irrational fears flitted through his mind as the taxi crawled on, but they were not his only cause for alarm. A vaguer apprehension had also been growing in the back of his mind since that morning: reports of fresh fighting had begun trickling into Saigon at about the time Joseph and Guy were breakfasting together at his villa in Cong Ly, and he had monitored the details during the hours he had spent in his JUSPAO office.

During the night Viet Cong units had carried out a rash of surprise attacks on seven cities north of Saigon in violation of the Tet cease-fire, and the American commander, General William Westmoreland, had decided to cancel the Tet truce and declare a state of maximum alert for U.S. forces throughout Vietnam. President Thieu had followed suit and put the South Vietnamese forces on a similar alert that morning, but by then half of his army were on leave for the holiday period. The centers that had come under assault — Da Nang, Nha Trang, Qui Nhon, Pleiku,

Hoi An, Kontum and Ban Me Thuot — were either on the coast or in the highlands north of Saigon, and the attacks, launched as the first Tet firecrackers were exploding, seemed to be a strategic innovation for Communist forces that hitherto had invariably operated deep in the jungles and hills. But although fighting had continued beyond dawn in the seven cities, the American and Vietnamese military commands up to the time of Joseph's departure from Saigon had remained skeptical about the prospect of any wider offensive. There had been countless "maximum alerts" before, senior officers had told him with a shrug, and nothing had happened; the attacks were very likely nothing more than standard Communist truce violations.

During Joseph's flight north, the Air Vietnam DC-4 had stayed above the clouds, and although he had peered often towards the ground he had not been able to detect any evidence of the reported fighting. After the drive from Phu Bai through the seemingly peaceful countryside, finding the historic Annamese capital still basking in its unruffled aura of the past had helped allay his fears, and he had felt more confident then that the official Saigon reaction was the right one. It was not until he heard the firecrackers begin exploding again in the streets of Gia Hoi that he remembered the famous Tet surprise victory won by an Annamese emperor in the eighteenth century; a force of one hundred thousand troops then had marched into Hanoi to massacre their Chinese enemies in the midst of the New Year revelries, and this sudden recollection brought all Joseph's apprehensions flooding back again. He leaned forward on his seat to urge the driver to try to push on faster through the crowded lanes, and the Vietnamese began sounding his horn continuously. When the taxi at last freed itself of the crowds thronging the market area, it headed along a dirt road close to the edge of the city, and Joseph stared out in dismay at the tumbledown shacks covered with roofs of corrugated tin.

"The soldiers call this 'The Street of the Emperor's Concubines,'" said the wizened driver in French, waving his hand vaguely towards the ramshackle dwellings of what was obviously the red light district. "Very convenient, you see, for the headquarters of the First Division."

Peering out through the window, Joseph caught a distant glimpse of the tower at the northeast corner of the red-walled fortress.

"But they're all closed tonight — even imperial concubines

must rest from their labors sometimes, *n'est-ce pas?*" The grinning driver stopped the car at a corner and gestured towards a big dilapidated building that looked like a converted rice warehouse with a crumbling wooden walkway running around the upper story. "But perhaps you are in luck. That's the address you seek, and look, somebody has waited for you."

Joseph could see that there were rows of doors leading off the walkway, and strings of gray washing flapped in the breeze along its length. Discolored paint was peeling and flaking from bulging walls that appeared to be on the point of collapse, but at the top of the steps the bent figure of an aged woman clad in dark clothes leaned over the rail watching the taxi.

"She may not be pretty, but she'll certainly be cheap, monsieur," said the taxi driver, leering around at him.

"Wait here," snapped Joseph angrily and flung himself out of the door without offering the driver any payment. As he ran up the steps two at a time, the crone on the balcony turned away and began hobbling towards a rickety door that stood ajar; but Joseph overtook her easily and seized her by the arm. He pulled from his pocket the photograph of his daughter that Guy had given him with her address and thrust it under the woman's nose.

"Chi Tuyet Luong co day khong?" he asked, speaking his Vietnamese, slowly and deliberately. "Is Tuyet Luong here?"

The woman stared at the picture, then shook her head once without looking at him. She struggled with surprising vigor to free herself from his grip, and when reluctantly he released her, she shuffled away and slammed her door behind her. Joseph walked slowly back along the balcony, rattling the handles of the other flimsy doors until he found one he could wrench open. It led him into a shabby cubicle that smelled sour and musty, and he recognized immediately the stale fumes of the opium pipe. Nothing more than a ragged curtain separated the flimsy, plywood cubicle from an internal corridor, and Joseph walked the length of the upper story, drawing back each curtain in turn. A rough plank bed, sometimes covered with a soiled sheet, and a wooden chair were the only furnishings in the sordid cubicles, and Joseph shuddered at their implication. As he turned away from his inspection of the last one, he noticed the dark figure of the old woman watching him curiously from the end of the corridor. He hurried back to her, pressed five thousand piastres into her hand and pulled out the picture of Tuyet again.

"I will come back at midnight," he said, speaking slowly and

619

deliberately in Vietnamese. "Tell Tuyet Luong she must meet me here. Tell her my name is Joseph Sherman. It's very important — a matter of life and death."

The wizened face of the woman had puckered with uncertainty but she nevertheless clutched the money tight in both hands. She stared at him quizzically for a long moment, then shuffled away into the shadows without giving any indication of whether she had understood him or not. Joseph had made the taxi driver take him to his hotel then and kept him waiting while he took his overnight bag to his room. He had paid off the taxi finally after it dropped him by the little bridge just as the sun was setting, and he continued into the Citadel on foot to appreciate better the splendor of the old pavilions and their ornamental gardens.

Out of respect for the imperial and Buddhist traditions of the historic city, the United States had always kept Hue off limits to its forces, apart from a handful of military advisers who occupied a compound south of the river. A small number of American civilians lived in the city to carry out consular and intelligence work and the main U.S. agencies also had representatives there; it was in accordance with Guy's written advice that Joseph went to the Citadel to report his presence in Hue to the office of CORDS, the Civil Operations Revolutionary Development Support agency which was then coordinating the American pacification program, and he found a female Vietnamese clerk staffing the CORDS office alone.

He gave her his name and the address of his hotel, saying simply that he had come for a two-day break to look at the palaces, and she wrote the information down in a book. One of the American staffers, an undercover CIA officer who had been warned by Guy to expect a senior JUSPAO man from Saigon, had left a telephone number and an invitation to join him for dinner, but Joseph felt in no mood for a social encounter and he returned alone on foot to his hotel. There he tried to eat some dinner in the restaurant overlooking the river, but the food remained virtually untouched on his plate and he spent an hour staring out through the window at the lantern-lit sampans clustered along the waterfront; to his increasing discomfort, fireworks continued to fill the darkness outside with unending volleys of noise, and he wandered out at last along the waterfront to kill time that was passing with such agonizing slowness.

Without meaning to, he found himself retracing his steps southward along the tree-lined streets that led to the Nam Giao, where so long ago he had watched the Sacrifice to Heaven with Lan; but he found that its high walls were overgrown with grass and weeds and parts of them had already crumbled. The ancient ceremonial edifice in the semi-darkness seemed unremarkable and lacking in charm, and he wandered aimlessly around the surrounding streets for a while. He began to feel despondent, and this mood deepened when he discovered he was unable to get a taxi in that part of Hue. At last he set off to walk all the way back to the ramshackle Gia Hoi brothel to keep his midnight appointment with the daughter who was not only a stranger to him but who had also been an avowed enemy of his country for the past fourteen years.

11

"Why have you come here?"

The sudden sound of the voice from behind him startled Joseph. He swung around but could make out no more than a shadowy outline of a slender woman dressed in black trousers and tunic. She had spoken in English, but her voice was filled with unconcealed hostility.

"Is that you, Tuyet?" He stepped eagerly into the deep shadow beneath the overhead walkway of the old rice depot, but she retreated a pace from him.

"Tell me why you've come!"

As his eyes accustomed themselves to the gloom, he was able to make out the shape of her face, and his breath caught in his throat. "Tuyet, I came to warn you! You must go away from here. Security agents are going to arrest you at dawn!" He stepped towards her again and stretched out his hands as if to take her by the shoulders.

"Please don't touch me!" She didn't move this time, but the coldness of her voice was sufficient to halt him in mid-stride, and they stood face to face, looking at one another with only the occasional splutter of the dying firecrackers of Tet punctuating the tense silence between them.

He had almost given up all hope of seeing her. The former rice depot had been locked and deserted at midnight; even the old crone had gone. He had waited and wandered irresolutely through the sordid neighborhood, losing all track of time, returning again and again to the corner outside the depot although he no longer had any real expectation of finding her there. It had been just before three A.M. when he returned for the last time, and after the long day of anxiety, her appearance in the shadows behind him had come as a shock.

"You've only got two hours, perhaps three," said Joseph desperately. "Let me help you to get to Saigon. We can take the first plane in the morning. I'll hide you until I find a way of getting you out of the country."

The sudden sound of her laughter from the darkness startled him. "Your security agents have chosen a very bad time to come and arrest me. It's not me who's in danger anymore, it's them — and you!"

Joseph moved closer, trying to read her expression in the gloom. "What do you mean?"

He saw her lift her wrist close in front of her face to check the luminous dial of the cheap watch she wore. "You and your Saigon friends have less than fifteen minutes to make *your* escape. After that Hue will fall into the hands of the people."

He stared at her in disbelief. "You mean the Communists are going to try to take the city?"

In the gloom he saw the flash of her teeth as she smiled. "Not just this city but a hundred cities of the South are about to be seized — including Saigon. Some attacks have already begun. Your puppet president, Thieu, and Air Marshal Ky will be assassinated, the radio stations will be taken over — a great general uprising of all the people of the South is getting under way."

"You can't be serious, Tuyet!"

She shrugged. "Perhaps you'll believe me when the representatives of the people come to the Imperial Hotel to arrest you. While you idled over your dinner there tonight, ten of our battalions were closing in all around the city."

"How did you know where I'm staying?"

"The girl in the CORDS office is one of us. Your name was added to the list of wanted Americans just after nine o'clock tonight."

Joseph stared at his daughter, aghast. "But, Tuyet, how can an attack like that succeed in Hue? There's a whole division of government troops quartered in the Citadel, and the U.S. Marines have three or four battalions standing by at Phu Bai — they could be here within minutes."

"At least half of the First Division are on leave for Tet, and most of the others are drunk and bloated with overeating!" Her voice was icy with contempt, and even in the half-darkness he saw her features twist with distaste as she waved her hand towards the old rice depot. "We've been planning this offensive for six months. I came to this awful place a year ago to organize an espionage center. With only twenty girls I've learned all that's worth knowing about the puppet troops and their commanders — and all the American military forces in the Hue region too. Now do you understand why it would've been better if you hadn't come?"

Joseph considered her words in silence, and when he spoke there was a catch in his voice. "Even now I don't regret coming, Tuyet. It's fourteen years since I saw you — but I've thought of you every day. Did you think I'd just forgotten you?"

"We've always lived in different worlds," she said fiercely. "You're no more important to me than the thousands of other overfed American aggressors who've trampled all over my country for so long."

Joseph stepped towards her and grasped her by the shoulders before she could move away. "I'm your father, Tuyet! And I've never given up hope that one day I would find you again."

She struggled to free herself, but he tightened his grip, and their faces came close together in the darkness. Suddenly, a brilliant flash of garish light illuminated the night sky above the Citadel and he saw her face clearly for the first time; the almond eyes, the high cheeks and the full, wide mouth were revealed to him as though through the lens of a camera for a fleeting, subliminal moment and her natural beauty was heightened and exaggerated by the glare. She looked startled and unsure of herself, and in the inky blackness that enveloped them in the wake of the flash, he felt her body relax suddenly in his grasp.

"Leave me alone and get away from here," she said in a low voice. "If you stay, they'll kill you when they come."

A flurry of explosions louder than any firecracker rent the night to the west and Joseph turned his head quickly in their direction. He listened for a moment, identifying the shriek of artillery rounds as well as rockets and mortar fire. By the time he turned back to her, the flashes of exploding shells were becoming continuous, and they were both able to see each other clearly by their glow.

"For fourteen years I've dreamed of this moment, Tuyet," said

623

Joseph quietly. "I'm not going to cut and run now — for anything or anybody."

Without warning he crushed her roughly against his chest and closed his eyes, abandoning himself to the surge of emotion that swept through him. For the briefest instant she clung to him in her turn, then she broke free and pushed him away. "Why don't you go? Do you want them to find me with you and kill me too? Do you want them to believe I'm a traitor?"

Joseph's hands fell limp at his sides and he looked at her uncertainly. "I can't turn my back on you, Tuyet. I can't leave you again just like that. . . ." He stopped in mid-sentence, distracted suddenly by a movement in the street behind her that led down to the river.

Sensing his alarm she turned to follow his gaze and saw the silhouetted figures of a dozen or more troops running rapidly in their direction. They hugged the shadows of the ramshackle huts as they came, but the light from the flames and the growing barrage being poured onto the city was bright enough by then for Joseph to recognize the distinctive flat helmets and square back-packs that the soldiers wore.

"They look like North Vietnamese troops," gasped Joseph.

"Yes — they're the vanguard of 804 Battalion of the People's Army," whispered Tuyet. "They've just crossed the river in inflatable boats."

Joseph tried to push Tuyet deeper into the shadows beneath the walkway, but the flares and artillery flashes that made the advancing troops visible to them were illuminating the whole street, and the attackers caught sight of them before they could take cover. The front rank immediately stopped and opened fire, and the long volley of shots splintered the crumbling wooden wall of the rice depot all around them. Joseph felt a sudden burning pain in his chest and he clutched at it with both hands as he sank to his knees. Almost immediately his fingers became sticky with blood and he stared up at Tuyet in astonishment.

For a moment she stood rooted to the spot, then she seized his arm and pulled him to his feet. Seeing the movement, the North Vietnamese troops began firing again, and more bullets thudded into the rotting wood above their heads. The troops began running faster as they drew near, and after glancing frantically over her shoulder, Tuyet dragged Joseph around the corner of the rice depot and hustled him across the street into the darkness of a narrow alley that led away through the heart of the shanty district towards the wharves of the River of Perfumes.

12

In his office on the fifth floor of the United States Embassy in Saigon, Guy Sherman was at that moment reading at his desk. He was CIA duty officer for the night and from time to time he lifted his head from the report he was scrutinizing to listen to the noise of the exploding firecrackers in the street outside. As the evening had worn on, the frequency of the explosions had gradually lessened and he was looking forward to the time when they would cease altogether. After a particularly loud detonation, he got up and went to the window to peer out across the rooftops, but he couldn't see much because the masonry rocket screen outside restricted his view.

Not for the first time he found himself patting the .38 automatic pistol he wore in a holster under his left armpit. Whether he did it for reassurance or to check that it was still there he wasn't sure, but he was already well aware that he wasn't the only man in the embassy that night whose nerves were being affected by the Tet firecrackers. Every time he had made his rounds, he'd noticed that the Marine guards in the front lobby and on the roof were tense and on edge. They were trying to disguise their unease by making wisecracks and pretending to go for their guns whenever particularly loud reports were heard, but it had been obvious that their humor was only a cover for the real disquiet they felt; they had heard reports of the widespread truce violations that had begun earlier in the day, and the continuing noise of the Tet celebrations in the streets was making it impossible for them to detect whether any new fighting was breaking out around Saigon. He'd tried to reassure them that all seemed peaceful as far as he could see, but he knew that this hadn't helped them much. When quiet at last returned, Guy left the window and sat down again to resume his inspection of a long report that had just come in from a newly recruited agent in the delta. It was poorly written and confused in content, and he had to concentrate hard in an effort to make anything of it; as a result the noise of the firecrackers faded gradually from his consciousness and soon he was scarcely aware of them at all.

As he settled to his task, inside a locked motor repair workshop on Phan Thanh Gian, half a mile west of the embassy, a tense group of twenty specially trained suicide commandos of the People's Liberation Armed Forces C-10 Battalion were gathered around a little one-ton Peugeot truck. On the oil-spattered concrete floor at their feet lay large baskets of rice and tomatoes inside which were concealed the disassembled parts of rocket launchers, antitank bazookas, machine guns, hand grenades, plastic explosives and thousands of rounds of ammunition; but for the moment the guerrillas were ignoring their weapons and giving all their attention to the political commissar, who was reading from a single sheet of typescript by the light of an unshaded bulb that hung from the cob-webbed ceiling. Because the flimsy walls and sack-covered windows would have betrayed any loud noise to the street outside, he spoke in a fierce whisper, emphasizing his words with exaggerated facial expressions.

" 'Move forward to achieve final victory!' — those are the words of Chairman Ho addressed from Hanoi to all cadres and combatants taking part in this historic general offensive. They are both a greeting for Tet and a combat order for our entire army and the whole population!"

The faces of the listening guerrillas were already taut with tension at the thought of the attack they were about to make; clad in loose shirts and trousers of black calico that to Western eyes resembled pajamas, they had put on red neckerchiefs and armbands to identify themselves when they were at close quarters with their enemy inside the walled compound of the U.S. Embassy. The youngest among them, Ngo Van Kiet, grandson of Jacques Devraux's one-time hunting camp "boy," licked his lips nervously and clenched his fists unseen at his sides to steady the fluttering sensation he felt in the pit of his stomach; at seventeen, he still had the round, hairless cheeks and innocent eyes of a child and when they wanted to tease him, his comrades still called him "Little Slug" as his dead father, Ngo Van Dong, had done when he was an infant. While listening to the commissar's voice Kiet scowled in the manner of the older men to disguise his extreme youth, and fingered the sash of red and gold silk that he had tied around his waist beneath his shirt. The sash was one of the old battle banderoles his father had worn when he stormed into the

French citadel at Yen Bay in 1930 alongside his grandfather, and it had been given to him when he was first made a member of the National Liberation Front's junior messenger corps at Moc Linh. Although he was immensely proud of the banderole, he had always been careful to obey his father's strict exhortation to keep it hidden beneath his clothes, since Communist Party dogmatists in the 1960s did not consider the past activities of old Quoc Dan Dang nationalists worthy of inclusion in the history of the Vietnamese revolution.

"In compliance with the attack order of the Presidium of the Liberation Front's Central Committee," said the commissar, reading slowly from the paper, "all cadres and combatants of the Liberation Armed Forces should now move forward to carry out direct attacks on the headquarters of the enemy. Our aim is to disrupt the American imperialists' will for aggression and to smash the puppet government and puppet army who are the lackeys of the United States. Our aim is also to restore power to the people, to liberate completely the fourteen million people of South Vietnam and fulfill our revolutionary task of establishing democracy throughout the country!"

The commissar raised his head and gazed round with glittering eyes at the faces of his twenty commandos. "The Tet General Offensive of 1968 will be the greatest battle ever fought throughout the long history of our country, comrades! It will bring forth worldwide change but will also require many sacrifices. It will decide the fate and survival of our Fatherland and will shake the world. . . . Our country has a history of four thousand years of fighting and defeating foreign aggression, particularly glorious battles such as Bach Dang, Chi Lang, Don Da and Dien Bien Phu. We defeated the so-called special war of the Americans and we are defeating their so-called limited war. Now we will move resolutely forward to defeat the American aggressors completely in order to restore independence and liberty in our country!"

The guerrillas gazed raptly at the commissar, visibly moved by the grandeur of his rhetoric; they knew he was a northerner who had fought through the First Indochina War against the French and had been wounded at Dien Bien Phu. Three fingers of his left hand were missing, and he walked with a pronounced limp from his wounds. They could see that he, too, was moved by the moment, and he made no effort to conceal the tears glistening in his eyes.

"Dear comrades," he continued, his voice breaking slightly,

627

"the American aggressors know they are losing. The call for assault to achieve independence has sounded! The mighty mountains of the Annamite Chain and the great Mekong River are moving to lend us their great force! Tonight, comrades, you must act as heroes of Vietnam. You must act with the spirit and pride of true combatants of the Liberation Army! You must seize the American Embassy! Kill all its occupants! Repulse all efforts to reoccupy it! You must fight to your last drop of blood — and never surrender!" He lowered the paper and gazed around slowly at each of them in turn with burning eyes. "Final victory, comrades, shall be with us!"

"Final victory shall be with us!" As one man, the twenty guerrillas repeated the final exhortation in a hoarse whisper, raising their clenched fists above their heads as they did so. The commissar stood looking around at them for a moment longer, then turned on his heel and walked quickly from the garage.

Immediately young Kiet and the other nineteen men began scooping rice and tomatoes from the baskets to uncover the weapons and ammunition that had been smuggled into the heart of Saigon during the previous week. They loaded the munitions with great care onto the back of the Peugeot and climbed up to crouch beside them. Four of the guerrillas got into a battered little blue Renault taxi parked at the back of the garage, and Kiet ran to haul on the squeaking chains that raised the door leading into the street. As soon as the two vehicles moved outside, he scrambled aboard the truck and two minutes after the commissar finished reading out the battle order, they were chugging one behind the other without lights, through the near-deserted streets of Saigon towards their target.

13

By chance Guy Sherman was standing at one of the windows in the CIA duty officer's room on the fifth floor of the embassy, and although his view was restricted by the rocket screens, he caught a fleeting glimpse of the unlit vehicles as they cruised eastward along Mac Dinh Chi. A moment later the truck and the taxi passed out of sight beneath the level of the embassy's ten-foot wall, but the fact that they showed no lights immediately aroused his suspicion. Snatching the duty officer's Beretta submachine gun from its rack, he ran out to the bank of elevators on the fifth floor landing and pressed to go down to the ground.

He was still inside the elevator on his way to the lobby when the four guerrillas in the little Renault poked their automatic rifles through its open windows and fired at the two American military policemen on sentry duty at the side entrance of the embassy in Mac Dinh Chi. They were not hit, but the shots drove them inside and they barred the tall steel gates. The truck and the taxi then swung into Thong Nhut Boulevard, which ran in front of the embassy's shuttered main entrance. The four South Vietnamese policemen standing formal guard in little windowed kiosks built into the high wall fled for cover at the sound of the first shot, and seeing this, young Kiet jumped lightly to the ground clutching a fifteen-pound charge of C-4 plastic explosive against his belly. He had been chosen for the task of blowing the first vital breech in the embassy wall because of the quick-fingered skill he had demonstrated in bomb-making training; he was also light on his feet and a fast runner, and he sped to a pre-selected spot a few yards from the junction of Thong Nhut Boulevard and Mac Dinh Chi. Although his fingers trembled a little, he set the ten-second fuse at the foot of the wall without difficulty, then dashed back to take cover with the other guerrillas behind the Peugeot truck.

The roar of the explosion shook the Chancery building, and Guy felt the blast rock his elevator in its shaft. Before the dust of the detonation had settled, the squat Vietnamese commanding the guerrilla platoon blew a loud blast on his whistle and led his force through the gaping hole in the wall at a run. Twenty-five yards away the two military policemen guarding the side gate were quick to recover from the shock of the explosion. Falling debris was still raining down around them when they opened fire with their machine pistols on the Vietnamese pouring through the hole in the wall; they saw one or two stumble and fall, but the other guerrillas flung themselves to the ground and began laying down a barrage of withering fire in their direction. One of the MPs was killed instantly, but the other scrambled for the guardpost radio and yelled over and over into the transmitter: "They're coming in! They're coming in! We need help!"

But a few seconds later the radio went dead as a hail of gunfire riddled the guardpost. The second MP was hit in the head and chest, and the C-10 commandos began lugging their rockets and bazookas unmolested across the compound towards positions where they could attack the front door of the Chancery from close range.

Inside the embassy, Guy stepped out of the elevator into the ground floor lobby in time to see a United States Marine sergeant dashing towards the open front entrance. It took him a second or two to swing the massive teak doors shut, and before he had finished shooting home the bolts, the glass of the barred windows beside the door was being shattered by repeated bursts of automatic rifle fire. The CIA man ran bent double to the sergeant's side and fired a rapid burst from the Beretta through the broken window; then he ducked down beneath the sill. "Sergeant, go and grab some weapons from the armory," he yelled above the rattle of the incoming fire. "We've got to make those bastards out on the lawn think there's a whole army in here."

As the Marine dashed away towards the armory, Guy heard the Marine corporal manning the switchboard of the guardpost telephoning frantically for help. Inside the beleaguered Chancery building at that moment, he knew there were fewer than a dozen Americans. In addition to the two Marines in the lobby, there was another Marine sergeant at a guardpost on the roof, four code and communication clerks on upper floors and a duty Foreign Service officer — that night a junior diplomat new to Saigon — who had a room on the fourth floor. To defend themselves they possessed between them only a few .38 pistols, one or two 12-gauge shotguns and half-a-dozen Italian submachine guns.

Outside on the lawn, young Kiet was helping to sight the first bazooka that had been maneuvered into position. The lights above the closed entrance were still on, and he and the two other gunners decided to aim their first missile at the eagle in the center of the Great Seal of the United States that was mounted in a thick slab of glazed granite beside the door. It was an easy target at close range, and they yelled delightedly as the rocket smashed through the center of the circular plaque. The other guerrillas had already taken up positions on the lawn behind big earth-filled concrete tubs ten or twelve feet in diameter that contained flowers; there they set up their rocket launchers and bazookas, and one by one began firing at the facade of the Chancery.

The first rocket that smashed the Great Seal passed through the wall behind it and detonated in the ceiling above the Marine guardpost. The corporal trying to call for help was badly wounded by fragments of burning metal, and the blast wrecked his communications radios, cutting contact with other Marine units in Saigon and the sergeant on the roof. Guy, shocked by the deafening explosion, rose unsteadily from his crouched position by one of the front windows and backed away, hugging the wall, but before he'd got very far, a second rocket punched through the teak doors to detonate deafeningly against the rear wall of the Chancery. A few seconds later, a third burst through a wall high up, and Guy flung himself full length on the floor behind a pillar at the rear of the lobby.

Behind the desk of the guardpost, the Marine sergeant who had returned from the armory with an armful of weapons was trying to administer first-aid to the wounded corporal; when he saw this, Guy rose and ran to his side. Turning to face the splintered front doors, he leveled the Beretta in their direction and waited, certain that the rocket barrage would be followed by an attempt to storm into the Chancery.

As the CIA officer crouched facing the doors, expecting the worst, the news that the Viet Cong had attacked and captured a vital acre of sovereign American territory in the heart of Saigon was shocking United States military commanders and diplomats from their beds all over the city. As they stumbled into their clothes, other reports began streaming in by telephone and radio indicating that coordinated surprise attacks were being launched against all major cities; in the middle of the night of January 31, 1968, South Vietnam was suddenly ablaze from end to end. Stunned foreign correspondents of the international wire services, newspapers and television tumbled from their beds to find that the puzzling conflict which they had previously been forced to search for deep in the jungles and mountains had come right to their doorsteps. One by one they discovered that only a few blocks from their hotels and apartments, the most sensational engagement of the whole war was just beginning; as the minutes passed they began to realize that the battle would probably be the first one of the conflict which they could make comprehensible to Americans at home.

They dashed to the scene to see for themselves, they telephoned and spoke to bewildered Americans on the upper floors of the besieged Chancery, and throughout the long night they cabled, telephoned and telexed their running stories in snatches to New York, London and Paris and thence to tens of thousands of radio and television stations and newspapers around the world; and the world watched, listened and read with fascination of this latest development in the unequal David-and-Goliath

631

conflict in Vietnam; they could scarcely believe that a small band of Communist guerrillas had seized the symbolic headquarters of the strongest military nation on earth and was resisting all efforts to recapture it.

But although Guy and the unwounded Marine guard waited anxiously minute by minute in the front lobby of the embassy for the final invasion assault, it didn't come. Unknown to them, the guerrillas had lost their leader in the first seconds of the raid as they plunged through the wall; he had been killed in the initial exchange of fire by one of the two American MPs on gate duty, and as a result, the leaderless platoon remained dug in indecisively around the protective flower tubs, content to fire their rocket launchers and machine guns intermittently at the embassy and at any Americans who appeared on rooftops in the streets outside. A Military Police unit sent to raise the siege from outside found both gates locked and was driven back by fire from the guerrillas when it tried to break the side gate open. Their commanding officer decided not to risk his men by attempting an attack over the wall in the darkness, and they failed to find the hole that the Viet Cong guerrillas had blown in the brickwork. So like the rest of the U.S. command, they spent the night wondering how the Viet Cong had got into the compound with their weapons and then locked two sets of gates behind them.

As the night wore on, the battle became more confused, and when it was decided that no U.S. defense units would try to enter the compound until daylight, troops were deployed in strength on surrounding rooftops. By the light of flares they poured fire onto the guerrillas, pinning them down and preventing any outright invasion of the main building. Helicopters were called in to try to land on the Chancery roof, but the Viet Cong were able to drive them off, firing from inside the protection of the concrete flower tubs which they had emptied of their earth.

Because the first rocket smashed the Marine guardpost's communications equipment in the front lobby, even the Americans trapped on the upper floors of the building didn't know what was going on below, and they spent the night waiting for their doors to burst open and admit Viet Cong commandos come to kill them. The duty foreign service officer retreated to the code room with a .38 pistol, where he was able to conduct direct telephone conversations with his State Department superiors in Washington — without knowing whether the next minute might be his last.

After waiting for nearly an hour to repel an attack through the front door that never came, Guy left the lobby and hurried back to his office on the fifth floor. He listened to the shortwave world news broadcasts from the BBC and the Voice of America and spent most of the next hour on the telephone trying to piece together an accurate assessment of the assault force's strength. A senior military intelligence officer at "Pentagon East," the Tan Son Nhut headquarters of General Westmoreland which was itself under attack by four Viet Cong battalions, told him that from the rooftops in Thong Nhut Boulevard, ten or a dozen bodies could be seen stretched out around the flower beds, apparently dead. A handful of guerrillas were still visible flitting among the concrete tubs returning fire, he told Guy. "The survivors seem determined to resist until the bitter end — but our guess is that no more than a platoon's involved. It's just a pipsqueak operation compared to what's going on in Hue, Da Nang and every other goddamned place."

"Okay," replied Guy impatiently, "so tell me why the hell you're not sending anybody in to flush them out. The longer the VC hold on to our sovereign territory, the bigger splash they'll make in the international press."

"Our commanders have decided not to risk their men until dawn," said the intelligence officer flatly. "There shouldn't be any problem mopping it up then."

"Jesus Christ, that's not soon enough!" snapped Guy. "I've been listening to the shortwave newscasts — the world's being told they're running wild through the whole fucking embassy and we can't get them out! Are we just going to sit back and let them score that kind of propaganda victory?"

"I'll try to get someone to correct that impression with the wire services," said the intelligence officer coolly. "Believe me, we have a fuller picture out here than you do. Just sit tight. Everything will work out fine."

"Goddamnit, a few determined GIs could clean them out in a few minutes," shouted Guy angrily, but the line had gone dead and he slammed down his receiver with a curse. When he went to look out of the window again he found that desultory small arms fire was still being exchanged by the Americans on the rooftops and the guerrillas in the gardens below under the light from occasional flares. He watched with growing impatience for half an hour, then hastened downstairs to the lobby again. He found there that the Marine sergeant had made his corporal comfortable on a stretcher and was trying to arrange by telephone to have him evacuated from the roof by helicopter as soon as a landing became possible. By his watch it was almost five A.M., and coming to a sudden decision, Guy picked up one of the sergeant's spare 12-gauge shotguns and filled his trouser pocket with a handful of shells. In his other hand he still carried his Beretta light machine gun, and bending double, he ran to the front door and peered out through the smashed window. He spent several minutes noting the positions of the remaining Viet Cong, then hurried towards one of the smaller exits at the back of the Chancery.

"What are you intending to do, sir?" called the Marine sergeant in a concerned tone as he passed his desk. "Can I give you any help?"

"No — you stay put, sergeant," said Guy, shaking his head. Then he grinned ruefully. "I just want to test out one of my father's old theories about the will to win."

14

Guy inched slowly out from the protection of the Chancery block, his body pressed close to the ground, moving forward on his elbows. He held the shotgun and the Beretta in front of him and stopped every few yards to rest; he was making for one of the concrete flower tubs close to the corner of the building, where by the light of a flare he had seen two guerrillas stretched on the grass, seemingly dead. He had calculated that the survivors still holding out behind two tubs thirty yards away would least expect to be fired on from positions occupied by their comrades.

Before leaving the Chancery he had made one last call to the intelligence officer at "Pentagon East," asking him to order the American forces outside the embassy to stop using flares above the compound because he knew that if he were caught in the open he would be lost. As a result of his survey through the broken Chancery windows, he believed there were no more than four or five guerrillas left alive, and they seemed to be grouped around tubs on either side of the walkway leading to the front entrance of the Chancery. In the pre-dawn darkness he could no longer see them, but as he moved silently across the lawn, in the intervals of quiet between the bursts of firing he once or twice heard the low mutter of their voices. When he reached the protection of the concrete urn he had singled out, he found that one of the two guerrillas there was already dead; the other, who lay in a pool of blood, was still breathing but unconscious.

For several minutes he remained motionless beside them, recovering from the exertion of his crawl; then he lifted his head and peered towards the next urn. From the embassy windows he had watched the men inside rise up above the concrete rim every few minutes to return fire towards a rooftop on the opposite side of Thong Nhut Boulevard, and anticipating that they would do so again, he raised the Beretta and took aim in their direction.

A hush had fallen over the compound and several minutes passed without movement. Guy's mouth was dry, and he recognized the same flutter of excitement stirring within him that he had experienced before in autumn dawns spent hunting in the mountains of West Virginia. As he crouched staring intently at the spot where he expected his quarry to raise their heads, he remembered suddenly that this feeling must have been inherited not from Senator Nathaniel Sherman but from an unknown French hunting guide who had stalked tiger and elephant in the colonial jungles of Vietnam. He remembered too in that same instant that his real father had been assassinated by Vietnamese nationalists, and he was seized then by an ecstatic conviction that hunting down the embassy invaders would be an historic act of personal vengeance for him.

Inside the concrete urn thirty yards away at that moment, young Kiet slammed his last full magazine into the breech of his AK-47 assault rifle and passed it to the Vietnamese lying beside him. Empty brass cartridge cases lay scattered all around them, and the older guerrilla, who had already expended his last rounds of ammunition, looked questioningly at Kiet.

"Take it, comrade," he said softly. "You are a far better shot than I." He rolled over onto his side and pointed to the two fragmentation grenades attached to his belt. "I still have these. I'm better with things that blow up violently."

Kiet's companion stared at him in alarm. The exhortation delivered by their commissar in the garage had suddenly returned to his mind with great vividness. "Act as heroes! Act with the spirit and pride of true combatants of the Liberation Army! Fight to your last drop of blood — and never surrender!" Was Kiet, he wondered, intending to use his grenades to blow them both to pieces now that the situation was hopeless and they were almost out of ammunition?

Kiet, sensing the unspoken fear behind his comrade's expression, shook his head. "Don't worry — they'll be used only to kill American imperialists who try to take us prisoner."

A long, speculative burst of fire from the opposite side of the street raked the line of flower tubs again, and Kiet felt his companion tense beside him; the guerrilla peered up through the gloom, trying to mark the rooftop position of the American rifleman in the darkness above them, and the moment the shooting died away, he raised himself on his elbows and loosed off three quick shots in reply.

From his hiding place thirty yards away, Guy squeezed the Beretta's trigger as soon as he saw the man's head and shoulders appear above the parapet of the flower tub. The weapon trembled in his hands as he held the burst, and the hail of bullets took the Vietnamese in the head and chest, killing him instantly. The noise and the nearness of the shots stunned Kiet for a moment, but when he heard Guy running across the lawn towards him, he rolled over and unhooked one of the fragmentation grenades from his belt. He withdrew its pin but didn't throw it; listening to the sound of Guy's feet, he began counting off the seconds remaining before the grenade detonated.

In the faint light of the coming dawn Guy saw Kiet twisting his body into position to lob the grenade and started to fire as he ran; the Vietnamese boy flattened himself desperately against the earth as the bullets thudded into the concrete above him, and when Guy was only a few feet away, he pushed the grenade over the low parapet with a flick of his wrist. The CIA man opened his mouth to let out a shout of fury as he charged and he was leaping onto the rim of the tub when the grenade arced onto the lawn. Kiet recoiled in terror when the blurred figure of the American appeared suddenly above him and he was rolling on his back at the moment bullets from the Beretta slammed into his chest. At almost the same instant, the grenade exploded deafeningly, and lethal shards of hot, jagged metal ripped through Guy's groin into his abdomen. For a moment he teetered on the parapet of the flower tub screaming in agony, then he pitched forward with outstretched arms on top of the Vietnamese and lay still.

When dawn broke it became clear to the Americans outside the embassy that the Viet Cong platoon had become depleted. After the hole in the wall was found, a Military Police jeep rammed through the locked front entrance while troops of the 101st

Airborne Division began landing by helicopter on the Chancery roof. The paratroopers raced through the six floors of the building wielding rifles, grenades and knives, expecting to find more Viet Cong inside the building — but to their surprise they found it was occupied only by the small band of Americans who emerged pale-faced and shaken from their hiding places.

Some skirmishing continued in and around other buildings as the few Viet Cong survivors resisted bitterly to the end, but the embassy was finally secured again just before nine-thirty A.M. when General Westmoreland arrived to inspect the scene. The Communists had held the compound for six and a half hours — a relatively brief occupation but one that shocked America deeply. Two of the original platoon of twenty Viet Cong were captured alive, although wounded. Nineteen other bodies were found strewn around the compound amidst the rubble and shattered masonry from the front of the damaged Chancery. Among them were several embassy drivers who might or might not have been Viet Cong, and even hardened journalists were appalled at the sight of the carnage and destruction when they were allowed in to question General Westmoreland about the embassy battle and the widespread Communist offensive then being pressed all over South Vietnam.

Guy Sherman and the young Ngo Van Kiet were found dead together, their bodies tangled in the moment of death. When they were dragged apart, their clothing was soaked in each other's blood and nobody noticed that the silk banderole beneath Kiet's shirt had originally been striped with gold too. Like the dead men themselves, neither the watching journalists nor the grim-faced Marines who eventually had to part their bodies would ever know that their deaths brought to an end a tangled skein of personal hatreds that had stretched back over forty long years to a colonial hunting camp that had once been pitched in the jungles of Cochin-China north of Saigon.

15

"Does it hurt very bad?"

The tiny voice speaking Vietnamese startled Joseph, and he opened his eyes to find a little girl aged about ten squatting on her haunches by his feet. She wore a pale, collarless tunic and trousers of cheap cotton and was barefooted, but her brow was crinkled in a worried frown and he realized then that he must have groaned aloud as he shifted his position in the bottom of the sampan; it was rocking only gently with the movement of the river, but the two worn coconut palm mats beneath his back did little to cushion the discomfort caused by the rough-hewn planks.

"It hurts a little, yes."

He gasped as he spoke and his breathing was labored; the dressing taped to the upper part of his bare chest was dark with dried blood, and he could move his right arm only with difficulty because of the stiffness. The bullet had passed between his top two ribs just beneath the collarbone on his right side and penetrated the pleural cavity, but from the wound beneath his armpit he guessed it had passed out of his body again. His right lung had collapsed, and after five days and nights he was becoming accustomed to the shortness of breath which went with having to manage on only one lung.

"Are you going to die?"

Joseph looked into the wide, wondering eyes; her ten-year-old face, unaware of its innocent, unformed beauty, was perfectly serious as she gazed at him, expectantly waiting for an answer. "No, I don't think so." He winced again as he raised himself on one elbow. "I'm going to get better sometime. And then maybe I'll take you and your Mamma away to a place where there isn't any war."

"Isn't any war?" The cherubic amber face crinkled with incomprehension. Outside, the distant rattle of rifle and machine-gun fire was continuous; occasionally the deeper roar of 90-millimeter tank cannon and the crump of mortar shells shook the earth and drowned out the lighter weapons, but the sound of small arms fire rarely died away altogether. The four Communist battalions that had stormed into Hue in the early hours of January 31 had seized the Citadel, Gia Hoi and most of the suburbs along the southern bank of the River of Perfumes within an hour or two, encountering only light resistance. American Marines of the First Battalion at Phu Bai had successfully fought their way through to the U.S. MACV compound opposite the Citadel within hours, but all their attempts to move out and clear the North Vietnamese and Viet Cong troops from the other areas south of the river had been resisted every step of the way. On the other bank, the depleted remnants of the First ARVN Division who had not been on leave when the Communists struck were trying to counterattack too, but they were making no progress against the Communists who now held the palaces in the heart of the Citadel. The U.S. Marines had taken to advancing along the streets crouched behind tanks in World War II fashion, but even these tactics, so unfamiliar to troops who had become accustomed to the jungle and hill warfare of Vietnam, were proving ineffective, and gains of a few yards only were being made each day; accurate bazooka fire was taking its toll of the tanks, and the jungle-trained enemy was proving suprisingly adept at house-to-house fighting. Low cloud and drizzle had made provision of close tactical air support impossible, and the fight for Hue raging all around the sampan that was moored among a clutter of similar boat dwellings was already proving to be a costly battle of attrition for both sides.

"There's always been fighting in your country ever since you were born," said Joseph speaking very quietly. "But it's not like that everywhere. Children in other countries play games all day, go swimming and take picnics. Would you like to do that?"

She looked at him uncertainly, resting her delicate chin on two tiny fists, and didn't answer. Once or twice during the past five days he had seen her peering shyly round the edge of the hanging mat that divided the cocoa palm fiber cabin into two compartments. Normally she had left the boat with Tuyet and her younger brother Chuong in the early morning each day and returned with them in the early evening, but for once she seemed to have stayed behind in the rear compartment of the sampan, and he assumed she had climbed through while he slept.

"Are you really my mamma's father?" Her little face contorted again in consternation.

"Yes, I am."

"But you're an American. How can that be?"

"Perhaps I'll explain later." Joseph winced and closed his eyes again. The slightest effort tired him still, and he felt dizzy whenever he moved. Due to the shock of the wound and the loss of blood, he had spent most of the first five days sleeping fitfully, slipping back and forth from unconsciousness to a dazed state of wakefulness, hearing only dimly the noise of the battle outside. Sometimes he had wakened to find Tuyet kneeling beside him tending his injury, and he had guessed from the odor of the dressings that it had become infected. It took her half an hour each day to free the bandages and clean the wound, using pots of warm water boiled on a little spirit stove in the rear of the boat;

but although her movements were always gentle and considerate, she had deliberately avoided his eyes, and her features had remained set always in a mask of indifference. Whenever he had tried to speak to her, she had motioned him to silence and refused to reply.

He had little recollection of how they had reached the sampan. He had stumbled somehow through the shanty district with her help and they had reached the river wharves without being detected. They had seen more North Vietnamese soldiers crossing the river in small boats, but then he had begun to feel faint and dizzy. They hid on the wharves for a while before taking to some kind of boat of their own, but then he had lost consciousness completely. He had come around to find her slapping his face in desperation, and with her help he had clambered onto the covered sampan. The first thing he remembered after that was waking to find her feeding him a thin rice gruel in the early light of morning.

"Won't your people find me here?" he had asked when he had become sufficiently clear-minded to realize they were in an occupied part of the city. "Aren't we still in danger?"

"The sampan has a safe conduct pass issued by the commander of the People's Liberation Armed Forces," she told him curtly. "It's well known that I've lived on the river ever since I came to Hue a year ago."

Joseph had watched her closely as she spoke, and despite the coldness of her manner he had sensed that she, too, was afraid that the boat might be searched.

"I'm very sorry, Tuyet," he had said softly. "I came here to warn you — not to put you in greater danger."

She had turned her back on him abruptly then, busying herself with the new dressing, and had made no acknowledgment of his apology.

When Joseph opened his eyes again, the little girl was still sitting silently beside him, watching him with mystified eyes. He glanced at his watch and discovered to his amazement that he had slept again for two hours. Through the worn fiber of the cabin roof he could see that it was growing dark outside, and there seemed for the first time to be a lull in the fighting.

"What is your name?" asked the girl impatiently, as though she had been waiting for all the two hours to put that question.

"Joseph Sherman."

She repeated an approximation of the name aloud several times in her little singsong Vietnamese voice. Then she stopped suddenly. "If you are my mamma's father, then you are also *my* grandpapa."

Her face was grave, as though she had been turning the awesome prospect over in her mind for some time, and Joseph felt tears start to his eyes. Unable to speak, he nodded and smiled tenderly at her.

She didn't return the smile but continued to stare at him, perplexed. "But how *can* that be — when you're an American?"

"It's difficult to explain." He continued to smile at her. "What's your name?"

She studied his face in silence for a long time, as though in doubt as to whether she should confide in him; then she drew an exasperated breath to indicate that she was yielding the information with reluctance. "My name is Trinh," she said firmly.

"That's a beautiful name — it means 'pure and virtuous,' doesn't it? I bet you're really a little angel in disguise."

She giggled suddenly, and her hand flew to her mouth, but she continued gazing at him, her eyes bright with merriment above her fingers; then she leaned forward and plucked at the hair growing on his forearm. "Why is it Americans have hair growing all over their bodies like monkeys?"

Her expression of innocent curiosity reminded Joseph with a sudden vividness of Lan at the age of ten in the garden of the governor general's palace, and he saw in a flash the inherited resemblance; feeling the lump in his throat grow, he beckoned to her to come closer to him, but at that moment the boat rocked from side to side under the weight of somebody stepping aboard from the quay and the smile melted from her face. Before she could move, the matting was drawn aside and Tuyet appeared. Her face clouded on seeing them together, and she admonished Trinh in Vietnamese so rapid that Joseph couldn't catch what she said. The startled girl immediately scrambled out of his compartment, and he heard Tuyet continuing to scold her behind the mat curtain.

When she brought his evening bowl of gruel and dried fish an hour later, Tuyet's face was dark with displeasure. She placed the food in front of him without speaking, then made to return to the rear of the sampan without inspecting the dressing on his wound. In the distance he heard the rattle of gunfire grow in volume again as another battle began.

"Tuyet, please stay and talk for a minute," said Joseph quietly. "I'd like to know what's happening in the city."

"Your imperialist troops and their puppet allies are trying to break the hold of the people — but they're not succeeding. The revolution in Hue is going to be victorious." She spoke with her back to him, but Joseph noticed there was not the same conviction in her words as previously and her shoulders seemed to sag.

"Tuyet, may I ask you where you go each day?"

"To help carry forward the revolution. There's much work to be done. In the occupied areas of the city our cadres have to walk the streets with megaphones calling on the corrupt officials of the Thieu government to give themselves up. We've set up many reeducation centers. . . ."

"I think your children grew lonely and frightened today when you left them here," he said, interrupting her deliberately. "You shouldn't scold Trinh for coming to talk to me."

She crawled back quickly along the sampan towards him, her eyes ablaze with anger. "Which is better? To go to work for the revolution as I am expected to do? Or stay away and have them come looking for me? And have them find *you* here?"

The lines of tension and fatigue in her face were clearly visible, and to his amazement he saw that she was on the verge of tears; in a blaze of realization he understood for the first time the weight of the dilemma with which she was struggling. "Tuyet, I'm sorry. I've been blind. I can see now how difficult I'm making things. It's too dangerous for me to stay here — for you and your children." He eased himself painfully into a sitting position. "I think I'm strong enough now to leave the sampan. I'll try to make my way through the darkness tonight to the American lines around the MACV compound."

"You won't get more than a few yards! With a collapsed lung you'll be able to walk only very slowly. You're weak from loss of blood — you would be taken before you'd gone a hundred yards."

Joseph threw back the blanket covering his legs and pushed himself to his knees. "That would be better than being found here. With me gone, you and the children will be safe again."

She snatched up the blanket to cover him once more then froze at the sudden sound of voices on the quay. They heard the piping voice of Trinh answering questions put to her in a guttural northern accent and the little girl's apprehension was evident from her replies.

"Who else lives on the sampan?"

"My mother, my brother, me and . . ."

Trinh stopped suddenly and they heard her cry out. Joseph pressed his eye to a slit in the palm fiber cabin wall and saw three North Vietnamese regulars in khaki uniforms and jungle-leaf hats. One of the soldiers had caught Trinh roughly by the wrist and she looked frightened.

"And who else? Come on, tell us quickly!"

Joseph felt the sampan rock and then saw Tuyet scramble onto the quay and run to her daughter's side. She held a paper in her hand which she thrust under the nose of the soldier. "I'm Tuyet Luong. I'm a political cadre working with the People's Liberation Armed Forces. Here's my safe conduct pass for the sampan, signed by our commander."

The North Vietnamese soldier looked Tuyet slowly up and down, then turned towards his companions and snorted derisively. "We can't always trust the judgment of our southern sisters, can we, comrades?" Joseph saw the soldier look Tuyet up and down once more, his gaze openly lascivious this time; then he grinned at his companions. "I think I must search the sampan anyway to make sure, comrades, don't you agree?" He dropped Trinh's wrist, took Tuyet by the arm and stepped towards the stern of the sampan.

"Wait!" Tuyet hung back, forcing the soldier to stop. "My son's already asleep. He's ill with a fever and mustn't be wakened." Joseph, watching through the torn cabin wall, saw the face of the North Vietnamese grow angry. Then Tuyet forced an artificial smile to her lips and put a hand on his arm, gesturing towards the neighboring sampan that, like most of the others moored along the bank, was empty because its inhabitants had fled. "Perhaps you should search the next boat," she said in a cajoling voice. "I'll help you if you like — then I can send my daughter to bed too." She waved Trinh hurriedly back onto their own boat, then drew the soldier smilingly towards the next craft.

Joseph heard the little girl scuttle back into the cabin and settle down beside her brother, who was already asleep. Through the torn cabin wall he saw the other two North Vietnamese saunter away, laughing obscenely, and he lay down himself and pulled the blanket up over his chest. The battle downstream died away again as quickly as it had begun, and calm returned to the river once more. Joseph tried hard to close his ears, but he could not blot out the sounds coming from the adjoining sampan. He heard the North Vietnamese soldier grunting and breathing noisily and once he thought he heard Tuyet cry out. When an hour later she returned alone to their sampan, he heard her sobbing quietly on her mat for a long time before she fell asleep.

16

The next morning Joseph woke late. Cold drizzle brought by the northeast monsoon was drifting down onto the embattled city from skies that seemed to press ever closer to the ground, and moisture was dripping steadily through the sampan's canopy onto his blanket. Before he was properly awake he found himself wondering vaguely why the previously distant rattle of gunfire seemed suddenly amplified, and it was some moments before he realized that the fighting was moving in the direction of his hiding place. As he lay there he strained his ears, hoping above the noise of the battle to hear voices or the sounds of movement in the curtained-off rear section of the sampan, but gradually it dawned on him that Tuyet and her children were no longer there. When he pushed himself up on one elbow to peer out through a slit in the cocoa palm fiber, the infected wound in his chest throbbed suddenly; he could feel the dressing was sticky with suppuration, and he began wondering how much longer he could hope to survive without proper treatment.

Through the slit he could see occasional puffs of white smoke from exploding rockets, and all along the waterfront, fires started by a heavy American artillery bombardment called in from eight miles outside the city the previous night were still smoldering and sending a pall of thick black smoke into the air. A corner tower of the Citadel was visible to him, its masonry shattered and scarred by American and South Vietnamese shells but still the ten-foot-thick walls were affording protection to North Vietnamese snipers who fired sporadically from high windows and parapets.

It was with a start that Joseph realized that the drenched flag he could see hanging limp on its staff above the fortified main gate was the gold-starred red and blue standard of the National Liberation Front. Although Tuyet had told him that the Communists had controlled most of the city for a week from their command post in the throne room of the Nguyen emperors, this symbolic proof of America's inability to dislodge them, hoisted above the historic ramparts, still came as a shock. He could see that the Communist forces had blown up the French-built Clemenceau Bridge, causing its massive steel arches to collapse into the river, but despite this obstacle he couldn't understand why the superior weight of American arms was not able to retake Hue quickly now that the enemy for the first time ever had done what Americans had always wanted — come out of their jungle and mountain hiding places to fight in the open.

As the day wore on, the pain in his chest grew more severe and he could only lie helplessly in the bottom of the dripping sampan, dozing during the lulls in the fighting. From time to time he caught a glimpse through the canopy of the distinctive palm-leaf helmets of the North Vietnamese troops; they seemed to be hurrying unheeding past the sampan, and he guessed they were retreating westward along the river in the face of the American advance. As the empty hours passed, a conviction grew in him that Tuyet had taken the children and fled. He considered trying to leave the sampan but decided it would be more dangerous to get caught in the cross fire between the two armies than to remain where he was. The whole of his body seemed to throb with the pain of the wound, making him feel sick and dizzy, and he wondered through the muzziness if he might be dying. He felt desperately tired, and as the feeling that Tuyet had gone forever strengthened, a mood of deep despondency settled in his mind, and he found he hardly cared what happened to him.

He fell asleep again as evening approached, and he imagined he was dreaming when he felt the boat rock and heard hushed whispers behind the mat curtain. The sounds of his daughter lighting the little stove and preparing a simple meal helped by the children seemed as real in his dream as they had done for seven nights past, but he continued dozing and only opened his eyes when Tuyet pulled the mat aside to bring in his usual dish of rice gruel and dried fish. After putting the bowl down in front of him, she retreated wordlessly, but he reached out and caught her by the arm.

"Tuyet, I thought you weren't coming back tonight." She turned her head towards him unprotesting, and he saw then that she was pale and trembling. "But I'm very glad you did because I wanted to thank you for last night. I had no right to expect that . . ."

He choked on his words and his voice died away altogether;

gently she pulled her wrist free of his grasp and sat back on her haunches, twisting her hands in her lap and staring fixedly at the floor. Outside there was a sudden exchange of fire much nearer than before.

"The fighting's coming closer, isn't it? Is that why you are worrying — because you are losing Hue?"

"I no longer care who wins and who loses!" She uttered her words with great vehemence, but although her expression was fierce her eyes brimmed with tears.

"Why, Tuyet?"

"I've grown tired of slaughter and bloodshed! Today I saw a hundred people murdered in cold blood. Some were shot in the head, others were battered to death with clubs and rifle butts." A shudder of horror shook her body at the memory. "Some of them were even buried alive."

Joseph stared at her aghast. "Who were these people? Who killed them?"

"My comrades." Her tone was suddenly bitter and contemptuous. "My comrades killed them because we were wrong."

"What do you mean?"

"We were wrong about the uprising. A great 'General Uprising' of all the people of South Vietnam was predicted. All over the South people should have swarmed onto the streets to welcome the triumphal entry of our forces — but they didn't; they've remained indifferent. So now the government leaders of Hue have been killed — along with a lot of minor functionaries."

There was a sudden loud explosion close to the sampan, and they both stopped and listened in alarm. The stutter of automatic rifle fire continued to grow louder, the low-pitched bark of the Russian-made AK-47 assault rifles contrasting sharply with the higher trilling of the American M-16.

"My job here was to help compile lists of government officials, army officers, religious leaders, teachers — people like that. We were told they would be taken away for reeducation. But they were really death lists all the time. Today, because the leadership can see we're going to be pushed out of Hue, they've embarked on a mass campaign of cold-blooded assassination." She stopped, and her voice sank to a whisper. "The names of three thousand people are on those lists — and all of them are to be murdered!"

She fell silent for a minute or two, then she looked up at him again. "There were foreigners among them — some German and French priests and several Americans. There was a tall young one, fair-haired like you. They tied his hands behind him, made him kneel beside a shallow grave, then shot him in the back of the neck. They buried him even before he had stopped moving."

Tears began trickling down her cheeks and she closed her eyes; she sat like this for a long time, her fingers flexing and unflexing convulsively in her lap, and at last Joseph leaned towards her. "Please let me take you all away to America, Tuyet," he pleaded. "You can put it all behind you there."

She shook her head quickly without opening her eyes. "It's impossible!"

"Nothing is impossible, Tuyet, if you want it badly enough. If you believe in it enough, it can become possible. I want more than anything to take you away from Vietnam."

She shook her head again and a little sob escaped her lips. "I've done many terrible things too." She opened her eyes to find him staring at her with an agonized expression; her lower lip trembled but she fought to regain her control. "Yes, I threw the bombs in Saigon to kill my husband's torturers, if that is the rumor you've heard. And I would do it again! By killing him they robbed me of the only happiness I had known in my whole life! And the desire for revenge didn't leave me for a long time. I fought as a platoon leader of the Liberation Army in the delta for two years. I killed many times — Americans as well as government troops."

"I knew about that." Joseph spoke very quietly, and she gazed at him open-mouthed in astonishment.

"You knew all that — but still you wanted to come?"

Joseph nodded silently.

Her eyes widened as though she was horrified suddenly by everything she had been saying; then, with a little moan of anguish, she slipped her arms around his neck and bent towards him until her forehead rested against his bare chest. Sobbing wracked her body for several minutes and Joseph wept silently too, his arms tight about her. Outside along the devastated waterfront the battle advanced steadily towards them.

While he was holding her, Joseph saw the frightened faces of little Trinh and her brother, Chuong, peer anxiously around the edge of the curtain and reluctantly he disengaged himself. "What will you do, Tuyet?" he asked softly. "This area will be in American hands within a few hours. Will you take a chance and stay with me? I'll get us all to America, I promise you." He glanced towards the frightened children and smiled. "All of us."

647

She drew back from him, clasping her arms tight around her own body as if to strengthen her resolve, and after a moment's pause she shook her head decisively. "I must stay here. Vietnam has been my only real mother and father. We'll all go to the North! My Uncle Kim has heard of me through my work for the Liberation Front." She shot a quick glance at Joseph. "He holds a high position in the Politburo of the Lao Dong, and he's a close confidant of Ho Chi Minh. He's offered to help me find a home near him in Hanoi."

She turned away hurriedly to usher the children back into the rear section, and he heard her banging about and giving whispered instructions as they packed their meager belongings. After a few minutes Trinh clambered through into his part of the sampan again and hurried to his side. She looked at him for a moment with sad eyes, then reached out and touched the dressing on his wound delicately with one finger.

"I hope you get better," she whispered, suddenly shy. She took a deep breath as if she was about to say something more, but the sound of her mother's voice calling urgently from beyond the mat curtain brought a look of alarm to her round child's face. After a quick glance over her shoulder to make sure her mother wasn't watching, she bent towards him. "*Thua Ong ngoai con di*," she whispered close to his ear; "I must go now, Grandpapa." She pressed her lips briefly against his bristly cheek, then scampered back to her mother.

Joseph lay waiting miserably for Tuyet to come and take her leave, and only when he felt the boat rock twice did he realize she had chosen deliberately to avoid an anguished farewell. Sick at heart, he yelled her name at the top of his voice and scrambled to his knees. He crawled frantically through the empty rear section and out onto the flat stern. The noise of mortar and small arms fire had become deafening and she was fifty yards away, moving fast in a westward direction along the riverbank. Already an anonymous figure in the gathering gloom, her loose black trousers ballooned around her legs as she ran balancing the pole on her left shoulder. The paniers were heavily laden with the cooking stove and all the other modest possessions from the sampan, and the two children clung desperately to her hands and clothing, half walking, half running beside her through the awful din of the battle that filled the night.

Although his eyes never left them, neither Tuyet nor the boy looked back. Only Trinh turned her head once in his direction, and he waved his uninjured arm sadly in farewell. The little girl raised her head to speak excitedly to her mother, pointing back towards him, but she stumbled in doing so and he saw Tuyet shake her angrily in admonition. Gradually the three frail figures were swallowed up in the misty half-darkness, and he sank slowly to his knees on the stern of the sampan, a cold knot of certainty that he would never see his daughter again tightening in the pit of his stomach.

A platoon of Marines advancing behind a tank found Joseph crouched on the sampan's stern half an hour later. He had crawled back into the interior to get his bloodstained shirt and he waved this slowly above his head to dissuade them from firing on him. A black sergeant with the butt of a dead cigar clenched between his teeth advanced from the darkness holding his M-16 unwaveringly on Joseph until he was certain he was not armed or hostile. Only then did he allow his astonishment to show.

"Jesus! You mean to say an American has been hiding out on one of these little fuckin' sampans for a whole week with that wound?" The sergeant laughed incredulously as he helped Joseph ashore, then stepping down into the boat, he got down onto his hands and knees to inspect the interior. A moment later he was back on the bank, wrinkling his nose.

"Guess you're glad to get off that thing, Mister Sherman, ain't yuh? Kinda stinks in there, don't it?"

Joseph looked at the sergeant but didn't reply; there was enough light left for him to see for the first time that the sampan had been moored only a hundred yards or so from the spot where he had spent that first enchanted night with Lan on the River of Perfumes thirty-two years before.

17

Captain Gary Sherman sat up in his dank, musty bunker at Firebase Birmingham and rubbed his eyes. Outside, twilight was falling over the flat coastal plains of Quang Ngai, three hundred miles north of Saigon. He had slept for half an hour but was still gray-faced with fatigue; only three hours earlier he had led his understrength Bravo Company back to base from its third

649

abortive "search-and-destroy" sweep of the week through the poor hamlets that lay scattered across the low-lying marshes of the province within sight of the sea. The mission had been routine; they had been out for two nights without once making contact with the Viet Cong, but mines and booby traps had again whittled away another half-dozen of his men.

By the end of the operation, the fatigued survivors were watching the wounded being hauled out by medivac helicopters with envious expressions in their eyes, and he knew that some of the frightened young draftees he was trying so painstakingly to mold into an efficient fighting force would have gladly swapped places with them. Two had suffered minor shrapnel wounds, another had lost a foot, and a third had all the fingers blown off his left hand. Three of them, however, had been killed outright, and as always happened with mines, the bodies of the victims had been horribly mutilated, and their departure by helicopter wrapped in their own rain ponchos had left the other men dull-eyed and silent with shock.

It was the third time in a week that Bravo Company had been caught in a minefield, and in all some thirty men had been lost; seven had been killed and many of the others had suffered severed limbs and mutilations that would leave them crippled and disfigured for life. The casualty rate was higher than normal because the winding paths through the hamlets of the region, like those all over rural South Vietnam, had been sown and resown with mines more intensively than ever before in the wake of the Tet Offensive that had proved so costly for the Communist forces. Although pictures of the street fighting in the major cities had shocked America deeply, the Viet Cong and the North Vietnamese losses by the time they retreated had mounted to thirty thousand dead and wounded against American and South Vietnamese losses of about ten thousand. As a result, as soon as the offensive ended, the severely weakened Communist battalions had reverted to their familiar guerrilla strategy once more, dodging and feinting in the jungles and mountains and rarely engaging their enemy openly.

Anxious to press home their advantage, the United States military commanders in South Vietnam were pushing their own troops hard in pursuit, and for this reason Gary's repeated requests to have his demoralized company stood down from active duty had been refused. General Westmoreland, the American commander in South Vietnam, had asked for a massive new commitment of troops from the United States to help bolster this new drive, but the Tet Offensive had greatly strengthened antiwar sentiment in America, and President Johnson had turned down his request; as a consequence no replacements were arriving for the casualties in Bravo Company either, and for a minute or two after waking Gary lay motionless on the inflated mattress covering his wooden plank bed, reflecting wearily on his predicament. He could see no end to the terrible attrition of the men under his command, and he couldn't think how he was going to lift the morale of the Bravo troops for yet another operation. He had barely been able to believe his ears when, after their return that afternoon, the colonel commanding the four-company Task Force Birmingham had announced that Bravo was being assigned a blocking role in a dawn assault by the entire force on the village of Quang To. High grade intelligence indicated the presence in the village of a large contingent of the Viet Cong's 42nd Light Force Battalion, the crew-cut colonel had announced with a smug grin. "The SOBs are hiding out in those bricked-up houses and the tunnels underneath," he had told his officers. "I guess all our guys need a boost — we've had too many frustrating weeks of noncontact. So you can go tell 'em tomorrow we're gonna give 'em a real chance to zap Victor Charlie's ass!"

Looking at his watch, Gary saw there was still a half an hour to go before briefing time, and he dragged himself reluctantly to his feet and began to wash. As he splashed water on his sleepy face from a hand bowl, the sudden sound of hysterical giggling reached his ears from outside and he stopped and looked out through the doorway. Two of the draftees in his company, both steelworkers from Indiana, were staggering back to their billets from the direction of the base "boom-boom shop," a collection of tumbledown shacks just off Highway One where peasant girls sold their favors under the beady-eyed gaze of an aged mama-san; they were passing a marijuana joint back and forth between them as they swayed along and one of them, a heavily built youth with fair hair, was tipping a can of American beer to his lips between giggles. Watching them go, Gary remembered that the last time he'd seen them in the field they had been helping lift one of the shattered bodies into a helicopter; they hadn't changed their clothes, and he could see that blood smears from some of the wounded had merged into the filth of their mud-spattered combat fatigues.

"Go get a fresh issue of clothing, you men," called Gary

sharply. "I want everybody shaped up for my briefing in an hour's time."

The soldiers stopped giggling long enough to turn and raise their hands in a sloppy salute, but as he went back into the bunker, he heard their shrill laughter start up again and they continued noisily on their way back to their billets. He stood thinking absently about the two stoned soldiers for a moment, then to take his mind off the briefing for the next day's operation, he pulled out an airmail pad and sat down to write a letter to his father.

"*Dear Dad*," he began,

Don't mistake my lateness in replying to your letter from London as evidence of anything at all except that I'm usually too damned busy and too tired these days to get around to letter-writing. During the four months since the Tet panic died down, life here has been one long hectic round of "search-and-destroy" missions in which we do a hell of a lot of searching and very little destroying. In return of course we get a steady debilitating toll of casualties from traps and mines. That may sound to you like "the mixture as before," but believe me, it's stronger medicine now than ever and just as unpleasant to swallow. Your letter arrived a week ago and I'm snatching a few minutes between sorties to scribble a line in reply because I wanted to tell you how delighted I was when I read those first few lines about Mark getting out of his hellhole in Hanoi soon.

Like you, I don't give a damn either which peace group goes to bring him home as long as he gets out okay after all he's been through. I'm sure the personal letter you wrote to Ho Chi Minh helped a hell of a lot although I wish you'd told me about it before — it might have helped me to behave more sensibly those last couple of times we met. Your other major revelation that you'd quietly married Miss Boyce-Lewis and decided to set up home in England also helped make me feel a little more ashamed of myself than I already did — which is saying something. Outside the Continental that night when I saw you together I was somewhat less than gracious and my conscience bothered me a hell of a lot afterwards. It's a load off my mind to let you know that and I offer a clumsy apology along with my really heartfelt congratulations to you both . . .

Gary stopped writing and listened when a long burst of what sounded like distant machine-gun fire broke the silence; but it went on and grew rapidly louder and he recognized then the rapid thump of helicopter engines. One of the other three Birmingham companies was obviously returning from an operation, and he listened absently until all the choppers had landed.

"I was going to say I hope your shoulder's mended," he continued when the last helicopter engine had cut.

But I guess it must be okay if you felt well enough to "walk up the aisle" at Caxton Hall. If you're embarking on a critique of our Vietnam policy in book form, as you say in your letter, you must be in fairly good shape, I guess — so I'll wish you luck with that too. A book of that kind from someone as knowledgeable as you on the subject must be assured of considerable sales — no doubt the libraries at the White House, the State Department and the Pentagon will be ordering advance copies to see what you say about their masters. As for myself, I feel I could contribute a few lines of "critique" myself right now about the situation here. (This will obviously have to be mailed clandestinely through civilian channels to reach you intact now that I've gotten onto this subject.) We've just done three missions in a week, and we're going out again at the crack of dawn tomorrow. We're badly under strength and morale among the remaining men is very low. Whether we'll have any more luck this time is open to serious doubt and I'm afraid I'm feeling pretty down in the mouth about it all. I find myself torn now between a strong desire to resign my commission and get the hell out, and a sense of duty that tells me that I ought to stay and do what I can to curb some of the worst things going on here. For instance, there's a rule that any Vietnamese who doesn't stop and identify himself in a village should be shot. Many run away out of sheer terror and then it's a question of "shoot first and ask questions afterwards." This, as you can imagine, leads to a lot of indiscriminate killing. Also you never know when you go into a village whether you're going to find just women and children, a few hidden snipers or a whole goddamned battalion of VC. So we've taken to laying down a heavy barrage of rocket and artillery fire every time just in case. It's madness, really. Civilian casualties on a big scale are unavoidable and "winning the hearts and minds of the people," as we're supposed to be doing, is impossible under these circumstances . . .

Gary stopped writing and glanced at his watch again; only five minutes remained before the briefing began, and he reluctantly shuffled the pages of the letter together. *"I've got to dash now to yet another 'war council,'"* he added hurriedly at the foot of the page on which he'd just been writing. *"So I'll just add for now those immortal words beloved by magazine serial writers, 'to be continued.'"* Without looking over what he'd written, he folded the pages together and slipped them into one of his breast pockets.

When he stepped out of the bunker, the darkness outside was moist and warm against his face and because of the heat he walked slowly towards base headquarters where the officers of the four companies were beginning to assemble. To take his mind off the dismal prospect of the briefing, he let his thoughts stray back to his father's letter and he found himself wondering as he walked how his brother Mark would cope with the problems of readjustment to freedom after his terrible imprisonment. He tried to imagine too what kind of life his father was leading with his new English wife, and it occurred to him suddenly that the lives of his brother, his father and himself had all been marked deeply by Vietnam. As he mused on this, the image of the game animals shot in the jungles of Cochin-China and Annam by his grandfather and his dead uncle forty years before flashed unbidden into his mind; he remembered how his father had tried to explain his aversion to the tableau during their unhappy meeting in the museum and the halting words he'd used then came back to him. ". . . Too often, Gary, we get carried away with the idea of wanting to win at all costs . . . We're all of us likely, God knows, to fall prey to the worst sides of our natures . . ."

For some reason the memory brought back the vague sense of foreboding he'd felt earlier on learning that he would have to go out again so soon with his exhausted draftees, and the feeling grew rapidly as he approached the briefing room. By the time he reported to Birmingham's colonel his mood had become deeply pessimistic.

As the American briefing got under way, fifteen miles to the north in the village of Quang To, two hundred guerrillas of the 42nd Light Force Battalion of the Liberation Army were settling down for the night in thatched "hootches" that all had concealed entrances leading into the network of subterranean passages beneath the village. The tunnels, which were two or three kilometers long, led to outlets on the seashore, and the guerrillas had many times rehearsed rapid withdrawal through them to test the speed and thoroughness with which they could vacate the village. On these occasions wives and families invariably stayed behind, and as the senior commissar of the battalion went from hut to hut that night giving whispered orders to the fighting men to retreat to the beach, he also warned their families to remain where they were on pain of punishment; they were told that spies at Firebase Birmingham had learned that an American raid was expected at dawn and they were instructed not to cooperate with the imperialist troops in any way. When their meal was finished the

Viet Cong guerrillas took leave of their families without fuss and slipped down into the tunnels. By midnight only women, children and old men beyond military age remained in Quang To.

Next morning Gary flew in the lead helicopter when Task Force Birmingham took off at first light. Looking back, he could see the rest of the first wave of the force strung out behind, a dozen wasp-like silhouettes seesawing in Indian file against the orange flare of the rising sun. Ahead of them he could see brilliant flashes and smoke bursts spreading all across the half-dozen hamlets of the target village, and Cobra gunships were plunging and rearing through the smoke, pouring rocket and machine-gun fire into the thatched huts. Although there was no sign of firing from the ground, the door gunners of all the troop-carrying helicopters opened up with their M-60s too, as they neared the selected landing zone in a paddy field two hundred yards to the south of Hamlet One. The two soldiers Gary had reprimanded the night before were flying with him in his lead helicopter alongside other members of their platoon; all of them were strained and tense, and they clutched their M-16s tightly in front of them, peering through the open door searching for signs of the 42nd Light Force which by reputation was a crack Viet Cong unit that hit hard and ruthlessly when it chose to engage.

"We're gonna get us a whole rack of yellow ass today, man," said the beefier of the two Indiana steelworkers, slapping the stock of his rifle loudly with his hand. "And it's about goddamned time, too."

His companion, who was dark and sparely built, nodded his agreement. "That's for sure — if the Alpha boys can drive the gooks our way, we'll turn them all into strawberry jam." He turned around and grinned at Gary. "We'll do that for you, captain — and for all the Bravo guys who got burned already."

Gary nodded curtly in acknowledgment, then turned his attention to the ground as they began dropping down into the landing zone. To get the task force's blood up, the colonel at the previous night's briefing had ordered his officers to stress the prospect of avenging dead friends. Gary had gone along reluctantly, unable to find any other way of repairing the shattered morale of his company, but he was still worrying at the problem, wondering if he had done right, as the ground rushed up to meet them. Then suddenly it no longer mattered, the men were pouring out through the open doors of the helicopter into the

655

waist-high grass, racing frantically for cover, and the sole thought in everybody's mind was survival.

Bravo's first job was to secure the landing zone, and Gary barked orders to his platoon lieutenants to spread the force in a wide circle. During the next fifteen minutes, helicopters roared in and out, ferrying in the assault companies, the thump of their rotors sending great waves racing through the tall grass whenever they landed and took off. Gary watched the troops of Alpha, Charlie and Delta swarming out of the choppers, as tense and jittery at the moment of landing as his own men had been; their pinched faces, too, bore telltale signs of fatigue, and they stared apprehensively at the ground ahead of them, watching for booby traps as they moved onto the paths leading into Hamlet One. Then the helicopters' engines faded into the distance and the sounds of the soldiers moving deeper into the hamlet lessened too; something approaching quiet descended over Quang To, and gradually the light of the rising sun changed from orange to a paler yellow glow.

Gary had begun moving his force in an arc to its blocking position in the southern quarter of the village when they heard the roar of an explosion and saw a fountain of black earth shoot up above the distant tree line. The detonation was followed by a lazy drift of smoke that climbed into view more slowly above the treetops.

"Motherfuckin' bastards," whispered the dark-haired boy from Indiana, who was moving in a crouch at Gary's side. "Another goddamned mine!"

A flurry of shots followed the explosion, and Gary ordered his men to freeze. The sound of shooting continued but it remained scattered and didn't develop into the heavy, sustained pattern of exchange fire that denoted two forces settling into an engagement. By the time Bravo Company was in position, the crackle of flames was audible and smoke from burning thatch began to blur the sky.

"They've found some goddamned action at last," breathed the Indiana boy beside Gary. "At last we're zapping yellow ass, captain."

The officer frowned; the radio of his RTO was crackling with messages, but no coherent picture of the sweep was emerging. "You'd better go take a look and see what's happening — then get straight back here," he told the youth sharply.

For a moment the young draftee looked dubious; then he

loped off obediently into the trees. It was five minutes before he returned, and then Gary noticed immediately that the expression on his face was a mixture of elation and horror. "Alpha Company's shooting up the whole fuckin' village, captain," he said in an awed voice. "They're just shooting every damned kind of gook and pushin' 'em into a ditch. They're burning the huts, and killin' the cattle. They're just wiping' the whole place out — kids, babies, women, old guys, the chickens, everythin'!"

Gary stared at him in disbelief. "Are you sure of what you're saying? Are there no VC?"

The boy shook his head rapidly from side to side.

"Who's doing the shooting?"

"Everybody! Sergeants, a lieutenant, all of 'em! They're rapin' the women too."

The young steelworker had been talking loudly and excitedly, and other men of the company, hearing what he was saying, came running over to listen. When Gary noticed this, he swung angrily on them. "Get back to your goddamned posts, all of you! This is a disciplined blocking force and we're staying here to do our job." He beckoned one of his lieutenants to him. "Take over here. I'm going into the village." Motioning to the two Indiana draftees to follow, he led them at a run into the trees.

In the first hamlet he approached through the scrub, Gary saw two Americans firing into a cowering crowd of women and children herded together near a ditch. One of the Americans was a lieutenant, the other a sergeant, and the screams of terror of the Vietnamese peasants died abruptly in their throats as bullets from a machine gun and an M-16 smashed into them. The moment they crumpled to the ground, another GI began kicking and knocking the bleeding corpses over the lip of the ditch; a movement among them caught Gary's eye and, turning, he saw a small boy burrowing into a pile of bodies either in search of somebody already dead or to hide from the bullets. When the sergeant noticed this, he fired repeatedly at the boy until he too rolled over and lay still.

Dry-mouthed with horror, Gary unslung his Armalite from his shoulder and fired a long burst above the heads of the two Americans. "Drop your weapons now — or I'll kill you both!" he yelled and lunged out of the trees towards them. The sensation of flying in the air was the next thing he felt and only when his body stopped rising and began to topple head first into the geyser of black earth being thrown up all around him did he realize he had detonated a mine. By then the whole front of his chest had been laid open by the blast. When his body came to rest on the ground, the two GIs from Indiana stared down at it in horror. They could see all his organs — his heart, his liver, his lungs — pumping and pulsating inside his cloven chest and his blood was gushing into the earth around their feet. It took five minutes for him to die, and they could only watch helplessly as he lay writhing and screaming on the ground. At last one of the steelworkers ran back to the lieutenant in charge of Bravo and all the men left their blocking positions to gather around the dead body of their company commander.

By the time the Bravo medic reached the scene and began trying to wrap Gary's shattered body in a poncho, many of his troops were sobbing openly. Others shrieked obscenities at the heavens like men insane, then gradually, one by one they moved off deeper into the village to join in the carnage. Many of them continued sobbing and screaming as they helped hunt down the rest of the Vietnamese villagers. They murdered them singly and in groups, burned and pillaged their homes and stabbed their cattle and buffalo to death with bayonets; a few recoiled in horror from what was happening and either hid themselves or tried to save an isolated peasant girl or an old woman, but their efforts had little effect on the rest of the men in the two companies. The slaughter went on without letup for several hours, and at the end of it, the heaps of bodies in and around Quang To were numbered in hundreds.

18

The anchorman of *Panorama*, Britain's most prestigious television current affairs program, held the newly published book aslant in his lap so that one of the studio cameras could switch its focus to a tight close-up of the picture on its dust jacket. As the screens of television sets in homes all over the country filled with the image of an agonized American Marine wounded in the Battle of Hue, the anchorman began to read an extract from the book's preface that rolled slowly across a teleprompt machine beneath the camera facing him.

"At the opening of the constitutional convention of the United

States of America in 1787, George Washington said, 'Let us raise a standard to which the wise and the honest can repair.' Since then most American leaders have aspired to govern our country in accordance with those simple principles but the standard that we're fighting under in Vietnam today has been raised and held aloft by successive American presidents over the last decade largely for reasons connected with their own personal vanity and a misplaced sense of pride. That same standard today flutters over the heads of more than half a million American troops in the field in Vietnam — but it's becoming clearer every day that honesty and wisdom have played little or no part in the decision-making process which led us into the war and keeps us fighting there although there's obviously no prospect now of ever winning any creditable victory. Instead of honesty and wisdom, shame and disgust are now widespread in the United States and elsewhere in the Western world because of what we're doing in Southeast Asia. The time has come, I believe, for all 'wise' and 'honest' men inside and outside the government to call a halt. We should terminate immediately our calamitous military involvement in Vietnam and stop the terrible hemorrhage of American lives and treasure that otherwise will continue indefinitely without any benefit whatsoever to the United States and the West . . ."

The face of the anchorman, stern, square-jawed and caked with flattering makeup, came back on camera, and he paused for a moment to let the dramatic import of the words sink in. "Those are the views of Joseph Sherman, author of this new book on the Vietnam war, entitled *The American Betrayal*, which is fast becoming the bible of the antiwar movement at present convulsing America. Mr. Sherman, a foreign correspondent in Asia in the 1950s and later a professor of Asian studies at Cornell University, resigned from his post as a special government adviser in Saigon just over a year ago to write this book, which is published here in London this week. On publication in America recently it sparked off enormous controversy, attracting bitter criticism from supporters of the United States role and winning high praise for its courage from the war's opponents . . ."

The camera pulled back from the anchorman to reveal Joseph seated beside him; he sat awkwardly in the studio chair, the shoulder wounded fourteen months before in Hue hunched unnaturally in a position which caused him the least discomfort. As the introductory statement continued, the director of the program, seated before a bank of monitors in the control gallery, switched the transmission picture to Joseph alone, and keeping pace with the grave and sonorous tones of the anchorman, the camera moved steadily into a very close shot that finally framed only his features from jaw to hairline; still noticeably gaunt from the pain and stress of his wound, Joseph's face was set in a grim, tight-lipped expression.

"Mr. Sherman recently married the British television journalist Naomi Boyce-Lewis and came to live here in England — but he's no detached armchair critic of America's Vietnam war. He was himself wounded in the shoulder during last year's Tet Offensive in Hue, and in fact his family's involvement in the conflict has been perhaps as tragic as that of any family in America." The anchorman paused, knowing what he was about to say could cause distress to the American sitting beside him. "Mr. Sherman's elder son, an infantry captain, died last year in a jungle ambush, and his younger son, an air force pilot, was until recent release held prisoner for three years in Hanoi. In addition, a brother working for the State Department was killed by Viet Cong guerrillas during their Tet raid on the U.S. embassy — so Mr. Sherman is perhaps uniquely qualified to comment on the agony Vietnam is causing America . . ."

The searching close-up shot of Joseph's face detected a quick movement of his jaw muscles and a narrowing of his eyes; millions of viewers saw him swallow hard under the bright glare of the studio lights, then his face became composed again.

"But perhaps nothing is more indicative of the way the Vietnam war is dividing the American nation," the anchorman continued, "than the fact that the author's own father has become one of the book's most prominent critics. And the dispute takes on more than usual significance because his father is none other than Nathaniel Sherman, Democratic senator from Virginia for the past forty-nine years, the senior member of the Upper House and one of America's most colorful and widely renowned political figures . . . Senator Sherman is at present in our Washington studio waiting to join us by satellite transmission, and he has kindly agreed to participate in our discussion . . ."

While the anchorman was speaking, a big screen above him came to life, revealing the head and shoulders of Nathanial Sherman seated in the BBC studio in Washington and listening carefully to the introduction. Although in his eighties, he was still of impressive appearance; his craggy features were florid but alert and his snowy-white hair and bushy eyebrows gave him a stern, patriarchal air. Dressed in an elegant suit of white linen, he clearly relished the role of venerable elder statesman, and the fact that he had lost his left arm was no longer noticeable since he had taken to wearing an artificial limb.

"Good evening, senator," said the anchorman, turning towards the screen. "Thank you for consenting to join us."

"The pleasure is wholly mine, sir. I'm delighted to have the opportunity of talking to you and your English viewers." The senator smiled and inclined his head a fraction in an aristocratic gesture of acknowledgment and as Joseph glanced up at the magnified image on the studio screen he realized that his father, ever the showman, was instinctively exaggerating his southern drawl for the benefit of the British audience.

"We'll be asking for your comments shortly, senator," said the anchorman respectfully, "but first I'd like to begin by putting a question to your son here in London." He turned to Joseph, glancing down at his clipboard list of prepared questions as he did so. "First, Mr. Sherman, I'd like to ask you to spell out in detail why you believe so ardently that America should get out of Vietnam. And perhaps you could also tell us whether this conclusion is based solely on a detailed analysis of the situation on the ground — or has it been influenced in any way by the personal suffering Vietnam has caused you?"

Joseph didn't reply immediately, and the anchorman, fearing suddenly that his first question might have been too blunt and unfeeling, glanced up anxiously at his American guest. To his surprise he found Joseph was still staring distractedly at the satellite picture of his father, but after a moment he seemed to gather himself and he turned to face him. "To lose one son blown up by a booby trap and have the other subjected to torture and degradation for three long years certainly helps focus the mind," said Joseph in a tight voice. "But the conclusion in my book that withdrawal is our only sensible option and the reasons that led me to it are based on knowledge and insights I've gained over many years of association with Vietnam. It's now painfully obvious that we, the people of the United States, let our country drift into our present nightmare because we didn't keep a close enough eye on our political and military leaders and their motives. None of us has been vigilant enough — but since I've known Vietnam intimately for most of my life, I came to feel my own negligence very keenly after the Tet Offensive. And because I've suffered a great deal of personal grief too, I felt an extra compulsion to try to redress the balance with this book."

Above Joseph's head the enlarged face of his father had been darkening in evident disagreement as he spoke, and as soon as he'd finished, the senator cut in smoothly without waiting to be invited. "If I may be allowed to offer a comment on that, sir," he said, addressing the anchorman in a voice that was at once both sorrowful and elaborately polite, "I'd like to make my standpoint clear from the very outset. I'm against all forms of 'bugging out,' whether they're advocated by the so-called doves in the United States Congress here in Washington — or by my own son sitting beside you there in England."

"I understand, senator, that you're very anxious to give your side of the argument," replied the anchorman quickly in an apologetic tone, "and we're equally anxious to hear it, but if you'll be kind enough to bear with us, I'd like to put one or two more questions to your son first. I'll come back to you in a moment." He swung in his swivel chair to face Joseph again. "It's very honest of you, Mr. Sherman, to admit that you can't entirely separate your emotional involvement from your objective arguments about Vietnam — but isn't there a danger that your belief that the war can't be won might have grown directly out of the double bereavement you've suffered — and the anxiety of having to stand by helplessly while your younger son languished as a prisoner of war in Hanoi?"

Again Joseph didn't reply immediately; his father's silky tones and the feigned regret in his voice as he spoke had not disguised the implacable hostility of what he said. When agreeing to take part in the program with him, Joseph had harbored a vague hope that perhaps the private grief they shared might help to personalize for outsiders the agony that Vietnam was causing in their country. At the same time, he realized suddenly, he had hoped that perhaps a public discussion of the issues which had such painful personal significance for them both might somehow draw them closer together, might lead them at this late stage in their lives to some kind of better understanding. But the tenor of the senator's intervention and the labored reference to his own presence in England made him suspect that his father had already planned and prepared his remarks with the same care that he gave to his calculated speeches in the Senate. These thoughts chased one another through his mind as he prepared to answer his interviewer's question, and when he finally spoke, his tone was more coldly dispassionate than it might otherwise have been.

"There's no danger at all that I've confused the deep sadness I feel at the deaths in our family with the glaring political mis-calculations that have brought them about," said Joseph quietly. "We've created and we support a government in Saigon that's supposedly democratic but which in fact is brutal and detested by the people it governs. The men who run it are natural successors to the hated mandarins who ruled under the French, and they wouldn't survive five minutes without American financial sup-port. In comparison the austere, self-sacrificing methods prac-ticed by the Viet Cong in the areas they administer seem highly attractive to the peasants of South Vietnam — so it's a fraud to pretend we're defending a democratic government. It's too late to try to change it now — that's why the war *can't* be won."

Joseph deliberately kept his eyes averted from the screen on which his father's face was visible and sat back warily in his chair, waiting for the next question. The anchorman, however, glanced up to check the senator's reaction and, seeing the look of impatience growing on his face, decided the moment had come when he might draw him into the discussion with maximum impact.

"Perhaps you'd like to tell us now, senator," he said crisply, "why it is you don't share your son's views about the impossibility of victory in Vietnam."

"I would indeed, sir." The older man leaned forward belliger-ently in his seat and cleared his throat in a theatrical fashion. "Things like death in the family affect different people in dif-ferent ways. With some it knocks the stuffing out of them, makes them want to give up. With others it stiffens their will and makes them more determined than ever to fight on to final victory." He paused dramatically, and his head jutted forward on his wrinkled neck. "During nearly five decades of public service I've been proud to serve on the Armed Services Committee of the United States Senate, and I'd like to remind your viewers that today we've got the greatest army, the greatest navy and the greatest air force in the whole world! But despite this fact we're still bogged down in Vietnam, suffering two thousand casualties every week because we're strangling our war effort with self-imposed restric-tions. If we were to kick off our shackles and release the full strength of our air and sea power, Ho Chi Minh would very quickly be forced to halt his war of aggression. The word 'victory' doesn't frighten me like it does some folks — but to achieve it we need to exert our national will to its fullest extent. Just because we've suffered a setback or two, there's no reason to abandon in the jungles and rice paddies of Vietnam, the principles of greatness, freedom and courage that have marked this country since its birth . . ."

As his father continued to elaborate his views with ringing phrases, Joseph was seized with a sudden urge to rise from his seat and excuse himself from the rest of the interview. Because he had flown directly to London to see Naomi after his discharge from the hospital in Saigon and stayed until they married, he and his father had not met for well over a year, and the discovery on the air that the senator's views and attitudes had not been modified in the least by the deaths of Guy and Gary shocked and saddened him. He found himself wondering illogically whether the senator remained resolutely deaf to the growing body of antiwar opinion out of real conviction or because he couldn't bear to concede that the son with whom he'd been at loggerheads all his life might this time have right on his side. As the resonant drawl of his father's voice continued, Joseph began to fear too that the three-way interview might in the end reveal more about the lifelong differences between them than about his advocacy of disengagement in Vietnam, and as he turned his attention back to what was being said from Washington, he realized to his horror that the senator's reply had already become acutely personal.

". . . Perhaps I should make it clear that my son Joseph and I haven't always seen eye to eye," he was saying, still smiling engagingly to take the sting from his words. "Vietnam isn't the first topic we've fallen out on. Temperamentally Joseph has always been more inclined to compromise than I have, so the line he's taken in this book doesn't really come as that much of a surprise — although I'm sorry to find a son of mine advocating that we should cut and run from a war in a way that will bring humiliation down on our country."

The anchorman, sensing the tension that had been growing in Joseph during his father's response, decided to interject no question. Instead he merely raised an eyebrow and turned an open palm in his direction, indicating that he was free to reply.

"I'd like to try to confine my comments to the issues," said Joseph in a strained voice. "And I think the most dangerous idea of all is the one that says we should try harder militarily. If we put a million American troops into South Vietnam, they would cause even more devastation and destroy what's left of the country. Our air attacks against North Vietnam don't contribute anything at all towards military success in the South, they don't protect our troops in any meaningful way, and they've made the people of North Vietnam even more determined to endure and defeat us . . ."

Before the British journalist had time to intervene, Nathaniel Sherman cut in sharply. "My disagreement, sir, with those remarks is total. If we're to confront Communist aggression successfully, we need to be resolute and call on all the strength of our great land. The people of Virginia whom I represent, like the vast majority of the American people, are patriots. Many thousands like me have lost sons and grandsons in Vietnam. Like me they don't believe it's wrong to oppose Communism, like me they believe the Vietnamese aggressors should be punished." He paused again, and his eyes glittered with the ardor of his words. "They aren't like my son! To them, pride in their country isn't a sin!"

Joseph stiffened in his chair, glaring up at the screen on which his father's picture was projected. "I've never condemned anyone simply for being proud of their country or opposing Communism," he said sharply. "But the kind of false, stubborn pride which makes it impossible for a man or a nation to admit they're wrong should be seen for what it is — a recipe for disaster!"

In Washington, Nathaniel Sherman drew thoughtfully on a long cigar that he'd just lit and considered its glowing end for a moment or two when the *Panorama* anchorman invited him to make a concluding comment. Then he glanced up at the camera again and the sorrowful smile that had flitted across his face throughout the discussion returned. "Sir, it won't be lost on anybody who reads *The American Betrayal* that all references to the enemy leaders Ho Chi Minh and General Giap are couched in respectful terms. The book also points out how its author met and worked alongside those men during his time with the OSS in Indochina in 1945. Some reviewers here in the United States have concluded that these influences have remained stronger in the writer's mind than more recent events, and others have pointed out that the book was published at a time when its author had already left the United States to live in Britain. One, I believe, even suggested the title referred more appropriately to the author's decision to turn his back on his own proud national heritage than to anything America was doing in Vietnam to halt the spread of Communism across the world." The senator paused and drew long on the cigar, then smiled into the lens of the camera once more. "As the author is my son, I'd like to be able to refute the accusations of those critics — but in all honesty I have to confess that on the face of it, they seem to have a point or two."

Because he was seething with anger, Joseph found himself unable to look at the screen which showed the still-smiling face of his father; knowing the camera was on him, he tried to hide his feelings, but his face turned pale and his knuckles whitened on the arms of his chair.

"Do you wish to reply to that very briefly, Mr. Sherman?" asked the anchorman hurriedly as the floor manager signaled to him that the fadeout signature tune of the program was about to begin.

Joseph shook his head grimly. "I've got nothing to add."

Before the anchorman could stop him, Joseph rose abruptly from his chair and strode away across the studio into the shadows. Naomi Boyce-Lewis, who had been watching the live transmission anxiously from a position inside the studio door, reached out a consoling hand towards him as he came up to her but he brushed it aside. Flinging the studio doors back on their hinges with a crash, he continued angrily into the darkened corridor outside without breaking his stride.

The program director, taken aback at first by Joseph's abrupt departure, recovered in time to order a cameraman to continue filming Joseph's dramatically empty chair; behind it loomed the satellite-borne image of Senator Nathaniel Sherman, and he remained resolutely under the glare of the studio lights in Washington, puffing on his cigar and smiling confidently at the camera until the credits had finished rolling.

19

Scores of buses parked bumper to bumper had been drawn up around the curbs outside the White House like covered wagons formed into a ring of siege in the old West. But instead of screaming Red Indians advancing on this barricade of transports in the heart of Washington, through the driving midnight hail and sleet of Friday, November 14, 1969, came a silent column of mourning Americans carrying guttering candles shielded inside little plastic drinking cups. They marched to the slow doleful beat of muffled drums, the last of forty thousand peace demonstrators taking part in a forty-hour "March Against Death," each one wearing around his or her neck a hand-lettered placard bearing the name of an American who had been killed in the war in Vietnam or a Vietnamese village that had been destroyed. Mark Sherman walked stiffly among them, moving like a zombie, his mouth open, a glazed and vacuous expression fixed on his face; the expression could have been interpreted as either a smile or a grimace of pain, and one of the anxious march organizers, noticing this, developed a worried frown when he saw a television cameraman filming the marchers up ahead. He hurried to the side of Mark's mother, who was walking with him, and whispered urgently in her ear. After he had moved away, Tempe put an arm gently around her son's shoulders and talked to him soothingly for several moments as though to a child; gradually, as he listened, his features slackened and he walked on, gazing expressionlessly ahead through the freezing rain.

On the placard hung with string around Mark's neck, the hand-painted letters of his brother Gary's name had begun to run and blur in the wet; Tempe's placard was daubed with the name of "Quang To," the village where he had died, and Joseph Sherman marched stolidly at his younger son's other shoulder, carrying a sign bearing Guy's name in full and the date of the raid on the Saigon embassy. Never by nature a political activist, Joseph had agreed to travel from England to take part in the rally only after Tempe had contacted him to say that because the event was likely to turn into the biggest political demonstration ever assembled in the United States, Mark was insisting on taking part. She had told Joseph she was worried about Mark's mental state, which had been deteriorating steadily since his release twelve months before; because he was the grandson of Senator Nathaniel Sherman and the son of the author of the most celebrated anti-Vietnam war book, he was being taken up with increasing enthusiasm by some activists in the peace movement.

Mark had gone to live with Tempe and her second husband on his return home, and his moods, she had told Joseph, were now fluctuating sharply between withdrawn sullenness and sudden lapses into half-demented rages. When he spoke of the war, he invariably condemned it in terms reminiscent of the confessions broadcast while he was still a prisoner in Hanoi, but he had

667

steadfastly refused to reveal anything at all about his imprisonment, either to air force analysts or the several psychiatrists called in by Joseph and Tempe after his discharge from the service. He had adopted the practice of accepting all the invitations he received to attend peace rallies and flew into uncontrollable fits of temper if anyone tried to stop him; as a result he had become an enigmatic and tragic public figure, and his presence at a number of peace demonstrations had been exploited to the full. From time to time as he strode along beside his son, Joseph glanced round at him ready to give a friendly smile of encouragement, but Mark showed the same indifference to him that he had done ever since his release and kept his head turned to the front. Even when Joseph tried to pass a conversational remark about the weather or the landmarks they were passing, he continued pointedly to ignore him.

Mark, Tempe and Joseph, along with a small group of other people related to men who had died in Vietnam, were marching in a special delegation around the angular, silver-haired figure of Dr. Benjamin Spock; a celebrated pediatrician who through his famous book on child care had counseled a whole generation of parents on how to bring up their young, Dr. Spock had become a prominent and passionate critic of the war that was claiming the lives of thousands of those young male adults he had helped guide successfully through the dangers of infancy. Now in the fall of 1969 he had suddenly become a symbolic father figure to the peace movement that was attracting growing numbers of young, white middle-class demonstrators and since dusk the previous day he had been leading the nonstop "March Against Death" through the nation's capital. Half-a-million other demonstrators who were flooding into Washington by road, rail and air were due to bring the demonstration to its climax with a rally around the Washington Monument the next day, and Joseph had agreed to address the throng alongside other celebrities from show business, the arts and politics; the somber, two-day protest march was being staged as a dramatic prelude to that rally, and for more than thirty hours little files of up to one hundred peaceful demonstrators had been setting out every few minutes from the Arlington National Cemetery on the southern bank of the Potomac River and butting across the windy Memorial Bridge on the first leg of their pilgrimage, shielding their guttering candles with their bodies as they went. Their four-mile trek took them along Constitution Avenue to the fence bordering the South Portico of the White House, and there within earshot of President Richard Nixon they were pausing to call out the names of the dead Americans written on the placards around their necks. This act of mourning for men who were total strangers to most of the demonstrators had caused tears to mingle with the rain on the cheeks of many of them, and they plodded on along Pennsylvania Avenue, visibly moved, before their eyes turned towards their next goal — the floodlit dome of the Capitol that floated like a pale ghost in the icy darkness above the city. Beneath the rotunda on the west lawn, twelve unvarnished pine-plank coffins were drawn up on trestles under floodlights, and there the marchers were stopping to remove the placards from their necks and place them reverently in the caskets in a poignant act of remembrance; at the same time they were also snuffing out the individual candles they had carried from Arlington to commemorate the forty-five thousand American lives that had been lost far away in Asia, and often the finality of this act caused fresh weeping among the men as well as the girls and women taking part.

As the Spock group approached the circle of bus barricades around the White House just after midnight on Friday, Tempe shot an anxious warning look at Joseph and moved close to Mark to take his arm. Joseph moved closer too and took his other elbow; Tempe had earlier confided to Joseph her fear that the calling of Gary's name might prove to be a moment of high emotional intensity for Mark, and they had agreed to do what they could to distract him. Flurries of icy rain were blowing in their faces as they approached the spot opposite the second-floor windows of the White House where other demonstrators ahead of them were already calling out names of the dead; the male voices tended to be hoarse and angry, those of the girls and women, softer, more restrained, but as the sad rhythm of the chants and the funeral drumbeats grew louder, Joseph felt his son grow tense at his side.

At first Mark complied with the strict orders of the march organizers; he stopped at the appointed place in the single-file line and turned to face the White House. He yelled "Gary Sherman! Charles County, Virginia!" in a loud, despairing voice then fell obediently silent while first Joseph then Tempe stopped to call out the names of Guy Sherman and Quang To village. But when one of the marshals supervising the protest motioned to Mark to move on, he appeared not to hear; the marshal called again more loudly and stepped towards him, but Mark would not turn and march away. His refusal immediately disrupted the steady, disciplined flow of the line, and the rhythm of the protest broke down. Both Joseph and Tempe tried to urge him on with gentle words, but suddenly he broke free from them and began screaming Gary's name over and over in a high-pitched, hysterical voice. At the same time he flung himself towards the White House railings and leaped to grab hold of the spikes at the top. For a moment or two he swung there, still screaming, then somehow managed to turn to face the other marchers, hanging by his arms from the top of the fence; several marshals converged rapidly on him and tried to pull him down, but he kicked and fought savagely to drive them off, and continued to hang spreadeagled from the top bars, his writhing body silhouetted against the backdrop of the floodlit White House.

Television kliegs added their glare to the scene as camera crews and news photographers arrived to record the incident and the marshals gave up trying to pull him off the fence by force. Joseph tried quietly to persuade his son to come down, but Mark ignored his efforts completely; Tempe also pleaded with him unsuccessfully for several minutes before giving up. In the end three policemen had to hammer repeatedly at his fingers with their nightsticks to break his grip on the railings and when he finally fell sobbing to the ground, only the intervention of a senior march marshal, who explained quietly to the police who Mark was, prevented his arrest.

Tempe, watched helplessly by Joseph, tried to talk Mark out of completing the march when he'd recovered, but with a sullen insistence he continued along Pennsylvania Avenue to the Capitol, occasionally sucking his bleeding fingers as he stumbled through the rain. In front of the pine caskets he had difficulty untangling the placard with Gary's name from his neck, and the white board became daubed with blood from his hands. Tempe, with tears in her eyes, finally lowered the placard into the coffin for him, and he stood staring at it for a long time. When his mother gently touched his elbow, he remembered the candle he carried for Gary and snuffed it out very slowly with his own fingers. Tempe tried to lead him away then, but he insisted on staying, and as fresh lines of marchers arrived at the coffins, Mark stepped forward to snuff out each of their candles in turn. He held his fingers in the flames longer each time before extinguishing them, and when Tempe finally was able to persuade him to leave, the skin of one hand had become blackened and charred.

"There's an awful lot, Tempe, that I'd have to apologize to you for if I ever got started," said Joseph sadly as he looked down at Mark's sleeping face. "If I hadn't been so damned stupid, maybe none of this would have happened."

"What do you mean?" Tempe asked the question in a barely audible whisper.

"If I hadn't left you, I don't think either of my sons would have chosen the careers they did. Perhaps Gary wouldn't be dead and Mark wouldn't be . . ." His voice trailed off, and they both stood looking down at Mark's pale, pinched face.

They had arrived back at his father's old Georgetown mansion just before two A.M., and a doctor close to the family had been summoned immediately to tend Mark's hands and administer a heavy sedative. The senator had been staying at the plantation house in Charles County for several weeks, and Joseph had suggested taking Mark to Georgetown after the demonstration to avoid the embarrassment of his meeting Tempe's husband. Before leaving, the doctor had told him that the sedation he had administered would ensure that Mark slept for at least twelve hours, and he had agreed to return later to examine him again. As he lay asleep before them, the gaunt, unnatural cast of Mark's features and his unhealthy pallor made him look more of an invalid than ever before, and Tempe had to close her eyes to blot out the sight.

"You put too much blame on yourself, Joseph," she said quietly as she turned away. "Haven't you ever thought that Gary's temperament made the army an ideal choice for him — and that Mark might have wanted to fly in the beginning because you were a pilot?"

"But that was something forced on me — I would never have gone in for flying if the war hadn't come along."

"I know," said Tempe, "but those old 'Flying Tiger' pictures that he saw all over the house when he was a boy caught his imagination. And one day he found this in a drawer and asked me if he could have it." She turned towards him, opening her hand, and Joseph stared at the old rabbit's foot lying on her palm. "He never went anywhere without it — and he was still carrying it with him tonight."

Joseph gazed at her in astonishment, and when she turned and walked from the bedroom he followed her in silence. In the drawing room she sank down wearily on a chesterfield and closed her eyes. In middle age her hair had begun to turn gray and her face was pale with fatigue, but she was still a handsome, composed woman, and despite her obvious distress Joseph couldn't help noticing that her air of calm good sense hadn't deserted her.

"I'm truly glad, Tempe, that you found happiness with someone else," he said quietly. "You deserve it."

She didn't reply or open her eyes to look at him, and at that moment a maid entered the room bringing the late edition of the *Washington Post* that was always delivered direct to the house from the *Post*'s plant by private messenger on the senator's orders. As she laid the newspaper on a low table, Joseph caught sight of the photograph on the front page, and he rose hurriedly to pick it up so that Tempe wouldn't see it.

The stark image of Mark spreadeagled in an attitude of crucifixion against the floodlit façade of the White House had been blown up to cover four columns, and the caption writer hadn't missed the tragic symbolism inherent in the picture. Joseph turned aside from Tempe and stood staring at the photograph, scarcely noticing the sound of a telephone ringing in the hall; when the maid came back to tell Tempe that there was a call for her, he didn't look up. A few moments later she returned to the room and came to stand beside him.

"That call was from the plantation house, Joseph," she said shakily. "It's your father — he's had a stroke. The doctor says he won't live more than a few hours, and he's asking for you to go to him."

Joseph stared at her blankly and said nothing.

"My car's outside," said Tempe softly. "I'll drive you there if you want."

20

Senator Nathaniel Sherman lay dying in the Robert E. Lee bed when Joseph and Tempe arrived at the plantation house overlooking the James River just after five o'clock in the morning. The left side of his body had become partially paralyzed as a result of the stroke, and his face had been affected, but he had remained aware enough of his surroundings to order the household staff to carry him to the east river view bedroom and put him in the historic four-poster in which the celebrated Confederate general had often slept.

"Taking his chance to play to the gallery for the last time, I suppose," commented Joseph grimly when his sister, Susannah, who greeted him at the door, directed him up the great staircase of carved walnut.

Susannah had frowned even while embracing him, then she'd led Tempe away to the drawing room so that he could go up alone. Although the news that his father was dying had not moved him unduly in Washington, the sight of the stricken body propped up on a bank of white pillows in the canopied bed shocked him when he entered the room. The old man's eyes were closed and he appeared to be sleeping, but the stroke had dragged down the left side of his face, making it grotesque; his cheeks were shrunken yellow hollows, and in comparison the old tentacles of scar tissue from the hunting accident stood out white and livid on his face and neck in the dull glow of a single bedside lamp. To Joseph they looked like grasping fingers spreading up from the wound that had severed his left arm, and the new facial disfigurement on that same side made him think that whatever malevolent force had inflicted the original injuries was now reaching out to snatch away the final prize that had eluded it so many years before.

Joseph shuddered at the thought and sat down on a chair already in place beside the bed; the nurse who had been on duty in the room tiptoed out, closing the door soundlessly behind her, and as he sat alone staring at the piteously sunken face, he wasn't surprised to find that the natural compassion he would have felt for any dying man was mixed, in the case of his own father, with feelings of anger. The memory of their bitter clash on television only months before was still painfully fresh in his mind and a clear sight of the hunting scars brought back with surprising force the sense of outrage he'd experienced on learning the true story behind Chuck's death.

During the drive from Washington, he had wondered several times whether he would find his father conscious; he had wondered, too, whether he would have one last chance to do what he had always failed to do before — confront him with his knowledge of Chuck's death. He had always felt vaguely that he owed it to Chuck, to the memory of his courage and good sense, to force some admission of guilt or regret from his father, and his failure to act on this impulse over the years had sometimes weighed heavily on his conscience. In the coldest moments of his anger he had also contemplated revealing the truth about Guy — but loyalty to his dead mother and the promise he'd made her had always stopped him. As the minutes ticked by at the bedside, he found himself wondering again whether he would have the courage to speak the truth if the dying man regained consciousness.

Lost in his own thoughts, Joseph failed at first to notice when his father's eyes opened, and it was the sound of his trying to speak that brought him back to the present with a start. Then he saw that his left eyelid, because of the paralysis, drooped over the iris, forcing him to squint at him with his right eye. The left side of his mouth drooped too, making clear speech difficult, and his first words were strangled and incoherent.

"Don't try to talk," said Joseph quietly. He was appalled by the disintegration taking place before his eyes, and he searched his mind frantically for some shred of comfort that he might offer. "Trust you to take to the old Robert E. Lee," he said, forcing a smile to his lips. "I guess you figured they'll have to rename it the 'Nathaniel Sherman Bed' now, huh?"

He didn't think his words had been heard at first, but suddenly the misshapen features on the snowy pillow lit up with an expression of delight and the head nodded feebly in agreement; then the smile faded as soon as it had come. "I'm going, Joseph . . . I know it." His speech was still slurred, but by bending closer, Joseph could make out his meaning. "That's why I wanted to talk to you." He lifted his remaining hand slowly from beneath the sheet and held it towards him, and Joseph took it reluctantly in both his own. "We've had our differences, Joseph," he continued in a croaking voice, "but I asked you to come because I wanted you to know . . . before I go, that I don't hold it against you . . . for disagreeing with me in public . . . There's no bad blood . . . I didn't want you to have that on your conscience."

Joseph stared wonderingly at his father. The fingers of his hand felt cold and limp, as if they might already be dead, but even the imminence of death had not dented the senator's unassailable arrogance. He had called him to his deathbed to offer forgiveness when he himself had condemned his own son in public with unpardonable and illogical bitterness.

"We've always had our differences, Father," said Joseph grimly.

The dying man nodded, gazing back at him with the one rheumy eye. "You were always different from Chuck and Guy . . . More sensitive, I guess . . . more like your mother . . . You always seemed far away from me." The cold hand twitched weakly in Joseph's grasp. "But you're strong in other ways. You're the only one who's survived. Chuck and Guy are dead . . ."

Joseph saw his chance and leaned closer suddenly. "Has the burden of Chuck's death been hard for you to bear all these years?"

The good eye fell closed, and for a moment the senator's ragged breathing was the only sound in the room. "I tried to save him. . . . I did everything I could . . ." The eyelid fluttered and the exposed eye gazed blearily at him. "You know that, Joseph, don't you?"

Joseph gazed back at his father in disbelief; then after a moment he turned his face away towards the uncurtained window. "Chuck had what it takes . . . He was strong . . . so damned strong and determined . . . he had the will to succeed — that's why his death was such a terrible loss. Never forget that, Joseph, will you? I guess he was a little headstrong . . . Like his old father . . . Like his brother Guy . . . But that's not the worst fault a man can have, I don't reckon."

His voice was rambling, rising and falling on each painful breath, and Joseph, feeling the anger in him reach a new peak, let go of his father's hand and stood up. "You're wrong to compare Chuck with Guy," he said in a whisper so fierce that it caused the dying face to turn quickly towards him. "You're more wrong than you've ever known."

The solitary eye regarded Joseph directly for a moment, then seemed to cloud over. "I know . . . I know . . . You don't have to tell me that, Joseph . . . there was never anybody to touch Chuck, was there? Nobody at all!"

A grimace of pain contorted his face suddenly and his head began rolling back and forth on the pillow. As he watched his father suffering his death agonies, Joseph felt the anger rush out of him like air from a deflated balloon, and the urge to wound was replaced in the same instant by an intense feeling of pity. Nathaniel Sherman had misled others for so long about his role in the death of his favorite son that in the end he might even have come to believe his own lies. Perhaps he'd had to do that to make his grief bearable, thought Joseph, but either way he remained impregnable behind the walls of his own illusions, as lonely and isolated as he lay dying as he had been all his life in the midst of his own family.

As he stood watching life fade from the stricken body, another thought struck Joseph with sickening force: he was not so different himself from the man he had been at odds with all his life. He had imagined himself wronged and misunderstood as a boy by a blind, insensitive father who had continued to see life simply through the eyes of ancestors who had tamed the raw, wild lands of America by unrelenting physical determination. He had always imagined that his own more sensitive nature was superior, yet he too in his turn had set his own sons and his brother Guy against himself; his own foolish romantic idealism had led him to believe that nothing was impossible if a man responded honestly to the innermost urgings of his soul, if he set his love of truth above all things — but these beliefs had brought disaster on himself in his own life that had exceeded even the scale of his father's.

Saddened more by these thoughts than by his father's imminent death, Joseph turned his back on the bed suddenly and walked across the room to the window. For a long time he stood looking out over the darkened boxwood lawns towards the river; the night was moonless but light from the uncurtained window on the ground floor cast a faint glow into the garden, and as his eyes accustomed themselves to the darkness he fancied he saw someone moving among the trees. But although he stared hard into the shadows, he couldn't be certain the light hadn't played a trick on him.

Standing there, he remembered how only two or three hours before he had stood beside another bed in Georgetown looking down at the face of his only surviving son who was as lost and remote from him now as his dying father, and he shivered involuntarily; dimly he became aware that in the four-poster behind him, the passage of air in and out of his father's lungs was becoming more noisy and labored, but something prevented him from turning around. Then a long, harsh, high-pitched scream split the darkness of the garden outside and Joseph recoiled instinctively as a dark shape rose from the blackness of the box-woods and soared upwards, passing close across the face of the window. The peacock screamed again as it settled on the chimney stack above the room, and its repeated cries rang eerily in the flue that rose from the big fireplace beside the bed. A shower of soot tumbled noisily into the hearth, and Joseph heard clearly the dry rattling sound of the peacock spreading the spines of its tail on the chimney top.

A moment later the rhythm of his father's breathing was interrupted suddenly; a long choking cough racked him and his breath gurgled loudly in his throat like water. Joseph rushed to the bedside, fell to his knees and seized the old man's hand again; the desire to utter some final words of consolation welled up in him with such force that tears started to his eyes — but he gazed in vain into the face that was now clenched and contorted in agony. Clearly beyond hearing or seeing, the senator's whole frame was trembling; then abruptly all movement ceased and the spent, white body seemed to sink and melt into the snowy pillows.

Joseph remained motionless on his knees beside the bed for a minute or two, holding the limp lifeless hand; then he rose and walked quietly to the door. On the landing outside he found Tempe waiting with one hand pressed to her mouth.

"What was that awful noise, Joseph?" she asked in a horrified whisper.

"Just one of the peacocks flying up to the chimney." He reached out and took her hand, relieved to find it warm to his touch. "There's nothing to worry about — he's gone."

PART EIGHT

Victory and Defeat

1972–1975

Richard Nixon won the presidential election of November 1968 largely on the strength of his campaign pledge to "end the war and win the peace" in Vietnam. This promise seemed highly attractive to an American nation that had been deeply shocked by the scale of the Tet Offensive the previous February; the Communist offensive, because it exploded the myth that the war was being won, left President Johnson's Vietnam policies in ruins and contributed directly to his decision not to run again for the presidency, but during the four years of his first term, President Nixon used his ambiguous campaign pledge to spread and escalate the war against Communism in Indochina. He ordered brief invasions of Cambodia and Laos, bombed those two countries over a longer period, resumed the bombing of North Vietnam halted by President Johnson, and eventually mined the approaches to the harbor of Haiphong in an attempt to stop seaborne supplies from the Soviet Union reaching North Vietnam. To pacify public opinion while intensifying the war in these new directions, he scaled down the country's direct involvement by gradually withdrawing American ground troops from Vietnam and arming, supplying and training a greatly expanded South Vietnamese army — a policy he called "Vietnamization." Contrived to satisfy both "doves" and "hawks" alike, this policy gradually cooled the passions of the most fervent antiwar protesters — those students who feared they would be drafted to Vietnam if the war continued until their deferments expired. In March 1969, some 540,000 American troops were fighting in Vietnam, but this peak figure was reduced by stages until only 27,000 "advisers" remained at the end of 1972. The policy of "Vietnamization" expanded President Thieu's army to a strength of more than a million men and increased the flood of American money and war materials into Saigon, but this did nothing to solve the chronic political and social problems that made South Vietnam so vulnerable to a Communist takeover; the new enlarged army was seen by the largely peasant population as a bigger and better force for terror and oppression, and the increased flow of aid led to greater corruption among the country's military rulers. The invasions of Cambodia and Laos in 1970 and 1971 by mixed American and South Vietnamese forces were designed to strike at Communist bases and supply routes, but neither met with much success; the large-scale bombing of these two countries bordering Vietnam also had tragic results, killing unknown numbers of their peasants, turning millions into refugees and ultimately hastening their fall to Communism in 1975. Although President Nixon succeeded in extracting American ground forces from the conflict step by step, 20,000 American fighting men were killed in Vietnam while he was commander in chief, and in the first two years of his presidency he dropped more bombs on Indochina than the United States had dropped in Europe and the Pacific in World War II. By May 1972 some three thousand tons of bombs were falling each day on Indochina at a daily cost of $20 million — but still the war dragged on. By then the remaining American troops fought only with great reluctance; drug-taking became rife in the ranks, and officers were frequently attacked by enlisted men with fragmentation grenades. The soldiers' attitudes were conditioned by the growing mood of disenchantment with the war at home which had been heightened dramatically by two separate events — the revelation in November 1969 that three hundred Vietnamese civilians had been massacred eighteen months earlier by American troops at the village of My Lai, and the publication in the summer of 1971 of leaked secret documents which became known as the Pentagon Papers. The Pentagon Papers were a detailed government study of American involvement in

Vietnam between 1945 and 1968, and they revealed most dramatically the extent of President Kennedy's intervention in the plot to overthrow Ngo Dinh Diem, and the dubious background to the Gulf of Tonkin Resolution which, it became clear, had been prepared in advance of the North Vietnamese attacks of August 1964 to give President Johnson a free hand to make war in Vietnam without a formal war declaration. Above all, the Pentagon Papers were a staggering catalogue of how Presidents Kennedy and Johnson had deliberately deceived the American people over Vietnam and they turned public attention increasingly to the long-drawn-out peace talks which had begun in Paris in May 1968. Elaborate and infinitely complex, the negotiations, which were to last five years, were often used by both sides for propaganda purposes, but they always centered around one issue: who should govern in Saigon. What began as talks between American and North Vietnamese diplomats were expanded later to include representatives of President Thieu's government and the National Liberation Front but something akin to a permanent stalemate was quickly reached; Hanoi and the Liberation Front demanded as their price for peace a complete American withdrawal and representation for the Front in a coalition government in South Vietnam, but President Thieu refused to countenance the idea of a coalition. As the talking continued inconclusively in Paris, the war went on, and in the spring of 1972, General Vo Nguyen Giap pushed three of North Vietnam's best divisions into South Vietnam supported by tanks and artillery. In response to this new offensive, President Nixon ordered giant American B-52 bombers to attack the regions around Hanoi and Haiphong for the first time since 1968 and he also seeded the Gulf of Tongking with mines to blockade Haiphong Harbor. The Communist thrust into South Vietnam lost momentum as a result and eventually the renewed American bombing and the mining of Haiphong forced the Communist leadership in Hanoi to modify their peace demands. In early October 1972 they dropped their insistence that the National Liberation Front be included immediately in a coalition government in Saigon; instead, in return for a cease-fire and an American withdrawal, they proposed that the government of President Thieu should continue temporarily in office while a joint "Council of National Reconciliation" discussed the problems of cooperation in the South. With the American presidential election due in November, President

Nixon and his National Security Adviser, Dr. Henry Kissinger, were anxious to clinch an early agreement — but President Thieu denounced the new proposals as a "disguised coalition" and refused to cooperate. Despite this setback, a partial bombing halt was observed by the United States in response and Dr. Kissinger ringingly declared that peace was "at hand" during a dramatic press conference in Washington on October 26. Two weeks later, on a wave of peace optimism, President Nixon was reelected for a second term by a landslide majority, but when the talks in Paris were resumed shortly after the election, they foundered again without any clear explanation being given as to what was holding up an agreement. President Nixon's critics promptly accused him of exploiting the peace talks for his own electoral advantage, and when the delegates began reassembling once more at the beginning of December in the anonymous villa in the suburbs of Paris where they had met over the years, there was an unprecedented mood of tension and expectation among the journalists waiting in the wintry streets outside. Their thoughts, like those of the delegates, were turned to peace, and with Christmas approaching, few of them anticipated the bloody act of wholesale destruction that would be carried out before American forces finally bowed out of Vietnam.

1

Joseph Sherman turned up the collar of his overcoat against the chill December wind blowing along the Avenue de Général Leclerc in Gif-sur-Yvette and stamped his feet to warm them. With thirty other journalists and photographers of many different nationalities, he was awaiting the arrival of Henry Kissinger, and as he stood there, shoulders hunched against the cold, he reflected that the setting for the final confrontation between the United States and its Vietnamese enemies was as surprising and bizarre as everything else had been during the baffling war that had spanned an entire decade. The whitewashed artist's cottage with its orange-tiled roof and green shutters, outside which the journalists had gathered, was an anonymous little dwelling standing behind stucco walls on the edge of the sleepy suburban town fifteen miles from the center of Paris; its address was 108 Avenue de Général Leclerc and it had first been chosen as a venue for peace talks late in 1969 when Dr. Kissinger and Hanoi's chief negotiator, Le Duc Tho, began holding secret meetings away from the public gaze focused on the formal peace negotiations taking place in the grandiose French government conference chamber on the Avenue Kleber. Originally owned by a left-wing French artist, Fernand Léger, the cottage had been bequeathed on his death to the French Communist Party which Ho Chi Minh had helped to found in the 1920s. Most prominent Vietnamese Communists of the older generation had cut their revolutionary teeth in Paris in the 'twenties and 'thirties and bonds of friendship developed then with French Communists still held in the 1970s; so the party had willingly loaned the painter's cottage to Hanoi as a diplomatic hideaway, and during the closing months of 1972, it had become the most frequently used of three North Vietnamese houses in and around Paris.

From conversations with acquaintances in the State Department, Joseph knew that framed cubist abstracts by Fernand Léger still hung on the walls of the long main room where a rectangular green baize table had been set up, and the American delegation always found little bottles of French mineral water and glasses set out in front of their half-dozen chairs whenever they arrived. In the days when the venue was still secret, Kissinger had often stepped across the threshold breathless after a 100 m.p.h.

dash through suburban Paris to throw off pursuing reporters, but since its location was now known, he had become accustomed to arriving more grandly in a white rented Mercedes, flanked by French police motorcycle outriders.

At that same green baize table on October 8, Kissinger had listened with barely suppressed excitement as Le Duc Tho abruptly reversed four long years of stubborn intransigence and told him that his government was ready at last to agree to a cessation of hostilities. Hanoi would release its American prisoners, he had said, in return for an undertaking that President Nixon would withdraw all remaining U.S. troops and allow South Vietnam to work out its own political future. This amounted to a virtual acceptance of earlier American proposals, and the absence of the habitual Communist demand for the National Liberation Front to be admitted into a coalition government in Saigon had electrified the Americans present. They realized that the North Vietnamese had their eyes fixed firmly on the date for the American presidential election, then one month away, and obviously expected to be able to pressure President Nixon into settling quickly so as to gain maximum advantage at the polls — but otherwise the sincerity of the Hanoi delegates seemed beyond doubt.

Two nerve-wracking months, however, had passed since that day. President Nixon had been reelected, but President Thieu had refused to give his approval to the deal, and when the negotiations resumed in mid-November, according to Joseph's informants, the Americans had found that the Communists had returned inexplicably to their old stubborn uncooperative ways. The American delegation had tried to persuade the Communists to meet some of President Thieu's objections but had made no headway at all, and Joseph was told that there had been no alternative but to break off the talks. Since the resumption on December 4, the new session had dragged on for ten days, and in their contacts with the journalists since then, the baffled American negotiators had admitted that they were becoming increasingly frustrated by the rude and sometimes contemptuous time-wasting tactics of the Communists.

The journalists had erected their own scaffold in the street opposite the cottage so that they could see over the wall into the garden around it, and occasionally in breaks between the talks they had caught glimpses of Kissinger or Le Duc Tho strolling and chatting with aides beneath the bare trees. Atmospheric pictures had been taken of them with telephoto lenses, but the windows of the cottage had always remained draped with frilled net curtains which successfully concealed those inside from the journalists' gaze. Covering the talks in this way was a frustrating assignment, but because hopes for a settlement were high, Joseph, like the others, had stuck doggedly to the task for the past ten days.

Flurries of sleet were beginning to dance in the cold wind on that afternoon of December 13 when the Kissinger entourage finally drove up the avenue and swung into the cottage garden past solid steel gates that were immediately slammed shut behind their cars. A dumpy figure in a white raincoat and heavy-rimmed spectacles, Henry Kissinger strode stern-faced to the front door of the cottage without acknowledging the appeals from the journalists on their scaffold to stop and pose for a photograph. Joseph, like all the other correspondents, was watching intently to see if the austere, white-haired figure of Le Duc Tho would appear to greet Kissinger at the door, and because his attention was fully absorbed, he didn't notice the curtains at an upper window shift briefly. In the event, Le Duc Tho made no appearance, and a buzz of disappointed comment rose from all round the viewing platform as gloomy predictions were exchanged about the early announcement of a cease-fire.

As he watched the journalists conversing from his place beside the window in one of the upstairs rooms, Tran Van Kim suddenly snapped his fingers at an aide standing behind him and called for a pair of binoculars. Kim wore the same kind of dark, high-necked tunic as Le Duc Tho, his manner towards the junior members of the North Vietnamese delegation was similarly distant and formal, and when his aide returned with the binoculars, he took them from him impatiently. He adjusted the lenses with care until the group of journalists on the scaffold came sharply into focus, then he stared hard at one of the faces.

"Fetch a list of the correspondents covering the talks," he said quietly to his aide at last without turning round. "Check particularly to see if there is an American named 'Sherman' among them. And hurry!"

The aide hastened from the room and returned a few minutes later bearing a sheaf of papers. "Yes, Comrade Kim," he said breathlessly, "there is a 'Joseph Sherman' among the listed Americans." He held out a telephoto close-up of Joseph taken by one of the delegation's intelligence operatives, and Kim eagerly took it from him. As Kim studied the picture, the aide began reading dutifully from Joseph's dossier.

"Professor of Asian studies at Cornell University, 1954 to 1967; senior adviser to the U.S. Joint Public Affairs Office in Saigon for three months, January to March 1968; thereafter resigned and wrote a book entitled *The American Betrayal* criticizing United States policy in Vietnam . . ."

"Yes, yes," broke in Kim testily, "the book's well known. But what's he doing now?"

The aide consulted his list again. "Because of the fame his book has brought him, Joseph Sherman, who is married to a British television journalist and lives in London, has currently been commissioned by *The Times* of London to write a series of special analytical articles on the peace negotiations and the war. So far two have been published." The aide handed over two press clippings attached to another sheet of paper. "At present he's staying at the Intercontinental Hotel at the corner of Rue de Rivoli and the Rue de Castiglione alongside the Tuileries Gardens. His room number is 4567."

Kim read carefully through the clippings, still standing by the window, then he sat down at a desk and pulled a blank sheet of paper towards him. With a ball-point pen that he took from a breast pocket of his tunic, he wrote in French in his own hand: "I have spotted you outside among the journalists. I will meet you at 7.30 A.M. tomorrow inside the gate of the Tuileries at the foot of Rue de Castiglione. Perhaps you would be interested to hear some news of your daughter, Tuyet — and the inside story of the deceitful intrigues which Kissinger and the American negotiators are pursuing inside this house — Tran Van Kim."

Kim sealed the note in an envelope and handed it to the aide. "Call one of our journalists on his car radio and ask him to come to the back of the house immediately. Give him this letter to deliver to Sherman. Tell him I shall be watching from the window."

When the leather-jacketed French Communist reporter, who was a stranger to Joseph, handed him the envelope on the scaffold, Tran Van Kim was able to see the frown of puzzlement that crossed the American's face. He watched him read the note but when Joseph raised his eyes to stare in surprise towards the cottage, Kim was careful to stand well back behind the net curtains so that he couldn't be seen. From the room below, the drone of Henry Kissinger's voice was clearly audible, speaking English with guttural German inflections; it rose and fell in blunt, irritated cadences as the National Security Adviser told an expressionless Le Duc Tho that because the North Vietnamese delegation was obviously now stalling and resorting to trickery for some ulterior motive, the United States was not prepared to continue the discussions and the negotiations were therefore suspended.

2

Tran Van Kim waved an arm vaguely towards the hosts of stone warriors, goddesses and orators fast becoming visible on the columned walls of the Palais du Louvre in the growing light. "The French, Monsieur Sherman, are a classic example of a people too clever for their own good," he said contemptuously as he walked beside Joseph through the light powdering of snow that covered the Tuileries Gardens. "I hope the same will not turn out to be true of the Americans." He flashed a brittle smile at Joseph, then quickly turned his head away again. "The French, you see, have never been able to contain the exuberance of their own conceit. Is it surprising that the poor people of Paris, confronted daily with these overlarge, overdecorated palaces, should have risen up in anger to cut off the heads of those insufferably arrogant aristocrats who built them? The very existence of such overpowering buildings in their midst was an intolerable provocation. But then the French have always lacked a sense of proportion — that's why they unfailingly exaggerate their own worth."

Joseph dug his hands deeper into his overcoat pockets but didn't reply. The sky was still heavy with snow and the sculpted figures on the massive baroque façades of the Louvre stood out like sentinels in the suffused glow of the dawn. From the Rue de Rivoli and the quays along the Seine the noise of the early morning traffic was only a distant hum, like the buzzing of flies dying with the onset of winter.

"See the angel with the outstretched wings and the clarion," said Kim, pointing to a cornice silhouetted on the south wing. "That is what the French are best at — blowing their own trumpet." He smirked at his own wit and glanced at Joseph. "You've seen the same ostentation on the front of the old Opera House in Saigon — and on the old palaces of the French governors. Their boastful architecture and their overbearing manner in Vietnam had the same effects on my countrymen as these palaces had on the poor people of France — they made us both revolutionaries." The Vietnamese closed his eyes as he walked and sucked the cold air deep into his lungs. "But just the same it's good to be back in Paris after all these years. We shouldn't forget that it was their arrogance and their desire to show off before a humble people that led the French *colons* to bring our best minds here to be educated — and that here we first studied the teachings of Marx and Lenin." He sighed again as he walked. "But despite our differences we still had some things in common. The French and the Vietnamese are both unsentimental people." He glanced quickly at Joseph once more. "Unlike the Americans, of course."

"Talking of being unsentimental, will you take the opportunity to visit your brother, Tam, while you're here?" asked Joseph suddenly. "I'm sure you know he's just arrived to join the Saigon delegation. I talked to him yesterday — it must be over thirty years since you last met." Joseph watched Kim's still deceptively youthful face, but it remained expressionless, and he didn't reply. Although in his late fifties, there was no trace of gray in his dark hair, and his round, almost cherubic, features still bore a strong resemblance to his brother's. "If you do want to talk to Tam, he's taken an apartment at number 3 Avenue Leopold II in the Sixteenth Arrondissement," added Joseph, still watching him carefully. "He once told me that despite the differences between you, he'd never be able to forget that you are his brother."

Kim turned away to gaze across the gardens, and Joseph was unable to see his face. For a while they walked in silence, then Kim shook his head dismissively. "I didn't come to Paris for family reasons, Monsieur Sherman. Nor, as you might imagine, did I come to discuss philosophy and history. I asked you to meet me because I wanted to tell you the real reasons behind the breakdown of the negotiations at Gif-sur-Yvette."

Joseph eyed him suspiciously. "Why tell me?"

"Because you're well known as an authoritative critic of your government — and you're writing now for an influential Western newspaper outside America. If you tell the truth in tomorrow's edition of *The Times*, perhaps the evil plans of your president will be thwarted."

"What 'evil plans' exactly are you talking about?"

Kim took a deep breath and turned to look at the American as they walked. "Soon no doubt your president or Dr. Kissinger will tell the world that we're responsible for breaking off the talks — but the truth is exactly the opposite! We proposed cease-fire terms in early October that amounted to acceptance of an earlier American outline. Kissinger was delighted to agree. Only when the Thieu regime in Saigon was consulted did Kissinger and your president begin to go back on that agreement. It's well known that Thieu would oppose any agreement at all on principle, since his dictatorship will be undermined by the slightest change. But now he's raised no less than sixty-nine objections to our draft proposal — and your president, instead of forcing him to accept the terms already agreed with us, is asking us now to reconsider all sixty-nine points. Nixon and Kissinger seem to fear above all else a public row with their puppet Thieu." He stopped talking, and his eyes glittered angrily. "Now we've just heard through Soviet intelligence sources in Washington that Nixon is preparing to send a massive fleet of bombers against our cities during the Christmas period to force us to accept these new changes — that's the truth behind the breakdown of the talks."

Joseph reflected on Kim's words in silence for a moment. "When did you arrive in Paris, Kim?"

"Only yesterday."

Joseph's expression grew thoughtful. "I wonder if you're telling the truth? Couldn't it be that you and the rest of the Politburo in Hanoi have suddenly realized too late that Le Duc Tho may have been overplaying your hand — and you want to try to use me or someone like me to get you off the hook?" Kim shook his head vigorously but Joseph ignored him. "I'm too long in the tooth not to recognize a deliberate leak when I hear one, Kim. I know you've always believed you'd be able to crack the Thieu regime wide open one day if you pressed hard enough — but if you're getting cold feet now on the idea, I'm not the one to help you. A critic of my government I may be — but I'm no Communist stooge!"

They walked on through the snow in silence, then a calculating expression flitted across the face of the Vietnamese. "Is it of no interest to you then, Monsieur Sherman, if Hanoi is bombed?"

Joseph stopped suddenly in his tracks and looked hard into Kim's face. "What the hell do you mean by that?"

Kim gazed steadily back at him. "Your daughter, Tuyet, and her children have lived in Hanoi for the past four years — or had you forgotten?"

689

Little flurries of powdery snow blew between the two men as they stared at one another; then Joseph took a quick step towards the Vietnamese. " 'Unsentimental' is the right word for you, Kim," he breathed, clenching and unclenching his fists at his sides. "You're so damned 'unsentimental' that common human decency seems to mean nothing to you. Do you think I imagine you had nothing to do with what happened to my son Mark? You and the rest of the Politburo must have sifted through the names of all the U.S. pilots you ever captured to see if there wasn't some political capital to be made out of them. You're nothing if not thorough."

Joseph was shaking with anger, but the Vietnamese remained unruffled. "My comrades and I don't have time to concern ourselves with minor details, Monsieur Sherman. We have many complicated duties to perform."

"I've got 'complicated duties' to perform too," said Joseph grimly. "And they don't include writing disguised propaganda on behalf of the Lao Dong — even under the threat of blackmail." He glared angrily at Kim, then turned abruptly on his heel and stalked away into the thickening snow.

Kim watched him go for a moment, then pulled a notebook from an inside pocket and wrote in it briefly. He waited until Joseph disappeared from view before making his way slowly to the Rue de Rivoli entrance of the Tuileries once more, and there he flagged down a passing taxi. After casting wary glances along the street in both directions, he got in and read to the driver from his notebook the address in the Sixteenth Arrondissement that Joseph had given him. Because the snow was getting heavier, he didn't spot the little radio car driven by the same black-jacketed French journalist who had delivered his message to Joseph at Gif-sur-Yvette. The car had been parked on the north side of the Rue de Rivoli alongside the Intercontinental, and the hard-faced North Vietnamese intelligence agent seated beside the Frenchman nodded once to indicate he should follow the taxi as it pulled away in the direction of the Place de la Concorde.

The radio car stayed a careful hundred yards behind the taxi all along the Seine to the Pont d'Iena where both cars crossed the river again. In the Rue La Fontaine beyond the broadcasting rotunda of the Maison de Radio Téléfusion Française, Kim stopped the taxi and instructed the driver to wait. The intelligence agent shadowing him ordered his driver to slow down, and they watched Kim walk around the corner out of sight into

Avenue Leopold II. As the agent's car pulled slowly across the junction, the men inside saw Kim pressing the bell of number 3, the corner apartment, and almost immediately the door was opened by a Vietnamese whose facial resemblance to Kim was striking. The agent took a photograph with his miniature camera as Tran Van Tam seized the hand of the brother he had not seen for thirty-six years and flung his other arm around his neck. Before Tam drew Kim inside, the agent managed to take a second picture, and after making a note of the address, he ordered the French journalist to turn around and drive the car past again so that he could take a further picture of the whole building.

Inside an apartment on the first floor, the two brothers who had not met since the day of the tennis championships in Saigon in 1936 stood looking at each other with tears brimming in their eyes. "I may only stay a few minutes," said Kim in a choked whisper. "And there must be absolutely no discussion of politics."

3

A full moon sailed high above Hanoi on the night of Monday, December 18, 1972, casting a ghostly, filtered light onto the city through ragged clouds that drifted lazily across the sky. Crowds of cyclists and pedestrians were thronging the streets as they had done every evening since late October when the partial bombing halt declared by the United States had once again put the area of the capital and the region seventy miles to the south off limits to American air raiders. The streets consequently were not blacked out and the people in them were relaxed, moving without haste or anxiety between their homes and the factories where they worked or the markets where they bought their supplies. In the industrial suburb of Kham Tien, Tuyet Luong and her two children were returning home from a local produce market, carrying vegetables and their meager monthly rice ration. They were heading for a drab, one-bedroom apartment in a twenty-year-old workers' housing project that had been assigned to them with Tuyet's job in a nearby munitions factory on her arrival in Hanoi in the spring of 1968. Since then Tuyet had spent twelve hours at the factory every day, screwing percussion caps onto artillery shells, and at the age of thirty-five her face was prematurely lined and gray with fatigue;

her shoulders sagged, too, as she walked, and the shabby black calico trousers and tunic she wore were frayed and threadbare.

Alongside her Trinh, grown tall and gangling at fourteen, and Chuong, her sprightly eleven-year-old son, chattered and chased one another up and down the curb, shrieking and giggling whenever one of them spilled the bag of vegetables they were carrying. Tuyet admonished them from time to time in a tired voice, but they were able to walk quietly for only a minute or two before their youthful high spirits prompted some new bout of mischief. The ear-splitting wail of the city's air raid sirens, however, stopped the children dead in their tracks just after eight o'clock. Within moments the streetlights and all the illuminations in the public buildings went out, plunging the capital into darkness. The droves of cyclists immediately began stampeding homewards, and Tuyet called both her children to her and began running towards the underground shelter beneath their own four-story housing block. They looked up into the night sky as they ran, but although the full moon was still bright, they couldn't see or hear anything, because the first wave of the biggest armada of strike aircraft ever assembled in the history of aerial warfare was streaking towards Hanoi at an altitude of nearly seven miles, which made it both invisible and inaudible to people on the ground.

All the eight-engined B-52 Stratofortresses in that first wave carried a massive load of explosives — forty-two 750-pound bombs stacked like fish roe in their long steel bellies and another twenty-four 500-pounders clamped beneath their broad wings. They were homing on their targets in Hanoi and Haiphong at six hundred miles an hour in packs of three, having been guided nearly three thousand miles across the Pacific from Guam or across the neck of the Indochina peninsula from Thailand, by bombardier navigators imprisoned in tiny windowless cabins on their lower decks. These navigators, who would never catch a glimpse of the country they were attacking, had plotted their courses blindly with maps and instruments and were at that moment preparing to release their bombs with the aid of radar screens and stopwatches. They were proud of their ability to dump their destructive loads to earth with surgical precision, and each formation of three B-52s could on an ideal mission destroy everything within a precise target area almost two miles long by one mile wide. Because the American negotiators had not been able to win their arguments in that little artist's cottage outside

Paris five days before, on the night of December 18 the B-52s were being sent for the first time to attack vital installations in the very heart of both Hanoi and Haiphong — docks, shipyards, roads, bridges, missile sites, airstrips, supply dumps, munitions factories and military barracks; targets on their outskirts had been attacked sometimes in the past, but this was the first substantial raid of the war directed against the city centers themselves.

Because the planes from which they fell could neither be seen nor heard, the explosion of the first stick of bombs petrified Tuyet and her children as they dashed towards their underground shelter. The night sky was lit first by a blinding flash of light which made the moon invisible, then the earth beneath their feet shook and the buildings on either side of the street trembled. A deafening roar engulfed them, followed by another blinding flash of light which lit the city like day, and it was succeeded in its turn by another flash, then another, until the glare, the explosions and the rumbling of the ground became continuous.

Tuyet, Trinh and Chuong stopped running and clutched fearfully at one another; at first they were not even sure bombs were falling. This was nothing like the fitful fighter-bomber attacks on the suburbs that had been launched in response to General Giap's Easter offensive in the South. The world seemed to be ending, the earth seemed to be heaving and exploding all around them in a blaze of light, and like all the other inhabitants of Hanoi and Haiphong they were gripped by the starkest terror. Only when the antiaircraft defenses around the capital began to open up and the long dark cylinders of Soviet surface-to-air missiles were seen lancing upwards into the heavens through the white glare of the exploding bombs, did Tuyet and her children realize that there were aircraft flying silently high above their heads; and only then did they recover their nerve sufficiently to run on to the shelter.

The first attack lasted about twenty minutes, and at the end of that time the elemental roar of the explosions ceased abruptly. After letting a few precautionary minutes pass, Tuyet and her children, along with thousands of others who had crowded into the underground shelters of Kham Tien, came out silently into the darkened street and gazed upward in horror; a blood-red glow lit the heavens all around the city and thick black smoke drifted across the face of the moon. Muted explosions filled the night as distant fuel depots and ammunition dumps continued to blow up, and each new blast sent fresh columns of fire leaping

693

towards the sky. In every direction they looked fires were burning — in the space of a few minutes Hanoi had become an inflamed bruise on the dark face of the earth.

Before the shock of the first attack had subsided, however, the sirens sounded again at nine P.M., and Tuyet and her children dashed once more into the underground shelter. Soon the foundations of the city were shaking again as the onslaught was resumed, and this second attack lasted another twenty minutes before another lull ensued; then at ten o'clock, eleven o'clock and midnight the sirens sounded and fresh waves of B-52s arrived overhead to rain their lethal explosives onto new targets. The giant bombers continued to sweep in over the city at hourly intervals throughout the night, laying down their mathematical carpets of destruction, and they continued to attack relentlessly on the hour every hour throughout the night for the next eleven days, with only a short pause on Christmas Day. In the daytime while their crews rested, smaller tactical aircraft, F-4 Phantoms, F-111s and U.S. Navy fighter-bombers from carriers in the Gulf of Tongking, continued the raids so as to give the antiaircraft defenses of the cities no respite, and as the days passed the planes systematically pulverized and flattened all their chosen targets.

At the same time, however, the awesome size of the attacking force paradoxically gave new encouragement to the defenders of Hanoi. In the previous seven years only one American B-52 had been lost over Indochina, but because the giant strategic bombers were attacking in such dense formations, fifteen were smashed from the sky by SAM-2 missiles. The bombers carried highly sophisticated electronic counterdevices that could jam the direction-finding radar in the Soviet missiles, but the North Vietnamese countered this by switching off the missiles' guidance systems and firing the SAM-2s blindly into the midst of the B-52 formations armed with proximity fuses. More than sixty American crewmen had to bail out of the stricken aircraft brought down in this way, and half of them survived to join other American prisoners of war in Hao Loa prison — which remained unscathed as the raiders intended in the center of Hanoi.

Although the B-52 crews were proud of their ability to pinpoint their targets, their bombardiers knew well enough that if they punched their bomb-release switches a few seconds too early or too late, their bombs would fall perhaps a few hundred yards outside their target area. Their commanders would later claim that with less than two thousand deaths claimed by the

Vietnamese themselves in a city of one million people, the raids were one of history's most accurate aerial campaigns. Hadn't sixty thousand people died in the British bombing of Dresden? Hadn't thirty thousand people died in the German blitz of London? Weren't such figures proof that America had mastered the art of bombing cities while showing consideration for the people in them? But despite these comparisons, at least one Hanoi hospital was hit, large swathes of houses were reduced to ruins, and each morning new groups of dazed Vietnamese could be found wandering blankly amidst the rubble of their former homes, weeping for lost relatives.

Among them on the morning after the last of the raids was the slender figure of Dang Thi Trinh. She stood in Kham Tien, outside what had once been the entrance to the underground shelter beneath her housing block, her awkward young body bent with anguish and her tears making pale streaks in the grime and dirt that coated her face. Only one wall of the building remained standing; the other three had collapsed as though punched by a mighty fist, and men, women and children were scrambling over the mountains of debris like automatons picking up pieces of broken furniture and ornaments. Others simply stood staring about them in blank disbelief, and Trinh was numbly watching a rescue team shoveling and manhandling stones from the shaft leading down into the shelter. Faint cries had been heard from beneath the rubble in the early hours of the morning, but they had long since ceased, and she had been waiting there for five or six hours, weeping and hugging herself in her grief.

By three A.M. on that last night of the raids, she had become accustomed to the constant roar of the attacks and because at that hour they had seemed to be moving away from the city, she had come out of the shelter with her mother and Chuong to watch the distant flashes of bombs falling on Haiphong. Chuong had squealed with delight when they saw a missile explode in a burst of orange flame high in the darkness and the silhouette of one of the great eight-engined American bombers had begun spiraling downwards in the glare. It seemed to fall for a very long time before it reached the ground several miles away, and they had watched until it exploded with an earthshaking rumble, sending a great new fountain of fire into the air.

A moment later, to their horror, a new "ladder" of bombs had begun falling half a mile away on the other side of the munitions factory where Tuyet worked, and everybody had begun screaming and dashing for the underground shelters again. Trinh had fallen and become separated from her mother and brother in the stampede and she had been hustled into a neighboring shelter by a party cadre who helped her up. Unknown to them, at that moment, forty thousand feet above them, a SAM-2 missile was racing towards an approaching trio of B-52s programmed to finish off the munitions factory. The first one dropped its thirty tons of bombs successfully on target and turned away, but the SAM-2 exploded two or three hundred feet above the second aircraft, rocking it violently at the moment when the navigator was reaching for his bomb-release switch. The B-52 pitched and yawed under the impact of the explosion, and the navigator was flung hard against the bulkhead of his cabin. By the time he'd gathered himself, the second hand of his stopwatch was five seconds past the release point and the little yellow signal light indicating "Bomb Doors Open" was winking furiously on the panel before him. He seized the release switch nevertheless, and one by one the lights beside the radar panel went out, indicating that first the 750-pounders, then the 500-pounders had slipped from the gray body of the plane. Forty seconds later the "Bombs Released" sign lit up in the cockpit and the pilot breathed a sigh of relief as he began to turn the nose of the plane back towards Guam.

The thirty tons of bombs that should have demolished the munitions factory, because of the five-second delay, stitched a row of craters across the southern end of the Kham Tien suburb; one of them smashed down three walls of the housing block in which Tuyet lived with her son and daughter and it exploded as it reached the ground floor, blasting a ten-foot crater into the underground shelter where a hundred people were crouching in the darkness. In mid-afternoon, Trinh watched the crumpled bodies of her mother and Chuong being dragged out together; they had been clutching one another when the bomb smashed into their refuge and they were still entwined. Sobbing hysterically, Trinh flung herself on her mother's body, and it took several minutes of pleading and cajoling before the rescue workers were able to lift her to her feet and lead her away.

4

A solemn hush fell over the sumptuously furnished main salon of the old Hotel Majestic on the Avenue Kleber. For several minutes the rustle of high-quality parchment paper and the rattle of winter rain flurries against the windows were the only sounds in the chamber. Silent, deferential American and North Vietnamese protocol aides stood respectfully beside Henry Kissinger and Le Duc Tho, who were seated facing each other across the baize-covered mahogany conference table, and one by one they turned the sixty or so pages of the bound cease-fire agreements so that their principals could scribble their initials on texts they had negotiated so laboriously over the previous four years. It was a quarter to one on the afternoon of Tuesday, January 23, 1973, and in the formal diplomatic surroundings of the Quai d'Osay's International Conference Center furnished with gilded mirrors, tasseled drapes and antique silk tapestries, the ten-year war that America had fought through the heat and slime of Vietnam's jungles and paddy fields was coming quietly to an end.

A little group of correspondents, photographers and television news cameramen had been invited into the chamber to observe the ceremony, and their cameras had begun to click and whirr the moment a discreet French protocol official hovering inside the door gave the sign that they might begin to record the scene. Tran Van Kim, who was seated beside Le Duc Tho, glanced up from watching the signing ritual and scanned the faces of the journalists until he caught Joseph Sherman's eye. The two men looked at one another for a moment, then the Vietnamese gave a little formal nod of recognition before turning his attention back to the typewritten agreements.

When the two chief negotiators at last laid aside their pens, their aides closed the bound documents and walked around the table with measured steps to exchange their copies. Through their interpreters, Dr. Kissinger and Le Duc Tho made brief, sonorous speeches referring to their mutual desire for peace and the historic nature of the moment; then the meeting broke up so that they could step out into the rainy street to be photographed by the rest of the waiting pressmen. The pavements were drenched, the skies overhead leaden, and the photographers had to use flash for their pictures as the American and the North Vietnamese clasped hands on the pavement's edge, smiling broadly at one another as if they were old friends. In the lobby leading to the street, the delegations and the pressmen milled together as they put on hats and raincoats; in the crush Joseph felt a tug on his sleeve and turned to find Tran Van Kim beside him.

"Perhaps we might meet briefly, Monsieur Sherman, before you leave Paris," said the Vietnamese in a low voice.

Joseph shrugged. "Isn't it a little late for fresh revelations about the secret machinations of the evil American negotiators?"

"I have information for you this time of a purely personal nature."

Kim spoke in a strangely subdued voice, and Joseph's manner softened at once. "Why don't we meet for a drink on the terrace at my hotel this evening? I'm at the Intercontinental."

The Vietnamese shook his head quickly. "I'd rather we met in private. I'll come to your room there at six o'clock." As soon as he'd spoken, Kim moved away, giving the American no opportunity to reply, and he was quickly swallowed up in the crowd.

Joseph lunched with a member of Kissinger's staff who explained in confidence the background to the two dozen new clauses embodied in the final agreements, and by mid-afternoon he was back in his hotel room, fitting a blank piece of paper into his typewriter to begin his final article for *The Times*. For an hour he wrestled with the task of trying to explain how the final accords differed from the terms reportedly agreed before the massive Christmas bombing raids on Hanoi and Haiphong. He thought back over what the aide had told him over lunch: there were changes in the definition of the Demilitarized Zone, the American right to continue military assistance to Saigon had been clarified, some offensive phrases had been dropped and other favorable clauses had been strengthened, the aide had told him — but all of that had seemed to Joseph little more than wrangling over semantics. President Thieu, he'd learned, had been forced to go along with the agreement against his will in the end because the U.S. government had threatened to cut off all future aid and leave him to Hanoi's mercy if he didn't — but nothing he'd been told seemed to explain why the furious Christmas bombing onslaught had been necessary.

Joseph himself had spent an uneasy Christmas holiday in England at the country house deep in the West Sussex Downs where he had lived with Naomi since their marriage in 1968. There he had listened round the clock to radio reports of the wholesale destruction wrought by the B-52s in North Vietnam. Harbor facilities, railways, bridges, roads, military dumps and factories had all been successfully destroyed, and Hanoi's capability to wage war had been severely curtailed, but side by side with the news had come furious, worldwide criticism of the massive raids; some ninety-five thousand tons of explosives had been dumped on Indochina over the Christmas period, more than Nazi Germany had dropped on Britain during the entire Second World War, and many newspapers and politicians throughout the Western world had condemned the bombing as barbarous. The raids had been called off finally on December 30 and the White House had then given an assurance to Hanoi that they would not be resumed as long as "serious negotiations" were taking place. Henry Kissinger had returned to Paris on January 8 to find that the bombing had left Le Duc Tho a greatly changed man; anxious to settle quickly, his manner was no longer obstructive as it had been during the round of talks in early December, and the final details of the cease-fire had been hammered out in less than a week.

In those first days of 1973, Joseph knew that already in the United States the war had been recognized almost universally as a tragic mistake for the nation. Some fifty-seven thousand American lives had been lost and $146 billion had been wasted on a conflict that had divided his countrymen more deeply than any other issue since the Civil War, but as he sat in his Paris hotel room on that wintry afternoon, he nevertheless found himself struggling to give the moment the right perspective for the next day's paper. Hour after hour he grappled unsuccessfully with his thoughts, and he was still sitting before a blank sheet of paper at six o'clock when Tran Van Kim knocked crisply on his door. On entering, the Vietnamese offered no greeting but held a large manila envelope wordlessly towards him.

"What's that?" asked Joseph, taking the packet warily.

"Photographs," replied Kim without looking at him.

"Photographs of whom?"

"Your daughter, Tuyet."

There was silence for a moment, then with a puzzled frown Joseph began opening the envelope.

"I'm afraid she's dead," added Kim quietly. "She was killed in the Christmas bombing."

Joseph stopped opening the envelope and stood still in the middle of the room. After a moment he dropped the package unopened on the table beside his typewriter and sat down with his back to the Vietnamese. Once or twice he rubbed his hand across his forehead as if to ease a pain, and all the time Kim stood waiting quietly just inside the door, his overcoat buttoned, his round face blank and expressionless.

"How did she die?"

"There was a direct hit on the underground shelter beneath her apartment block. She was found with a hundred other people buried in the rubble."

"Were they all killed?"

"Fortunately a large proportion of the workers quartered in Kham Tien had already been evacuated from the city. But almost the whole of that suburb was atomized by the ferocity of the bombing on the last night — not a single dwelling was left standing."

"I meant Tuyet and her family," said Joseph dully. "Were they all killed?"

"Her son Chuong died with her. The girl Trinh by chance had taken cover in another shelter. She survived."

Joseph put his hands to his head and sat staring in front of him. Then his eye fell on the envelope again and he finished opening it and spread the half-dozen photographs inside across the table-top. There was one of Tuyet he had taken himself outside the Lycée Marie-Curie in Saigon; she had been a willowy sixteen-year-old then, dressed in a pale *ao dai*, and even wearing a faintly sullen expression, her youthful face was still strikingly beautiful. Another, apparently taken on her wedding day, showed her smiling and holding the arm of a handsome, fierce-eyed Vietnamese youth who seemed uncomfortable in a crumpled suit. A third picture showed Tuyet and Lan together, wearing their elegant national dress; both were slender and graceful, obviously mother and daughter, but they stood apart, neither touching nor looking at one another. There were others too of Tuyet and the children and the last one, showing Trinh and her brother Chuong, grown taller than in Hue, had apparently been taken sometime during the past four years.

Among the prints there was a short note scrawled in French on a sheet of rice paper; it was signed with Trinh's name, and Joseph felt a lump come to his throat as he read it.

My mother, I know, wanted you to have these photographs. She didn't talk of you often but I made her tell me all about you after Hue. I think she didn't like to talk too much about it because it always made her cry. She once told me you'd never seen most of these pictures and I thought my great-uncle Kim would know how to get them to you. I hope you don't mind, but I've kept for myself one of you and my mother outside her school in Saigon. Goodbye — Trinh.

Joseph dropped the note on the desk and covered his face with his hands; he sat like this for a long time, ignoring the Vietnamese.

"She was very insistent that I pass them to you. Otherwise I wouldn't have made contact."

Joseph started at the sound of Kim's voice; again he recognized the subdued, almost confiding tone in which the Vietnamese had spoken at the Avenue Kleber earlier in the day, and he swung round in his chair. "What will become of Trinh?"

"The party will look after her welfare!" His quick response had a hollow ring to it, and as though suddenly embarrassed by what he'd said, Kim took a hesitant step towards Joseph. "I'll take a close interest in her too, myself, of course. Tuyet wasn't just your daughter, remember — she was also the child of my sister."

"Were you close to her?" asked Joseph in a surprised tone.

"She was very conscious of her mixed blood after she came to Hanoi, and I think this made her distant with me. But I was able to help her in small ways without her knowing. As you can see from her note, Trinh is less inhibited — she thinks of me rightly as her great-uncle."

Joseph nodded ruefully. "If Lan had kept her promise to marry me, we would have been brothers-in-law, Kim."

The Vietnamese raised his eyebrows in surprise. "Tuyet once told me that you had asked my sister to marry you — but she said nothing of Lan's wishes."

"Lan accepted when I first proposed to her," replied Joseph, his face downcast. "But in the end her loyalty to your father was too great. It was the same week that you quarreled with him, and after you'd gone she changed her mind. She said your father needed her loyalty more than ever then."

Kim lowered his eyes and said nothing, and an uncomfortable silence lengthened between them.

"You don't have any family of your own, do you?" said Joseph quietly. "I can sense it."

"No, I never married. I decided like our late president to devote my life to our revolution." Kim spoke almost defiantly, but Joseph could see that there was a trace of embarrassment in his manner.

"Is that the only reason?"

"Perhaps my quarrel with my father had something to do with my decision," he replied slowly, dropping his eyes again. "Perhaps because of it I became skeptical about our stifling family traditions in Vietnam. Perhaps in the end, that wasn't the wisest decision of my life."

Joseph could see that the admission of his own error hadn't been made easily, and he felt a sudden twinge of sympathy for the stiff-faced man before him. "It's ironic, Kim, isn't it, that we should find ourselves talking together in Paris on a day like this. It's more than forty years since we first met, and both of us have suffered greatly because of the wars in your country. Your father, your sister and her daughter are dead and you cut yourself adrift from your family long ago. I've lost my elder son, my brother and a daughter — but for what?"

"For freedom — the people of Vietnam have always been determined to be free." Kim's words were uttered almost sorrowfully, and he unbuttoned his coat and lowered himself wearily into a chair as he spoke. "A conflict between those who collaborated with France and our country's true patriots was always inevitable. There was no way to stop brother fighting brother in Vietnam. The United States should have had enough sense to leave well alone. Then at least you wouldn't have shared in the tragedy."

Joseph sat staring at the blank sheet of paper in his typewriter, then turned to look at the Vietnamese as a thought struck him. "You'll probably never understand, Kim, but we came to Vietnam for noble motives. We were afraid Communism would swamp the world and change it beyond recognition if we didn't act. The trouble was, we went on fighting long after it became clear we'd been wrong about that. But we'd never understood the complicated background to your war, and in our frustration we used terror and methods of mass destruction which betrayed all our own dearest principles. In the end we were trying to win just to satisfy our national vanity. That's why the war has torn my country apart."

The Vietnamese nodded. "Bad mistakes are always costly for those who make them. Your country has paid its price."

Joseph considered his response in silence for a moment. "Have you never regretted, Kim, doing what you did in 1936? Haven't you ever regretted turning your back on your father and dividing your family?"

"It's often made me very sad," replied the Vietnamese in a

halting voice. "I brought great sorrow to my mother and Lan, I know. I paid a high price for my political beliefs — but I always knew there was much more at stake than just my own relations with my family."

"Hasn't the terrible destruction in your country ever given you second thoughts? Didn't you ever wonder whether you made the right choice?"

Kim was silent for a moment, then he shook his head slowly. "It was perhaps impossible for my father to see things my way, I realize that now. He couldn't comprehend that history was about to change the world. He thought the lands granted to him unjustly by the French would remain in our hands forever. Your intervention in Vietnam stemmed the tide of history for a while and prolonged those vain hopes, but today's agreement has set history in motion again. Very soon my brother Tam's rice lands will be taken from him and he will realize at last that like my father he chose the wrong side." Kim paused and sighed quietly. "My father said to me that last day that Marxism would destroy our family and our country — but he was wrong about our country. What's happened here in Paris today has made me more convinced than ever that I made the right choice in 1936. My sacrifice has been worthwhile."

"But you're a lonely man, Kim, I can see that."

"Yes, I don't deny it — that's why I'll be pleased to do what I can for Trinh." He looked up quickly at Joseph with an embarrassed smile. "When I look at Trinh, sometimes I see Lan as she was as a young girl when she and Tam and I were all happy together. The memory is sweet and painful at the same time — but as a man gets older his memories become more important if he has nothing else."

Joseph stood up and crossed to the window to stare out into the wintry darkness. The rain had turned to snow and big flakes were spinning silently to earth through the pools of light cast by the lamps in the Tuileries. The bleakness of the scene seemed suddenly to echo Joseph's own feelings, and he spoke over his shoulder in a dispirited voice. "Back home the military are very proud of the Christmas bombing. Killing only sixteen hundred people while destroying all the strategic targets in two major cities is a cause for celebration for them. But even one death is too many — if it's your daughter." Joseph continued to gaze unseeing into the falling snow. "That bombing was our form of torture. You wrung propaganda confessions out of our pilots although

703

everybody knew they were meaningless. Because Le Duc Tho wouldn't say what we wanted him to say in December, we launched the biggest air strike in history. We tightened our 'ropes' until Le Duc Tho rushed back to the Avenue Kleber to 'bao cao' and sign the agreements. We both know you signed to stop the pain of the bombs — and we both know when you've recovered you'll take South Vietnam as you've intended to all along."

Kim stood up, his face impassive, buttoning his coat. "You're right, Monsieur Sherman. We shan't rest until we achieve our goal. Our country will be reunited one day — we haven't fought all our lives just for a compromise."

Joseph turned from the window and stepped towards Kim, holding out his hand. The Vietnamese, taken aback, looked down at it with a startled expression on his face.

"We can't pretend we've always been friends, Kim, but we have known each other for nearly half a century — and today should be a day of reconciliation. Thank you for bringing the photographs. And thank you for telling me about Tuyet — I would rather have known."

They shook hands briefly and the Vietnamese turned away towards the door. Joseph walked ahead of him, then hesitated before opening it, a quizzical look on his face. "Tell me one other thing, Kim — did you meet with your brother Tam while you were both in Paris?"

A defensive look came into Kim's eyes and he fumbled awkwardly with his gloves. "I visited him briefly at the address you gave me — but it was painful for both of us to have to part again so soon." For a second or two he stared at his shoes, then he looked up anxiously at Joseph again. "Nobody knows about this except you. Please don't mention it to anybody."

"I won't." Joseph opened the door and stood aside. "But before you go I have something else to thank you for."

"What's that?"

"Before you arrived I didn't know what to write about today's events. Now I do. I shall write about the news you've given me — and the sadness it's caused me."

The eyes of the Vietnamese widened in surprise. "You'll tell of the death of your daughter?"

Joseph nodded without hesitation. "Yes — and about my attachment to Vietnam over the years."

"It will be an article of considerable interest," said the

Vietnamese slowly. "Goodbye." He grasped Joseph's hand once more, then hurried out of the room.

Joseph sat down at his typewriter and tapped the keys nonstop for the next hour. He described in detail his family's long involvement with Vietnam, beginning with Chuck's death during the 1920s hunting expedition and ending with a brief description of how Tuyet was killed in the Christmas bombing; in the course of the article he tried to spell out how events in Vietnam had influenced his own life, then he got up and paced the room deep in thought for several minutes before sitting down again and adding one final paragraph. "Looking back over those fifty years to that early personal tragedy in the jungles of Annam, I realize now that my family's worst error was never to admit openly to ourselves that my brother's death might have been avoided with greater foresight. Not facing up to that fact kept destructive tensions simmering beneath the surface for many years. In seeking to defend the 'honor' of the United States in Vietnam, successive presidents and other national leaders, I believe, have made similar mistakes and brought unprecedented tragedy down upon our nation. Only if we admit this and resolve never to make the same errors again, will all those Americans who died in Vietnam have made some worthwhile sacrifice."

Joseph tugged the last sheet of paper from the typewriter, read it over to himself and zipped the machine into its case. He gathered up the photographs of Tuyet that had lain beside his elbow on the table all the time he was writing and slipped them quickly into his case. He took his article down to the telex room on the ground floor of the hotel, handed it in for immediate transmission to *The Times* office in London and carried his typewriter and overnight bag out into the street to wait for a taxi that would take him to the airport for his London flight. There were no taxis available immediately and he stood hatless on the pavement, oblivious to the falling snow; his shoulders sagged, his face was set in lines of deep sadness, and as he stood there the shoulder wound he'd received in Hue began to throb dully. Suddenly he felt old, and with flecks of white snow settling on his hair, he looked every one of his sixty-three years.

5

An aging Tory Member of Parliament with a jovial, patrician face raised his glass of claret in Naomi Boyce-Lewis's direction at the head of the table then passed it slowly back and forth beneath his nose, teasing his olfactory senses with its bouquet. "The whole world, Naomi, my sweet, may be tipping suddenly on its ear this Easter weekend — but while you and Joseph continue to serve this magnificent Château Latour, so wisely laid down here for you by your dear departed father in the year of your birth, I, for one, shan't be convinced it's all up with us." The M.P. closed his eyes and sipped the wine with an expression of near-ecstasy on his face.

"Shame on you, Toby, old boy," cried a male voice from down the table, "giving away a lady's age like that on her birthday!"

The M.P. opened his eyes wide, stared for a moment at one of the Latour labels with its clearly marked 1936 vintage, then smote his forehead with his free hand in a theatrical gesture of mock anguish. His act drew a quick roar of laughter from the company, but Naomi, looking radiantly beautiful in a simple white Corrèges gown which left her suntanned shoulders bare, was obviously happy and content to be thirty-nine, even publicly. Not in the least ruffled, she raised an affectionately admonishing eyebrow at the M.P., then smiled warmly at Joseph who was seated at the other end of the table.

Flickering candles in silver holders bearing the crest of the Boyce-Lewis family shone on the starched white shirt fronts and décolleté necklines of two dozen men and women whose faces were well known in British politics, the City, the London theater, and print and television journalism; most of the wives and mistresses wore discreetly expensive jewelry that flashed and sparkled in the candlelight whenever they turned their head or moved their hands, and on the walls behind them, gilt-framed portraits of several generations of Boyce-Lewises who had dwelled in the fashionable Belgrave Square house in London's West End gazed down with what appeared to be approval on the privileged gathering.

"I don't want to put the damper on your birthday party, Naomi," said the M.P., his face becoming serious, "but even on this happy occasion we can't ignore the fact, can we, that there's hardly been a time in the recent past when we've had so much damned bad news all at once. With Kissinger getting the thumbs-down sign from the Egyptians *and* the Israelis after all that shuttling, and King Faisal getting himself murdered, the Middle East must go up again in flames soon. The new cabinet in Portugal's being stuffed with Communists, so we've got official Commie spies in NATO, and to cap it all the North Vietnamese hordes have come from nowhere again and look like reaching Saigon within the week."

"It'll probably take a bit longer than that," protested Joseph with a smile. "Hanoi may have thrown eighteen divisions into the offensive but Thieu's regrouping his forces along the coast and around Saigon."

"Whatever happened to Nixon's 'Vietnamization' program that was supposed to make the South self-reliant? It's only two years since Kissinger negotiated those tricky Paris agreements — surely they were meant to prop Thieu up longer than that?"

"Vietnamization only increased the size of the army and the amount of weaponry at their disposal. Morale never got any better, and the soldiers were no better trained. But why Thieu suddenly decided to retreat from the central highlands is anybody's guess." Joseph shrugged his shoulders. "Perhaps he was haunted by the French experience at Dien Bien Phu — he had a horror of the North Vietnamese cutting off his 23rd Division a long way from their supply bases. Now the retreat's touched off a panic and soldiers and civilian refugees are fleeing southward together like lemmings."

"Dreadful bloody mess." The M.P. turned back to Naomi. "It's your old stamping ground too, of course, my dear, isn't it? Are you going to dash back to cover the death throes?"

"My office has been having panic discussions all day today about a final documentary — some sort of 'Farewell to Saigon.' They've asked me to do it — but so far I'm hedging." She smiled affectionately down the table at Joseph again. "I'm not sure now that I want to go all that way and leave my poor husband here to fend for himself."

The M.P. snorted. "Poor husband, indeed! Look at that California suntan. He hasn't been here through our foul winter — spent his time out there playing tennis and swimming, I shouldn't wonder. All that stuff about writing a new book on America's future role in Asia is just a cover for living the good life, if you ask me. He's as fit as a flea." He eyed the three uniformed women in black satin frocks, white caps and pinafores who had been serving at table and were beginning to clear the last of the dishes. "And as for fending for himself, he wouldn't have to do much of that. Look — if you decide to go and he really needs looking after, I'll come round here or pop down to that lovely country house of yours in Sussex and help open a bottle of the Latour from time to time." The M.P.'s shoulders shook and he guffawed so infectiously at his own humour that the rest of the table joined in.

In the hall outside the dining room a telephone rang, and a moment later the door opened and one of the maids came to Naomi's chair to whisper in her ear. As she hurried out, a butler appeared with a tray of port decanters and liqueurs and while they were circulating the same maid returned to tell Joseph that Naomi wished to consult him for a moment or two in private about the telephone call. He excused himself apologetically and found her waiting for him in his book-lined study that was furnished with many of his oriental artworks and mementos from Cornell.

"That was the studio — they're getting in a state about the Vietnam story. They've just had news that Thieu's forces have surrendered Hue without a fight. Da Nang's going to be next. The government troops have started fighting each other with hand grenades to get on the evacuation aircraft. They say half the South Vietnamese forces have now either been killed, wounded, taken prisoner or forced to retreat without their equipment."

Joseph shook his head in disbelief. "So if you're going to Saigon you'd better hurry."

"Yes, that's why they were ringing — they want to get a crew and a director off first thing tomorrow morning."

"What did you tell them?"

"I said I'd ring them back in ten minutes." She took one of his hands in both her own. "What do you think I should do?"

"You should go. You want to, don't you? Saigon's always had a great fascination for you."

She squeezed his fingers and smiled fondly into his eyes. "I think 'had' may be the operative word. I'm not so sure anymore — I've got you now." She paused and frowned. "I'm torn between going — and staying with you."

"But you'll only be away for a couple of weeks."

She stroked the back of his hand with her fingers and lowered her eyes. "I know. But it's not just that, Joseph. Even if I go I've decided this will be my last film. I suppose on her thirty-ninth birthday a girl gets around to thinking one or two deep thoughts. Like whether it isn't time she gave up rushing around the world and thought about — well, other things, before it's too late."

"Other things?" asked Joseph with an inquisitive smile.

"It's becoming quite the fashion, you know. Several friends from my year at Sherbourne have suddenly started doing it — even those with already grown up families."

"Doing what?" Joseph's frown of mystification deepened.

She shot him an exasperated smile. "Having babies, darling! In their late thirties or early forties. I know I'm practically a senior citizen but they can do all kinds of tests and things now to make sure it's all right. Do you think I could still manage it?"

Joseph laughed and ran an affectionate hand over one of her long, satin-clad thighs. "I'm absolutely sure you could do anything you chose," he said softly. "But I'm darned sure this old monkey is too far gone for such tricks."

"What nonsense!" She pulled away from him and scrutinized his face for a moment. His hair was gray right through now but he was still lean and straight in his elegant Savile Row dinner jacket and his deep tan from his winter in California made him look younger than his years again. "You're in better shape than a lot of men half your age, darling, and you know it — even with a bullet hole in your left shoulder." She laughed and caressed his cheek with her hand. "It's me we've got to worry about."

A fire was burning low in the study fireplace, and Joseph turned from her and picked up a poker to stir the logs. Bright flames rose immediately, casting an orange glow on his face, and he remained kneeling on the rug watching the charred wood burn, his expression suddenly wistful. The flames died away quickly, and when he spoke his voice betrayed an inner sadness. "I sometimes feel a bit like these logs, Naomi — glowing bright on the outside, maybe, but kind of hollow and burned out in the middle."

"Joseph!" She dropped to her knees beside him and took his face in her hands, staring at him in astonishment. "You mustn't feel like that — my darling, you mustn't!"

"I'm sorry." He shook himself and stood up. "Why don't we discuss it all after you get back. If you don't go, you'll always regret it." He smiled at her again. "It will at least give me a chance to go down to the country and get on with my book — and think about your latest bombshell in between chapters."

She returned his smile, then her face became serious again. "Joseph, couldn't you come to Saigon? Not to work — just to be there with me?"

Joseph shook his head. "There's nothing but painful ghosts of the past in Saigon for me now, Naomi, you know that."

She looked at him in silence for a moment, then nodded understandingly. He followed her towards the door, but she stopped and turned to him before opening it. Putting her hands against the satin-faced lapels of his jacket, she smiled mischievously into his face. "When our guests have gone, darling, even though you haven't had a chance to think about it between chapters, do you think as a birthday treat we could go straight to bed and start trying out my new idea? Or at least just pretend."

Aroused by her words he took her in his arms and pressed the softness of her long body against himself. He let his cheek rest against her blond hair for a moment, inhaling with closed eyes the delicate fragrance of her perfumed skin. Then they broke apart smiling tenderly at one another and he returned to the dining room to find the port decanters still circling the table amidst loud laughter and thick clouds of cigar smoke. As he closed the hall door behind him, he heard Naomi on the telephone telling the studio she would be ready to fly out to the doomed city of Saigon at noon next day.

6

Once Naomi had left for Vietnam to cover the spectacular southward advance of Hanoi's eighteen divisions, Joseph retreated sixty miles south of London to their country house in West Sussex. There, surrounded by the green, rolling hills of the South Downs, he tried to settle to his writing; but as the days passed he found himself increasingly distracted by the news from Saigon. Only forty-eight hours after Naomi had left, the Communist forces smashed into Qui Nhon, Nha Trang and Dalat, encountering little resistance from the dispirited government forces, and as he listened to the radio news roll call of cities falling one after the other to the North Vietnamese onslaught, Joseph's mind was flooded with memories; he recalled the desperate journey he had made with Lan beside him in the OSS jeep in 1945, driving nonstop northwards along the old Mandarin Way above the beautiful white beaches and azure seas of Nha Trang and Qui Nhon. The fall of Dalat on April 2 plunged him into a new bitter-sweet bout of reminiscence as he recalled the exhilaration they'd shared at the Lang-Biang Palace in 1954, and this in turn stirred stark recollections of her awful death before his eyes in Saigon only a few weeks later. Eventually these thoughts became oppressive, inducing in him a dark sense of foreboding about Naomi's safe return, and he found himself waiting with increasing anxiety for her telephone calls. She rang him two or three times a week from the Continental Palace, but the calls were invariably subject to frustrating delays and over the crackling line she was able to say little of what she'd seen of the fighting. In the end she confined herself to repeated assurances that she was safe and keeping out of danger, but as time passed these stilted conversations, instead of setting his fears at rest, made Joseph more uneasy.

By the end of the first week in April, the Communists were tightening a military noose around Saigon. Less than a hundred thousand battle-ready government troops faced some three hundred thousand North Vietnamese, whose spearhead had moved to within forty miles of the capital at Xuan Loc, and as far as Joseph could see the only hope seemed to lie in the possibility that Hanoi might prefer to negotiate and have their troops appear in the streets as liberators rather than military conquerors. From Washington he listened anxiously to reports that President Ford was trying to persuade Congress that a fresh 750-million-dollar dose of military aid might save Saigon — but as the days slipped by the legislators on Capitol Hill remained adamant, fiercely protective of their new power in the wake of Richard Nixon's "imperial presidency."

Listening to news of this calamitous train of events hour by hour on his shortwave radio amidst the hills of southern England, Joseph became too distracted to work. He began rising before dawn and driving the few miles to the ancient cathedral city of Chichester to buy extra newspapers as soon as they arrived at the railway station. Ill-at-ease, he wandered restlessly through the paddocks and formal gardens of the eighteenth-century manor house between news broadcasts and telephone calls from Naomi, and after President Thieu's resignation on April 21 had signaled the end was near, he began to take longer walks outside the grounds, tramping blindly across the surrounding hills, oblivious to the green shoots of spring speckling the branches of the trees above his head and the ground around his feet. A frown of anxiety became a permanent expression on his suntanned face, and he walked with hunched shoulders and the jerky, uncoordinated stride of a man abstracted by events beyond his control.

*

Unknown to Joseph, in those same days many thousands of miles away in Hanoi, the brother of the girl who had first made his spirit a hostage to Vietnam's fortunes four decades before was suffering similar symptoms of anxiety. While Joseph strode daily through the South Downs, Tran Van Kim was pacing anxiously back and forth across the uncarpeted floor of one of the austere offices set aside for the use of Politburo members in the Party Headquarters of the Lao Dong. His fears, however, although shaped by the same events, were for his own safety.

The realization that his career and possibly his life were in jeopardy had come to him only gradually. The frantic day and night round of meetings and consultations that had followed the unexpected success of the Ho Chi Minh offensive in late March and early April had proved exhausting and at first he had been too tired to read the warning signals. He had taken a full part in the early discussions, and with experience born of long observation of his old mentor Ho Chi Minh, who had died in September 1969, he had been careful not to commit himself fully to either of the two extreme views which had quickly polarized the Politburo. One faction wanted to hazard everything at once in an all-out drive on Saigon, while the remaining members advocated caution and restraint, and seeing that opinion was equally divided, he had managed to praise and criticize both points of view equally. Because he was so confident that he was pursuing the wisest course, he didn't take it amiss that he was never called on to make an unequivocal statement of his views, and it was some days before he realized that he was no longer being asked to voice any opinion at all.

After the victory of the Khmer Rouge in Cambodia and the resignation of Nguyen Van Thieu, the tempo of the meetings had increased dramatically. The corridors of the Party Headquarters were filled at all hours of the day and night with bustling functionaries in high-collared tunics who rushed frantically from one meeting to another bearing sheafs of top-secret papers. It was then, when his own schedule of meetings slackened abruptly, that he had felt the first stab of sickening fear; he was being excluded completely from all top-level counsels about future policy in the South — and that could mean only one thing!

Left idle in his room for hours on end, he began frantically to search his memory for some unconscious transgression. His relationship with Ho Chi Minh had been personal and intimate for more than thirty years and he had always known that he owed his place in the Politburo to this fact above all else. He had anticipated a gradual diminution of his influence in the years following Ho's death, but he had always felt confident that the prestige and intimate knowledge of party affairs he had gained during three decades as the leader's close confidant would guarantee his position. He had been aware that the amount of time he had spent with Ho had been a cause of envy among other Politburo members, and General Vo Nguyen Giap in particular, in the later years of Ho's life, had begun to treat him with a cold reserve. As he paced his office at the beginning of the last week in April 1975, Kim concluded that the direct threat would almost certainly come from the defense minister who was supervising the overall strategy for the offensive; he tried obliquely to approach one or two members of the party's ruling body who had been most friendly to him in the past in an effort to discover if he was being linked with others in some large-scale purge; but all cold-shouldered him, confirming his worst apprehensions — he was alone, suddenly and inexplicably a political outcast!

Barely able to sleep or eat, it came almost as a relief on the morning of Tuesday, April 21, when he received a summons to the office of the head of the party's Control Commission who was responsible for internal party discipline. The thin-faced cadre, who had always shown him great deference while Ho Chi Minh was alive, didn't rise when he entered his office or invite him to be seated; instead he addressed him in a curt voice without looking up from his papers.

"Your fellow members of the Politburo of the great and glorious Lao Dong Party have instructed me to make certain things known to you, comrade," said the cadre. "As you know, the party is on the brink of an historic victory which will bring our southern brethren under our control for the first time. This is a period when the highest self-discipline will be required of all comrades at all levels. Many difficulties and hazards lie ahead, and it will not be an easy task to change the capitalist ways of the southern people and bring them into line with the discipline of our own socialist society. It has been agreed unanimously that anybody who lacks total dedication to the cause cannot be tolerated in the highest echelons of our party at a time like this. It has been further agreed that anybody who is likely to betray our goals in the South because of misguided personal loyalties is not to be trusted and must be discarded at once!"

Kim stared at the bowed head of the cadre, who was reading

everything he said in a toneless voice from a typewritten sheet on the desk before him. He knew he was being invited to condemn himself from his own mouth, but he couldn't understand why. "I've dedicated my whole life to the party," he said in an injured tone. "Of what am I accused?"

Without replying, the cadre pushed across the desk a type-written report to which two photographs were fastened. Kim picked them up, but at first the Paris apartment building at the corner of Avenue Leopold II and Rue La Fontaine shown in the top one meant nothing to him. Then in the second picture he recognized the backview of himself stepping into the doorway to be greeted by his brother Tam, and with his heart hammering at his ribs he turned to the report and read the agent's account of how he had been followed to the Sixteenth Arrondissement.

"It was nothing more than a personal meeting," he said in a barely audible whisper as he let the report fall onto the desk top. "There was no discussion whatsoever of political matters . . ."

The cadre looked blankly back at him. "It has been decided that you will present yourself at the Party Interrogation Center at Phuc Yen at four o'clock this afternoon for further examination of the facts. A car will be provided for your convenience but no driver will be available. You must drive yourself — take the northern route. That is all."

Kim returned slowly to his own office, moving along the gloomy corridors like a somnambulist. Whether the evidence shown to him was the real reason for his fall from favor, he didn't know; perhaps it was being used to cover some personal spite or other, some lingering envy of his past prominence. Bitter feuds at the top party level, he knew from experience, were often rooted in personal dislikes, and he cursed himself for his foolishness in giving potential enemies sufficient ammunition to condemn him. For half an hour he sat hunched at his desk, staring dully at his empty wooden document trays; then gathering himself, he glanced at his watch and found it was already two o'clock. After a moment's thought, he drew two sheets of blank paper from a drawer and began writing rapidly. When he had covered both pages in closely spaced scrawl, he sealed them in an envelope and used a telephone to summon a junior aide from an adjoining office.

"Take this to my niece, Trinh, at the munitions factory," he told the youth sharply. "Deliver it in person without fail at once. Tell her it's most urgent."

"Yes, Comrade Kim." The youth acknowledged the order in an anxious voice and made to leave, but at the door he halted and turned to look uncertainly at his superior. "Is anything wrong, Comrade Kim? You look unwell."

Kim stared at him hopelessly for a moment. "Go quickly. And when you've delivered the note don't come back here. Go somewhere you won't be found!"

The youth's face turned pale. "Why, Comrade Kim? Why?"

"Because I've been ordered to Phuc Yen for interrogation. Now go — before it's too late."

Half an hour later Kim walked down to the motor compound at the rear of the building and stepped into a Russian-made Moskwa saloon that had been brought to the door for him by an overalled mechanic. He drove the car carefully through the city and across the Red River Bridge, heading for Phuc Yen which lay thirty miles northwest of Hanoi on the slopes of the Red River valley. As he drove alongside the Lake of the Restored Sword, he wondered briefly whether he would ever see the twin pagodas on their little islands again — then he noticed in his rearview mirror another Moskwa with three plainclothes security men following him openly. All along the winding highway that climbed steeply up the valley, they remained at an even distance behind him, making no effort at all to conceal their presence, and his hands began to tremble on the wheel. As he drove he kept a constant watch in his rearview mirror — but the trail of oil dripping from the puncture made in the Moskwa's hydraulic system by the overalled mechanic was too fine to detect, and he remained unaware that his brakes had been rendered useless.

Because of the long gradient, he didn't try to slow the car until he was running down a long steep slope on the far side of the first big hill outside the city. The road swung sharply away from a high cliff, and he applied his foot to the brake for the first time as the Moskwa sped down towards the bend. To his horror, the unresisting pedal went right down to the floorboards without altering his speed, and the car raced on towards a yawning gap in the retaining fence that he could see, from the freshly broken wood, had been made very recently. In the instant before the vehicle hurtled out over the cliff edge, Kim remembered the last words his father had spoken to him on that night long ago in Saigon when he had flung the ten-piastre note contemptuously in his face. ". . . In the end, Kim, if Bolshevism succeeds you'll bring down ruination on your country, your family — and yourself . . ."

The car spun in the air and fell a hundred feet before it struck a projecting spur of rock and exploded. It bounced against the cliff face again lower down then sprang outwards, showering debris and burning petrol in all directions before the turbulent waters of the Red River finally swallowed it up and quenched the angry flames.

Three days later at the old manor house in a fold of the South Downs, Joseph was woken from a troubled sleep at three A.M. by the ringing of his bedside telephone. When he lifted the receiver he recognized Naomi's excited voice at once but had difficulty understanding her on the poor line.

"Darling, there's . . . been . . . a . . . purge . . . in . . . the . . . Lao Dong . . . Politburo," she said, pausing deliberately after each word because of the crackling line. "A French journalist in Hanoi has been given the story by a very unusual source."

Joseph rubbed his bleary eyes and sat up in bed. "Very interesting," he shouted back. "But why wake me in the middle of the night to tell me this?"

"Please listen, Joseph! This is very important. It's Tran Van Kim who's been purged — he may even be dead. The journalist got the story from a distraught Vietnamese girl who came to his office. She asked him privately to contact you. She said her name was Trinh and she's traveling south to Saigon in three days' time. She said she needs your help."

Joseph sat bolt upright suddenly as the significance of Naomi's words sank in. "Trinh, did you say? Tuyet's daughter?"

"Yes," shouted Naomi, "it seems so. What do you want me to do — I'll do anything you say."

Joseph's knuckles whitened on the telephone receiver. "Don't do anything," he shouted. "Nothing at all."

"Why not?" asked Naomi in a puzzled voice. "Why on earth not?"

"Because *I'm* coming to Saigon myself!"

He slammed down the telephone, dressed quickly and ran to the study where he kept his passport. Without waiting to pack a bag or turn out the lights of the house, he hurried outside to the garage. Within ten minutes of receiving Naomi's call, he was driving fast through the country lanes of Sussex heading for London to catch the first available flight to the Far East. The dawn of Friday, April 25, 1975, was breaking over the western reaches of the capital as he took off four hours later from

Heathrow Airport on the first leg of his journey to the beleaguered city of Saigon that had only five days left to live.

7

Three days later on the afternoon of Monday, April 28, 1975, a heavy pall of saturated air blanketed the capital of South Vietnam. The ominously dark clouds that heralded the first monsoon downpour of the new wet season had been growing blacker hour by hour since dawn, but although it seemed constantly to be on the point of explosion, the gathering storm stubbornly refused to break. As a result, an electric tension descended on the streets, and in the luminous, gray light three and a half million people caught fast in the tightening circle of Communist armor were able to see clearly the telltale lines of fear etched deep into one another's faces. Hurrying on foot through the heart of the city towards Doc Lap Palace, Joseph could hear the distant rumble of an artillery barrage being laid down on the main South Vietnamese airbase of Bien Hoa, eighteen miles away. The noise of the barrage was interspersed from time to time with sounds of thunder that grew gradually louder, and Joseph noticed that the people he passed gazed up constantly at the sky, obviously wondering when the bombardment of the capital would begin.

After weeks of growing apprehension the people trapped in Saigon had become openly fearful because they knew that with twenty-one Communist divisions ringing the city, the single remaining division of disciplined ARVN troops would have no hope of defending them. Faced with this hopeless military situation, South Vietnam's tottering government was preparing to swear in its second new president in the space of six days in the hope that he might prove more acceptable to the Communists; but rumors of the move had already spread through the streets and few who'd heard it held out much hope that this last desperate political gamble would succeed in saving the city. Hanoi's leaders had augmented their forces and maneuvered them into position with slow deliberation during the second half of April so as to give themselves time to destroy South Vietnam's political leadership beyond repair; to ensure that President Thieu didn't flee abroad and set up a government in exile which might compromise their eventual control of the South, they had given hints through their Camp Davis representatives at Tan Son Nhut that they might accept a negotiated settlement if he stepped down formally from the presidency. But after tricking Washington into forcing him to resign, they had immediately made new demands: they insisted that the vice-president who succeeded Thieu should in turn be replaced by the neutralist figure General Duong Van Minh, and because this seemed to offer a slender hope of preventing the total destruction of Saigon, the South Vietnamese had hastily agreed.

The swearing-in ceremony for Big Minh had been set for the late afternoon, and Joseph reached Doc Lap Palace just after five o'clock in time to watch the ineffectual Buddhist general, who had played a leading role in the American-inspired overthrow of Ngo Dinh Diem, march sad-faced into the main reception hall. The brocade and plush chamber hung with huge crystal chandeliers was already filled with an audience of two hundred Vietnamese army officers and politicians who had records of opposition to the Thieu regime, and they watched with silent apprehension as President Minh stepped onto a podium decorated with his own personal crest — a representation of *Yin* and *Yang*, the symbolic harmonious opposites of Asian philosophy that emphasized his wish for reconciliation with his Communist enemies. Joseph pushed his way through the crowd of a hundred or so journalists at the back of the hall to where Naomi stood tense beside her camera crew, directing the filming of the proceedings. A steel helmet dangled from her left hand, and she still wore an olive green flak jacket like most of the other correspondents who were dashing to and from the front lines of a war that had moved to within a few minutes' drive of their city center hotels. Together they listened to Big Minh in an agony of concentration, trying to assess whether this last-ditch change of leadership would give Joseph a few extra hours to find Trinh.

"You must have realized that the situation is very critical," Minh began, speaking in a voice that cracked frequently with emotion. "Tragic things are occurring minute by minute, second by second in our country, and we're paying dearly for our mistakes with our blood. I'm deeply distressed by these events and I feel a responsibility now to seek a cease-fire and bring peace on the basis of the Paris Agreements. . . . The coming days will be very difficult. I cannot promise you much. . . ."

Joseph shook his head in frustration and Naomi, glancing

around, saw that his face was gray with fatigue. During the forty-eight hours since his arrival in Saigon, he had barely slept. Day and night he had roamed the city, searching out the haunts of old Viet Minh and Viet Cong contacts among the maze of back alleys and shanty slums lining the canals. He had begun by offering substantial bribes to the venal waiters and doormen at the Continental Palace, the Caravelle and other big hotels; these men, he knew, were Viet Cong informers of long standing, and he promised them more money if they could tell him how he could contact Dang Thi Trinh, an important new cadre of the Provisional Revolutionary Government who had left Hanoi five days ago to come south to take up special duties in Saigon. He had slipped hundred-dollar bills unobtrusively into their hands and sometimes discreetly showed them copies of his old OSS photographs taken with Ho Chi Minh and Vo Nguyen Giap in 1945. In his desperation to find Trinh, he lied blatantly without any sense of shame. He was a writer sympathetic to the Communist cause, he said, and he had reason to believe that Comrade Trinh bore important confidential information that the leadership of the Lao Dong in Hanoi wished him to receive; it was of vital importance to the party that she contact him the moment she arrived from the north.

The waiters had watched and listened with suspicious eyes, then after holding out for further bribes, had supplied names and addresses that took him with agonizing slowness along secret chains of command that led through the muddy lanes and into the reeking boat dwellings of the city slums. Wary eyes and monosyllabic grunts had greeted his inquiries everywhere in the dark and dingy meeting places. Careless of his own safety he even went at night into villages beyond the city limits when contacts were arranged there, certain he was moving higher up the secret Viet Cong hierarchy; but frustratingly he came to a halt on the second night at what he judged was the middle level of command — and none of the contacts admitted to any knowledge of Trinh's existence.

On Sunday he had ostentatiously attended all the services at Saigon Cathedral, where over the years Viet Cong go-betweens had made surreptitious contacts with foreign journalists whenever it suited them; but not once had he been approached. On Monday morning, growing ever more desperate, he had driven out to Tan Son Nhut airport and visited Camp Davis, the fortified compound where as a result of the 1973 Paris Agreements a representational contingent of two hundred troops of the People's Army of North Vietnam was stationed along with a smaller group of Viet Cong officials of the Provisional Revolutionary Government. In theory they were there to supervise the 1973 cease-fire, but it was common knowledge that the North Vietnamese officers were disguised political cadres from Hanoi, and for two years they had given bizarre press conferences every Saturday morning to promote Hanoi's propaganda line. On his way there Joseph saw for the first time the growing crowds of Vietnamese waiting for evacuation flights on big U.S. Air Force C-130s that were lifting off the runway at regular intervals. The gymnasium of the American Defense Attaché's Office had been turned into a refugee processing center, and the sight of anxious men, women and children clutching bags of possessions as they waited to leave the country had heightened Joseph's own feelings of alarm. On an impulse he had decided to reveal the real nature of his interest in Trinh to the Hanoi colonel who commanded Camp Davis, and he sent in a short note with his OSS photograph giving Trinh's full name and his reasons for wishing to find her. The narrow-eyed officer who received him half an hour later had listened impassively to his story, then shaken his head. "I have no knowledge of any of these things of which you speak," he told him coldly, then summoned an aide to show him out.

The ranks of refugees lining up to leave had been swollen considerably by the time Joseph left Tan Son Nhut, and the small contingent of United States Marines that had been flown in a week before to police the evacuation was having difficulty persuading panicky Vietnamese not to block the approaches to the airport with their abandoned vehicles. On his way back into Saigon, Joseph had become trapped in an impenetrable traffic jam of army trucks and other military vehicles and had parked his rented car and begun to walk. Before long he found himself in Bui Phat, one of the areas where Communist rockets had struck the city at dawn that day, leveling a whole street of huddled tin roof shanties; smoke was still rising from ruins which had been swept by swathes of fire, and dead bodies and the mutilated living were still being unearthed from the wrecked homes. Small groups of sobbing relatives and stunned onlookers stood watching, and as he approached the corner of the ruined street, Joseph saw one badly burned victim of the raid being dragged from beneath the shattered remains of a corrugated lean-to hut.

He watched with a growing sense of horror as two soldiers

tugged at a pair of charred ankles and the rest of the body came free with a faintly audible groan. Convinced suddenly that the victim was a young girl, he ran forward with an involuntary cry; the trunk and limbs were black and blistered, all the hair had been burned from the head, and clear brown eyes, wide with agony, were rolling uncontrollably. The charred lips were moving without making any sounds, and Joseph grabbed a water bottle from one of the soldiers and made them lower their burden while he poured a few drops of liquid into the scorched throat. There was another faint moan of agony as a spasm of pain shook the body, and Joseph saw then that most of the victim's clothing had been burned to nothing in the all-consuming fire. What he had imagined were black trousers were in reality blistered skin, and he saw then that the dying Vietnamese was a male youth, and despite his deep feelings of horror, a flood of relief swept over him. A moment later the youth shuddered and moaned one last time before he died, and the two South Vietnamese soldiers, who had been waiting with expressions of impatient hostility on their faces, continued their gruesome task of disposing of the anonymous corpse.

Joseph stood for a long time among the ruins created by the rockets, as stunned suddenly as the local people all around him by the realization that the war was closing inexorably at last on the city that for most of the past thirty years had led a charmed existence amid the bloody battles being fought all around it. With the exception of the Tet Offensive seven years earlier and an isolated rocket attack in 1971, the capital of South Vietnam had always remained an island of relative peace in a restless sea of war, but as the day wore on and the monsoon clouds darkened over the city, the certainty that the end was near seemed to become something tangible in the air. The vision of that charred male corpse returned to haunt Joseph's memory hour by hour as he continued his search for Trinh, and it gradually became a recurring symbol of fear and dread. He began thinking of it again as he listened to Duong Van Minh's despairing speech because it was soon clear from what he said that the mind of South Vietnam's new president must also be filled with similar thoughts. Addressing the "Provisional Revolutionary Government of South Vietnam" directly by its own declared name for the first time, he said that all the people now wanted "reconciliation" above all else; but the tone of his voice suggested he held out little hope that the Viet Cong or the North Vietnamese would make many concessions now that outright military victory was within their grasp.

"Reconciliation requires that each element of the nation respect the other's right to live," said Minh, struggling to inject conviction into his words. "We should all sit down together and work out a solution. I propose from this podium that we stop all aggression against each other forthwith." The burly general paused and drew a long breath without looking at his audience, well aware that he was speaking via the live television broadcast to many ears beyond the hall. "I hope with all my heart that this suggestion will meet with approval. . . ."

At that moment the whole palace was shaken by an elemental explosion; brilliant flashes lit the sky outside and curtained doors leading to the patios were blown open. A mighty rush of wind lashed rain into the chamber as the first monsoon storm broke with great violence, and when the doors had been secured again President Minh had to raise his voice to make himself heard above the continuing crash of thunder.

"In past days, fellow citizens," he said, his face more stricken than before, "you may have noticed that many people have been quietly leaving the country. Well, I want to remind all our citizens that this is our beloved land. Please be courageous; stay and accept the fate of God. . . ." Thunder crashed and rolled deafeningly once again, and Minh had to wait until it died away; then he raised his eyes beseechingly to the audience once more. "Please remain and stay together — rebuild South Vietnam! Build an independent Vietnam, democratic and prosperous, so Vietnamese will live with Vietnamese in brotherhood." He paused one last time and gazed around the hall, a brave man fully aware that he was about to be engulfed by one of history's irresistible tides. "Thank you very much," he added quietly at last, but the words never reached the ears of his listeners because they were drowned in another thunderclap.

As the gathering began to break up, Naomi moved to Joseph's side and squeezed his arm consolingly; his face was drawn and he raised his shoulders in a resigned shrug. Many times since his arrival he had quizzed Naomi about the message she had received from the French journalist, and she had gone over it patiently again and again for him: a girl called Trinh had contacted the Agence France Presse representative in Hanoi to tell him of Kim's disappearance after his dismissal from the Politburo. In exchange for the information, she had asked that he contact

Joseph Sherman in confidence and say that her great-uncle had arranged for her to be infiltrated to the South as a cadre of the Provisional Revolutionary Government; she feared for her future in the North, she had said, with Kim in disgrace. As the North Vietnamese army was likely to win victory in the South any day, she had felt she would have no future there either; that was why she wanted Joseph to help her get out of Vietnam. There had been no party announcement about Kim, but the French journalist had later learned from a reliable informant that he had died in a car crash.

"Please don't look so worried, Joseph," said Naomi quietly. "Perhaps Trinh's been delayed on the journey. It's probably chaos on the roads in the Communist areas too."

Joseph didn't answer. He was staring over her shoulder at the crowd of National Assembly delegates milling beneath the great chandeliers, discussing Minh's speech.

"What is it?" she asked, turning to follow his gaze.

"Tran Van Tam! Look there, chatting with the new prime minister. Still the perfect political chameleon! Somehow he must have managed to make the transition from Thieu's regime to the neutralists." Joseph hurried over to the Vietnamese, and when Tam turned to find him at his elbow, he offered his hand.

"So you've come to witness the final act of our national tragedy, Joseph, have you?" He spoke quietly so that his voice did not carry to those around him and smiled sadly. "We've done all we can but we've got no bargaining power left. At most the swearing-in of the new president will win us a little time."

Joseph nodded. "But what about your personal plans, Tam? Will you be among those answering the call to stay and accept the fate of God?"

The Vietnamese giggled nervously and glanced around him again before answering "I'd like to respond patriotically, but like many others I'm afraid of what the Communists will do. I've already taken the precaution of sending my wife and family out of the country to Thailand."

"Have you managed to export some of your wealth too?" asked Joseph quietly.

Tam giggled again with embarrassment. "Certain precautions have been taken, yes."

"And how do you plan to get out yourself? The crowds are growing at the airport."

"Your ambassador has always been a good friend to me."

Tam's face creased into a calculated smile. "I've always done my best, you see, to give him my independent view of the affairs of our government. As a token of his gratitude he's offered to guarantee me a seat on one of his helicopters if a sudden evacuation becomes necessary."

"And how did you manage to escape being tarred permanently with President Thieu's brush?"

"A judicious resignation from my post at the Ministry of Information a few weeks ago — when it became clear which way the wind was blowing," Tam allowed himself another smile. "But tell me, are you writing another book? Is that what's brought you back to Saigon again at this dangerous time?"

Joseph shook his head. "No, Tam, as a matter of fact I came because of what happened to your brother, Kim, in Hanoi. I was sorry to hear the news."

Tam sighed and shook his head. "The circumstances of his death are very strange, but I don't understand how it affects you."

"Perhaps you didn't know, but Tuyet and her son were killed in the 1972 Christmas bombing. Her daughter Trinh survived. Your brother, Kim, was her only relative in Hanoi, and now that he's gone she's alone and frightened. Kim told her beforehand, it seems, how to get a message to me through a French journalist in Hanoi and also arranged papers for her so that she could be quietly infiltrated into Saigon with other northern cadres."

Tam's eyes widened. "And you've come here to look for her to take her out of Vietnam?"

Joseph nodded grimly. "But I can't find her, Tam. I've tried all the contacts I know. There's no trace of her." An edge of desperation had entered his voice. "Do you know anybody on the other side who might help?"

A defensive expression came into the eyes of the Vietnamese. "I don't think so — I'm very sorry. Like many others I have affairs of my own still to arrange."

Tam made as if to move off, but Joseph seized him by the shoulders and swung him around. "Trinh's your flesh and blood too, Tam! A man like you must have private contacts with the Viet Cong." Joseph paused and his expression hardened suddenly. "Maybe I should mention that to the ambassador and have him cancel your helicopter seat!"

Tam's face turned pale and he laughed nervously. For a moment he stared at Joseph in alarm, then his face brightened.

"Why don't you consult your friend in the 'white room'?"

Joseph stared at Tam, thunderstruck. "What do you know about the man in the white room?"

"Your brother Guy told me he took you to the cell to try to identify him. He thought you recognized him from the old days in Tongking but refused to reveal what you knew."

Joseph shook his head in disbelief; seven years had passed since he had visited that blinding white cell where the shivering skeleton of Dao Van Lat had been incarcerated. "Is he still there?" he asked in an incredulous voice.

Tam nodded. "Yes, and still his will hasn't been broken — they gave up interrogating him long ago. He's never divulged anything about the Liberation Front's organization but now that the end is near perhaps he might make an exception — for an old comrade-in-arms who showed him loyalty in the past."

"It's worth trying!" Joseph grasped Tam by the shoulders. "Arrange with your security people for me to visit him — with the cameras and microphones switched off."

Tam nodded quickly. "I'll make some telephone calls at once. Please wait at your hotel until you hear from me."

8

Twenty-four hours later in the early evening of Tuesday, April 29, Joseph was squatting on his heels beside the white stool in the center of the white room, staring with increasing desperation into the face of the shrunken skeleton that its prisoner had become. The skin on Lat's face and body seemed to have contracted during the long years in the chilled atmosphere, drawing itself tight across his bones and making his face skull-like. His hair had turned white like everything else in the room, his eyes were unnaturally large and luminous in their hollow sockets, and he leaned forward at the waist, hugging himself with his sticklike arms just as he had done when Joseph had last seen him in 1968. He still wore only a ragged pair of shorts and his wasted body seemed to have barely enough flesh on it to sustain life, but as before he seemed totally oblivious to his suffering and sat unmoving and incurious on his stool, his gaze fixed blankly on the white wall in front of him.

725

"Please listen to me, Lat. The war's almost over," said Joseph patiently, repeating himself for the second time. "The microphones have already been switched off, and you and all the other political prisoners are going to be set free later this evening by President Minh. Your forces are certain to win total victory within twenty-four hours. They're approaching the outskirts of Saigon already — but you must help me before they get here!"

Joseph sat back on his haunches to study Lat's face again, but the Vietnamese gave no sign that he had heard; instead he continued to stare straight in front of him, his eyes unblinking, and Joseph wondered with a stab of alarm if he had lost his reason entirely.

"Your nephew Tran Van Kim is dead, Lat." Joseph leaned closer, straining every nerve in his body to break the trancelike state into which the Vietnamese seemed to have sunk. "He was dismissed in disgrace from the Politburo and died in a car crash a week ago. That's why I need your help." He tugged from his pocket again the photographs of Tuyet as a young girl that he'd held up twice already before Lat's eyes. "I fell in love with Kim's sister, Lan — your niece — in the 'thirties. We had a daughter, Tuyet. She grew up to become Tuyet Luong, who served your cause well in the delta. Maybe you never knew she was related to you — but look, here she is, standing with me outside her school in Saigon!"

Joseph again pushed the photographs in front of Lat's eyes and waited. He had shown him the pictures of himself with Ho and Vo Nguyen Giap as soon as he arrived and recalled how they themselves had first met in Hue in 1925. He had reminded the Vietnamese how he had poled him downriver on a raft to the Pac Bo caves after his Warhawk had crashed, but Lat had still not betrayed the slightest sign of comprehension.

"Tuyet Luong was killed in the Christmas bombing of Hanoi three years ago," continued Joseph, speaking slowly as though to a child, "but she had a daughter, Trinh, who survived — you're her great-great-uncle. Kim cared for her after her mother was killed, but now Kim's dead she has nobody in the North. She's asked me to help her — she wants to leave Vietnam with me but I can't trace her. Kim arranged for her to be infiltrated into Saigon as a cadre of the Provisional Revolutionary Government but I need the name of the P.R.G. security chief so that I can ask him to find her for me. Can't you help?"

Joseph gazed imploringly into Lat's face as he finished

speaking, but the Vietnamese remained motionless on his stool as though he were alone in the cell, and Joseph stood up with a snort of exasperation. Glancing at his watch he saw that it was already after six o'clock, and forgetting for a moment that the cell was sound-proofed, he strained his ears, trying to hear the engines of the American helicopters from the Seventh Fleet that had begun their massive final evacuation operation at midday. As he hurried to the old Sûreté Générale headquarters from his hotel, he had seen the Sea Stallions, Chinooks and Jolly Green Giants lumbering across the rooftops, lifting out load after load of the thousand or so Americans still stranded in Saigon. Two departure areas had been set up — one on a tennis court at Tan Son Nhut, the other on the lawn inside the United States Embassy compound — and the helicopters were shuttling back and forth to the forty American ships cruising offshore in the South China Sea. Smaller, silver-painted helicopters of the CIA's airline, Air America, had been visible darting among the vapor trails of the bigger aircraft, plucking from rooftops little knots of Americans and Vietnamese who feared that they faced death or imprisonment at the hands of the Communists because of their close links with the United States. As it became obvious that many Vietnamese who wanted to leave would be left behind, signs of panic had become visible everywhere in the city, and remembering this, Joseph began pacing agitatedly back and forth across the white cell.

Within minutes of the swearing-in of President Minh the previous afternoon, it had become evident that this last humiliating political concession had been made in vain. Before the politicians had even dispersed from Doc Lap Palace, captured aircraft flown by North Vietnamese pilots had begun dive-bombing the Tan Son Nhut airbase, destroying within a few minutes South Vietnam's last vestige of air power. The same planes had then swooped on the center of Saigon and the deafening roar of aircraft rushing low across the rooftops with their wing cannons pumping had plunged the capital into chaos. Antiaircraft guns had opened up from the palace grounds and anyone in possession of an automatic rifle had begun shooting indiscriminately in the streets, convinced that the Viet Cong had launched their final assault by stealth. With the bewildering noise of warfare filling the tree-lined boulevards, Joseph and Naomi had taken shelter with hundreds of others on the stone floor of the cathedral. A twenty-four-hour curfew had been declared, trapping them there until the late evening, and when they emerged they discovered that through their spokesmen at Camp Davis, the Communists had again made fresh political demands which quite clearly sounded the death knell for Saigon. President Minh's government must "declare its support for the revolution," they had said, and all Americans must withdraw immediately from Vietnam. They had indicated contemptuously that the final attack on Saigon would begin at midnight on Tuesday, April 29, and any American not evacuated by then would have to suffer the consequences.

A few hours later the North Vietnamese forces had launched their heaviest rocket barrage of the war against Tan Son Nhut. One of the fleet of giant C-130 aircraft of the United States Air Force that had been ferrying out refugees to Guam was destroyed on the runway, there were many casualties among the thousands of Vietnamese still waiting in the processing center, and two young American Marines of the evacuation security force were killed by the rockets. It was these American combat deaths coming two years after the United States' withdrawal from Vietnam that had caused an anxious President Ford in Washington to abandon the airlift with fixed-wing planes from Tan Son Nhut and order the immediate launching of the helicopter evacuation, code-named "Operation Frequent Wind."

As a result the sound of axes and saws attacking the gnarled bole of the ancient tamarind tree on the front lawn of the American Embassy at midmorning had symbolized the United States' final admission that its efforts to save South Vietnam from Communism had failed. The lawn was the only area within the embassy where the great helicopters could put down with safety, and Joseph had watched the tamarind fall as he left the Chancery building at about ten-thirty that morning. Inside the embassy he had contacted people he knew manning the CIA station on the upper floors to secure a promise of a place in one of the last helicopters for himself and Trinh, and soon afterwards the prearranged secret signal for the start of the evacuation had been broadcast over the American Armed Forces radio. Every fifteen minutes the announcer intoned: "The temperature in Saigon is 105 degrees and rising," and the announcement was followed immediately by Bing Crosby singing "White Christmas."

Immediately all those foreigners who had been pre-warned by the evacuation organizers at the U.S. Embassy — journalists, businessmen, civilian engineers, contractors — had hurried to their appointed assembly areas around the city; some boarded buses for the airport, others climbed to the flat roofs of apartment buildings where the Air America helicopters could land. Shortly before eleven A.M. the exodus of the international press corps had begun and doors had started banging like gunfire suddenly in the corridors of the Continental Palace, the Caravelle, the Majestic and other hotels as Americans representing the *New York Times*, the *Washington Post*, *Time*, *Newsweek* and the television networks rushed out lugging portable typewriters and camera equipment. Other newspapers and television reporters from a dozen other Western countries — "TCNs" or "Third Country Nationals" in the jargon of the airlift organizers — went too, trooping to their assembly points through streets and squares left eerily deserted by the twenty-four-hour curfew.

Most of the American journalists had visited Joseph's room before they left, shaking their heads apologetically; as soon as he arrived in Saigon he had asked them all to let him know if they were contacted by a young Vietnamese girl asking for him, and as they prepared to leave, one after the other they came to shake hands and wish him well. After a lot of heated argument Joseph had insisted that Naomi leave with the members of her camera crew, and he had watched from a window of the Continental as the little procession of correspondents hurried away across the burning asphalt of Lam Son Square. Naomi turned once or twice, casting anxious eyes up at the window, but Joseph, unable to bear the thought of waving goodbye to her, had stepped quickly back out of sight. Feeling waves of tiredness sweep over him, he had stretched out on the bed then and fallen immediately into an exhausted sleep.

As they marched through empty streets, Naomi and the rest of the journalists warily eyed the South Vietnamese police and the holstered weapons on their belts; they had begun stringing barbed-wire barricades across the baking pavements and the journalists knew that their own raggle-taggle departure with all their equipment was providing undeniable confirmation that the United States was finally pulling out. Every Westerner in Saigon knew that Brigadier Nguyen Ngoc Loan, the Saigon chief of security who had shot a Viet Cong suspect in the head before television cameras in 1968, had issued a warning that if the Americans tried to leave alone, they wouldn't reach the airport alive. None of them knew then that Brigadier Loan was too busy arranging his own escape to carry out his bloody threat, but the expressions of resentment on the faces of the policemen as they passed were enough to make the journalists feel ashamed and uneasy. At some helicopter departure points they found South Vietnamese soldiers had set up machine gun nests on adjoining rooftops and the little groups of press refugees immediately began searching for safer takeoff zones.

Because discipline among the police and the army was crumbling, the curfew was only patchily enforced, and around the ten-foot-high walls of the United States Embassy, a crowd of about two thousand Vietnamese had gathered by early afternoon. Yelling and screaming hysterically, many of them scrambled up the high steel gates, pleading with the Marine guards that they faced slaughter at the hands of the Communists if they did not get on the evacuation helicopters — but none were allowed in without proper authorization. While the Marines held the frightened crowd at bay at the front gates, high-ranking Vietnamese ministers and army officers waving special passes slipped through a rear door of the compound to take their places quietly among the crowd of privileged evacuees waiting inside. From there they could see plumes of black smoke rising above Tan Son Nhut, which was still coming under intermittent rocket and mortar attack, and sounds of firing began to echo through the streets as order broke down all over Saigon. The giant Sikorsky Sea Stallions and Chinooks started fluttering in and out of the embassy compound in midafternoon, collecting loads of sixty and seventy people at a time, and it was not long before scattered shots were being directed at them from among the crowd outside. Cobra gunships bristling with weapons were called in to protect the landing zone, and Joseph, from his hotel window, had been able to watch them hovering ominously above the Chancery as the afternoon wore on.

When Tam's call finally came about five-thirty, Joseph had dashed straight to the security headquarters at the top of the Rue Catinat. The chief of police was already on his way out to the Seventh Fleet, Tam had explained, and a subordinate had been ordered to release all of the three hundred political prisoners still in custody at seven o'clock that evening. Tam had called the duty officer and arranged for Joseph to see the man in the white room alone — that was as much as he could do. Perhaps they would meet again in the United States, Tam had said with another characteristic giggle. He was leaving that moment for the embassy compound to catch his own flight, and he wished Joseph luck in his search.

Joseph had hung up without replying and run out of the room. In the streets he could hear that the rocket bombardment of Tan Son Nhut was being stepped up; little jeeploads of South Vietnamese troops were rushing back and forth, the radios in the open vehicles crackling with angry fretful exchanges, and although Saigon had been cordoned off against refugees for more than two weeks to prevent a repetition of the chaos that had occurred farther north, crowds of peasants, with frightened children at their heels, were beginning to appear in the city center. Pushing mattresses on handcarts, clutching suitcases or carrying poles hung with pots and pans, they were running blindly, not caring where they were going as long as they were getting away from the firestorms ignited by the Communist rockets around their old homes.

At the former French Sûreté headquarters Joseph had been conducted into the cellars by a hawk-faced security officer who was still in uniform. When he opened the door to the white cell for him, Joseph had waited before entering to see that he didn't stay to observe or reactivate the spy cameras and microphones which had been turned off. Once inside, it had taken Joseph a few seconds to get over the shock of Lat's appearance, and he had spent a quarter of an hour crouched beside him going over his story, first in French, then in Vietnamese and finally in English.

It was while he was pacing back and forth across the dazzling room, fighting down his growing despair, that Lat spoke for the first time. He didn't raise his head or change the attitude of his hunched body and he uttered the words so softly that Joseph wondered at first whether he had imagined hearing them.

"Even if Tuyet Luong was your daughter, why should I help you?"

At the sound of his voice, Joseph rushed to squat at Lat's side. For a long moment he gazed at him, at a loss for words, then he gripped his arm gently. "I was brought here to identify you seven years ago, Lat, don't you remember? I recognized you at once and you recognized me. But because the paths of our lives had crossed long ago I found I couldn't speak. You saved me when my plane crashed, and my OSS medic was able to save the life of Ho Chi Minh — we'd been comrades-in-arms together for a while and it's hard to forget that." Joseph tightened his grip on the scrawny arm of the silent prisoner. "But that's all behind us now. Soon you'll be free, your cause has triumphed. Saigon will be yours within a few hours and I've got no way of forcing you to

731

help me. But, Lat, I'm asking you for the sake of a young girl's life. Trinh's the daughter of *my* daughter, Tuyet — and she's your flesh and blood too!"

To Joseph's astonishment the eyes of the Vietnamese moistened and looking directly into Joseph's face for the first time, he spoke in a cracked voice. "Is what you say really true? Are the forces of the people really on the verge of victory today?"

Joseph nodded anxiously. "Yes, Lat, what I'm telling you is the truth."

The ravaged face of the Vietnamese relaxed suddenly and as he turned away again, his mouth opened wide to reveal toothless gums. He sat like this for a long time before Joseph recognized the expression as a smile, but he said nothing more, and in desperation Joseph grabbed his arm again and shook it. "Lat, who can help me find Trinh? You must tell me now!"

The fixed, half-demented smile did not waver. "Go to 15 Phong Phu, Cholon. There is a Chinese merchant who calls himself Wang. Say there that you've spoken with Nguoi Hiem Doc Ran — the Serpent Who Strikes Silently. Say that I command him to help you find my great-niece Dang Thi Trinh."

Joseph seized one of Lat's skeletal hands and held it fast in his own for a moment. Then he rose and ran from the cell. Even after Joseph's departure Lat continued sitting motionless on the stool, the features of his skull-like head frozen in the same unchanging grimace of triumph.

9

The drive to Cholon, although it was only four miles, took Joseph nearly an hour. The evening monsoon storm flooded the streets as he set out, slowing all traffic to a crawl, and the growing number of barbed-wire barricades forced him to halt and turn constantly. The helicopters carrying fleeing Americans out to the navy armada off the coast were still clattering through the murk overhead, but already the houses and apartments that had belonged to United States personnel were being looted by yelling mobs of Vietnamese. Smashed crockery and furniture thrown from upstairs windows littered the streets through which Joseph drove and he had to swerve frequently to avoid groups of ragged children hauling home stolen refrigerators, washing machines and air-conditioning units; he saw men running from the broken doors of American apartments with armfuls of whisky and champagne while women staggered under the weight of gauze-wrapped sides of meat that they had obviously snatched from abandoned deep-freeze cabinets. Joseph was driving the battered Pontiac that Naomi had rented to transport her camera crew, and several times he had to turn and reverse quickly when police fired in his direction without warning. Some South Vietnamese soldiers were stripping off their uniforms openly in the streets, tossing their rifles aside and running anonymously through the storm in their underpants in search of a hiding place, and he saw others stopping cars and siphoning gasoline from their tanks while they held the drivers at gunpoint.

It was dark when Joseph finally located Phong Phu, a narrow unpaved alley that the rain had turned into a sea of mud, and because the strain of the past few days had brought him to the brink of exhaustion he stumbled frequently in the gloom. It took him some time to discover that number 15 was a dingy, two-story villa from which the stucco was peeling, but his knock was answered immediately by a scowling Vietnamese youth who led him wordlessly into a shadowy, candlelit room where the air was heavy with the scent of burning joss sticks. He was left alone there for several minutes before an unsmiling, white-haired Chinese appeared in the doorway. Joseph launched immediately into his story and his listener heard him out impassively, betraying no sign of surprise that he brought instructions from a commander of the Liberation Front who had been held prisoner in solitary confinement for the past eight years.

"My informant inside the central police station had already advised me of your meeting with the Serpent Who Strikes Silently before your arrival," the Chinese said in an uninterested voice when Joseph had finished. "I've been expecting your visit."

"Then you can help me find Dang Thi Trinh?" asked Joseph.

A mirthless smile parted the lips of the Chinese and he shook his head slowly, as though astounded at Joseph's stupidity. "Mr. Sherman, you seem to think that Comrade Trinh is the only cadre from Hanoi who's been infiltrated into Saigon in the past two weeks. I can assure you we've brought in many thousands of cadres and civilian commandos during that time."

"But you must know where Trinh has been assigned," protested Joseph, his voice tight with tension.

There was a flash of gold teeth in the candlelight as the face of the Chinese relaxed into another pitying smile. "Full lists of individual cadres are kept only by local commanders, Mr. Sherman."

"Can't they be contacted to check?"

The Chinese studied Joseph's anxious face in silence. "The forces of the National Liberation Army and our northern brothers are on the brink of an historic victory, Mr. Sherman, after thirty years of bloody struggle. The fate of a single female cadre is of little consequence on a night like this. . . ."

Joseph gazed helplessly at the Chinese. "But Hiem Doc Ran commanded you to trace her for me."

"Hiem Doc Ran can give his command easily — but it can't easily be carried out. And maybe it can't be carried out at all before the battle begins." The Chinese continued to regard Joseph with unblinking eyes, then he nodded. "But I will see what can be done. Wait here please."

He left the room as silently as he had entered and descended a long flight of steps at the rear of the building into a cellar. Opening a soundproofed door leading into a tunnel, he passed beneath Phong Phu into a brightly lit underground communications center where half-a-dozen Vietnamese wearing headphones crouched over powerful Russian-made two-way radios, transmitting and receiving a constant stream of messages. The Chinese spoke with the Vietnamese supervising the radio operators for a minute or two, then returned to his own house and mounted the stairs again to the candlelit room where Joseph waited.

"All unit commanders will be contacted, Mr. Sherman," he said quietly. "It will take several hours. There are many more important messages to be transmitted and received. Return to your hotel and wait there — you'll be contacted."

"But if it takes several hours it may be too late!"

"That's the best that can be done." The note of finality in the voice of the Chinese made it clear there was no point in putting further questions, and when the scowling youth reappeared a moment later, Joseph followed him out without protest.

The rain had stopped when Joseph stepped wearily into the muddy lane once more but the noise of rocket and mortar fire was growing louder all around the city. He could see the glow of flames spreading across the sky to the northwest above the airport and the roar of the big evacuation helicopters and their American jet fighter escorts filled the night. As he turned the nose of the Pontiac back towards the Continental, a small Air America helicopter passed overhead unseen, carrying the emaciated prisoner from the cellars of the old French Sûreté headquarters whom he had first met almost exactly fifty years before in the gilded throne room of the Emperor Khai Dinh in the Palace of Perfect Concord. Crouched on the floor of the bucking aircraft, Dao Van Lat's wrists were still manacled and he still wore the same ragged pair of shorts. The hawk-faced security guard who had shown Joseph into the white cell two hours earlier was seated opposite him, dressed now in the anonymous short-sleeved shirt and dark trousers of a Vietnamese civilian, and his lips twisted in a smile as he addressed a second South Vietnamese security man hunched on one of the aircraft's small seats. "I don't think our silent prisoner can believe his good fortune," he said sarcastically. "He can't believe he's really being flown to freedom."

Lat stared out into the rushing void beyond the open door of the helicopter and said nothing. His eyes were wary and apprehensive and there was no sign of the exultant expression which had lit his ravaged features a few hours before when he learned the war was ending. Shortly after Joseph left the white room, the order to release all three hundred political prisoners in the cells had come through, but Lat's name had not been among them and he had been taken under close guard to another cell adjoining the rear courtyard. The other prisoners were freed without him, and when the evacuation helicopter fluttered down into the courtyard half an hour later his head had been covered with a blanket to prevent recognition and he'd been hustled aboard a moment before it took off again.

As the aircraft rose above the rooftops, the hawk-faced guard had smiled sourly at him. "There's no need to worry, comrade," he said in a mocking tone. "The American CIA provided your special accommodation for the past eight years and they've given special instructions about how your imprisonment shall end. Just relax."

The night had grown fully dark by the time the helicopter passed over the coast, heading for the brightly lit ships of the Seventh Fleet, and as they came in sight, the guard prodded Lat's bony shoulder once more and urged him to look out of the open door. "There are the ships, comrade, that will take us to a new life in America. And there below is the South China Sea — the great, wide, free spaces of the sea! That's much better than the terrible white cell where you've lived for eight long years, isn't it? Won't you break your silence now and talk to us — tell us what you think of all this?"

The only light inside the helicopter was the pale glow from the instrument panel, but it was sufficient for the guard to see Lat turn his hate-filled gaze on him. From his expression it was clear that he understood what his final fate was to be.

"I think you've guessed what's coming, comrade, haven't you?" said the guard softly. "And you've probably guessed why. You may not have given anything away, but our American friends have decided you know too much. Many Vietnamese who've worked secretly for America are being left behind — and because you know who they are, you must be given the freedom of the seas!"

Reaching out suddenly, the guard hauled Lat into a crouching position by the open doorway; grasping the waistband of Lat's ragged shorts, he tore them off. "You won't need such clothing for swimming, will you, comrade?"

Lat's shrunken body, mutilated by his own hand in a frenzy of patriotic fervor forty-five years earlier, teetered on the brink of the black void outside the speeding helicopter, and both guards watched his face intently, waiting for fear to show. But even in the final moments of his life Lat gazed at the darkness ten thousand feet above the ocean with the same blank, stubborn expression of resistance that he had always shown his captors, and when the hawk-faced guard lashed at him with his foot he still did not cry out. For a second or two his hands scrabbled at the door frame, trying instinctively to cling on, then his frail, fleshless body tumbled soundlessly into the black abyss of the night. Turning and twisting slowly like a sycamore leaf in the invisible air currents, he fell without uttering a sound, and the shock of his plunge from ten thousand feet killed him long before the black foaming sea smashed and swallowed his lifeless corpse.

10

When he opened the door of his room on his return to the Continental Palace, Joseph had expected to find it empty and he was shocked to find her sitting there, pale and disheveled, waiting for him. As soon as she saw him she rose and flung herself into his arms. Outside the din of a new rocket barrage pulverizing Tan Son Nhut filled the night, and through the windows the crimson streaks of rocket trajectories intercrossed with tracers lit the sky like a fireworks display.

"For God's sake, why did you come back?" gasped Joseph, his arms tightening around her.

"I just couldn't leave without you." Naomi buried her face in his shoulder and her voice became muffled. "I couldn't bear to think of losing *you* to Saigon, too. If something awful's going to happen, I want to be with you." They clung to one another without speaking, listening to the noise of the war rising to a crescendo outside. "The evacuation was awful," said Naomi, her head still pressed against his chest. "ARVN soldiers started firing at our bus just down the street from here. They ran alongside banging on the windows and screaming for us to take them with us. The Marines guarding us had to fire over their heads." She shuddered at the memory. "At Tan Son Nhut the gate guards opened fire at us. Luckily our driver was American. He just put his foot down and crashed through, but a lot of the Vietnamese drivers turned back. Then we had to wait two hours in one of those old American bunkers, and shells were raining down around us all the time. The Air America terminal went up in flames, and when the time came for us to make a dash for it, we had to throw away our bags and my crew lost their equipment and all our film. I got halfway to the helicopter ramp then stopped — I knew I couldn't bear to arrive back in London without you. All the Vietnamese buses were turning back at the gate by this time because their own troops were firing at them and I ran out and jumped on one. They're all trying to get into the embassy now."

Joseph closed his eyes and breathed deeply. "Jesus! Why did it have to end like this?"

Naomi pulled away from him and poured two glasses of whisky. "It's the way it's always been, I suppose, isn't it? Muddle — well-meaning, well-intentioned muddle." She shrugged hopelessly and sipped her drink. "Hundreds of Vietnamese employees of your agencies have been abandoned all over town. A lot of them have been waiting hours for helicopters or buses that never come. They're just standing there, so trusting, looking up at the sky watching for the helicopters, clutching their children and those pathetic little bags. . . ."

Seeing her shoulders tremble, Joseph went to her and took her in his arms.

"The embassy's like a madhouse. I went there first looking for you. It took me a quarter of an hour to fight my way in. Somebody told me the White House and Kissinger are screaming for the ambassador to wind up the evacuation by midnight. But there are a thousand Vietnamese at least inside the compound and more keep slipping over the walls all the time. The Marines are herding them into groups of sixty and jamming them into the helicopters as fast as they get back from the ships. God only knows how many they'll have to leave behind. . . ."

Her voice broke then, and Joseph held her in silence while they finished their drinks. Outside, the red glow of incendiary fires was lighting the horizon in an arc that spread right around the city's nothern perimeter from east to west. The Communists were at that moment overrunning Bien Hoa and Long Binh where resistance had finally collapsed, and long columns of their tanks and trucks were beginning to head down Highway One towards the capital. It was just after ten o'clock and the North Vietnamese field commander of the Ho Chi Minh offensive, General Van Tien Dung, was studying the flow of reports with his staff officers in a dugout at Ben Cat thirty miles north of the Continental Palace Hotel. Within two hours he would issue his final order of the war to the fifteen attacking divisions and send them thundering in for the kill.

"Have you had no news of Trinh at all?" asked Naomi when she had recovered her composure.

"I've done everything I can. I hope to get a message here telling me where she is. I just have to wait." Joseph's face was haggard with strain but he tried to smile as he put his hands on her shoulders. "You'd better wait for me inside the embassy. I'll take you there now . . ."

A light knock at the door made him turn and he wrenched it open to find one of the Continental's white-jacketed floor waiters grinning apologetically. "Excuse me, Mr. Sherman, but there's a Vietnamese downstairs looking for an American. . . ."

Joseph rushed past him into the hall before he could finish and ran down the nearest staircase. When he reached the front lobby, however, it was empty, and he halted in bafflement. A moment later the little waiter who had followed him down, panted up behind him.

"No, no, Mr. Sherman, outside." He waved frantically towards the front doors and Joseph ran to the entrance.

On the pavement a large Vietnamese family stood waiting, clutching bags and cases. The mother held a small baby and three other small children clung around her legs. An older boy and girl approached with their father, a thin, anxious-looking man wearing a sweat-stained shirt and baggy trousers. The father immediately seized Joseph's arm, jabbering hysterically in broken English, and Joseph stared at him and the anonymous faces of his family in bewilderment.

"You must help us, please . . . Please help us. For fifteen years I've worked for your country! The Communists will kill us all. . . ."

Joseph turned to find the little waiter standing behind him on the steps. "You were mistaken," he told him in a desperate voice. "I don't know them."

The waiter shook his head violently. "No mistake, Mr. Sherman. They tell me they looking for an American — any American."

The mother had seized Joseph's other arm and she began pleading with him too while the children stared up at him, round-eyed with fright. He tried to free himself but they clung to his clothes with desperate hands.

"I'm sorry, I can't help you," gasped Joseph. "You must try the embassy." He put his hand into his pocket, intending without thinking to give them some dollars. Then he checked himself and began trying to back away into the door of the hotel. The man let go of him suddenly and his expression changed in an instant from pleading to one of contempt.

"We've tried to get into your embassy — it's impossible. We waited twelve hours to be collected — but the buses never came . . ." His head jerked suddenly and a stream of spittle stained Joseph's jacket.

The mother began weeping bitterly, and with one last hate-filled glance over his shoulder, the man shepherded the forlorn little group away from the hotel. Joseph stood watching them, and when Naomi came up beside him to take his arm, she found him trembling and unable to speak. They stood in the doorway until the family finally disappeared from view around the corner of Lam Son Square. "We'd better get *you* to the embassy now," said Joseph thickly, without looking at her.

Before they left Joseph called the little waiter to him and thrust two one-hundred-dollar bills into his hand. "Go to my room now and wait there until I come back," he said, speaking slowly and emphatically. "Don't leave it even if a bomb falls on the hotel. Take down carefully any telephone message which comes for me."

The waiter stared in amazement at the banknotes, then nodded quickly and rushed towards the stairs. As they hurried across the cathedral square a lull in the rocket attack on Tan Son Nhut brought an eerie quiet to the city and the shouts of the crowd milling outside the United States Embassy reached them long before they arrived there. In the sky above the flat-roofed Chancery they could see the shadowy bulk of a Cobra helicopter gunship hovering like a basking shark, its machine guns that could fire six thousand rounds a minute trained constantly on the surrounding rooftops and the seething mob below. Occasionally an F-5 jet of the U.S. Navy or Air Force roared overhead, but otherwise Saigon seemed suddenly to be holding its breath in fearful anticipation of the war's end.

When they reached the embassy, they found that even on the outer edges of the crowd the mood of the Vietnamese was ugly. As they pushed their way towards the rear gate they were jostled and spat on, and Joseph had to put both arms around Naomi at times to ensure that they weren't pulled apart. As they neared the high wall they saw that barbed-wire obstacles had been strung along the top and the younger men in the crowd were scrambling up lamp stanchions, trying to climb over the entanglements. One youth who had become caught fast by the front gate was dangling upside down, bleeding profusely, but other Vietnamese ignored him, stretching frantic hands up towards the Marines, waving letters from their American employers or telegrams from relatives abroad. Whenever persistent climbers reached the top of the wall, the Marines were stamping viciously on their fingers with their heavy boots or using the butts of their M-16 rifles to send them tumbling back into the street, and each time this happened a new roar of anger rose from the crowd.

A few yards short of the gate an hysterical Vietnamese youth suddenly flourished a long-bladed knife in front of Joseph and seized Naomi by the hair. "Take me with you," he screamed, "or your wife won't get in alive." His eyes were rolling with fear, and Naomi cried out in pain. Gritting his teeth, Joseph jabbed his fist into the youth's face, and to his relief he staggered and fell, dropping the knife. Breathing heavily from the exertion, Joseph pushed Naomi in front of him, and a Marine, who had been watching them approach, leaned down and dragged her up beside him. Clinging precariously to the top of the gate she turned and looked beseechingly at Joseph as he turned back into the crowd. "Please be careful," she shouted, "and for God's sake hurry back!"

11

It was just after two o'clock in the morning when Joseph's telephone finally rang and he recognized the voice of the Cholon Chinese the moment he picked up the receiver.

"Comrade Trinh arrived in Saigon seven hours ago," he announced in a neutral voice. "She traveled all the way from Hanoi by truck. She's a member of Infiltration Brigade Nineteen now in place at Bien Hoa Bridge. She's been contacted and told to wait. Nineteen Brigade has concealed itself in a concrete culvert a hundred yards south of the bridge. You'll find her there if you go now."

The line clicked and went dead without any further formality, and Joseph grabbed the little waiter by the arm and rushed him down the stairs. Crouched in the front passenger seat of the Pontiac, the waiter held on to the dashboard tightly with both hands and every so often he fingered the little wedge of hundred-dollar bills that Joseph had pushed into the breast pocket of his white jacket to persuade him to accompany him. In his Ben Cat headquarters, General Dung, the Communist field commander, had already given the final order to attack Saigon at midnight precisely: "Make deep thrusts! Advance to the predetermined points!" he had told his forces proudly and the artillery batteries brought up from the coast had immediately begun raining 130-millimeter shells on the Tan Son Nhut headquarters of South Vietnam's Joint Chiefs of Staff.

The noise of this continuous artillery barrage became deafening as Joseph guided the Pontiac carefully through the refugees swarming into the northeastern suburbs, but as he drove he noticed the flame trees in his headlights and remembered that this was the same road out of the city along which his father, Chuck and himself had traveled with Jacques Devraux on that first hunting trip half a century before; now, however, the road was choked with abandoned jeeps and trucks left there by fleeing ARVN troops who had perhaps begun to realize that most of their generals had already fled to the ships of the U.S. Seventh Fleet anchored off Vung Tau. Because of the panic and confusion the short drive took Joseph more than half an hour, and the hands of his watch showed two forty-five A.M. when he extinguished the headlights and swung the car off the road a quarter of a mile short of the Bien Hoa Bridge. As he leaned across and pushed open the passenger door, the little waiter was still fingering his wad of American bills, possibly agonizing over whether the risk he was about to take was worth it.

"Take off your white jacket — or you'll be visible a mile away," said Joseph sharply. "Put the money in your trouser pocket if you want to take it with you. But hurry." He helped the Vietnamese pull the jacket off his shoulders, then pushed him out into the darkness. "The culvert is about a hundred yards from the bridge! Call her name softly — 'Comrade Dang Thi Trinh' — and hurry!"

"Dang Thi Trinh — okay." The little waiter repeated the name in a frightened voice then scampered away into the darkness.

Looking through the windshield, Joseph found he could see beyond the bridge, not more than a mile or two away, a long column of North Vietnamese trucks and tanks advancing confidently with their headlights blazing. As he watched the spearhead move nearer he was seized with a sudden fear; the waiter would simply disappear into the darkness with the money and keep running — back in the direction of Saigon! What a fool he'd been! For ten minutes he sat behind the wheel in an agony of suspense; he was sure that an American revealing himself to a Communist infiltration team so close to the battle zone would be taken captive, but he knew he would have to take the risk and try to find Trinh himself if the waiter didn't reappear. He looked at his wristwatch every few moments as the minutes ticked by and he had opened the driver's door and was climbing out of the car to begin creeping towards the culvert when two shadows materialized silently from the darkness beside him.

"It's us, Mr. Sherman," whispered the waiter shakily. "Here's Comrade Trinh."

Joseph clapped the waiter ecstatically on the shoulder and bundled him into the back of the Pontiac; then he led the other figure towards the front passenger seat. She turned to face him as he opened the door for her, and in the red glow from the fires raging beyond the city he saw that her face was strained but composed. She wore the dusty black trousers and tunic of a peasant but her straw hat was pushed back on her shoulders and her hair fell loose about her cheeks. His heart lurched when he saw how she had grown into a young woman of seventeen; she looked back at him wide-eyed, her expression apprehensive and shy, her features combining unmistakably traces of Lan's beauty and Tuyet's proud strength. He resisted a fierce urge to throw his arms around her, and instead said softly in Vietnamese: "Trinh, I'm so happy that I've found you in time."

She looked at him anxiously for a moment, then turned her gaze in the direction of the advancing North Vietnamese tanks. "I'm very glad, too — but we must hurry, mustn't we?"

Joseph smiled and motioned her into the car. "Don't worry. We'll make it all right."

He ran to the driver's door, slipped behind the wheel again and turned quickly in the direction of the city. He had to sound the Pontiac's horn continuously to clear a path through the running crowds, and when the car was under way he lifted his wrist close to his face; the glow of the fires, bright enough to drive by, was also sufficient to illuminate his watch dial, and he saw that it showed just after three. "There's still time for us to get to my embassy — and there we'll find a helicopter to fly out of Vietnam."

As he drove he felt a light touch on his arm and turned his head to find Trinh's fingers on his sleeve; she had a wondering look in her eyes and she removed her hand with a little embarrassed smile when she found him looking at her.

Inside the United States Embassy on Thong Nhut Boulevard at that moment the last American ambassador to Saigon was folding the United States flag and tucking it into a plastic bag to carry with him to the ships of the Seventh Fleet. His face was gray and crumpled in the aftermath of a debilitating attack of pneumonia, and he watched anxiously as the giant CH-53 helicopters continued to sweep into the embassy compound to pick up fresh loads of evacuees. Their pilots now were red-eyed with fatigue and the five or six hundred Vietnamese still waiting seemed to sense that the end of the airlift might be approaching. From the rooftop pad smaller CH-47 helicopters were evacuating the last of the thousand or so embassy staff and their dependents but not many remained by three-fifteen A.M., and those still waiting stood

743

around in irresolute little groups on an upper floor inside the Chancery watching with dismay the final defeat and humiliation of their country and its Asian ally.

Naomi Boyce-Lewis waited with them, rarely leaving her place by the windows; she scanned the streets outside constantly, watching for a sign of Joseph, but as her turn to leave drew near, she was ushered firmly into a line drawn up before an internal stairwell. She tried to hang back but the diplomats around her confided that in Washington President Ford was becoming increasingly impatient with the ambassador's reluctance to wind up "Operation Frequent Wind." The embassy's secret communications equipment was being smashed, they told her, and the last direct messages had already been sent to Washington. The helicopter radio links with the commanders of the Seventh Fleet were the only surviving channels of contact between Saigon and Washington, and orders were expected from the White House at any time, they said, to curtail the airlift as soon as the last U.S. diplomat was airborne. After that there was no certainty that anybody else would get out.

Naomi took a last look out of the window then reluctantly moved up the stairwell behind the other waiting Americans. When she stepped out onto the Chancery roof it was almost four A.M. and the CH-47 that was to take her and twenty-four others to the U.S.S. *Blue Ridge*, the flagship of the evacuation fleet, was just settling onto the pad. Because time was precious it did not cut its rotors, and they continued to spin as Marine guards urged the first group of passengers forward into its open hatches. Suddenly Naomi realized that from the top of the six-story building she could see the rivers of North Vietnamese armor flowing down the two main highways towards Saigon with their driving lights shining, and her heart sank; then in the next instant she lowered her gaze to the street outside the embassy walls and saw Joseph's Pontiac nosing through the crowd towards the side gate.

The desperate Vietnamese were swarming frenziedly around the slow-moving car, imagining somehow that it might be their last chance of salvation, and Naomi stepped aside to let other diplomats board the helicopter ahead of her. Her hand flew to her mouth when she saw a dozen or more youths scramble onto the Pontiac's roof, hoping to spring from there over the gate when it got near enough. Others smashed at its windows, and gradually the dense throng halted the car. In their anger they began rocking it and Naomi let out a little cry when it toppled slowly onto its side. Men and boys attacked it with their feet, shattering its windshield and side windows, and it was then that Naomi saw for the first time the terrified face of Trinh as she struggled to force open the passenger door that was suddenly above her head.

Inside the car, the screams of the crowd were deafening; Joseph, who had fallen awkwardly when the car went over, was fighting to free his legs from the controls and trying to calm Trinh at the same time. As she began trying to climb out of the car he seized her arm, motioning for her to wait, and pulled his passport from inside his jacket. "If we become separated, show this to the soldiers on the top of the wall and they'll let you in," he yelled, thrusting it into her hand.

She nodded frantically and clambered out of the wrecked car clutching the passport. The crowd had begun to surge wildly back and forth and almost at once she was carried away from him along the foot of the wall. A volley of shots rang out from among the crowd, directed at the helicopter that had just landed on top of the Chancery, and this was greeted with hysterical cheers; then the heavier bark of a machine gun firing from a roof on the other side of Thong Nhut suddenly broke in on the clamor and half-a-dozen men and women crumpled to the ground. As Joseph pulled himself from the Pontiac screams of "Viet Cong! Viet Cong!" rose all around him and there was a concerted rush at the walls. The American Marines standing shoulder to shoulder on the parapet, wearing flak jackets and steel helmets, stamped on the climbers' hands with their heavy combat boots and brandished their bayonets, and again the crowd fell back screaming abuse. The Cobra gunship that had been hovering overhead suddenly dropped like a hawk and the roar of its multibarreled weapons blotted out everything else for several seconds while it fired at the Communist machine gun nest on the rooftop opposite.

In the thick of the crowd Joseph craned his neck in desperation, trying to spot Trinh, but he couldn't see her. Then he heard a distant voice shrieking his name, and he looked up to see Naomi gesticulating frantically from the Chancery roof. She was pointing along the wall, and following her directions, he saw Trinh scrambling up a lightpole with two or three other youths. He shouldered his way through the crowd and began climbing the same lattice-iron stanchion; halfway up, he found himself gasping for breath and he stopped. As he rested he saw a Marine guard appear above him, and the soldier clubbed savagely at the two Vietnamese youths ahead of Trinh with his M-16 to clear the way for Joseph. They fell backwards with a yell, sweeping Trinh to the ground, and she rose sobbing and holding her arms beseechingly towards Joseph.

"*Ong ngoai! Ong ngoai!*" she screamed, reverting in her despair to "Grandpapa," the childish term of endearment she had first used for him seven years before in the sampan on the River of Perfumes, "*Vui long giup toi!* — Please help me!"

The Marine was calling repeatedly for Joseph to climb up alone but he ignored him and leaned back into the crowd, stretching out his arms towards Trinh. She tried to grab his hand, but the fear-crazed mob surged wildly around her and she was swept away. The Cobra gunship which had failed to silence the Viet Cong machine gun had begun dropping flares to expose its position, and by their ghostly light Joseph saw her struggling to her feet again. Feeling his strength ebbing he decided not to venture back into the melee; instead he yelled her name repeatedly and waved her in his direction. When she saw him she began fighting her way towards the light stanchion once more, but before she reached it a dark blob flew in an arc above the heads of the crowd. The flash of the grenade exploding blinded Joseph for a few seconds and when his vision cleared he saw Trinh lying still among the mass of bodies crumpled on the pavement.

From the top of the Chancery, Naomi couldn't see what had happened outside the compound, but from the hunched, rigid position of Joseph's body as he clung to the lightpole she sensed that something was wrong. At that moment a yelling Marine grabbed her by the shoulders and hustled her towards the open door of the helicopter that was waiting to leave. She tried to struggle and shouted for him to release her but her words were torn away in the noise of the helicopter's fast-spinning rotor blades. In the end he lifted her bodily into the aircraft alongside the other passengers and slammed the door. As the helicopter shuddered into the air she saw Joseph release his hold on the lightpole and slip back into the crowd, and she buried her face in her hands.

When Joseph reached Trinh's side she was lying quite still, with her eyes closed, but there was no sign of injury on her face or body. With the growing pandemonium of the Communist bombardment filling his ears, he knelt to pick her up and, summoning his fading strength, he staggered back to the foot of the wall. The explosion of the grenade had scattered the crowd and he signaled to a Marine sergeant on top of the gate to take Trinh from him. The sergeant leaned down and hauled her over the gate with one arm before passing her to one of his waiting men inside; then he climbed down to help Joseph scramble over.

Trinh was still unconscious when Joseph took her from the Marine and carried her unsteadily across the darkened embassy compound to the landing zone on the lawn. He persuaded the colonel supervising the evacuation to let them board the last Sikorsky Sea Stallion, and he squeezed in among the seventy or so frightened Vietnamese who were already crowded inside. He had to crouch on the floor, cradling Trinh's head against his chest, and as the helicopter rose and pulled slowly away from the glare of the embassy area, she opened her eyes and gazed around at the sea of faces in terror.

"Don't worry, Trinh," he said, speaking close to her ear. "You're safe — everything's going to be all right."

Postscript

While researching the background to this novel I received invaluable guidance from history scholars in Paris, London, Washington and at Harvard University; a number of journalists and writers with a deep knowledge of Vietnam also kindly shared their perceptions of the past with me. In Paris, my early enthusiasms were nourished by French historian Philippe Devillers and foreign correspondent Edith Lenart, who has covered Indochina with distinction for many years. In London Dr. Ralph B. Smith, Reader in the History of Southeast Asia at the School of Oriental and African Studies, steered me towards scores of stimulating sources, including the once-secret Sûreté Générale files now accessible in the French Ministry of Colonies. In Washington, author William R. Corson, a splendid friend and a man of perhaps unrivaled military and intelligence experience in Southeast Asia, was an unfailing inspiration and helpmate; Professor Allan W. Cameron of the Fletcher School of Law and Diplomacy, a specialist in the diplomatic history of Indochina, gave endless hours of his time to discussing Vietnam with me; Frank Snepp, author of *Decent Interval*, the inside story of Saigon's final fall, provided many fresh insights; Douglas Pike, who has written several authoritative works on the Viet Cong, helped me generously and Bruce Martin, research facilities officer at the Library of Congress, constantly rendered assistance far beyond the call of duty.

In libraries and archives in Paris, London and Washington over a three-year period I consulted several hundred books and thousands of documents relating to Vietnam; all contributed something to my efforts to re-create the Vietnam of decades past but among them a few books stood out as beacons of enlightenment. *The Three Kingdoms of Indo-China* by Harold J. Coolidge, Jr. and Theodore Roosevelt, published in 1933, provided fascinating glimpses of what big game hunting was like in Cochin-China and Annam in colonial times; *Little China* by Alan Houghton Brodrick, published in 1942, and *East of Siam* by American travel writer Harry A. Franck (1939) were indispensable guides to Vietnamese and colonial customs in the early years of this century. Ngo Vinh Long in his work *Before the Revolution; The Vietnamese Peasants Under the French* documented as nobody else has done the privations suffered by some of his countrymen on the rubber plantations and in the World War II famine, and Virginia Thompson's wide-ranging survey *French Indo-China* (1937) brought the rigors and problems of life in the French colonial territories sharply into focus for me. Among the several biographies of Ho Chi Minh, Charles Fenn's, published in 1973, stood out because of its author's personal contacts with the enigmatic Vietnamese leader during World War II. Little has been written about Britain's brief but crucial involvement in Indochina in 1945 and George Rosie's brave little paperback, *The British in Vietnam* is so far the sole published guide to those controversial events. Jules Roy's *The Battle of Dien Bien Phu* and Bernard Fall's *Hell in a Very Small Place* were compelling reading for anyone wishing to reconstruct authentically the climactic battle of the French Indochina war. Of the books written during the 1960s David Halberstam's *The Making of a Quagmire* and Malcolm W. Browne's *The New Face of War* proved invaluable guides to Saigon and South Vietnam in that period and Don Oberdorfer's *Tet!* was an essential companion for understanding fully the historic Communist offensive of 1968.

At a practical level my warmest thanks are also due to my research assistant in Washington, Sally Weston, to my typist Jean Johnson who tirelessly worked and reworked successive drafts of the novel in both London and Washington — and ultimately to my tenacious editor in Boston, William D. Phillips. In acknowledging my debt of gratitude to those specialists who have aided me, I don't, however, mean to suggest that they necessarily approve in every case of the manner in which I have portrayed the events of the past fifty years. In the end the novelist's viewpoint remains, uniquely, his own.

Anthony Grey
The Chinese Assassin £1.95

When an airliner crashes in Mongolia the Chinese government keep suspiciously quiet regarding its contents. Yet a year later they claim one of the victims was Lin Piao, Chinese Defence Minister, fleeing to Russia after an abortive attempt to assassinate Mao and seize power. How did Lin Piao die? Was it an accident or was it murder? As the secret services of Russia, China and America clash the most destructive earthquake since the fifteenth century rocks China, and the dying Mao comes face to face with a deadly assassin.

'Chillingly authentic' YORKSHIRE POST

Wilbur Smith
The Angels Weep £2.95

The destiny of the Ballantynes would be the destiny of their land of Rhodesia for as long as the red sun burned. Through the bloodsoaked aftermath of the Matabele wars to the savage betrayal of the Jameson Raid, the chronicle of Zouga Ballantyne and his dynasty was the chronicle of Africa's turbulent times, leaping almost a century to its dark and ironic coda, when a new generation of Ballantynes is locked in the bitter struggle for mastery of the land soon to be reborn as Zimbabwe.

George MacDonald Fraser
Flashman and the Redskins £1.95

'Harry Flashman is back . . . a Forty-Niner on the Rio Grande and Santa Fe trail, helping his old doxy move her bawdy-house from New Orleans to California . . . best man at Geronimo's wedding . . . twenty-seven years later he is bak, mixing with President Grant and mountain men like Kit Carson as the Sioux and Cheyenne are chiselled out of their hunting grounds and Custer drops his clanger at Little Big Horn' OBSERVER

Fiction

☐	**The Chains of Fate**	Pamela Belle	£2.95p
☐	**Options**	Freda Bright	£1.50p
☐	**The Thirty-nine Steps**	John Buchan	£1.50p
☐	**Secret of Blackoaks**	Ashley Carter	£1.50p
☐	**Lovers and Gamblers**	Jackie Collins	£2.50p
☐	**My Cousin Rachel**	Daphne du Maurier	£2.50p
☐	**Flashman and the Redskins**	George Macdonald Fraser	£1.95p
☐	**The Moneychangers**	Arthur Hailey	£2.95p
☐	**Secrets**	Unity Hall	£2.50p
☐	**The Eagle Has Landed**	Jack Higgins	£1.95p
☐	**Sins of the Fathers**	Susan Howatch	£3.50p
☐	**Smiley's People**	John le Carré	£2.50p
☐	**To Kill a Mockingbird**	Harper Lee	£1.95p
☐	**Ghosts**	Ed McBain	£1.75p
☐	**The Silent People**	Walter Macken	£2.50p
☐	**Gone with the Wind**	Margaret Mitchell	£3.95p
☐	**Wilt**	Tom Sharpe	£1.95p
☐	**Rage of Angels**	Sidney Sheldon	£2.50p
☐	**The Unborn**	David Shobin	£1.50p
☐	**A Town Like Alice**	Nevile Shute	£2.50p
☐	**Gorky Park**	Martin Cruz Smith	£2.50p
☐	**A Falcon Flies**	Wilbur Smith	£2.50p
☐	**The Grapes of Wrath**	John Steinbeck	£2.50p
☐	**The Deep Well at Noon**	Jessica Stirling	£2.95p
☐	**The Ironmaster**	Jean Stubbs	£1.75p
☐	**The Music Makers**	E. V. Thompson	£2.50p

Non-fiction

☐	**The First Christian**	Karen Armstrong	£2.50p
☐	**Pregnancy**	Gordon Bourne	£3.95p
☐	**The Law is an Ass**	Gyles Brandreth	£1.75p
☐	**The 35mm Photographer's Handbook**	Julian Calder and John Garrett	£6.50p
☐	**London at its Best**	Hunter Davies	£2.90p
☐	**Back from the Brink**	Michael Edwardes	£2.95p

☐	**Travellers' Britain**	⎱ Arthur Eperon	£2.95p
☐	**Travellers' Italy**	⎰	£2.95p
☐	**The Complete Calorie Counter**	Eileen Fowler	90p
☐	**The Diary of Anne Frank**	Anne Frank	£1.75p
☐	**And the Walls Came Tumbling Down**	Jack Fishman	£1.95p
☐	**Linda Goodman's Sun Signs**	Linda Goodman	£2.95p
☐	**The Last Place on Earth**	Roland Huntford	£3.95p
☐	**Victoria RI**	Elizabeth Longford	£4.95p
☐	**Book of Worries**	Robert Morley	£1.50p
☐	**Airport International**	Brian Moynahan	£1.95p
☐	**Pan Book of Card Games**	Hubert Phillips	£1.95p
☐	**Keep Taking the Tabloids**	Fritz Spiegl	£1.75p
☐	**An Unfinished History of the World**	Hugh Thomas	£3.95p
☐	**The Baby and Child Book**	Penny and Andrew Stanway	£4.95p
☐	**The Third Wave**	Alvin Toffler	£2.95p
☐	**Pauper's Paris**	Miles Turner	£2.50p
☐	**The Psychic Detectives**	Colin Wilson	£2.50p

All these books are available at your local bookshop or newsagent, or
can be ordered direct from the publisher. Indicate the number of copies
required and fill in the form below   12

....

Name..
(Block letters please)

Address..

....

Send to CS Department, Pan Books Ltd, PO Box 40, Basingstoke, Hants
Please enclose remittance to the value of the cover price plus:
35p for the first book plus 15p per copy for each additional book ordered
to a maximum charge of £1.25 to cover postage and packing
Applicable only in the UK

While every effort is made to keep prices low, it is sometimes
necessary to increase prices at short notice. Pan Books reserve
the right to show on covers and charge new retail prices which
may differ from those advertised in the text or elsewhere